D1263688

WAGNER,
the Wehr-Wolf

George W. Reynolds

Illustrated by
Henry Anelay

Introduction by
E. F. Bleiler

DOVER PUBLICATIONS, INC.
Mineola, New York

Copyright

Copyright © 1975 by Dover Publications, Inc.
All rights reserved.

Bibliographical Note

Wagner, the Wehr-Wolf, first published by Dover Publications, Inc., in
1975 and reprinted in 2015, is an unabridged and unaltered reprint of the
work published in book form by [the author and] John Dicks, London [n.d.;
originally serialized in *Reynolds' Miscellany,* 1846–7]. The Introduction and
Bibliography were written for the 1975 Dover edition by E. F. Bleiler. The
original pagination of the work, in which the main text begins on page 3
rather than page 1, has been retained for this edition.

International Standard Book Number
ISBN-13: 978-0-486-79929-2
ISBN-10: 0-486-79929-8

Manufactured in the United States by RR Donnelley
79929801   2015
www.doverpublications.com

CONTENTS

INTRODUCTION TO THE DOVER EDITION

On the evening of May 13, 1840, a young man who looked something like Lewis Carroll superimposed on Horace Greeley happened to walk past the chapel on Aldersgate Street, London. The sidewalk was crowded, and a meeting was going on. Impelled by the curiosity that was one of his characteristics, the young man, George William MacArthur Reynolds (26), entered the chapel, where he found J. H. Donaldson, a noted temperance lecturer, haranguing his listeners on temperance, or as it is better described, teetotalism.

Reynolds, who had spent his formative years as a wealthy young man in France and knew the vintages well, listened with growing displeasure. Then, "fortified by the bastard kind of courage engendered by wine, although he had not drunk to any excess," Reynolds interrupted Donaldson, and challenged him to a public debate. Donaldson agreed, and the two men argued the issue on several occasions. Reynolds, despite his membership in several French learned societies, soon found that he was getting the worse of the argument. He tried to establish that coffee and tobacco were more harmful than wine, tried to argue for moderation instead of abstinence, but failed, and on May 30, 1840, confessed defeat. He signed the pledge with the London United Temperance Association, and presumably sealed his wine cellars.

The incidents narrated above, and those to come in the next few paragraphs, are on the trivial side, but they do offer exact details, otherwise lacking, to a pattern that appeared many times in the life of G. W. M. Reynolds, and, indeed, had a certain share in creating modern England.

G. W. M. Reynolds, if he is remembered at all today, is considered a sensational novelist who sometimes operated in the same range as the penny dreadfullers of Salisbury Square, the world of the British counterpart to the American dime novel.

Yet Reynolds was really a remarkable man. He was the most popular English author of the middle nineteenth century; one of his books, *The Mysteries of London*, sold over a million copies in ten years. It was translated, immediately after British publication, into French, German, Italian, and Spanish. It even enjoyed a wide circulation (in German) in the Russian Empire, where it was officially banned. In America his name was so important as a sales document that generations of unscrupulous publishers in New York issued novels by other men under his name. Reynolds was one of the best journalists and editors in England, the founder of a newspaper that rose to a circulation of over 600,000 copies, and survived until the 1950's. He was also an indefatigable worker for social reform, and at one time led the Chartist movement, the working-class upheaval of the middle century. A man of great ability, incredible energy and efficiency, he literally risked his liberty at the time of the agitation of 1848–9. If his emotional constitution had been somewhat different, his name might now be as familiar as Gladstone's or Palmerston's.

After being converted to temperance, Reynolds immediately threw himself into the cause with impetuosity and violent enthusiasm. In a very short time he was recognized as one of the leaders of the London organization, and directed the joys and responsibilities of the movement. One of the exercises of London temperance was a river excursion: the Teetotalers would board the steam packets *Eclipse* and *Vivid*, and proceed up the river to Richmond, where they would disembark and march (banners and music) to Vauxhall Gardens. There they feasted and sang, Reynolds in the lead.

Almost immediately after joining the temperance society, Reynolds began to explore the financial side of temperance. In a matter of weeks he floated a stock company and founded *The Teetotaler, a Weekly Journal Devoted to Temperance, Literature and Science*, first issue June 27, 1840. Reynolds assumed the editorship.

Reynolds opened the first issue of *The Teetotaler* with an installment of his novel, *The Drunkard's Tale*, the theme of which the reader can easily guess. He also filled the periodical with sensational fiction showing the evils of alcohol, very competent essays, scientific articles, good book reviews, and temperance news. The magazine was capably handled. High points of its short life were *Noctes Pickwickianae*, a series of conversations between Mr. Pickwick and Sam Weller about temperance, and a novel, *Pickwick Married*, in which Mr. Pickwick is finally trapped. Reynolds's emphasis on Pickwick is not surprising, since he had already (1837–9) written a near best-seller entitled *Pickwick Abroad*.

Reynolds then started to publish a serious study of alcoholism, which was to cover the history of noted criminals who had acted under the influence, trade disorders, human spontaneous combustion (a topic which fascinated the Victorians), and the physiological effects of drink. He also offered the temperance people a brief history of the Ottoman Empire, a topic that obviously delighted him, judging from its

perpetual recurrence in his fiction. No copy of either work is known to survive.

But soon the typical end to the pattern came: On September 25, 1841, the journal published an acrimonious note by Reynolds, and suspended publication. He had quarreled with his fellow stockholders and temperance associates, and walked out. His financial loss was considerable.

This exemplifies the pattern that dominated the life of G. W. M. Reynolds in both letters and politics: initial disinterest or hostility, traumatic conversion, enthusiastic participation, financial involvement, attempts at personal advancement, disagreements with his fellows, a bitter quarrel, and dissociation. Intellectually brilliant, imaginative, industrious, obstinate, smug, somewhat arrogant, aggressive, humorless, self-advancing, vain, probably greedy, hot-headed, yet kindly, compassionate, self-sacrificing, he presented a strange mixture of psychic ingredients. He was the model of a Victorian social reformer.

George William MacArthur Reynolds (1814–79) came of a prominent, wealthy family, being the oldest son of Captain George Reynolds, flag officer in the Royal Navy, recipient of knighthood and orders from both the King and foreign powers. Captain Reynolds died before G. W. M. R.'s majority, leaving his son some £12,000 and a guardianship. To follow family traditions, young George was sent to the Royal Military Institute at Sandhurst, where he stayed for about two and a half years. But Sandhurst and G. W. M. R. did not agree, and in 1830 he was released. He left for France, then a haven for British expatriates, where he remained for about eight years.

We do not know too many details of his early life, but a little can be reconstructed. He was in Paris during the Revolution of 1830, his sympathies strongly with Louis Philippe. Was he at the barricades with the students? Among his associates at Calais was Beau Brummell. Was it from Brummell that he acquired the almost pathological hatred that he later displayed for the Prince Regent? Some of Reynolds's time may have been spent in high living, but his basic seriousness and organization emerged even at this early date. He studied the sciences intensively. He was also a close student of French culture, and by the time he returned to England was a confirmed Francophile, a good political analyst, and almost certainly the Englishman with the largest knowledge of French letters.

During this early period, in 1832, Reynolds published his first book, a small 40-page volume, which in later life he preferred not to mention. This was *The Errors of the Christian Religion Exposed, by a Comparison of the Gospels of Matthew and Luke* (London, 1832). "I am now eighteen years old, and till this year have been a firm believer in Christianity. . . . About six months ago I perused the *Age of Reason*, and this entirely opened my eyes to the errors in which I had so lately trodden." Young Reynolds attacks the prophecies of Isaiah, advocates Deism, and as a foretaste of his later mode of life, promises his readers a sequel!

In 1835 and 1836, Reynolds, now in control of his inheritance, ventured into publishing in Paris. Together with associates he founded the *London and Paris Courier*, a newspaper intended to rival Galignani's for the expatriate or tripper Englishman. Reynolds, who assumed editorship after a few months, drove the circulation high, almost putting Galignani out of business, but he quarreled with his associates in August 1836, and stormed away. Among his contributors had been one W. M. Thackeray, who later stated that the first money he had ever earned by writing came from Reynolds.

Reynolds also entered book publishing in Paris, his most noteworthy publication being a novel that he later characterized as "the first original English work of any consequence published in France." This was *The Youthful Imposter*, by G. W. M. Reynolds (1835). It does not really deserve such high praise, since it was mostly a steal from Bulwer. Reynolds seems to have lost most of his capital in this venture.

By the end of 1837 George William Mac-Arthur Reynolds was back in London, considerably poorer, but equipped with a wife, Susannah Frances, who was also a writer. Reynolds now made his bid for fame by assuming the editorship of the *Monthly Magazine*, an unbelievably dull, moribund journal of considerable age. Within an issue or two Reynolds turned it into one of the most interesting periodicals of the day. With excellent factual articles on the current events and culture of the Continent, reasonably good popular fiction, good book reviews, and a really fine summary in digest form of scientific, artistic and literary achievements, it deserved more than the early death it suffered.

During his editorship of the *Monthly Magazine*, in which he was aided by his wife, Reynolds began two major projects: *Pickwick Abroad* and *The Modern Writers of France*. *Pickwick Abroad* has been called the most successful imitation of Dickens's *Pickwick Papers*. Reynolds took Pickwick, Weller, Tupman and Winkle to Paris, where they had adventures among sleazy Anglo-French remittance men, French courtesans, and assorted scoundrels. Among the characters was Vidocq, the celebrated detective, whom the travelers visited to regain a stolen watch. Reynold's contemporaries enjoyed *Pickwick Abroad*, perhaps because the other Pickwickian pastiches by other authors are so much worse, but a reader in the 1970's is likely to find it essentially monotonous and unimaginative.

The Modern Writers of France, which was published in book form in 1839, was superior to *Pickwick Abroad*, although it has now been completely forgotten. In it Reynolds made the first good survey of the literary boom that followed the Revolution of 1830; he covered Sand, Balzac, Kock, Sue, Dumas Sr., Hugo and others. It is particularly significant since Reynolds's own sensational fiction was based so much on French prototypes.

In December 1838, however, the end came. Reynolds quarreled with his superiors and left the journal. Judging by the direction that the *Monthly Magazine* took after his departure, we can guess that his superiors did not like his politics, his editorial personality, his self-advertisement in planted articles, or his bumptiousness. Or the dispute may simply have been about money. In any case the *Monthly Magazine* lasted only a couple of years after his departure.

What happened to G. W. M. R. between December 1838, when he was out of a job, and May 1840, when he bearded the temperance lecturer, we do not know, beyond the fact that he finished *Pickwick Abroad, The Modern Writers of France* and *The Steam Packet, A Tale of the River and Ocean*, another novel derivative from the *Pickwick Papers*. Nor do we know what happened to him during the longer period between September 1841, when he had denounced his fellow teetotalers as cheap, scheming chiselers, and the end of 1844. *A Sequel to Don Juan* (1843) and a patched up novel, *Master Timothy's Bookcase* (1841), are all that we have from this period, from which we might have expected renewed editorial work and at least two or three new novels. In *A Sequel to Don Juan* Reynolds continued in verse the adventures of Byron's hero, with episodes that were considered improper by British standards of the day. Here and in his sensational fiction Reynolds consciously took the French position on questions of sex:

> That political articles . . . may more or less guide the public mind and teach the indolent and careless to think for themselves, is certain; but that works abounding with voluptuousness and licentiousness can produce the same results, is a speculation . . . palpably false. . . . The French author paints the truth in all its nudity, and this development of the secrets of nature shocks the English reader. . . . It is much better, says the French writer, to prepare a youth for that life in which he is about to embark, by a bold and naked display of the truth, than to expose him to all the bitterness of disappointment. (*The Modern Writers of France*, preface to the first edition)

In the fall of 1844 Reynolds began the work that was to make him the most popular author in Great Britain. This was *The Mysteries of London*. Published in weekly penny parts, it ran for about two years, with ever increasing sales, and perpetual reprint of the early installments. For George Vickers, the publisher of *The Mysteries of London*, Reynolds also edited a new periodical which featured his work. This was the *London Journal*, which began in March 1845.

Until 1845, despite his overestimation of his own work, and some small financial success from his part novels, Reynolds had been a minor figure in the literary world. But with *The Mysteries of London* and the *London Journal*, almost overnight he became the dominant personality in the popular literature of the decade.

Mayhew, who surveyed the slums and back alleys and small factories and public places where Reynolds's fiction was sold, is a witness, a couple of years later, to this phenomenon:

> It may appear anomalous to speak of the literature of an uneducated body, but even the costermongers have their tastes for books. They are very fond of hearing any one read aloud to them, and listen very attentively. . . . What they love best to listen to—and, indeed, what they are most eager for—are Reynolds's periodicals, especially the "Mysteries of the Court." "They've got tired of Lloyd's blood-stained stories," said one man, who was in the habit of reading to them, "and I'm satisfied that, of all London, Reynolds is the most popular man among them. They stuck to him in Trafalgar-square,[1] and would again. They all says he's a 'trump'. . . . The costermongers . . . are very fond of illustrations. I have known a man, what couldn't read, buy a periodical what had an illustration, just that he might learn from some one, who *could* read, what it was all about. . . . Now here," proceeded my friend, "you see's an engraving of a man hung up, burning over a fire,[2] and some costers would go mad if they couldn't learn what he'd been doing, who he was, and all about him. . . . Here's one of the passages that took their fancy wonderfully," my informant observed:

> 'With glowing cheeks, flashing eyes, and palpitating bosom, Venetia Trelawney rushed back into the refreshment-room, where she threw herself into one of the arm-chairs already noticed. But scarcely had she thus sunk down upon the flocculent cushion, when a sharp click, as of some mechanism giving way, met her ears; and at the same instant her wrists were caught in manacles which sprang out of the arms of the treacherous chair, while two steel bands started from the richly-carved back and grasped her shoulders. A shriek burst from her lips—she struggled violently, but all to no purpose: for she was a captive—and powerless!

> 'We should observe that the manacles and the steel bands which had thus fastened upon her, were covered with velvet, so that they inflicted no positive injury upon her, nor even produced the slightest abrasion of her fair and polished skin.'[3]

Here all my audience," said the man to me, "broke out with—'Aye, that's the way the harristocrats hooks it. There's nothing o' that sort among us. The rich has all that barrikin to themselves.' 'Yes, that's the b—— way the taxes goes in,' shouted a woman."

The year 1846 was an important one for Reynolds. Despite the success of *The Mysteries of Lon-*

---

[1] See below, page xii.

[2] Probably the illustration in *Pope Joan, or The Female Pontiff*.

[3] From *The Mysteries of the Court of London, Second Series*.

don, Reynolds and Vickers quarreled; Reynolds left the *London Journal*, although he did fulfill his contract on the novel. The reason seems to have been money: Reynolds wanted more than £5 per installment, which was a good price for penny fiction, but still not enough for a best-seller. Reynolds cast about and finally came up with a business arrangement that was stable, and lasted (in various forms) for the remainder of his life. This was with John Dicks of London, who undertook the printing of a new periodical that Reynolds projected and assumed publication of Reynolds's fiction. The periodical, *Reynolds's Magazine* (soon retitled *Reynolds's Miscellany*) was quite successful, running from November 1846 through 1869. In it Reynolds published much of his new fiction; what was not printed in the magazine was published in weekly penny parts by Dicks. Both men became wealthy by this arrangement.

During the next ten years or so, 1847–57, Reynolds wrote some thirty novels, many of which are extremely long, as well as a great deal of ephemeral prose. This productivity must be a record of some sort, since it totals to something like thirty-five or forty million words of fiction. Other writers in the popular traditions of England, France and America have written comparable amounts, and a few have written a little more; but in all other cases that I know about, the writing has been spread out over many more years. Yet Reynolds did not employ a stable of writers, as did Alexandre Dumas, Sr. The secret, Reynolds once revealed not without smugness, was organization and diligence. He would spend about seven hours on each story installment of ten thousand words, without working too far in advance. This would leave him five or six days free in each week for other activities.

G. W. M. R. maintained this fantastic writing program until 1857, at which time his production decreased. 1859 witnessed the appearance of his last novel, *Mary Stuart, Queen of Scotland*. So far as is known, he wrote no more fiction, except for two trivial pieces. Why he stopped writing we do not know. Possibly he was simply tired of writing—there are hints that he had difficulty preparing *Mary Stuart*; possibly he found his other projects more interesting; possibly he had some sort of conversion away from his earlier sensationalism; possibly his health, which had been somewhat fragile for a time, was giving out. Or, most probably, there were no longer financial drives for him to write. In any case, his place as lead novelist in *Reynolds's Miscellany* was taken by James Malcolm Rymer ("Malcolm Errym"), the author of the famous *Varney the Vampyre*.

Until now we have considered G. W. M. R. as a writer, but to describe him apart from the causes he fought for is simply a partial statement, and to consider his literary and editorial work without mentioning his social and political activities is to provide a picture without a frame. There was always some movement or cause in Reynolds's life, and while the immediate road may have changed often enough, his destination seems to have been fairly permanent: social equality, cultural freedom, economic security for all, and universal tolerance.

Throughout his life Reynolds lived in movement after movement, carrying everything before him at first, what with his drive and intelligence, but dropping out of the "game" when met with opposition. If Reynolds had had the long-term persistence, accommodativeness, and resilience of, say, Jack Wilkes; if he had been able to utilize his one-time position as de facto leader of the "official" counterculture of mid-Victorian England, the Chartists; if his fellow Chartists had followed his insistence on a direct confrontation with Parliament, British history might have been different in large ways.

Reynolds's first love, it would seem, was French politics, both in the sense of supporting liberalism and economic amelioration in France, and in creating a rapprochement between England and France. He translated French literature and historical works extensively (probably much more than can be documented), wrote in praise of French customs and institutions, and on French political history, and for a time was French correspondent for the London (Weekly) *Dispatch*. He eventually quit this position since the editors supported the conservatives, and Reynolds did not wish the readers to assume that he agreed.

Other areas, too, engaged his support. The preface to his lurid *Grace Darling, or The Heroine of the Fern Islands* (1839) could well serve as a modern feminist tract, and he often contrasted the lot of women in England with their more elevated position in France. Succeeding this came teetotalism, as has already been described, and in the late 1840's, "Jewish liberation," as Reynolds termed it. The Second Series of *The Mysteries of London* may well have been the strongest attack to date, in fiction, on anti-Semitism. Elements of this are to be found in *Wagner, the Wehr-wolf*.

The Chartists were the group that attracted Reynolds longest, and in which he rose highest before withdrawing. Chartism in general—it had many divagations, sidestreams, schisms and time-changes—was a reform movement with its strength in the working classes, but with a fair number of radical liberal intellectuals, among whom Reynolds may be counted. Its main issue was electoral reform. Reynolds later, in his *Reynolds's Political Instructor* (Nov. 10, 1849), summarized the Chartist objectives: universal suffrage, vote by ballot, annual Parliament, equal electoral districts, paid representatives, and no property qualification. (Reynolds added to the platform recognition of the rights of labor and abolition of the laws of primogeniture.) These ideas were incorporated into three great petitions, which were to be signed by several million persons, and then presented to Parliament. Reynolds was concerned with the Third Petition.

In 1843 Reynolds had scoffed at the Chartists, since he cared less about electoral change than about social reform: unemployment insurance, pensions for the aged, social medicine, land reform and similar topics; but he was active in several organizations that might be termed social service. In 1845 he was a member of the Metropolitan Labourer's Suburban Dwelling Society council, together with Earl Grey, Mr. Ricardo the economist and Douglas Jerrold. Its purpose was to buy land outside the cities and resettle workers in cooperative communities. He was also associated with the National Parliamentary and Financial Reform Association, a middle-class organization, many of whose members he alienated by advocating support of the Hungarian liberation movement. Especially interesting to Americans is his leadership of the Potters' Joint Stock Emigration Society, which had established a cooperative community on the Fox River, Wisconsin; unfortunately, we know little about it.

The year 1848, however, seems to have witnessed Reynolds's sudden conversion to the Charter, perhaps because a strong group within the Chartists now shared his interests. The sequence of events parallels in essence his involvement with the Teetotalers.

By March 1848 the French Revolution was a fait accompli, and the British government was apprehensive. The Chartists had announced a full meeting in Trafalgar Square, March 6, 1848, to vote support for the French. The government feared armed rebellion and prohibited the meeting. Wellington was placed in charge of the defenses of London; clerks in the public buildings built bullet shields out of piles of the London *Times*; and the city was overrun with about 150,000 special police.

As the mobs rolled around Trafalgar Square —anywhere from 20,000 to 200,000, depending upon one's politics—the Charter leadership held back, hesitant to disobey the proclamation. Reynolds thereupon came to the front, mounted the pillar, introduced himself as a publisher who had sympathy for the working man, and was declared chairman of the meeting. He urged the crowds to defy the government and not to yield. The Chartists paraded him home enthusiastically, and he had to give another speech from the balcony of his home. While the anticipated insurrection never took place, sporadic riots and/or police repressions continued for three or four days.

As a result of Trafalgar, Reynolds was accepted as a leading figure among the Chartists, and soon became a member of the Executive. He took part in further meetings, including Kennington Common, where he urged the Chartists to declare themselves the government, if the Petition was rejected.

Reynolds's political activities also took other forms than organization. In November 1849 he and Dicks founded a weekly political paper, *Reynolds's Political Instructor*, which was issued for about six months. In this semiofficial organ for the Chartists, Reynolds developed Proudhon's thesis, "Property is theft," and also demanded legislation to improve the lot of labor: "to regulate the duties of the employer towards the employed, acknowledging the rights of Labour, recognizing it as capital, and providing not only for its fair remuneration but also for its constant employment—these details of a sound policy would soon alter the face of the land and the aspect of society, and lay a solid foundation for those farther and more complete changes when all property shall be national, and consequently no property is robbery." Reynolds also editorialized against capital punishment, for mine safety, for abolishing the peerage and disestablishing the state church. *Reynolds's Political Instructor* ceased publication in May 1850, to be followed in August by *Reynolds's Weekly Newspaper*.

Reynolds's Weekly Newspaper proved to be highly viable. Before a decade had passed, it reached the enormous circulation of half a million, and it was accepted as the news organ for the "radical working man." Reynolds also stumped the industrial Midlands and the North, the sources of Chartist strength, where he made many speeches. During the party elections of 1850 he had the largest vote, and for a time he was the leading personality within the movement. It is remarkable that he was never tried for sedition, as were some of his associates.

History reveals, however, that the Petition was rejected by Parliament, and the Chartists gradually collapsed. Some members emigrated; others joined other organizations; others lost interest as the government quietly moved to a few reforms. Faction and personality clashes arose. Reynolds had planned to stand for Parliament in 1851 as a Chartist; he withdrew and resigned from the Executive.

Reynolds's remaining associations with the declining movement were in reporting obituaries and in feuding with Ernest Jones, a former associate who conducted a rival labor newspaper, the *People's Journal*. Among the writers for Jones's paper was a German exile who wrote under the name Charles Marx. It would be a nice story if I could say that G. W. M. R. and Marx feuded with one another, but unfortunately there are no files of *Reynolds's Weekly Newspaper* in the United States, and I do not know.

The remainder of Reynolds's life, until his death in June 1879, is not known in any detail. He wrote no fiction that has been traced; he worked no more in politics. In the early 1860's he sold his literary rights to Dicks, for what is said to have been a fortune, and he lived in wealthy retirement, doing only a certain amount of editorial work on Dicks's *Bow Bells*. It is said that in his last days Reynolds "got religion," and died a churchwarden in a London church, now destroyed. It has not been possible to confirm this sad end, and I hope that it is not true.

After Reynolds's death the *Bookseller* printed an obituary. Conceding that Reynolds had been a bothersome radical, the *Bookseller* went on to say that the news media, including the *Times* (which Reynolds usually referred to as "the infamous *Times*"), out of political rancor, had not mentioned his death. "If we bestow more space than is our wont on the deceased, it is because the passing away of so notorious a writer deserves some record ... Dickens and Thackeray and Lever had their thousands of readers, but Mr. Reynolds's were numbered by the hundreds of thousands, perhaps millions."

II

Wagner, the Wehr-wolf began as a serial in the November 8, 1846 issue of *Reynolds's Magazine of Romance, General Literature, Science and Art*. But it probably appeared on the portable pamphlet scaffolds of the hawkers and on the bookstands ten days earlier; price one penny. Each issue of the magazine contained several pages of the novel, plus a woodcut illustration. It was the lead story for each of the early issues.

Along with the sensational *Wagner, the Wehr-wolf*—to offer medicament with the spices—appeared educational material: "The Anatomy and Physiology of Ourselves Popularly Considered" by James Johnson, M.R.C.S.; papers on popular science; a cooking and housekeeping section by Mrs. Reynolds; and a series of "Letters to the Industrious Classes." Each letter is addressed to an occupational group (governesses, weavers, etc.) and each is concerned with improving the financial lot of the working man.

Pride of place, however, went to *Wagner, the Wehr-wolf*, which seems to have been extremely popular. Novelty may have been an element in this popularity, since Reynolds was using a concept alien to English literature, the werewolf. The word "werewolf" is known from earlier English letters, but no early English werewolf story survives, and Reynolds offers the first significant use of the motif in English. The werewolf stories that were written before Reynolds's novel can be counted on one's fingers: "Hughes the Werewolf" by Sutherland Menzies (1838), "*The Wehr-wolf*" (*The Story-Teller*, 1833), Appel's "The Boar Wolf" (translated from German, available in English by 1843, and possibly earlier), and the werewolf story in Captain Marryat's *Phantom Ship* (1839). Whether Reynolds read these earlier tales is impossible to say, but it is reasonable to assume that he knew Marryat's popular story, which shares ideas with *Wagner, the Wehr-wolf*.

In addition to the werewolf belief, which Reynolds treated simply as far as its manifestations go, Reynolds used other popular motives: the Rosicrucians, the Turks, Italian intrigue and desert-island adventures. Italians and desert islands are topics too large and too obvious to be discussed, but Reynolds may well have picked up his story of Christian Rosenkreuz and his eternal lamp from Godwin's books, to cite the most obvious source. As for Turks and Turkish expansion, Reynolds was obviously attracted to aspects of Turkish culture, since Turkey appears in so much of his work. My own guess is that he liked the simple monotheism, the social democracy, the luxurious harems, and the efficacious means by which Sultans rid themselves of enemies.

Reynolds wrote two other important supernatural novels besides *Wagner, the Wehr-wolf*: *Faust* and *The Necromancer*. *Faust* (1845–6) is loosely antecedent to *Wagner, the Wehr-wolf*. The introduction to *Wagner, the Wehr-wolf*, as Reynolds's followers would have recognized, brings Faust to Wagner's hut; the guarded comments about the shattering events of 1517 refer to Faust's horrible death. Yet Wagner does not appear in *Faust*, and was presumably an afterthought, the name suggested by the classic Faust legend, in which Faust's servant was called Wagner.

Faust interprets the old Renaissance legend in a novel way. While in prison Wilhelm Faust is visited by the Devil, who offers him 24 years of power and indulgence in exchange for his soul. Faust accepts, and has adventures in Germany, where he makes use of the Vehm, and in Italy, where he meets Lucretia Borgia. But Faust does not keep all aspects of his bargain with the Devil—which includes sacrificing his first-born child—and he is thrown into Vesuvius, a fate comparable to that of Varney in (the earlier) *Varney the Vampyre*.

Reynolds's third supernatural novel, *The Necromancer* (1852), is also concerned with the diabolic contract, but more in the manner of Maturin's *Melmoth the Wanderer* or Ainsworth's *Revelations of London* (*Auriol*). In the 1380's Lord Danvers sold his soul to the Devil, receiving in exchange an elixir of youth, 150 years of life, immunity from weapons, and the power of instant translocation. He also has an escape clause: if he can find six virgins who love him more than their souls, and if he can sacrifice them, he will escape the Devil. Most of the novel is devoted to Danvers's attempt to convince Number Six. He fails.

Smaller elements of fantasy occur in certain of the other novels. In *The Coral Island* (1848–9) a curse pursues the ruling house of Naples in the fourteenth century; every third member is born a leper. The curse is broken when one of the leprous family finds on a South Pacific island a curative oil. In *Omar* (1855–6) the White Lady who haunts the Hohenzollerns appears; a spae wife is a character in *Kenneth* (1851), which is otherwise more Gothic than Reynolds's other fiction; clairvoyance is a topic in *The Empress Eugenie's Boudoir* (1857); while the frame for *Master Timothy's Bookcase* (1841) is based on a genie-like being. *The Bronze Statue* (1849–50) involves an extended supernatural sequence set in Hussite Bohemia: a girl has been consecrated to the Devil, and cannot be released until she finds a champion who, not for love, but from pure benevolence, will joust with the Devil. This sequence is later rationalized. *The Pixy* (1848) is concerned with a child ghost, and minor elements of fantasy occur scattered in other stories. On the whole, however, it might be said that Reynolds's strength did not lie in fantasy, but elsewhere.

For Reynolds's remaining forty to fifty million words of fiction little more need be done than indicate a few of the directions it took. Reynolds built on Dickens's *Pickwick Papers* in two minor works and two novels: *Pickwick Abroad* (1837–9) and *The Steam Packet* (1840), in which a similar drinking club takes a voyage. Reynolds's contemporaries liked *Pickwick Abroad*, but I find *The Steam Packet* superior. Reynolds also drew on current events for his themes: In *Grace Darling* (1839) he combined the idea of the Beauchamp murder in Kentucky with an act of heroism at sea that had recently achieved wide publicity. The Russo-Turkish and Crimean Wars furnished background for several novels: *Rosa Lambert* (1853–4), *Omar* (1855–6), and *Leila* (1856), while *The Loves of the Harem* (1855), set in early nineteenth-century Turkey, is really a detective story of a sort. The Sultan's minister must solve the mystery of the headless corpses found floating in the Bosphorus.

A very large share of Reynolds's work, particularly in his later period, is "costume opera," or sensationalism against a historical setting; this often incorporates historical persons and events. Among such works are *Mary Stuart* (1859); *Canonbury House, or The Mysteries of the Court of Queen Elizabeth* (1857–8); *The Rye House Plot* (1853–4), set in the times of Charles II; *Margaret* (1856–7), in medieval Scotland; *The Massacre of Glencoe* (1852–3), also Scotland. *The Days of Hogarth* (1847–8) is letterpress written about the engravings of Hogarth, which are usually reproduced with the text. The story is essentially A Rake's Progress. The later historical novels are by no means as sensational as his earlier works, and lack their exuberant vitality.

Another major grouping of novels purports (although this is not always sustained) to have a social or societal point. *The Seamstress* (1850), which tells of the seduction and tragic end of a working girl, in fairly realistic terms, is the purest member of this form. Other such novels include *Joseph Wilmot* (1853–5), which offers a little social protest as Joseph becomes a footman, many melodramatic situations, and the eventual revealment that Joseph is a misplaced baby and a peer of the realm. It is heavily indebted to Dickens for characterizations. *Mary Price* (1852) is concerned with a working girl, while *The Soldier's Wife* (1852–3) treats of brutality in the

army. *Rosa Lambert* (1853–4), with its complicated depravities and revealments, might well serve as the model for a modern soap opera.

Reynolds's contemporaries considered the series *The Mysteries of London* (1844–8) and its fellow series *The Mysteries of the Courts of London* (1848–55) his most successful work, and with this I would agree. These six gigantic novels, almost as long as the collected works of Dickens, constitute a vast shifting panorama of characters and roles, sometimes realistic, sometimes naturalistic, sometimes sentimental, sometimes romantic. Reynolds himself claimed the novels to be a moral document, a document showing how power had corrupted the aristocracy. In one sense it is such a document, despite its sensationalism. As Thackeray put it, "Prejudice against the great is only a rude expression of sympathy with the poor." In another sense, however, it is simply a succession of thrillers ultimately based on French prototypes of the Human Comedy sort. It would be pointless to try to isolate an exact parallel or source: Balzac, Hugo, Sue, Kock, Dumas fils, Dumas père have all been drawn upon, even the novels of Vidocq.

The First Series of *The Mysteries of London* (1844–6) conveys an idea of the complexity of Reynolds's mind; his passionate outbursts against injustice of all sorts; his strange fancies; his curious emphasis on erotic elements, both sensual and puritanical; and his knowledge of both under and upper world of London crime. It is the story of two brothers, two women, and a professional criminal, the Resurrection Man. One of the brothers is honest, and after many misfortunes, including an undeserved prison sentence, becomes a grandee in an Italian principate. The other brother takes the easy path, resolving to make fast money by any means. After temporary successes in swindling and confidence rackets, he comes to ruin and a sordid death.

Around them swirls London, with dozens of other characters, high life and low life, lords and riverboat pirates, bawds and duchesses, lascivious clergymen and virtuous working girls, coal miners and sophisticators of liquor, dishonest undertakers who work with resurrection men, burglars and assassins, fraudulent insane-asylum keepers, conmen and card sharps, high-minded political exiles, protofascist dictators in Italy, revolutionaries, Queen Victoria and Prince Albert, kept women and stockbrokers, Gypsies, members of Parliament, crooked bankers— rising to fortune, sinking to the gutter, thieving and deceiving, seducing, kidnapping, selling their bodies to avoid starvation, bearing illegitimate children, being swindled and murdered, starving in poverty, maintaining elaborate harems with Circassian girls (one of Reynolds's penchants)—in hovels, palaces, gambling dens, ruins, fashionable residences. The ingenuity which it takes to keep this vast human orrery in motion can be admired.

Yet besides being a vast cosmos of human sensation *The Mysteries of London* is many other things. In a sense it is education for the masses, and it is also propaganda. Reynolds may spend a couple of pages explaining quite accurately how dice can be controlled; how beer is adulterated; how rotten meat is disguised and sold to the poor at high prices; exactly how a graverobber works (very differently and more systematically than Baron Frankenstein's servitors); what percentage of prostitutes comes from various occupational groups; how wealth is distributed in the British Isles; how the various slums are geographically constituted; how fake auctions work; how prisons fail to train inmates for life outside; and a host of other topics that may well have been very important to the Londoner with a low income, who had to live with his guard up.

Occasionally Reynolds incorporated such material because it was germane to his story or intrinsically interesting, but at other times he obviously used the thriller as a vehicle for his social ideas. Brief biographies of criminals, scattered through the vast mechanism, reveal how a nineteenth-century recidivist was formed and educated. Unsentimental, this often sounds quite modern. Similarly, a whole series of adventures in Italy are obviously designed to show the horrors of a state without a constitution, when a despot assumes ultimate authority. In the Second Series of *The Mysteries of London* (1846–8) Reynolds reintroduces one of the heroes of the First Series and describes a political utopia that he set up.

Reynolds was not content, however, with recording the minor pilferings and peccadillos of society—in which he was surprisingly accurate for a sensationalist; he aimed higher. The general theme of *The Mysteries of London* and *The Mysteries of the Courts of London* is corruption of the higher social classes. In the First Series and Second Series of the *Courts*, for example, Reynolds attacked the memory of the Prince Regent with a frenzy that is indescribable, and must be read to be appreciated. He accused George IV of almost every crime, luridly described in full detail, from rape and swindling to seduction, subverting civil liberties, and procuring murder.

It is no marvel that Reynolds's contemporaries regarded him as a renegade, for in all probability never before or since has the British aristocracy undergone a more violent, more sustained and systematic fictional attack. To quote Reynolds from *The Seamstress*: "The British aristocracy, male and female, is the most loathsomely corrupt, demoralized and profligate class of persons that ever scandalized a country." The establishment, which never forgave him, saw it otherwise:

> He was a person with a mission—the exposure of a bloated and criminal aristocracy. Fearless was he—fearless in enterprise, indomitable in offence. While he lived, the upper classes had in him a critic of the most merciless habit, the most desperate and bloody-minded disposition. True it is that he imagined many of his facts, but what surprising facts they were . . . how colossal his invention, how sublime his effrontery, his purpose how relentless and how dark! (*The Saturday Review*, 1886)

For about a decade the *Mysteries* cycles were read by young people, shop girls, working men, tradesmen, and even by the aristocracy (who, according to Reynolds, borrowed the parts from their footmen, since they were too proud or too cheap to buy them!). These hundreds of thousands of readers may have devoured the serial parts for thrills and for the projection of their own hates and sorrows, but subliminally, along with the blood and eroticism, they must have picked up many of the ideas that Reynolds embodied in his novels. To call it an education would be too strong; but to call it a pointing would be just.

III

Today, despite the importance of G. W. M. Reynolds to the Victorian middle-world, he is almost forgotten except in the marginal world of collecting "bloods." He has never received formal treatment from a literary point of view; his bibliography has been neglected and garbled; and he has become only a name wandering vaguely through Chartist anecdotes, many of which are not accurate.

History, in her silence, has been too harsh on Reynolds. He obviously had flaws, both as a person and as a writer, but he also had remarkable abilities. As a social figure, despite extravagances of the nonce, he probably worked much good. Much of what he agitated for has come to pass, and his words may well have formed a background for the succeeding generation. Unfortunately, here in the United States we cannot judge his social and political thought, since files of his newspapers are not available. In England he has been criticized for certain paradoxes in his thought: he proclaims his sympathy for the poor, yet when he describes the poor he often equates poverty with criminality, and his ultimate aim for the poor man, it has been charged, is to gift him with bourgeois wealth and position. I do not consider these valid criticisms, however, for Reynolds makes clear that terminal poverty is a source of crime, and one can wonder what else, in Victorian England, Reynolds could have wished for the poor but a share of the creature comforts.

A more puzzling note for the modern reader is the heavy sensual, erotic element in Reynolds's fiction and poetry, a note for which he was often criticized by the clergy of his time. At an early age, he tried to justify this element on the grounds of social expediency, as was indicated in the quotation given above from *The Modern Writers of France*. But a reader wonders, as he works his way through *The Mysteries of London* and *The Mysteries of the Courts of London*, to say nothing of *Rosa Lambert* and *Grace Darling*, at the steady succession of voyeuristic scenes, and it is a temptation to identify this as Reynolds personally, not Reynolds the crypto-social-theorist. To

cite only one example from *The Mysteries of the Court of London*, Fourth Series: young Ashton wanders along a strand, watching the bathers emerge from their bathing machines. Reynolds describes in gloating detail the sexual antics and coquetry, the nudity on the part of the men, the parting of female garments—after which Ashton reflects in shocked horror at this scene of depravity. It is a strange combination of titillation and puritanism.

As literature Reynolds is an even stranger phenomenon. If he is to be judged by the same technical standards as general literature, he shows peculiar weaknesses and some unexpected strengths. His characters segregate themselves into good and bad, and the good are impossible. Occasionally the lower criminal types assume credibility, but after a novel has ended, no character ever remains with the reader. Reynolds's plot details, too, are tawdry, despite the fervor with which they are emitted, and are ultimately repetitious. His incredible schedule forced him to compose many purple and sentimental episodes that I am sure would have embarrassed him if he had taken the pains to consider quality rather than quantity. Obviously, Reynolds had little power of self-criticism, a defect which he shared with many of the Victorian novelists, particularly Collins.

Behind these deficiencies, however, stands what must be one of the most remarkable structural abilities in English letters. His clear linear style, which carefully avoids entanglements of thought, while preserving an exceptionally large and colorful vocabulary, carries the reader along easily. Reynolds conveys information neatly, economically and with complete clarity. He also had the ability to work through the most complex fictional paths, through the most tangled relationships and intricate developments—often incorporating extraneous stories or little essays—without losing narrative speed or the original concept of the story. A common precept given to young Victorian writers was, "Characterize like Dickens, plot like Reynolds." All of these abilities are more marked in *The Mysteries of the*

Courts of London than in much of the minor fiction. In this respect Reynolds stands head and shoulders above the other writers of bloods and penny dreadfuls and shilling shockers.

The closest counterpart to Reynolds lies not in the field of letters but in art: the French illustrator Gustave Doré, whom Reynolds probably knew through their mutual friends, the Jerrolds. Both men displayed incredible prolificness and industry, unmatched powers of visualization, the ability to handle large scapes without losing composition, social concerns, and on the side of weaknesses, a primitive element, patches of vulgarity, mawkishness and sentimentality. If Reynolds had an intellectual component which Doré lacked, Doré had a less pedestrian imagination.

Reynolds seems to have had more influence on his colleagues, however, than Doré did on his. To Reynolds primarily is due the expansion of the Gothic heart situation to fit the more modern novel of manners and ultimately the domestic novel; to Reynolds the first true "soap opera," as exemplified in the sufferings of *Rosa Lambert*, seduced daughter of a dissipated clergyman; the

first real sensational novels in the later sense, of extravagant melodramatic situations against a fairly realistic social background. Some authorities have considered Wilkie Collins the beginning of the sensational novel; others have selected Miss Braddon or Mrs. Wood. All these authors as sensationalists, however, were pallid reflections of the exuberant Reynolds. The ladies who push their husbands down wells; second wives who burn their stepchildren to death; aristocratic squires who swindle their near relatives, are sugar-coated rehashes of what Reynolds had done a decade earlier.

When nineteenth-century literature eventually achieves a necessary reunderstanding and reinterpretation, G. W. M. Reynolds will probably receive a fairly large share of attention on historical and ideological grounds. He does not have the freshness or imagination of Dickens, or the profundity of Hardy, or the disquieting perceptions of LeFanu, but it must be remembered that he was striving for something different: to reach the multitudes on their own level. In this, he succeeded.

E. F. BLEILER

WAGNER,
the Wehr-Wolf

"'THE WORDS I AM ABOUT TO UTTER ARE SOLEMNLY IMPORTANT.'" (See p. 8.)

WAGNER, THE WEHR-WOLF.

PROLOGUE.

It was the month of January, 1516.

The night was dark and tempestuous;—the thunder growled around;—the lightning flashed at short intervals;—and the wind swept furiously along, in sudden and fitful gusts.

The streams of the great Black Forest of Germany bubbled in playful melody no more, but rushed on with deafening din, mingling their torrent-roar with the wild creaking of the huge oaks, the rustling of the firs, the howling of the affrighted wolves, and the hollow voices of the storm.

The dense black clouds were driven restlessly athwart the sky; and when the vivid lightning gleamed forth with rapid and eccentric glare, it seemed as if the dark jaws of some hideous monster, floating high above, opened to vomit flame.

And as the abrupt but furious gusts of wind swept through the forest they raised strange echoes—as if the impervious mazes of that mighty wood were the abode of hideous fiends and evil spirits, who responded in shrieks, moans, and lamentations, to the fearful din of the tempest.

It was indeed an appalling sight!

An old—old man sat in his little cottage on the verge of the Black Forest.

He had numbered ninety years: his head was completely bald—his mouth was toothless—his long beard was white as snow—and his limbs were feeble and trembling.

He was alone in the world: his wife—his children—his grand-children—all his relations, in fine, *save one*—had preceded him on that long last voyage from which no traveller returns.

And that *one* was a grand-daughter—a beauteous girl of sixteen, who had hitherto been his solace and his comfort, but who had suddenly disappeared—he knew not how—a few days previously to the time when we discover him seated thus lonely in his poor cottage.

But perhaps she also was dead? An accident might have snatched her away from him, and sent her spirit to join those of her father and mother, her sisters, and her brothers, whom a terrible pestilence—*the Black Death*—hurried to the tomb a few years before?

No: the old man could not believe that his darling grand-daughter was no more—for he had sought her throughout the neighbouring district of the Black Forest, and not a trace of her was to be seen. Had she fallen down a precipice, or perished by the ruthless murderer's hand, he would have discovered her mangled corpse: had she become the prey of the ravenous wolves, certain signs of her fate would have doubtless somewhere appeared.

The sad—the chilling conviction therefore went to the old man's heart, that the only being left to solace him on earth, had deserted him; and his spirit was bowed down in despair.

Who now would prepare his food, while he tended his little flock? who was there to collect the dry branches in the forest, for the winter's fuel, while the aged shepherd watched a few sheep that he possessed? who would now spin him warm clothing to protect his weak and trembling limbs?

"Oh! Agnes," he murmured, in a tone indicative of a breaking heart, "how couldst thou have thus abandoned me? Didst thou quit the old man to follow some youthful lover, who will buoy thee up with bright hopes, and then deceive thee? O Agnes—my darling! hast thou left me to perish without a soul to close my eyes?"

It was painful how that aged shepherd wept.

Suddenly a loud knock at the door of the cottage aroused him from his painful reverie; and he hastened, as fast as his trembling limbs would permit him, to answer the summons.

He opened the door; and a tall man, apparently about forty years of age, entered the humble dwelling. His light hair would have been magnificent indeed, were it not sorely neglected; his blue eyes were naturally fine and intelligent, but fearful now to meet, so wild and wandering were their glances;—his form was tall and admirably symmetrical, but prematurely bowed by the weight of sorrow;—and his attire was of costly material, but indicative of inattention even more than it was travel-soiled.

The old man closed the door, and courteously drew a stool near the fire for the stranger who had sought in his cottage a refuge against the fury of the storm.

He also placed food before him: but the stranger touched it not—horror and dismay appearing to have taken possession of his soul.

Suddenly the thunder, which had hitherto growled at a distance, burst above the humble abode; and the wind swept by with so violent a gust, that it shook the little tenement to its foundation, and filled the neighbouring forest with strange, unearthly noises.

Then the countenance of the stranger expressed such ineffable horror, amounting to a fearful agony, that the old man was alarmed, and stretched out his hand to grasp a crucifix that hung over the chimney-piece: but his mysterious guest made a forbidding sign of so much earnestness, mingled with such proud authority, that the aged shepherd sank back into his seat without touching the sacred symbol.

The roar of the thunder past—the shrieking, whistling, gushing wind became temporarily lulled into low moans and subdued lamentations amidst the mazes of the Black Forest;—and the stranger grew more composed.

"Dost thou tremble at the storm?" inquired the old man.

"I am unhappy," was the evasive and somewhat impatient reply. "Seek not to know more of me—beware how you question me. But you, old man, are *you* happy? The traces of care seem to mingle with the wrinkles of age upon your brow."

The shepherd narrated, in brief and touching terms, the unaccountable disappearance of his much-loved grand-daughter Agnes.

The stranger listened abstractedly at first; but afterwards he appeared to reflect profoundly for several minutes.

"Your lot is a wretched one, old man," he said, at length: "if you live a few years longer, that period must be passed in solitude and cheerlessness;—if you suddenly fall ill, you must die the lingering death of famine, without a soul to place a morsel of food, or the cooling cup to your lips;—and when you shall be no more, who will follow you to the grave? There are no habitations nigh: the nearest village is half-a-day's journey distant;—and ere the peasants of that hamlet or some passing traveller might discover that the inmate of this hut had breathed his last, the wolves from the forest would have entered and mangled your corpse."

"Talk not thus!" cried the old man, with a visible shudder: then, darting a half-terrified, half-curious glance at his guest, he said, "But who are you that speak in this awful strain—this warning voice?"

Again the thunder rolled, with crashing sound above the cottage; and once more the wind swept by, laden, as it seemed, with the shrieks and groans of human beings in the agonies of death.

The stranger maintained a certain degree of composure only by means of a desperate effort; but he could not altogether subdue a wild flashing of the eyes and a ghastly change of the countenance—signs of a profoundly-felt terror.

"Again, I say, ask me not who I am!" he exclaimed, when the thunder and the gust had passed. "My soul recoils from the bare idea of pronouncing my own accursed name! But—unhappy as you see me—crushed, overwhelmed with deep affliction as you behold me—anxious, but unable, to repent for the past as I am, and filled with appalling dread for the future as I now proclaim myself to be—still is my power far, far beyond that limit which hems mortal energies within so small a sphere. Speak, old man—wouldst thou change thy condition? For to me—and to me alone of all human beings—belong the means of giving thee new life—of bestowing upon thee the vigour of youth—of rendering that stooping frame upright and strong—of restoring fire to those glazing eyes, and beauty to that wrinkled, sunken, withered countenance, of endowing thee, in a word, with a fresh tenure of existence, and making that existence sweet by the aid of treasures so vast that no extravagance can dissipate them!"

A strong though indefinite dread assailed the old man as this astounding proffer was rapidly opened, in all its alluring details, to his mind;—and various images of terror presented themselves to his imagination;—but these feelings were almost immediately dominated by a wild and ardent hope, which became the more attractive and exciting in proportion as a rapid glance at his helpless, wretched, deserted condition led him to survey the contrast between what he then was, and what, if the stranger spoke truly, he might so soon become.

The stranger saw that he had made the desired impression;—and he continued thus:—

"Give but your assent, old man,—and not only will I render thee young, handsome, and wealthy; but I will endow thy mind with an intelligence to match that proud position. Thou shalt go forth into the world to enjoy all those pleasures—those delights—and those luxuries, the names of which are even now scarcely known to thee!"

"And what is the price of this glorious boon?" asked the old man, trembling with mingled joy and terror throughout every limb.

"There are two conditions," answered the stranger, in a low, mysterious tone. "The first is, that you become the companion of my wanderings for one year and a half from the present time—until the hour of sunset on the 30th of July, 1517—when we must part for ever,—you to go whithersoever your inclinations may guide you—and I——But of that, no matter!" he added, hastily, with a sudden motion, as if of deep mental agony, and with wildly flashing eyes.

The old man shrank back in dismay from his mysterious guest: the thunder rolled again—the rude gust swept fiercely by—the dark forest rustled awfully—and the stranger's torturing feelings were evidently prolonged by the voices of the storm.

A pause ensued; and the silence was at length broken by the old man, who said, in a hollow and tremulous tone, "To the first condition I would willingly accede. But the second?"

"That you prey upon the human race, whom I hate—because of all the world I alone am so deeply, so terribly accurst!" was the ominously fearful yet only dimly significant reply.

The old man shook his head—scarcely comprehending the words of his guest, and yet daring not to ask to be more enlightened.

"Listen!" said the stranger, in a hasty, but impressive voice. "I require a companion—one who has no human ties, and who will minister to my caprices,—who will devote himself wholly and solely to watch me in my dark hours, and endeavour to recall me back to enjoyment and pleasure,—who, when he shall be acquainted with

my power, will devise new means in which to exercise it for the purpose of conjuring up those scenes of enchantment and delight that may for a season win me away from thought. Such a companion do I need for a period of one year and a half; and you are, of all men, the best suited to my design. But the Spirit whom I must invoke to effect the promised change in thee, and by whose aid you can be given back to youth and comeliness, will demand some fearful sacrifice at your hands. And the nature of that sacrifice—the nature of the condition to be imposed—I can well divine!"

"Name the sacrifice—name the condition!" cried the old man, eagerly. "I am so miserable—so spirit-broken—so totally without hope in this world, that I greedily long to enter upon that new existence which you promise me! Say, then—what is the condition?"

"That you prey upon the human race, whom *he* hates as well as I," answered the stranger.

"Again those awful words!" ejaculated the old man, casting trembling glances around him.

"Yes—again those words!" echoed the mysterious guest, looking with his fierce, burning eyes into the glazed orbs of the aged shepherd. "And now learn their import!" he continued, in a solemn tone. "Knowest thou not that there is a belief in many parts of our native land, that at particular seasons certain doomed men throw off the human shape, and take that of ravenous wolves?"

"Oh! yes—yes—I have indeed heard of those strange legends in which the Wehr-Wolf is represented in such appalling colours!" exclaimed the old man, a terrible suspicion crossing his mind. "'Tis said that at sunset on the last day of every month the mortal to whom belongs the destiny of the Wehr-Wolf, must change his natural form for that of the savage animal; in which horrible shape he must remain until the moment when the morrow's sun dawns upon the earth."

"The legend that told thee this, spoke truly," said the stranger. "And now dost thou comprehend the condition which must be imposed upon thee?"

"I do—I do!" murmured the old man, with a fearful shudder. "But he who accepts that condition makes a compact with the Evil One, and thereby endangers his immortal soul!"

"Not so," was the reply. "There is naught involved in this condition which——But hesitate not," added the stranger, hastily: "I have not time to waste in bandying words. Consider all I offer you: in another hour you shall be another man!"

"I accept the boon—and on the conditions stipulated!" exclaimed the shepherd.

"'Tis well, Wagner——"

"What! you know my name!" cried the old man.

"And yet, meseem, I did not mention it to thee."

"Canst thou not already perceive that I am no common mortal?" demanded the stranger, bitterly. "And who I am—and whence I derive my power,—all, all shall be revealed to thee so soon as the bond is formed that must link us for eighteen months together! In the meantime, await me here!"

And the mysterious stranger quitted the cottage abruptly, and plunged into the depths of the Black Forest.

One hour elapsed ere he returned,—one mortal hour, during which Wagner sat bowed over his miserably scanty fire, dreaming of pleasure—youth—riches—and enjoyment;—converting, in imagination, the myriad sparks which shone upon the extinguishing embers into piles of gold, and allowing his now uncurbed fancy to change the one single room of the wretched hovel into a splendid saloon, surrounded by resplendent mirrors and costly hangings.—while the untasted fare spread for the stranger on the rude fir-table, became transformed, in his idea, into a magnificent banquet laid out on a board glittering with plate, lustrous with innumerable lamps, and surrounded by an atmosphere fragrant with the most exquisite perfumes.

The return of the stranger awoke the old man from this charming dream, during which he had never once thought of the conditions whereby he was to purchase the complete realization of the vision.

"Oh! what a glorious reverie you have dissipated!" exclaimed Wagner. "Fulfil but one tenth part of that delightful dream——"

"I will fulfil it all!" interrupted the stranger; then, producing a small phial from the bosom of his doublet, he said, "Drink!"

The old man seized the bottle, and greedily drained it to the dregs.

He immediately fell back upon the seat, in a state of complete lethargy.

But it lasted not for many minutes; and when he awoke again, he experienced new and extraordinary sensations. His limbs were vigorous—his form was upright as an arrow—his eyes, for many years dim and failing, seemed gifted with the sight of an eagle—his head was warm with a natural covering—not a wrinkle remained upon his brow nor on his cheeks—and, as he smiled with mingled wonderment and delight, the parting lips revealed a set of brilliant teeth. And it seemed, too, as if by one magic touch, the long-fading tree of his intellect had suddenly burst into full foliage; and every cell of his brain was instantaneously stored with an amount of knowledge, the accumulation of which stunned him for an instant, and in the next appeared as familiar to him as if he had never been without it.

"Oh! great and powerful being, whosoever thou art!" exclaimed Wagner, in the full melodious voice of a young man of twenty-one, "how can I manifest to thee my deep—my boundless gratitude for this boon which thou hast conferred upon me?"

"By thinking no more of thy lost grand-child Agnes, but by preparing to follow me whither I shall now lead thee," replied the stranger.

"Command me: I am ready to obey in all things," cried Wagner. "But one word ere we set forth——who art thou, wondrous man?"

"Henceforth I have no secrets from thee, Wagner," was the answer, while the stranger's eyes gleamed with unearthly lustre; then, bending forward, he whispered a few words in the other's ear.

Wagner started with a cold and fearful shudder as if at some appalling announcement; but he uttered not a word of reply—for his master beckoned him imperiously away from the humble cottage.

CHAPTER I.

THE DEATH-BED.—THE OATH.—THE LAST INJUNCTIONS.

OUR tale commences in the middle of the month of November, 1520, and at the hour of midnight.

In a magnificently-furnished chamber, belonging to one of the largest mansions of Florence, a nobleman lay at the point of death.

The light of the lamp suspended to the ceiling played upon the ghastly countenance of the dying man, the stern expression of whose features was not even mitigated by the fears and uncertainties attendant on the hour of dissolution.

He was about forty-eight years of age, and had evidently been wondrous handsome in his youth; for though the frightful pallor of death was already upon his cheeks, and the fire of his large black eyes was dimmed with the ravages of a long-endured disease, still the faultless outlines of the aquiline profile remained unimpaired.

The most superficial observer might have read the aristocratic pride of his soul in the haughty curl of his short upper lip,—the harshness of his domineering character in the lines that marked his forehead,—and the cruel sternness of his disposition in the expression of his entire countenance.

Without absolutely scowling as he lay on that bed of death, his features were characterized by an inexorable severity which seemed to denote the predominant influence of some intense passion—some evil sentiment deeply rooted in his mind.

Two persons leant over the couch to which death was so rapidly approaching.

One was a lady of about twenty-five: the other was a youth of nineteen.

The former was eminently beautiful: but her countenance was marked with much of that severity—that determination—and even of that sternness which characterized the dying nobleman. Indeed, a single glance was sufficient to show that they stood in the close relationship of father and daughter.

Her long, black, glossy hair now hung dishevelled over the shoulders that were left partially bare by the hastily negligence with which she had thrown on a loose wrapper:—and those shoulders were of the most dazzling whiteness.

The wrapper was confined by a broad band at the waist; and the slight drapery set off, rather than concealed, the rich contours of a form of matured but admirable symmetry.

Tall, graceful, and elegant, she united easy motion with fine proportion; thus possessing the lightness of the Sylph and the luxuriant fulness of the Hebe.

Her countenance was alike expressive of intellectuality and strong passions. Her large black eyes were full of fire; and their glances seemed to penetrate the soul. Her nose, of the fine aquiline development,—her lips, narrow, but red and pouting, with the upper one short and slightly projecting over the lower, and her small, delicately rounded chin, indicated both decision and sensuality: but the insolent gaze of the libertine would have quailed beneath the look of sovereign hauteur which flashed from those brilliant eagle eyes.

In a word, she appeared to be a woman well adapted to command the admiration—receive the homage—excite the passions—and yet repel the insolence of the opposite sex.

But those appearances were to some degree deceitful: for never was homage offered to her—never was she courted nor flattered.

Ten years previously to the time of which we are writing—and when she was only fifteen—the death of her mother, under strange and mysterious circumstances, as it was generally reported, made such a terrible impression on her mind, that she hovered for months on the verge of dissolution; and when the physician who attended upon her communicated to her father the fact that her life was at length beyond danger, that assurance was followed by the sad and startling declaration, that she had for ever lost the sense of hearing and the power of speech.

No wonder, then, that homage was never paid nor adulation offered to Nisida—the deaf and dumb daughter of the proud Count of Riverola!

Those who were intimate with this family ere the occurrence of that sad event,—especially the physician, Dr. Duras, who had attended upon the mother in her last moments, and on the daughter during her illness,—declared that, up to the period when the malady assailed her, Nisida was a sweet, amiable, and retiring girl; but she had evidently been fearfully changed by the terrible affliction which that malady left behind. For if she could no longer express herself in words, her eyes darted lightnings upon the unhappy menials who had the misfortune to incur her displeasure; and her lips would quiver with the violence of concentrated passions, at the most trifling neglect or error of which the female dependants immediately attached to her own person might happen to be guilty.

Towards her father she often manifested a strange ebullition of anger—bordering even on inveterate spite, when he offended her; and yet, singular though it were, the Count was devotedly attached to his daughter. He frequently declared that, afflicted as she was, he was proud of her; for he was wont to behold in her flashing eyes—her curling lip—and her haughty air, the reflection of his own proud—his own inexorable spirit.

The youth of nineteen to whom we have alluded, was Nisida's brother; and much as the father appeared to dote upon the daughter, was the son proportionately disliked by that stern and despotic man.

Perhaps this want of affection—or rather this complete aversion—on the part of the Count of Riverola towards the young Francisco, owed its origin to the total discrepancy of character existing between the father and son. Francisco was as amiable, generous hearted, frank, and agreeable as his sire was austere, stern, reserved, and tyrannical. The youth was also unlike his father in personal appearance, his hair being of a rich brown, his eyes of a soft blue, and the general expression of his countenance indicating the fairest and most endearing qualities which can possibly characterize human nature.

We must, however, observe, before we pursue our narrative, that Nisida imitated not her father in her conduct towards Francisco;—for she loved him—she loved him with the most ardent affection—such an affection as a sister seldom manifests towards a brother. It was rather the attachment of a mother for her child; inasmuch as Nisida studied all his comforts—watched over him, as it were, with the tenderest solicitude—was happy when he was present—melancholy when he was absent,—and seemed to be constantly racking her imagination to devise new means to afford him pleasure.

To treat Francisco with the least neglect was to arouse the wrath of a Fury in the breast of Nisida; and every unkind look which the Count inflicted upon his son, was sure, if perceived by the daughter, to evoke the terrible lightnings of her brilliant eyes.

Such were the three persons whom we have thus minutely described to our readers.

The Count had been ill for some weeks at the time when this chapter opens; but on the night which marks that commencement, Dr. Duras had deemed it his duty to warn the nobleman that he had not many hours to live.

The dying man had accordingly desired that his children might be summoned; and when they entered the apartment, the physician and the priest were requested to withdraw.

Francisco now stood on one side of the bed, and Nisida on the other; while the Count collected his remaining strength to address his last injunctions to his son.

"Francisco," he said, in a cold tone, "I have little inclination to speak at any great length; but the words I am about to utter are solemnly important. I believe you entertain the most sincere and earnest faith in that symbol which now lies beneath your hand."

"This crucifix!" ejaculated the young man; "Oh! yes, my dear father—it is the emblem of that faith which teaches us how to live and die."

"Then take it up—press it to your lips—and swear to obey the instructions which I am about to give you," said the Count.

Francisco did as he was desired; and, although tears were streaming from his eyes, he exclaimed, in an emphatic manner, "I swear most solemnly to fulfil your commands, my dear father—so confident am I that you will enjoin nothing that involves aught dishonourable!"

"Spare your qualifications," cried the Count, sternly: "and swear without reserve—or expect my dying curse, rather than my blessing."

"Ah! my dear father," ejaculated the youth, with intense anguish of soul; "talk not of so dreadful a thing as bequeathing me your dying curse! I swear to fulfil your injunctions—without reserve!"

And he kissed the holy symbol.

"You act wisely," said the Count, fixing his glazing eyes upon the handsome countenance of the young man, who now awaited in breathless suspense, a communication thus solemnly prefaced. "This key," continued the nobleman, taking one from beneath his pillow as he spoke, "belongs to the door in yonder corner of the apartment."

"That door which is never opened!" exclaimed Francisco, casting an anxious glance in the direction indicated.

"Who told you that the door was never opened?" demanded the Count, sternly.

"I have heard the servants remark——" began the youth, in a timid but still frank and candid manner.

"Then, when I am no more, see that you put an end to such impertinent gossiping," said the nobleman, impatiently; "and you will be the better convinced of the propriety of thus acting as soon as you have learnt the nature of my injunctions. That door," he continued, "communicates with a small closet, which is accessible by no other means. Now my wish—my command is this:—Upon the day of your marriage, whenever such an event may occur—and I suppose you do not intend to remain unwedded all your life—I enjoin you to open the door of that closet. You must be accompanied by your bride—and by no other living soul. I also desire that this may be done with the least possible delay after the matrimonial ceremony,—the very day—the very morning —within the very hour after you quit the church. That closet contains the means of elucidating a mystery profoundly connected with me—with you—with the family, —a mystery, the development of which may prove of incalculable service alike to yourself and to her who may share your title and your wealth. But should you never marry, then must the closet remain unvisited by you; nor need you trouble yourself concerning the eventual discovery of the secret which it contains, by any persons into whose hands the mansion may fall at your death. It is also my wish that your sister should remain in complete ignorance of the instructions I am now giving you. Alas! poor girl—she cannot hear the words which fall from my lips: neither shall you communicate their import to her by writing, nor by the language of the fingers. And remember that while I bestow upon you my blessing —my dying blessing,—may that blessing become a withering curse—the curse of hell upon you—if in any way you violate one tittle of the injunctions which I have now given you."

"My dearest father," replied the weeping youth, who had listened with the most profound attention to these extraordinary commands; "I would not for worlds act contrary to your wishes. Singular as they appear to me, they shall be fulfilled to the very letter."

He received from his father's hands the mysterious key, which he secured about his person.

"You will find," resumed the Count, after a brief pause, "that I have left the whole of my property to you. At the same time my will specifies certain conditions relative to your sister Nisida, for whom I have made due provision only in the case—which is, alas! almost in defiance of every hope!—of her recovery from that dreadful affliction which renders her so completely dependent upon your kindness."

"Dearest father, you know how sincerely I am attached to my sister—how devoted she is to me——"

"Enough—enough!" cried the Count: and, overcome by the efforts he had made to deliver his last injunctions, he fell back insensible on his pillow.

Nisida, who had retained her face buried in her hands during the whole time occupied in the above conversation, happened to look up at that moment: and perceiving the condition of her father, she made a hasty sign to Francisco to summon the physician and the priest from the room to which they had retired.

This commission was speedily executed; and in a few minutes the physician and the priest were once more by the side of the dying noble.

But the instant that Dr. Duras—who was a venerable looking man of about sixty years of age—approached the bed, he darted, unseen by Francisco, a glance of earnest inquiry towards Nisida, who responded by one of profound meaning, shaking her head gently, but in a manner expressive of deep melancholy, at the same time.

The physician appeared to be astonished at the negative thus conveyed by the beautiful mute; and he even manifested a sign of angry impatience.

But Nisida threw upon him a look of so imploring a nature, that his temporary vexation yielded to a feeling of immense commiseration for that afflicted creature; and he gave her to understand by another rapid glance, that her prayer was accorded.

This interchange of signs of such deep mystery scarcely occupied a moment, and was altogether unobserved by Francisco.

Doctor Duras proceeded to administer restoratives to the dying nobleman—but in vain!

The Count had fallen into a lethargic stupor, which lasted until four in the morning, when his spirit passed gently away.

The moment Francisco and Nisida became aware that they were orphans, they threw themselves into each other's arms, and renewed by that tender embrace the tacit compact of sincere affection which had ever existed between them.

Francisco's tears flowed freely: but Nisida did not weep!

A strange—an almost portentous light shone in her brilliant black eyes; and though that wild gleaming denoted powerful emotion, yet it shed no lustre upon the unfathomable depths of her soul—afforded no clue to the real nature of those agitated feelings.

Suddenly withdrawing himself from his sister's arms, Francisco conveyed to her by the language of the fingers the following tender sentiment:—"You have lost a father, beloved Nisida, but you have a devoted and affectionate brother left to you."

And Nisida replied, through the same medium, "Your happiness, dearest brother, has ever been my only study —and shall continue so."

The physician and Father Marco, the priest, now advanced, and taking the brother and sister by the hands, led them from the chamber of death.

"Kind friends," said Francisco, now Count of Riverola, "I understand you. You would withdraw my sister from a scene too mournful to contemplate. Alas! it is hard to lose a father; but especially so at my age, inexperienced as I am in the ways of the world!"

"The world is indeed made up of thorny paths and devious ways, my dear young friend," returned the physician; "but a stout heart and integrity of purpose will ever be found faithful guides. The more exalted and the wealthier the individual, the greater the temptations he will have to encounter. Reflect upon this, Francisco: it is advice which I, as an old—indeed, the oldest friend of your family—take the liberty to offer."

With these words, the venerable physician wrung the hands of the brother and sister, and hurried from the house, followed by the priest.

The orphans embraced each other, and retired to their respective apartments.

CHAPTER II.

NISIDA.—THE MYSTERIOUS CLOSET.

THE room to which Nisida withdrew, between four and five o'clock on that mournful winter's morning, was one of a suite entirely appropriated to her own use.

This suite consisted of three apartments, communicating with each other, and all furnished in the elegant and tasteful manner of that age.

The innermost of the three rooms was used by Nisida as her bed-chamber; and when she now entered it, a young girl, beautiful as an angel, but dressed in the

—her proud forehead supported on her delicate hand—her lips apart, and revealing the pearly teeth—her lids with their long black fringes half-closed over the brilliant eyes—and her fine form cast in voluptuous abandonment upon the soft cushions of the chair,—she indeed seemed a magnificent creature!

But when, suddenly awaking from that profound meditation, she started from her seat with flashing eyes —heaving bosom—and an expression of countenance denoting a fixed determination to accomplish some deed from which her better feelings vainly bade her to abstain; when she drew her tall—her even majestic form

"POINTED TO THE PAPER IN A SIGNIFICANT MANNER." (See p. 11.)

attire of a dependant, instantly rose from a seat near the fire that blazed on the hearth, and cast a respectful but inquiring glance towards her mistress.

Nisida gave her to understand, by a sign, that all was over.

The girl started—as if surprised that her lady indicated so little grief; but the latter motioned her with an impatient gesture to leave the room.

When Flora—such was the name of the dependant—had retired, Nisida threw herself into a large arm-chair near the fire, and immediately became buried in a deep reverie.

With her splendid hair flowing upon her white shoulders

up to its full height, the drapery shadowing forth every contour of undulating bust and exquisitely modelled limb,—while her haughty lip curled in contempt of any consideration save her own indomitable will,—she appeared rather a heroine capable of leading an Amazonian army, than a woman to whom the sighing swain might venture to offer up the incense of love.

There was something awful in the aspect of this mysterious being,—something ineffably grand and imposing in her demeanour,—as she thus suddenly rose from her almost recumbent posture, and burst into the attitude of a resolute and energetic woman.

Drawing the wrapper around her form, she lighted a

lamp, and was about to quit the chamber, when her eyes suddenly encountered the mild and benignant glance which the portrait of a lady appeared to cast upon her.

This portrait, which hung against the wall precisely opposite to the bed, represented a woman about thirty years of age,—a woman of beauty much in the same style as that of Nisida, but not marred by anything approaching to a sternness of expression. On the contrary, if an angel had looked through those mild black eyes, their glances could not have been endowed with a holier kindness; the smiles of good spirits could not be more plaintively sweet than those which the artist had made to play upon the lips of that portrait.

Yet in spite of this discrepancy between the expression of Nisida's countenance and that of the lady who had formed the subject of the picture, it was not difficult to perceive a certain physical likeness between the two; nor will the reader be surprised when we state that Nisida was now gazing on the portrait of her deceased mother!

And that gaze—oh! how intent—how earnest—how enthusiastic it was! It manifested something more than love—something more impassioned and ardent than the affection which a daughter might exhibit towards even a living mother: it showed a complete devotion—an adoration—a worship!

Long and fixedly did Nisida gaze upon that portrait: till suddenly from her eyes, which shot such burning glances, gushed a torrent of tears.

Then probably fearful lest this weakness on her part might impair the resolution necessary to execute the purpose which she had in view—Nisida dashed away the tears from her long lashes, and hastily quitted the room.

Having traversed the two other apartments of her own suite, she cast a searching glance along the passage which she now entered; and, satisfied that none of the domestics were about,—for it was not yet six o'clock on that winter's morning,—she hastened to the end of the corridor.

The lamp flared with the speed at which she walked; and its uncertain light enhanced the pallor that now covered her countenance.

At the bottom of the passage she cautiously opened the door, and entered the room with which it communicated.

This was the sleeping apartment of her brother.

A single glance convinced her that he was wrapt in the arms of slumber.

He slept soundly too—for he was wearied with the vigil which he had passed by the death-bed of his father—worn out also by the thousand conflicting and unsatisfactory conjectures that the last instructions of his parent had naturally excited in his mind.

He had not, however, been asleep a quarter of an hour when Nisida stole, in the manner described, into his chamber.

A smile of mingled joy and triumph animated her countenance, and a carnation tinge flushed her cheeks, when she found he was fast locked in the embrace of slumber.

Without a moment's hesitation, she examined his doublet, and clutched the key that his father had given to him scarcely six hours before.

Then, light as the fawn, she left the room.

Having retraced her steps half-way up the passage, she paused at the door of the chamber in which the corpse of her father lay.

For an instant—a single instant she seemed to revolt from the prosecution of her design: then, with a stern contraction of the brows, and an imperious curl of the lip—as if she said within herself "Fool that I am to hesitate!"—she entered the room.

Without fear—without compunction, she approached the bed. The body was laid out: stretched in its winding-sheet, stiff and stark did it seem to repose on the mattress—the countenance rendered more ghastly than even death could make it, by the white band which tied up the under-jaw.

The nurses who had thus disposed the corpse, had retired to snatch a few hours of rest; and there was consequently no spy upon Nisida's actions.

With a fearless step she advanced towards the closet—the mysterious closet relative to which such strange injunctions had been given!

CHAPTER III.

THE MANUSCRIPT.—FLORA FRANCATELLI.

NISIDA'S hand trembled not as she placed the key in the lock: but when it turned, and she knew that in another instant she might open that door if she chose, she compressed her lips firmly together—she called all her courage to her aid,—for she seemed to imagine that it was necessary to prepare herself to behold something frightfully appalling.

And now again her cheeks were deadly pale; but the light that burned in her eyes was brilliant in the extreme.

White as was her countenance, her large black orbs appeared to shine—to glow—to burn, as if with a violent fever.

Advancing the lamp with her left hand, she half-opened the door of the closet with her right.

Then she plunged her glances with rapidity into the recess.

But, holy God! what a start that courageous, bold and energetic woman gave,—a start as if the cold hand of a corpse had been suddenly thrust forth to grasp her.

And, oh! what horror convulsed her countenance—while her lips were compressed as tightly as if they were an iron vice!

Rapid and instantly recoiling as that glance was, it had nevertheless revealed to her an object of interest as well as of horror; for, with eyes now averted, she seized something within the closet, and thrust it into her bosom.

Then, hastily closing the door, she retraced her way to her brother's chamber.

He still slept soundly: Nisida returned the key to the pocket whence she had taken it, and hurried back to her own room, from which she had scarcely been absent five minutes.

And did she now seek her couch? did she repair to rest?

No:—that energetic woman experienced not weariness—yielded not to lassitude.

Carefully bolting the door of her innermost chamber, she seated herself again in the arm-chair, and drew from her bosom the object which she had taken from the mysterious closet.

It was a manuscript, consisting of several small slips of paper, somewhat closely written upon.

The writing was doubtless familiar to her: for she paused not to consider its nature, but greedily addressed herself to the study of the meaning which it conveyed.

And of terrible import seemed that manuscript to be: for while Nisida read, her countenance underwent many and awful changes: and her bosom heaved convulsively at one instant, while at another it remained motionless, as if respiration were suspended.

At length the perusal was completed; and grinding her teeth with demoniac rage, she threw the manuscript upon the floor. But at the same moment her eyes, which she cast wildly about her, caught the mild and benign countenance of her mother's portrait; and, as oil stills the fury of the boiling billows, did the influence of that picture calm in an instant the tremendous emotions of Nisida's soul.

Tears burst from her eyes; and she suddenly relapsed from the incarnate fiend into the subdued woman.

Then stooping down, she picked up the papers that lay scattered on the floor; but as she did so she averted her looks, with loathing and disgust, as much as possible from the pages that her hands collected almost at random.

And now another idea struck her—an idea the propriety of which evidently warred against her inclination.

She was not a woman of mere impulses—although she often acted speedily after a thought had entered her brain. But she was wondrously quick at weighing all her reasons for or against the suggestions of her imagination; and thus, to any one who was not acquainted with her character, she might frequently appear to obey the first dictates of her impetuous passions.

Scarcely three minutes after the new idea had struck her, her resolution was fixed.

Once more concealing the papers in her bosom, she repaired with the lamp to her brother's room—purloined the key a second time—hastened to the chamber of death—opened the closet again—and again sustained the shock of a single glance at its horrors, as she returned the manuscript to the place whence she had originally taken it.

Then, having once more retraced her way to Francisco's chamber, she restored the key to the folds of his doublet—for he continued to sleep soundly; and Nisida succeeded in regaining her own apartments just in time to avoid the observation of the domestics, who were now beginning to move about.

Nisida sought her couch, and slept until nearly ten

o'clock, when she awoke with a start—doubtless caused by some unpleasant dream.

Having ascertained the hour by reference to a water-clock, or clepsydra, which stood on the marble pedestal near the head of the bed, she rose—unlocked the door of her apartment—rang a silver bell—and then returned to her bed.

In a few moments Flora, who had been waiting in the adjoining room, entered the chamber.

Nisida, on regaining her couch had turned her face towards the wall, and was, therefore, unable to perceive anything that took place in the apartment.

The mere mention of such a circumstance would be trivial in the extreme, were it not necessary to record it in consequence of an event which now occurred.

For, as Flora advanced into the room, her eyes fell on a written paper that lay immediately beneath the arm-chair; and conceiving, from its appearance, that it had not been thrown down on purpose, as it was in no wise crushed nor torn, she mechanically picked it up and placed it on the table.

She proceeded to arrange the toilet-table of her mistress, preparatory to that lady's rising; and, while she is thus employed, we will endeavour to make our readers a little better acquainted with her than they can possibly yet be.

Flora Francatelli was the orphan daughter of parents who had suddenly been reduced from a condition of affluence to a condition of extreme poverty. Signor Francatelli could not survive this blow: he died of a broken heart;—and his wife shortly afterwards followed him to the tomb—also the victim of grief. They left two children behind them: Flora, who was then an infant, and a little boy named Alessandro, who was five years old. The orphans were entirely dependent upon the kindness of a maiden aunt—their departed father's sister. This relative, whose name was, of course, also Francatelli, performed a mother's part towards the children; and deprived herself not only of comforts, but at times even of necessaries in order that they should not want. Father Marco, a priest belonging to one of the numerous monasteries of Florence, and who was a worthy man, took compassion upon this little family; and not only devoted his attention to teach the orphans to read and write—great accomplishments amongst the middle classes in those days—but also procured from a fund at the disposal of his abbot, certain pecuniary assistance for the aunt.

The care which this good relative took of the orphans, and the kindness of Father Marco, were well rewarded by the veneration and attachment which Alessandro and Flora manifested towards them. When Alessandro had numbered eighteen summers, he was fortunate enough to procure, through the interest of Father Marco, the situation of secretary to a Florentine noble who was charged with a diplomatic mission to the Ottoman Porte; and the young man proceeded to Leghorn, whence he embarked for Constantinople, attended by the prayers, blessings, hopes of the aunt and sister, and of the good priest, whom he left behind.

Two years after his departure, Father Marco obtained for Flora a situation about the person of the Lady Nisida; for the monk was confessor to the family of Riverola, and his influence was sufficient to secure that place for the young maiden.

We have already said that Flora was sweetly beautiful. Her large blue eyes were fringed with dark lashes, which gave them an expression of the most melting softness: her dark brown hair, arranged in modest bands, seemed of even a deeper hue when contrasted with the brilliant and transparent clearness of her complexion; and though her forehead was white and polished as alabaster, yet the rose-tint of health was upon her cheeks, and her lips had the rich redness of coral. Her nose was perfectly straight; her teeth were white and even; and the graceful arching of her swan-like neck imparted something of nobility to her tall, sylph-like, and exquisitely-proportioned figure.

Retiring and bashful in her manners, every look which fell from her eyes—every smile which wreathed her lips, denoted the chaste purity of her soul. With all her readiness to oblige—with all her anxiety to do her duty as she ought, she frequently incurred the anger of the irascible Nisida: but Flora supported those manifestations of wrath with the sweetest resignation, because the excellence of her disposition taught her to make every allowance for one so afflicted as her mistress.

Such was the young maiden whom the nature of the present tale compels us thus particularly to introduce to our readers.

Having carefully arranged the boudoir, so that its strict neatness might be welcome to her mistress when that lady chose to rise from her couch, Flora seated herself near the table, and gave way to her reflections.

She thought of her aunt, who inhabited a neat little cottage on the banks of the Arno, and whom she was usually permitted to visit every Sabbath afternoon: she thought of her absent brother, who was still in the service of the Florentine Envoy to the Ottoman Porte, where that diplomatist was detained by the tardiness that marked the negotiations with which he was charged;—and then she thought—thought, too, with an involuntary sigh—of Francisco, Count of Riverola.

She perceived that she had sighed—and, without knowing precisely wherefore, she was angry with herself.

Anxious to turn the channel of her meditations in another direction, she rose from her seat to examine the clepsydra. That movement caused her eyes to fall upon the paper which she had picked up a quarter of an hour previously.

In spite of herself, the image of Francisco was still uppermost in her thoughts; and in the contemplative vein thus encouraged, her eyes lingered, unwittingly—and through no base motive of curiosity—upon the writing which that paper contained.

Thus she actually found herself reading the first four lines of the writing, before she recollected what she was doing.

The act was a purely mechanical one, which not the most rigid moralist could blame.

And had the contents of the paper been of no interest, she might even have continued to read more in that same abstracted mood;—but those four first lines were of a nature which sent a thrilling sensation of horror through her entire frame; the feeling terminating with an icy coldness at the heart.

She shuddered without starting—shuddered as she stood;—and not even a murmur escaped her lips.

The intenseness of that sudden pang of horror deprived her alike of speech and motion during the instant that it lasted.

And those lines, which produced so strange an impression upon the young maiden, ran thus:—

"*merciless scalpel hacked and hewed away at the still almost palpitating flesh of the murdered man, in whose breast the dagger remained deeply buried,—a ferocious joy—a savage hyena-like triumph——*"

Flora read no more: she could not even if she had wished.

For a minute she remained rooted to the spot: then she threw herself into the chair, bewildered and dismayed at the terrible words which had met her eyes.

She thought that the handwriting was not unknown to her; but she could not recollect whose it was. One fact was, however, certain—it was not the writing of her mistress.

She was still musing upon the horrible and mysterious contents of the paper, when Nisida rose from her couch.

Acknowledging with a slight nod of the head the respectful salutation of her attendant, she hastily slipped on a loose wrapper, and seated herself in the arm-chair which Flora had just abandoned.

The young girl then proceeded to comb out the long raven hair of her mistress. But this occupation was most rudely interrupted; for Nisida's eyes suddenly fell upon the manuscript page on the table; and then she started up in a paroxysm of mingled rage and alarm.

Having assured herself by a second glance that it was indeed a portion of the writings which had produced so strange an effect upon her a few hours previously, she turned abruptly towards Flora: and imperiously confronting the young maiden, pointed to the paper in a significant manner.

Flora immediately indicated by a sign that she had found it on the floor, beneath the arm-chair.

"And you have read it!" was the accusation which, with wonderful rapidity, Nisida conveyed by means of her fingers—fixing her piercing, penetrating eyes on Flora's countenance at the same time.

The young maiden scorned the idea of a falsehood; and, although she perceived that her reply would prove far from agreeable to her mistress, she unhesitatingly admitted, by the language of the hands, "I read the four first lines, and no more."

A crimson glow instantly suffused the face, neck, shoulders, and bosom of Nisida; but, instantly compressing her lips—as was her wont when under the influence of her boiling passions—she turned her flashing eyes once more upon the paper, to ascertain which leaf of the manuscript it was.

That rapid glance revealed to her the import—the dread, but profoundly mysterious import—of the first four lines on that page; and again darting her soul-searching looks upon the trembling Flora, she demanded, by the rapid play of her delicate, taper fingers, "Will you swear that you read no more?"

"As I hope for salvation!" was the symbolic answer.

The penetrating, imperious glance of Nisida dwelt long upon the maiden's countenance; but no sinister expression—no suspicious change on that fair and candid face contradicted the assertion which she had made.

"I believe you: but beware how you breathe to a living soul a word of what you *did* read!"

Such was the injunction which Nisida now conveyed by her usual means of communication; and Flora signified implicit obedience.

Nisida then secured the page of writing in her jewel-casket; and the details of the toilette were resumed.

CHAPTER IV.

THE FUNERAL.—THE INTERRUPTION OF THE CEREMONY.

EIGHT days after the death of the Count of Riverola, the funeral took place.

The obsequies were celebrated at night, with all the pomp observed amongst noble families on such occasions. The church in which the corpse was buried, was hung with black cloth; and even the innumerable wax tapers which burnt upon the altar and around the coffin, failed to diminish the lugubrious aspect of the scene.

At the head of the bier stood the youthful heir of Riverola; his pale countenance of even feminine beauty contrasting strangely with the mourning garments which he wore, and his eyes bent upon the dark chasm that formed the family-vault into which the remains of his sire were about to be lowered.

Around the coffin stood Dr. Duras, and other male friends of the deceased: for the females of the family were not permitted, by the custom of the age and the religion, to be present on occasions of this kind.

It was eleven o'clock at night; and the weather without was stormy and tempestuous.

The wind moaned through the long aisles, raising strange and ominous echoes, and making the vast folds of sable drapery wave slowly backwards and forwards, as if agitated by unseen hands. A few spectators, standing in the background, appeared like grim figures on a black tapestry; and the gleam of the wax tapers, oscillating on their countenances, made them seem death-like and ghastly.

From time to time the shrill wail of the shrieking owl, and the flapping of its wings against the diamond-paned windows of the church, added to the awful gloom of the funeral scene.

And now suddenly arose the chant of the priests—the parting hymn for the dead!

Francisco wept: for though his father had never manifested towards him an affection of the slightest endearing nature, yet the disposition of the young Count was excellent: and, when he gazed upon the coffin, he remembered not the coldness with which its inmate in his lifetime had treated him—he thought only of a parent whom he had lost, and whose remains were there!

And truly on the brink of the tomb no animosity should ever find a resting-place in the human heart. Though elsewhere men yield to the influence of their passions and their feelings, in pursuing each his separate interests,—though, in the great world, we push and jostle each other, as if the earth was not large enough to allow us to follow our separate ways,—yet when we meet around the grave to consign a fellow-creature to his last resting place, let peace and holy forgivenesss occupy our souls. There let the clash of interest and the war of jealousies be forgotten; and let us endeavour to persuade ourselves, that, as all the conflicting pursuits of life must terminate at this points at last, so should our feelings converge to the one focus of amenity and Christian love. And, after all, how many who have considered themselves to be antagonists, must, during a moment of solemn reflection, become convinced that when toiling in the great workshop of the world, they have been engaged, in unconscious fraternity, in building up the same fabric!

The priests were in the midst of their solemn chant—a deathlike silence and complete immovability prevailed amongst the mourners and the spectators—and the wind was moaning beneath the vaulted roofs, awaking those strange and tomb-like sounds which are only heard in large churches—when light but rushing footsteps were heard on the marble pavement; and in another minute a female, not clothed in a mourning garb, but splendidly attired as for a festival, precipitated herself towards the bier.

There her strength suddenly seemed to be exhausted; and, with a piercing scream, she sank senseless on the cold stones.

The chant of the priests was immediately stilled, and Francisco, hurrying forward, raised the female in his arms, while Dr. Duras asked for water to sprinkle on her countenance.

Over her head the stranger wore a white veil of rich material, which was fastened above her brow by a single diamond of unusual size and of brilliant lustre. When the veil was drawn aside, shining auburn tresses were seen depending in wanton luxuriance over shoulders of alabaster whiteness: a beautiful but deadly pale countenance was revealed; and a splendid purple velvet dress delineated the soft and flowing outlines of a form modelled to the most perfect symmetry.

She seemed to be about twenty years of age,—in the full splendour of loveliness, and endowed with charms which presented to the gaze of those around a very incarnation of the ideal beauty which forms the theme of raptured poets.

And now, as the vacillating and uncertain light of the wax candles beamed upon her, as she lay senseless in the arms of the Count of Riverola, her pale, placid face appeared that of a classic marble statue; but nothing could surpass the splendid effects which the funereal tapers produced on the rich redundancy of her hair, which seemed dark where the shadow rested on it, but glittering as with a bright glory where the lustre played on its shining masses.

In spite of the solemnity of the place and the occasion, the mourners were struck by the dazzling beauty of that young female, who had thus appeared so strangely amongst them: but respect still retained at a distance those persons who were merely present from curiosity to witness the obsequies of one of the proudest nobles of Florence.

At length the lady opened her large hazel eyes, and glanced wildly around, a quick spasm passing like an electric shock over her frame at the same instant: for the funeral scene burst upon her view, and reminded her where she was, and why she was there.

Recovering herself almost as rapidly as she had succumbed beneath physical and mental exhaustion, she started from Francisco's arms; and, turning upon him a beseeching—inquiring glance, exclaimed in a voice which ineffable anguish could not rob of its melody, "Is it true—Oh! tell me, is it true that the Count of Riverola is no more?"

"It is, alas! too true, lady," answered Francisco, in a tone of the deepest melancholy.

The heart of the fair stranger rebounded at the words which thus seemed to destroy a last hope that lingered in her soul; and a hysterical shriek burst from her lips as she threw her snow-white arms, bare to the shoulders, around the head of the pall-covered coffin.

"Oh! my much-loved—my noble Andrea!" she exclaimed, a torrent of tears now gushing from her eyes.

"That voice!—is it possible?" cried one of the spectators, who had hitherto been standing, as before said, at a respectful distance: and the speaker—a man of tall, commanding form, graceful demeanour, wondrously handsome countenance, and rich attire—immediately hurried towards the spot where the young female still clung to the coffin, no one having the heart to remove her.

The individual who had thus stepped forward gave one rapid but searching glance at the lady's countenance; and, yielding to the surprise and joy which suddenly animated him, he exclaimed, "Yes—it is, indeed, the lost Agnes!"

The young female started when she heard her name thus pronounced in a place where she believed herself to be entirely unknown; and astonishment for an instant triumphed over the anguish of her heart.

Hastily withdrawing her snow-white arms from the head of the coffin, she turned towards the individual who had uttered her name; and he instantly clasped her in his arms, murmuring, "Dearest—dearest Agnes: art thou restored——"

But the lady shrieked, and struggled to escape from that tender embrace, exclaiming, "What means this insolence? will no one protect me?"

"That will I," said Francisco, darting forward, and tearing her away from the stranger's arms. "But, in the name of heaven! let this misunderstanding be cleared up elsewhere. Lady—and you, signor—I call on you to remember where you are, and how solemn a ceremony ye have both aided to interrupt!"

"I know not that man!" ejaculated Agnes, indicating the stranger. "I came hither because I heard but an hour ago—that my noble Andrea was no more. And I would not believe those who told me. Oh! no—I could not think that heaven had thus deprived me of all I loved on earth!"

"Lady, you are speaking of my father," said Francisco, in a somewhat severe tone.

"Your father!" cried Agnes, now surveying the young Count with interest and curiosity. "Oh! then, my lord, you can pity—you can feel for me, who in losing your father have lost all that could render existence sweet."

"No—you have not lost all!" exclaimed the handsome, noble looking stranger, advancing towards Agnes, and speaking in a profoundly impressive tone. "Have you not one single relative left in the world? Consider, Nisida—an old, old man—a shepherd in the great Black Forest of Germany——"

"Speak not of him!" cried Agnes, wildly. "Did he know all, he would curse me—he would spurn me from him—he would discard me for ever! Oh! when I think of that poor old man, with his venerable white hair,—that aged, helpless man who was so kind to me—who loved me so well—and whom I so cruelly abandoned—— But tell me, signor," she exclaimed, in a suddenly altered tone, while her breath came with the difficulty of acute suspense,—"tell me, signor, does that old man still live?"

"He lives, Agnes," was the reply. "I know him well: —at this moment he is in Florence!"

"In Florence!" repeated Agnes, and so unexpectedly came this announcement that her limbs seemed to give way under her, and she would have fallen on the marble pavement, had not the stranger caught her in his arms.

"I will bear her away," he said: "she has a sincere friend in me."

And he was moving off with his senseless burden, when Francisco, struck by a sudden idea, caught him by the elegantly slashed sleeve of his doublet, and whispered thus, in a rapid tone:—"From the few, but significant, words which fell from that lady's lips, and from her still more impressive conduct, it would appear, alas! that my deceased father had wronged her. If so, signor, it will be my duty to make her all the reparation that can be afforded in such a case."

"'Tis well, my lord," answered the stranger, in a cold and haughty tone. "To-morrow evening I will call upon you at your palace."

He then hurried on with the still senseless Agnes in his arms; and the Count of Riverola retraced his steps to the immediate vicinity of the coffin.

This scene, which so strangely interrupted the funeral ceremony, and which has taken so much space to describe, did not actually occupy ten minutes from the moment when the young lady first appeared in the church until that when she was borne away by the handsome stranger.

The funeral obsequies were completed: the coffin was lowered into the family vault: the spectators dispersed, and the mourners, headed by the young Count, returned in procession to the Riverola mansion, which was situate at no great distance.

CHAPTER V.
THE READING OF THE WILL.

WHEN the mourners reached the palace, Francisco led the way to an apartment where Nisida was awaiting their coming.

Francisco kissed her affectionately upon the forehead; and then took his seat at the head of the table, his sister placing herself on his right hand.

Dressed in deep mourning, and with her countenance unusually pale, Nisida's appearance inspired a feeling of profound interest in the minds of those who did not perceive that, beneath her calm and mournful demeanour, feelings of painful intensity agitated within her breast. But Dr. Duras, who knew her well,—better, far better

than even her own brother, noticed an occasional wild flashing of the eye—a nervous motion of the lips—and a degree of forced tranquillity of mien, which proved how acute was the suspense she in reality endured!

On Francisco's left hand the Notary-General, who had acted as one of the chief mourners, took a seat. He was a short, thin, middle-aged man, with a pale complexion, twinkling grey eyes, and a sharp expression of countenance. Before him lay a sealed packet, on which the eyes of Nisida darted at short intervals, looks the burning impatience of which were comprehended by Dr. Duras alone: for next to Signor Vivaldi the Notary-General—and consequently opposite to Nisida—sat the physician.

The remainder of the company consisted of Father Marco and those most intimate friends of the family who had been invited to the funeral; but whom it is unnecessary to describe more particularly.

Father Marco having recited a short prayer, in obedience to the custom of the age and the occasion, the Notary-General proceeded to break the seals of the large packet which lay before him: then, in a precise and methodical manner, he drew forth a sheet of parchment closely written on.

Nisida leant her right elbow upon the table, and half-buried her countenance in the snowy cambric handkerchief which she held.

The Notary-General commenced the reading of the will.

After bestowing a few legacies, one of which was in favour of Dr. Duras, and another in that of Signor Vivaldi himself, the testamentary document ordained that the estates of the late Andrea, Count of Riverola, should be held in trust by the Notary-General and the physician, for the benefit of Francisco, who was merely to enjoy the revenues produced by the same until the age of thirty. at which period the guardianship was to cease, and Francisco was then to enter into full and uncontrolled possession of those immense estates.

But to this clause there was an important condition attached; for the testamentary document ordained that should the Lady Nisida—either by medical skill, or the interposition of heaven—recover the faculties of hearing and speaking at any time during the interval which was to elapse ere Francisco would attain the age of thirty, then the whole of the estates, with the exception of a very small one in the northern part of Tuscany, were to be immediately made over to her; but without the power of alienation on her part.

It must be observed that, in the middle ages, many titles of nobility depended only on the feudal possession of a particular property. This was the case with the Riverola estates; and the title of "Count of Riverola" was conferred simply by the fact of the ownership of the landed property. Thus, supposing that Nisida became possessed of the estates, she would have enjoyed the title of "Countess," while her brother Francisco would have lost that of "Count."

We may also remind our readers that Francisco was now nineteen; and eleven years must consequently elapse ere he could become the lord and master of the vast territorial possessions of Riverola.

Great was the astonishment experienced by all who heard the provisions of this strange will—with the exception of the Notary-General and Father Marco, the former of whom had drawn it up, and the latter of whom was privy to its contents (though under a vow of secrecy) in his capacity of father-confessor to the late Count.

Francisco was himself surprised, and, in one sense, hurt; because the nature of the testamentary document seemed to imply that the property would have been inevitably left to his sister, with but a very small provision for himself, had she not been so sorely afflicted as she was; and this fact forced upon him the painful conviction that even when contemplating his departure to another world, his father had not softened towards his son!

But, on the other hand, Francisco was pleased that such consideration had been shown towards a sister whom he so devotedly loved; and he hastened, as soon as he could conquer his first emotions, to request the Notary-General to permit Nisida to peruse the will, adding in a mournful tone, "For all that your Excellency has read, has been, alas! unavailing in respect to her."

Signor Vivaldi handed the document to the young Count, who gently touched his sister's shoulder and placed the parchment before her.

Nisida started, as if convulsively; and raised from her

handkerchief a countenance so pale—so deadly pale, that Francisco shrank back in alarm.

But instantly reflecting that the process of reading aloud a paper had been as it were a kind of mockery in respect to his afflicted sister, he pressed her hand tenderly, and made a sign for her to peruse the document.

She mechanically addressed herself to the task; but ere her eyes—now of burning, unearthly brilliancy—fell upon the parchment, they darted one rapid, electric glance of ineffable anguish towards Dr. Duras, adown whose cheeks large tears were trickling.

In a few minutes Nisida appeared to be absorbed in the perusal of the will; and the most solemn silence prevailed throughout the apartment.

At length she started violently, tossed the paper indignantly back to the Notary-General, and hastily wrote on a slip of paper these words:—"*Should medical skill or the mercy of heaven restore my speech and faculty of hearing, I will abandon all claim to the estates and title of Riverola to my dear brother Francisco.*"

She then handed the slip to the Notary-General, who read the contents aloud.

Francisco darted upon his sister a look of ineffable gratitude and love, but shook his head—as much as to imply that he would not accept the boon, even if circumstances enabled her to confer it.

She returned the look with another, expressive of impatience at his refusal; and her eyes seemed to say, as eloquently as eyes ever yet spoke, "Oh! that I had the power to give verbal utterance to my feelings!"

Meantime the Notary-General had written a few words beneath those penned by Nisida, to whom he handed back the slip; and she hastened to read them, thus:—"*Your ladyship has no power to alienate the estates, should they come into your possession.*"

Nisida burst into an agony of tears and rushed from the room.

Her brother immediately followed to console her; and the company retired, each individual to his own abode.

But of all that company who had been present at the reading of the will, none experienced such painful emotions as Dr. Duras.

CHAPTER VI.

THE PICTURES.—AGNES AND THE UNKNOWN.—MYSTERY.

WHEN Agnes awoke from the state of stupor in which she had been conveyed from the church, she found herself lying upon an ottoman, in a large and elegantly furnished apartment.

The room was lighted by two silver lamps suspended to the ceiling, and which being fed with aromatic oil of the purest quality, imparted a delicious perfume to the atmosphere.

The walls were hung with paintings representing scenes of strange variety and interest, and connected with lands far—far away. Thus, one depicted a council of Red Men assembled round a blazing fire, on the border of one of the great forests of North America: another showed the interior of an Esquimaux hut amidst the eternal ice of the Pole;—a third delineated, with fearfully graphic truth, the writhings of a human victim in the folds of the terrible anaconda in the island of Ceylon;—a fourth exhibited a pleasing contrast to the one previously cited, by having for its subject a family meeting of Chinese on the terraced roof of a high functionary's palace at Pekin; a fifth represented the splendid Court of King Henry the Eighth in London;—a sixth showed the interior of the harem of the Ottoman Sultan.

But there were two portraits amongst this beautiful and varied collection of pictures, all of which, we should observe, appeared to have been very recently executed—two portraits which we must pause to describe. One represented a tall man of about forty years of age, with magnificent light hair—fine blue eyes, but terrible in their expression—a countenance indisputably handsome, though every lineament denoted horror and alarm—and a symmetrical form, bowed by the weight of sorrow. Beneath this portrait was the following inscription:—"*F., Count of A., terminated his career on the 1st of August, 1517.*"

The other portrait alluded to was that of an old—old man, who had apparently numbered ninety winters. He was represented as cowering over a few embers in a miserable hovel, while the most profound sorrow was depicted on his countenance. Beneath this picture was the ensuing inscription:—"*F. W., January 7th, 1516. His last day thus.*"

There was another feature in that apartment to which we must likewise direct our reader's attention, ere we pursue the thread of our narrative. This was an object hanging against the wall, next to the second portrait just now described. It also had the appearance of being a picture—or at all events a frame of the same dimensions as the others; but whether that frame contained a painting, or whether it were empty, it was impossible to say, so long as it remained concealed by the large black cloth which covered it, and which was carefully fastened by small silver nails at each corner.

This strange object gave a lugubrious and sinister appearance to a room in other respects cheerful, gay, and elegant.

But to resume our tale.

When Agnes awoke from her stupor, she found herself reclining on a soft ottoman of purple velvet, fringed with gold; and the handsome stranger, who had borne her from the church, was bathing her brow with water which he took from a crystal vase on the marble table.

As she languidly and slowly opened her large hazel eyes, her thoughts collected themselves in the same gradient manner; and when her glance encountered that of her unknown friend, who was bending over her with an expression of deep interest on his features, there flashed upon her mind a recollection of all that had so recently taken place.

"Where am I?" she demanded, starting up, and casting her eyes wildly around her.

"In the abode of one who will not injure you," answered the stranger, in a kind and melodious tone.

"But who are you? and wherefore have you brought me hither?" exclaimed Agnes. "Oh! I remember—you spoke of that old man—my grandfather—the shepherd of the Black Forest——"

"You shall see him—you shall be restored to him," answered the stranger.

"But will he receive—will he not spurn me from him?" asked Agnes, in a wildly impassioned—almost hysterical tone.

"The voice of pity cannot refuse to heave a sigh for thy fall," was the response. "If thou wast guilty in abandoning one who loved thee so tenderly, and whose only earthly reliance was on thee, he, whom you did so abandon, has not the less need to ask pardon of thee. For he speedily forgot his darling Agnes—he travelled the world over, yet sought her not—her image was as it were effaced from his memory. But when accident——"

"Oh! signor, you are mistaken—you know not the old man whom I deserted, and who was a shepherd on the verge of the Black Forest!" interrupted Agnes, in a tone expressive of bitter disappointment. "For he, who loved me so well, was old—very old, and could not possibly accomplish those long wanderings of which you speak. Indeed, if he be still alive—but *that* is scarcely possible——"

And she burst into tears.

"Agnes," cried the stranger, "the venerable shepherd of whom you speak, accomplished those wanderings in spite of the ninety winters which marked his age. He is alive, too——"

"He is alive!" ejaculated the lady, with reviving hope.

"He is alive—and at this moment in Florence!" was the emphatic answer. "Did I not ere now tell thee as much in the church?"

"Yes—I remember—but my brain is confused!" murmured Agnes, pressing her beautiful white hand upon her polished brow. "Oh! if he be indeed alive—and so near me as you say—delay not in conducting me to him: for he is now the only being on earth to whom I dare look for solace and sympathy."

"You are even now beneath the roof of your grandfather's dwelling," said the stranger, speaking slowly, and anxiously watching the effect which this announcement was calculated to produce upon her to whom he addressed himself.

"Here!—this my grandsire's abode!" she exclaimed, clasping her hands together, and glancing upward, as if to express gratitude to heaven for this welcome intelligence. "But how can that old man, whom I left so poor, have become the owner of this lordly place? Speak, signor!—all you have told me seems to involve some mystery," she added with breathless rapidity. "Those wanderings of which you ere now spoke—wanderings over the world, performed by a man bent down by age; —and then this noble dwelling—the appearances of wealth which present themselves around—the splendour—the magnificence——"

"All—all are the old man's," answered the stranger, "and may some day become thine!"

"Holy Virgin!" exclaimed Agnes, sinking upon the ottoman from which she had ere now risen, "I thank thee that thou hast bestowed these blessings on my relative in his old age. And yet," she added, again overwhelmed by doubts, "it is scarcely possible—no—it is too romantic to be true! Signor, thou art of a surety mistaken in him whom thou supposest to be my grandsire!"

"Give me thine hand, Agnes—and I will convince thee," said the stranger.

The young lady complied mechanically; and her unknown friend led her towards the portrait of the old man of ninety.

Agnes recognised the countenance at a single glance, and would have fallen upon the floor had not her companion supported her in his arms.

Tears again came to her relief; but, hastily wiping them away, she extended her arms passionately towards the portrait, exclaiming, "Oh! now I comprehend you, signor!—my grandsire lives in this dwelling indeed—beneath this roof—but lives only in that picture! Alas! alas! it was thus, no doubt that the poor old man seemed when he was abandoned by me—the lost, the guilty Agnes! It was thus that he sat in his lonely dwelling, crushed and overwhelmed by the black ingratitude of his grand-daughter! Oh! that I had never seen this portrait—this perpetuation of so much loneliness and so much grief! Ah! too faithful delineation of that sad scene which was wrought by me—by me, wanton that I was—vainly penitent that I am!"

And covering her face with her hands, she threw herself on her knees before the portrait, and gave way to all the bitterness and all the wildness of her grief.

The stranger interrupted her not for some minutes: he allowed the flood of that anguish to have its full vent; —but, when it was partially subsiding, he approached the kneeling penitent, raised her gently, and said, "Despair not! your grandsire lives."

"He lives!" she repeated, her countenance once more expressing radiant hope, as the sudden gleam of sunshine bursts forth amidst the last drops of the April shower.

But, almost at the same instant that she uttered those words, her eyes caught sight of the inscription at the foot of the picture; and, bounding forward, she read it aloud.

"Holy Virgin! I am deceived—basely, vilely deceived!" she continued, all the violence of her grief, which had begun to ebb so rapidly, now flowing back upon her soul: then, turning abruptly round upon the stranger, she said in a hoarse hollow tone, "Signor, wherefore thus ungenerously trifle with my feelings—my best feelings? Who art thou? what wouldst thou with me? and wherefore is that portrait here?"

"Agnes—Agnes!" exclaimed her companion, "compose yourself, I implore you! I do not trifle with you—I do not deceive you! Your grandsire, Fernand Wagner, is alive—and in this house. You shall see him presently; but, in the meantime, listen to what I am about to say."

Agnes placed her finger impatiently upon the inscription at the bottom of the portrait; and exclaimed in a wild, hysterical tone, "Canst thou explain this, signor? 'January 17th, 1516'—that was about a week after I abandoned him: and, Oh! well indeed might those words be added—'His last day thus!'"

"You comprehend not the meaning of that inscription," ejaculated the stranger, in an imploring tone, as if to beseech her to have patience and listen to him. "There is a dreadful mystery connected with Fernand Wagner—connected with me—connected with these two portraits—connected also with——"

He checked himself suddenly, and his whole form seemed convulsed with horror as he glanced towards the black cloth covering the neighbouring frame.

"A mystery!" repeated Agnes. "Yes—all is mystery; and vague and undefinable terrors oppress my soul!"

"Thou shalt soon—too soon be enlightened!" said the stranger, in a voice of profound melancholy: "at least, to a certain degree," he added, murmuringly. "But contemplate that other portrait for a few moments—that you may make yourself acquainted with the countenance of a wretch who, in conferring a fearful boon upon your grandsire, has plunged him into an abyss of unredeemable horror!"

Agnes cast her looks towards the portrait of the tall man with the magnificent hair, the flashing blue eyes,

the wildly expressive countenance, and the symmetrical form bowed with affliction; and, having surveyed it for some time with repugnance strangely mingled with an invincible interest and curiosity, she suddenly pointed towards the inscription.

"Yes—yes: this is another terrible memorial!" cried the stranger. "But art thou now prepared to listen to a wondrous—an astounding tale—such a tale as even nurses would scarcely dare narrate to lull sleepless children——"

"I am prepared," answered Agnes. "I perceive there is a dreadful mystery connected with my grandsire—with you also—and perhaps with me; and better learn at once the truth, than remain in this state of intolerable suspense."

Her unknown friend conducted her back to the ottoman, whereon she placed herself.

He took a seat by her side, and after a few moments' profound meditation addressed her in the following manner.

CHAPTER VII.
REVELATIONS.

"You remember, Agnes, how happily the time passed when you were the darling of the old man in his poor cottage. All the other members of his once numerous family had been swept away by pestilence, malady, accident, or violence; and you only were left to him. When the trees of the great Black Forest were full of life and vegetable blood, in the genial warmth of summer, you gathered flowers which you arranged tastefully in the little hut; and those gifts of Nature, so culled and so dispensed from your hands, gave the dwelling a more cheerful air than if it had been hung with tapestry richly fringed. Of an evening—when the setting sun, with its sheen, overflowed the western plains as with glowing gold—you were wont to kneel by the side of that old shepherd; and together ye chanted a hymn giving thanks for the mercies of the day, and imploring the renewal of them for the morrow. Then did the music of your sweet voice, as it flowed upon the old man's ears in its melting, silvery tones, possess a charm for his senses, which taught him to rejoice and be grateful that, though the rest of the race were swept away, thou, Agnes, was left!

"When the winter came, and the trees were stripped of their verdure, the poor cottage had still its enjoyments: for though the cold was intense without, yet there were warm hearts within; and the cheerful fire of an evening when the labours of the day were passed, seemed to make gay and joyous companionship.

"But suddenly you disappeared;—and the old man found himself deserted. You left him, too, in the midst of winter—at a time when his age and infirmities demanded additional attentions. For two or three days he sped wearily about, seeking you everywhere in the neighbouring district of the Black Forest. His aching limbs were dragged up rude heights, that he might plunge his glances down into the hollow chasms;—but not a trace of Agnes! He roved along the precipices overlooking the rushing streams, and searched—diligently searched the mazes of the dark wood:—but still not a trace—not a trace of Agnes! At length the painful conviction broke upon him that he was deserted—abandoned; and he would sooner have found thee a mangled and disfigured corse in the forest, than have adopted that belief. Nay—weep not now: it is all past:—and if I recapitulate these incidents, it is but to convince thee how wretched the old man was, and how great is the extenuation for the course he was so soon persuaded to adopt."

"Then, who art thou that knowest all this?" exclaimed Agnes, casting looks of alarm upon her companion.

"Thou shalt soon learn who I am," was the mysterious reply.

Agnes still gazed upon him in mingled terror and wonder; for his words had gone to her heart, and she remembered how he had embraced her when she first encountered him in the church. His manner, too, was so kind—so mild—so paternal towards her; and yet he seemed but a few years older than herself!

"You have gazed upon the portrait of the old man," he continued, "as he appeared on that memorable evening which sealed his fate!"

Agnes started wildly.

"Yes—sealed his fate, but spared him his life!" said the unknown, emphatically. "As he is represented in that picture, so was he sitting mournfully over the sorry fire, for the morrow's renewal of which there was no wood! At that hour a man appeared—appeared in the midst of the dreadful storm which burst over the Black Forest. This man's countenance is now known to thee: it is perpetuated in the other portrait to which I directed thine attention."

"There is something of a wild and fearful interest in the aspect of that man," said Agnes, casting a shuddering glance behind her, and trembling lest the canvas had burst into life, and the countenance whose lineaments were depicted thereon, was peering over her shoulder.

"Yes—and there was much of wild and fearful interest in his history," was the reply: "but of that I cannot speak—no, I dare not. Suffice it to say that he was a being possessed of superhuman powers, and that he proffered his services to the wretched—the abandoned—the deserted Wagner. He proposed to endow him with a new existence—to restore him to youth and manly beauty—to make him rich—to embellish his mind with wondrous attainments—to enable him to cast off the wrinkles of age——"

"Holy Virgin! now I comprehend it all!" shrieked Agnes, throwing herself at the feet of her companion: "and you—you——"

"I am Fernand Wagner!" he exclaimed, folding her in his embrace.

"And can you pardon me—can you forgive my deep, deep ingratitude?" cried Agnes.

"Let us forgive each other!" said Wagner. "You can now understand the meaning of the inscription beneath my portrait. '*His last day thus*' signifies that it was the last day on which I wore that aged, decrepit, and sinking form."

"But wherefore do you say, '*Let us forgive each other?*'" demanded Agnes, scarcely knowing whether to rejoice or weep at the marvellous transformation of her grandsire.

"Did I not ere now inform thee that thou wast forgotten until accident threw thee in my way to-night?" exclaimed Fernand. "I have wandered about the earth and beheld the scenes which are represented in those pictures—aye, and many others equally remarkable. For eighteen months I was the servant—the slave of him who conferred upon me this fatal boon——"

"At what price then have you purchased it?" asked Agnes, with a cold shudder.

"Seek not to learn my secret, girl!" cried Wagner, almost sternly: then, in a milder tone, he added, "By all you deem holy and sacred I conjure you, Agnes, never again to question me on that head; I have told thee as much as it is necessary for thee to know——"

"One word—only one word!" exclaimed Agnes, in an imploring voice. "Hast thou bartered thine immortal soul——"

"No—no!" responded Wagner, emphatically. "My fate is terrible indeed—but I am not beyond the pale of salvation. See, Agnes—I kiss this crucifix—the symbol of faith and hope!"

And, as he uttered these words, he pressed to his lips an ivory crucifix of exquisite workmanship which he took from the table.

"The Virgin be thanked that my fearful suspicion should prove unfounded!" ejaculated Agnes.

"Yes—I am not altogether lost," answered Wagner. "But *he*—the unhappy man who made me what I am—And yet I dare not say more," he added, suddenly checking himself. "For one year and a half did I follow him as his servitor—profiting by his knowledge—gaining varied information from his experience—passing with the rapidity of thought from clime to clime—surveying scenes of ineffable bliss—and studying all the varieties of misery that it is the lot of human nature to endure. When he—my master—passed away——"

"On the 1st of August, 1517," observed Agnes, quoting the inscription beneath the portrait of the individual alluded to.

"Yes:—when he had passed away," continued Wagner, "I continued my wanderings alone until the commencement of last year, when I settled myself in Florence. The mansion to which I have brought you, is mine. It is a somewhat secluded spot—on the banks of the Arno, and is surrounded by gardens. My household consists of but few retainers; and they are elderly persons—docile and obedient. The moment that I entered this abode, I set to work to paint those portraits to which I have directed your attention,—likewise these pictures," he added, glancing around, "and in which I have represented scenes that my own eyes have witnessed. Here, henceforth, Agnes, shalt thou dwell; and let the past be forgotten. But there are three conditions which I must impose upon thee."

"Name them," said Agnes. "I promise obedience beforehand."

"The first," returned Fernand, "is that you henceforth look upon me as your brother, and call me such when we are alone together or in the presence of strangers. The second is that you never seek to remove the black cloth which covers yon place——"

Agnes glanced towards the object alluded to, and shuddered—as if that dark veil concealed some new mystery.

"And the third condition is that you revive not on any future occasion the subject of our present conversation, nor ever question me in respect to those secrets which it may suit me to retain in my own breast."

Agnes promised obedience, and, embracing Wagner, said, "Heaven has been merciful to me in my present affliction, in that it has given me *a brother!*"

"Thou speakest of this affliction, Agnes!" exclaimed Wagner; "this is the night of revelations and mutual confidence—and this night once past, we will never again allude to the present topics, unless events should render their revival necessary. It is now for thee to narrate to me all that has befallen thee since the winter of 1516."

Agnes hastened to comply with Fernand's request, and commenced her history in the following manner.

CHAPTER VIII.

THE HISTORY OF AGNES.

"WHEN you, dear brother—for so I shall henceforth call you—commenced your strange and wondrous revelations ere now, you painted in vivid colours the happiness which dwelt in our poor cottage on the borders of the Black Forest. You saw how deeply your words affected me—I could not restrain my tears. Let me not, however, dwell upon this subject; but rather hasten to explain those powerful causes which induced me to quit that happy home.

It was about six weeks before my flight, that I one day went into the forest to gather wood. I was in the midst of my occupation, gaily trilling a native song, when the sound of a horse's feet upon the hard soil of the beaten path suddenly interrupted me. I turned round, and beheld a cavalier of strikingly handsome countenance, though somewhat stern withal,—and of noble mien. He was in reality forty-four years of age,—as I afterwards learnt; but he seemed scarcely forty, so lightly did time sit upon his brow. His dress was elegant, though of strange fashion; for it was the Italian costume that he wore. The moment he was close to the spot where I stood, he considered me for a short while, till I felt my cheek glowing beneath his ardent gaze. I cast down my eyes; and the next instant he had leaped from his horse and was by my side. He addressed me in gentle terms; and when I again looked at him his countenance no longer seemed stern. It appeared that he was staying with the Baron von Nauemberg, with whom he had been hunting in the Black Forest, and from whom and his suite he was separated in the ardour of the chase. Being a total stranger in those parts he had lost his way. I immediately described to him the proper path to pursue; and he offered me gold as a recompense. I declined the guerdon; and he questioned me concerning my family and position. I told him that I lived hard by with an only relative—a grandsire, to whom I was devotedly attached. He lingered long in conversation with me; and his manner was so kind—so condescending—and so respectful, that I thought not I was doing wrong to listen to him. At length he requested me to be on the same spot at the same hour on the morrow; and he departed.

"I was struck by his appearance—dazzled by the brilliancy of his discourse; for he spoke German fluently, although an Italian. He had made a deep impression on my mind; and I felt a secret longing to meet him again. Suddenly it occurred to me that I was acting with impropriety, and that you would be angry with me. I therefore resolved not to mention to you my accidental encounter with the handsome cavalier; but I determined at the same time, not to repair to the forest next day. When the appointed hour drew near, my good genius deserted me: and I went. He was there—and he seemed pleased at my punctuality. I need not detail to you the nature of the discourse which he held towards me. Suffice it to say, that he declared how much he had been struck with my beauty, and how fondly he would love me: then he dazzled me still more by revealing his haughty name: and I found that I was beloved by the Count of Riverola.

"You can understand how a poor girl, who had hitherto dwelt in the seclusion of a cottage on the border of a vast wood, and who seldom saw any person of higher rank than herself, was likely to be dazzled by the fine things which that great nobleman breathed in her ear. And I *was* dazzled—flattered—excited—bewildered.

whither important affairs called him sooner than he had anticipated. He urged me to accompany him: I was bewildered—maddened by the contemplation of my duty on the one hand, and of my love on the other. My guardian saint deserted me; I yielded to the persuasion of the Count—I became guilty—and there was now no alternative save to fly with him!

"Oh! believe me when I declare that this decision cost me a dreadful pang: but the Count would not leave me time for reflection. He bore me away on his fleet steed, and halted not until the tall towers of Nauemberg Castle appeared in the distance. Then he stopped

GRIFFIN & DUVERGIER

"SHE FOUND HERSELF RECLINING ON A SOFT OTTOMAN." (See p. 14.)

I consented to meet him again: interview followed interview, until I no longer required any persuasion to induce me to keep the appointments thus given. But there were times when my conscience reproached me for my conduct, which I knew you would blame: and yet I dared not unburden my soul to you!

"Six weeks thus passed away: I was still innocent—but madly in love with the Count of Riverola. He was the subject of my thoughts by day—of my dreams by night; and I felt that I could make any sacrifice to retain his affection. That sacrifice was too soon demanded! At the expiration of the six weeks he informed me that on the following day he must return to Italy

at a poor peasant's cottage, where his gold ensured me a welcome reception. Having communicated the plan which he proposed to adopt respecting our journey to Florence, he took an affectionate leave of me, with a promise to return early on the ensuing morning. The remainder of the day was passed wretchedly enough by me: and I already began to repent of the step I had taken. The peasants who occupied the cottage vainly endeavoured to cheer me; my heart was too full to admit of consolation. Night came at length, and I retired to rest; but my dreams were of so unpleasant a nature—so filled with frightful images—that never did I welcome the dawn with more enthusiastic joy. Shortly after day break the Count appeared at the cottage attended by only one of the numerous suite—a faithful dependant on whom he could rely implicitly. They were mounted on good steeds: and Antonio—such was the name of the servitor—led a third by the bridle This one the Count had purchased at an adjacent hamlet, expressly for my use. He had also procured a page's attire; for in such disguise was it agreed that I should accompany the Count to Italy.

"I should observe that the nobleman, in order to screen our amour as much as possible, had set out from Nauemberg Castle, attended by Antonio alone, alleging as an excuse that certain affairs compelled him to travel homeward with as much celerity as possible. The remainder of his suite were therefore ordered to follow at their leisure.

"Oh! with what agonizing emotions did my heart beat, as, in a private chamber of the cottage, I laid aside my peasant's garb and donned the doublet, hose, cap, and cloak of a youthful page. I thought of you —of your helplessness—your age—and also of my native land, which I was about to quit—perhaps for ever! Still I had gone too far to retreat, and regrets were useless. I must also confess that when I returned to the room where the Count was waiting for me, and heard the flattering compliments which we'e paid me on my appearance in that disguise, I smiled—yes, I smiled, and much of my remorse vanished!

"We set out upon our journey towards the Alps: and the Count exerted all his powers of conversation to chase away from my mind any regrets or repinings that might linger there. Though cold and stern—forbidding and reserved—haughty and austere in his bearing towards others, to me he was affectionate and tender. To be brief,—yet with sorrow must I confess it, at the expiration of a few days I could bear to think without weeping, of the fond relative whom I had left behind me in the cottage of the Black Forest.

"We crossed the Alps in safety, but not without having experienced much peril: and in a short time glorious Italy spread itself at our feet. The conversation of the Count had already prepared me to admire——"

At this moment Agnes's narrative was interrupted by a piercing shriek which burst from her lips; and extending her arms towards the window of the apartment, she screamed hysterically—"Again that countenance!" —and fell back on the ottoman.

CHAPTER IX.

CONCLUSION OF THE HISTORY OF AGNES.

In order that the reader may understand how Agnes could perceive any object outside the window in the intense darkness of that tempestuous night — or rather morning, for it was now past one o'clock—we must observe that not only was the apartment in which Wagner and herself were seated brilliantly lighted by the silver lamps, but that, according to Florentine custom, there were also lamps suspended outside to the verandah, or large balcony belonging to the casements of the room above.

Agnes and Wagner were moreover placed near the window, which looked into a large garden attached to the mansion; and thus it was easy for the lady, whose eyes happened to be fixed upon the casement in the earnest interest with which she was relating her narrative, to perceive the human countenance that suddenly appeared at one of the panes.

The moment her history was interrupted by the ejaculation of alarm which broke from her lips, Wagner started up and hastened to the window: but he could see nothing save the waving evergreens in his garden, and the lights of a mansion which stood at a distance of about two hundred yards from his own abode.

He was about to open the casement and step into the garden, when Agnes caught him by the arm exclaiming wildly, "Leave me not—I could not bear to remain here alone!"

"No—I will not quit you, Agnes," replied Wagner, conducting her back to the sofa and resuming his seat by her side. "But wherefore that ejaculation of alarm? Whose countenance did you behold? Speak, dearest Agnes!"

"I will hasten to explain the cause of my terror," returned Agnes, becoming more composed. "Ere now I was about to detail the particulars of my journey to Florence, in company with the Count of Riverola, and

attended by Antonio: but as those particulars are of no material interest, I will at once pass on to the period when we arrived in this city."

"But the countenance at the window?" said Wagner, somewhat emphatically.

"Listen—and you will soon know all," replied Agnes. "It was in the evening when I entered Florence for the first time. Antonio had proceeded in advance to inform his mother—a widow who resided in a decent house, but in an obscure street near the cathedral—that she was speedily to receive a young lady as a guest. This young lady was myself, and accordingly, when the Count assisted me to alight from my horse at the gate of Dame Margaretha's abode, the good widow had everything in readiness for my reception. The Count conversed with her apart for a few minutes; and I observed that he also placed a heavy purse in her hand—doubtless to ensure her secrecy relative to the amour, with the existence of which he was of course compelled to acquaint her. Having seen me comfortably installed in Dame Margaretha's best apartment, he quitted me with a promise to return on the morrow."

Agnes paused for a few moments—sighed and continued her narrative in the following manner:

"Fortunately for me, Dame Margaretha was a German woman who had married an Italian: and we were therefore able to converse together: otherwise my position would have been wretched in the extreme. She treated me with kindness, mingled with respect; for though but a poor peasant girl, I was beloved and protected by one of the most powerful nobles of Florence. I retired early to rest:—sleep did not, however, immediately visit my eyes. Oh! no—I was in Florence, but my thoughts were far away—in my native Germany, and on the borders of the Black Forest. At length I fell into an uneasy slumber; and when I awoke, the sun was shining through the lattice. I rose to dress myself: and to my ineffable delight, I found that I was no longer to wear the garb of a page. That disguise had been removed while I slept; and in its place were costly vestments, which I donned with a pleasure that triumphed over the gloom of my soul. In the course of the morning rich furniture was brought to the house, and in a few hours the two apartments allotted to me were converted, in my estimation, into a little paradise. The Count arrived soon afterwards; and I now—pardon me the neglect and ingratitude which my words confess,—I now felt very happy. The noble Andrea enjoined me to go abroad but seldom, and never without being accompanied by Dame Margaretha; he also besought me not to appear to recognise him, should I chance to meet him in public at any time,—nor to form any acquaintances; in a word, to live as retired and secluded as possible, alike for his sake and my own. I promised compliance with all he suggested: and he declared in return that he would never cease to love me.

"Dwell not upon details, Agnes," said Wagner, "for although I am deeply interested in your narrative, my curiosity is strangely excited to learn the meaning of that terror which overcame you are now."

"I will confine myself to material facts as much as possible," returned Agnes. "The time glided rapidly away; weeks—months flew by,—and, with sorrow and shame must I confess, that the memories of the past— the memories of the days of my innocence—intruded but little on the life which I led. For, though he was so much older than I, yet I loved the Count of Riverola devotedly—Oh! heaven knows how devotedly! His conversation delighted—fascinated me; and he seemed to experience a pleasure in imparting to me the extensive knowledge which he had acquired. To me he unbent as doubtless to human being he never unbent before: in my presence his sternness—his sombre moods—his gloomy thoughts vanished. It was evident that he *had* much preying upon his mind; and perhaps he loved me thus fondly, because—by some unaccountable whim or caprice, or strange influence—he found solace in my society. The presents which he heaped upon me, but which have been nearly all snatched from me, were of immense value! and when I remonstrated with him on account of a liberality so useless to one whom he had allowed to want for nothing, he would reply, ' *But remember, Agnes, when I shall be no more, riches will constitute your best friend —your safest protection; for such is the order of things in this world.*'—He generally spent two hours with me every day, and frequently visited me again in the evening. Thus did time pass; and at length I come to that incident which will explain the terror I ere now experienced."

Agnes cast a hasty glance towards the window, as if to assure herself that the object of her fears was no longer there; and satisfied on this head, she proceeded in the following manner:—

"It was about six months ago, that I repaired as usual on the Sabbath morning to mass, accompanied by Dame Margaretha, when I found myself the object of some attention on the part of a lady, who was kneeling at a short distance from the place which I occupied in the church. The lady was enveloped in a dark, thick veil, the ample folds of which concealed her countenance, and meandered over her whole body's splendidly symmetrical length of limb in such a manner as to aid her rich attire in shaping, rather than hiding, the contours of that matchless form. I was struck by her fine proportions, which gave her, even in her kneeling attitude, a queen-like and majestic air; and I longed to obtain a glimpse of her countenance—the more so as I could perceive by her manner and the position of her head, that from beneath her dark veil her eyes were intently fixed upon myself. At length the scrutiny to which I was thus subjected began to grow so irksome—nay, even alarming, that I hurriedly drew down my own veil, which I had raised through respect for the sacred altar whereat I was kneeling. Still I knew that the stranger-lady was gazing on me: I *felt* that she was. A certain uneasy sensation—amounting almost to a superstitious awe—convinced me that I was the object of her undivided attention. Suddenly the priests, in procession, came down from the altar, and as they passed us, I instinctively raised my veil again through motives of deferential respect. At the same instant I glanced towards the stranger-lady she also drew back the dark covering from her face. Oh! what a countenance was then revealed to me!—a countenance of such sovereign beauty, that, though of the same sex, I was struck with admiration; but, in the next moment, a thrill of terror shot through my heart—for the fascination of the basilisk could scarcely paralyze its victim with more appalling effect than did the eyes of that lady. It might be conscience qualms, excited by some unknown influence—it might even have been imagination; but it nevertheless appeared as if those large, black, burning orbs shot forth lightnings which seared and scorched my very soul! For that splendid countenance, of most unearthly beauty, was suddenly marked by an expression of such vindictive rage—such ineffable hatred—such ferocious menace, that I should have screamed had I not been as it were stunned—stupefied!

"The procession of priests swept past: I averted my head from the stranger-lady: in a few moments I again glanced shudderingly towards the place which she had occupied—but she was gone. Then I felt relieved! On quitting the church I frankly narrated to old Margaretha these particulars as I have now unfolded them to you; and methought that she was for a moment troubled as I spoke. But, if she were, she speedily recovered her composure—endeavoured to soothe me by attributing it all to my imagination, and earnestly advised me not to cause any uneasiness to the Count by mentioning the subject to him. I readily promised compliance with this injunction; and in the course of a few days ceased to think upon the incident which had made so strange but evanescent an impression on my mind."

"Doubtless Dame Margaretha was right in her conjecture," said Wagner; "and your imagination——"

"Oh! no—no—it was not fancy!" interrupted Agnes, hastily. "But listen—and then judge for yourself. I informed you ere now that it was about six months ago when the event which I have just related took place. At that period, also, my noble lover—the ever-to-be-lamented Andrea—first experienced the symptoms of that internal disease which has, alas! carried him to the tomb!"

Agnes paused, wiped away her tears, and continued thus:—

"His visits to me consequently became less frequent;—I was more alone—for Margaretha was not always a companion who could solace me for the absence of one so dearly loved as my Andrea;—and repeated fits of deep despondency seized upon my soul. At those times I felt as if some evil—vague and undefinable, but still terrible—were impending over me. Was it my lord's approaching death of which I had a presentiment? I know not! Weeks passed away: the Count's visits occurred at intervals growing longer and longer—but his affection towards me had not abated. No: a malady that preyed upon his vitals, retained him much at home;—and at last, about two months ago, I received, through Antonio,

the afflicting intelligence that he was confined to his bed. My anguish now knew no bounds: I would fly to him—oh! I would fly to him:—who was more worthy to watch by his couch than I, who so dearly loved him? But Dame Margaretha represented to me how painful it would be to his lordship were our amour to transpire through any rash proceeding on my part—the more so, as I knew that he had a daughter and a son! I accordingly restrained my impetuous longing to hasten to his bed-side:—I could not so easily subdue my grief!

"One night I sat up late in my lonely chamber—pondering on the melancholy position in which I was placed,—loving so tenderly, yet not daring to fly to him whom I loved,—and giving way to all the mournful ideas which presented themselves to my imagination. At length my mind grew bewildered by those sad reflections; vague terrors gathered around me—multiplying in number and augmenting in intensity,—until at length the very figures on the tapestry with which the room was hung, appeared animated with power to affright me. The wind moaned ominously without, and raised strange echoes within; oppressive feelings crowded on my soul. At length the gale swelled to a hurricane—a whirlwind, seldom experienced in this delicious clime. Howlings in a thousand tones appeared to flit through the air: and piercing lamentations seemed to sound down from the black clouds that rolled their mighty volumes together, veiling the moon and stars in the thickest gloom. Overcome with terror, I retired to rest—and I slept. But troubled dreams haunted me throughout the night, and I awoke at an early hour in the morning. But—holy angels protect me! what did I behold? Bending over me, as I lay, was that same countenance which I had seen four months before in the church,—and now, as it was *then*, darting upon me lightnings from large black eyes that seemed to send shafts of flame and fire to the inmost recesses of my soul! Yet—distorted as it was with demoniac rage—that face was still endowed with queen-like beauty—the majesty of loveliness, which had before struck me, and which even lent force to those looks of dreadful menace that were fixed upon me. There were the high forehead—the proud lip, curled in scorn,—the brilliant teeth, glistening between the quivering vermilion,—and the swan-like arching of the dazzling neck;—there also was the dark glory of the luxuriant hair.

"For a few moments I was spell-bound—motionless—speechless. Clothed with terror and sublimity, yet in all the flush of the most perfect beauty, a strange—mysterious being stood over me: and I knew not whether she were a denizen of this world, or a spirit risen from another. Perhaps the transcendant loveliness of that countenance was but a mask, and the wondrous symmetry of that form but a disguise, beneath which all the passions of hell were raging in the brain and in the heart of a fiend. Such were the ideas that flashed through my imagination: and I involuntarily closed my eyes, as if that action could avert the malignity that appeared to menace me. But dreadful thoughts still pursued me—enveloping me, as it were, in an oppressive mist wherein appalling though dimly seen images and forms were agitating: and again I opened my eyes. The lady—if an earthly being she really were—was gone. I rose from my couch, and glanced nervously around—expecting almost to behold an apparition come forth from behind the tapestry, or the folds of the curtains. But my attention was suddenly arrested by a fact more germane to worldly occurrences. The casket wherein I kept the rich presents made to me at different times by my Andrea, had been forced open, and the most valuable portion of its contents were gone. On a closer investigation I observed that the articles which were left were those that had been purchased new; whereas the jewels that were abstracted were old ones, which, as the Count had often informed me, had belonged to his deceased wife.

"On discovering this robbery, I began to suspect that my mysterious visitress, who had caused me so much alarm, was the thief of my property; and I immediately summoned old Margaretha. She was, of course, astounded at the occurrence which I related; and, after some reflection, she suddenly remembered that she had forgotten to fasten the house-door ere she retired to rest on the preceding evening. I chided her for a neglect which had enabled some evil-disposed woman to penetrate into my chamber, and not only terrify but also plunder me. She implored my forgiveness, and besought me not to mention the incident to the Count when next we met. Alas! my noble Andrea and I never met again!

"I was sorely perplexed by the event which I have

just related. If the mysterious visitress were a common thief, why did she leave any of the jewels in the casket? and wherefore had she on two occasions contemplated me with looks of such dark rage and infernal menace? A thought struck me. Could the Count's daughter have discovered our amour? and was it she who had come to regain possession of jewels belonging to the family. I hinted my suspicions to Margaretha; but she speedily convinced me that they were unfounded. '*The Lady Nisida is deaf and dumb,*' she said, '*and cannot possibly exercise such faculties of observation, nor adopt such means of obtaining information as would make her acquainted with all that has occurred between her father and yourself. Besides—she is constantly in attendance on her sire, who is very—very ill.*' I now perceived the improbability of a deaf and dumb female discovering an amour so carefully concealed; but, to assure myself more fully on that head, I desired Margaretha to describe the Lady Nisida. This she readily did; and I learnt from her that the Count's daughter was of a beauty quite different from the lady whom I had seen in the church and in my own chamber. In a word it appears that Nisida has light hair, blue eyes, and a delicate form; whereas the object of my interest, curiosity, and fear, is a woman of dark Italian loveliness.

"I have little more now to say. The loss of the jewels and the recollection of the mysterious lady were soon absorbed in the distressing thoughts which the serious illness of the Count forced upon my mind. Weeks passed away, and he came not: but he sent repeated messages by Antonio, imploring me to console myself, as he should soon recover, and urging me not to take any step that might betray the existence of our amour. Need I say how religiously I obeyed him in this latter respect? Day after day did I hope to see him again, for I knew not that he was dying; and I used to dress myself in my gayest attire—even as now I am apparelled—to welcome his expected visit. Alas! he never came; and his death was concealed from me, doubtless that the sad event might not be communicated until after the funeral, lest in the first frenzy of anguish I should rush to the Riverola palace to imprint a last kiss upon the cheek of the corpse. But a few hours ago I learnt the whole truth from two female friends of Dame Margaretha who called to visit her, and whom I had hastened to inform that she was temporarily absent. My noble Andrea was dead, and at that very moment his funeral obsequies were being celebrated in the neighbouring church—the very church in which I had first beheld the mysterious lady! Frantic with grief—unmindful of the exposure that would ensue—reckless of consequences, I left the house—I hastened to the church—I intruded my presence amidst the mourners. You know the rest, Fernand. It only remains for me to say that the countenance which I beheld ere now at the window—strongly delineated and darkly conspicuous amidst the blaze of light outside the casement—was that of the lady whom I had thus seen for the third time! But, tell me, Fernand, how could a stranger thus obtain admittance to the gardens of your mansion?"

"You see yon lights, Agnes?" said Wagner, pointing towards the mansion which, as we stated at the commencement of this chapter, was situate at a distance of about two hundred yards from Fernand's dwelling, the backs of the two houses thus looking towards each other. "Those lights," he continued, "are shining in a mansion the gardens of which are separated from my own by a simple hedge of evergreens that would not bar even the passage of a child. Should any inmate of that mansion possess curiosity sufficient to induce him or her to cross the boundary, traverse my gardens, and approach the casements of my residence, that curiosity may be easily gratified."

"And to whom does yon mansion belong?" asked Agnes.

"To Dr. Duras, an eminent physician," was the reply.

"Dr. Duras, the physician who attended my noble Andrea in his illness!" exclaimed Agnes. "Then the mysterious lady of whom I have spoken so much, and whose countenance ere now appeared at the casement, must be an inmate of the house of Dr. Duras; or, at all events, a visitor there! Ah! surely there is some connexion between that lady and the family of Riverola?"

"Time will solve the mystery, dearest sister—for so I am henceforth to call you," said Fernand. "But, beneath this roof, no harm can menace you. And now let me summon good Dame Paula, my housekeeper, to conduct you to the apartments which have been prepared for your reception. The morning is far advanced, and we both stand in need of rest."

Dame Paula—an elderly, good-tempered—kind-hearted matron—shortly made her appearance: and to her charge did Wagner consign his newly-found relative, whom he now represented to be his sister.

But as Agnes accompanied the worthy woman from the apartment, she shuddered involuntarily as she passed the frame which was covered with the black cloth, and which seemed darkly ominous amidst the blaze of light that filled the room.

CHAPTER X.
FRANCISCO, WAGNER, AND NISIDA.

ON the ensuing evening, Francisco, Count of Riverola, was seated in one of the splendid saloons of his palace, pondering upon the strange injunctions which he had received from his deceased father relative to the mysterious closet, when Wagner was announced.

Francisco rose to receive him, saying, in a cordial though melancholy tone, "Signor, I expected you."

"And let me hasten to express the regret which I experience at having addressed your lordship coldly and haughtily last night," exclaimed Wagner. "But—at the moment—I only beheld in you the son of him who had dishonoured a being very dear to my heart."

"I can well understand your feelings on that occasion, signor," replied Francisco. "Alas! the sins of the fathers are too often visited upon the children in this world. But in whatever direction our present conversation may turn, I implore you to spare as much as possible the memory of my sire."

"Think not, my lord," said Wagner, "that I should be so ungenerous as to reproach you for a deed in which you had no concern, and over which you exercised no control. Nor should I inflict so deep an injury upon you as to speak in disrespectful terms of him who was the author of your being, but who is now no more."

"Your kind language has already made me your friend," exclaimed Francisco. "And now point out to me in what manner I can in any way repair—or mitigate—the wrong done to that fair creature in whom you express yourself interested."

"That young lady is my sister," said Wagner, emphatically.

"Your sister, signor! And yet, meseems, she recognised you not——"

"Long years have passed since we saw each other," interrupted Fernand: "for we were separated in our childhood."

"And did you not both speak of some relative—an old man who once dwelt on the confines of the Black Forest of Germany, but who is now in Florence?" asked Francisco.

"Alas! that old man is no more," returned Wagner. "I did but use his name to induce Agnes to place confidence in me, and allow me to withdraw her from a scene which her wild grief so unpleasantly interrupted; for I thought that were I then and there to announce myself as her brother, she might not believe me—she might suspect some treachery or snare in a city so notoriously profligate as Florence. But the subsequent explanations which took place between us cleared up all doubts on that subject."

"I am well pleased to hear that the poor girl has found so near a relative and so dear a friend, signor," said Francisco. "And now acquaint me. I pray thee, with the means whereby I may, to some extent, repair the injury your sister has sustained at the hands of him whose memory I implore you to spare!"

"Wealth I possess in abundance—oh! far greater abundance than is necessary to satisfy all my wants!" exclaimed Wagner, with something of bitterness and regret in his tone: "but, even were I poor, gold would not restore my sister's honour. No—let that subject, however, pass. I would only ask you, Count, whether there be any scion of your family—any lady connected with you—who answers this description?"

And Wagner proceeded to delineate, in minute terms, the portraiture of the mysterious lady who had inspired Agnes on three occasions with so much terror, and whom Agnes herself had depicted in such glowing language.

"Signor! you are describing the Lady Nisida, my sister!" ejaculated Francisco, struck with astonishment at the portrait thus verbally drawn.

"Your sister, my lord!" cried Wagner. "Then has

Dame Margaretha deceived Agnes in representing the Lady Nisida to be rather a beauty of the cold north than of the sunny south."

"Dame Margaretha!" said Francisco: "do you allude, signor, to the mother of my late father's confidential dependent, Antonio?"

"The same," was the answer. "It was at Dame Margaretha's house that your father placed my sister Agnes, who has resided there nearly four years."

"But wherefore have you made those inquiries relative to the Lady Nisida?" inquired Francisco.

"I will explain the motive with frankness," responded Wagner.

He then related to the young Count all those particulars relative to the mysterious lady and Agnes, with which the reader is already acquainted.

"There must be some extraordinary mistake—some strange error, signor, in all this," observed Francisco. "My poor sister is, as you seem to be aware, so deeply afflicted that she possesses not faculties calculated to make her aware of that amour which even I, who possess those faculties in which she is deficient, never suspected, and concerning which no hint ever reached me until the whole truth burst suddenly upon me last night at the funeral of my sire. Moreover, had accident revealed to Nisida the existence of that connexion between my father and your sister, signor, she would have imparted the discovery to me; such is the confidence and so great is the love that exists between us. For habit has rendered us so skilful and quick in conversing with the language of the deaf and dumb, that no impediment ever exists to the free interchange of our thoughts."

"And yet, if the Lady Nisida had made such a discovery, her hatred of Agnes may be well understood," said Wagner; "for her ladyship must naturally look upon my sister as the partner of her father's weakness—the dishonoured slave of his passions."

"Nisida has no secret from me," observed the young Count, firmly.

"But wherefore did Dame Margaretha deceive my sister in respect to the personal appearance of the Lady Nisida?" inquired Wagner.

"I know not. At the same time——"

The door opened, and Nisida entered.

She was attired in deep black: her luxuriant raven hair, no longer depending in shining curls, was gathered up in massy bands at the sides, and in a knot behind, whence hung a rich veil *that meandered over her body's splendidly symmetrical length of limb in such a manner as to aid her attire in shaping rather than hiding the contours of that matchless form.* The voluptuous development of her bust was shrouded, not concealed, by the stomacher of black velvet which she wore, and which set off in strong relief the dazzling whiteness of her neck.

The moment her lustrous dark eyes fell upon Fernand Wagner, she started slightly: but this movement was imperceptible alike to him whose presence caused it, and to her brother.

Francisco conveyed to her, by the rapid language of the fingers, the name of their visitor, and at the same time intimated to her that he was the brother of Agnes, —the young and lovely female whose strange appearance at the funeral, and avowed connexion with the late noble, had not been concealed from the haughty lady.

Nisida's eyes seemed to gleam with pleasure when she understood in what degree of relationship Wagner stood towards Agnes; and she bowed to him with a degree of courtesy seldom displayed by her to strangers.

Francisco then conveyed to her in the language of the dumb all those details already related in respect to the "mysterious lady" who had so haunted the unfortunate Agnes.

A glow of indignation mounted to the cheeks of Nisida; and more than usually rapid was the reply she made through the medium of the alphabet of the fingers.

"My sister desires me to express to you, signor," said Francisco, turning towards Wagner, "that she is not the person whom the Lady Agnes has to complain against. My sister," he continued, "has never, to her knowledge, seen Lady Agnes; much less has she ever penetrated into her chamber;—and indignantly does she repel the accusation relative to the abstraction of the jewels. She also desires me to inform you that last night, after the reading of our father's last testament, she retired to her chamber, which she did not quit until this morning at the usual hour; and that therefore it was not her countenance which the Lady Agnes beheld at the casement of your saloon."

"I pray you, my lord, to let the subject drop now, and for ever!" said Wagner, who was struck with profound admiration—almost amounting to love—for the Lady Nisida: "there is some strange mystery in all this, which time alone can clear up. Will your lordship express to your sister how grieved I am that any suspicion should have originated against her in respect to Agnes?"

Francisco signalled the remarks to Nisida; and the latter, rising from her seat, advanced towards Wagner, and presented him her hand in token of her readiness to forget the injurious imputations thrown out against her.

Fernand raised that fair hand to his lips, and respectfully kissed it; but the hand seemed to burn as he held it, and when he raised his eyes towards the lady's countenance, she darted on him a look so ardent and impassioned that it penetrated into his very soul.

That rapid interchange of glances seemed immediately to establish a kind of understanding—a species of intimacy between those extraordinary beings: for, on the one side, Nisida read in the fine eyes of the handsome Fernand all the admiration expressed there; and he, on his part, instinctively understood that he was far from disagreeable to the proud sister of the young Count of Riverola. While *he* was ready to fall at her feet and do homage to her beauty, *she* experienced the kindling of all the fierce passions of sensuality in her breast.

But the unsophisticated and innocent-minded Francisco observed not the expression of these emotions on either side, for their manifestation occupied not a moment. The interchange of such feelings is ever too vivid and electric to attract the notice of the unsuspecting observer.

When Wagner was about to retire, Nisida made the following signal to her brother:—"Express to the signor that he will ever be a welcome guest at the palace of Riverola; for we owe kindness and friendship to the brother of her whom our father dishonoured."

But, to the astonishment of both the Count and the Lady Nisida, Wagner raised his hands, and displayed as perfect a knowledge of the language of the dumb as they themselves possessed.

"I thank your ladyship for this unexpected condescension," he signalled by the rapid play of the fingers; "and I shall not fail to avail myself of this most courteous invitation."

It were impossible to describe the sudden glow of pleasure and delight which animated Nisida's splendid countenance, when she thus discovered that Wagner was able to hold converse with her; and she hastened to reply thus:—"We shall expect you to revisit us soon."

Wagner bowed low, and took his departure, his mind full of the beautiful Nisida.

CHAPTER XI.

NISIDA AND WAGNER.—FRANCISCO AND FLORA.—THE APPROACH OF SUNSET.

UPWARDS of two months had passed away since the occurrences related in the preceding chapter, and it was now the 31st of January, 1521.

The sun was verging towards the western hemisphere; but the rapid flight of the hours was unnoticed by Nisida and Fernand Wagner, as they were seated together in one of the splendid saloons of the Riverola mansion.

Their looks were fixed upon each other's countenance— the eyes of Fernand expressing tenderness and admiration —those of Nisida beaming with all the passions of her ardent and sensual soul.

Suddenly the lady raised her hands, and by the rapid play of the fingers, asked—"Fernand, do you indeed love me as much as you would have me believe that I am beloved?"

"Never in this world was woman so loved as you," he replied, by the aid of the same language.

"And yet I am an unfortunate being—deprived of those qualities which give the greatest charm to the companionship of those who love."

"But you are eminently beautiful, my Nisida; and I can fancy how sweet—how rich toned would be your voice could your lips frame the words—'*I love thee!*'"

A profound sigh agitated the breast of the lady; and at the same time her lips quivered strangely—as if she were essaying to speak.

Wagner caught her to his breast: and she wept long and plenteously. Those tears relieved her—and she returned his warm, impassioned kisses with an ardour that convinced him how dear he had become to that afflicted, but transcendently beautiful being. On her side, the blood in her veins appeared to circulate like molten lead; and her face—her neck—her bosom were suffused with burning blushes.

At length, raising her head, she conveyed this wish to her companion:—"Thou hast given me an idea which may render me ridiculous in your estimation; but it is a whim—a fancy—a caprice engendered only by the profound affection I entertain for thee. I would that thou shouldst say, in thy softest—tenderest tones, the words—'I love thee!'—and by the wreathing of thy lips I shall perceive enough to enable my imagination to persuade itself that those words have really fallen upon my ears!"

Fernand smiled assent; and while Nisida's eyes were fixed upon him with the most enthusiastic interest, he said, "I love thee!"

The sovereign beauty of her countenance was suddenly lighted up with an expression of ineffable joy—of indescribable delight; and signalling the assurance—"I also love thee, dearest, dearest Fernand,"—she threw herself into his arms.

But almost at the same moment voices were heard in the adjacent room; and Wagner, gently disengaging himself from Nisida's embrace, hastily conveyed to her an intimation of the vicinity of others.

The lady gave him to understand by a glance that she comprehended him; and they remained motionless, gazing fondly upon each other.

"I know not how it has occurred, Flora," said the voice of Francisco, speaking in a tender tone, in the adjoining room—"I know not how it has occurred that I should have addressed you in this manner—so soon, too, after the death of my lamented father, and while these mourning garments yet denote the loss which myself and sister have sustained——"

"Oh! my lord, suffer me to retire," exclaimed Flora Francatelli, in a tone of beseeching earnestness: "I should not have listened to your lordship so long in the Gallery of Pictures—much less have accompanied your lordship hither!"

"I requested thee to come with me to this apartment, Flora, that I might declare—without fear of our interview being interrupted—how dear, how very dear thou art to me, and how honourable is the passion with which thou hast inspired me. O Flora," exclaimed the young Count, "I could no longer conceal my love for thee! My heart was bursting to reveal its secret; and when I discovered thee alone ere now in the Gallery of Pictures, I could not resist the favourable opportunity which accident seemed to have afforded for this avowal."

"Alas! my lord," murmured Flora, "I know not whether to rejoice or to be sorrowful at the revelation which has this day met my ears."

"And yet you said ere now that you could love me—that you did love me, in return!" ejaculated Francisco.

"I spoke truly, my lord," answered the bashful maiden: "but, alas! how can the humble, obscure, portionless Flora become the wife of the rich, powerful, and honoured Count of Riverola? There is an inseparable gulf fixed between us, my lord!"

"Am I not my own master? Can I not consult my happiness in that most solemn and serious of this world's duties—marriage?" cried Francisco, with all the generous ardour of youth and of his own noble disposition.

"Your lordship is free and independent in point of fact," said Flora, in a low, tender, and yet impressive tone; "but your lordship has relations—friends——"

"My relations will not thwart the wishes of him whom they love," answered Francisco; "and those who place obstacles in the way of my felicity cannot be denominated my friends."

"Oh! my lord—could I yield myself up to the hopes which your language inspires!" cried Flora.

"You can—you may, dearest girl!" exclaimed the young Count. "And now I know that you love me! But many months must elapse ere I can call thee mine; and, indeed, a remorse smites my heart that I have dared to think of my own happiness, so soon after the mournful ceremony which consigned a parent to the tomb! Heaven knows that I do not the less deplore his loss——But wherefore art thou so pale—so trembling, Flora?"

"Meseems that a superstitious awe, as if of evil omens, has seized upon my soul," returned the maiden, in a tremulous tone. "Let us retire, my lord: the Lady Nisida may require my services elsewhere."

"Nisida!" repeated Francisco, as if the mention of his sister's name had suddenly awakened new ideas in his mind.

"Ah! my lord," said Flora, sorrowfully, "you now perceive that there is at least one relative who may not learn with satisfaction the alliance which your lordship would form with the poor and humble dependant!"

"Nay, by my patron saint, thou hast misunderstood me!" exclaimed the young Count, warmly. "Nisida will not oppose her brother's happiness; and her strong mind will know how to despise these conventional usages which require that high birth should mate with high birth, and wealth ally itself to wealth. Yes—Nisida will consult my felicity alone; and when I ere now repeated her name as it fell from your lips, it was in a manner reproachful to myself, because I have retained my love for thee a secret from her. A secret from Nisida—oh! I have been cruel, unjust, not to have confided in my sister long ago! And yet," he added, more slowly, "she might reproach me for my selfishness in bestowing a thought on marriage so soon—so very soon after a funeral! Flora, dearest maiden—circumstances demand that the avowal which accident and opportunity have this day led me to make, should exist as a secret known only unto yourself and me. But, in a few months, I will explain all to my sister, and she will greet thee as her brother's chosen bride. Art thou content, Flora, that our mutual love should remain thus concealed until the proper time shall come for its revelation?"

"Yes, my lord—and for many reasons," was the reply.

"For many reasons, Flora?" exclaimed the young Count.

"At least for more than one," rejoined the maiden. "In the first instance, it is expedient that your lordship should have due leisure to reflect upon the important step which you propose to take—a step conferring so much honour upon myself, but which may not insure your happiness."

"If this be a specimen of thy reasons, dear maiden," exclaimed Fransisco, laughing, "I need hear no more. Be well assured," he added seriously, "that time will not impair the love I experience for you."

Flora murmured a reply which did not reach Wagner; and immediately afterwards the sound of her light steps were heard retreating from the adjacent room. A profound silence of a few minutes occurred: and then Francisco also withdrew.

Wagner had been an unwilling listener to the preceding conversation; but while it was in progress, he from time to time threw looks of love and tenderness on his beautiful companion, who returned them with impassioned ardour.

Whether it were that her irritable temper was impatient of the restraint imposed upon herself and her lover by the vicinity of others—or whether she was annoyed at the fact of her brother and Flora being so long together—(for Wagner had intimated to her who their neighbours were the moment he had recognised their voices)—we cannot say: but Nisida showed an occasional uneasiness of manner, which she, however, studied to subdue as much as possible, during the scene that took place in the adjoining apartment.

Fernand did not offer to convey to her any idea of the nature of the conversation which occupied her brother and Flora Francatelli; neither did she manifest the least curiosity to be enlightened on that head.

The moment the young lovers had quitted the next room, Wagner intimated the fact to Nisida; but at the same instant, just as she was bestowing upon him a tender caress—a dreadful — an appalling reminiscence burst upon him with such overwhelming force, that he fell back stupefied on the sofa.

Nisida's countenance instantly assumed an expression of the deepest solicitude; and her eloquent—speaking eyes, implored him to tell her what had assailed him.

But, starting wildly from his seat, and casting on her a glance of such bitter—bitter anguish, that the appalling emotions thus expressed struck terror to her soul—Fernand rushed from the room.

Nisida sprang to the window; and, though the obscurity of evening now announced the last flickerings of the setting sunbeams in the west, she could perceive her lover dashing furiously on through the spacious gardens that surrounded the Riverola palace.

On—on he went towards the River Arno; and in a few moments he was out of sight.

Alas! intoxicated with love, and giving himself wholly up to the one delightful idea—that he was with the beauteous Nisida—then, absorbed in the interest of the discourse which he had overheard between Francisco and Flora—Wagner had forgotten until it was nearly too late *that the sun was about to set on the last day of the month!*

CHAPTER XII.

THE WEHR-WOLF.

'TWAS the hour of sunset.

The eastern horizon, with its gloomy and sombre twilight, offered a strange contrast to the glorious glowing hues of vermilion, and purple, and gold, that blended in long streaks athwart the western sky.

For even the winter sunset of Italy is accompanied with resplendent tints—as if an Emperor, decked with a refulgent diadem, were repairing to his imperial couch.

The declining rays of the orb of light bathed in molten gold the pinnacles, steeples, and lofty palaces of proud Florence, and toyed with the limpid waves of the Arno, on whose banks innumerable villas and casinos already sent forth delicious strains of music, broken only by the mirth of joyous revellers.

And by degrees, as the sun went down, the palaces of the superb city began to shed light from their lattices set in richly sculptured masonry; and here and there where festivity prevailed, grand illuminations sprang up with magical quickness,—the reflection from each separate galaxy rendering it bright as day,—far—far around.

Vocal and instrumental melody floated through the still air, and the perfume of exotics, decorating the halls of the Florentine nobles, poured from the widely opened portals, and rendered that air delicious.

For Florence was gay that evening—the last day of each month being the one which the wealthy lords and high-born ladies set apart for the reception of their friends.

The sun sunk behind the western hills; and even the hot-house flowers closed up their buds—as if they were eye-lids weighed down by slumber, and not to awake again until the morning should arouse them again to welcome the return of their lover—that glorious sun!

Darkness seemed to dilate upon the sky like an image in the midst of a mirage, expanding into superhuman dimensions,—then rapidly losing its shapeliness, and covering the vault above densely and confusedly.

But by degrees countless stars began to stud the colourless canopy of heaven, like gems of orient splendour; for the last—last flickering ray of the twilight in the west had expired in the increasing obscurity.

But, hark! what is that wild and fearful cry?

In the midst of a wood of evergreens on the banks of the Arno, a man—young, handsome, and splendidly attired—has thrown himself upon the ground, where he writhes like a stricken serpent.

He is the prey of a demoniac excitement: an appalling consternation is on him;—madness is in his brain—his mind is on fire.

Lightnings appear to gleam from his eyes—as if his soul were dismayed, and withering within his breast,

"Oh! no—no!" he cries, with a piercing shriek, as if wrestling madly—furiously—but vainly, against some unseen fiend that holds him in his grasp.

And the wood echoes to that terrible wail: and the startled bird flies fluttering from its bough.

But, lo! what awful change is taking place in the form of that doomed being? His handsome countenance elongates into one of savage and brute-like shape;—the rich garment which he wears becomes a rough, shaggy, and wiry skin;—his body loses its human contours—his arms and limbs take another form; and, with a frantic howl of misery, to which the woods give horribly faithful reverberations, and with a rush like a hurling wind, the wretch starts wildly away—no longer a man, but a monstrous wolf!

On—on he goes: the wood is cleared—the open country is gained. Tree—hedge—and isolated cottage appear but dim points in the landscape—a moment seen, the next left behind: the very hills appear to leap after each other.

A cemetery stands in the monster's way; but he turns not aside:—through the sacred enclosure, on—on he goes. There are situate many tombs, stretching up the slope of a gentle acclivity, from the dark soil of which the white monuments stand forth with white and ghastly gleaming; and on the summit of the hill is the church of St. Benedict the Blessed.

From the summit of the ivy-grown tower the very rooks, in the midst of their cawing, are scared away by the furious rush and the wild howl with which the Wehr-Wolf thunders over the hallowed ground.

At the same instant a train of monks appear round the angle of the church—for there is a funeral at that hour; and their torches, flaring with the breeze that is now springing up, cast an awful and almost magical light upon the dark grey walls of the edifice,—the strange effect being enhanced by the prismatic reflection of the lurid blaze from the stained glass of the oriel window.

The solemn spectacle seemed to madden the Wehr-Wolf. His speed increased—he dashed through the funeral train—appalling cries of terror and alarm burst from the lips of the holy fathers, and the solemn procession was thrown into confusion. The coffin-bearers dropped their burden—and the corpse rolled out upon the ground—its decomposing countenance seeming horrible by the glare of the torchlight.

The monk who walked nearest the head of the coffin was thrown down by the violence with which the ferocious monster cleared its passage; and the venerable father—on whose brow sat the snow of eighty winters—fell with his head against a monument, and his brains were dashed out.

On—on fled the Wehr-Wolf—over mead and hill, through valley and dale. The very wind seemed to make way: he clove the air—he appeared to skim the ground—to fly.

Through the romantic glades and rural scenes of Etruria the monster sped—sounds resembling shrieking howls, bursting ever and anon from his foaming mouth—his red eyes glaring in the dusk of the evening like ominous meteors—and his whole aspect so full of appalling ferocity, that never was seen so monstrous—so terrific a spectacle!

A village is gained—he turns not aside—but dashes madly through the little street formed by the huts and cottages of the Tuscan vine-dressers.

A little child is in his path—a sweet, blooming, ruddy, noble boy, with violet-coloured eyes and flaxen hair,—disporting merrily at a short distance from his parents who are seated at the threshold of their dwelling.

Suddenly a strange and ominous rush—an unknown trampling of rapid feet falls upon their ears: then with a savage cry, a monster sweeps past.

"My child! my child!" screams the affrighted mother; and simultaneously the shrill cry of an infant in the sudden agony of death carries desolation to the ear!

'Tis done—'twas but the work of a moment: the wolf has swept by—the quick rustling of his feet is no longer heard in the village. But those sounds are succeeded by awful wails and heartrending lamentations; for the child—the blooming, violet-eyed, flaxen-haired boy—the darling of his poor but tender parents, is weltering in his blood!

On—on speeds the destroyer, urged by an infernal influence which maddens the more intensely because its victim strives vainly to struggle against it:—on—on, over the beaten road—over the fallow field—over the cottager's garden—over the grounds of the rich one's rural villa!

And now, to add to the horror of the scene, a pack of dogs have started in pursuit of the wolf,—dashing—crushing—hurrying—pushing—pressing upon one another in all the anxious ardour of the chase.

The silence and shade of the open country, in the mild starlight, seem eloquently to proclaim the peace and happiness of a rural life:—but now that silence is broken by the mingled howling of the wolf and the deep baying of the hounds,—and that shade is crossed and darkened by the forms of the animals as they scour so fleetly—oh! with such whirlwind speed along!

But that Wehr-Wolf bears a charmed life;—for though the hounds overtake him—fall upon him—and attack him with all the courage of their nature,—yet does he hurl them from him—toss them aside—spurn them away—and at length free himself from their pursuit altogether!

And now the moon rises with unclouded splendour, like a maiden looking from her lattice screened with purple curtains; and still the monster hurries madly on with unrelaxing speed.

For hours he has pursued his way thus madly;—and, on a sudden, as he passes the outskirts of a sleeping town, the church bell is struck by the watcher's hand, to proclaim midnight.

Over the town—over the neighbouring fields—through the far-off forest, clanged that iron tongue; and the Wehr-Wolf sped all the faster—as if he were with ominous flapping, like the wings of the fabulous Simoorg.

But, in the midst of appalling spasmodic convulsions,

—with direful writhings on the soil, and with cries of bitter anguish,—the Wehr-Wolf gradually threw off his monster shape; and at the very moment when the first sunbeam penetrated the wood and glinted on his face, he rose a handsome—young—and perfect man once more!

CHAPTER XIII.

NISIDA'S EMOTIONS.—THE DISGUISE.—A PLOT.

WE must now return to Nisida, whom we left gazing from the window of the Riverola mansion, at the moment when Wagner rushed away from the vicinity of his lady-love on the approach of sunset.

The singularity of his conduct—the look of ineffable horror and anguish which he cast upon her ere he darted from her presence—and the abruptness of his departure, filled her mind with the most torturing misgivings, and with a thousand wild fears.

Had his senses suddenly left him? was he the prey to fits of mental aberration which would produce so extraordinary an effect upon him? had he taken a sudden loathing and disgust to herself? or had he *discovered* anything in respect to her which had converted his love into hatred!

She knew not—and conjecture was vain!

To a woman of her excitable temperament the occurrence was particularly painful. She had never known the passion of love until she had seen Wagner: and the moment she did see him, she loved him. The sentiment on her part originated altogether in the natural sensuality of her disposition: there was nothing pure—nothing holy—nothing refined in her affection for him; —it was his wonderful personal beauty that had made so immediate and so profound an impression upon her heart.

There was consequently something furious and raging in that passion which she experienced for Fernand Wagner,—a passion capable of every extreme—the largest sacrifices, or infuriate jealousies—the most implicit confidence, or the maddest suspicion! It was a passion which would induce her to ascend the scaffold to save him; or to plunge the vengeful dagger into his heart did she fancy that he deceived her!

To one, then, whose soul was animated by such a love, the conduct of of Fernand was adapted to wear even an exaggerated appearance of singularity; and as each different conjecture swept through her imagination, her emotions were excited to an extent which caused her countenance to vary its expression a hundred times in a minute.

The fury of the desolating torrent—the rage of the terrific volcano—the sky cradled in the blackest clouds —the ocean heaving tempestuously in its mighty bed— the chafing of a tremendous flood against an embankment which seems ready every moment to give way and allow the collected waters to burst forth upon the broad plains and into the peaceful valleys,—all these occurrences in the physical world were imaged by the emotions that now agitated within the breast of the Italian lady.

Her mind was like a sea put in motion by the wind :— and her eyes flashed fire—her lip quivered—her bosom heaved convulsively—her neck arched proudly, as if she were struggling against ideas that forced themselves upon her and painfully wounded her boundless patrician pride.

For the thought that rose uppermost amidst all the conjectures which rushed to her imagination, was that Fernand had suddenly conceived an invincible dislike towards her.

Wherefore did he fly thus—as if eager to place the greatest possible distance between herself and him?

Then did she recall to mind every interchange of thought that had passed between them through the language of the fingers; and she could fix upon nothing which, emanating from herself, had given him offence?

Had he then really lost his senses?

Madly did he seem to be rushing towards the Arno, on whose dark tide the departing rays of the setting sun glinted with oscillating and dying power.

She still continued to gaze from the window, long after he had disappeared: obscurity was gathering rapidly around—but, even had it been noon-day, she would now have seen nothing. Her ideas grew bewildered: mortification—grief—anger—suspicion—burning desire, all mingled together, and at length produced a

species of stunning effect upon her—so that the past appeared to be a dream and the future was wrapt in the darkest gloom and uncertainty.

This strange condition of her mind did not however last long: the natural energy of her character speedily asserted its empire over that intellectual lethargy which had seized upon her;—and, awaking from her stupor, she resolved to waste not another instant in useless conjectures as to the cause of her lover's conduct.

Hastening to her own apartments, she dismissed Flora Francatelli, whom she found there, with an abruptness of gesture and a frowning expression of countenance amounting to an act of cruelty towards that resigned and charming girl; so that as the latter hastened from the room, tears started from her eyes, and she murmured to herself, " Can it be possible that Donna Nisida suspects the attachment her brother has formed towards me? Oh! if she do, the star of an evil destiny seems already to rule my horoscope !"

Scarcely had Flora disappeared in this sorrowing manner, when Nisida secured the outer door of her own suite of apartments, and hurried to her bed-chamber. There she threw aside the garb belonging to her sex, and assumed that of a cavalier, which she took from a press opening with a secret spring. Then, having arranged her hair beneath a velvet tocque shaded with waving black plumes, in such a manner that the disguise was as complete as she could render it, she girt on a long rapier of finest Milan steel; and, throwing the short cloak, edged with costly fur, gracefully over her left shoulder, she quitted her chamber by a private door opening behind the folds of the bed curtains.

A narrow and dark staircase admitted her into the gardens of the Riverola mansion. These she crossed with a step so light and free, that had it been possible to observe her in the darkness of the evening, she would have been taken for the most elegant and charming cavalier that ever honoured the Florentine Republic with his presence.

In about a quarter of an hour she reached the abode of Dr. Duras; but, instead of entering it, she passed round one of its angles, and opening a wicket by means of a key which she had about her, gained access to the gardens in the rear of the mansion.

She traversed these grounds with hasty steps, passed the boundary which separated them from the gardens of Wagner's dwelling, and then relaxing her pace, advanced with more caution to the windows of that very apartment where Agnes had been so alarmed two months previously, by observing the countenance at the casement.

But all was now dark within: Wagner was not in his favourite room—for Nisida *knew* that this *was* her lover's favourite apartment.

Perhaps he had not yet returned?

Thus thought the lady; and she walked slowly round the spacious dwelling, which like the generality of the patrician mansions of Florence in those times—as indeed is now the case to a considerable extent—stood in the midst of extensive gardens.

There were lights in the servants' offices; but every other room seemed dark. No :—one window in the front, on the ground-floor, shone with the lustre of a lamp.

Nisida approached it, and beheld Agnes reclining in a pensive manner on a sofa in a small but elegantly furnished apartment. Her countenance was immediately overclouded; and for an instant she lingered to gaze upon the sylph-like form that was stretched upon that ottoman. Then she hastily pursued her way; and having perfected the round of the building, once more reached the windows of her lover's favourite room.

Convinced that he had not returned, and fearful of being observed by any of the domestics who might happen to pass through the gardens, Nisida retraced her way towards the dwelling of Dr. Duras. But her heart was now heavy; for she knew not how to act.

Her original object was to obtain an interview with Wagner that very night, and learn, if possible, the reason of his extraordinary conduct towards her; for the idea of remaining in suspense for many long—long hours was painful in the extreme to a woman of her excitable nature.

She was however compelled to resign herself to this latter alternative; and having let herself through the wicket belonging to the physician's gardens, she directed her steps homeward.

On her way she passed by the gate of the Convent of Carmelite Nuns—one of the wealthiest, most strictly disciplined, and celebrated monastic establishments in the Florentine Republic.

It appeared that a sudden thought here struck her; for ascending the steps leading to the gate, she paused beneath the lamp of the deep Gothic portico, took out her tablets, and hastily wrote the following words :—

"Donna Nisida of Riverola requests an interview with the Lady Abbess Maria to-morrow at mid-day, on a matter seriously regarding the spiritual welfare of a young female who has shown great and signal disregard for the rites and ordinances of the most Holy Catholic

her. Fearful that they might be domestics belonging to the household she hastily and noiselessly retreated within the deep shade of the wall of the mansion; and there she remained motionless.

We must now detail the conversation which was passing between the two individuals whose presence in the garden had thus alarmed the Lady Nisida.

"But are you sure of what you say, Antonio?" demanded one of the men.

"By Saint Jacopo! I cannot be mistaken," was the reply. "The closet has been locked up for years and years—and the old Count always used to keep the key

Church; and in respect to whom the most severe measures must be adopted. Donna Nisida will visit the holy Mother to-morrow at mid-day."

Having written these words, Nisida tore off the leaf and thrust it through a small square grating set in the massive door of the convent. Then ringing the bell to call attention to the gate, she hastily pursued her way homeward.

She had gained the gardens of the Riverola mansion, and was advancing towards the door of the private staircase leading to her chamber, when she suddenly perceived two dark figures standing within a few yards of

in an iron chest, which was also carefully locked and chained round. What can the place possibly contain but a treasure?"

"After all, it is only conjecture on your part; and, that being the case, it is not worth while to risk one's life——"

"You are a coward, Stephano!" exclaimed Antonio, angrily. "The closet has got a heavy—massive door, and a prodigiously strong lock; and if those precautions were not adopted to protect a hoard of wealth, why were they taken at all, let me ask you?"

"There is something in what you say," replied Stephano: "but you do wrong to call me a coward. If it were not that we are cousins and linked by a bond of long-maintained friendship, I would send my rapier through your doublet in a twinkling."

"Nay—I did not mean to anger thee, Stephano," cried the valet. "But let us speak lower: chafe not, I pray thee!"

"Well—well," said the other, gloomily, "go on, in the name of your patron saint! Only keep a guard over your tongue, for it wags somewhat too freely; and remember that a man who has been for fifteen years the captain of as gallant a band as ever levied contributions on the lieges of the Republic, is not to have 'coward' thrown in his teeth."

"Let it pass, good Stephano!" urged the valet. "I tell thee that the closet whereof I have spoken, can contain naught save a treasure—perhaps in gold—perhaps in massive plate."

"We can dispose of either to our advantage," observed the bandit, with a hoarse chuckle.

"Will you undertake the business?" demanded Antonio.

"I will," was the resolute answer; "and as much to convince you that Stephano is not a coward, as for any other reason. But when is it to be done? and why did you make an appointment to meet me here, of all places in Florence?"

"It can be done when you choose," replied Antonio; "and, as for the other question, I desired you to meet me here, because I knew that you would not refuse a fine chance; and suspecting this much, it was necessary to show you the geography of the place."

"Good!" observed the robber-chief. "To-morrow night I have a little affair in hand for a reverend and holy father, who is sure to be chosen Superior of his Order if his rival in the candidature be removed; and in four-and-twenty hours the said rival must be food for the fishes of the Arno."

"Then the night after that?" suggested Antonio.

"Pre-engaged again," returned the bandit-captain, coolly. "A wealthy Countess has been compelled to pledge her diamonds to a Jew: on Sunday next she must appear with her husband at the Palace of the Medici; and on Saturday night, therefore, the diamonds must be recovered from the Jew."

"Then the husband knows not that they are so pledged?" said Antonio.

"Scarcely," answered the brigand. "They were deposited with the Jew for a loan which the Countess raised to accommodate her lover. Now do you understand?"

"Perfectly. What say you to next Monday night?"

"I am at your service," responded Stephano. "Monday will suit me admirably—and midnight shall be the hour. And now instruct me in the nature of the locality."

"Come with me, and I will show you by which window you and your comrades must effect an entry," said Antonio.

The valet and the robber-chief now moved away from the spot where they had stood to hold the above conversation; and the moment they had turned the adjacent angle of the mansion, Nisida hastened to regain her apartment by the private staircase—resolving, however, to see Wagner as early as possible in the morning.

CHAPTER XIV.

THE LAST MEETING OF AGNES AND THE STRANGER LADY.

WHILE all Nature was wrapt in the listening stillness of admiration at the rising sun, Fernand Wagner dragged himself painfully along towards his home.

His garments were besmeared with mud and dirt: they were torn, too, in many places; and here and there were stains of blood, still wet, upon them.

In fact, had he been dragged by a wild horse through a thicket of brambles, he could scarcely have appeared in a more wretched plight.

His countenance was ghastly pale—terror still flashed from his eyes—and despair sat on his lofty brow.

Stealing through the most concealed part of his garden, he was approaching his own mansion with the air of a man who returns home in the morning after having perpetrated some dreadful deed of turpitude under cover of the night.

But the watchful eyes of a woman have marked his coming from the lattice of her window; and in a few minutes Agnes, light as a fawn, came bounding towards him, exclaiming, "Oh! what a night of uneasiness have I passed, Fernand! But at length thou art restored to me—thou, whom I have ever loved so fondly; although," she added, mournfully, "I abandoned thee for so long a time!"

And she embraced him tenderly.

"Agnes!" cried Fernand, repulsing her with an impatience which she had never experienced at his hands before: "wherefore thus act the spy upon me? Believe me, that although we pass ourselves off as brother and sister, yet I do not renounce that authority which the real nature of those ties that bind us together——"

"Fernand! Fernand! this to me!" exclaimed Agnes, bursting into tears. "Oh! how have I deserved such reproaches?"

"My dearest girl—pardon me—forgive me!" cried Wagner, in a tone of bitter anguish. "My God! I ought not to upbraid thee for that watchfulness during my absence, and that joy at my return, which prove that you love me! Again I say, pardon me, dearest Agnes."

"You need not ask me, Fernand," was the reply. "Only speak kindly to me——"

"I do—I will, Agnes," interrupted Wagner. "But leave me now! Let me regain my own chamber alone: —I have reasons—urgent reasons for so doing;—and this afternoon, Agnes, I shall be composed—collected again. Do you proceed by that path—I will take this."

And, hastily pressing her hand, Wagner broke abruptly away.

For a few moments Agnes stood looking after him in vacant astonishment at his extraordinary manner, and also at his alarming appearance, but concerning which latter she had not dared to question him.

When he had entered the mansion by a private door, Agnes turned and pursued her way along a circuitous path shaded on each side by dark evergreens, and which was the one he had directed her to take so as to regain the front gate of the dwelling.

But scarcely had she advanced a dozen paces, when a sudden rustling amidst the trees alarmed her; and in another instant a female form—tall, majestic, and with a dark veil thrown over her head—stood before her.

Agnes uttered a faint shriek; for—although the lady's countenance was concealed by the veil—she had no difficulty in recognising the stranger who had already terrified her on three previous occasions, and who seemed to haunt her.

And, as if to dispel all doubt as to the identity, the majestic lady suddenly tore aside her veil, and disclosed to the trembling, shrieking Agnes, features already too well known.

But, if the lightnings of those brilliant, burning, black eyes had seemed terrible on former occasions, they were now absolutely blasting; and Agnes fell upon her knees, exclaiming, "Mercy! mercy! how have I offended you?"

For a few moments those basilisk-eyes darted forth shafts of fire and flame—and the red lips quivered violently—and the haughty brow contracted menacingly; and Agnes was stupefied—stunned—fascinated,—terribly fascinated by that tremendous rage, the vengeance of which seemed ready to explode against her.

But only a few moments lasted that dreadful scene;—for the lady, whose entire appearance was that of an avenging fiend in the guise of a beauteous woman, suddenly drew a sharp poniard from its sheath in her bodice, and plunged it into the bosom of the hapless Agnes.

The victim fell back; but not a shriek—not a sound escaped her lips. The blow was well aimed—the poniard was sharp and went deep—and death followed instantaneously.

For nearly a minute did the murderess stand gazing on the corpse—the corpse of one erst so beautiful: and her countenance, gradually relaxing from its stern, implacable expression, assumed an air of deep remorse—of bitter, bitter compunction.

But—probably yielding to the sudden thought that she must provide for her own safety—the murderess drew forth the dagger from the white bosom in which it was buried—hastily wiped it upon a leaf—returned it to the sheath—and replacing the veil over her countenance, hurried rapidly away from the scene of her fearful crime.

CHAPTER XV.

THE SBIRRI.—THE ARREST.

SCARCELY ten minutes had elapsed since the unfortunate Agnes was thus suddenly cut off in the bloom of youth and beauty, when a lieutenant of police, with his guard of sbirri, passed along the road skirting Wagner's garden.

They were evidently in search of some malefactor; for stopping in their course, they began to deliberate on the business which they had in hand.

"Which way could he possibly have gone?" cried one, striking the butt-end of his pike heavily upon the ground.

"How could we possibly have missed him?" exclaimed another.

"Stephano is not so easily caught, my men," observed the lieutenant. "He is the most astute and cunning of the band of which he is the captain. And yet I wish we had pounced upon him, since we were so nicely on his track."

"And a thousand ducats offered by the State for his capture," suggested one of the sbirri.

"Yes—'tis annoying!" ejaculated the lieutenant: "but I could have sworn he passed this way."

"And I would bear the same evidence, signor," observed the first speaker. "May be he has taken refuge in those bushes."

"Not unlikely. We are fools to grant him a moment's vantage-ground. Over the fence, my men—and beat amongst those gardens."

Thus speaking, the lieutenant set the example by leaping the railing, and entering the grounds belonging to Wagner's abode.

The sbirri, who were six in number, including their officer, divided themselves into two parties, and proceeded to search the gardens.

Suddenly a loud cry of horror burst from one of the sections; and when the other hastened to the spot, the sbirri composing it found their comrades in the act of raising the corpse of Agnes.

"She is quite dead," said the lieutenant, placing his hand upon her heart. "And yet the crime cannot have been committed many minutes—as the corpse is scarcely cold, and the blood still oozes forth."

"What a lovely creature she must have been!" exclaimed one of the sbirri.

"Cease your profane remarks, my man," cried the lieutenant. "This must be examined into directly. Does any one know who dwells in that mansion?"

"Signor Wagner, a wealthy German," was the reply given by a sbirri.

"Then come with me, my man," said the lieutenant; "and let us lose no time in searching his house. One of you must remain here by the corpse—and the rest may continue their search after the bandit, Stephano."

Having issued these orders, the lieutenant, followed by the sbirro whom he had selected to accompany him, hastened to the mansion.

The gate was opened by an old porter, who stared in astonishment when he beheld the functionaries of justice visiting that peaceful dwelling. But the lieutenant ordered him to close and lock the gate; and having secured the key, the officer said, "We must search this house: a crime has been committed close at hand."

"A crime!" ejaculated the porter: "then the culprit is not here—for there is not a soul beneath this roof who would perpetrate a misdeed."

"Cease your prating, old man!" said the lieutenant, sternly. "We have a duty to perform—see that we be not molested in executing it."

"But what is the crime, signor, of which——"

"Nay—*that* you shall know anon," interrupted the lieutenant. "In the name of his Serene Highness, the Duke, I command you in the first place to lead me and my follower to the presence of your master."

The old man hastened to obey this mandate; and he conducted the sbirri into the chamber where Wagner, having thrown off his garments, was partaking of that rest which he so much needed.

At the sound of heavy feet and the clanking of martial weapons, Fernand started from the slumber into which he had fallen only a few minutes previously.

"What means this insolent intrusion?" he exclaimed, his cheeks flushing with anger at the presence of the police.

"Pardon us, signor," said the lieutenant, in a respectful tone: "but a dreadful crime has been committed close by—indeed, within the enclosure of your own grounds——"

"A dreadful crime!" ejaculated Wagner.

"Yes, signor—a crime——"

The officer was interrupted by an ejaculation of surprise which burst from the lips of his attendant sbirro;

and turning hastily round, he beheld his follower intently scrutinizing the attire which Fernand had ere now thrown off.

"Ah! blood-stains!" cried the lieutenant, whose attention was directed towards those marks by the finger of his man. "Then is the guilty one speedily discovered! Signor," he added, turning once more towards Wagner, "are those your garments?"

An expression of indescribable horror convulsed the countenance of Fernand; for the question of the officer naturally reminded him of his dreadful fate—the fate of a Wehr-Wolf,—although, we should observe, he never remembered, when restored to the form of a man, what he might have done during the long hours that he wore the shape of a ferocious monster.

Still, as he knew that his garments had been soiled—torn—and blood-stained in the course of the preceding night, it was no wonder that he shuddered and became convulsed with mental agony when his terrible doom was so forcibly recalled to his mind.

His emotions were naturally considered to be corroborative evidence of guilt; and the lieutenant, laying his hand upon Wagner's shoulder, said in a stern, solemn manner, "In the name of his Highness, our Prince, I arrest you for the crime of murder!"

"Murder!" repeated Fernand, dashing away the officer's arm; "you dare not accuse me of such a deed!"

"I accuse you of murder, signor," exclaimed the lieutenant. "Within a hundred paces of your dwelling, a young lady——"

"A young lady!" cried Wagner, thinking of Agnes whom he had left in the garden.

"Yes, signor—a young lady has been most barbarously murdered!" added the officer in an impressive tone.

"Agnes! Agnes!" almost screamed the unhappy man, as this dreadful announcement fell upon his ears. "Oh! is it possible that thou art no more, my poor Agnes?"

He covered his face with his hands, and wept bitterly.

The lieutenant made a sign to his follower, who instantly quitted the room.

"There must be some mistake in this, signor," said the old porter, approaching the lieutenant, and speaking in a voice tremulous with emotions. "The master whom I serve, and whom you accuse, is incapable of the deed imputed to him."

"Yes—God knows how truly you speak!" ejaculated Wagner, raising his head. "That girl——Oh, sooner than have harmed one single hair of her head——But how know you that it is Agnes who is murdered?" he cried, abruptly turning towards the lieutenant.

"It was you who said it, signor," calmly replied the officer, as he fixed his dark eyes keenly upon Fernand.

"Oh! it was a surmise—a conjecture—because I parted with Agnes a short time ago in the garden——" exclaimed Wagner, speaking in hurried and broken sentences.

"Behold the victim!" said the lieutenant, who had approached the window, from which he was now looking.

Wagner sprang from his couch, and glanced forth into the garden beneath.

The sbirri were advancing along the gravel pathway, bearing amongst them the corpse of Agnes, upon whose pallid countenance the morning sunbeams were dancing as if in mockery even at death.

"Holy Virgin! it is indeed Agnes!" cried Wagner, in a tone of the most profound—heartrending anguish, and he fell back senseless in the arms of the lieutenant.

An hour afterwards, Fernand Wagner was the inmate of a dungeon beneath the palace inhabited by the Duke of Florence.

CHAPTER XVI.

NISIDA AND THE CARMELITE ABBESS.

PUNCTUALLY at mid-day, the Lady Nisida of Riverola proceeded, alone and unattended, to the Convent of Carmelite Nuns, where she was immediately admitted into the presence of the Abbess.

The superior of this monastic establishment was a tall, thin, stern-looking woman, with a sallow complexion, an imperious compression of the lips, and small grey eyes that seemed to flicker with malignity rather than to beam with the pure light of Christian love.

She was noted for the austerity of her manners, the rigid discipline which she maintained in the convent, and the inexorable disposition which she showed towards those who, having committed a fault, came within her jurisdiction.

Rumour was often busy with the affairs of the Carmelite Convent : and the grandams and gossips of Florence would huddle together around their domestic hearths, on the cold winter evenings, and venture mysterious hints and whispers of strange deeds committed within the walls of that sacred institution,—how from time to time some young and beautiful nun had suddenly disappeared, to the surprise and alarm of her companions, —how piercing shrieks had been heard to issue from the interior of the building, by those who passed near it at night,—and how the inmates themselves were often aroused from their slumbers by strange noises resembling the rattling of chains, the working of ponderous machinery, and the revolution of huge wheels.

Such food for scandal as these mysterious whispers supplied, was not likely to pass without exaggeration; and that love of the marvellous which inspired the aforesaid gossips, led to the embellishment of the rumours just glanced at,—so that one declared with a solemn shake of the head, how spirits were seen to glide around the convent walls at night,—and another averred that a nun, with whom she was acquainted, had assured her that strange and unearthly forms were often encountered by those inmates of the establishment who were hardy enough to venture into the chapel, or to traverse the long corridors or gloomy cloisters after dusk.

These vague and uncertain reports did not, however, prevent some of the wealthiest families in Florence from placing their daughters in the Carmelite Convent. A nobleman or opulent citizen who had several daughters, would consider it a duty to devote one of them to the service of the Church ; and the votive girl was most probably compelled to perform her noviciate and take the veil in this renowned establishment. It was essentially the convent patronised by the aristocracy ; and no female could be received within its walls save on the payment of a considerable sum of money.

There was another circumstance that added to the celebrity and augmented the wealth of the Carmelite Convent. Did a young unmarried lady deviate from the path of virtue,—or did a husband detect the infidelity of his wife,—the culprit was forthwith consigned to the care of the Abbess, and forced to take up her abode in that monastic institution. Or again—did some female openly neglect her religious duties, or imprudently express an opinion antagonistic to the Roman Catholic Church, the family to which she belonged would remove her to the spiritual care of the Abbess.

The convent was therefore considered to be an institution recognised by the State as a means of punishing immorality, upholding the interests of the Catholic religion — persuading the sceptical — confirming the waverer—and exercising a salutary terror over the ladies of the upper class, at that time renowned for their dissolute morals. The aristocracy of Florence patronised and protected the institution—because its existence afforded a ready means to get rid of a dishonoured daughter or an unfaithful wife ; and it was even said that the Abbess was invested with extraordinary powers by the rescript of the Duke himself,—powers which warranted her interference with even the liberty of young females who were denounced to her by their parents, guardians, or others who might have a semblance of a right to control or coerce them.

Luther had already begun to make a noise on Germany ; and the thunders of his eloquence had reverberated across the Alps to the Italian States. The priesthood were alarmed, and the conduct of the Reformer was an excuse for rendering the discipline of monastic institutions more rigid than ever. Nor was the Abbess Maria a woman who hesitated to avail herself of this fact as an apology for strengthening her despotism, and widening the circle of her influence.

The reader has now heard enough to make him fully aware that the Carmelite Convent was an establishment enjoying an influence, exercising an authority, and wielding a power, which—if these were misdirected—constituted an enormous abuse in the midst of a State bearing the name of a Republic. But the career of the Medici was then hastening towards a close ; and, in proportion as the authority of the Duke became circumscribed, the encroachments of the ecclesiastical orders grew more extensive.

The Abbess Maria, who was far advanced in years, but was endowed with one of those vigorous intellects against which Time vainly directs its influence, received the Lady Nisida in a little parlour plainly furnished. The praying-desk was of the most humble description ; and above it rose a cross of wood, so worm-eaten and decayed, that it

seemed as if the grasp of a strong hand would crush it into dust. But this emblem of the creed had been preserved in the Carmelete Convent since the period of the second Crusade, and was reported to consist of a piece of the actual cross on which the Saviour suffered in Palestine.

Against the wall hung a scourge, with five knotted throngs, whereon the blood-stains denoted the severity of that penance which the Abbess frequently inflicted upon herself. On a table stood a small loaf of coarse bread and a pitcher of water ; for although a sumptuous banquet was every day served up in the refectory, the Abbess was never known to partake of the delicious viands, nor to place her lips in contact with wine.

When Nisida entered the presence of the Abbess, she sank on her knees, and folded her arms meekly across her bosom. The holy mother gave her a blessing, and made a motion for her to rise. Nisida obeyed, and took a seat near the Abbess at the table.

She then drew forth her tablets, and wrote a few lines, which the superior read with deep attention.

Nisida placed a heavy purse of gold upon the table, and the Abbess nodded an assent to the request contained in the lines inscribed on the tablet.

The interview was about to terminate, when the door suddenly opened, and an elderly nun entered the room.

"Ursula," said the Lady Abbess, in a cold but reproachful tone, "didst thou not know that I was engaged ? What means this abrupt intrusion ?"

"Pardon me, holy mother !" exclaimed the nun ; "but the rumour of such a frightful murder has just reached us——"

"A murder !" ejaculated the Abbess. "Oh ! unhappy Florence, when wilt thou say farewell to crimes which render thy name detestable amongst Italian States !"

"This deed, too, holy mother, is one of inordinate blackness," continued Sister Ursula. "A young and beautiful lady——"

"We know not personal beauty within these walls, daughter," interrupted the Abbess, sternly.

"True, holy mother ! and yet I did but repeat the tale as the porteress ere now related it to me. However," resumed Ursula, "it appears that a young female, whom the worldly-minded outside these sacred walls denominate beautiful, was barbarously murdered this morning—shortly after the hour of sunrise——"

"Within the precincts of Florence ?" inquired the Abbess.

"Within a short distance of the convent, holy mother," answered the nun. "The dreadful deed was accomplished in the garden attached to the mansion of a certain Signor Wagner, whom the worldly-minded style a young man wondrously handsome."

"A fair exterior often conceals a black heart, daughter," said the Abbess. "But who was the hapless victim ?"

"Rumour declares, holy mother——"

The nun checked herself abruptly, and glanced at Nisida, who, during the above conversation had approached the windows which commanded a view of the convent garden, and whose back was therefore turned towards the Abbess and Ursula.

"You may speak fearlessly, daughter," said the Abbess ; "that unfortunate lady hears you not—for she is both deaf and dumb."

"Holy Virgin succour her !" ejaculated Ursula, crossing herself. "I was about to inform your ladyship," she continued, "that rumour represents the murdered woman to have been the sister of that Signor Wagner of whom I spoke ; but it is more than probable that there was no tie of relationship between them—and that——"

"I understand you, daughter," interrupted the Abbess. "Alas ! how much wickedness is engendered in this world by the sensual, fleshly passion which mortals denominate Love ! But is the murderer detected ?"

"The murderer was arrested immediately after the perpetration of the crime," responded Ursula : "and at this moment he is a prisoner in the dungeons of the palace."

"Who is the lost man that has perpetrated such a dreadful crime ?" demanded the Abbess, again crossing herself.

"Signor Wagner himself, holy mother," was the reply.

"The pious Duke Cosmo bequeathed gold to this institution," said the Abbess, "that masses might be offered up for the souls of those who fall beneath the weapon of the assassin. See that the lamented Prince's instructions be not neglected in this instance, Ursula."

"It was to remind your ladyship of this duty that I ventured to break upon your privacy," returned the nun, who then withdrew.

The Abbess approached Nisida, and touched her upon the shoulder to intimate to her that they were again alone together.

She had drawn down her veil; and was leaning her forehead against one of the iron bars which protected the window—apparently in a mood of deep thought.

When the Abbess touched her, she started abruptly round—then, pressing the Superior's hand with convulsive violence, hurried from the room.

ducal palace, was that gloomy prison, having no window, save a grating in the massive door to admit the air.

A lamp burnt dimly upon the table, whereon stood also the coarse prison fare provided for the captive, but which was untouched.

The clanking of the weapons of the sentinels, who kept guard in the passage from which the various dungeons opened, fell mournfully upon Fernand's ears, and every moment reminded him of the apparent impossibility of escape—even if such an idea possessed him.

The lamp had burnt throughout the day in his dungeon; for the light of heaven could not penetrate to that

"HE DASHED THROUGH THE FUNERAL TRAIN." (See p. 23.)

The old porteress presented the alms-box as she opened the gate of the convent; but Nisida pushed it rudely aside, and hurried down the steps as if she were escaping from a lazar-house rather than issuing from a monastic institution.

CHAPTER XVII.

WAGNER IN PRISON.—A VISITOR.

It was evening; and Wagner paced his narrow dungeon with agitated steps.

Far beneath the level of the ground, and under the

horrible subterranean cell—and it was only by the payment of gold that he had induced his gaoler to permit him the indulgence of the artificial substitute for the rays of the glorious sun.

"Oh! wretched being that I am!" he thought within himself, as he paced the stone floor of his prison-house: "the destiny of the accursed is mine! Ah! fool—dotard that I was to exchange the honours of old age for the vicissitudes of a renewed existence! Had Nature taken her course, I should probably now be sleeping in the quiet grave—and my soul might be in the regions of the blessed! But the tempter came and dazzled me with prospects of endless happiness, and I succumbed! O

Faust! would that thou hadst never crossed the threshold of my humble cottage in the Black Forest! How much sorrow—how much misery should I have been spared! Better—better to have remained in poverty—solitude—helplessness—worn down by the weight of years, and crushed by the sense of utter loneliness,—oh, better to have endured all this than to have taken on myself a new tenure of that existence which is so marked with misery and woe!"

He threw himself upon a seat, and endeavoured to reflect on his position with calmness; but he could not.

Starting up, he again paced the dungeon in an agitated manner.

"Holy God!" he exclaimed, aloud, "how much wretchedness has fallen upon me in a single day! Agnes murdered; Nisida, perhaps, for ever estranged from me—myself accused of a dreadful crime, whereof I am innocent—and circumstances all combining so wonderfully against me! But who could have perpetrated the appalling deed? Can that mysterious lady, whom Agnes spoke of so frequently, and who, by her description, so closely resembled my much-loved Nisida—can she——"

At that moment the bolts were suddenly drawn back from the door of the dungeon—the clanking chains fell heavily on the stone pavement outside—and the gaoler appeared, holding a lamp in his hand.

"Your brother, signor, has come to visit you," said the turnkey. "But pray let the interview be a brief one—for it is as much as my situation and my own liberty are worth, to have admitted him without an order from the Chief Judge."

With these words the gaoler made way for a cavalier to enter the dungeon: and as he closed the door, he said, "I shall return shortly to let your brother out again."

Surprise had hitherto placed a seal on Wagner's lips; but even before the visitor had entered the cell, a faint suspicion—a wild hope had flashed to his mind that Nisida had not forgotten him—that Nisida would not abandon him!

But this hope was destroyed almost as soon as formed, by the sudden recollection of her affliction; for how could a deaf and dumb woman succeed in bribing and deceiving one so cautious and wary as the gaoler of a criminal prison?

Nevertheless, the moment the visitor had entered the cell, and in spite of the deep disguise which she wore, the eyes of the lover failed not to recognise the object of his adoration in that elegant cavalier who now stood before him.

Scarcely had the gaoler closed and bolted the massive door again, when Fernand rushed forward to clasp Nisida in his arms; but, imperiously waving her hand, she motioned him to stand back.

Then with the language of the fingers, she rapidly demanded, "Will you swear upon the cross that the young female who has been murdered was not your mistress?"

"I swear," answered Fernand, in the same symbolic manner; and, as the light of the lamp played on his handsome countenance, his features assumed so decided an expression of truth, frankness, and sincerity, that Nisida was already more than half convinced of the injustice of her suspicions.

But still she was determined to be completely satisfied; and, drawing forth a small but exquisitely sculptured crucifix from her doublet, she presented it to her lover.

He sank upon one knee, received it respectfully, and kissed it without hesitation.

Nisida then threw herself into his arms, and embraced him with a fondness as warm—as wild—as impassioned as her suspicions had ere now been vehement and fearfully resentful.

Her presence caused Fernand to forget his sorrow—to forget that he was in a dungeon—to forget also the tremendous charge that hung over his head. For never had his Nisida appeared to him so marvellously beautiful as he now beheld her, disguised in the graceful garb of a cavalier of that age. Though tall, majestic, and of rich proportions for a woman, yet in the attire of the opposite sex, she seemed slight, short, and eminently graceful. The velvet cloak set so jauntily on her sloping shoulder, the doublet became her symmetry so well, and the rich lace-collar was so arranged as to disguise the prominence of the chest—that voluptuous fulness which could not be compressed!

At length a sudden thought struck Fernand, and he inquired in the usual manner how Nisida had gained access to him?

"A faithful friend contrived this interview for me," she replied, with her wonted rapidity of play upon the fingers. "He led the gaoler to believe that I was a German, and totally unacquainted with the Italian tongue. Thus not a word was addressed to me: and gold has opened the doors which separated me from you. The same means shall secure your escape."

"Dearest Nisida," signalled Wagner, "I would not escape were the door of my dungeon left open and the sentinels removed. I am innocent, and that innocence must be proved!"

The lady exhibited extraordinary impatience at this reply.

"You do not believe me guilty?" asked Wagner.

She shook her head in a determined manner, to show how profound was her conviction of his innocence.

"Then do not urge me, beloved one, to escape and be dishonoured for ever," was the urgent prayer he conveyed to her.

"The evidence against you will be overwhelming," she gave him to understand; then with an air of the most heart-appealing supplication, she added, "Escape, dearest Fernand—for my sake!"

"But I should be compelled to fly from Florence; and wouldst thou accompany me?"

She shook her head mournfully.

"Then will I remain here—in this dungeon! If my innocence be proved, I may yet hope to call the sister of the Count of Riverola my wife; if I be condemned——"

He paused;—for he knew that, even if he were sentenced to death, he could not die,—that some power, of which, however, he had only a vague notion, would rescue him,—that the compact, which gave him renewed youth and a long life on the fatal condition of his periodical transformation into a horrid monster, must be fulfilled; and though he knew not—understood not how all this was to be, still he knew that it *would* happen if he should really be condemned!

Nisida was not aware of the motive which had checked her lover as he was conveying to her his sense of the dread alternatives before him; and she hastened to intimate to him the following thought :—"You would say, that if you be condemned you will know how to meet death as becomes a brave man? But think of *me*—of Nisida, who loves you!"

"Would you continue to love a man branded as a murderer?"

"I should only think of you as my own dear Fernand!"

He shook his head—as much as to say, "It cannot be!"—and then once more embraced her fondly—for he beheld, in her anxiety for his escape, only a proof of her ardent affection.

At this moment the gaoler returned; and while he was unbolting the door, Nisida made one last, imploring appeal to her lover to give his assent to escape, if the arrangements were made for that purpose.

But he conveyed to her his resolute determination to meet the charge, with the hope of proving his innocence : and for a few moments Nisida seemed convulsed with the most intense anguish of soul.

The gaoler made his appearance, and Wagner, to maintain the deceit which Nisida informed him to have been practised on the man, said a few words aloud in German, as if he were really taking leave of a brother.

Nisida embraced him tenderly : and, covering her countenance as much as possible with her slouched hat, the waving plumes of which she made to fall over her face, this extraordinary being issued from the cell.

CHAPTER XVIII.

FLORA FRANCATELLI.—THE THREE NUNS.—THE CHAIR.

NISIDA regained her apartment, by the private staircase, without any molestation. Having laid aside her male attire, she assumed a loose wrapper, and then, throwing herself into an arm-chair, gave way to her reflections.

These were apparently of no pleasurable nature; for they were frequently interrupted by convulsive starts and rapid glancings around the room—as if she were fearful lest some terrible spectre was present to scare her.

Once or twice her eyes lingered upon her mother's portrait; and then profound sighs escaped her bosom.

Presently the beautiful Flora Francatelli entered the apartment; but Nisida made her a sign of dismissal.

The maiden withdrew : and we must now follow her to her own chamber.

On reaching her bed-room, Flora did not immediately retire to rest. She felt that should not sleep, even were she to seek her pillow : for she had much—very much to ponder upon !

There was a marked—an undisguised reserve about her mistress which materially affected her. Although she could not control her affections, yet she felt as if she were acting with duplicity towards the Lady Nisida, in having listened to the love-tale of Francisco, and retaining that revelation of affection a secret in her own breast.

Yet had he not implored, had he not enjoined her to keep that avowal to herself? Yes :—and when she looked at the matter, as it were face to face, she could not justly reproach herself :—nevertheless, that secret love weighed upon upon her conscience like a crime !

She could not understand wherefore Nisida's manner had changed towards her. Francisco had assuredly made no communication to his sister ; and nothing had transpired to excite a suspicion of the real truth in her mind. Still there was a coolness on the part of that lady ; or might it not be that Flora's imagination deceived her ?

There was another, and even a more serious cause of grief weighing on her mind. Despatches had been received by the nobleman in whose suite her brother Alessandro had repaired to Constantinople ; and the Secretary to the Council of Florence had intimated to Signora Francatelli (Flora's aunt) that Alessandro had abjured the faith of his forefathers and had embraced the Mussulman creed. It was also stated that the young man had entered the service of the Grand Vizier ; but whether he had become a renegade through love for some Turkish maiden, or with the hope of ameliorating his condition in a worldly point of view, whether, indeed, self-interest or a conscientious belief in the superiority of the Moslem doctrines over those of Christianity, had swayed Alessandro, no one could say.

His aunt was almost heart-broken at the news ; Father Marco, through whose influence he had obtained the post of Secretary to the Florentine envoy, was shocked and grieved : and Flora was not the less afflicted at an event which, as she had been taught to believe, must inevitably place her much-beloved brother beyond the hope of spiritual salvation.

Amidst the gloomy reflections excited by the Lady Nisida's coolness, and the disagreeable tidings which had been received concerning her brother, there was nevertheless one gleam of consolation for Flora Francatelli.

This was the love which Francisco entertained for her—and which she so tenderly, so sincerely reciprocated.

Yes—a maiden's first love is ever a source of solace amidst the gloom of affliction, because it is so intimately intertwined with hope ! For the soul of the innocent, artless girl who fondly loves, soars aloft in a heaven of their own creation, dove-like on the wings of faith !

It was already late when Flora began to unbraid and set at liberty her dark brown tresses, preparatory to retiring to rest,—when a low knock at the chamber-door startled her in the midst of her occupation.

Thinking it might be the Lady Nisida who required her attendance, she hastened to open the door ; and immediately three women, dressed in religious habits, and having black veils thrown over their heads so as completely to conceal their faces, entered the room.

Flora uttered a faint scream—for the sudden apparition of those spectre-like figures, at such a late hour of the night, was well calculated to alarm even a person of maturer age and stronger mind than Signora Francatelli.

"You must accompany us, young lady," said the foremost nun, advancing towards her. "And beware how you create any disturbance, for it will avail you nothing."

"Whither am I to be conducted?" asked Flora, trembling from head to foot.

"That we cannot inform you," was the reply. "Neither must you know at present ; and, therefore, our first duty is to blindfold you."

"Pity me—have mercy upon me !" exclaimed Flora, throwing herself upon her knees before the nun who addressed her in so harsh, so stern a manner. "I am a poor, unprotected girl ; have mercy upon me !"

But the three nuns seized upon her, and, while one held the palm of her hand forcibly over her mouth, so as to check her utterance, the others hastily blindfolded her.

Flora was so overcome by this alarming proceeding, that she fainted.

When she came to her senses, she found herself lying on a hard and sorry couch in a large apartment almost entirely denuded of furniture, and lighted by a feebly-burning lamp suspended to the low ceiling.

For a moment she thought she was labouring under the influence of a hideous dream ; but, glancing around, she started with affright, and a scream burst from her lips, when she beheld the three nuns standing by the bed.

"Why have you brought me hither?" she demanded, springing up in the couch and addressing the recluses with frantic wildness.

"To benefit you in a spiritual sense," replied the one who had before acted as spokesman ; "to purge your mind of those mundane vanities which have seized upon it, and to render you worthy of salvation. Pray, sisters —pray for this at present benighted creature !"

Then, to the surprise of the young maiden, the three nuns all fell upon their knees around her, and began to chant a solemn hymn in most lugubrious notes.

They had thrown aside their veils, and the flickering light of the dim lamp gave a ghastly and unearthly appearance to their pale and severe countenances. They were all three elderly persons, and their aspect was of that cold, forbidding nature, which precludes hope on the part of anyone who might have to implore mercy.

The young maiden was astounded—stupefied :—she knew not what to conjecture. Where was she? who were those nuns that had treated her so harshly? why was she brought to that cold, cheerless apartment? what meant the hymn that seemed chanted expressly on her account?

She could not bear up against the bewilderment and alarm produced by the questions which she asked herself, and none of which she could solve. An oppressive sensation came over her ; and she was about to sink back upon the couch upon which she had risen, when the hymn suddenly ceased—the nuns rose from their suppliant posture, and the foremost, addressing the poor girl, in a reproachful tone, exclaimed, "Oh, wicked—worldly-minded creature,—repent—repent—repent !"

There was something so awful—so appalling in this strange conduct on the part of the nuns, that Flora began to doubt whether she were not labouring under some terrible delusion. She feared lest her senses were leaving her ; and, covering her face with her hands, so as to close her eyes against external objects, she endeavoured to look inwards, as it were, and scrutinize her own soul.

But there was not allowed time to reflect ; for the three nuns seized upon her, the foremost saying, "You must come with us."

"Mercy ! mercy !" screamed the wretched girl, vainly struggling in the powerful grasp of the recluses.

Her long hair, which she had unbraided before she was carried off from the Riverola mansion, floated over her shoulders, and enhanced the expression of ineffable despair which her pallid countenance now wore.

Wildly she glanced around her, as she was being hurried from the room, and frantic screams escaped her lips. But there was no one nigh to succour her—no one to melt at the outbursts of her anguish !

The three nuns dragged rather than conducted her into an adjacent apartment, which was lighted by a lamp of astonishing brilliancy, and hung in a skylight raised above the roof.

On the floor, immediately beneath this lamp, stood an arm-chair of wicker-work, and from this chair two stout cords ascended to the ceiling, through which they passed by means of two holes perforated for the purpose.

When Flora was dragged by the nuns to the immediate vicinity of the chair, which her excited imagination instantly converted into an engine of torture, that part of the floor on which the chair stood seemed to tremble and oscillate beneath her feet, as if it were a trap-door.

The most dreadful sensations now came over her. She felt as if her brain were reeling—as if she must go mad.

A fearful scream burst from her lips, and she struggled with the energy of desperation as the nuns endeavoured to thrust her in the chair.

"No, no !" she exclaimed, frantically ; "you shall not torture me—you dare not murder me ! What have I done to merit this treatment ? Mercy, mercy !"

But her cries and her struggles were alike useless, for she was now firmly bound to the chair, into which the nuns had forced her to seat herself.

Then commenced the maddening scene, which will be found in the ensuing chapter.

CHAPTER XIX.

THE DESCENT.—THE CHAMBER OF PENITENCE.

HAVING bound Flora Francatelli to the chair, in the manner just described, the three nuns fell back a few paces, and the wretched girl felt the floor giving way under her.

A dreadful scream burst from her lips as slowly, slowly the chair sank down; while the working of hidden machinery in the roof, and the steady, monotonous revolution of wheels, sounded with ominous din upon her ears.

An ice-stream seemed to pour over her soul. Wildly she cast around her eyes; and then more piercing became her shrieks, as she found herself gradually descending into what seemed to be a pit or well, only that it was square instead of round.

The ropes creaked, the machinery continued its regular movement, and the lamp fixed in the skylight overhead became less and less brilliant.

And bending over the mouth of this pit into which she was descending were three nuns, standing motionless and silent, like hideous spectres, on the brink of the aperture left by the square platform, or trap, whereon the chair was fixed.

"Mercy, mercy!" exclaimed Flora, in a voice expressive of the most acute anguish.

And, stretching forth her snowy arms (for it was round the waist and by the feet that she was fastened to the chair), she convulsively placed her open palms against the wooden walls of the pit, as if she could by that spasmodic movement arrest the descent of that terrible apparatus that was bearing her down into that hideous, unknown gulf.

But the walls were smooth and even, and presented nothing to which she could cling—nothing whereon she could fix her grasp.

Her brain reeled, and for a few minutes she sat motionless in dumb, inert despair.

Then again, in obedience to some mechanical impulse, she glanced upwards. The light of the lamp was now dimly seen, like the sun through a dense mist; but the dark figures were still bending over the brink of the abyss, thirty yards above.

The descent was still progressing, and the noise of the machinery still reached her ears, with buzzing, humming, monotonous indistinctness.

She shrieked not now—she screamed not any more; but it was not resignation that sealed her lips—it was despair.

Suddenly she became aware of the gradual disappearance of the three nuns. As she descended, the wall seemed to rise slowly upwards, and cover them from her view.

Then, for an instant, there was a slight shock given to the platform whereon the chair was placed, as if it rested on something beneath.

But, no; the fearful descent still went on: for, when she again stretched forth her hand to touch the walls, they appeared to be slowly rising, rising.

She was now involved in almost total darkness; but far, far overhead the dim lustre of the lamp was seen: and the four walls of the gulf now appeared to touch the ceiling of the room above, and to enclose that faint but still distinct orb within the narrow square space thus shut in.

The noise of the machinery also reached her still; but merely with a humming sound that was only just audible.

For an instant she doubted whether she was still descending; but, alas! when her arms were a third time convulsively stretched forth, her fair hands felt the walls slipping away from her touch—gliding upwards, as it were, with steady motion.

Then she knew that the descent had not ceased.

But whither was she going?—to what awful depth was she progressing?

Already, she conjectured, was she at least sixty yards beneath that dim yellow orb which every instant appeared to shine as through a deeper, deepening mist.

For what fate was she reserved, and where was she?

Suddenly it struck her she was an inmate of the Carmelite Convent; for the rumours alluded to in a preceding chapter had often met her ears, and her imagination naturally associated them with the occurrences of that dreadful night.

The piercing shrieks, the noise of machinery, the disappearance from time to time of some member of that monastic institution—all the incidents, in fine, to which those rumours had ever pointed, now seemed to apply to her own case.

These reflections flashed with lightning rapidity through her brain, and paralyzed her with horror.

Then she lost all further power of thought; and, though not absolutely fainting, she was stunned and stupefied with the tremendous weight of overwhelming despair.

How long she remained in this condition she knew not; but she was suddenly aroused by the opening of a low door in the wall in front of her.

Starting as from a dreadful dream, she stretched forth her arms, and became aware that the descent had stopped; and at the same moment she beheld a nun, bearing a lamp, standing on the threshold of the door which had just opened.

"Sister, welcome to the Chamber of Penitence!" said the recluse, approaching the terrified Flora.

Then, placing the lamp in a niche near the door, the nun proceeded to remove the cords which fastened the young maiden to the chair.

Flora rose, but fell back again on the seat—for her limbs were stiff in consequence of the length of time they had been retained in one position. The nun disappeared by the little door for a few minutes; and, on her return, presented the wretched girl a cup of cold water. Flora swallowed the icy beverage and felt refreshed.

Then by the light of the lamp in the niche she hastily examined the countenance of the nun; but its expression was cold—repulsive—stern; and Flora knew that it was useless to seek to make a friend of her. A frightful sense of loneliness, as it were, struck her like an ice-shaft penetrating to her very soul; and, clasping her hands together, she exclaimed, "Holy Virgin, protect me!"

"No harm will befall you, daughter," said the nun, "if you manifest contrition for past errors and a resolution to devote your future years to the service of Heaven."

"My past errors!" repeated Flora, with mingled indignation and astonishment. "I am not aware that I ever injured a living soul by word or deed—nor entertained a thought for which I need to blush. Neither have I neglected those duties which manifest the gratitude of mortals for the bounties bestowed upon them by Providence."

"Ah! daughter," exclaimed the nun; "you interpret not your own heart rightly. Have you never abandoned yourself to those carnal notions—those hopes—those fears—those dreams of happiness, which constitute the passion that the world calls love?"

Flora started, and a blush mantled on her cheeks, before so pale.

"You see that I have touched a chord which vibrates to your heart's core, daughter," continued the nun, on whom that sudden evidence of emotion was not lost. "You have suffered yourself to be deluded by the whisperings of that feeling whose tendency was to wean your soul from Heaven."

"And is it possible that a pure and virtuous love can be construed into a crime?" demanded the young maiden, her indignation overpowering her fears.

"A love that is founded on, and fostered by ambition, is a sin," replied the nun. "Marriage is doubtless an institution ordained by Heaven; but it becomes a curse, and is repulsive to all pious feelings, when it unites those whose passion is made up of sensuality and selfishness."

"You dare not impute such base considerations to me!" exclaimed Flora, her cheeks again flushing, but with the glow of conscious innocence shamefully outraged by the most injurious suspicions.

"Nay, daughter," continued the nun, unmoved by the manner of the young maiden; "you are unable to judge rightly of your own heart. You possess a confidence in integrity of purpose, which is but a mental blindness on your part."

"Of what am I accused, and wherefore am I brought hither?" asked Flora, beginning to feel bewildered by the sophistry that characterized the nun's discourse.

"Those who are interested in your welfare," replied the nun, evasively, "have consigned you to the care of persons devoted to the service of Heaven, that your eyes may be opened to the vanity of the path which you have been pursuing, but from which you are so happily rescued."

"And where am I? Is this the Convent of the Carmelites? Why was I subjected to all the alarms—all the mental tortures through which I have just passed?" demanded the young maiden, wildly and rapidly.

"Think not that we have acted towards you in the spirit of persecution," said the nun. "The mysteries which have alarmed you will be explained at a future period, when your soul is prepared, by penitence, self-mortification, and prayer, to receive the necessary revelation. In the meantime, ask no questions; forget the world—and resolve to embrace a life devoted to the service of Heaven."

"To embrace a conventual existence?" almost shrieked the wretched girl. "Oh, no—never!"

"Not many days will elapse ere your mind will undergo a salutary change," said the nun, composedly. "But if

At the foot of the altar knelt five women, half naked, and holding scourges in their hands.

"These are the Penitents," whispered the nun to Flora. "Pause for a moment, and contemplate them."

A minute elapsed, during which the five penitents remained motionless as statues, with their heads bowed upon their bosoms, and their arms hanging down by their sides, as if those limbs were lifeless—save in respect to the hands that held the scourges. But suddenly one of them—a young and beautiful woman—exclaimed, in a tone of piercing anguish, "It is my fault! it is my

"THE BLOW WAS WELL AIMED." (See p. 26.)

you will now follow me—as you appear to be somewhat recovered—I will conduct you to your cell adjoining the Chamber of Penitence."

Flora, perceiving that any further attempt to reason with the recluse would be fruitlessly made, arose and followed her into a long, narrow, dark passage, at the end of which was a door standing half open.

The nun extinguished her lamp, and led the way into a large apartment, hung with black. At the farther end there was an altar, surmounted by a crucifix of ebony, and lighted up with four wax candles, which only served to render the gloom of the entire scene more apparent.

fault! it is my fault!" and the others took up the wail in voices equally characteristic of heartless woe.

Then they lacerated their shoulders with the hard leathern thongs of their scourges; and a faintness came over Flora Francatelli when she observed the blood appear on the back of the young and beautiful penitent who had given the signal for this self-mortification.

The nun, perceiving the effect thus produced upon the maiden, touched her upon the shoulder as a signal to follow whither she was about to lead; and, opening one of several doors communicating with the Chamber of Penitence, she said, in a low whisper, "This is your cell. May the Virgin bless you!"

Flora entered the little room allotted to her, and the nun retired, simply closing, but not bolting the door behind her.

A taper burnt before a crucifix suspended to the wall; and near it hung a scourge, from which last-mentioned object Flora averted her eyes with horror.

A bed, a simple toilette-table, a praying-desk, and a single chair, completed the furniture of the cell, which was of very narrow dimensions.

Seating herself on the bed, Flora burst into an agony of tears.

What would her aunt think when she received the news of her disappearance? for she could not suppose that any friendly feeling on the part of her persecutors would induce them to adopt a course which might relieve that much-loved relative's mind concerning her. What would Francisco conjecture? Oh! these thoughts were maddening!

Anxious to escape from them, if possible, the almost heart-broken girl proceeded to lay aside her garments and retire to rest.

Physical and mental exhaustion cast her into a deep sleep; but the horrors of her condition pursued her even in her dreams, so that when she awoke she was not startled to find herself in that gloomy cell.

Casting her eyes around, she observed two circumstances which showed her that someone had visited her room during the hours she slept; for a new taper was burning before the crucifix, and her own garments had been removed, the coarse garb of a penitent now occupying their place on the chair.

"Oh! is it possible that I am doomed to bid farewell to the world for ever?" exclaimed Flora, in the voice of despair, as she clasped her hands convulsively together.

CHAPTER XX.

FRANCISCO AND NISIDA.—DR. DURAS AND THE LETTER.

THE greatest confusion prevailed in the Riverola palace when, in the morning, the disappearance of Flora Francatelli was discovered.

Nisida hastened at an early hour to her brother's apartment, and intimated to him the fact that she was nowhere to be found.

Francisco, who was already dressed, was overwhelmed with grief at this announcement, and, in the first access of excitement, conveyed to her his intention of seeking the young maiden throughout the city.

He was hastening to quit the room, when Nisida held him back, and intimated to him that his anxiety in this respect would create suspicions injurious alike to his reputation and that of Flora Francatelli—the more so as she was but a menial in the household.

Francisco paused, and reflected for a few moments. Then, having tenderly embraced his sister, he hastily addressed her by the symbolic language in which they were accustomed to converse.

"Pardon me, beloved Nisida, for having kept a secret from thee—the only one that my heart has ever so selfishly cherished."

Nisida appeared to be profoundly astonished at this communication, and made an impatient sign for him to proceed.

"You will not be surprised at my anxiety to seek after the missing girl," he continued, "when I intimate to you that I love her, and that, next to yourself, she is dearer to me than I can express."

"Your passion can scarcely be an honourable one, Francisco," was the reproach conveyed by Nisida, while her countenance wore a corresponding expression.

"I would sooner die than harbour an injurious thought in respect to that virtuous and beautiful creature!" responded the young Count, his face flushing with the glow of generous emotions. "My happiness is intimately connected with this attachment, Nisida; and I feel convinced that you would rather forward my views than oppose them."

"Yes, dear brother," was the reply which she conveyed to him; "your happiness is my only consideration."

But, as she gave this assurance, an ill-subdued sigh escaped her breast; and she compressed her lips tightly to crush the emotions that were agitating her. A cloud evanescently appeared on the broad and marble forehead; the pencilled brows contracted; and the eyes flashed brightly—oh! far more brightly than glanced the ray of the morning sun through the windows upon the glossy surface of her luxuriant hair. A momentary spasm seemed to convulse that full and rounded form; and the small and elegantly-shaped foot which peered from beneath her flowing robe, tapped the floor twice with involuntary movement.

Mistress as she usually was of even her most intense feelings, and wonderfully habituated by circumstances to exercise the most complete command over her emotions, she was now for an instant vanquished by the gush of painful sentiments which crowded on her soul.

Francisco did not, however, observe that transitory evidence of acute feeling on the part of his sister—a feeling which seemed to partake of the nature of a remorse, as if she were conscience-stricken!

For she loved her brother deeply, tenderly, but after the fashion of her own wild and wonderful disposition—a love that was not calculated always to prove friendly to his interests.

Francisco paced the room in an agitated manner.

At length he stopped near where his sister was standing, and intimated to her that Flora might perhaps have repaired to the residence of her aunt.

Nisida conveyed to him this answer: "The moment that I missed Flora ere now, I despatched a domestic to her aunt's cottage; but she has not been there since Sunday last."

"Some treachery is at work here, Nisida," was the young Count's response. "Flora has not willingly absented herself."

At this moment Francisco's page entered the apartment to announce that Dr. Duras was in the reception-room.

The young Count made a sign to his sister to accompany him; and they proceeded to the elegant saloon where the physician was waiting.

Having saluted the Count and Nisida with his usual urbanity, Dr. Duras addressed himself to the former, saying, "I have just learnt from your lordship's page that the favourite attendant on your sister has most unaccountably disappeared."

"And both Nisida and myself are at a loss what to conjecture or how to act," replied Francisco.

"Florence is at this moment the scene of dreadful crimes," observed the physician. "Yesterday morning a young female was murdered by a near neighbour of mine——"

"I was astounded when I heard of the arrest of Signor Wagner on such a charge," interrupted the Count. "He was latterly a frequent guest at this house—although, I believe, you never happened to meet him here?"

"No," answered the physician. "But I saw him at the funeral of your lamented father, and once or twice since in the gardens attached to his mansion; and I certainly could not have supposed, from his appearance, that he was a man capable of so black a crime. I was, however, about to observe, that Florence is at this moment infested by a class of villains who hesitate at no deed of turpitude. This Signor Wagner is a foreigner, possessed of immense wealth, the sources of which are totally unknown; and, moreover, it is declared that the sbirri, yesterday morning, actually traced the robber-captain, Stephano, to the vicinity of his mansion. All this looks black enough, and it is more than probable that Wagner was in league with the redoubtable Stephano and his banditti. Then the mysterious disappearance of Flora is, to say the least, alarming; for, I believe, she was a well-conducted — virtuous — estimable young woman."

"She was—she was, indeed!" exclaimed Francisco. "At least," he added, perceiving that the physician was somewhat astonished at the enthusiasm with which he spoke—"at least, such is my firm impression; such, too, is the opinion of my sister."

"The motive which brought me hither this morning," said Doctor Duras, "was to offer you a little friendly advice, which my long acquaintance with your family, my dear Count, will prevent you from taking amiss."

"Speak, doctor—speak your thoughts!" cried Francisco, pressing the physician's hand gratefully.

"I would recommend you to be more cautious how you form an intimacy with strangers," continued Dr. Duras. "Rumour has a thousand tongues—and it is already reported in Florence, that the alleged murderer was on familiar terms with the noble Count of Riverola and the Lady Nisida."

"The Duke himself is liable to be deceived in respect to the real character of an individual," said Francisco, proudly.

"But his Highness would not form hasty acquaintances," replied the physician. "After all, it is with the best possible feeling that I offer you my counsel—knowing your generous heart, and also how frequently generosity is imposed upon.''

"Pardon the impatience with which I answered you, my dear friend,'' exclaimed the young Count.

"No pardon is necessary,'' exclaimed the physician; "because you did not offend me. One word more—and I must take my leave. Crimes are multiplying thickly in Florence, and Stephano's band becomes each day more and more daring; so that it is unsafe to walk alone in the city after dusk. Beware how you stir abroad unattended, my dear Francisco, at unseasonable hours.''

"My habits are not of that nature,'' replied the Count. "I, however, thank you cordially for your well-meant advice. But you appear to connect the disappearance of Flora Francatelli,'' he added, very seriously, "and the dreadful deed supposed to be committed by Signor Wagner!''

"I merely conjecture that this Wagner is associated with that lawless horde who have become the terror of the Republic,'' answered the physician; "and it is natural to suppose that these wretches are guilty of all the enormous crimes which have lately struck the city with alarm.''

Francisco turned aside to conceal the emotions which these remarks excited within him; for he now began to apprehend that she whom he loved so fondly had met with foul play at the hands of the bravoes and banditti, whom Stephano was known to command.

Dr. Duras seized that opportunity to approach Nisida, who was standing at the window; and as he thrust into her hand a note, which she immediately concealed in her dress, he was struck with surprise and grief at the acute anguish that was depicted upon her countenance.

Large tears stood on her long, dark lashes, and her face was ashy pale.

The physician made a sign of anxious inquiry; but Nisida, subduing her emotions with an almost superhuman effort, pressed his hand violently, and hurried from the room.

Dr. Duras shook his head mournfully; but also in a manner that showed that he was at a loss to comprehend that painful manifestation of feeling on the part of one whom he well *knew* to be endowed with almost miraculous powers of self-control.

His meditations were interrupted by Francisco, who, addressing him abruptly, said, "In respect to the missing young lady, whose absence will be so acutely felt by my sister, the only course which I can at present pursue is to communicate her mysterious disappearance to the Captain of Police.''

"No time should be lost in adopting that step,'' responded the doctor. "I am about to visit a sick nobleman in the neighbourhood of the Captain's office. We will proceed so far in each other's company.''

The young Count summoned his page to attend upon him, and then quitted the mansion in company with the physician.

* * * * * *

In the meantime Nisida had retired to her own apartment, where she threw herself into a seat, and gave vent to the dreadful emotions which had for the last half-hour been agitating within her bosom.

She wept—oh! she wept long and bitterly! It was terrible and strange to think how that woman of iron mind now yielded to the outpourings of her anguish.

Some time elapsed ere she even attempted to control her feelings; and then her struggle to subdue them was as sudden and energetic as her grief had a moment previously been violent and apparently inconsolable.

Then she recollected the note which Dr. Duras had slipped into her hand, and which she had concealed in her bosom; and she hastened to peruse it.

The contents ran as follow:—

"In accordance with your request, my noble-hearted and much-enduring friend, I have consulted eminent lawyers in respect to the will of the late Count of Riverola. The substance of their opinion is unanimously this:—'The estates are unalienably settled on yourself, should you recover the faculties of hearing and speaking at any time previously to your brother's attainment of the age of thirty; and should you enter into the possession of the estates and allow your brother to enjoy the whole or greater part of the revenues, in direct contradiction to the spirit of your father's will, the estates would become liable to confiscation to his Highness the Duke. In this case your brother and yourself would alike be ruined.'

"Now, the advice that these lawyers give is this:—'A memorial should be addressed to his Highness, exhibiting that you refuse to undergo any surgical treatment or operation for the restoration of the faculties of hearing and speech, inasmuch as you would not wish to deprive your brother of the enjoyment of the estates, nor of the title conferred by his possession; that you, therefore, solicit a decree confirming his title of nobility, and dispensing with the prerogative of confiscation on the part of the Prince, should you recover the faculties of hearing and speech, and act in opposition to the will of your late father in respect to the power of alienating the estates from your own possessions.'

"Such, my generous-minded friend, is the counsel offered by eminent advocates: and by the memory of your sainted mother—if not for the sake of your own happiness—I implore you to act in accordance with these suggestions. You will remember that this advice pretty accurately corresponds with that which I gave you, when, late on the night that the will was read, you quitted your sleepless couch and came to my dwelling to consult me on a point so intimately connected with your felicity in this world.

"Your sincerely devoted friend,
"JERONYMO DURAS.''

While Nisida was occupied in the perusal of the first paragraph of this letter dark clouds lowered upon her brow; but as she read the second paragraph, wherein the salutary advice of the lawyers was conveyed to her, those clouds rapidly dispersed, and her splendid countenance became lighted up with joyous, burning, intoxicating hope.

It was evident that she had already made up her mind to adopt the counsel proffered her by the eminent advocates whom the friendly physician had consulted on her behalf.

CHAPTER XXI.

THE SUBURB OF ALLA CROCE.—THE JEW.—THE ROBBER CHIEF'S LOVE.

IT was past the hour of ten on Saturday night, when a tall, powerfully-built man emerged from what might be termed the fashionable portion of the city of Florence, and struck into the straggling suburb of Alla Croce.

This quarter of the town was of marvellously bad reputation, being infested by persons of the worst description, who, by herding, as it were, together in one particular district, had converted the entire suburb into a sort of sanctuary where crime might take refuge, and into which the sbirri, or police-officers, scarcely dared to penetrate.

The population of Alla Croce was not, however, entirely composed of individuals who were at variance with the law; for poverty, as well as crime, sought an asylum in that assemblage of forbidding-looking dwellings, which formed so remarkable a contrast with the marble palaces, noble public buildings, and handsome streets of the city of Florence itself.

And not only did the denizens of penury and crushing toil—the artizans, the vine-dressers, the gardeners, the water-carriers, and the porters of Florence—occupy lodgings in the suburb of Alla Croce; but even wealthy persons—yes, men whose treasures were vast enough to pay the ransom of princes—buried themselves and their hoards in this horrible neighbourhood.

We allude to that undeservedly persecuted race—the Jews,—a race endowed with many virtues and generous qualities, but whose characters have been blackened by a host of writers whose narrow minds and illiberal prejudices have induced them to preserve all the exaggerations and misrepresentations which tradition hands down in the Christian world relative to the cruelly-treated Israelite.

The enlightened commercial policy of those merchant-princes, the Medici, had, during the primal glories of their administrative sway in the Florentine Republic, relaxed the severity of the laws against the Jews; and, recognising in the persecuted Israelites those grand trading and financial qualities which have ever associated the idea of wealth with their name, permitted them to follow unmolested their specific pursuits.

But at the time of which we are writing—the year 1521—the Prince who held the reins of Florentine Government had yielded to the representations of a bigoted and intolerant clergy, and the Jews had once more become the subjects of persecution. The dissipated nobles extorted from them by menace those loans which would not have been granted on the security proffered; and the wealthy members of the "scattered race" actually began to discover that they could repose greater confidence in the refuse of the Florentine population than in the brilliant aristocracy, or even in the famous sbirri themselves. Thus had many rich Jews established themselves in the quarter of Alla Croce; and by paying a certain sum to the Syndic, or magistrate of this suburb—a functionary elected by the inhabitants themselves, and in virtue of a law of their own enactment—the persecuted Israelites enjoyed comparative security and peace.

We now return to the man we left plunging into the suburb of which we have offered a short account.

This individual was dressed in a simple attire, but composed of excellent materials. His vest was of dark velvet, slashed, but not embroidered; and on his breast he wore a jazeran, or mailed cuirass, which was not only lighter than a steel corslet, but was equally proof against poniard or pike. In his broad leather belt were stuck two pairs of pistols, and a long dagger: a heavy broadsword also hung by his side. His black boots came up nearly to the knee—in contravention of the prevailing fashion of that age, when those articles of dress seldom reached above the swell of the leg. A large slouched hat, without plumage or any ornament, was drawn down as much as possible over his features; and the broad *mantello*, or cloak, was gathered round the body in such a manner that it covered all the left side and the weapons fastened in the belt, but left the sword arm free for use in any sudden emergency.

Behind the wayfarer stretched the magnificent city of Florence—spreading over deep vale, on both sides of the Arno, and, as usual, brilliant with light like a world of stars shining in mimic rivalry of those that studded the purple vault above.

Before him were the mazes of the Alla Croce, the darkness of which suburb was only interrupted by a few straggling and feeble lights gleaming from houses of entertainment, or from huts whose poverty required not the protection of shutters to the casements.

And now—as one of those faint lights suddenly fell upon the wayfarer's countenance, as he passed the abode in which it shone—let us avail ourselves of the opportunity afforded by that glimpse, to state that this man's features were handsome, but coarse, and bearing the traces of a dissolute life. His age was apparently forty: it might have been been a few years more matured—but his coal-black hair, moustachio, and bushy whiskers, unstreaked by silver, showed that time sat lightly on his head, in spite of the evident intimacy with the wine-cup above alluded to.

Having threaded the greater portion of the suburb, which was almost knee-deep in mud—for it had been raining nearly all day, and had only cleared up after sunset—the individual whom we have been describing stopped at the corner of a street, and gave a shrill whistle.

The signal was immediately answered in a similar fashion: and in a few minutes a man emerged from the darkness of the bye-street. He also was well-armed, but much more plainly dressed than the other; and his countenance was such as would not have proved a very friendly witness in his favour in a court of justice.

"Lomellino?" said the first individual whom we have described in this chapter.

"Captain Stephano?" responded the other, in a low tone.

"All right, my fine lad," returned the bandit-captain. "Follow me."

The two robbers then proceeded in silence, until they reached a house larger and stronger in appearance than any other in the same street. The shutters which protected the casements, were massive and strengthened with iron bars and huge nails, somewhat after the fashion of church-doors. The walls were of solid grey stone, whereas those of the adjacent huts were of mud or wood. In a word, this dwelling seemed a little fortress in the midst of an exposed and unprotected town.

Before this house the robbers stopped.

"Do you remain on the other side of the street, Lomellino," said the bandit-chief: "and, is need be, you will answer to my accustomed signal."

"Good! Captain!" was the reply; and Lomellino crossed over the way to the deep shade of the houses on that side.

Stephano then gave a low knock at the door of the well-defended dwelling above described.

Several minutes elapsed: and no sounds were heard within.

"The old usurer is at home, I know," muttered Stephano to himself; for the moment he had knocked a gleam of light, peeping through a crevice in an upper casement, had suddenly disappeared.

He now rapped more loudly at the door with the handle of his heavy broadsword.

"Ah! he comes," muttered the bandit-chief, after another long pause.

"Who knocks so late?" demanded a weak and tremulous voice from within.

"I—Stephano Verrina!" cried the brigand, pompously; "open—and fear not!"

The bolts were drawn back—a chain fell heavily on the stone floor inside—and the door opened, revealing the form of an old and venerable-looking man, with a long white beard. He held a lamp in his hand; and by its fitful glare, his countenance, of the Jewish cast, manifested an expression denoting the terror which he vainly endeavoured to conceal.

"Enter, Signor Stephano," said the old man. "But wherefore here so late?"

"Late do ye call it, Signor Isaachar?" ejaculated the bandit, crossing the threshold. "Meseems there is yet time to do a world of business this night, for those who have the opportunity and the inclination."

"Ah! but you and yours turn night into day," replied the Jew, with a chuckle intended to be of a conciliatory nature; "or rather you perform your avocations at a time when others sleep."

"Every one to his calling, friend Isaachar," said the brigand-chief. "Come! have you not made that door fast enough yet? you will have to open it soon again—for my visit will be none of the longest."

The Jew having replaced the chains and fastened the huge bolts which protected the house-door, took up the lamp and led the way to a small and meanly furnished room at the back of his dwelling.

"What business may have brought you hither to-night, good Captain Verrina?" he inquired, in a tone of ill-subdued apprehension.

"Not to frighten thee out of thy wits, good Isaachar," responded Stephano, laughing.

"Ah! ha!" exclaimed the Jew, partially reassured: "perhaps you have come to pay me the few crowns I had the honour to lend you—without security, and without interest——"

"By my patron saint! thou wast never more mistaken in thy life, friend Isaachar," interrupted the robber-chief. "The few crowns you speak of, were neither more nor less than a tribute paid on consideration that my men should leave unscathed the dwelling of worthy Isaachar ben Solomon: in other words, that thy treasure should be safe at least from them."

"Well—well! be it so!" cried the Jew. "Heaven knows I do not grudge the amount in question—although," he added, slowly, "I am compelled to pay almost an equal sum to the Syndic."

"The Syndic of Alla Croce and the Captain of the banditti are two very different persons," remarked Stephano. "The magistrate protects you from those over whom he has control; and I, on my side, guarantee you against the predatory visits of those over whom I exercise command. But let us to business."

"Aye—to business!" echoed the Jew, anxious to be relieved from the state of suspense into which this visit had thrown him.

"You are acquainted with the young, beautiful, and wealthy Countess of Arestino, Isaachar?" said the bandit.

The Jew stared at him in increased alarm, now mingled with amazement.

"But, in spite of all her wealth," continued Stephano, "she was compelled to pledge her diamonds to thee, to raise the money wherewith to discharge a gambling debt contracted by her lover, the high-born, handsome, but ruined Marquis of Orsini."

"How knowest thou all this?" anxiously inquired the Jew.

"From her ladyship's own lips," responded Stephano. "At least, she told me that she had raised the sum to accommodate a very particular friend. Now, as the transaction is unknown to her husband, and as I am well assured that the Marquis of Orsini is really on most excellent terms with her ladyship,—moreover, as this same Marquis did pay a certain heavy gambling debt within an hour after the diamonds were pledged to you,—it requires but little ingenuity to put all these circumstances together, to arrive at the result which I have mentioned. Is it not so, Isaachar?"

"I know not the motive for which the money was raised," answered the Jew, wondering what was coming next.

"Oh! then the money *was* raised with you," cried Stephano; "and consequently you hold the diamonds."

"I did not say so—I——"

"A truce to this fencing with my words!" ejaculated the bandit, impatiently. "I have an unconquerable desire to behold these diamonds——"

"You, good Captain!" murmured Isaachar, trembling from head to foot.

"Yes—I! And wherefore not? Is there anything so marvellous in a man of my refined taste and exquisite notions, taking a fancy to inspect the jewels of one of the proudest beauties of gay Florence? By my patron saint! you should thank me that I come in so polite a manner to request a favour, the granting of which I could so easily compel without all this tedious circumlocution."

"The diamonds!" muttered the Jew, doubtless troubled at the idea of surrendering the security which he held for a very considerable loan.

"Perdition seize the man!" thundered Stephano, now waxing angry. "Yes—the diamonds, I say; and fortunate will it be for you if they are produced without farther parley."

Thus speaking, the bandit suffered his cloak to fall from over his belt, and the Jew's quick eye recoiled from the sight of those menacing weapons with which his visitor was armed as it were to the teeth.

Then, without further remonstrance, but with many profound sighs, Isaachar proceeded to fetch a small iron box from another room; and in a few moments the diamond-case, made of sandal-wood inlaid with mother-of-pearl, was in the bandit captain's hands.

"Let me convince myself that it is all right?" exclaimed Stephano, examining the lid of the case. "Yes—there are the arms of Arestino, with the cyphers of the Countess, G. A.—Giulia Arestino—a very pretty name, by my troth! Ah! how the stones sparkle!" he cried, as he opened the case. "And the inventory is complete—just as it was described to me by her ladyship. You are a worthy man, Isaachar—a good man: you will here restored tranquillity to the mind of this beautiful Countess," continued Stephano, in a bantering tone; "and she will be enabled to appear at court to-morrow, with her husband. Good-night, Isaachar: my brave men shall receive orders to the effect that the first who dares to molest you, may reckon upon swinging to the highest tree that I can find for his accommodation."

"You violate your compact, Signor Verrina!" exclaimed the Jew, his rage now mastering his fears. "Wherefore should I pay you tribute to protect me, when you enter my house and rob me thus vilely?"

"In this case a lady is concerned, good Isaachar," responded the bandit, calmly: "and you know that with all true cavaliers the ladies are pre-eminent. Once more, a fair night's repose, my much respected friend!"

Thus saying, Stephano Verrina rose from the seat on which he had been lounging; and the Jew, knowing that altercation and remonstrance were equally useless, hastened to afford the means of egress to so unwelcome a visitor.

Stephano lingered a moment opposite the house until he heard the door bolted and chained behind him: then, crossing the street, he rejoined his follower Lomellino.

"All right, Captain?" said the latter, inquiringly.

"All right," answered Stephano, "Poor Isaachar is inconsolable, no doubt; but the Countess will be consoled at his expense. Thus it is with the world, Lomellino: what is one person's misery is another's happiness."

"Dost grow sentimental, good Captain?" exclaimed the man, whose ears were entirely unaccustomed to such language on the part of his chief.

"Lomellino, my friend," answered Verrina, "when a man is smitten in a certain organ, commonly called the heart, he is apt to give utterance to that absurdity which the world denominates sentiment. Such is my case."

"You are then in love, Captain?" said Lomellino, as they retraced their way through the suburb of Alla Croce.

"Just so," replied the bandit-chief. "I will tell you how it happened. Yesterday morning, when those impertinent sbirri gave me a harder run than I have ever yet experienced, I was fain to take refuge in the garden of that very same Signor Wagner——"

"Who was yesterday arrested for murder?" interrupted Lomellino.

"The identical one," returned Stephano. "I concealed myself so well that I knew I might bid defiance to those bungling sbirri—although their scent was sharpened by the hope of the reward set on my head by the Prince. While I thus lay hidden, I beheld a scene that would have done good to the heart of even such a callous fellow as yourself—I mean callous to female qualifications. In a word, I saw one woman stab another as effectually as——"

"But it was Wagner who killed the woman!" ejaculated Lomellino.

"No such thing!" said Stephano, quietly. "The murderess is of the gentle sex—though she can scarcely be gentle in disposition. And such a splendid creature, Lomellino! I beheld her countenance for a few minutes, as she drew aside her veil that her eyes might glare upon her victim; and I whispered to myself, '*That woman must be mine: she is worthy of me!*' Then the blow descended—her victim lay motionless at her feet—and I never took my eyes off the countenance of the murderess. '*She is an incarnate fiend,*' I thought; '*and admirably fitted to mate with the Bandit-Captain.*'—Such was my reflection then; and the lapse of a few hours has only served to strengthen the impression. You may now judge whether I have formed an unworthy attachment!"

"She *is* worthy of you, Captain!" exclaimed Lomellino. "Know you who she is?"

"Not a whit," replied Stephano. "I should have followed her when she left the garden, and complimented her on her proficiency in handling a poniard: but I was not so foolhardy as to stand the chance of meeting the sbirri. Moreover, I shall speedily adopt measures to discover who and what she is; and when I present myself to her, and we compare qualifications, I do not think there can arise any obstacle to our happiness, as lovers are accustomed to say."

"Then it was *she* who murdered the Lady Agnes?" said Lomellino.

"Have I not told you so? Signor Wagner is as innocent of that deed as the babe unborn; but it is not for me to step forward in his behalf, and thereby criminate a lady on whom I have set my affections."

"That were hardly to be expected, Captain," returned Lomellino.

"And all that I have now told thee, thou wilt keep to thyself," added Stephano: "for to none else of the band do I speak so freely as to thee."

"Because no one is so devoted to his Captain as I," rejoined Lomellino. "And now that we are about to separate," added the man, as they reached the verge of the suburb, which was then divided by a wide, open space from the city itself, and might even be termed a detached village,—"now that we are about to separate, Captain, allow me to ask whether the affair for Monday night still holds good?"

"The little business at the Riverola palace, you mean?" said Stephano. "Most assuredly! You and Piero will accompany me. There is little danger to be apprehended; and Antonio has given me the necessary information. Count Francisco sleeps at a great distance from the point where we must enter; and as for his sister—she is as deaf as if she had her ears sealed up."

"But what about the pages—the lacqueys——"

"Antonio will give them all a sleeping draught. Everything," added the robber-chief, "is settled as cleverly as can be."

"Antonio is your cousin, if I err not?" asked Lomellino.

"Something of the kind," replied Stephano: "but what is better and more binding—we are friends. And yet, strange to say, I never was within the precincts of the Riverola mansion until the night before last; and—more singular still—I have never, to my knowledge, seen any members of the family in whose service Antonio has been so long."

"Why, Florence is not honoured by your presence during the daytime," observed Lomellino; "and at night the great lords and high-born ladies who happen to be abroad, are so muffled up—the former in their cloaks, and the latter in their veils——"

"True—true; I understand all you would say, Lomellino," interrupted the Captain; "but you know how to be rather tedious at times. Here we separate,—I to repair to the Arestino palace—and you——"

"To the cavern," replied Lomellino; "where I hope to sleep better than I did last night," he added.

"What! a renewal of those infernal shriekings and

screamings that seem to come from the bowels of the earth?" exclaimed the Captain.

"Worse than ever," answered Lomellino. "If they continue much longer, I must abandon my office of treasure-keeper, which compels me to sleep in the innermost room——"

"That cannot be allowed, my worthy friend," interrupted the Captain; "for I should not know whom to appoint in your place. If it were not that we should betray our own stronghold," continued Stephano, emphatically, "we would force our way into the nest of our noisy neighbours, and levy such a tribute upon them as would put them on their good behaviour for the future."

"The scheme is really worth consideration," remarked Lomellino.

"We will talk more of it another time," said the Captain. "Good-night, Lomellino. I shall not return to the cavern until very late."

The two banditti then separated—Lomellino striking off to the right, and Stephano Verrina pursuing his way towards the most aristocratic quarter of Florence.

Upon entering the sphere of marble palaces, brilliantly lighted villas, and gay mansions, the robber-chief covered his face with a black mask—a mode of disguise so common at that period, not only amongst ladies, but also with cavaliers and nobles, that it was not considered at all suspicious, save as a proof of amatory intrigue, with which the sbirri had no right of interference.

CHAPTER XXII.

THE COUNTESS OF ARESTINO.

WE must now introduce our readers to a splendid apartment in the Arestino palace.

This room was tastefully decorated and elegantly furnished. The tapestry was of pale blue; and the ottomans, ranged round the walls in oriental style, were of rich crimson satin embroidered with gold. In the middle stood a table covered with ornaments and rich trinkets lately arrived from Paris—for France already began to exercise the influence of its superior civilization and refinement over the south of Europe.

The ceiling of that room was a masterpiece of the united arts of sculpture and painting. First, the hand of the sculptor had carved it into numerous medallions, on which the pencil of the painter had then delineated the most remarkable scenes in early Florentine history. Round the sides, or cornices, were, beautifully sculptured in marble, the heads of the principal ancestors of the Count of Arestino.

It was within a few hours of midnight, and the beautiful Giulia Arestino was sitting restlessly upon an ottoman,—now holding her breath to listen if a step were approaching the private door behind the tapestry—then glancing anxiously towards a clepsydra on the mantel.

"What can detain him thus? will he deceive me?" she murmured to herself. "Oh, how foolish—worse than foolish—mad—to confide in the promise of a professed bandit! The jewels are worth a thousand times the reward I have pledged myself to give him. Wretched being that I am!"

And with her fair hand she threw back the dark masses of hair that had fallen too much over her polished brow; —and on this polished brow she pressed that fair hand—for her head ached with the intensity of mingled suspense and alarm.

Her position was indeed a dangerous one, as the reader is already aware. In the infatuation of her strong—unconquerable—but not less guilty love for the handsome spendthrift, Orsini, she had pledged her diamonds to Isaachar ben Solomon for an enormous sum of money, every ducat of which had passed without an hour's delay into the possession of the young Marquis. Those diamonds were the bridal gift of her fond and attached, but, alas! deceived husband, who, being many years older than herself, studied constantly how to afford pleasure to the wife of whom he was so proud. He was himself an extraordinary judge of the nature, purity, and value of precious stones; and being immensely rich, he had collected a perfect museum of curiosities in that particular department. In fact, it was his amateur study, or, as we should say in these times, his peculiar hobby;—and hence the impossibility of imposing on him by the substitution of a hired or false set of diamonds for those which he had presented to his wife.

It was therefore absolutely necessary to get these diamonds back from Isaachar, by fair means or foul. The fair means were to redeem them by the payment of the loan advanced upon them; but the sum was so large, that the Countess dared not make such a demand upon her husband's purse, because the extravagances of her lover had lately compelled her to apply so very, very frequently to the Count for a replenishment of her funds. The foul means were therefore resorted to —an old woman, who had been the nurse of the Countess in her infancy, and to whom in her distress she applied for advice, having procured for the patrician lady the services of Stephano Verrina, the bandit-captain.

It is not to be wondered at, then, if the Countess of Arestino were a prey to the most poignant anxiety, as each successive quarter of an hour passed without bringing either Stephano or any tidings from him. Even if she feigned illness, so as to escape the ceremony of the following day, the relief would only be temporary—for the moment she should recover, or affect to recover, her husband would again require her to accompany him to the receptions of the Prince.

Giulia's anguish had risen to that point at which such feelings become intolerable and suggest the most desperate of remedies—suicide, when a low knock behind the pale-blue arras suddenly imparted hope to her soul.

Hastily raising the tapestry on that side whence the sound had emanated, she drew back the bolt of a little door communicating with a private staircase (usually found in all Italian mansions at that period); and the robber-chief entered the room.

"Have you succeeded?" was Giulia's rapid question.

"Your ladyship's commission has been executed," replied Stephano, who, we should observe, had laid aside his black mask ere he appeared in the presence of the Countess.

"Ah! now I seem to live—to breathe again!" cried Giulia, a tremendous weight suddenly removed from her mind.

Stephano produced the jewel-case from beneath his cloak; and as the Countess hastily took it—nay, almost snatched it from him, he endeavoured to imprint a kiss upon her fair hand.

Deep was the crimson glow which suffused her countenance—her neck—even all that was revealed of her breast, as she drew back haughtily, and with a sublime patrician air of offended pride.

"I thank you—thank you from the bottom of my soul, Signor Verrina," she said in another moment: for she felt how completely circumstances had placed her in the power of the bandit-chief, and how useless it was to offend him. "Here is your reward;"—and she presented him a heavy purse of gold.

"Nay—keep that jingling metal, lady," said Stephano: "I stand in no need of it—at least for the present. The reward I crave is of a different nature, and will even cost you less than you proffer me."

"What other recompense can I give you?" demanded Giulia, painfully alarmed.

"A few lines, written by that fair hand to my dictation," answered Stephano.

Giulia cast upon him a look of profound surprise.

"Here, lady—take my tablets, for I see that your own are not at hand," cried the chief. "Delay not—it grows late—and we may be interrupted."

"We may indeed," murmured Giulia, darting a rapid look at the water-clock. "It is within a few minutes of midnight."

She might have added—"And at midnight I expect a brief visit from Manuel d'Orsini, ere the return of my husband from a banquet at a friend's villa." But of course this was her secret: and anxious to rid herself of the company of Stephano, she took the tablets with trembling hands and prepared to write.

"*I, Giulia Countess of Arestino,*" began the brigand, dictating to her, "*confess myself to owe Stephano Verrina a deep debt of gratitude for his kindness in recovering my diamonds from the possession of the Jew Isaachar, to whom they were pledged for a sum which I could not pay.*"

"But wherefore this document?" exclaimed the Countess, looking up in a searching manner at the robber-chief; for she had seated herself at the table to write, and he was leaning over the back of her chair.

"'Tis my way at times," he answered, carelessly, "when I perform some service for a noble lord or a great lady, to solicit an acknowledgment of this kind in preference to gold." Then, sinking his voice in a low whisper, he added, with an air of deep meaning, "Who knows but that this document may some day save my head?"

Giulia uttered a faint shriek—for she comprehended in a moment how cruelly she might sooner or later be compromised through that document, and how entirely she was placing herself in the bandit's power.

But Stephano's hand clutched the tablets whereon the Countess had, almost mechanically, written to his subtle dictation; and he said, coolly, "Fear not, lady: I must be reduced to a desperate strait indeed, when my safety shall depend on the use I can make of this fair handwriting."

Giulia felt partially relieved by this assurance; and it was with ill-conditioned delight that she acknowledged the ceremonial bow with which the bandit-chief intimated his readiness to depart.

But at that moment three low and distinct knocks were heard at the little door behind the arras.

Giulia's countenance became suffused with blushes; then, instantly recovering her presence of mind, she said, in a rapid, earnest tone, "*He* who is coming knows nothing concerning the jewels, and will be surprised to find a stranger with me. "Perhaps he may even recognise you—perhaps he knows you by sight——"

"What would you have me do, lady?" demanded Stephano. "Speak—and I obey you."

"Conceal yourself—here—and I will soon release you."

She raised the tapestry on the opposite side to that by which Stephano had entered the room; and the robber-chief hid himself in the wide interval between the hangings and the wall.

All this had scarcely occupied a minute; and Giulia now hastened to open the private door, which instantaneously gave admittance to the young, handsome, and dissipated Marquis of Orsini.

CHAPTER XXIII.

THE LOVE OF WOMAN.—GIULIA AND HER LOVER.

SILENCE, and calmness, and moonlight were without the walls of the Arestino villa; for the Goddess of Night shone sweetly but coldly on the city of Florence, and asserted her empire even over the clouds that ere now had seemed laden with storm. Nor beamed she there alone—that fair Diana; for a countless host of handmaidens—the silver-faced stars—had spread themselves over the deep purple sky; and there—there they all shone in subdued and modest glory—those myriads of beacons floating on the eternal waves of that far-off and silent sea!

Shine on, sweet Regent of the Night—and ye, too, silver-faced stars, whose countenances are reflected and multiplied endlessly, as they are rocked to and fro, on the deep blue bosom of the Arno! while on the banks of that widely-famed stream, Nature herself, as if wearied of her toils, appears to be sleeping.

Would that the soul of man could thus lie down in its night of sorrow or of racking passion, on the margin of the waters of Hope,—confident that the slumber of contentment and peace will seal his eyelids heavy with long vigils in a world where conflicting interests need constant watchings, and that the stillness of the unfathomable depths of those waters will impart its influence unto him!

For, Oh! if calmness, silence, and moonlight prevail without the walls of the Arestino villa,—yet within there be hearts agitated by passions and emotions from which the gentle Genius of Slumber shrinks back aghast.

In the brilliantly-lighted apartment, to which we have already introduced our readers, the Countess Giulia receives her lover, the dissipated but handsome Marquis of Orsini:—the bandit-captain is concealed behind the richly-worked tapestry;—and at the door—not the little private one of that room—an old man is listening;—an old man whose ashy pale countenance, clenching hands, quivering white lips, and wildly rolling eyes, indicate how terrible are the feelings which agitate within his breast.

This old man was the Count of Arestino—one of the mightiest nobles of the Republic. Naturally his heart was good, and his disposition kind and generous:—but then he was an Italian—and he was jealous! Need we say more to account for the change which had now taken place in his usually calm, tranquil, yet dignified demeanour?

Or shall we inform our readers, that at the banquet to which he had been invited at a friend's villa that evening, he had overheard two young nobles, in a conversation which the generous wine they had been too freely imbibing rendered indiscreetly loud, couple the names of Giulia Arestino—his own much-loved wife—and Manuel d'Orsini in a manner which suddenly excited a fearful—a blasting suspicion in his mind. Stealing away unperceived from the scene of revelry, the Count had returned unattended to the immediate vicinity of his mansion; and from the shade of a detached building, he had observed the Marquis of Orsini traverse the gardens, and enter the portico leading to the private staircase communicating with that wing of the palace which contained the suite of apartments occupied by Giulia.

This was enough to strengthen the suspicion already excited in the old nobleman's mind; but not quite sufficient to confirm it. The Countess had several beautiful girls attached to her person; and the Marquis might have stooped to an intrigue with one of them. The Lord of Arestino was therefore resolved to act with the caution of a prudent man; but he was also prepared to avenge, in case of the worst, with the spirit of an Italian.

He hurried round to the principal entrance of his palace, and gave some brief but energetic instructions to a faithful valet, who instantly departed to execute them: the Count then ascended the marble staircase—traversed the corridors leading towards his lady's apartments—and placed himself against the door of that one wherein Giulia has already received her lover.

Thus, while silence, and calmness, and moonlight reign without—yet within the walls of the Arestino mansion a storm has gathered, to explode fearfully.

And all through the unlawful, but not less ardent love of Giulia for the spendthrift Marquis of Orsini!

Sober-minded men—philosophic reasoners—persons of business-habits—stern moralists,—all these may ridicule the poet or the novelist who makes Love his everlasting theme: they may hug themselves in the apathy of their own cold hearts, with the belief that all the attributes of the passion have been immensely exaggerated; but they are in error—deeply, profoundly, indisputably in error! For Love, in its various phases, amongst which are Jealousy, Suspicion, Infidelity, Rivalry, and Revenge, has agitated the world from time immemorial—has overthrown empires—has engendered exterminating wars, and has extended its despotic sway alike over the gorgeous city of a consummate civilisation, and the miserable wigwam of a heathen barbarism? Who, then, can wonder if the theme of Love be universal—that it should have evoked the rude and iron evidence of the Scandinavian Scald, as well as the soft and witching poesy of the bards of more genial climes; or that its praises or its sorrows should be sung on the banks of the Arno, the Seine, or the Thames, as well as amidst the pathless forests of America, or the burning sands of Africa, or in the far-off islands of the Southern Seas?

But alas! it is thou, O Woman! who art called on to make the most cruel sacrifices at the altar of this imperious deity—Love! If thou lovest honourably, 'tis well: but if thou lovest unlawfully, how wretched is thy fate! The lover, for whose sake thou hast forgotten thy duties as a wife, has sacrificed nothing to thee, whilst thou hast sacrificed everything to him. Let the amour be discovered—and who suffers? Thou! *He* loses not caste—station—name—nor honour: thou art suddenly robbed of all those! The gilded saloons of fashion throw open their doors to the *seducer*: but bars of adamant defend that entrance against the *seduced!* For *his* sake thou risketh costumely—shame—reviling—scorn—and the lingering death of a breaking heart: for *thee* he would not risk one millionth part of all that! Shouldst thou be starving, say to him, "*Go forth and steal to give me bread: dare the dishonour of the deed—and make the sacrifice of thy good name for me. Or go and forge—or swindle—or lie foully, so that thou bringest me bread; for have not I dared dishonour, made the sacrifice of my good name, and done as much—aye, far more than all that for thee?*" Shouldst thou, poor seduced, weak one, address thy seducer thus, he will look upon thee as a fiend-like tempter—he will rush from thy sight—he will never see thee more—his love will be suddenly converted into hatred! Yes—man demands that Woman should dishonour herself for *his* sake; but he will not allow a speck to appear upon what he calls *his good name*—no, not to save that poor, confiding, lost creature from the lowest depths and dregs of penury into which her frailty may have plunged her!

Such is the selfishness of man! Where is his chivalry?

But let us return to the Arestino palace.

The moment Manuel d'Orsini entered the apartment

by means of the private door, he embraced Giulia with a fondness which was more than half affected—at least on that occasion; and she herself returned the kiss less warmly than usual—but this was because she was constrained and embarrassed by the presence of the bandit-captain, who was concealed behind the tapestry.

"You appear cool—distant, Giulia," said Manuel, casting upon her an inquiring glance.

"And you either love me less—or you have something on your mind," returned the Countess, in a low tone.

"In the first instance you are wrong—in the second you are right, well beloved," answered the Marquis. "But tell me——"

"Speak lower, Manuel—we may be overheard—some of my dependants are in the adjacent room, and——"

"And you wish me to depart as soon as possible, no doubt?" said the Marquis, impatiently.

"Oh! Manuel—how can you reproach me thus?" asked Giulia, in a voice scarcely above a whisper; for that woman who dared be unfaithful to her husband revolted at the thought that a coarse-minded bandit should be in a position to overhear her conversation with her lover;—"how can you reproach me thus, Manuel?" she repeated;—"have I not given thee all the proofs of tenderest love which woman can bestow? have I not risked everything for thee?"

"I do not reproach you, Giulia," he replied, pressing his hand to his brow: "but I am unhappy—miserable!"

And he flung himself upon the nearest ottoman.

"Oh! what has occurred to distract thee thus!" exclaimed the Countess, forgetting the presence of Stephano Verrina in the all-absorbing interest of her lover's evident—too evident grief. "Am I ever to find thee oppressed with care—thee, who art so young—and so gloriously handsome?" she added, her voice suddenly sinking to a whisper.

Manuel gazed for a few moments, without speaking, on the countenance of his mistress as she leant over him: then in a deep and hollow tone—a tone the despair of which was too real and natural to be in the slightest degree affected, he said, "Giulia, I am a wretch—unworthy of all this sweet love of thine! I have broken the solemn vow which I pledged thee—I have violated my oath——"

"O Manuel!" ejaculated the Countess, still forgetting the presence of the bandit: "thou hast——"

"Gambled once more—and lost!" cried the Marquis, wildly. "And the sum that I am bound in honour to pay on Monday—by noon—is nearly equal in amount to that which thy generosity lent me the other day."

"Holy Virgin aid you, my unhappy Manuel!" said Giulia.

"For thou canst not?" exclaimed the young noble, with a profound sigh. "Oh! I am well aware that I have no claim upon thee——"

"Ah! wherefore that reproach?—for a reproach it is!" interrupted the Countess. "No claim on me! Hast thou not my heart? and in giving thee that, Manuel, I laid at thy feet a poor offering, which, though so poor, yet absorbs all others of which I may dispose! Do not reproach me, Manuel—for I would lay down my life to save thy soul from pain, or thy name from dishonour!"

"Now art thou my own Giulia!" cried the Marquis, pressing her hand to his lips. "An accursed fatality seems to hang over me! This habit of gaming entraps me as the wine-cup fascinates the bibber who would fain avoid it, but cannot. Listen to me for one moment, Giulia. In the public casino—which, as thou well knowest, is a place of resort where fortunes are lost and won in an hour—aye, sometimes in a minute—I have met a man whose attire is good and whose purse is well filled, but whose countenance I like as little as I should that of the Captain of the Sbirri, or his Lieutenant, if I had committed a crime. This individual of whom I speak—for I know not his name—was the favoured votary of Dame Fortune who won of me that sum which thy kindness, Giulia, alone enabled me to pay but a few days past. And now am I a second time this man's debtor. An hour ago he entered the casino—he stayed but for ten minutes—and in that time——"

"Oh! Manuel, is not this conduct of thine something bordering on madness?" interrupted the Countess. "And if thou art thus wedded to the fatal habit, how canst thou find room in thy heart for a single gleam of affection for me?"

"Now dost thou reproach me in thy turn, Giulia!" exclaimed the young Marquis. "But believe me, my

angel!" he continued, exerting all his powers to bend her to his purpose,—"believe me when I declare—Oh! most solemnly declare, by all that I put faith in, and by all I hope for hereafter—that could I be relieved from this embarrassment—extricated from this difficulty——"

"Heavens! how can it be done?" interrupted the Countess, casting her eyes wildly around: for the time was passing—she suddenly remembered that the bandit was still concealed in the room—and then, her husband might return earlier than was expected!

"Oh! if you despair of the means, Giulia," said the Marquis, "I must fly from Florence—I must exile myself for ever from the city of my birth, and which is still more endeared to me, because," he added, sinking his voice to a tender tone,—"because, my well-beloved, it contains thee!"

"No, Manuel—you must not quit Florence, and leave a dishonoured name behind thee!" exclaimed this loving woman, who was thus sublimely careful of the reputation of him for whom she had so long compromised her own. "What can be done? would that I had the means to raise this sum——"

"It is with shame that I suggest——" continued Manuel.

"What? Speak—speak! The means?"

"The jewels, dearest—thy diamonds——"

"Merciful heavens! if you did but know all!" cried Giulia, almost frantically. "Those diamonds were pledged to the Jew Isaachar ben Solomon, to raise the sum with which thy last debt was paid, Manuel; and—but forgive me if I did not tell all this before—not half an hour has elapsed since——"

She stopped short; for she knew that the bandit overheard every syllable she uttered.

Nor had she time, even if she possessed the power, to continue her most painful explanation; for scarcely had she thus paused abruptly, when the door burst open, and the Count of Arestino stood in the presence of the guilty pair.

CHAPTER XXIV.

THE INJURED HUSBAND, THE GUILTY WIFE, AND THE INSOLENT LOVER.

In fury of heart and agony of mind, rushed the old Lord into that apartment. Oh! how had he even been able to restrain himself so long, while listening at the door? It was that the conversation between his wife and the Marquis had, as the reader is aware, been carried on in so low a tone—especially on the side of the Countess, that he had not been able to gather sufficient to place beyond all doubt the guilt of that fair creature; and, even in the midst of his Italian ire, he had clung to the hope that she might have been imprudent—but not culpable as yet!

Oh! in this case, how gladly would that old Lord have forgiven the past, on condition of complete reformation for the future! He would have removed his young wife far away from the scene of temptation—to a distant estate which he possessed; and there, by gentle remonstrance and redoubled attention, he would have sought to bind her to him by the links of gratitude and respect, if not by those of love.

But this dream—so honourable to that old man's heart—was not to be realized; for scarcely was it conceived, when the discourse of the youthful pair turned upon the diamonds—those diamonds which he had given her on their bridal day!

Giulia spoke clearly and plainly enough then—in spite of the presence of the bandit in that chamber; for she was about to explain to her lover how willingly she would comply with his suggestion to raise upon the jewels the sum he again required,—a readiness on her part which might be corroborated by the fact that she had already once had recourse to this expedient, and for him;—but that she dared not adopt the same course again, as her husband might detect the absence of the valuables ere she could obtain funds to redeem them.

When she acknowledged to her lover that "these diamonds were pledged to the Jew Isaachar ben Solomon, to raise the sum with which his last debt was paid," it flashed to the old nobleman's mind that his wife had exhibited some little confusion when he had spoken to her a day or two previously concerning her jewels; and now it was clear that they had been used as the means to supply the extravagances of an unprincipled spendthrift. How could he any longer cling to the hope that Giulia was imprudent only, and not guilty? Must she not be guilty, to have made so large a sacrifice and run so great a risk for the sake of the Marquis of Orsini?

It was under the influence of these excited feelings that the Count of Arestino burst into the room.

Fortunately—so far as outward appearance went—there was nothing more to confirm the old nobleman's suspicions;—the youthful pair were not locked in each other's arms; their hands were not even joined. Manuel was seated on the sofa—and Giulia was standing at a short distance from him.

But conscious guilt elicited a faint scream from her

who was himself so taken by surprise at this unembarrassed mode of address, that he began to fancy his ears must have deceived him and his suspicions beguiled him; "on what business could you possibly have needed my services at this late hour?"

"I will explain myself," returned Orsini, who was a perfect adept in the art of dissimulation, and who, never losing his presence of mind, embraced at a glance the whole danger of Giulia's position and his own, and the probability that their conversation might have been overheard: "I was explaining to her ladyship the temporary embarrassment under which I lay, and from

"HE SANK UPON ONE KNEE." (See p. 30.)

lips; and the boiling blood, after rushing to her countenance, seemed to ebb away as rapidly again—leaving her beauteous face as pale as marble; while she clung to the mantel-piece for support.

"I am glad that your lordship is returned," said the Marquis, rising from his seat and advancing towards the Count in a manner so insolently cool and apparently self-possessed, that Giulia was not only astonished but felt her courage suddenly revive: "I was determined—however uncourteous the intrusion, and unseemly the hour—to await your lordship's coming; and as her ladyship assured me that you would not tarry late——"

"My Lord Marquis," interrupted the old nobleman,

which I hoped that your friendship might probably release me——"

"And her ladyship spoke of her diamonds—did she not?" demanded the Count, addressing himself to the Marquis, but fixing a keen and penetrating glance on Giulia.

"Her ladyship was remonstrating with me on my extravagance," hastily replied the Marquis, "and was repeating to me—I must say in a manner too impressive to be agreeable—the words which my own sister had used to me a few days ago, when explaining, as her motive for refusing me the succour which I needed, that she had been compelled to pledge her diamonds——"

"Ah! they were your sister's diamonds that were pledged to Isaachar the Jew?" said the Count, half ironically and half in doubt; for he was fairly bewildered by the matchless impudence of the young Marquis.

"Yes, my lord—my dear sister, who, alas! is ruining herself to supply me with the means of maintaining my rank. And as my sister and her ladyship, the Countess, are on the most friendly terms, as you are well aware, it is not surprising if she should have communicated the secret of the diamonds to her ladyship, and also begged her ladyship to remonstrate with me——"

"Well, my lord," interrupted the Count, impatiently, "your own private affairs have no particular interest for me—at this moment: and as for any business on which you may wish to speak to me, I shall be pleased if you postpone it until to-morrow."

"Your lordship's wishes are commands with me," said Manuel, with a polite salutation; and having made a low bow to Giulia, he quitted the room—not by the private door, be it well understood, but by that which had ere now admitted the Count of Arestino.

The moment the door had closed behind the Marquis of Orsini, the Count approached his wife, and said, in a cold, severe manner, "Your ladyship receives visitors at a late hour."

He glanced, as he spoke, towards the dial of the clepsydra, and Giulia followed his look in the same direction: it was half an hour after midnight.

"The Marquis explained to your lordship—or partially so—the motive of his importunate visit," said Giulia, endeavouring to appear calm and collected.

"The Marquis is an unworthy—reckless—unprincipled young man," exclaimed the Count, fixing a stern, searching gaze upon Giulia's countenance, as if with the iron of his words he would probe the depths of her soul. "He is a confirmed gamester—is overwhelmed with debts—and has tarnished, by his profligacy, the proud name that he bears. Even the friendship which existed for many, many years between his deceased father and myself, shall no longer induce me to receive at this house a young man whose reputation is all but tainted, even in a city of dissipation and debauchery, such, as, alas! the once glorious Florence has become! For his immorality is not confined to gaming and wanton extravagance," continued the Count, his glance becoming more keen as his words fell like drops of molten lead upon the heart of Giulia: "but his numerous intrigues amongst women—his perfidy to those confiding and deceived fair ones——"

"Surely, my lord," said the Countess, vainly endeavouring to subdue the writhings of torture which this language excited, "surely the Marquis d'Orsini is wronged by the breath of scandal!"

"No, Giulia: he is an unprincipled spendthrift," returned the Count, who never once took his eyes off his wife's countenance while he was speaking;—"an unprincipled spendthrift," he added emphatically—"a man lost to all sense of honour—a ruined gamester—a heartless seducer—a shame, a blot, a stigma upon the aristocracy of Florence;—and now that you are acquainted with his real character, you will recognise the prudence of the step which I shall take to-morrow—that is, to inform him that henceforth the Count and Countess of Arestino must decline to receive him again at their villa. What think you, Giulia?"

"Your lordship is the master to command, and it is my duty to obey," answered the Countess: but her voice was hoarse and thick—the acutest anguish was rending her soul, and its intensity almost choked her utterance.

"She is guilty!" thought the Count within himself; and to subdue an abrupt explosion of his rage, until he had put the last and most certain test to his lady's faith, he walked twice up and down the room:—then, feeling that he had recovered his powers of self-control, he said, "To-morrow, Giulia, is the reception-day of his Highness the Duke; and I hope thou hast made suitable preparations to accompany me in a manner becoming the wife of the Count of Arestino."

"Can your lordship suppose for an instant that I should appear in the ducal presence otherwise than as meet and fitting for her who has the honour to bear your name?" said Giulia, partially recovering her presence of mind, as the conversation appeared to have taken a turn no longer painful to her feelings:—for, Oh! cannot the reader conceive the anguish—the moral anguish she had ere now endured, when her husband was heaping ashes on the reputation of her lover!

"I do not suppose that your ladyship will neglect the preparation due to your rank and to that name which you esteem it an honour to bear, and which no living being should dishonour with impunity!"

Giulia quailed—writhed beneath the searching glance which now appeared literally to glare upon her.

"Nevertheless," continued the Count, "I was fearful you might have forgotten that to-morrow is the reception-day! And while I think of it, permit me to examine your diamonds for a few minutes—to convince myself that the settings are in good order—as you know," he added, with a strange, unearthly kind of laugh, "that I am skilled in the jeweller's craft."

The old man paused; but he thought within himself, "Now, what subterfuge can she invent, if my suspicions be really true, and if my ears did not ere now deceive me?"

How profound, then, was his astonishment, when Giulia, with the calm and tranquil demeanour which innocence usually wears, but with the least, least curl of the upper lip, as if in haughty triumph, leisurely and deliberately drew the jewel-case from beneath a cushion of the ottoman whereon she was seated, and, handing it to him, said, "Your lordship perceives that I had not forgotten the reception which his Highness holds to-morrow, since I ere now brought my diamonds hither to select those which it is my intention to wear."

The Count could have pressed her hand as he took the case in his own—he could have fallen at her feet and demanded pardon for the suspicions which he had entertained—for it now seemed certain beyond all possibility of doubt that the explanation volunteered by the Marquis was the true one :—yes—he could have humbled himself in her presence; but his Italian pride intervened, and he proceeded to examine the diamonds with no other view than to gain time to reflect how he should account for the abrupt manner in which he had entered the room ere now, and for the chilling behaviour he had maintained towards his wife.

On her side, Giulia, relieved of a fearful weight of apprehension, was only anxious for this scene to have a speedy termination, that she might release the robber-captain from his imprisonment behind the tapestry.

Three or four minutes of profound silence now ensued.

But suddenly the Count started, and uttered an ejaculation of mingled rage and surprise.

Giulia's blood ran cold to her very heart's core—she scarcely knew why.

The suspense was not, however, long—though most painful; for, dashing the jewel-case with its contents upon the table, the old nobleman approached her with quivering lips, and a countenance ghastly white, exclaiming, "Vile woman! thinkest thou to impose upon me thus? The diamonds I gave thee are gone—*the stones set in their place are counterfeit!*"

Giulia gazed up towards her husband's countenance for a few moments in a manner expressive of blank despair; then, falling on her knees before him, and clasping her hands together, she screamed frantically—"Pardon, pardon!"

"Ah; then it is all indeed too true!" murmured the unhappy nobleman, staggering as if with a blow: but, recovering his balance, he stamped his foot resolutely upon the floor, and drawing himself up to his full height, while he half averted his eyes from his kneeling wife, he exclaimed, "Lost—guilty—abandoned woman, how canst thou implore pardon at my hands? For pardon is mercy—and what mercy hast thou shown to me? Giulia, I am descended from an old and mighty race—and tradition affords no room to believe that any one who has borne the name of Arestino has dishonoured it—until now! Oh! fool—dotard—idiot that I was to think that a young girl could love an aged man like me! For old age is a weed, which, when twined round the plant of love, becomes like the deadly nightshade, and robs the rose-bush of its health! Alas! alas! I thought that in my declining years I should have one to cheer me —one who might respect, if she could not love me—one who would manifest some gratitude for the proud position I have given her, and the boundless wealth that it would have been my joy to leave her. And now that hope is gone — withered—crushed — blighted, woman, by thy perfidy! Oh! wherefore did you accompany the old man to the altar—if only to deceive him? wherefore did you consent to become his bride, if but to plunge him into the depths of misery? You weep! Ah! weep on: and all those tears—be they even so scalding as to make seams on that too fair face—cannot wipe away the stain which is now affixed to the haughty name of Arestino! Weep on, Giulia: but thy tears cannot move me now!"

And the old lord's tone changed suddenly from the deep, touching pathos of tremulousness to a stern, fixed, cold severity which stifled the germs of hope that had taken birth in the heart of his guilty wife.

"Mercy! mercy!" she shrieked, endeavouring to grasp his hand.

"No!" thundered the Count of Arestino; and he rang violently a silver bell which stood upon the table.

"Holy Virgin! what will become of me? for what fate am I destined?" implored Giulia, frantically.

The old nobleman approached her — gazed on her sternly for nearly a minute—then, bending down, said in a hollow, sepulchral tone, "Thou art doomed to eternal seclusion in the Convent of the Carmelites!"

He then turned hastily round and advanced to the door, to which steps were already distinctly heard drawing near in the corridor.

For an instant Giulia seemed paralyzed by the dreadful announcement that had been made to her: but suddenly a ray of hope flashed on her mind—and, darting towards that part of the tapestry behind which the robber was concealed, she said, in a low and rapid tone, "Thou hast heard the fate that awaits me: I charge thee to seek Manuel d'Orsini, and let him know all."

"Fear not, lady! you shall be saved!" answered Stephano in a scarcely audible but yet profoundly emphatic whisper.

She had only just time to turn away, when the Count's faithful valet, accompanied by *three nuns* wearing their black veils over their faces, entered the room.

Half-an-hour afterwards the Carmelite Convent received another inmate!

CHAPTER XXV.

THE MARQUIS OF ORSINI.

UPON quitting the Arestino palace, the Marquis of Orsini suddenly lost that bold, insolent, self-sufficient air with which he had endeavoured to deceive the venerable Count whose wife he had dishonoured.

For dishonour now menaced *him*.

Where could he raise the sum necessary to liquidate the debt which he had contracted with the stranger at the Casino, or gaming-house? And as the person to whom he found himself thus indebted *was* a stranger—a total stranger to him, he had no apology to offer for a delay in the payment of the money due.

"Perdition!" he exclaimed aloud, as he issued rapidly from the grounds contingent to the Arestino mansion: "is there no alternative save flight? Giulia cannot assist me—her jewels are gone—they are pledged to the Jew Isaachar—she was telling me so when the Count broke in upon us. What course can I adopt? what plan pursue? Shall the name of Orsini be dishonoured —that proud name which for three centuries has been maintained spotless? No—no: this must not be!"

And in a state of the most painful excitement—so painful, indeed, that it amounted almost to a physical agony—the Marquis hastened rapidly through the mazes of the sleeping city—reckless whither he was going, but experiencing no inclination to repair to his own abode.

The fact of the diamonds of his mistress having been pledged to Isaachar ben Solomon was uppermost in his mind:—for the reader must remember that he was unaware of the circumstance of their restoration to Giulia —as it was at the moment when she was about to give him this explanation that the old Lord of Arestino had interrupted their discourse.

The diamonds, then, constituted the pivot on which his thoughts now revolved. They seemed to shine like stars amidst the deep haze which hung upon his mind. Could he not possess himself of them? The name of Orsini would be dishonoured if the gambling debt were not paid; and one bold—one desperate step might supply him with the means to save himself from the impending ruin—the imminent disgrace.

But as the thoughts encouraged by those simple words —"*the diamonds*"—assumed a more palpable shape in his imagination, he shrank dismayed from the deed which they suggested: for gamester—debauchee—spendthrift as he was, he had never yet perpetrated an act that could be termed a *crime*. The seduction of the Countess of Arestino was not a crime in his estimation;—Oh! no— because a man may seduce, and yet not be dishonoured in the eyes of the world. It is his victim, or the partner

of his guilty pleasure, only who is dishonoured. Such is the law written in society's conventional code. Vile— detestable—unjust law!

To weigh and balance the reason for or against the perpetration of a crime,—to pause only for an instant to reflect whether the deed shall or shall not be done,—this is to yield at once to the temptation. The desperate man who hovers hesitatingly between right and wrong invariably adopts the latter course.

And Manuel of Orsini was not an exception to the general rule.

Silence, and calmness, and moonlight were still spread over the City of Flowers, while the Marquis pursued the path leading to the suburb of Alla Croce. And the silver-faced stars shone on—shone on, brightly and sweetly, as the young nobleman knocked at the well-protected door of Isaachar ben Solomon.

For a long time his summons remained unanswered; and he repeated it several times ere it received the slightest attention.

At last a casement was opened slowly on the upper storey; and the Jew demanded who sought admittance at that hour,

"'Tis I—the Marquis of Orsini!" exclaimed the nobleman.

"A thousand pardons, my lord: I come directly," answered the Jew, not daring to offend a scion of the omnipotent aristocracy of Florence, yet filled with sore misgivings—the more painful because they were so vague and undefined.

In a few moments Manuel was admitted into the abode of Isaachar ben Solomon, who carefully barred and bolted the door again ere he even thought of alleviating his acute suspense by inquiring the nobleman's business.

"Deign to enter this humble apartment, my lord," said the Jew, at length, as he conducted the Marquis into the same room where he had a few hours previously received the bandit captain.

"Isaachar," exclaimed Manuel, flinging himself upon a seat, "you behold a desperate man before you."

"Alas! my lord—what can a poor, aged, and obscure individual like myself do to assist so great and powerful a noble as your lordship?" said the Jew, in a trembling tone.

"What can you do?" repeated the Marquis: "much— everything, old man! But listen patiently—for a few moments only. A noble lady's fame—honour—reputation are at stake; and I am the guilty—unhappy cause of danger that threatens her. To minister to my necessities, she has pledged her jewels——"

"Yes—yes, my lord—I understand," said Isaachar, trembling from head to foot: "'tis a plan by no means unusual now-a-days in Florence."

"Her husband suspects the fact, and has commanded her to produce the diamonds to-morrow——"

"Her diamonds!" articulated the Jew in a stifling tone.

"Yes—*her diamonds*," exclaimed Manuel emphatically: "and they are in your possession. Now do you understand me?"

"I—I—my lord——"

"Let us not waste time in idle words, Isaachar," cried the Marquis. "Will you permit this scandal to be discovered, and involve the Countess of Arestino—myself— aye, and *yourself*, old man, in danger, and perhaps ruin? Perhaps, did I say? Nay—that ruin is certain to fall upon *her*,—certain also to overwhelm *you*,—for the Count of Arestino is a Councillor of State, and," added Manuel, with slow, measured emphasis, "*the dungeons of the Inquisition open at his commands to receive the Heretic or the Jew!*"

Isaachar ben Solomon vainly endeavoured to reply; fear choked his utterance; and he sank, trembling and faint, upon a low ottoman, where he sat, the picture of dumb despair.

"Ruin, then, awaits the Countess,—ruin, and the Inquisition yawn to engulf you,—and dishonour—the dishonour of having involved that noble lady in such a labyrinth of peril attends upon me," continued Orsini, perceiving that his dark threats had produced the effect which he had desired.

"My lord—my lord," gasped the unfortunate Israelite, who could not close his eyes against the truth—the terrible truth of the prospect submitted to his contemplation.

"It is for you to decide between the ruin of one—two —three persons, yourself being he who will, if possible, suffer most," resumed the Marquis impressively,—"it is, I say, for you to decide between exposure and the Inquisition on one hand, and the surrender of those paltry diamonds on the other!"

"The diamonds—the diamonds—they are gone!" exclaimed the Jew, his voice becoming almost frantic with the wild hope that suddenly struck him of being able to shift the danger from his own head to that of another. "The captain of the banditti—Stephano Verrina—was here a few hours ago,—here, in this very room,—and he sat where your lordship now sits."

"Well—well?" cried the Marquis, impatiently: for his heart began to grow sick with the fear of disappointment in respect to his plan of obtaining the diamonds of his mistress.

"And Stephano Verrina took them from me—basely, vilely wrenched them as it were from my grasp!" continued the Jew.

"'Tis false!—a miserable subterfuge on your part!" ejaculated the Marquis, starting from his seat and striding in a menacing manner towards Isaachar ben Solomon.

"'Tis true! I will give your lordship the proof!" cried the Jew: and Manuel fell back a few paces. "Stephano came and told me all. He said that the Countess had pledged her jewels for the sake of her lover—of you, my lord—you, the Marquis of Orsini. 'Twas to pay a gambling debt which your lordship had contracted; and that debt was paid within an hour or two from the moment when the sum was advanced on the diamonds. Moreover," continued Isaachar, still speaking in a rapid, excited tone,—"moreover, Stephano was hired by the Countess to regain them from me!"

"Liar!" thundered the Marquis, again rushing towards the defenceless old man.

"Patience, my lord—patience for an instant;—and you will see that I am no utterer of base falsehoods. The robber-captain examined the diamonds carefully—yes, most carefully; and, while occupied in the scrutiny, he let drop expressions which convinced me that he was hired by the Countess. '*The inventory is complete*,' he said, '*just as it was described to me by her ladyship. You are a worthy man, Isaachar*,' he added *you will have restored tranquillity to the mind of this beautiful Countess; and she will be enabled to appear at Court tomorrow with her husband.*' Now does your lordship believe me?"

The Marquis was staggered; for several minutes he made no answer. Was it possible that the Countess of Arestino could have employed the dreaded chieftain of the Florentine banditti to wrest her diamonds from the possession of Isaachar? or had the Jew invented the tale for an obvious purpose? The latter alternative scarcely seemed feasible. How could Isaachar have learnt that the sum raised was for the payment of a gambling debt? Giulia would not have told him so. Again, how had he learnt that this debt had been paid within an hour or two after the money was procured? and how had he ascertained that the Countess actually required her diamonds to accompany her husband to Court?

"Perdition!" ejaculated Orsini, bewildered by conflicting ideas, suspicions, and alarms: and he paced the room with agitated steps.

Nearly a quarter of an hour thus elapsed—the silence being occasionally broken by some question which the Marquis put to the Jew, and to which the latter had his reply ready. And each question thus put, and every answer thus given, only served to corroborate Isaachar's tale, and banish hope still further from the breast of the ruined nobleman.

At length the latter stopped short—hesitated for a few moments, as if wrestling with some idea or scheme that had taken possession of his mind;—then, turning abruptly towards the Jew, he said, in a deep hollow tone, "Isaachar, I need gold!"

"Gold—gold, my lord!" ejaculated the Jew, all his fears returning: "surely—surely, my lord, her ladyship will supply you with——"

"Fool—dolt!" cried the Marquis, terribly excited: "do you not see that she herself is menaced with ruin—that the villain Stephano must have kept the diamonds for himself! that is, granting your tale to be true——"

At that moment there was an authoritative knock at the house door.

"This is Stephano Verrina himself," exclaimed the Jew: "I know his manner of knocking with the rude handle of his sword. What can he want? what will become of me?"

"Stephano Verrina, say you?" cried the Marquis, hastily. "Then admit him by all means: and the pos-

session of the diamonds of the Countess shall be disputed between him and me at the sword's point."

Manuel d'Orsini was naturally brave; and the desperate position in which he was placed rendered his tone and bearing so resolute—so determined, that Isaachar feared lest blood should be shed in his dwelling,

"My lord—my lord," he said, in an imploring tone, "depart—or conceal yourself——"

"Silence, signor!" ejaculated the Marquis; "and hasten to admit the Captain of Banditti. I have heard much of Stephano Verrina, and would fain behold this formidable chieftain."

The Jew proceeded, with trembling limbs and ghastly countenance, to obey the orders of the Marquis; and in a few moments he returned to the room, accompanied by Stephano Verrina.

CHAPTER XXVI.

A COMBAT.—THE DESPISED AND PERSECUTED ISRAELITE.

ISAACHAR had taken away the lamp with him to give admission to the bandit, and the Marquis had remained for a few instants in the dark,

When the Jew reappeared, bearing the light, Orsini's first and natural impulse was to cast a rapid, searching glance at the brigand captain. At the same moment this individual burst into a loud, coarse, and joyous laugh; and the Marquis, to his profound surprise, recognised in Stephano Verrina the person with whom he had twice played so unsuccessfully at the gambling-house.

"Good, my lord!" exclaimed Verrina, flinging himself on the ottoman which the Jew had ere now occupied; "there is not in all Florence a man whom I would rather have encountered than yourself."

"You are somewhat pressing for the trifle—the miserable trifle in which I am indebted to you, signor," said the Marquis, haughtily; "seeing that scarce two hours have elapsed since I lost the amount at the casino."

"Pshaw! who alluded to the affair save yourself!" cried Stephano. "It was for another motive——"

"Yes: and I also wished to see Signor Stephano Verrina for another motive," exclaimed Manuel, emphatically.

"Ah! then you know me, my lord," said the bandit. "And yet methought I was a stranger to you—although you were none to me—at the casino?"

"You were a stranger until now," returned Orsini: "but Isaachar knew by the knock which you dealt so lustily on his door, who was his visitor."

"And your lordship was desirous to see me?"

"Very much so. I believe you expressed a similar wish?"

"Precisely, my lord," returned Stephano. "But as you hold the higher rank in the world, precedence in the way of explanation belongs to your lordship."

"It is rather an explanation which I seek than one which I have to give," rejoined Manuel, in a cold but resolute manner. "In a word, my business with thee is touching the diamonds of the Countess of Arestino."

"And my business with your lordship is touching the Countess herself," observed Verrina, also in a cool and deliberate manner.

"Ah!" cried the Marquis, with a sudden start.

"Yes, my lord. But this is no place for explanations on *that* head," added Stephano, glancing towards the Jew.

"I understand you, signor, we must confer *alone*," said the Marquis. "We will go out together presently: but in the meantime, one word concerning the diamonds which the Countess of Arestino——"

"Employed me to procure for her," exclaimed Stephano, finishing the nobleman's sentence for him. "I presume that old Isaachar here has informed you of the particulars of my previous visit to him this night—or rather last night, for it is now the Sabbath morning."

"I am well informed of those particulars, Sir Captain," returned Manuel; "but I would fain know what has become of the jewels which you obtained from Isaachar."

"I might with reason question your lordship's right to catechise me——"

"Ah! villain—would you dare?" exclaimed the Marquis, his countenance becoming flushed with rage; for he imagined that the robber-chief was trifling with him. "Far as you are beneath me—wide as is the gulf that separates the Marquis of Orsini from the proscribed bravo—yet will I condescend to wreak upon thee, base-born as thou art, that vengeance which the law has not yet been able to inflict!''

And Manuel unsheathed his weapon with such rapidity, that the polished blade of Milan steel flashed like lightning in the glare of the lamp.

"Since that is your object, I will bear with your humour," muttered Stephano, starting from his seat and drawing his heavy sword.

"My lord—good Signor Verrina—in mercy—not here —I implore——" ejaculated the Jew, speaking in a piteous tone, and wringing his hands in alarm at this hostile demonstration.

was made at him by his opponent, and at the next moment wounded the Marquis in the sword-arm.

The weapon fell from Manuel's hand, and he stood at the mercy of his conqueror.

"You are wounded, my lord—and the blood is flowing!" cried Stephano. "Hasten, friend Isaachar—fetch water—bandages——"

"It is nothing—a mere scratch," exclaimed the Marquis, tearing away with his left hand the right sleeve of his doublet, and displaying a tolerable severe gash which run down the fore-arm lengthways, and from which the blood trickled on the floor. "Be kind

"AT THE FOOT OF THE ALTAR KNELT FIVE WOMEN." (See p. 33.)

"Stand back!" thundered the bandit-chief; the Jew retreated into the most remote corner of the room, where he fell upon his knees and began to offer up prayers that no blood might be spilt—for he was a humane and kind-hearted man.

The Marquis and the Captain of Banditti crossed their weapons; and the combat began. The former was lighter, younger, and therefore more active than his opponent: but the latter was far more experienced in the use of his sword; and, moreover, the space was too narrow to enable the Marquis to gain any advantage from his superior agility. The fight lasted for about ten minutes, when the bandit parried a desperate thrust that

enough to bind it with my scarf, Signor Verrina, and let us continue in a more peaceful manner the discourse which has been somewhat rudely interrupted.''

Isaachar, however, supplied water in an ewer, and linen bandages: and the old man, forgetting the object of Manuel's predatory visit to his abode, hastened himself to wash and bind up the wounded arm.

"Thou art a good Jew—and hast something of the feelings of the Christian in thee," said the Marquis, when the operation was completed.

"Didst thou ever suppose that different creeds make different hearts, my lord?" asked the old man, in a half-melancholy, half-reproachful tone.

"Isaachar, I shall not forget this kindness on your part," said the Marquis, blushing with shame at himself when he reflected on the purpose for which he had sought the Jew's dwelling. "Heaven knows it is not in my power to reward you with gold; but whenever I may henceforth hear your race traduced, reckon upon me as its champion."

The old man cast a look of gratitude upon the Marquis; and, after some little hesitation, he said in a tremulous tone, "Your lordship hinted ere now—at least methought I understood as much—that you required gold. I take Father Abraham above to witness that I am not so rich as ye Christians deem me to be: but since your lordship can say a kind word of the Jew—I—I will lend you such sum as you may need — without interest — without bond——"

Orsini, in whose breast all generous feelings had not been entirely crushed by the vices which had proved his ruin, extended his left hand—for his right now hung in a sling—to the kind-hearted Jew, exclaiming, "There is the signor to whom I am indebted, worthy Isaachar: it is for him to say whether he will press me immediately for the sum that I have fairly lost to him with the dice."

"Not I!" ejaculated Stephano, in his blunt, coarse manner. "And therefore your lordship need not lay yourself under an obligation to the Jew, who, after all, is a worthy signor in his way."

"Yes," exclaimed the Marquis, "I shall *ever* lie under an obligation to him; nor shall I be ashamed to proclaim the fact in the presence of all Florence."

"And now, my lord," resumed Stephano, "I will give you that explanation relative to the diamonds which you might have had without bloodshed; but patience and aristocracy are as much at variance as a thief and the headsman. Read this paper, my lord: it is not the worst testimonial which I could produce in proof of good character."

And he handed to the Marquis the document which he had compelled the Countess of Arestino to sign.

Manuel read it with astonishment.

"Then she *has* the diamonds in her possession!" he exclaimed; "and you must have seen her since I was there!"

"My lord," replied Stephano, as he received back the paper, "I was at the Arestino palace now, at the same time, and in the same room, as yourself. But this is a mystery I will explain presently. As for the diamonds—Isaachar here can tell your lordship what *he* has done with the *real* stones, for those that I received from him and which I handed to her ladyship were *false!*"

Orsini glanced towards the Jew, who was now pale and trembling.

"It was to make inquiries on this point," continued Stephano, "that I came here on the present occasion. And, to speak truly, it was also with the intention of making the old Israelite disgorge his plunder."

"Plunder!" repeated the Jew, in a tone almost of indignation, in spite of the terror with which the bandit-captain inspired him. "Did I not lend my good golden ducats upon those diamonds? and must I be blamed, if, knowing—ah! knowing too well, the base artifices of which many of even the best-born Florentine nobles and great ladies are capable,—must I be blamed, I say, if, aware of all this, I adopted a device which the wickedness of others, and not our own, has rendered common amongst those of our race who traffic in loans upon jewels and precious stones?"

"Isaachar speaks naught save the pure truth," remarked Orsini, blushing at the justice which dictated these reproaches against that aristocracy whereof he was a member. "Signor Verrina," he continued, "you are a brave man—and I believe you to be a generous one. Confirm this opinion on my part, by refraining from farther molestation towards the Jew; and thou wilt doubly render me thy debtor."

"Be it as you will, my lord," grumbled the bandit-chief. "And now let us depart—for I have much to communicate to your lordship."

"I am ready to accompany you," returned the Marquis, putting on his plumed hat, and settling his cloak with his left hand.

"One word, my lord," said Isaachar, in his habitually nervous and trembling tone: "should the Countess of Arestino *really* need her diamonds—*really* need them, my lord—I—I should not object—that is, my lord," he added in a firmer voice, as if ashamed at the hesitation with which he was expressing his readiness to do a good

action,—"I will at once give them up, trusting to her ladyship's honour to pay me my moneys at her most befitting convenience."

"Her ladyship does not require them *now*," exclaimed the bandit-chief, emphatically.

The Marquis looked at Stephano inquiringly; for there was something ominously mysterious in his words: but the brigand stalked in a dogged manner towards the door, as if anxious to hurry the departure so long protracted; and Manuel, having renewed the expressions of his gratitude towards Isaachar ben Solomon, hastily followed Verrina from the house.

CHAPTER XXVII.

STEPHANO AND THE MARQUIS.—THE STRONGHOLD OF THE BANDITTI.

THE moment Stephano and the Marquis were alone together, in the open street, the former related all the incidents which had occurred at the Arestino palace after the departure of Manuel himself; and the young nobleman now learnt, with feelings of mingled remorse and sorrow, that the unfortunate Countess had been hurried away to the Convent of the Carmelites, that species of Inquisition the gates of which so seldom opened more than *once* for each new female victim!

"But you promised to save her, signor?" he exclaimed with enthusiastic warmth.

"I gave that pledge, in the manner I have described to your lordship," returned Verrina; "and I shall not swerve from it."

"Think you that her liberation can be effected?" demanded Manuel. "Remember that the Convent is protected by the highest personages in the State,—that violence never will succeed in accomplishing the object—for, should an armed man dare to pass that sacred threshold, every soldier—every sbirro in Florence would fly to the spot——"

"It is then your lordship who is afraid of attempting the rescue of the Countess?" interrupted Stephano, in a contemptuous tone.

"That observation is hardly fair, Signor Verrina," said the young nobleman: "considering that my right arm is disabled, and that the wound was received in combat with yourself."

"I crave your lordship's pardon," exclaimed the bandit-captain. "My remark was most uncourteous—particularly to one who has ere now given no equivocal proof of his valour. But I pretend not to courtly manners: and such as I am, you will find me faithfully devoted to your service and to that of the Lady Giulia. The attempt to rescue her will be somewhat hazardous: it is, however, tolerably sure of success. But it can only be undertaken on certain conditions; and these regard your lordship's self. Indeed, had I not so opportunely met you at the Jew's house, I should have sent one of my fellows to you to-morrow."

"In what way do the conditions that you speak of regard myself," inquired the Marquis.

"To this extent," returned the robber-chief; "that you accompany me to our stronghold, wherever it may be—that you join us in any project or plan that may be undertaken with a view to liberate the Countess of Arestino—and that you remain with us until such project or plan be attempted: then, whether it succeed or fail, you shall be at liberty to take your departure."

"Agreed!" exclaimed Manuel: "and now permit me to ask you one question :—On what ground do you manifest this interest in behalf of the Countess and myself? You are well aware that from me you have little to hope in the shape of reward; and that the Countess will be in no better condition than myself to recompense you, even if you should succeed in effecting her rescue."

"I am aware of all this, my lord," answered Stephano; "and I will give you an explanation of my motives as frankly as you solicit it. In the first place, it suits my projects to make friends as much as possible with nobles and great ladies; as no one can say how or when such interest may be available to me or to those connected with me. Secondly, I am not sorry to have an excuse for paying a visit to the Carmelite Convent: and in case of failure, it will be as well to have a Florentine noble amongst us. Because the statutes of our most glorious Republic are somewhat unequal in their application: thus, for instance, if a plebeian commit sacrilege, he is punished with death; but a patrician is merely reprimanded by the Judge and mulcted in a sum which is devoted to religious purposes. In this latter case, too, the companions of the patrician are punished only as he himself is. Now, therefore, your lordship's presence amongst us will be a guarantee for our safety. Lastly—for I have another and less selfish motive—I admire the spirit with which your lordship spends money, drinks a flagon of good wine, and loses your thousands at dice : for, saving your lordship's presence, there is much in all those feats which finds sympathy with my own inclinations. Thus, everything considered, Stephano Verrina and fifty as gallant fellows as ever wore the name of banditti, are completely at your lordship's service—and at that of the dear lady who has the good taste to prefer a dashing, roystering blade like yourself, to a gentleman no doubt very worthy of esteem, but certainly old enough to be her father."

The Marquis made no reply to this tirade ; but he reflected profoundly upon all that the robber-chieftain said, as they walked somewhat leisurely along, through the suburb of Alla Croce, and towards the city.

He reflected, because he now saw all the dangers that were associated with the step he was taking,—the chance of being arrested with the whole band of lawless freebooters, and the dishonour that would attach itself to his name were such an event to occur. But on the other hand, Giulia was immured in a terrible prison-house,—immured in consequence of her love for him ; and his naturally chivalrous disposition triumphed over selfish considerations. Could her liberation be effected, he would fly with her into another State ; and the revenues arising from her own little patrimony, which had been settled on herself at her marriage, would enable them to live comfortably, if not affluently. And who could tell but that her husband might die intestate ?—and then all his wealth would become hers by law.

Thus did he reason with himself.

"Well, my lord—you do not reply ?" exclaimed the robber-captain, impatient of the long silence which had followed his explanations. "Are you content to abide by the conditions I ere now proposed ?"

"Perfectly content," answered the Marquis.

He knew that it was useless to reason with the brigand against that spoliation of the Convent which he had more than hinted at ; for it was not likely that the robbers would incur so great a risk as that involved in the sacrilegious invasion of the sacred establishment, unless it were with the hope of reaping an adequate reward.

The bandit-chief and the young nobleman had now reached the boundary of the city ; but, instead of entering the streets, they turned abruptly to the right Stephano acting as guide, and plunged into a thick grove of evergreens.

"Here, my lord," said Stephano, stopping short, "you must consent to be blindfolded."

"And wherefore ?" demanded Manuel, indignantly. "Think you that I shall betray the secrets of your dwelling, wherever and whatever it may be ?"

"I entertain no such base suspicion," returned Verrina. "But we banditti are governed by a code of laws which none of us—not even I, the chief—dare violate. To the observance of this code we are bound by an oath of so deadly—so dreadful, a nature, that bold and reckless as we are, we could not forget *that*. And I should alike break our laws and depart from my oath, were I to conduct an uninitiated stranger to our stronghold, otherwise than blindfolded."

"I offer no farther opposition, Signor Verrina," said the Marquis. "Fix on the bandage."

Stephano tied his scarf over the nobleman's eyes, and then conducted him slowly through the mazes of the grove.

In this manner they proceeded for nearly a quarter of an hour, when they stopped, and Stephano, quitting Manuel's hand, said in a low tone, "Stand still just where you are for a moment, while I give the signal ; and do not move a single step—for it is a dangerous neighbourhood."

About half a minute elapsed, during which it struck Manuel that he heard a bell ring, far—far under ground. The sound was very faint ; but still he felt convinced that he *did* hear it, and that it appeared to come from the bowels of the earth.

But he had not much time for reflection ; for Stephano once more took his hand, saying, "You are now about to descend a flight of steps."

They proceeded downward together for some distance, when the steps ceased, and they pursued their way on a flat surface of pavement ; but the echoes of their footsteps convinced the Marquis that he was threading a subterranean cavern or passage.

Presently a huge door, sounding as it were made of iron, was closed behind them ; and Stephano exchanged a few words in a whisper with some one who spoke to him at that point. Then they descended a few more steps, and at the bottom another door was banged heavily, when they had passed its threshold,—the echoes rebounding like pistol-shots throughout the place.

For a few minutes more did they proceed on another level paved floor ; and then the gurgling rush of a rapid stream met the ears of the Marquis.

"Be careful in following me," said Stephano ; "for you are about to cross a narrow bridge, my lord—and one false step is destruction !"

Slowly they passed over the bridge, which seemed to be a single plank of about thirty feet in length, and excessively narrow he had no doubt, both from the caution which he had received and the elasticity of that dangerous pathway.

On the opposite side, the level paved surface was continued ; and at the expiration of another minute, heavy folding-doors closed behind them.

"Take off the bandage, my lord," said Stephano, as he untied the knot which fastened the scarf at the back of the young nobleman's head.

The Marquis of Orsini gladly availed himself of this permission ; and when the bandage fell from his eyes, he found himself in a spacious cavern, paved with marble, hung with rich tapestry, and lighted by four chandeliers of massive silver.

Six pillars of crystal supported the roof, and rendered the lustre of the chandeliers almost insupportably brilliant by means of reflection.

In the midst of this subterranean apartment, stood a large table, covered with flagons, empty wine flasks, and drinking cups ; but the revellers had retired to rest—and the Marquis and Stephano were alone in that banqueting-hall.

"Follow me, my lord," said the bandit-captain ; "and I will conduct you to a place where you will find as dainty a couch as even a nobleman so accustomed to luxury as your lordship need not despise."

Thus speaking, Stephano opened an iron door at the end of the hall, and led the way along a narrow and low corridor, lighted by lamps placed in niches at short intervals. At the end of this corridor, he knocked at another door, which was opened in a few moments by a man who had evidently been aroused from his slumber.

"I bring a guest, Lomellino," said Verrina. "See that his lordship be well cared for."

Stephano then retraced his way along the corridor, and Lomellino closed and bolted the iron door.

But no pen can describe the astonishment of the Marquis when he found himself in a spacious room heaped all around with immense riches. Massive plate—splendid chandeliers—gorgeous suits of armour and martial weapons encrusted with gold or set with precious stones —chalices and dishes of silver—bags of money piled in heaps—an immense quantity of jewellery spread upon shelves—and an infinite assortment of the richest wearing apparel,—all these, suddenly bursting on the young nobleman's view by the light of a lamp suspended to the roof, produced an effect at once brilliant and astounding.

When Lomellino addressed him with a request to follow whither he should lead, it seemed as if some rude voice were suddenly awaking him from a delicious dream —save that the cause of his pleasure and wonder was still present. Then ashamed at having allowed himself to be so attracted by the spectacle of boundless wealth around him, he followed Lomellino to an alcove at the farther end of the caverned room, and the entrance of which was covered by a purple velvet curtain, richly fringed with gold.

Within were two beds, having a screen between them. These conches were of the most comfortably description, and such as in those times were not usually seen elsewhere than in the dwellings of the wealthy. Near each bed stood a toilet-table and washing-stand, with ewers of massive silver and towels of fine linen : and to the walls hung two large mirrors—articles of exclusive luxury at that period. The floor was richly carpeted ; and a perfumed lamp burnt in front of the dial of a water-clock.

Lomellino respectfully informed the Marquis that one division of the alcove was at his service ; and Manuel was too much wearied by the adventures of the evening not to avail himself of the information.

The brigand, seeing that he was wounded, but without asking any questions as to the cause, proffered his aid to divest the Marquis of his upper clothing; and at length the young nobleman was comfortably stretched in one of the voluptuous beds.

Sleep had just closed his eye-lids, and he had even already entered upon a vision of fairy enchantment,—doubtless conjured up to his imagination by the gorgeous spectacle of the treasure-chamber,—when he was startled by screams which appeared to issue from the very wall of the alcove at the head of his bed.

He listened—and those screams became more and more piercing in their nature, although their tone was subdued as if by the existence of a thick intervening partition.

"Holy Virgin! what sounds are those!" he exclaimed, more in pity than in fear—for they were unmistakably female shrieks which he heard.

"Perdition seize on those Carmelite nuns!" cried Lomellino: "they seem to have got another victim!"

"*Another victim!*" murmured the Marquis, falling back in his bed, a prey to the most torturing feelings: and then his lips framed the sweet and tender name of "GIULIA!"

CHAPTER XXVIII.

A FEARFUL ACCUSATION.

FAIR and beauteous art thou, O City of Flowers! with thy domes, and spires, and turrets overlooking the Arno's silver stream, and crowding together in that river's classic vale,—surrounded, too, by oak-covered hills, and cypress groves, and gardens of olives and ever-greens,—and presenting to the view of the spectator who stands on the rocky summit of Monte Senario, so vast an assemblage of palaces as to justify the saying of Ariosto that it seemed as if the very soil produced them!

Or seen from the olive-crowned hills of Fiesole, consecrated by the genius of Milton, how glorious is thy rich combination of beauty, thou Athens of Etruria!

The sun dawned upon the eventful night, the incidents of which have occupied so many chapters. The golden flood poured upon that Florentine scene so fair even in winter,—bathing in yellow lustre the mighty dome of the Cathedral of Saint Mary, the Ducal Palace on its left, and the cupola of the Medicean chapel on its right,—and bringing out into strong relief against the deep foliage of the evergreens, the marble fronts of palaces, villas, and convents, seated amidst the hills or scattered through the vale,—the whole affording a rich and varied view, as if eternal summer reigned in that delightful region, and beneath the purple canopy of that warm Italian sky

Alas! that the selfish interest—dark passions—conflicting feelings—clashing aims and black, black crimes of men should mar the serenity and peace which ought to maintain an existence congenial to this scene!

Scarcely had the orient beams penetrated through the barred casements of the Jew Isaachar's house in the suburb of Alla Croce, when the old man was awakened from a repose to which he had only been able to withdraw a couple of hours previously, by a loud and impatient knocking at his gate.

Starting from his couch, he glanced from the window, and, to his dismay, beheld the Lieutenant of Police, accompanied by half a dozen of his terrible sbirri, and by an individual in the plain, sober garb of a citizen.

A cold tremor came over the unhappy Israelite: for he knew that this official visit could bode him no good; and the dread of having incurred the resentment of the Count of Arestino immediately conjured up appalling scenes of dungeons, chains, judgment-halls, and tortures, to his affrighted imagination.

The dark hints which Manuel d'Orsini had dropped relative to the possibility of the Count's discovering the affair of the diamonds, and the certain vengeance that would ensue, flashed to the mind of Isaachar ben Solomon; and he stood as it were paralyzed at the window, gazing with the vacancy of despair upon the armed men on whose steel morions and pikes the morning sunbeams now fell in radiant glory.

The knocking was repeated more loudly and with greater impatience than before; and Isaachar, suddenly restored to himself, and remembering that it was dangerous as well as useless to delay the admittance of those who would not hesitate to force a speedy entry, huddled on his garments, and descended to the door.

The moment it was opened, the sbirri and the citizen entered: and the lieutenant, turning shortly round upon the Jew, said, "His Excellency the Count of Arestino demands, through my agency, the restoration of certain diamonds which his lordship has good reason to believe are in your possession. But think not that his lordship is desirous of plundering you of those jewels which you hold as a security for certain moneys advanced: for here is the gold to repay thee."

Thus speaking, the lieutenant produced from beneath his cloak a heavy bag of gold; and Isaachar, now considerably relieved of his apprehensions, led the way into the apartment where he had received the Marquis of Orsini and Stephano de Verrina during the night just past.

"Hast thou heard my message, Israelite?" demanded the lieutenant.

"Yes—yes; and his lordship is a worthy man—an estimable man. No oppressor of the poor defenceless Jew is he! Would that Florence abounded in such nobles as the Count of Arestino!"

"Cease thy prating, Jew; and let us despatch this business," cried the officer. "You see," he added, glancing towards his men, "that with these at my disposal, the ransacking of your dwelling would be a light and easy matter."

"I will not render it necessary," returned the Jew. "Tarry ye here a few moments, and the diamonds shall be delivered up."

Isaachar proceeded into another apartment, the lieutenant following him as far as the passage to see that he did not escape. When the old man returned, he held a small rosewood case in his hand; and from this box he produced the stones which he had extracted from the settings the very day the jewels were first mortgaged to him.

"Now, signor," said the lieutenant, turning to the citizen in the plain sober garb, "as you are the diamond merchant of whom his lordship the Count originally purchased the precious stones which have been traced to the possession of Isaachar, it is for you to declare whether those be the true diamonds or not."

The citizen examined the stones, and having pronounced them to be the genuine ones, took his departure, his services being no longer required.

The lieutenant secured the rosewood case with its valuable contents about his person, and then proceeded to settle with interest the amount claimed by the Jew as the sum which he had advanced on the jewels.

While this transaction was in progress, the notice of one of the sbirri was attracted by the marks of blood which appeared upon the floor, and which, as the reader will recollect, had been caused by the wound that the Marquis of Orsini had received from the robber Stephano.

"It is decidedly blood," whispered one sbirro to his companions.

"Not a doubt of it," observed another. "We must mention it to the lieutenant when he has done counting out that gold."

"Do you know what I have heard about the Jews?" asked the first speaker, drawing his comrades still further aside.

"What?" was the general question.

"That they kill Christian children to mix the blood in the dough with which they make the bread used at their religious ceremonies," answered the sbirro.

"Depend upon it, Isaachar has murdered a Christian child for that purpose!" said one of his companions.

The atrocious idea gained immediate belief amongst the ignorant sbirri: and as the Jew now quitted the room for a few minutes to secure the gold which he had just received, in his coffer in the adjacent apartment, the police-officers had leisure to point out to their superior the traces of blood which they had noticed, and the suspicion which these marks had engendered.

The lieutenant was not further removed beyond the influence of popular prejudice and ridiculous superstition than even his men; and, though by no means of a cruel disposition, yet he thought it no sin nor injustice to persecute the Hebrew race, even when innocent and unoffending. But now that suspicion—or what he chose to consider suspicion—pointed at Isaachar ben Solomon as a dreadful criminal, the lieutenant did not hesitate many moments how to act.

Thus, when the Jew returned to the room with the fond hope of seeing his visitors take their speedy departure, he was met by the terrible words, uttered by the officer of the sbirri—"*In the name of the Most Holy Inquisition, Isaachar, do I make you my prisoner.*"

The unhappy Jew fell upon his knees, stunned—terrified by this appalling announcement; and although he assumed this attitude of supplication, he had not the power to utter a syllable of intercession nor of prayer. Horror had for the moment stricken him dumb: and a thousand images of terror, conjured up by the fearful words—"THE INQUISITION"—suddenly sprang up to scare, bewilder, and overwhelm him.

"Bind him—gag him!" ejaculated the lieutenant: and this order was immediately obeyed: for whenever a prisoner was about to be conveyed to the dungeon of the Inquisition, he was invariably gagged in order that no

was remarkable for the stern and gloomy grandeur of its architecture. Its massive and heavy tower, crowned with embattled and overhanging parapets, seemed to frown in sullen and haughty defiance at the lapse of Time. The first range of windows were twelve feet from the ground, and were grated with enormous bars of iron, producing a sombre and ominous effect. Within were the apartments of the Duke's numerous dependants; and the lower portion of the palace had been rendered thus strong to enable the edifice to withstand a siege in those troublous times when the contentions of the Guelphs and Ghibelines desolated Florence. On the second floor

"'FEAR NOT, LADY, YOU SHALL BE SAVED!'" (See p. 43.)

questions on his part might evoke answers at all calculated to afford him a clue to the cause of his arrest.

This precaution was originally adopted in reference to those only who were ignorant of the charges laid against them: but it had subsequently become common in all cases of arrests effected in the name, or on the part, of the Holy Brotherhood.

The Palazzo del Podesta, or Ducal Palace, was one of the most celebrated edifices in Florence. In strong contrast with the beautiful specimens of composite Tuscan combined with a well-assimilated portion of the Grecian character, which abounded in Florence, the Ducal Palace

there was in front a plain and simple architrave, and on that storey the windows were high and arched; for those casements belonged to the ducal apartments. The upper storeys were in the same style: but the general aspect was stern and mournful to a degree.

This palace was built—as indeed nearly all the Florentine mansions then were, and still are—in the form of a square; and around this court, which was of an antique and gloomy cast, were numerous monumental stones, whereon were inscribed the names of the nobles and citizens who had held high offices in the State previous to the establishment of the sway of the Medici.

It was beneath the Palazzo del Podesta that the

dungeons of the criminal prison and also those of the Inquisition were situated.

In a cell belonging to the former department, Fernand Wagner was already a captive: and Isaachar ben Solomon now became the inmate of a narrow, cold, and damp stone chamber, in that division of the subterranean which was within the jurisdiction of the Holy Office.

CHAPTER XXIX.

THE VISIT OF THE BANDITTI TO THE RIVEROLA PALACE.

It was Monday night—and within an hour of the time appointed by Stephano for the meditated invasion of the Riverola palace.

Francisco had already retired to rest—for he was wearied with vain and ineffectual wanderings about the city and its environs, in search of some trace that might lead him to discover his lost Flora.

Indeed, the few days which had now elapsed since her mysterious disappearance had been passed by the young Count in making every possible inquiry, and adopting every means which imagination could suggest, to obtain a clue to her fate. But all in vain; and never for a moment did he suspect that she might be an inmate of the Carmelite Convent for, although he was well aware of the terrible power wielded by that institution, yet, feeling convinced that Flora herself was incapable of any indiscretion, it never struck him that the wicked machinations of *another* might place her in the custody of the dreaded Carmelite Abbess.

We said that Francisco had retired to rest somewhat early on the above-mentioned night; and the domestics, yielding to the influence of a soporific which Antonio, the faithless valet, had infused into the wine which it was his province to deal out to them under the superintendence of the head-butler, had also withdrawn to their respective chambers.

Nisida had dismissed her maids shortly before eleven; but *she* did not seek her couch. There was an expression of wild determination—of firm resolve in her dark black eyes and her compressed lips, which denoted the courage of her dauntless but impetuous mind: for of that mind the large piercing eyes seemed an exact transcript.

Terrible was she in the decision of her masculine —oh! even more than masculine character; for beneath that glorious beauty with which she was arrayed, beat a heart that scarcely knew compunction—or that, at all events, would hesitate at nothing calculated to advance her interests or projects.

Though devoured with ardent passions, and of a temperament naturally voluptuous and sensual even to an extreme, she had hitherto remained chaste, as much for want of opportunity to assuage the cravings of her mad desires, as through a sentiment of pride :—but since she had loved Wagner—the first and only man whom she had ever loved—her warm imagination had excited those desires to such a degree, that she felt capable of making any sacrifice—save one—to secure him to herself!"

And that *one* sacrifice which she could not make, was not her honour :—no—of that she now thought but little in the whirlwind of her impetuous ardent heated imagination. But madly as she loved Fernand Wagner,—that is, *loved* him after the fashion of her own strange and sensual heart,—she loved her brother still more; and this attachment was at least a pure—a holy sentiment, and a gloriously redeeming trait in the character of this wondrous woman of a mind so darkly terrible.

And for her brother's sake it was that there was *one* sacrifice—the sacrifice of a tremendous, but painfully persevered in, project—which she would not make even to her love for Fernand Wagner! No—rather would she renounce *him* for ever—rather would she perish, consumed by the raging desires of her own ungratified passions— than sacrifice one tittle of what she deemed to be her brother's welfare to any such selfish feeling of her own.

Wherefore do we dwell upon this subject now?

Because such was the resolution which Nisida vowed within her own heart, as she stood alone in her chamber, and fixed her eyes upon a document, bearing the Ducal Seal, that lay upon the table.

The document contained the decision of his Highness in respect to the memorial which she had privately forwarded to him in accordance with the advice given her a few days previously by Dr. Duras. The Duke lost no time in vouchsafing a reply : and this reply was unfavourable to the wishes and adverse to the hopes of Nisida. His Highness refused to interfere with the provisions of the late Count's will; and this decision was represented to be final.

Therefore was it that Nisida solemnly vowed within herself to persevere in a course long ago adopted and ever faithfully—steadily—sternly adhered to since the day of its commencement;—and, as if to confirm herself in the strength of this resolution, she turned her eyes with adoring—worshipping look towards the portrait of her maternal parent,—those eloquent speaking orbs seeming almost to proclaim the words which her lips could not utter,—"Yes, MOTHER—SAINTED MOTHER! THOU SHALT BE OBEYED!"

Then she hastily secured the ducal missive in an iron box where she was in the habit of keeping her own private papers, and which opened with a secret spring.

But did she, then, mean to renounce her love for Wagner? did she contemplate the terrible alternative of abandoning him in his misfortune—in his dungeon?

No :—far from that! She would save him, if she could ;—she would secure him to herself, if such were possible :—but she would not sacrifice to these objects the *one* grand scheme of her life—that scheme which had formed her character as we now find it, and which made her stand alone as it were amongst the millions of her own sex.

And it was to put into execution the plan which she had devised to effect Wagner's freedom, that she was now arming herself with all the resolution—all the magnanimity—all the firmness of which her masculine soul was capable.

The dial on the mantel in the chamber marked the hour of eleven; and Nisida commenced her preparations.

Having divested herself of her upper garment, she put on a thin but strong, and admirably formed corslet, made so as to fit the precise contour of her ample bust, and completely to cover her bosom. Then she assumed a black velvet robe, which reached up to her throat, and entirely concealed the armour beneath. Her long flexible dagger was next thrust carefully into a sheath formed by the wide border of her stomacher; and her preparations for defence in case of peril were finished.

She now took from a cupboard six small bags, which were nevertheless heavy; for they were filled with gold; and these she placed on a table. Then seating herself at that table, she wrote a few lines on several slips of paper; and these she thrust into her bosom.

Having accomplished her arrangements thus far, the Lady Nisida took a lamp in her hand, and quitted her apartments.

Ascending a staircase leading to the upper storey, she paused at one of several doors in a long corridor, and slowly and noiselessly drew the bolt by which that door might be fastened outside.

This was Antonio's room : and thus by Nisida's precaution, was he made a prisoner.

She then retraced her way to the floor below, and proceeded to the apartment in which her father breathed his last, and where the mysterious closet was situate.

No one until now had entered that room since the day of the late Count's funeral; and its appearance was gloomy and mournful in the extreme—not on account of the dark, heavy hangings of the bed, and the drawn curtains of the windows, but also from the effect of the ideas associated with that chamber.

And as Nisida glanced towards the closet-door, even *she* trembled and her countenance became ashy pale : for not only did she shudder at the thought of the horrors which that closet contained; but through her brain also flashed the dreadful history revealed to her by the manuscript of which, however, only a few lines have as yet been communicated to the reader.

But *she* knew all—*she* had read the whole : and well— oh! well might she shudder and turn pale.

For terrible indeed must have been the revelations of a manuscript whereof the few lines above alluded to gave promise of such appalling interest,—those lines which ran thus :—" *merciless scalpel hacked and hewed away at the still almost palpitating flesh of the murdered man, in whose breast the dagger remained deeply buried—a ferocious joy—a savage hyena-like triumph——*"

But we are to some extent digressing from the thread of our narrative.

Nisida placed the lamp in the chimney, in such a way that its light was concealed so as to leave all the immediate vicinity of the door in a state of complete darkness; and she seated herself in a chair close by, to await the expected events of midnight.

Slowly—slowly passed the intervening twenty minutes:

and the lady had ample leisure to reflect upon all the incidents of her life,—aye, and to shudder too at *one* which had dyed her hand in blood—the blood of Agnes !

Yet, though she shuddered thus—she did not look upon it with that unbounded, tremendous horror, that would be experienced by a lady similarly placed in these times ; for jealousy was a feeling that, by the tacit convention of a vitiated society, was an excuse for even murder—and, moreover, she possessed the true Italian heart which deemed the death of a rival in love a justifiable act of vengeance.

But she felt some compunction, because she had learnt, when it was too late, that Agnes was not the mistress of Fernand Wagner ; and she was convinced that in affirming this much, he had uttered the strictest truth.

Thus was she rather grieved at the fatal mistake than appalled by the deed itself ;—and she shuddered because she knew that her fearful impetuosity of disposition had led to the unnecessary deed which had entailed so dark a suspicion and so much peril upon her lover.

She was in the midst of these and other reflections connected with the various salient features of her life, when the door of the room was slowly and cautiously opened, and a man entered, bearing a lantern in his hand.

Two others followed close behind him.

"Shut the door, Lomellino," said the foremost.

"But are you sure that this is the room ?" asked the man thus addressed.

"Certain," was the reply. "Antonio described its situation so clearly——"

"Then why did he not join us ?"

"How do I know ? But that need not prevent us——"

Nisida at this moment raised the lamp from the fireplace, and the light flashing at that end of the room produced a sudden start and ejaculation on the part of the banditti.

"Perdition !" cried Stephano : "what can this mean."

Nisida advanced towards the robbers in a manner so calm—so dignified—so imperious—and so totally undaunted by their presence, that they were for a moment paralyzed and rooted to the spot as if they were confronted by a spectre.

But at the next instant, Stephano uttered an exclamation of mingled surprise and joy, adding, " By my patron saint ! Lomellino, this is the very lady of whom I spoke to you the other evening !"

"What ! the one who did the business so well——"

"Yes—yes," cried Stephano, hastily : "you know what I mean—in Wagner's garden ! But——"

Nisida had in the meantime drawn from her bosom one of the slips of paper before alluded to : and, handing it to the bandit-chief, she made a hasty and imperious motion for him to read it.

He obeyed her with the mechanical submission produced by astonishment and curiosity, mingled with admiration for that bold and daring woman whom he already loved and resolved to win :—but his surprise was increased a hundred-fold, when he perused these lines :—
" I am the Lady Nisida of Riverola. Your design is known to me : it matters not how. Rumour has doubtless told you that I am deaf and dumb : hence this mode of communicating with you. You have been deluded by an idle knave ; for there is no treasure in the closet yonder. Even if there had been, I should have removed it the moment your intended predatory visit was made known to me. But you can serve me ; and I will reward you well for your present disappointment."

"What does the paper say ?" demanded Lomellino and Piero, the Captain's two companions, almost in the same breath.

"It says just this much," returned Stephano : and he read the writing aloud.

"The Lady Nisida !" ejaculated Lomellino. "Then it is she who used her dagger so well in Wagner's garden."

"Peace, silly fool !" cried Stephano. "You have now let out the secret to Piero. True, 'tis no matter—as he is as stanch to me as you are ; and therefore he may as well know that this lady here was the murderess of the young female in Wagner's garden : for I saw her do the deed when I was concealed amongst the evergreens there. She is as much in our power as we are in hers ; and we will let her know it if she means any treachery."

"But how could *she* have discovered that we meant to come here to-night, and what our object was ?" asked Piero.

"Antonio must have peached—that's clear !" returned Stephano : "and therefore he did not join us, as he agreed, in the hall down stairs. But no matter. It seems there's gold to be earned in this lady's service ; and even if there wasn't, I have such an affection for her, I would cut the throat of the Duke or the Cardinal-Archbishop himself merely to give her pleasure."

Then turning towards Nisida, whose courage seemed partially to have abandoned her—for her countenance was ghastly pale and her hand trembled so that it could scarcely hold the lamp,—Stephano made a low bow, as much as to imply that he was entirely at her service.

Nisida exerted a powerful effort to subdue the emotions that were agitating her : and, advancing towards the door, she made a sign for the banditti to follow her.

She led them to her own suite of apartments, and to the innermost room—her own bed-chamber,—having carefully secured the several doors through which they passed.

The banditti stood round the table, their eyes wandering from the six tempting looking money-bags to the countenance of Nisida, and then back to the little sacks :—but Stephano studied more the countenance than the other object of attraction ; for Nisida's face once more expressed firm resolution—and her haughty, imperious, determined aspect, combined with her extraordinary beauty, fired the robber-chieftain's heart.

Taking from her bosom another slip of paper, she passed it to Stephano, who read its contents aloud for the benefit of his companions :—*" The trial of Fernand Wagner will take place this day week. If he be acquitted your services will not be required. If he be condemned, are ye valiant and daring enough (sufficiently numerous ye are—being upwards of fifty in all) to rescue him on his way back from the Judgment Hall to the prison of the Ducal Palace ? The six bags of gold now upon the table are yours, as an earnest of reward, if ye assent. Double that amount shall be yours, if ye succeed."*

" 'Tis a generous proposition," observed Lomellino.

"But a dangerous one," said Piero.

"Nevertheless, it shall be accepted, if only for her fair self's sake," exclaimed Stephano, completely dazzled by Nisida's surpassing majesty of loveliness ;—then, with a low bow, he intimated his readiness to undertake the enterprise.

Nisida handed him a third paper, on which the following lines were written :—*" Take the gold with you, as a proof of the confidence I place in you. See that you deceive me not ; for I have the power to avenge as well as to reward. On Sunday evening next let one of you meet me, at ten o'clock, near the principal entrance of the Cathedral of Saint Mary ; and I will deliver the written instructions of the mode of proceeding which circumstances may render necessary."*

"I shall keep this appointment myself," said Stephano to his companions ; and another obsequious but somewhat coarse bow denoted full compliance with all that Nisida had required through the medium of the slips of paper.

She made a sign for the banditti to take the bags of gold from the table—an intimation which Piero and Lomellino did not hesitate to obey.

The private staircase leading into the gardens then afforded them the means of an unobserved departure ; and Nisida felt rejoiced at the success of her midnight interview with the chiefs of the Florentine Banditti.

CHAPTER XXX.

FLORA'S CAPTIVITY.—A COMPANION.—THE LIVING TOMB.

SIX days had now elapsed since Flora Francatelli became an inmate of the Carmelite Convent.

During this period she was frequently visited in her cell by Sister Alba, the nun who had received her at the bottom of the pit or well into which she had descended by means of the chair ; and that recluse gradually prepared her to fix her mind upon the necessity of embracing a conventual life.

It was not, however, without feelings of the most intense—the most acute—the most bitter anguish, that the unhappy maiden received the announcement that she was to pass the remainder of her existence in that monastic institution.

All the eloquence—all the sophistry—all the persuasion of Sister Alba, who presided over the department of the Penitents, failed to make her believe that such a step was necessary for her eternal salvation.

"No," exclaimed Flora, "the good God has not formed

this earth so fair that mortals should close their eyes upon its beauties. The flowers—the green trees—the smiling pastures—the cypress groves were not intended to be gazed upon from the barred windows of a prison-house."

Then the nun would reason with her on the necessity of self-denial and self-mortification; and Flora would listen attentively; but if she gave no reply, it was not because she was convinced.

When she was alone in her cell, she sat upon her humble pallet, pondering upon her mournful condition, and sometimes giving way to all the anguish of her heart, or else remaining silent and still in the immovability of dumb despair.

Her suspicions often fell upon the Lady Nisida as the cause of her terrible immurement in that living tomb—especially when she remembered the coldness with which her mistress had treated her a day or two previously to her forced abduction from the Riverola palace. Those suspicions seemed confirmed, too, by the nature of the discourse which Sister Alba had first addressed to her, when she upbraided her with having given way to "those carnal notions—those hopes—those fears—those dreams of happiness, which constitute the passion that the world calls Love."

The reader will remember that Flora had suspected the coolness of Nisida to have arisen from a knowledge of Francisco's love for the young maiden; and every word which Sister Alba had uttered in allusion to the passion of love seemed to point to that same fact.

Thus was Flora convinced that it was this unfortunate attachment—in which for a moment she had felt herself so supremely blest—that was the source of her misfortunes. But, then, how had Nisida discovered the secret? This was an enigma defying conjecture; for Francisco was too honourable to reveal his love to his sister, after having so earnestly enjoined Flora herself not to betray that secret.

At times a gleam of hope would dawn in upon her soul, even through the massive walls of that living tomb to which she appeared to have been consigned. Would Francisco forget her? Oh! no—she felt certain that he would leave no measure untried to discovered her fate—no means unessayed to effect her deliverance.

But, alas! then would come the maddening thought that he might be deceived with regard to her real position,—that the same enemy or enemies who had persecuted her, might invent some specious tale to account for her absence, and deter him from persevering in his inquiring concerning her.

Thus was the unhappy maiden a prey to a thousand conflicting sentiments,—unable to settle her mind upon any conviction save the appalling one which made her feel the stern truth of her captivity.

Oh! to be condemned so young to perpetual prisonage, was indeed hard—too hard,—enough to make reason totter on its throne and paralyze the powers of even the strongest intellect!

Sister Alba had sketched out to her the course of existence on which she must prepare to enter. Ten days of prayer and sorry food in her own cell were first enjoined as a preliminary, to be followed by admission into the number of Penitents who lacerated their naked forms with scourges at the foot of the altar. Then, the period of her penitence in this manner would be determined by the manifestations of contrition which she might evince, and which would be proved by the frequency of her self-flagellation—the severity with which the scourge was applied—and the anxiety which she might express to become a member of the holy sisterhood. When the term of penitence should arrive, the maiden would be removed to the department of the Convent inhabited by the professed nuns; and then her flowing hair would be cut short, and she would enter on her noviciate previously to taking the veil,—that last, last step in the conventual régimé which would for ever raise up an insuperable barrier between herself and the great—the beautiful—the glorious world without!

Such was the picture spread for the contemplation of this charming but hapless maiden.

Need we wonder if her glances recoiled from the prospect, as if from some loathsome spectre, or from a hideous serpent preparing to dart from his coils and twine its slimy folds around her?

Nor was the place in which she was a prisoner calculated to dissipate her gloomy reflections.

It seemed a vast cavern hollowed out of the bowels of the earth, rendered solid by masonry, and divided into various compartments. No windows were there to admit the pure light of day: an artificial lustre, provided by lamps and tapers, prevailed eternally in that earthly purgatory.

Sometimes the stillness of death—the solemn silence of the tomb reigned throughout that place: then the awful tranquillity would be suddenly broken by the dreadful shrieks, the prayers, the lamentations, and the scourges of the Penitents.

The spectacle of these unfortunate creatures,—with their naked forms writhing and bleeding beneath the self-inflicted stripes, which they doubtless rendered as severe possible in order to escape the sooner from that terrible preparation for their noviciate,—this spectacle, we say, was so appalling to the contemplation of Flora, that she seldom quitted her own cell to set foot in the Chamber of Penitence. But there were times when her thoughts became so torturing, and the solitude of her stone-chamber so terrible, that she was compelled to open the door and escape from those painful ideas and that hideous loneliness, even though the scene merely shifted to a reality from which her gentle spirit recoiled in horror and dismay.

But circumstances soon gave her a companion in her cell. For, on the second night of her abode in that place, the noise of the well-known machinery was heard;—the revolution of wheels and the play of the dreadful mechanism raised ominous echoes throughout the subterranean. Another victim came: all the cells were tenanted; and the new-comer was therefore lodged with Flora, whose own grief was partially forgotten—or at all events mitigated—in the truly Christian task of consoling a fellow-sufferer.

Thus it was that the Countess of Arestino and Flora Francatelli became companions in the Carmelite Convent.

At first the wretched Giulia gave way to her despair and refused all comfort. But so gentle—so winning—so softly fascinating were the ways of the beautiful Flora,—and so much sincerity did the charming girl manifest in her attempt to revive that frail but drooping flower which had been thrown as it were at her feet—at the feet of her, a pure though also drooping rosebud of innocence and beauty,—so earnest did the maiden seem in her disinterested attentions, that Giulia yielded to the benign influence, and became comparatively composed.

But mutual confidence,—that outpouring of the soul's heavy secrets which so much alleviates the distress of the female mind,—did not spring up between the Countess and Flora; because the former shrank from revealing the narrative of her frailty—and the latter chose not to impart her love for the young Count of Riverola. Nevertheless, the Countess gave her companion to understand that she had friends without, who were acquainted with the fact of her removal to the Carmelite Convent, and on whose fidelity as well as resolute valour she could reckon;—for the promise made her by the robber-captain, and the idea that the Marquis of Orsini would not leave her to the dreadful fate of eternal seclusion in that place, flashed to her mind when the first access of despair had passed.

Flora was delighted to hear that such a hope animated the Countess of Arestino; and throwing herself at her feet, she said, "Oh! lady, shouldst thou have the power to save me——"

"Thinkest thou that I would leave thee here, in this horrible dungeon?" interrupted the Countess, raising Flora from her suppliant position on the cold pavement of the cell, and embracing her. "No: if those on whom I rely fulfil the hope that we have entertained, we shall go forth together. And, oh!" added the Countess, "were all Florence to rise up against this accursed institution—pillage it—sack it—and raze it to the ground, so that not one stone shall remain upon another, heaven could not frown upon the deed! For surely demons in mortal shape must have invented that terrible engine by means of which I was consigned to this subterranean!"

The recollection of the anguish she had suffered during the descent,—a mental agony that Flora could herself fully appreciate, she having passed through the same infernal ordeal,—produced a cold shudder which oscillated throughout Giulia's entire form.

But we shall not dwell upon this portion of our tale; for the reader is about to pass to scenes of so thrilling a nature, that all he has yet read in the preceding chapters are as nothing to the events which will occupy those that are to follow.

We said, then, at the opening of this chapter, that six days had elapsed since Flora became an inmate of the

Convent,—and four since circumstances had given her a companion in the person of Giulia of Arestino.

It was on the sixth night, and the two inmates of the gloomy cell were preparing to retire to their humble pallet, after offering up their prayers to the Virgin,—for adversity had already taught the Countess to pray, and to pray devoutly too,—when they were startled and alarmed by the sudden clang of a large bell fixed in some part of the subterranean.

The echoes which it raised, and the monotonous vibration of the air which it produced, struck terror to their souls.

A minute elapsed—and again the bell struck.

Flora and the Countess exchanged glances of terror and mysterious doubt—so ominous was that sound !

Again a minute passed—and a third time clanged that heavy iron tongue.

Then commenced a funeral hymn, chanted by several female voices, and emanating as yet from a distance,—sounding, too, as if the mournful melody were made within the very bowels of the earth.

But by degrees the strain became louder, as those who sang approached nearer ; and in a short time the sounds of many light steps on the stone pavement of the Chamber of Penitence, were heard by Giulia and her companion in their cell.

Again did they exchange terrified glances, as if demanding of each other what this strange interruption of night's silence could mean. But at that instant the hymn ceased—and again the loud bell clanged, as if in some far-off gallery hollowed out of the earth.

Oh ! in that convent where all was mysterious, and where a terrific despotism obeyed the dictates of its own wild will, such sounds as that funeral chant and that deafening bell were but too fully calculated to inspire the souls of the innocent Flora and the guilty Giulia with the wildest apprehensions !

Suddenly the door opened ; and Sister Alba, who presided over the Chamber of Penitence, appeared on the threshold.

"Come forth, daughters !" she exclaimed: "and behold the punishment due to female frailty."

The Countess of Arestino and Flora Francatelli mechanically obeyed this command ; and a strange—a heartrending sight met their eyes.

The Chamber of Penitence was filled with nuns in their convent-garbs, and the Penitents in a state of semi-nudity. On one side of the apartment, a huge door with massive bolts and chains stood open, allowing a glimpse, by the glare of the lamps, tapers, and torches, of the interior of a small cell that looked like a sepulchre. Near the entrance to that tomb—for such indeed it was —stood the Lady Abbess ; and on the pavement near her knelt a young and beautiful girl, with hands clasped and countenance raised in an agony of soul which no human pen can describe.

The garments of this hapless being had been torn away from her neck and shoulders, doubtless by the force used to drag her thither ;—and her suppliant attitude—the despair that was depicted by her appearance—her extreme loveliness—and the wild glaring of her deep blue eyes, gave her the appearance of something unearthly in the glare of that vacillating light.

"No, daughter," said the Abbess, in a cold, stern voice : "there is no mercy for you on earth !"

Then echoed through the Chamber of Penitence a scream—a shriek so wild—so long—so full of agony—that it penetrated to the hearts of Flora, the Countess, and some of the Penitents—although the Abbess and her nuns seemed unmoved by that appalling evidence of female anguish.

At the same instant the bell struck again ; and the funeral hymn was re-commenced by the junior recluses.

Sister Alba now approached Flora and the Countess, and said in a low whisper, "The vengeance of the conventual discipline is terrible on those who sin ! That miserable girl completed that noviciate five months ago ; and the night before she was to take the veil, she escaped. This awful crime she committed for the sake of some man whom she had known ere she first entered the convent, and for whom she thus endangered her immortal soul. But her justly incensed relations yesterday discovered her retreat ; and she was restored to this house of penitence and peace. Alas ! the effects of her frailty were but too apparent ; and that benighted girl would become a mother—*had she long enough to live !*"

These last words were uttered with terrible significancy ; and the nun turned aside, leaving Flora and the Countess each a prey to the most unspeakable horror.

In the meantime the helpless victim of ecclesiastical vengeance, the poor erring creature, who had dared and sacrificed everything for the love of her seducer,—had risen from her suppliant posture, and flown wildly—madly round to the elderly nuns in succession,—imploring mercy, and rending the very roof of the subterranean with her piercing screams. But those to whom she appealed, turned a deaf ear ; for a convent is a tomb in which all human sympathies are immured—a vortex wherein all the best feelings that concrete in the mortal heart are cruelly engulfed !

And while that wretched girl—for she was scarcely yet a woman, although, were life spared her, on the way to maternity—was thus fruitlessly imploring the mercy of hearts that were stern and remorseless, the hymn continued, and the bell tolled at short intervals.

Suddenly, at a particular verse in the funeral chant, the *three nuns*, who usually did the bidding of the Lady Abbess, glided noiselessly—but surely, like black serpents —towards the victim—seized her in their powerful grasp —and bore her to the cell in which she was to be immured —and the bell now clanged quickly with its almost deafening note ;—and those human and metallic sounds combined to deaden the screams that burst from the miserable girl, on whom the huge door at length closed with fearful din.

The massive bolts were drawn—the key turned harshly in the lock—and still the shrieks came from within the sepulchre where a human being was *entombed alive!*

So sickening a sensation came over Flora and the Countess, when the last act of the awful tragedy was thus concluded, that they reeled back to their cell with brains so confused, and such horrible visions floating before their eyes, that their very senses appeared to be abandoning them.

When they were enabled to collect their scattered ideas, and the incidents of the last half-hour assumed a defined shape in their memories, the sounds of hymn and bell had ceased—the Chamber of Penitence was deserted—the silence of death reigned throughout the subterranean— nor did even the faintest shriek or scream emanate from the cell in which the victim was entombed.

CHAPTER XXXI.
THE BANDITTI.

THE night of which we are speaking was destined to be one pregnant with alarms for the Countess of Arestino and Signora Francatelli.

Scarcely had they recovered from the effects of the appalling tragedy which had just been enacted: when their attention was drawn to a strange noise on one side of the cell.

They listened, and the noise continued—resembling an attempt to remove the massive masonry of that part of the stone chamber.

"Merciful heavens !" said Flora in a subdued whisper ; "what new terror can now be in store for us ?"

But scarcely were those words uttered, when a considerable portion of the masonry fell in with a loud crash ; and had not the Countess and Flora already withdrawn to the vicinity of the door, when the mysterious sound first began, they would either have been killed or seriously hurt by the falling of the huge stones.

A faint scream burst from Flora's lips ; and she would have rushed from the cell, had not an ejaculation of joy escaped the Countess.

For at the aperture formed by the falling in of the masonry, and by the glare of the light that shone on the other side, as well as by the dim taper that burnt before the crucifix in the cell, Giulia had in an instant recognised the countenance of the Marquis of Orsini.

"Manuel—dearest Manuel !" she exclaimed, rushing towards the aperture ; "art thou come to save me ?"

"Yes, Giulia," responded the Marquis. "But by what good fortune art thou the very first whom it is my destiny to encounter ? and who is thy companion ?"

"A good—a generous-hearted girl, whom you must save also from this dreadful place," answered the Countess. "And as for this accidental, but most fortunate encounter, I can tell you no more than that this is our cell. It is rather for me to ask——"

"We have no time to waste in idle talk, my lord," said Stephano, who now appeared at the aperture. "Pardon my roughness, noble lady, but every moment is precious. Is there any danger of an alarm being given ?"

"None, that I am aware of," returned the Countess. "The place where we now are must be a hundred yards below the surface of the earth——"

"No, my lady—that is impossible!" interrupted Stephano; "a hundred feet at the most—and even that is above the mark. But stand back, my lady, while we remove some more of this solid masonry."

Giulia obeyed the robber-chief, and turned to embrace Flora with the liveliest manifestations of joy, which the young maiden sincerely shared—for escape now indeed appeared to be at hand.

The aperture was rapidly enlarged by those who worked on the other side, and in a few minutes it was spacious enough to admit the passage of a human form. Then Giulia and Flora quitted their dismal cell, and entered the innermost chamber of the robbers' hold, but from which the treasures described in a previous chapter had all been removed away.

Giulia embraced the Marquis with grateful affection; but Stephano exclaimed, "Come, my lord! Remember your oath, and join us in this expedition to the end!"

At that moment the awful tragedy of the night flashed back to Flora's memory, from which nothing could have dispelled it even for an instant, save the thrilling excitement attendant on escape from the convent; and, in a few hurried words, she told the dreadful tale.

But what was the astonishment of all present when Piero, one of the banditti, exclaimed, in a tone of mingled rage and grief, "'Tis Carlotta! the victim can be none other—the dates you have mentioned, signora, convince me! Yes, five months ago she fled from that accursed convent—and yesterday she disappeared. Ah! my poor Carlotta!"

And the rude but handsome brigand wept.

Flora forgetting the danger of re-entering the walls of the terrible institution exclaimed, "Follow me: it may not be too late—I will show you the cell——"

And she once more passed through the aperture, closely followed by Stephano, Piero, Lomellino, and a dozen other banditti. The Marquis of Orsini stayed behind for a few instants to breathe a re-assuring word to Giulia, whom he left in the treasure-chamber (as that apartment of the robbers' hold was called), and then hastened after those who had penetrated into the subterranean of the Convent.

The party entered the Chamber of Penitence, where the long wax-candles were still burning before the altar; and Flora having hastily given Stephano as much information as she could relative to the geography of the place, that chieftain placed sentinels around. Flora had already pointed out the door of the dungeon to which Carlotta had been consigned; and Piero hastened to call upon his mistress to answer him.

It was a touching spectacle to behold that lawless and bold bad man melting into tenderness beneath the influence of Love!

But no reply came from within that dungeon; and though the bolts were easily drawn back, yet the lock was strong, and the key was not there!

By this time, the Penitents, who slept in the various cells adjoining the Chamber, had become alarmed by the heavy tread and the voices of men, and had opened their doors. But they were desired to keep back by the sentinels, whom Stephano had posted around to maintain order and prevent a premature alarm, but who, nevertheless, gave assurances of speedy escape for those who might choose to profit by the opportunity.

Suddenly a door, which Flora had never noticed before in the Chamber of Penitence, opened, and two recluses, appeared on the threshold.

"The Abbess!" ejaculated Flora, yielding to a sudden impulse of alarm.

But almost at the same instant Stephano sprang forward, caught the Abbess by the arm, and dragged her into the Chamber; then, rushing up a flight of narrow stone steps, with which that door communicated, and which the other recluse had already turned to ascend, he brought her forcibly back also.

This latter nun was Sister Alba, the presiding authority of the Chamber of Penitents.

Her astonishment, as well as that of the Lady Abbess, at the spectacle of a number of armed men in the most private part of the entire establishment, may well be conceived: nor was this disagreeable surprise unmixed with intense alarm.

But they had little time for reflection.

"The key of that door!" cried Stephano, in a fierce and menacing tone, as he pointed towards Carlotta's dungeon.

The Abbess mechanically drew forth the key from beneath her convent-habit; and Piero, rushing forward, snatched it eagerly.

In a few minutes it turned in the lock:—the next moment the door stood open.

But what a spectacle met the view of Piero, Flora, and those who were near enough to glance within!

Stretched upon the stone floor of the narrow cell lay the victim motionless and still! Drops of gore hung to her lips: in the agony of her grief she had burst a blood-vessel—and death must have been almost instantaneous.

Flora staggered back sick at the frightful sight: and she would have fallen to the ground, had not the Marquis of Orsini suddenly sprang forward to sustain her.

"This is no place for you, young lady," he said. "Permit me to conduct you back to the companionship of the Countess of Arestino."

Flora leant upon his arm; and he half carried rather than led her away from the Chamber of Penitence into the robbers' hold.

But as they passed through the aperture formed by the removal of the masonry, a terrible menace met their ears.

"Vengeance!" cried Piero, furiously; "vengeance on the murderess of Carlotta!"

"Yes—vengeance shalt thou have, comrade," returned the deep, sonorous voice of Stephano,

But scarcely were those words uttered, when the loud clanging of the bell struck up; and the Abbess exclaimed joyfully, "We are saved! we are saved!"

CHAPTER XXXII.

THE MYSTERY OF THE CHAIR.—THE CATASTROPHE.

THE reader will recollect that when Flora Francatelli was released from the chair at the bottom of the pit or well, Sister Alba had led her along a narrow dark passage communicating with the Chamber of Penitence.

In a small dome-like cavity, hollowed out of the roof of the passage, hung a large bell; and in a cell opening from the side of the passage immediately beneath this dome, dwelt an old nun, who, for some dreadful misdeed committed in her youth, had voluntarily consigned herself to the Convent of Carmelites, and, having passed through the ordeal of the Chamber of Penitence, had accepted the office of sextoness in that department of the establishment.

It was her duty to keep the Chamber of Penitence clean, maintain tapers constantly burning before the altar, supply also the cells of the Penitents themselves with lights, and toll the bell whenever occasion required. She it was who had visited Flora's cell the first night of her arrival at the Convent, to renew the taper that burnt before her crucifix, and to exchange the maiden's attire for the conventual garb.

This old nun it was, then, who suddenly tolled the bell, at the moment when Piero and Stephano were menacing the Abbess and Sister Alba with their vengeance, and when the Marquis of Orsini was bearing away Flora to the robbers' hold, that she might have the companionship of Giulia.

The way in which the old nun rang the bell was such that the inmates of the Convent would perceive it to be an alarm; and, moreover so startling was its sudden clang, that Stephano and Piero abandoned their hold on the Abbess and Sister Alba, and retreated a few paces, uncertain how to act:—hence the joyous exclamation of the Superior of the Convent:—"We are saved! we are saved!"

But little did that stern, imperious woman know of the desperate characters of those with whom she had now to deal. Ashamed of their momentary hesitation, Stephano and Piero rushed on the Abbess and Sister Alba, and dragged them—in spite of their deafening screams—into the fatal cell, where they threw them headlong over the lifeless corse of their victim.

Scarcely, however, had they closed the door on the wretched women, when the Marquis of Orsini returned; and, too well divining what had passed, he exclaimed, "In the name of heaven, Captain!—by all that is holy, Piero! I implore you not to consummate this dreadful crime!"

"My lord," said Stephano, "ere we entered on this expedition to-night, you bound yourself by an oath to obey me as the leader. I command you, then, not to interfere with our proceedings; but, on the contrary, go and ascertain whence comes the clanging of that infernal bell!"

The Marquis turned aside—sick at heart at the deed of vengeance which was in progress, but unable to remonstrate farther, in consequence of the oath which he had taken. It was, however, a relief for him to move away from the vicinity of the *living tomb*, whence emanated the shrieks of the Abbess and the nun; and, guided by the sound of the bell, he rushed—with whirling brain and desperate resolution—into the passage leading from the Chamber of Penitence.

In a few moments the clanging of the bell ceased—for the Marquis had discovered the old sextoness in her cell, and compelled her to desist.

All the events yet recorded in the preceding and the present chapter had occurred with a rapidity which the reader can scarcely comprehend, because their complicated nature and variety have forced us to enter into minute details requiring a considerable time to peruse. Those events which we are now about to describe, also succeeded each other with marvellous speed, and occupied an incredibly short space of time, although our narrative must necessarily appear prolix in comparison.

Extraordinary was the excitement that now prevailed in all the subterranean departments of the Convent. The victims of a stern but just vengeance were sending forth appalling screams from the fatal dungeon: and some of the Penitents in their cells, which were still guarded by the sentinels, were also giving vent to their affright by means of piercing shrieks, though others remained tranquil in hope of the promised release.

Stephano had entirely recovered his presence of mind, and now issued his orders with wondrous rapidity.

Pointing to the door by which the Abbess and Sister Alba had entered the Chamber of Penitence, he said, "Lomellino, this is the way to the upper part of the Convent—there can be no doubt of it! Take Piero and half-a-dozen of the men—and hasten up that staircase. Secure the front gate of the building, and possess yourself of the plate and treasure. But no violence remember—no violence to the nuns!"

Lomellino, Piero, and six of the banditti hastened to obey these commands, while Stephano remained below, to act as circumstances might require. He went the round of the five cells belonging to the Penitents, and enjoined those who were yielding to their terrors to hold their peace, as they had nothing to fear, but much to gain—at least, he observed, if they valued their freedom; and to those who were tranquil, he repeated the assurances of speedy liberation already given by his men.

In the meantime the Marquis of Orsini had, as we before said, discovered the sextoness in her cell, and had recommended her to cease ringing the alarum.

For thirty years the old woman had not seen a being of the male sex; and she was terrified by the appearance of an armed man in that place which she had so long deemed sacred against the possibility of such intrusion.

"Fear nothing," said the Marquis: "no one will harm you. But what will be the effect of that alarum which you have rung?"

"Merely to warn those above that something unusual is taking place below," answered the old woman.

"And by what means can access be obtained to this subterranean?" demanded Manuel.

"There is a staircase leading from the Chamber of Penitence up into the hall of the Convent——"

"Of the existence of that staircase I am aware," interrupted the Marquis, who had seen the Abbess and Sister Alba enter the Chamber of Penitence a few minutes previously, as stated in the preceding chapter; "but are there no other means of ingress or egress?"

"Yes: follow me," said the sextoness, overawed by the authoritative manner in which she was questioned.

Taking up a lamp from the table in her cell, she led the way to the farther end of the passage, threw open a door, and thrusting forth the light beyond the opening, exclaimed in a tone denoting a reminiscence the bitterness of which long years had scarcely mitigated,—"That is the road whereby I came hither; and many—many others have travelled the same downward path."

The Marquis seized the lamp, and beheld, a few paces from him, a wicker chair, to which two ropes, hanging perpendicularly down, were fastened. He raised his eyes, following the direction of the ropes; but as there was now no other light in the pit than the feeble flickering one shed by the lamp which he held, his glances could not penetrate the dense obscurity that prevailed above.

"What means this chair with its two ropes? and for what purpose is this narrow square compartment, the mouth of which is shrouded in darkness?" inquired Manuel.

"That is the method of descent to this region, for all those who come to the Convent either as willing Penitents, or who are sent hither against their inclina-

tion," returned the sextoness. "And though I came a willing Penitent, yet never—never while the breath shall animate this poor weak form, and reason shall remain, can I forget the mental agony—the intense anguish of that fearful descent. Ah! it is a cruel engine of torture, although it tears not the flesh, nor racks the limbs, nor dislocates the joints. And even though thirty long years have passed since I made that dread journey," she continued, glancing upwards,—"thirty years since I last saw the light of day—and though I have since learned and seen how much of the horror of that descent is produced by the delusion of mechanical ingenuity,—yet still I shudder, and my blood runs cold within me."

"To me, old woman," said the Marquis, "your words are an enigma. But you have excited my curiosity: speak quickly, and explain yourself—for I may not linger here."

"Behold this basket," returned the nun, without further preface:—"these ropes connect it with complicated machinery in some chamber adjoining the well itself. In that basket those who are doomed to pass the ordeal of penitence are lowered from an apartment above. This apartment is really but a short distance overhead; but the art of the mechanist has so contrived the four wooden walls of the well, that when the descent of the basket ceases, those walls rise slowly upwards—and thus the descent appears to be continued. Then, when the affrighted female stretches forth her hands wildly, she encounters the ascending walls—and she believes that she is still going down—down—down! Oh! signor—it is most horrible—but a fitting prelude to the terrors of that place!"

And she pointed back, towards the chamber of Penitence.

The Marquis was about to make some observation in reply to the strange disclosures of the old sextoness, when suddenly the din of a tumult, occurring, as it seemed, in that department of the Convent far overhead, reached his ears,—commencing with the rushing of many feet—the ejaculations of hostile bands—and then continuing with the clash of arms—and the shrieks of affrighted women—until, in a few moments, those ominous sounds were broken in upon and dominated by the wild—terrific cry of "Fire, fire!"

"Oh! wherefore have I tarried here so long?" exclaimed the Marquis; and he was about to return to the Chamber of Penitence, when a sudden blaze of light appeared at the mouth of the pit, thirty yards above.

Looking hastily up, he beheld the flames rolling over the entrance of that well at the bottom of which he stood—and, in another minute the forked fire burst from the sides—forcing for itself a way through the wooden walls:—and the old dry timber and planks yielded to the devouring element as if they had been steeped in oil.

But while the Marquis was still standing at the bottom, looking up the pit, the clash of weapons, the tread of many steps, and the vociferations of combatants appeared to grow nearer; and in another moment he became aware that the hostile sounds came down the well, and proceeded from the room far above, where the fire as well as the war was raging.

Manuel had again turned round to hurry back to the Chamber of Penitence, when a loud cry of despair came vibrating down, and in another instant the heavy form of a man was precipitated into the well.

The wicker chair fortunately broke his fall, and he rose with a dreadful imprecation.

"Piero!" cried the Marquis.

"Ah! my lord—is it you?" said the bandit, faintly, as he staggered back and fell heavily on the floor. "This is a bad business—the sbirri were alarmed, and broke in—Lomellino has got away—but the rest who were with me are slain——"

"And you are wounded, Piero," ejaculated the Marquis, rushing forward to assist the bandit, from whose breast he now perceived the blood to be flowing.

"Never mind me, my lord!" said Piero faintly, "Haste and tell Verrina that—our men fought well—it was not their fault—nor mine—the nuns must have given the —alarm——"

His voice had grown fainter and fainter as he spoke; and, while the Marquis was endeavouring to raise him, he fell back again and expired, with the name of Carlotta upon his tongue.

The combat had ceased above—but the flames had increased in the well to such an extent that the Marquis was compelled to beat a rapid retreat towards the Chamber of Penitence, whither the old sextoness had already fled.

At the entrance of that apartment he met Stephano, who, alarmed by the clashing of arms and the cries of "Fire" that had reached his ears, and which seemed to come from the direction of the passage, was hurrying thither to learn the cause.

In a few words the Marquis informed him of all that had occurred.

"Back to the cavern, my friends!" cried Stephano, in a loud tone: "if the sbirri discover us there, we will resist them to the death!"

And, followed by the Marquis and two or three of his men, the Captain passed through the aperture made from the cell recently occupied by Flora and the Countess, into the treasure-chamber.

But scarcely had those few individuals effected their retreat in this manner, when a tremendous crash was heard—cries and shrieks of horror and dismay burst from those who had not as yet passed through the opening—and then the roof of the Chamber of Penitence and all the adjacent cells gave way with a din as of a thousand cannon,—burying beneath their weight the sextoness, the five Penitents, the inmates of Carlotta's cell, and seven of the banditti.

Those who were in the treasure-chamber felt the ground shake beneath their feet: the sides—although hollowed from the solid rock—appeared to vibrate and groan:—and the aperture leading into the subterranean of the Convent was closed up by the massive masonry that had fallen in.

Flora and Giulia threw themselves into each other's arms, weeping bitterly; for they saw how dearly their freedom had been purchased; and they trembled for the result.

But the Marquis of Orsini, although greatly shocked at the terrible sacrifice of human life which had occurred, exerted himself to console and re-assure the two terrified ladies.*

CHAPTER XXXIII.

LOMELLINO'S ESCAPE—STEPHANO'S INTENTIONS.

STEPHANO VERRINA was not the man to allow his energies to be paralysed by the reverse he had just sustained. He immediately commanded a general muster of his men to be held in the banqueting-hall, that he might accurately ascertain the loss his corps had sustained.

Giulia and Flora were left in the treasure-chamber to snatch a few hours' repose, if they could—as it was now much past two o'clock in the morning; and the Marquis accompanied Stephano to the banqueting hall.

Scarcely were the men mustered, when the usual signals announcing the approach of a member of the band were heard; and in a few moments Lomellino appeared amongst the troop.

All crowded round him to hear the account which he had to give of his expedition and its failure.

His tale was soon told. It seemed that on reaching what might properly be termed the main building of the Convent, he found the greatest alarm and confusion prevailing amongst the nuns,—the shrieks of the Abbess, Sister Alba, and the Penitents, and the alarm of the bell having reached the ears of the recluses. Their consternation was increased almost to madness when they suddenly perceived several armed men emerging from the private staircase leading to the subterranean department; and Lomellino found it impossible to tran-

---

* "It was in the early part of February, 1521, that Florence, or, indeed, all Italy, was astounded by the intelligence that a band of robbers, commanded by a noted chief of desperate character, had penetrated into the convent of Carmelites by some subterranean passage known, most probably, only to themselves, and had committed the most unheard-of atrocities. The ducal bodyguard, however, received timely information of this most sacrilegious invasion into so respectable a sanctuary, and entering the building, encountered the depredators hand to hand. But in the midst of the combat, the Convent was found to be in flames; and so rapidly did the fire rage that in short time the roof fell in, and many nuns, sbirri, and banditti perished. When the ruins were subsequently visited, some strange machinery was discovered, whereof the uses can only be conjectured. Also in a subterranean cell were found the skeletons of a female and a child; and in two other cells, likewise under ground, were found massive chains fastened to rings in the wall."—*Guicciardini*, Vol. II.

quillize them either by threats or fair speaking. A guard of sbirri must have been passing at the time: for loud knocks resounded at the gate, which the old porteress immediately opened before Lomellino or any of his men could interfere to prevent her. A number of police officers rushed in: and then commenced a terrific combat between the banditti and the sbirri, the former of whom were forced into an apartment the door of which was originally locked, but was burst open in the deadly struggle. There the strife was continued; when suddenly the cry of "Fire" arose: and the flames, which had caught a bed in the apartment, spread rapidly to the cumbrous and time-worn wood-work that supported the ceiling. How the fire originated, Lomellino knew not; but as some of the nuns carried lamps in their hands, and rushed wildly about in all directions in their terror, it was not very difficult to hazard a conjecture as to the cause of the conflagration. From that apartment, where the fire began, the flames drove the combatants into an inner room; and then Lomellino saw his comrade Piero hurled down some steep place, he himself being too sorely pressed by his assailants to be able to repair to his assistance. At length, seeing that all his companions were slain, Lomellino had fought his way desperately through the police officers, and had succeeded in escaping from the Convent, though closely pursued by three of the sbirri. They were rapidly gaining upon him, when an awful crash suddenly met their ears, as they were hurrying along the street leading to the wood: and, looking back, Lomellino beheld a tremendous pillar of flame shoot up from the place where the Convent had stood, to the very sky—rendering, for the space of a minute, everything as light as day around. The building had fallen in—and heaven only knows how many of the nuns and sbirri had escaped, or how many had perished beneath the ruins! Those officers who were in pursuit of Lomellino, were so astounded by the sudden din and the column of flame, that they remained rooted to the spot where they had turned to gaze on the evidence of the catastrophe: and Lomellino had succeeded in effecting a safe and unobserved return to the stronghold.

This account was particularly welcome to the robbers, inasmuch as it convinced them that the sbirri had no clue to the secret entrance of their stronghold, and that none of their band had been captured in the conflict;—for they would rather hear of the death of their comrades than that they had been taken prisoners; because, were the latter the case, the tortures of the rack or the exhortations of the priest might elicit confessions hostile to the interests of the corps.

Stephano Verrina now proceeded to count his men, who had mustered fifty strong previously to the expedition of that fatal night, which, it was ascertained, had reduced the number to thirty-six,—seven, including Piero, having been slain by the sbirri, and as many having perished by the falling in of the Chamber of Penitence.

The Captain then addressed the troop in the following manner:—

"Worthy comrades,—Our number is sadly reduced; but regrets will not bring back those gallant fellows who are gone. It, therefore, behoves us to attend to our own interest; and, for that purpose I demand your attention for a few minutes. In pursuance of the resolution to which we came the night before last, at the general council that was held, the treasures and possessions amassed during many years of adventure and perils have been fairly divided, and each man's portion has been settled by lot. The fourteen shares that revert to us by the death of our comrades shall be equally subdivided to-morrow; and the superintendance of that duty, my friends, will be the last act of my chieftainship. Yes, brave comrades,—I shall then leave you, in accordance with the announcement I made the night before last. It will grieve me to part from you; but you will choose another Captain——"

"Lomellino! Lomellino!" exclaimed the banditti with one accord; "he shall succeed our gallant Verrina!"

"And you could not have made a better choice," continued Stephano. "Lomellino will——"

"Pardon me, Captain," interrupted the individual thus alluded to; "but is not that little expedition to take place on Monday—in case the lady requires it? We have received her gold as an earnest——"

"And double that amount was promised if the affair should turn out successful," added Stephano. "But I have reasons of my own—which *you* may perhaps understand, Lomellino—for desiring that all idea of that business should be abandoned. And, in order that the band may not be losers by this change of intentions, I will give you from my own share of our long accumulated property——"

"No! no!" cried the banditti enthusiastically; "we will not receive our gallant Stephano's gold! Let him act according to his own wishes!"

"I thank you, my friends, for this generosity on your part," said Stephano.

The meeting then broke up; and the robbers sat down to the banqueting-table, to luxuriate in the rich wines with which the stronghold was well stored.

"And therefore I mean to turn honest man," observed Verrina, also laughing. "In truth, I am not sorry to have found a good excuse to quit a mode of life which the headsman yearns to cut short. Not that I reck for peril; but, methinks, twenty years of danger and adventure ought to be succeeded by a season of tranquillity."

"Love has a marvellous influence over you, Signor Verrina," said the Marquis; "for love alone could have inspired such sentiments in your breast."

"I am fain to confess that your lordship is not far wrong," returned the bandit. "I have discovered a

"THE FIGHT LASTED FOR ABOUT TEN MINUTES." (See p. 45.)

The Marquis of Orsini was compelled, through fear of giving offence, to share in the festival.

"This resolution to abandon the command of your gallant band, is somewhat sudden, meseems, Signor Stephano," he said: for, not having been present at the council held two nights previously, he was unaware of the Captain's intention until it was alluded to in that individual's speech on the present occasion.

"Yes, my lord," was the reply: "the resolution *is* sudden. But," he added, sinking his voice to a whisper, "a certain little blind god is at the bottom of it."

"Ah! signor, you are in love!" said the Marquis, laughing.

woman who is worthy of me—although she may not consider me to be altogether deserving of her. But of that no matter; for I am not accustomed to consult the inclinations of others when mine own are concerned. And now a word in respect to yourself, my lord. When do you propose to quit this place; for, according to my promise, you are now the master of your actions."

"The mysterious assault made upon the Convent—the destruction of the entire establishment—and the lives that have been lost, will doubtless create a terrible sensation in Florence," replied the nobleman; "and should it transpire that I was in any way implicated——"

"That is impossible, my lord," interrupted Stephano.

"These men whom you behold around you, could alone betray that secret; and you must have seen enough of them——"

"To know that they are stanch and true," added the Marquis. "Yes—on reflection, I perceive that I have nothing to fear; and therefore, with your leave, the Countess, her young companion, and myself will take our departure to-morrow."

"In the evening—when it is dusk," said Stephano. "But your lordship will not remain in Florence?"

"The news which you brought me, a few days ago, of the arrest of that poor Israelite on a ridiculous but most monstrous charge, have affected me strangely," observed Manuel; "and as it is in my power to explain away that charge, I must tarry in Florence the necessary time to accomplish this object. The Count of Arestino will imagine that his wife has perished in the ruins of the Convent; and hence her temporary concealment in the city will be easily effected."

"Well, my lord," said Stephano, "it is not for me to dictate nor advise. But, as I always entertain an esteem for a man with whom I have measured weapons—and as I have somehow formed a liking for your lordship—pardon my boldness—I should recommend you not to remain in Florence on account of the Jew. The Lady Giulia might be discovered by her husband, and you would lose her again. To tell your lordship the truth," he added in a low confidential tone, "a friend of mine, who commands a trading vessel, sails in a few days from Leghorn for the Levant; and I intend to be a passenger on board, in company, I hope, with the sweet lady whom I have honoured with my affections. What says your lordship? will it suit your lordship to embark in that vessel?"

"A thousand thanks, Signor Verrina," replied the Marquis; "but I must remain at Florence to prove the innocence of that poor, persecuted Jew."

Stephano offered no further remonstrance: and the conversation which ensued possessed not the least interest for our readers.

On the following evening the Marquis, Giulia, and Flora quitted the robbers' stronghold—all three carefully blindfolded, and safely conducted amidst the dangers of the egress by Stephano, Lomellino, and another bandit.

When in the grove with which the entrance of the stronghold communicated, the bandages were removed from their eyes, and the two ladies, as well as the Marquis, were once more enabled to rejoice in their freedom.

According to a previous arrangement between them, and in consequence of the intention of the Marquis to remain a few days in Florence, Giulia accompanied Flora to the dwelling of the young maiden's aunt, who was rejoiced to behold the re-appearance of her niece, and who willingly accorded an asylum to the Countess.

The Marquis having conducted the two ladies to the hospitable cottage of this good woman, returned to his own dwelling, his protracted absence from which had caused serious apprehensions amongst the few domestics whom his means permitted him to maintain.

Ere we conclude this chapter, we shall observe in a few words that the greatest excitement prevailed in Florence relative to the attack on the Convent and its destruction. Many of the nuns had escaped from the building at the commencement of the fire: and these took up their abode in another institution of the same Order. But the thrilling events which occurred in the Chamber of Penitence did not transpire; nor was it ascertained who were the sacrilegious invaders of the establishment, nor by what means they had obtained an entry.

CHAPTER XXXIV.

THE ABDUCTION.

It was originally Stephano Verrina's intention to observe good faith with Nisida in respect to the service on which she had intimated her desire to employ him and his band.

But so dazzled was he by her almost supernatural majesty of beauty on that night when he and his companions encountered her in the Riverola palace, that he would have promised, or indeed undertaken, anything calculated to please or benefit her.

When, however, he came to reflect calmly upon the service in which Nisida had enlisted him, he began to suspect that some motive more powerful than the mere desire to effect the liberation of an innocent man, in-

fluenced that lady. Had she not put to death a beautiful creature who had resided in the same dwelling with Fernand Wagner? and did not that deed bear upon its aspect the stamp of an Italian woman's vengeance? Thus thought Stephano; and he soon arrived at the very natural conclusion that Nisida loved Fernand Wagner.

Wagner was therefore his rival; and Verrina did not consider it at all in accordance with his own particular views in respect to Nisida, to aid in effecting that rival's liberation, should he be condemned by the tribunal.

Again Stephano reflected that as Wagner's acquittal was within the range of probability, it would be expedient to possess himself of Nisida *before* the trial took place;—and what opportunity could be more favourable than the one which that lady herself afforded by the appointment she had given him for the Sunday evening at the gate of St. Mary's Cathedral?

All these considerations had determined the bandit to adopt speedy and strenuous measures to possess himself of Nisida, of whom he was so madly enamoured that the hope of gratifying his passion predominated even over the pride and delight he had hitherto experienced in commanding the Florentine robbers.

The appointed evening came; and Stephano, disguised in his black mask, repaired a few minutes before ten to the immediate vicinity of the old Cathedral.

At the corner of an adjacent street, two men, mounted on powerful horses, and holding a third steed by the bridle, were in readiness; and crouched in the black darkness formed by the shade of a huge buttress of the Cathedral, two other members of the troop which Lomellino now commanded, lay concealed;—for the new Captain of the Banditti had lent some of his stanchest followers to further the designs of the ex-chieftain.

A heavy rain had fallen in the early part of the day: but it ceased ere the sun went down; and the stars shone forth like Beauty's eyes when the tears of grief have been wiped away by the lips of the lover.

Stephano paced the arena in front of the sacred edifice; and at length a gentle tread and a rustling of velvet met his ears.

Then, in a few moments, as if emerging from the darkness, the majestic form of Nisida appeared: and when Stephano approached her, she drew aside her veil for an instant—only for a single instant, that he might convince himself of her identity with the lady for whom he was waiting.

But as the light of the silver stars beamed for a moment on the countenance of Nisida, that mild and placid lustre was outvied by the dazzling brilliancy of her large black eyes; and mental excitement had imparted a rich carnation hue to her cheeks, rendering her so surpassingly beautiful, that Stephano could almost have fallen on his knees to worship and adore her!

But, oh! what lovely skins do some snakes wear!—and into what charming shapes does Satan often get!

Nisida had replaced her veil while yet Verrina's eyes were fixed on her bewitching countenance: then, placing her finger lightly upon his arm—oh! how that gentle touch thrilled through him!—she made a sign for him to follow her towards a niche in the deep gateway of the Cathedral; for in that niche was an image of the Madonna, and before it burnt a lamp night and day.

To gain that spot it was necessary to pass the buttress in whose shade the two banditti lay concealed.

Stephano trembled, as he followed that lady, whom he knew to be as intrepid—bold—and desperate as she was beautiful:—he trembled—perhaps for the first time in his life,—because never until now had he felt himself overawed by the majesty of loveliness and the resolute mind of a woman.

But he had gone too far to retreat—even if that temporary and almost unaccountable timidity had prompted him to abandon his present design:—yes—he had gone too far—for at the moment when Nisida was passing the huge buttress, the two brigands sprang forth; and, though her hand instantly grasped her dagger, yet so suddenly and effectually was she overpowered, that she had not even time to draw it from its sheath.

Fortunately for the scheme of Stephano, the great square in front of the Cathedral was at that moment completely deserted by the usual evening loungers; and thus did he and his companions experience not the slightest interruption as they bore Nisida firmly and rapidly along to the corner of the street where the horses were in attendance.

The lady's hands were already bound—and her dagger had been taken from her; and thus the resistance she was enabled to make was very slight, when Stephano, having sprung upon one of the horses, received the charming burden from the banditti, and embraced that fine voluptuous form in his powerful arms.

The two men who had waited with Stephano's horse were already mounted on their own, as before stated; and the little party was now in readiness to start.

"No farther commands, signor?" said one of the banditti who had first seized upon Nisida.

"None, my brave fellow. Tell Lomellino that I sent him my best wishes for his prosperity. And now for a rapid journey to Leghorn!"

"Good night, signor."

"Good night. Farewell—farewell, my friends!" cried Verrina: and, clapping spurs to his steed, he struck into a quick gallop, his two mounted companions keeping pace with him, and riding one on either side, so as to prevent any possibility of escape on the part of Donna Nisida of Riverola.

In a few minutes the little party gained the bank of the Arno, along which they pursued their rapid way, lighted by the lovely moon, which now broke forth from the purple sky, and seemed, with its chaste beams playing on the surface of the water, to put a soul into the very river as it ran!

———

CHAPTER XXXV.

WAGNER AND THE TEMPTER—PHANTASMAGORIA.

WHILE Stephano was bearing away the Lady Nisida in the manner described in the preceding chapter, Fernand Wagner was pacing his solitary cell, conjecturing what would be the result of the morrow's trial.

Nisida had visited him a second time on the preceding evening—disguised, as on the former occasion, in male attire; and she had implored him, in the language of the deaf and dumb, but far more eloquently with her speaking eyes and the expression of her beauteous countenance, to allow measures to be that night adopted to effect his immediate escape. But he had resolutely persisted in his original determination to undergo his trial: for, by pursuing this course, he stood the chance of an acquittal; and he knew on the other hand that if he were sentenced to die, the decree of the human tribunal could not be carried into execution. How his escape from that fate (should death be indeed ordained) was to be accomplished was beyond his power of comprehension; but that he possessed a superhuman protector, he knew full well!

Without revealing to Nisida his motives for meeting the criminal judges, he refused to yield to her silently but eloquently pleaded prayer that he would escape should gold induce the jailers to throw open the door of his cell; but he conveyed to her the assurance that the deep interest she manifested in his behalf only bound him the more sincerely and devotedly to her.

During the eight or nine days of his imprisonment, he had reflected deeply upon the murder of Agnes. He naturally associated that black deed with the mystery of the strange lady who had so alarmed Agnes on several occasions; and he had of course been struck by the likeness of his much-loved Nisida to her whom his dead grand-daughter had so minutely described to him. But, if ever suspicion pointed towards Nisida as the murderess of Agnes, he closed his eyes upon the bare idea—he hurled it from him; and he rather fell back upon the satisfactory belief that the entire case was wrapped in a profound mystery, than entertain a thought so injurious to her whom he loved so tenderly.

We said that Nisida had visited him on the Saturday night. She had determined to essay her powers of mute persuasion once more, ere she finally arranged with the banditti for his rescue. But that arrangement was not to take place; for on the Sabbath evening she was carried away, in the manner already described.

And it was now, also, on the Sabbath evening that Wagner was pacing his dungeon,—pondering on the probable result of his trial, and yet never ceasing to think of Nisida.

His memory re-travelled all the windings, and wanderings, and ways which his feet had trodden during a long —long life, and paused to dwell upon that far back hour when he loved the maiden who became the wife of his first period of youth—for he was now in *a second period of youth*;—and he felt that he did not then love her so devotedly—so tenderly—so passionately as he loved Nisida now.

Suddenly, as he paced his dungeon and pondered on the past as well as on the present, the lamp flickered; and, before he could replenish it with oil, the wick died in its socket.

He had the means of procuring another light; but he cared not to avail himself thereof; and he was about to lay aside his vesture, preparatory to seeking his humble pallet, when he was struck by the appearance of a dim and misty lustre which seemed to emanate from the wall facing the door.

He was not alarmed; he had seen and passed through too much in this world to be readily terrified:—but he stood gazing, with intense curiosity and profound astonishment, upon that phenomenon for which his imagination suggested no natural cause.

Gradually the lustre became more powerful; but in the midst of it there appeared a dark cloud, which by degrees assumed the appearance of a human form;—and in a few minutes Wagner beheld a tall, strange-looking figure standing before him.

But assuredly that was no mortal being; for, apart from the mysterious mode in which he had introduced himself into the dungeon, there was on his countenance so withering—bitter—scornful—sardonic a smile, that never did human face wear so sinister an expression.

And yet this being wore a human shape and was attired in the habiliments of that age,—the long doublet, the tight hose, the trunk breeches, the short cloak, and the laced collar, but his slouched hat, instead of having a large and gracefully waving plume, was decorated with but a single feather.

Fernand stood with fascinated gaze fixed upon the being whose eyes seemed to glare with subdued lightnings, like those of the basilisk.

There was something awful in that form—something wildly and menacingly sinister in the sardonic smile that curled his lips, as if with ineffable contempt, and with the consciousness of his own power!

"Wagner!" he said, at length breaking silence, and speaking in a deep sonorous voice, which reverberated even in that narrow dungeon like the solemn tone of the organ echoing amidst cloistral roofs; "Wagner, knowest thou who the being is who now addresseth thee?"

"I can conjecture," answered Fernand boldly. "Thou art the Power of Darkness."

"So men call me," returned the Demon, with a scornful laugh. "Yes—I am he whose delight it is to spread desolation over a fertile and beautiful earth—he, whose eternal enmity against Man is the fruitful source of so much evil! But, of all the disciples who have ever yet aided me in my hostile designs on the human race, none was so serviceable as Faust—that Count of Aurana, whose portrait thou hast so well delineated, and which now graces the wall of thy late dwelling."

"Would that I had never known him!" ejaculated Wagner fervently.

"On the contrary!" resumed the Demon; "thou shouldst be thankful that, in the wild wanderings, of his latter years, he stopped at thy humble cottage in the Black Forest of Germany. Important to thee were the results of that visit—and still more important may they become!"

"Explain thyself, fiend!" said Wagner, nothing dismayed.

"Thou wast tottering with old age—hovering on the brink of the tomb—suspended to a thread which the finger of a child might have snapped," continued the Demon; "and in one short hour thou wast restored to youth, vigour, and beauty."

"And by how dread a penalty was that renovated existence purchased!" exclaimed Wagner.

"Hast thou not been taught by experience that no human happiness can be complete?—that worldly felicity must ever contain within itself some element of misery and distress?" demanded the fiend. "Reflect—and be just! Thou art once more young—and thy tenure of life will last until that age at which thou wouldst have perished, had no superhuman power intervened to grant thee a new lease of existence! Nor is a long life the only boon conferred upon thee hitherto. Boundless wealth is ever at thy command; the floor of this dungeon would be strewed with gold, and jewels, and precious stones at thy bidding—as thou well knowest! Moreover, thou wast ignorant—illiterate—uninformed: now all the sources of knowledge—all the springs of learning—all the fountains of science and art, are at thy disposal, and with whose waters thou canst slake the thirst of thine intellect. Endowed with a youthfulness and a vigour of form that will yield not to the weight of years —that will defy the pressure of time—and that no malady can impair, possessed of wealth having no limit, —and enriched with a mind so stored with knowledge that the greatest sage is as a child in comparison with thee,—how darest thou complain or repent of the compact which has given to thee all these, though associated with the destiny of a Wehr-Wolf?"

"It is of this fatal—this terrible destiny that I complain and that I repent," answered Wagner. "Still do I admit that the advantages which I have obtained by embracing that destiny, are great——"

"And may be far greater!" added the Demon, impressively. "Handsome, intelligent, and rich—all that thou dost require is POWER!"

"Yes," exclaimed Wagner eagerly—and now manifesting, for the first time since the appearance of the fiend in his cell, any particular emotion: "I have need of *power*! —power to avert those evils into which my sad destiny may plunge me,—power to dominate, instead of being subject to the opinions of mankind,—power to prove my complete innocence of the dreadful crime now imputed to me,—power to maintain an untarnished reputation, to which I cling most lovingly,—power too," he added in a slower and also a subdued tone,—"power to restore the lost faculties of hearing and speech to her whom I love!"

Strange was the smile that curled the Demon's lips, as Wagner breathed these last words.

"You require power—power almost without limit," said the fiend, after a few moments' pause: "and that aim is within your reach. Handsome—intelligent—and rich," he continued, dwelling on each word with marked emphasis, "how happy mayst thou be when possessed of the power to render available, in all their glorious extent, the gifts—the qualities wherewith thou art already endowed! When in the service of Faust—during those eighteen months which expired at the hour of sunset on the 30th July, 1517——"

"Alas!" cried Wagner, his countenance expressing emotions of indescribable horror: "remind me not of that man's fate! Oh; never—never can I forget the mental agony—the profound and soul-felt anguish which *he* experienced, and which he strove not to conceal, when at the gates of Vienna on that evening he bade me farewell—for ever!"

"But thou wast happy—supremely happy in his service," said the Demon; "and thou didst enjoy a fair opportunity of appreciating the value of the power which he possessed. By his superhuman aid wast thou transported from clime to clime—as rapidly as thought is transfused by lovers' glances; and in that varied bustling, busied life wast thou supremely happy. The people of Europe spoke of that western world, the discovery of which recently rewarded the daring venture of great navigators; and you were desirous to behold that new continent. Your master repeated the wish: and by my invisible agency, ye stood in a few moments in the presence of the Red Men of North America. Again—you accompanied your master to the eternal ice of the northern pole, and from the doorway of the Esquimaux hut ye beheld the wondrous play of the Boreal Lights. On a third occasion, and in obedience to your wish, you stood with your master in the Island of Ceylon, where the first scene that presented itself to your view was an occurrence, which, though terrible, is not uncommon in that reptile infested clime. Afterwards, my power— although its active agency was but partially known to you—transported you and the Count your master—*now my victim*—to the fantastic and interesting scenes in China,—then to the court of the wife-slaying tyrant of England,—and subsequently to the most sacred privacy of the imperial palace of Constantinople. How varied have been thy travels!—how varied thy movements! And that the scenes which thine eyes did thus contemplate made a profound impression upon thy mind is proved by the pictures now hanging to the walls of thy late dwelling."

"But wherefore this recapitulation of everything I know so well already?" demanded Wagner.

"To remind thee of the advantages of that power which Faust, thy master, possessed, and which ceased to be available to thee when the term of his compact with myself arrived. "Yes," continued the Demon emphatically; "the power which he possessed may be possessed by thee—and thou mayst, with a single word, at once and for ever shake off the trammels of thy present doom —the doom of a Wehr-Wolf!"

"Oh! to shake off those trammels were indeed a boon to be desired!" exclaimed Wagner.

"And to possess the power to gratify thy slightest whim," resumed the Demon,—"to possess the power to transport thyself at will to any clime, however distant, —to be able to defy the machinations of men and the

combinations of adverse circumstances, such as have plunged thee into this dungeon,—to be able, likewise, to say to thy beloved Nisida, '*Receive back the faculties which thou hast lost——*'"

And again was the smile sinister and strange that played upon the lips of the Demon.

But Wagner noticed it not; his imagination was excited by the subtle discourse to which he had lent so ready an ear.

"And hast *thou* the power," he cried, impatiently, "to render *me* thus powerful?"

"I have," answered the Demon.

"But the terms—the conditions—the compact?" exclaimed Wagner, in feverish haste, though with foreboding apprehension.

"THINE IMMORTAL SOUL!" responded the fiend, in a low but sonorous and horrifying whisper.

"No—no!" shrieked Wagner, covering his face with his hands. "Avaunt, Satan—I defy thee! Ten thousand, thousand times preferable is the doom of the Wehr-Wolf!—appalling even though *that* be!"

With folded arms and scornful countenance, did the Demon stand gazing upon Wagner, by the light of the supernatural lustre which filled the cell.

"Dost thou doubt my power?" he demanded, in a slow imperious tone. "If so, put it to the test, unbelieving mortal that thou art! But, remember—shouldst thou require evidence of that power which I propose to make available to thee, it must not be to give thee liberty, nor aught that may enhance thine interest."

"And any other evidence thou wilt give me?" cried Wagner interrogatively, a sudden idea striking him.

"Yes," answered the Demon, who doubtless divined his thoughts—for again did a scornful smile play upon his lips. "I will convince thee, by any manifestation thou mayst demand subject to the condition ere now named,—I will convince thee that I am he whose power was placed at the disposal of thy late master, Faust—and by means of which thou wast transported, along with him, to every climate of the earth."

"I will name my wish," said Wagner.

"Speak!" cried the fiend.

"Show me the Lady Nisida as she now is," exclaimed Fernand, his heart beating with the hope of beholding her whom he loved so devotedly; for, with all the jealousy of a lover, he was anxious to convince himself that she was thinking of him.

"Ah! 'tis the same as with Faust and his Theresa," murmured the Demon to himself:—then aloud, he said, "Rather ask me to show thee the Lady Nisida as she will appear four days hence."

"Be it so!" cried Wagner, moved by the strange and mysterious warning which those words appeared to convey.

The Demon then extended his right arm, and chanted in his deep sonorous tones, the following incantation:—

> "Ye Powers of Darkness! who obey
> Eternally my potent sway,
> List to thy sovereign master's call!
> Transparent make this dungeon wall;
> And now annihilated be
> The space 'twixt Florence and the sea.
> Let the bright lustre of the morn
> In golden glory steep Leghorn;
> Show where the dancing wavelets sport
> Round the gay vessels in the port,—
> Those ships whose gilded lanterns gleam
> In the warm sun's refulgent beam;
> And whose broad pennants kiss the gale
> Woo'd also by the spreading sail!—
> Now let this mortal's vision mark,
> Amidst that scene, the Corsair's bark,
> Clearing the port with swan-like pride;—
> Transparent make the black hull's side,
> And show the curtain'd cabin, where
> Of earth's fair daughters the most fair
> Sits like an image of despair.—
> Mortal, behold! thy Nisida is there!"

The strange phantasmagorian spectacle rapidly developed itself in obedience to the commands of the Demon.

First it appeared to Wagner that the supernal lustre which pervaded the dungeon gathered like a curtain on one side and occupied the place of the wall. This wondrous light became transparent, like a thin golden mist; and then the distant city of Leghorn appeared, producing an effect similar to that of the dissolving views now familiar to every one. The morning sun shone brightly upon the fair scene; and a forest of masts stood out in bold relief against the western sky. The gilded lanterns on the poops of the vessels—the flags and streamers of various hues—the white sails of those ships that were preparing for sea—and the richly painted pinnaces that were shooting along in the channel between the larger craft, rendered the scene surpassingly gay and beautiful.

But amidst the shipping Wagner's eyes were suddenly attracted by a large galley with three masts—looking most rakish with its snow-white sails, its tapering spars,

foreboding apprehension; but now an ejaculation of mingled rage and grief burst from his lips, when, on a sofa in that cabin, he beheld his love—his dearly loved Nisida, seated "like an image of despair," motionless and still, as if all the energies of her haughty soul, all the powers of her strong mind, had been suddenly paralysed by the weight of misfortune!

Wagner stood gazing—unable to utter another word beyond that one ejaculation of mingled rage and grief—gazing—gazing, himself a kindred image of despair, upon this mysterious and unaccountable scene.

But gradually the interior of the cabin grew more and

"'THERE IS NO MERCY FOR YOU ON EARTH.'" (See p. 53.)

its large red streamer, and its low—long and gracefully sweeping hull, which was painted jet black. On its deck were six pieces of brass ordnance; and stands of fire-arms were ranged round the lower part of the masts. Altogether, the appearance of that vessel was as suspicious and menacing as it was gallant and graceful; from the incantation of the Demon, Wagner gleaned its real nature.

And now—as that corsair-ship moved slowly out of the port of Leghorn—its black side suddenly seemed to open, or at least to become transparent; and the interior of a handsomely fitted up cabin was revealed.

Fernand's heart had already sunk within him through

more indistinct, until it was again completely shut in by the black side of the galley, which moved slowly from the mouth of the harbour—her dark hull disappearing by degrees, and melting away in the distance.

Wagner dashed his opened palm against his forehead, exclaiming, "Oh! Nisida—Nisida! who hath torn thee from me!"

And he threw himself upon a seat, where he remained absorbed in a painful reverie, with his face buried in his hands—totally unmindful of the presence of the Demon.

Two or three minutes passed—during which Fernand was deliberating within himself whether he were the sport of a wild and fanciful vision, or whether he had actually received a warning of the fate which hung over Nisida.

"Art thou satisfied with that proof of my power?" demanded a deep voice, sounding ominously upon his ear.

He raised his head with a spasmodic start:—before him stood the Demon, with folded arms and scornful expression of countenance, and, though the phantasmagorian scene had disappeared, the supernatural lustre still pervaded the dungeon.

"Fiend!" cried Wagner, impatiently: "thou hast mocked—thou hast deceived me!"

"Thus do mortals ever speak, even when I give them glimpses of their own eventual fate, through the medium of painful dreams and hideous nightmares," said the Demon, sternly.

"But who has dared—or rather, who *will* dare—for that vision is a prospective warning of a deed to happen four days hence—who, then, I ask, will dare to carry off the Lady Nisida—my own loved and loving Nisida?" demanded Wagner with increased impatience.

"Stephano Verrina, the formidable Captain of the Florentine Banditti, has this night carried away thy lady-love, Wagner," replied the Demon. "Thou hast yet time to save her: though the steed that bears her to Leghorn be fleet and strong, I can provide thee with a fleeter and a stronger. Nay, more—become mine—consent to serve me as Faust served me—and within an hour, within a minute, if thou wilt, Nisida shall be restored to thee—she shall be released from the hands of her captors —thou shalt be free—and thy head shall be pillowed on her bosom, in whatever part of the earth it may suit thee thus to be united to her. Reflect, Wagner—I offer thee a great boon—nay, many great boons:—the annihilation of those trammels which bind thee to the destiny of a Wehr-Wolf—power unlimited for the rest of thy days—and the immediate possession of that Nisida whom thou lovest so fondly, and who is so beautiful—so exceedingly beautiful!"

Desperate was the struggle that took place in the breast of Wagner. On one side was all he coveted on earth; on the other was the loss of his immortal soul. Here the possession of Nisida—there her forced abduction by a brigand: here his earthly happiness might be secured at the expense of his eternal welfare—there his eternal welfare must be renounced if he decided in favour of his earthly happiness. What was he to do? Nisida was weighing in the balance against his immortal soul: to have Nisida, he must renounce his God!

Oh! it was maddening—maddening, this bewilderment.

"An hour—an hour to reflect!" he cried, almost frantically.

"Not a quarter of an hour," returned the Demon. "Nisida will be lost to you—haste—decide!"

"Leave me—leave me for five minutes only!"

"No—not for a minute. Decide—decide!"

Wagner threw up his arms in the writhings of his ineffable anguish:—his right hand came in contact with a crucifix that hung against the wall; and he mechanically clutched it—not with any motive prepense— but wildly, unwittingly.

Terrific was the expression of rage which suddenly distorted the countenance of the Demon; the lightnings of ineffable fury seemed to flash from his eyes and play upon his contracting brow;—and yet a strong spasmodic shuddering at the same time convulsed his awful form: for as Wagner clung to the crucifix to prevent himself from falling at the feet of the malignant fiend, the symbol of Christianity was dragged by his weight from the wall—and, as Wagner reeled sideways, the cross which he retained with instinctive tenacity in his grasp waved across the Demon's face.

Then, with a terrific howl of mingled rage and fear, the fiend fell back and disappeared through the earth— as if a second time hurled down in headlong flight before the thunderbolts of heaven.

Wagner fell upon his knees and prayed fervently.

CHAPTER XXXVI.

THE TRIAL OF FERNAND WAGNER.

ON the ensuing morning Wagner stood before the judge of the Criminal Tribunal of the Republic.

The Judgment Hall was a large and lofty room on the Palazzo del Podesta, or Ducal Palace. The judges sat in antique and richly carved chairs, placed on a platform beneath a canopy of purple velvet fringed with gold.

On the left, at a handsome desk covered with papers, was seated the Procurator Fiscal, or Attorney-General of the Republic, distinguished in attire from the judges only by the fact of the ermine upon his scarlet robe being narrower than theirs. Opposite to this functionary was a bench whereon the witnesses were placed. The prisoner stood between two sbirri in a small pew, or dock, in the centre of the court.

Defendants in civil cases were alone permitted, in that age and country, to retain counsel in their behalf: persons accused of crimes were debarred this privilege. Wagner was therefore undefended.

The proceedings of the tribunal were usually conducted privately; but about a dozen gentlemen and twice as many ladies had obtained orders of admission on this occasion, the case having produced a considerable sensation in Florence on account of the reputed wealth of the accused. Perhaps, also, the rumour that he was a young man endowed with extraordinary personal attraction had exercised its influence upon the susceptible hearts of the Florentine ladies. Certain it is that when he was conducted into the Judgment Hall, his strikingly handsome exterior—his air of modest confidence—his graceful gait—and his youthful appearance, so far threw into the background the crime imputed to him, that the ladies present felt their sympathies deeply enlisted in his behalf.

The usher of the tribunal having commanded silence in a loud voice, the Chief Judge began the usual interrogatory of the prisoner.

To the questions addressed to him, the accused replied that his name was Fernand Wagner; that he was a native of Germany; that he had no profession, avocation, nor calling; that he was possessed of a large fortune: and that, having travelled over many parts of the world, he settled in Florence, where he had hoped to enjoy a tranquil and peaceful existence.

"The murdered female was reputed to be your sister," said the Chief Judge, "Was such the fact?"

"She was a near relative," answered Wagner.

"But was she your sister?" demanded the Procurator Fiscal.

"She was not."

"Then in what degree of relationship did she stand towards you?" asked the Chief Judge.

"I must decline a reply to that question."

"The tribunal infers, therefore, that the murdered female was not related to you at all," observed the Judge. "Was she not your mistress?"

"No, my lord!" cried Wagner, emphatically. "As truly as Heaven now hears my assertion, it was not so?"

"Was she your wife?" demanded the Judge.

A negative answer was given.

The Chief Judge and the Procurator Fiscal then by turns questioned and cross-questioned the prisoner in the most subtle manner, to induce him to state the degree of relationship subsisting between himself and Agnes; but he either refused to respond to their queries, or else answered direct ones by means of a positive denial.

The lieutenant of the sbirri was at length called upon to give an account of the discovery of the dead body and the suspicious circumstances which had led to the arrest of Wagner. Two of these circumstances appeared to be very strong against him. The first was the soiled and blood-stained appearance of the garments which were found in his chamber: the other was the exclamation— "*But how know you that it is Agnes who is murdered?*" —uttered before any one had informed him *who* had been murdered.

Wagner was called upon for an explanation.

He stated that he had been out the whole night; that the blood upon his garments had flowed from his own body, which had been scratched and torn in the mazes of the woods; that on his return home, he met Agnes in the garden; that he had left her there; and that when he was told a young lady had been assassinated in the vicinity of his dwelling, he immediately conceived that the victim must be Agnes.

When questioned concerning the motives of his absence from home during the entire night, he maintained a profound silence; but he was evidently much agitated and excited by the queries thus put to him.

He said nothing about the stranger-lady who had so frequently terrified Agnes; because, in relating the proceeding of that mysterious female in respect to his deceased grand-daughter—especially the incident of the abstraction of the antique jewels which the late Count of Riverola had given to her—he would have been compelled to enter into details concerning the amour between those who were no more. And this subject he was solicitous to avoid, not only through respect for the memory of the murdered Agnes, but also to spare the feelings of Count Francisco and Donna Nisida.

The Judge and the Procurator Fiscal, finding that they could elicit nothing from Wagner relative to the cause of his absence from home during the night preceding the murder, passed on to another subject.

"In the apartment belonging to your residence," said the Chief Judge, "there are several pictures and portraits."

Wagner turned pale, and trembled.

The Judge made a signal to an officer of the court; and that functionary quitted the Judgment Hall. In a few minutes he returned, followed by three subordinates bearing the two portraits mentioned in the sixth chapter of this tale, and also the large frame covered over with the large piece of black cloth.

On perceiving this last object, Wagner became paler still, and trembled violently.

"There are six other pictures in the room whence these have been taken," said the Judge: "but those six are not of a character to interest the tribunal. We however, require explanations concerning the two portraits and the frame with the black cloth cover, now before us."

The greatest excitement prevailed amongst the audience.

"On one of the portraits," continued the Chief Judge, "there is an inscription to this effect:—'F. Count of A. terminated his career on the 1st of August, 1517.'—What does this inscription mean?"

"It means that Faust, Count of Aurana, was a nobleman with whom I travelled during a period of eighteen months," replied Wagner; "and he died on the day mentioned in that inscription."

"The world has heard strange reports relative to Faust," said the Chief Judge, in a cold voice and with unchanged manner; although the mention of that name had produced a thrill of horror on the part of his brother-judges and the audience. "Art thou aware that rumour ascribes to him a compact with the Evil One?"

Wagner gazed round him in horrified amazement: for the incident of the preceding night returned with such force to his mind that he could scarcely subdue an agonizing ebullition of emotions.

The Chief Judge next recited the inscription on the other portrait:—"F. W., January 7th, 1516. His last day thus."

But Wagner maintained a profound silence; and neither threats nor entreaties could induce him to give the least explanation concerning the inscription.

"Let us then proceed to examine this frame with the black cloth cover," said the Chief Judge.

"My lord," whispered one of his brother-judges, "in the name of the blessed Virgin! have naught to do with this man. Let him go forth to execution:—he is a monster of atrocity—evidently a murderer—doubtless leagued with the Evil One, as Faust, of whose acquaintance he boasts, was before him——"

"For my part, I credit not such idle tales," interrupted the Chief Judge; "and it is my determination to sift this matter to the very foundation. I am rather inclined to believe that the prisoner is allied with the banditti who infest the Republic, than with any preterhuman power. His absence from home during the entire night, according to his own admission—his immense wealth, without any ostensible resources—all justified my suspicion. Let the case proceed," added the Chief Judge aloud; for he had made the previous observations in a low tone. "Usher, remove the black cloth from that picture?"

"No! no!" exclaimed Wagner wildly; and he was about to rush from the dock, but the sbirri held him back.

The usher's hand was already on the black cloth.

"I beseech your lordship to pause!" whispered the assistant-judge who had before spoken.

"Proceed!" exclaimed the presiding functionary, in a loud and authoritative tone; for he was a bold and fearless man.

And scarcely were the words uttered, when the black cloth was stripped from the frame; and the usher who had removed the covering, recoiled with a cry of horror, as his eyes obtained a glimpse of the picture which was now revealed to view.

"What means this folly?" ejaculated the Chief Judge. "Bring the picture hither."

The usher, awed by the manner of this great functionary, raised the picture in such a way that the

Judges and the Procurator Fiscal might obtain a full view of it.

"A Wehr-Wolf!" ejaculated the assistant-judge, who had previously remonstrated with his superior; and his countenance became as pale as death.

The dreadful words were echoed by other tongues in the court; and a panic fear seized on all save the Chief Judge and Wagner himself.

The former smiled contemptuously: the latter had summoned all his courage to aid him to pass through this terrible ordeal without confirming by his conduct the dreadful suspicion which had been excited in respect to him.

For, oh! the subject of that picture was indeed awful to contemplate! It had no inscription: but it represented, with the most painful and horrifying fidelity, the writhings and agonizing throes of the human being during the process of transformation into the lupine monster. The countenance of the unhappy man had already *elongated into one of savage and brute-like shape*; and so admirably had art counterfeited nature, that the rich garments seemed changed into a *rough, shaggy, and wiry skin!*

The effect produced by that picture was indeed of thrilling and appalling interest?

"A Wehr-Wolf!" had exclaimed one of the assistant-judges; and while the voices of several of the male spectators in the body of the court echoed the words mechanically, the ladies gave vent to screams, as they rushed towards the doors of the tribunal.

In a few moments that part of the court was entirely cleared.

"Prisoner!" exclaimed the Chief Judge, "have you aught more to advance in your defence relative to the charge of murder?"

"My lord, I am innocent!" said Wagner, firmly, but respectfully.

"The Tribunal pronounces you *Guilty*," continued the Chief Judge; then, with a scornful smile towards his assistants, and also to the Procurator Fiscal—who all three, as well as the sbirri and the officers of the court, were pale and trembling with vague fears—the presiding functionary continued thus:—"The Tribunal condemns you, Fernand Wagner, to death by the hand of the common headsman; and it is now my duty to name the day and fix the hour for your execution. Therefore I do ordain *that the sentence just pronounced be carried into effect precisely at the hour of sunset on the last day of the present month!*"

"My lord! my lord!" exclaimed the Procurator Fiscal; "the belief is that on the last day of each month —and at the hour of sunset——"

"I am aware of the common superstition," interrupted the Chief Judge, coldly and sternly; "and it is to convince the world of the folly of putting faith in such legends that I have fixed that day and that hour in the present instance.—Away with the prisoner to his dungeon!"

And the Chief Judge waved his hand imperiously, to check any further attempt at remonstrance;—but his assistant functionaries, the Procurator Fiscal, and the officers of the court, surveyed him with mingled surprise and awe, uncertain whether they ought to applaud his courage or tremble at his rashness.

Wagner had maintained a calm and dignified demeanour during the latter portion of the proceedings; and, although the sbirri who had charge of him ventured not to lay a finger upon his person, he accompanied them back to the prison of the Palazzo del Podesta.

CHAPTER XXXVII.

THE SHIPWRECK.

TEN days had elapsed since the incidents related in the preceding chapter.

The scene changes to an island in the Mediterranean Sea.

There, seated on the strand, with garments dripping wet, and with all the silken richness of her raven hair floating wildly and dishevelled over her shoulders—the Lady Nisida gazed vacantly on the ocean, now tinged with living gold by the morning sun.

At a short distance a portion of the shipwrecked vessel lay upon the shore, and seemed to tell her tale.

But where were the desperate, daring crew who had manned that gallant bark? where were those fearless freebooters who six days previously had sailed from Leghorn on their piratical voyage? where were those who hoisted the flag of peace and assumed the demeanour of honest traders when in port, but who on the broad bosom of the ocean carried the terrors of their black banner far and wide? where, too, was Stephano Verrina, who had so boldly carried off the Lady Nisida?

The gallant bark had struck upon a shoal, during the tempest and the obscurity of the night, and the pilot knew not where they were. His reckoning was lost—his calculations had all been set at naught by the confusion produced by the fearful storm which had assailed the ship and driven her from her course.

The moment the corsair galley struck, that confusion was increased to such an extent that the captain lost all control over his men; the pilot's voice was unheeded likewise.

The crew got out the long-boat, and leapt into it, forcing the captain and the pilot to enter it with them. Stephano Verrina, who was on deck when the vessel struck, rushed down into the cabin appropriated to Nisida, and by signs endeavoured to convey to her a sense of the danger which menaced them. Conquering her ineffable aversion for the bandit, Nisida followed him hastily to the deck. At the same instant that her eyes plunged as it were into the dense obscurity which prevailed around, the lightning streamed in long and vivid flashes over the turbulent waters: and with the roar of the billow suddenly mingled deafening shrieks and cries—shrieks and cries of wild despair, as the long boat, which had been pushed away from the corsair-bark went down at a little distance. And as the lightning played upon the raging sea, Nisida and Verrina caught hurried but frightful glimpses of many human faces, whereon was expressed the indescribable agony of the drowning!

"Perdition!" cried Verrina: "all are gone save Nisida and myself! And shall we too perish ere she has become mine?—shall death separate us ere I have revelled in her charms? Fool that I was to be over-awed by her impetuous signs,—or melted by her silent though strong appeals!"

He paced the deck in an excited manner as he uttered these words aloud.

"No! no!" he exclaimed wildly, as the tempest seemed to increase, and the ship was thrown farther on the shoal: "she shall not escape me thus, after all I have done and dared in order to possess her! Our funeral may take place to-night—but our bridal shall be first! Ha! ha!"—and he laughed with a kind of despairing mockery, while the fragments of the vessel's sails flapped against the spars with a din as if some mighty demon were struggling with the blast.

The sense of appalling danger seemed to madden Stephano only because it threatened to separate him for ever from Nisida; and, fearfully excited, he rushed towards her, crying wildly, "You shall be mine! you shall be mine!"

But how terrible was the yell which burst from his lips, when, by the glare of a brilliant flash of lightning, he beheld Nisida cast herself over the side of the vessel!

For a single instant he fell back, appalled—horror-struck: but at the next, he plunged with insensate fury after her.

And the rage of the storm redoubled.

*　　*　　*　　*　　*　　*

*　　*　　*　　*　　*　　*

When the misty shades of morning cleared away, and the storm had passed, Nisida was seated alone upon the strand—having miraculously escaped that eternal night of death which leads to no dawn.

But where was Stephano Verrina?

She knew not; although she naturally conjectured, and even hoped, that he was numbered with the dead.

CHAPTER XXXVIII.

THE ISLAND IN THE MEDITERRANEAN SEA.

FAIR and beauteous was that Mediterranean isle whereon the Lady Nisida had been thrown.

When the morning mists had dispersed, and the sunbeams tinged the ridges of the hills and the summits of the tallest trees, Nisida awoke as it were from the profound lethargic reverie in which she had been plunged for upwards of an hour since the moment when the billows had borne her safely to the shore.

The temperature of that island was warm and genial: for there eternal summer reigned; and thus, though her garments were still dripping wet, Nisida experienced not cold.

She rose from the bank of sand whereon she had been seated, and cast anxious, rapid, and searching glances around her.

Not a human being met her eyes; but in the woods that stretched, with emerald pride, almost down to the golden sands, the birds and insects—Nature's free commoners—sent forth the sounds of life, and welcomed the advent of the morn with that music of the groves.

The scenery which now presented itself to the contemplation of Nisida was indescribably beautiful. Richly wooded hills rose towering above each other with amphitheatrical effect; and behind the verdant panorama were the blue outlines of pinnacles of naked rock.

But not a trace of the presence of human beings was to be seen,—nor a hamlet—nor a cottage—nor the slightest sign of agriculture!

At a short distance lay a portion of the wreck of the corsair-ship. The fury of the tempest of the preceding night had thrown it so high upon the shoal whereon it had struck, and the sea was now comparatively so calm, that Nisida was enabled to approach close up to it.

With little difficulty she succeeded in reaching the deck,—that deck whose elastic surface lately vibrated to the tread of many daring, desperate men—but now desolate and broken in many parts.

The cabin which had been allotted to her, or rather to which she had been confined, was in the portion of the wreck that still remained; and there she found a change of raiment, which Stephano had provided ere the vessel left Leghorn. Carefully packing up these garments in as small and portable a compass as possible, she fastened the burden upon her shoulders by means of a cord, and quitting the vessel, conveyed it safe and dry to the shore.

Then she returned again to the wreck in search of provisions, considerable quantities of which she fortunately found to be uninjured by the water; and these she was enabled to transport to the strand by means of several journeys backward and forward between the shore and the wreck

The occupation was not only necessary, in order to provide the wherewith to sustain life; but it also abstracted her thoughts from a too painful contemplation of her position.

It was long past the hour of noon when she had completed her task; and the shore in the immediate vicinity of the wreck was piled with a miscellaneous assortment of objects,—bags of provisions, weapons of defence, articles of the toilet, clothing, pieces of canvas, cordage, and carpenter's tools.

Then, wearied with her arduous toils, she laid aside her dripping garments, bathed her beauteous form in the sea, and attired herself in dry apparel.

Having partaken of some refreshment, she armed herself with weapons of defence, and, quitting the shore, entered upon the vast amphitheatre of verdure to which we have already slightly alluded.

The woods were thick and tangled; but though, when seen from the shore, they appeared to form one dense uninterrupted forest, yet they in reality only dotted the surface of the island with numerous detached patches of grove and copse; and in the intervals were verdant plains or delicious valleys, exhibiting not the slightest signs of culture, but interspersed with shrubs and trees laden with fruits rich and tempting.

Nature had indeed profusely showered her bounties over that charming isle: for the trees glowed with their blushing or golden produce, as if gems were the fruitage of every bough.

Through one of the delicious valleys which Nisida explored, a streamlet, smooth as a looking-glass, wound its way. To its sunny bank did the lady repair: and the pebbly bed of the river was seen as plainly through the limpid water as an eye-ball through a tear.

Though alone was Nisida in that vale, and though many bitter reflections, deep regrets, and vague apprehensions crowded upon her soul, yet the liveliness of the scene appeared to diminish the intenseness of the feeling of utter solitude, and its soft influence partially lulled the waves of her emotions.

For never had mortal eyes beheld finer fruits upon the trees nor lovelier flowers upon the soil; all life was rejoicing, from the grasshopper at her feet to the feathered songster in the myrtle, citron, and olive groves;—and the swan glided past to the music of the stream.

Above, the heaven was more clear than that of even her own Italian clime,—more blue than any colour that tinges the flowers of the earth.

She roved along the smiling bank which fringed the stream, until the setting sun dyed with the richest purple the rocky pinnacles in the distance, and made the streamlet glow like a golden flood.

And Nisida—alone in the radiance and glory of her own charms,—alone, amidst all the radiance and glory of the charms of nature,—the beauteous Nisida appeared to be the Queen of that Mediterranean isle.

But whether it were really an island, or a portion of Nature appeared to be the undisputed Empress of that land; and Nisida returned to the shore with the conviction that she was the sole human inhabitant of this delicious region.

And now, once more seated upon the strand, while the last beams of the sun played upon the wide blue waters of the Mediterranean, Nisida partook of her frugal repast, consisting of the bread supplied by the wreck and a few fruits which she had gathered in the valley.

The effects of the tempest had totally disappeared in respect to the sea, which now lay stretched in glassy stillness. It seemed as if a holy calm, soft as an infant's

"THERE WAS SOMETHING AWFUL IN THAT FORM." (See p. 59.)

one of the three continents which hem in that tideless ocean, the lady as yet knew not.

Warned by the splendours of the setting sun to retrace her way, she turned and sped back to the strand where the stores she had saved from the wreck were heaped up.

When first she had set out upon her exploring ramble, she had expected every moment to behold human forms —her fellow-creatures—emerge from the woods; but the more she saw of that charming spot, whereon her destinies had thrown her, the fainter grew the hope or the fear—we scarcely know which to term the expectation. For no signs of the presence of man were there:

sleep, lay upon the bosom of the Mediterranean, now no longer terrible with storm, but a mighty emblem of mild majesty and rest.

Nisida thought of the fury which had lately convulsed that sea now so placid, and sighed at the conviction which was forced upon her—that no such calm was for the mortal breast when storms had once been there!

For she pondered on her native land, now, perhaps, far—oh! how far away; and the images of those whom she loved appeared to rise before her,—Francisco, in despair at his sister's unaccountable disappearance—and Fernand perchance already doomed to die!

And tears flowed down her cheeks and trickled upon her snowy bosom, gleaming like dew amongst lilies.

Of what avail was the energy of her character in that land along whose coast stretched the adamantine barrier of the sea?

Oh! it was enough to make even the haughty Nisida weep, and to produce a terrible impression on a mind hitherto acting ever in obedience to its own indomitable will.

Though the sun had set some time, and no moon had yet appeared in the purple sky, yet was it far from dark. An azure mantle of twilight seemed to wrap the earth—the sea—the heavens: and so soft—so overpowering was the influence of the scene and of the night, that slumber gradually stole upon the lady's eyes.

There now, upon the warm sand slept Nisida; and when the chaste advent of the moon bathed all in silver as the sun had for twelve hours steeped all in gold, the beams of the goddess of the night played on her charming countenance without awakening her.

The raven masses of her hair lay upon her flushed cheeks like midnight on a bed of roses; her long black lashes reposed on those cheeks, so surpassingly lovely with their rich carnation hues.

For she dreamt of Fernand; and her vision was a happy one. Imagination played wild tricks with the shipwrecked, lonely lady—as if to recompense her for the waking realities of her sad position. She thought that she was reposing in the delicious valley which she had explored in the afternoon,—she thought that Fernand was her companion—that she lay in his arms—that his lips pressed hers—that she was all to him as he was all to her—and that love's cup of enjoyment was full to the very brim.

But oh! when she slowly awoke, under the influence of the delightful vision, raised her eyes in the dewy light of voluptuous languor to the blue sky above her,—the sunbeams that were heralding in another day, cruelly dispelled the enchanting illusions of a warm and excited fancy; and Nisida found herself alone on the sea-shore of the island.

Thus the glory of that sunrise had no charms for her: although never had the orb of day come forth with greater pomp, nor to shine on a lovelier scene. No words can convey an idea of the rapid development of every feature in the landscape—the deeper and deepening tint glowing sky—the roseate hue of mountain peaks as they stood out against the cloudless orient—and the rich emerald shades of the woods sparkling with fruits.

The fragrant rose and the chaste lily—the blushing peony and the gaudy tulip—and all the choicest flowers of that delicious clime, expanded into renewed loveliness to greet the sun: and the citron and orange, the melon and the grape, the pomegranate and the date drank in the yellow light to nourish their golden hues.

Nisida's eyes glanced rapidly over the vast expanse of waters, and swept the horizon; but there was not a sail nor even a cloud which imagination might transform into the white wing of a distant ship.

And now upon the golden sand the lovely Nisida put off her garments one by one; and set at liberty the dark masses of her shining hair, which floated like an ample veil of raven blackness over the dazzling whiteness of her skin.

Imagination might have invested her forehead with a halo, so magnificent was the lustrous effect of the sun upon the silken glossiness of that luxuriant hair.

The Mediterranean was the lady's bath; and in spite of the oppressive nature of the waking thoughts which had succeeded her delicious dream,—in spite of that conviction of loneliness which lay like a weight of lead upon her soul, she disported in the waters like a mermaid.

Now she plunged beneath the surface, which glowed in the sun like a vast lake of quicksilver: now she stood in a shallow spot, where the waters rippled no higher than her middle, and combed out her dripping tresses:—then she waded farther in, and seemed to rejoice in allowing the little wavelets to kiss her snowy bosom.

No fear had she—indeed, no thought—of the monsters of the deep: could the fair surface of the shining water conceal aught dangerous or aught terrible?

Oh! yes—even as beneath that snowy breast, beat a heart stained with crime, often agitated by the most ardent and impetuous passions and devoured by raging desires!

For nearly an hour did Nisida disport in Nature's mighty bath, until the heat of the sun became so intense that she was compelled to return to the shore and resume her apparel.

Then she took some bread in her hand, and hastened to the groves to pluck the cooling and delicious fruits whereof there was so marvellous an abundance.

She seated herself on a bed of wild flowers, on the shady side of a citron and orange grove, and surrounded by a perfumed air. Before her stretched the valley, like a vast carpet of bright green velvet fantastically embroidered with flowers of a thousand varied hues. And in the midst meandered the crystal stream, with stately swans and an infinite number of other aquatic birds floating on its bosom.

And the birds of the groves, too, how beautiful were they, and how joyous did they seem! What variegated plumage did they display, as they flew past the Lady Nisida, unscared by her presence! Some of them alighted from the overhanging boughs, and as they descended swept her very hair with their wings: then, almost as if to convince her that she was no unwelcome intruder in that charming land, they hopped round her, picking up the crumbs of bread which she scattered about to attract them.

For the loneliness of her condition had already attuned the mind of this strange being to a susceptibility of deriving amusement from incidents which a short time previously she would have looked upon as the most inane triflings;—thus was the heaviness of her thoughts relieved by disporting in the water, as we ere now saw her, or by contemplating the playfulness of the birds.

Presently she wandered into the vale, and gathered a magnificent nosegay of flowers: then the whim struck her that she would weave herself a chaplet of roses; and as her work progressed she improved upon it, and fashioned a beauteous diadem of flowers to protect her head from the scorching noon-day sun.

But, think not, O reader! that while thus diverting herself with trivialities of which you would scarcely have deemed the haughty—imperious—active disposition of Nisida of Riverola to be capable,—think not that her mind was altogether abstracted from unpleasant thoughts. No—far, very far from that! She was merely relieved from a portion of that weight which oppressed her; but the entire burden could not be removed from her soul.

There were moments when her grief amounted almost to despair. Was she doomed to pass the remainder of her existence in that land? was it really an island, and unknown to navigators? She feared so: for did it join a continent, its loveliness and fruitfulness would not have permitted it to remain long unoccupied by those who must of necessity discover it.

And oh! what would her brother think of her absence? what would Fernand conjecture? And what perils might not at that moment envelope her lover, while she was not near to succour him by means of her artifice, her machinations, or her gold?

Ten thousand—thousand maledictions upon Stephano, who was the cause of all her present misery! Ten thousand—thousand maledictions on her own folly for not having exerted all her energies and all her faculties to escape from his power, ere she was conveyed on board the corsair-ship and it was too late!

But useless now were regrets and repinings; for the past could not be recalled, and the future might have much happiness in store for Nisida.

For oh! sweetest comes the hope which is lured back because its presence is indispensable; and oppressed as Nisida was with the weight of her misfortunes, her soul was too energetic—too sanguine—and too impetuous to yield to despair.

Day after day passed; and still not a ship appeared. Nisida did not penetrate much further into the island than the valley which we have described, and whither she was accustomed to repair to gather the flowers that she wove into diadems. She lingered for the most part near the shore on which she had been thrown, fearful lest, should she remain long away, a ship might pass in her absence.

Each day she bathed her beauteous form in the Mediterranean; each day she devoted some little time to the adornment of her person with wreaths of flowers. She wove crowns for her head—necklaces—bracelets—and scarfs,—combining the flowers so as to form the most wild and fanciful devices, and occasionally surveying herself in the natural mirror afforded her by the limpid stream.

Purposely wearing an attire as scanty as possible, on account of the oppressive heat which prevailed during each day of twelve long hours, and which was not materially moderated at night, she supplied to some extent the place of the superfluous garments thus thrown aside, by means of tissues of cool, refreshing, fragrant flowers.

Thus, by the time she had been ten or twelve days upon the island, her appearance seemed most admirably to correspond with her new and lonely mode of life, and the spot where her destinies had cast her. Habited in a single linen garment, confined round the slender waist with a cestus of flowers,—and with light slippers upon her feet,—but with a diadem of roses on her head, and with wreaths round her bare arms, and her equally bare ankles,—she appeared to be the goddess of that island—the genius of that charming clime of fruits, and verdure, and crystal streams, and flowers.

The majesty of her beauty was softened, and thus enhanced by the wonderful simplicity of her attire; the dazzling brilliancy of her charms was subdued by the chaste—the innocent—the primitive aspect with which those fantastically woven flowers invested her. Even the extraordinary lustre of her fine dark eyes was moderated by the gaudy yet elegant assemblage of hues formed by those flowers which she wore.

Was it not strange that she, whose soul we have hitherto seen bent on deeds or schemes of stern and important nature,—who never acted without a motive, and whose mind was far too deeply occupied with worldly pursuits and cares to bestow a thought on trifles,—who, indeed, would have despised herself had she wasted a moment in toying with a flower, or watching the motions of a bird,—was it not strange that Nisida should have become so changed as we now find her in that island of which she was the queen?

Conceive that same Nisida who planned dark plots against Flora Francatelli, now tripping along the banks of the sun-lit stream, bedecked with flowers and playing with the swans. Imagine that same being, who dealt death to Agnes, now seated beneath the shade of myrtles and embowering vines, distributing bread or pomegranate seeds to the birds that hopped cheerfully around her. Picture to yourself that woman of majestic beauty, whom you have seen clad in black velvet and wearing a dark thick veil, now weaving for herself garments of flowers, and wandering in the lightest possible attire by the sea shore, or by the rippling stream, or amidst the mazes of the fruit-laden groves.

And, sometimes, as she sat upon the yellow sand, gazing upon the wavelets of the Mediterranean, that were racing one after another, like living things from some far-off region, to that lovely but lonely isle, it would seem as if all the low and sweet voices of the sea—never loud and sullen now, since the night of the storm which cast her on that strand—were heard by her, and made delicious music to her ears!

In that island must we leave her now for a short space—leave her to her birds, her flowers, and her mermaid sports in the sea,—leave her also to her intervals of dark and dismal thoughts, and to her long but ineffectual watchings for the appearance of a sail in the horizon!

CHAPTER XXXIX.
THE WEHR-WOLF.

It was the last day of the month; and the hour of sunset was approaching.

Great was the sensation that prevailed throughout the city of Florence.

Rumour had industriously spread, and with equal assiduity exaggerated, the particulars of Fernand Wagner's trial—and the belief that a man, on whom the horrible destiny of a Wehr-Wolf had been entailed, was about to suffer the extreme penalty of the law, was generally prevalent.

The great square of the ducal palace, where the scaffold was erected, was crowded with the Florentine populace; and the windows were literally alive with human faces.

Various were the emotions and feelings which influenced that mass of spectators. The credulous and superstitious—forming more than nine-tenths of the whole multitude—shook their heads, and commented amongst themselves in subdued whispers, on the profane rashness of the Chief Judge who dared to doubt the existence of such a being as a Wehr-Wolf. The few who shared the scepticism of the Judge, applauded that high functionary for his courage in venturing so bold a stroke in order to destroy what they deemed to be an idle superstition.

But the great mass were dominated by a profound and indeed most painful sensation of awe: curiosity induced them to remain, though their misgivings prompted them to fly from the spot which had been fixed upon for the execution. The flowers of Florentine loveliness—and never in any age did the Republic boast of so much female beauty—were present; but bright eyes flashed forth uneasy glances, and snowy bosoms beat with alarms, and fair hands trembled in the lovers' pressure.

In the midst of the square was raised a high platform covered with black cloth, and presenting an appearance so ominous and sinister that it was but little calculated to revive the spirits of the timid. On this scaffold was a huge block; and near the block stood the headsman, carelessly leaning on his axe, the steel of which was polished and bright as silver.

A few minutes before the hour of sunset, the Chief Judge, the Procurator Fiscal, the two Assistant-Judges, and the lieutenant of sbirri, attended by a turnkey and several subordinate police-officers, were repairing in procession along the corridor leading to the doomed prisoner's cell.

The Chief Judge alone was dignified in manner; and he alone wore a demeanour denoting resolution, and at the same time complete self-possession. Those who accompanied him were, without a single exception, a prey to the most lively fear; and it was evident that had they dared to absent themselves, they would not have been present on this occasion.

At length the door of the prisoner's cell was reached: and there the procession paused.

"The moment is now at hand," said the Chief Judge, "when a monstrous and ridiculous superstition—imported into our country from that cradle and nurse of preposterous legends, Germany—shall be annihilated for ever. This knave who is about to suffer, has doubtless propagated the report of his lupine destiny in order to inspire terror, and thus prosecute his career of crime and infamy with the greater security from chances of molestation. For this end he painted the picture which appalled so many of you in the Judgment Hall, but which, believe me, my friends, he did not always believe destined to retain its sable covering. Well did he know that the curiosity of a servant or of a friend would obtain a peep beneath the mystic veil; and he calculated that the terror with which he sought to invest himself, would be enhanced by the rumours and representations spread abroad by those who thus penetrated into his feigned secrets. But let us not waste that time which now verges towards a crisis whereby doubt shall be dispelled and a ridiculous superstition destroyed for ever."

At this moment a loud—a piercing—and an agonizing cry burst from the interior of the cell.

"The knave has overheard me, and would fain strike terror to your hearts!" exclaimed the Chief Judge: then, in a still louder tone, he commanded the turnkey to open the door of the dungeon.

But when the man approached, so strange—so awful—so appalling were the sounds which came from the interior of the cell, that he threw down the key in dismay, and rushed from the dreaded vicinity.

"My lord, I implore you to pause!" said the Procurator Fiscal, trembling from head to foot.

"Would you have me render myself ridiculous in the eyes of all Florence?" demanded the Chief Judge, sternly.

Yet, so strange were now the noises which came from the interior of the dungeon—so piercing the cries of agony—so violent the rustling and tossing on the stone-floor, that for the first time this bold functionary entertained a partial misgiving, as if he had indeed gone too far.

But to retreat was impossible: and, with desperate resolution, the Chief Judge picked up the key, and thrust it into the lock.

His assistants, the Procurator Fiscal, and the sbirri, drew back with instinctive horror, as the bolts groaned in the iron work which held them: the chain fell with a dismal, clanking sound; and as the door was opened, a horrible monster burst forth from the dungeon with a terrific howl.

Yells and cries of despair reverberated through the long corridor; and those sounds were for an instant broken by that of the falling of a heavy body.

'Twas the Chief Judge—hurled down and dashed violently against the rough, uneven masonry, by the mad careering of the Wehr-Wolf as the monster burst from his cell.

On—on he sped, with the velocity of lightning, along

the corridor—giving vent to howls of the most horrifying description.

Fainting with terror, the Assistant-Judges, the Procurator Fiscal, and the sbirri, were for a few moments so overcome by the appalling scene they had just witnessed, that they thought not of raising the Chief Judge, who lay motionless on the pavement. But at length some of the police-officers so far recovered themselves as to be able to devote attention to that high functionary:—it was however too late—his skull was fractured by the violence with which he had been dashed against the wall —and his brains scattered on the pavement.

Those who now bent over his disfigured corpse exchanged looks of unutterable horror.

In the meantime, the Wehr-Wolf had cleared the corridor—rapid as an arrow shot from the bow—he sprang bounding up a flight of steep stone stairs as if the elastic air bore him on—and rushing through an open door, burst suddenly upon the crowd that was so anxiously waiting to behold the procession issue thence !

Terrific was the yell that the multitude sent forth,—a yell formed of a thousand combining voices,—so long—so loud—so wildly agonizing, that never had the welkin rung with so appalling an ebullition of human misery before !

Madly rushed the wolf amidst the people—dashing them aside—overturning them—hurling them down— bursting through the mass too dense to clear a passage of its own accord—and making the scene of horror more horrible still by mingling his hideous howlings with the cries—the shrieks—the screams that escaped from a thousand tongues.

No pen can describe the awful scene of confusion and death which now took place. Swayed by no panic fear, but influenced by terrors of dreadful reality, the people exerted all their force to escape from that spot ; and thus the struggling—crushing—pushing—crowding—fighting —and all the oscillations of a multitude set in motion by the direst alarms, were succeeded by the most fatal results. Women were thrown down and trampled to death—strong men were scarcely able to maintain their footing—females were literally suffocated in the pressure of the crowd—and mothers with young children in their arms excited no sympathy.

Never was the selfishness of human nature more strikingly displayed than on this occasion : no one bestowed a thought upon his neighbour—the chivalrous Florentine citizen dashed aside the weak and helpless female who barred his way, with as little remorse as if she were not a being of flesh and blood—and even husbands forgot their wives, lovers abandoned their mistresses, and parents waited not an instant to succour their daughters.

Oh ! it was a terrible thing to contemplate—that dense mass, oscillating furiously like the waves of the sea— sending up to heaven such appalling sounds of misery,— rushing furiously towards the avenues of egress,— falling back, baffled and crushed, in the struggle where only the very strongest prevailed,—labouring to escape from death, and fighting for life,—fluctuating, and rushing, and wailing in maddening excitement, like a raging ocean,—oh ! all this wrought a direful sublimity, with those cries of agony and that riot of desperation !

And all this while the wolf pursued its furious career, amid the mortal violence of a people thrown into horrible disorder, pursued its way with savage howls, glaring eyes, and foaming mouth—the only living being there that was infuriate and not alarmed—battling for escape, and yet unhurt !

As a whirlpool suddenly assails the gallant ship— makes her agitate and rock fearfully for a few moments, and then swallows her up altogether,—so was the scaffold in the midst of the square shaken to its very basis for a little space, and then hurled down—disappearing altogether amidst the living vortex.

In the balconies and at the windows overlooking the square the awful excitement spread like wild-fire ; and a real panic prevailed amongst those who were at least beyond the reach of danger. But horror paralyzed the power of sober reflection ; and the hideous spectacle of volumes of human beings battling—and roaring—and rushing—and yelling in terrific frenzy, produced a kindred effect, and spread the wild delirium amongst the spectators at those balconies and those windows.

At length, in the square below, the crowds began to pour forth from the gates,—for the Wehr-Wolf had by this time cleared himself a passage, and escaped from the midst of that living ocean so fearfully agitated by the storms of fear.

But even when the means of egress were thus obtained, the most frightful disorder prevailed—the people rolling in heaps upon heaps,—while infuriate and agile men ran on the tops of the compact masses, and leapt in their delirium as if with barbarous intent.

On—on sped the Wehr-Wolf, dashing like a whirlwind through the streets leading to the open country—the white flakes of foam flying from his mouth like spray from the prow of a vessel,—and every fibre of his frame vibrating as if in agony.

And oh ! what dismay—what terror did that monster spread in the thoroughfares through which he passed ; how wildly,—how madly flew the men and women from his path—how piteously screamed the children at the house-doors in the poor neighbourhoods !

But as if sated with the destruction already wrought in the great square of the palace, the wolf dealt death no more in the precincts of the city :—as if lashed on by invisible demons, his aim—or his instinct was to escape.

The streets are threaded—the suburbs of the city are passed—the open country is gained ; and now along the bank of the Arno rushes the monster—by the margin of that pure stream to whose enchanting vale the soft twilight lends a more delicious charm.

On the verge of a grove, with its full budding branches all impatient for the Spring, a lover and his mistress were murmuring fond language to each other. In the soft twilight blushed the maiden, less in bashfulness than in her own soul's emotion,—her countenance displaying all the magic beauty not only of feature but of feeling ; and she raised her large blue eyes in the dewy light of a sweet enthusiasm to the skies, as the handsome youth by her side pressed her fair hand and said, " We must now part until to-morrow, darling of my soul ! How calmly has this day, with all its life and brightness, passed away into the vast tomb of eternity ! It is gone without leaving a regret on our minds,—gone, too, without clouds in the heavens or mists upon the earth—most beautiful even at the moment of its parting. To-morrow, beloved one, will unite us again in your parents' cot— and renewed happiness——"

The youth stopped—and the maiden clung to him in speechless terror ; for an ominous sound, as of a rushing animal—and then a terrific howl, burst upon their ears.

No time had they for flight—not a moment even to collect their scattered thoughts.

The infuriate wolf came bounding over the green sward : the youth uttered a wild and fearful cry—a scream of agony burst from the lips of the maiden as she was dashed from her lover's arms—and in another moment the monster had swept by.

But what misery—what desolation had his passage wrought. Though unhurt by his glistening fangs— though unwounded by his sharp claws,—yet the maiden —an instant before so enchanting in her beauty, so happy in her love—lay stretched on the cold turf, the chords of life snapped suddenly by that transition from perfect bliss to the most appalling terror !

And still the wolf rushed madly—wildly on.

    *   *   *   *   *   *

      *   *   *   *   *

It was an hour past sunrise ; and from a grove in the immediate neighbourhood of Leghorn, a man came forth.

His countenance, though wondrously handsome, was deadly pale,—traces of mental horror and anguish remained on those classically chiselled features and in those fine, eloquent eyes.

His garments were soiled, blood-stained, and torn.

This man was Fernand Wagner.

He entered the city of Leghorn, and purchased a change of attire, for which he paid from a purse well filled with gold. He then repaired to a hostel, or public tavern, where he performed the duties of the toilette, and obtained the refreshment of which he appeared to stand so much in need.

By this time his countenance was again composed ; and the change which new attire and copious ablution had made in his appearance, was so great that no one who had seen him issue from the grove and beheld him now, would have believed in the identity of person.

Quitting the hostel, he repaired to the port, where he instituted inquiries relative to a particular vessel which he described, and which had sailed from Leghorn upwards of a fortnight previously.

He soon obtained the information which he sought ; and an old sailor, to whom he had addressed himself, not only hinted that the vessel in question was suspected, when in the harbour, to be of piratical character, but also declared that he himself had seen a lady conveyed on board during the night preceding the departure of the ship. Farther inquiries convinced Wagner that the lady spoken of had been carried by force, and against her will, to the corsair-vessel; and he was now certain that the Demon had not deceived him,—that he had indeed obtained a trace of his lost Nisida!

His mind was immediately resolved how to act; and his measures were as speedily taken.

Guided by the advice of the old sailor from whom he had gleaned the information he sought, he was enabled to purchase a fine vessel and equip her for sea within the space of a few days. He lavished his gold with no niggard hand—and gold is a wondrous talisman to remove obstacles and facilitiate human designs.

In a word, on the sixth morning after his arrival at Leghorn, Fernand Wagner embarked on board his ship, which was manned with a gallant crew, and carried ten pieces of ordnance.

A favouring breeze prevailed at the time; and the gallant bark set sail for the Levant.

CHAPTER XL.

WAGNER IN SEARCH OF NISIDA.

THE reader may perhaps be surprised that Fernand Wagner should have been venturous enough to entrust himself to the possibilities of a protracted voyage, since every month his form must undergo a frightful change—a destiny which he naturally endeavoured to shroud in the profoundest secrecy.

But it must be recollected that the Mediterranean is dotted with numerous islands; and he knew that, however changeable or adverse the winds might be, it would always prove an easy matter to make such arrangements as to enable him to gain some port a few days previously to the close of the month.

Moreover, so strong—so intense was his love for Nisida, that, even without the prospect afforded by this calculation, he would have dared all perils—incurred all risks—opposed himself to all hostile chances, rather than have remained inactive while he believed her to be in the power of a desperate—ruthless bandit.

For, oh! ever present to his mind was the image of the lost fair one;—by day, when the sun lighted up with smiles the dancing waves over which his vessel bounded merrily—merrily; and by night, when the moon shone like a silver lamp amidst the curtains of heaven's pavilion.

His was not the love which knows only passionate impulses; it was a constant, unvarying—tender sentiment; far—far more pure, and therefore more permanent, than the ardent and burning love which Nisida felt for him. His was not the love which possession could satiate and enjoyment cool down: it was a feeling that had gained a soft, yet irresistible empire over his heart.

And this love of his was nurtured and sustained by the most generous thoughts. He pictured to himself the happiness he should experience in becoming the constant companion of one whose loss of hearing and of speech cut her off as it were from that communion with the world which is so grateful to her sex:—he imagined to himself, with all the fond idolatry of sincere affection, how melodiously soft—how tremulously clear would be her voice, were it restored to her, and were it first used to articulate the delicious language of love. And then he thought how enchanting—how fascinating—how fraught with witching charms would be the conversation of a being endowed with so glorious an intellect,—were she able to employ the faculty of speech.

Thus did her very imperfections constitute a ravishing theme for his meditations; and the more he indulged in dreams like these, the more resolute did he become never to rest until he had discovered and rescued her.

Seven days had elapsed since the ship sailed from Leghorn; and Sicily had already been passed by, when the heavens grew overclouded, and everything portended a storm.

The captain, whom Wagner had placed in charge of his vessel, adopted all the precautions necessary to encounter the approaching tempest; and soon after the sun went down on the seventh night, a hurricane swept the surface of the Mediterranean.

The ship bent to the fury of the gust—her very yards were deep in the water. But when the rage of that dreadful squall subsided, the gallant bark righted again, and bounded triumphantly over the foaming waves.

A night profoundly dark set in; but the white crests of the billows were visible through that dense obscurity; while the tempest rapidly increased in violence, and all the dread voices of the storm—the thunder in the heavens, the roaring of the sea, and the gushing sounds of the gale—proclaimed the fierceness of the elemental war.

The wind blew not with that steadiness which the skill of the sailor and the capacity of the noble ship were competent to meet; but in long and frequent gusts of intermittent fury.

Now rose the gallant bark on the waves, as if towering towards the starless sky in the utter blackness of which the masts were lost: then it sank down into the abyss, the foam of the boiling billows glistening far above, on all sides amidst the obscurity.

What strange and appalling noises are heard on board a ship labouring in a storm,—the cracking of timbers—the creaking of elastic planks—the rattling of the cordage—the flapping of fragments of sails—the falling of spars—the rolling of casks, got loose—and at times a tremendous crash throughout the vessel, as if the whole frame-work were giving way and the very sides collapsing!

And amidst those various noises and the dread sounds of the storm, the voices of the sailors were heard,—not in prayer nor subdued by terror, but echoing the orders issued by the captain, who did not despair of guiding—nay, fighting, as it were, the ship through the tumultuous billows and against the terrific blast.

Again a tremendous hurricane swept over the deep: it passed—but not a spar remained to the dismantled bark. The tapering masts—the long graceful yards were gone, the cordage having snapped at every point where its support was needed,—snapped by the fury of the tempest as if wantonly cut by a sharp knife.

The boats,—the crew's last alternative of hope—had likewise disappeared.

The ship was now completely at the mercy of the wild raging of the winds and the fury of the troubled waters: it no longer obeyed its helm—and there were twenty men separated, all save *one*, from death only by a few planks and a few nails!

The sea now broke so frequently over the vessel, that the pumps could scarcely keep her afloat: and at length while it was yet dark, though verging towards the dawn, the sailors abandoned their task of working at those pumps. Vainly did the captain endeavour to exercise his authority—vainly did Wagner hold out menaces and promises by turns:—death seemed imminent—and yet these men, who felt that they were hovering on the verge of destruction, flew madly to the wine-stores.

Then commenced a scene of the wildest disorder amidst those desperate men; and even the captain himself, perceiving that they could laugh and shout—and sing in the delirium of intoxication, rushed from the side of Wagner, and joined the rest.

It was dreadful to hear the obscene jests—the ribald song—and the reckless execration sent forth from the cabin, as if in answer to the awful voices in which Nature was then speaking to the world.

But scarcely had a faint—faint gleam appeared in the orient sky,—not quite a gleam, but a mitigation of the intenseness of the night,—when a tremendous wave—a colossus amongst giants—broke over the ill-fated ship—while a terrible crash of timbers was for a moment heard in unison with the appalling din of the welming billows.

Wagner was the only soul on deck at that instant; but the fury of the waters tore him away from the bulwark to which he had been clinging—and he became insensible.

* * * * * *

When he awoke from the stupor into which he had been plunged, it was still dusk, and the roar of the ocean sounded in his ears with deafening din.

But he was on land—though where he knew not.

Rising from the sand on which he had been cast, he beheld the billows breaking on the shore at the distance of only a few paces; and he retreated farther from their reach.

Then he sat down, with his face towards the east, anxiously awaiting the appearance of the morn, that he might ascertain the nature and the aspect of the land on which he had been cast.

By degrees the glimmering which had already subdued the blackness of night into the less profound obscurity of duskiness, grew stronger; and a yellow lustre, as of a far-distant conflagration, seemed to struggle against a thick fog. Then a faint roseate streak tinged the eastern horizon—growing gradually deeper in hue, and spreading higher and wider—the harbinger of sunrise; while, simultaneously, the features of the land on which Wagner was thrown began to develop themselves like spectres stealing out of complete obscurity; till at length the orient lustre was caught successively by a thousand lofty pinnacles of rock;—and finally the majestic orb itself appeared, lightning up a series of verdant plains—delicious groves—glittering lakes—pellucid streams,—as well as the still turbulent ocean and the far-off mountains which had first peeped from amidst the darkness.

Fair and delightful was the scene that thus developed itself to the eyes of Wagner: but, as his glance swept the country which rose amphitheatrically from the shore, not a vestige of the presence of man could he behold. No smoke curled from amidst the groves—no church-spire peeped above the trees: nor had the wildness of nature been disturbed by artificial culture.

He turned towards the ocean: there was not a trace of his vessel to be seen. But farther along the sand lay a dark object, which he approached with a shudder—for he instinctively divined what it was.

Nor was he mistaken: it was the swollen and livid corpse of one of the sailors of the lost ship!

Wagner's first impulse was to turn away in disgust; but a better feeling almost immediately animated him; and hastening to the nearest grove, he broke off a large bough, with which he hollowed a grave in the sand.

He deposited the corpse in the hole, threw back the sand which he had displaced, and thus completed his Christian task.

During his visit to the grove he had observed with delight that the trees were laden with fruits, and he now returned thither to refresh himself by means of the banquet thus bountifully supplied by nature.

Having terminated his repast, he walked farther inland. The verdant slopes stretched up before him, variegated with flowers, and glittering with morning dew. As he advanced, the development of all the features of that land,—lakes and woods—hills undulating like the sea in sunset, after hours of tempest—rivulets and crystal streams, each with the most luxurious fruits of the tropics, and valleys carpeted with the brightest green, varied with nature's own embroidery of flowers, —the development of this scene was inexpressibly beautiful, far surpassing the finest efforts of creative fancy.

Wagner seated himself on a sunny bank, and fell into a profound meditation.

At length, glancing rapidly around, he exclaimed aloud, as if in continuation of the chain of thoughts which had already occupied his mind. "Oh! if Nisida were here—here in this delicious clime, to be my companion! What happiness, what joy! Never should I regret the world from which this isle, for an isle it must be—is separated; never should I long to return to that communion with men from which we should be cut off! Here would the eyes of my Nisida cast forth rays of joy and gladness upon everything around; here would the sweetest transition of sentiment and feeling take place! Nisida should be the Island Queen; she should deck herself with these flowers which her fair hands might weave into wildly fantastic arabesques! Oh! all would be happiness—a happiness so serene, that never would the love of mortals be more truly blest! But, alas!" he added, as a dreadful thought broke rudely upon this delightful vision, "I should be compelled to reveal to her my secret—the appalling secret of my destiny—that when the period for transformation came round, she might place herself in safety——"

Wagner stopped abruptly, and rose hastily from his seat on the sunny bank.

The remembrance of his dreadful fate had spoilt one of the most delicious waking dreams in which he had ever indulged: and, dashing his hands against his forehead, he rushed wildly towards the chain of mountains that intersected the island.

But suddenly he stopped short, for on the ground before him lay the doublet of a man,—a doublet, of the fashion then prevalent in Italy.

He lifted it up, examined it—but found nothing in the pockets: then, throwing it on the ground, he stood contemplating it for some minutes.

Could it be possible that he was in some part of Italy? that the ship had been carried back to the European continent during the tempest of the night? No—it was impossible that so lovely a tract of land would remain uninhabited, if known to men.

The longer he reflected, the more he became convinced that he was on some island hitherto unknown to navigators, and on which some other shipwrecked individual had probably been cast. Why the doublet should have been discarded he could well understand, as it was thick and heavy and the heat of the sun was already intense, although it was not yet near the meridian.

Raising his eyes from the doublet which had occasioned these reflections, he happened to glance towards a knot of fruit trees at a little distance; and his attention was drawn to a large bough which hung down as if almost broken away from the main stem.

He approached the little grove; and several circumstances now confirmed his suspicion that he was not the only tenant of the island at that moment. The bough had been forcibly torn down—and very recently too: several of the fruits had been plucked off, the little sprigs to which they had originally hung still remaining and bearing evidence to the fact. But if additional proof were wanting of human presence there, it was afforded by the half-eaten fruits that were strewed about.

Wagner now searched for the traces of footsteps, but such marks were not likely to remain in the thick rich grass, which, if trampled down, would rise fresh and elastic again with the invigorating dew of a single night.

The grove, where Wagner observed the broken bough and the scattered fruits, was farther from the shore than the spot where he had found the doublet; and he reasoned that the man whoever he might be, had thrown away his garment, when overpowered by the intensity of the heat, and had then sought the shade and refreshment afforded by the grove.

He therefore concluded that he had gone inland—most probably towards the mountains, whose rocky pinnacles of every form now shone with every hue in the glorious sun-light.

Overjoyed at the idea of finding a human being in a spot which he had at first deemed totally uninhabited,—and filled with hope that the stranger might be able to give him some information relative to the geographical position of the isle, and even perhaps aid him in forming a raft by which they might together escape from that oasis of the Mediterranean,—Wagner proceeded towards the mountains.

By degrees the wondrous beauty of the scene became wilder—more imposing, but less bewitching: and when he reached the acclivities of the hills, the groves of fruits and copses of myrtles and citrons, of vines and almond shrubs, were succeeded by woods of mighty trees.

Farther on still, the forests ceased: and Fernand entered on a region of almost universal desolation—yet forming one of the sublimest spectacles that nature can afford.

The sounds of torrents, as yet concealed from his view, and resembling the murmur of ocean's waves, inspired feelings of awe; and it was now for the first time since he entered on the region of desolation, having left the clime of loveliness nearly a mile behind, that his attention was drawn to the nature of the soil, which was hard and bituminous in appearance.

The truth almost immediately struck him: there was a volcano amongst those mountains up which he was ascending; and it was the lava which had produced that desolation, and which, cold and hardened, formed the soil whereon he walked.

It was now past mid-day; and he seated himself once more to repose his limbs, wearied with the fatigues of the ascent, and overcome by the heat that was there intolerable.

At the distance of about two hundred yards on his right was a solitary tree—standing like a sign to mark the tomb of nature's vegetation. Upon this tree his eyes were fixed listlessly—and he was marvelling within himself how that single scion of the forest could have been spared when the burning lava, whenever the eruption might have taken place, had hurled down and reduced to cinders all its verdant brethren.

Suddenly his attention was more earnestly riveted upon the dense and wide-spreading foliage of that tree; for the boughs were shaken in an extraordinary manner—and something appeared to be moving about amongst the canopy of leaves.

In another minute a long, unmistakable, appalling object darted forth,—a monstrous snake,—suspending itself by the tail to one of the lower boughs, and disporting playfully with its hideous head towards the ground. Then, with a sudden coil, it drew itself back into the tree, the entire foliage of which was shaken with the horrible gambollings of the reptile,

Wagner remembered the frightful spectacle which he had beholden in Ceylon; and an awful shudder crept through his frame:—for, although he knew that he bore a charmed life, yet he shrank with loathing from the idea of having to battle with such a horrible serpent.

Starting from the ground, he rushed—flew, rather than ran, higher up the acclivity, and speedily entered on a wild scene of rugged and barren rocks;—but he cared not whither the windings of the natural path which he now pursued might lead him, since he had escaped from the vicinity and from the view of the hideous boa-constrictor gambolling in the solitary tree.

Wearied with his wanderings, and sinking beneath the oppressive heat of the sun, Wagner was rejoiced to find a cavern in the side of a rock, where he might shelter and repose himself. He entered, and lay down upon the hard soil: the sounds of the torrents, which rolled still unseen amidst the chasms towards which he had approached full near, produced a lulling influence upon him;—and in a few minutes his eyes were sealed in slumber.

When he awoke, he found himself in total darkness.

He started up—collected his scattered ideas—and advanced to the mouth of the cavern.

The sun had set:—but outside the cave an azure twilight prevailed, and the adjacent peaks of the mountains stood darkly out from the partially though faintly illuminated sky.

While Wagner was gazing long and intently upon the sublime grandeur of the scene, a strange phenomenon took place.

First a small cloud appeared on the summit of an adjacent hill: then gradually this cloud became more dense and assumed a human shape.

Oh! with what interest—what deep enthusiastic interest did Fernand contemplate that spectacle; for his well-stored mind at once suggested to him that he was now the witness of that wondrous optical delusion called the Mirage.

Some human being in the plain on the other side of that range of mountains was the subject of that sublime scene:—might it not be the individual of whom he was in search—the owner of the doublet?

But, ah! wherefore does Wagner start with surprise?

The shadow of that human being, as it gradually assumed greater density and a more defined shape,—in a word, as it was now properly developed by the refraction of twilight—wore the form of a female!

Were there, then, many inhabitants on the opposite side of the mountains? or was there only one female—she, whose reflected image he now beheld?

He knew not; but at all events the pleasure of human companionship seemed within his reach: the presence of the doublet had convinced him that there was another man upon the island—and now the Mirage showed him the semblance of a woman!

Vast—colossal—like a dense, dark, shapely cloud, stood that reflected being in the sky: for several minutes it remained thus—and though Wagner could trace no particular outline of features, yet it seemed to him as if the female were standing in a pensive attitude.

But as the twilight gradually subsided, or rather yielded to the increasing obscurity, the image was absorbed likewise in the growing gloom; until the dusky veil of night made the entire vault above of one deep, uniform, purple hue.

Then Wagner once more returned to the cavern, with the resolution of crossing the range of hills on the ensuing morn.

CHAPTER XLI.

THE ISLAND QUEEN.

Oh! how beautiful—how enchantingly beautiful seemed Nisida, as her delicate feet bore her glancingly along the sunny banks of the crystal stream, to the soft music of its waters.

How the slight drapery which she wore set off the rich undulations of that magnificent form!—how the wreaths and the garlands of fantastically woven flowers became the romantic loveliness of her person—that glowing Hebe of the south!

Holding in her fair hand a light slim wand, and moving through the delicious vale with all the self abandonment of gait and limb which feared no intrusion on her solitude, she appeared that Mediterranean Island's Queen.

What though the evening breeze, disporting with her raiment, lifted it from her glowing bosom?—she cared not: no need for sense of shame was there! What though she laid aside her vesture to disport in the sea at morn?—no furtive glance did she cast around—no haste did she make to resume her garments; for whose eye, save that of God, beheld her?

But was she happy?

Alas! there were moments when despair seized upon her soul; and, throwing herself on the yellow sand, or on some verdant bank, she would weep—oh! she would weep such bitter, bitter tears, that those who have been forced to contemplate her character with aversion, must now be compelled to pity her.

Yes: for there were times when all the loveliness of that island seemed but a hideous place of exile, an abhorrent monotony which surrounded her—grasped her—clung to her—hemmed her in, as if it were an evil spirit having life and the power to torture her.

She thought of those whom she loved—she pondered upon all the grand schemes of her existence—and she felt herself cut off from a world to which there were so many ties to bind her, and in which she had so much to do!

Then she would give way to all the anguish of her soul—an anguish that amounted to the blackest, deepest despair, when her glances wildly swept the cloudless horizon, and beheld not a sail—no! nor a speck on the ocean to engender hope.

But when this tempest of grief and passion was past, she would be angry with herself for having yielded to it; and in order to distract her thoughts from subjects of gloom, she would bound towards the groves, light as a fawn—the dazzling whiteness of her naked and polished ankles gleaming in contrasts with the verdure of the vale.

*   *   *   *   *   *
*   *   *   *   *   *

One morning—after Nisida had been many, many days in the island—she was seated on the sand, having just completed her simple toilette on emerging from the mighty bath that lay stretched in glassy stillness far as the eye could reach, when she suddenly sprung upon her feet, and threw affrighted looks around her.

Had she possessed the faculty of hearing, it would be thought that she was thus startled by the sounds of a human voice which had at that instant broken upon the solemn stillness of the isle,—a human voice emanating from a short distance behind her.

As yet she saw no one;—but in a few moments a man emerged from the nearest grove, and came slowly towards her.

He was dressed in a light jerkin, trunk-breeches, tight hose, and boots,—in all as an Italian gentleman of that day, save in respect to hat and doublet, of which he had none. Neither wore he a sword by his side, nor carried any weapons of defence; and it was evident that he approached the Island Queen with mingled curiosity and awe.

Perhaps he deemed her to be some goddess, endowed with the power and the will to punish his intrusion on her realms:—or peradventure his superstitious imagination dwelt on the tales which sailors told in those times,—how mermaids who fed on human flesh dwelt on the coasts of uninhabited islands, and assuming the most charming female forms, allured into their embrace the victims whom shipwreck cast upon their strand, and instead of lavishing on them the raptures of love, made them the prey of their ravenous maws.

Whatever were his thoughts, the man drew near with evident distrust.

But, now—why does Nisida's countenance become suddenly crimson with rage? why rushes she towards the stores which still remained piled up on the strand? and wherefore, with the rapidity of the most feverish impatience, does she hurl the weapons of defence into the sea—all save one naked sword, with which she arms herself?

Because her eagle glance—quicker than that of the man who is approaching her—has recognised *him*, ere he has ever been struck with a suspicion relative to who *she* is: and that man is Stephano Verrina.

Now, Nisida! summon all thine energies to aid thee:—for a strong—a powerful—a remorseless man, is near;—and thou art so ravishingly beautiful in thy aërial drapery and thy wreaths of flowers, that an anchorite could not view thee with indifference!

Ah! Stephano starts—stops short—advances:—the suspicion has struck him! That aquiline countenance—those brilliant, large dark eyes—that matchless raven hair—that splendid symmetrical maturity of form—and, withal, that close compression of the vermilion lips—O Nisida!—have been scanned in rapid detail by the brigand!

"Nisida!" he exclaimed: "yes—it is she!"

And he bounded towards her with outstretched arms.

But the sharp sword was presented to his chest; and the lady stood with an air of such resolute determination, that he stopped short—gazing upon her with mingled wonderment and admiration.

Heavens! he had never beheld so glorious a specimen of female loveliness as that whereon his eyes were fastened,—fastened beyond the possibility of withdrawal.

How glossy black was that hair with its diadem of white roses!—how miserably poor appeared the hues of the carnations and the pinks that formed her necklace, when in contrast with her flushing cheeks!—how dingy were the lilies at her waist when compared with her heaving breast!

The reason of the brigand reeled—his brain swam round—and for a moment it seemed to him that she was not a being of this world:—not the Nisida he had known and carried off from Italy,—but a goddess—another and yet the same in all the glory of those matchless charms which had heretofore ravished—no, maddened him!

And now the spirit of this bold and reckless man was subdued,—subdued, he knew not how nor wherefore; but still subdued by the presence of her whom he had deemed lost in the waves, but who seemed to stand before him —with flowers upon her brow and a sharp weapon in her hand—radiant, too, with loveliness of person, and terrible with the fires of hatred and indignation!

Yes! he was subdued—overawed—rendered timid as a young child in her presence; and sinking upon his knees, he exclaimed, forgetful that he was addressing Nisida the Deaf and Dumb, "Oh! fear not, I will not harm thee! But, my God! take compassion on me—spurn me not—look not with such terrible anger upon one who adores, who worships you! How is it that I tremble and quail before you—I, once so reckless, so rude! But, oh! to kiss that fair hand—to be your slave—to watch over you —to protect you,—and all this but for thy smiles in return—I should be happy—supremely happy! Remember —we are alone on this island, and I am the stronger: I might compel you by force to yield to me—to become mine: but I will not harm you—no, not a hair of your head, if you will only smile upon me! And you will require one to defend and protect you—yes, even here in this island apparently so secure and safe;—for there are terrible things in this clime, dreadful beings, far more formidable than whole hordes of savage men—monsters so appalling that not all thy courage, nor all thine energy would avail thee a single moment against them. Yes, lady—believe me when I tell thee this! For many—many days have I dwelt, a lonely being, on the other side of this isle—beyond that chain of mountains,—remaining on that shore to which the wild waves carried me on the night of the shipwreck. But I hurried away at last, I dared all the dangers of mighty precipices, of yawning chasms, and roaring torrents, the perils of yon mountains, —rather than linger on the other side. For the anaconda, lady, is the tenant of this island, the monstrous snake, the terrible boa, whose dreadful coils, if wound around that fair form of yours, would crush it into a hideous, loathsome mass!"

Stephano had spoken so rapidly, and with such fevered excitement, that he had no time to reflect whether he were not wasting his words upon a being who could not hear them: until, exhausted and breathless with the volubility of his utterance, he remembered that he was addressing himself to Nisida the Deaf and Dumb.

But haply his appealing and his suppliant posture had softened the lady; for towards the end of his long speech a change came over her countenance, and she dropped the point of her sword towards the ground.

Stephano rose, and stood gazing on her for a few moments with eyes that seemed to devour her.

His mind had suddenly recovered much of its wonted boldness and audacity. So long as Nisida seemed terrible as well as beautiful, he was subdued:—now that her eyes had ceased to dart forth lightnings, and the expression of her countenance had changed from indignation and resolute menace to pensiveness and a comparatively mournful softness, the bandit as rapidly regained the usual tone of his remorseless mind.

Yes: he stood gazing on her for a few moments, with eyes that seemed to devour her:—then, in obedience to a maddening impulse, he rushed upon her, and in an instant wrenched the sword from her grasp.

But, rapid as lightning, Nisida bounded away from him, ere he could wind his arms around her; and, fleet as the startled deer, she hastened towards the groves.

Stephano, still retaining the sword in his hand, pursued her with a celerity which was sustained by his rage that she had escaped him.

But the race was as unequal as that of a lion in chase of a roe; for Nisida seemed borne along as it were upon the very air.

Leaving the groves on her left, she dashed into the vale. Along the sunny bank of the limpid stream she sped,—on, on towards a forest that bounded the valley at the farther end, and rose amphitheatrically up towards the region of the mountains!

Stephano Verrina still pursued her—though losing ground rapidly: but still he maintained the chase.

And now the verge of the forest is nearly gained; and in its mazes Nisida hopes to be enabled to conceal herself from the ruffian whom, by a glance hastily cast behind from time to time, she ascertains to be upon her track.

But, Oh! whither art thou flying thus wildly, beauteous Nisida?—into what appalling perils art thou rushing, as it were blindly?

For there, in the tallest tree on the verge of the forest to which thou art near,—*there*, amidst the bending boughs and the quivering foliage—one of the hideous serpents which infest the higher region of the isle, is disporting— the terrible anaconda—the monstrous boa, *whose dreadful coils, if wound around that fair form of thine, would crush it into a loathsome mass!*

CHAPTER XLII.
THE TEMPTATION.—THE ANACONDA.

In the meantime Fernand Wagner was engaged in the attempt to cross the chain of mountains which intersected the island whereon the shipwreck had thrown him.

He had clambered over rugged rocks and leapt across many yawning chasms in that region of desolation,—a region which formed so remarkable a contrast with the delicious scenery which he had left behind him.

And now he reached the basis of a conical hill, the summit of which seemed to have been split into two distinct parts; and the sinuous traces of the lava-streams, now cold and hard, and black, adown its sides, convinced him that this was the volcano, from whose rent crater had poured the bituminous fluid so fatal to the vegetation of that region.

Following a circuitous and naturally formed pathway round the base, he reached the opposite side; and now for a height of three hundred feet above the level of the sea, his eyes commanded a view of a scene as fair as that behind the range of mountains.

He was now for the first time convinced of what he had all along suspected—namely, that it was indeed an island on which the storm had cast him.

But though from the eminence where he stood, his view embraced the immense range of the ocean, no speck in the horizon—no sail upon the bosom of the expanse, imparted hope to his soul.

Hunger now oppressed him; for he had eaten nothing since the noon of the preceding day, when he had plucked a few fruits in the grove on the other side of the island. He accordingly commenced a descent towards the new region which lay stretched before him, fair as—even fairer than—the one which had just greeted his eyes.

But he had not proceeded many yards amidst the defiles of the rugged rocks which Nature had piled together around the base of the volcano, when he found his way suddenly barred by a vast chasm on the verge of which the winding path stopped.

The abyss was far too wide to be crossed save by the wing of the bird; and in its unfathomable depths boiled and roared a torrent, the din of whose eddies was deafening to the ear.

Wagner retraced his way to the very base of the volcano, and entered another defile: but this also terminated on the edge of the same precipice.

Again and again did he essay the various windings of that scene of rock and crag; but with no better success than at first;—and after passing a considerable time in these fruitless attempts to find a means of descent into the plains below, he began to fear that he should be compelled to retrace his way into the region of verdure which he had quitted the day before, and which lay behind the range of mountains.

But the thought of the hideous snake which he had seen in the tree, caused a cold shudder to pass over him:

—then, in the next moment, he remembered that if the region on one side of the mountains were infested with reptiles of that terrible species, it was not probable that the forest which he beheld as it were at his feet, were free from the same source of apprehension.

Still he had hoped to find human companionship on the side of the mountains which he had so far succeeded in reaching,—the companionship of the man who had cast away the doublet, and of the woman whom he had seen in the Mirage.

And was it not strange that he had not as yet overtaken, or at least obtained a trace of, the man who thus lation?" were the words which, uttered in a mild, benignant tone, met his ears.

He turned and beheld an old man of venerable appearance, and whose beard, white as snow, stretched down to the rude leathern belt which confined the palmer's gown that he wore.

"Holy anchorite!" exclaimed Wagner,—"for such I must deem thee to be—the sound of thy voice is most welcome in this solitude, amidst the mazes of which I vainly seek to find an avenue of egress."

"Thus is it oft with the troubles and perplexities of

"HOLDING IN HER HAND A LIGHT, SLIM WAND." (See p. 71.)

occupied a portion of his thoughts? If that man were still amongst the mountains, they should probably meet: if he had succeeded in descending into the plains below, the same pathway that conducted him thither would also be open to Wagner.

Animated with these reflections, and in spite of the hunger which now sorely oppressed him, Wagner prosecuted with fresh courage his search for a means of descent into the lovely region that lay stretched before him: when he was suddenly startled by the sound of a human voice near him.

"My son, what dost thou amidst this scene of deso-

the world, my son," answered the hermit,—"that world which I have quitted for ever."

"And dost thou dwell in this desolate region?" asked Fernand.

"My cave is hard by," returned the old man. "For forty years have I lived in the heart of these mountains, descending only into the plains at long intervals, to gather the fruits that constitute my food;—and then," he added in a tone which, despite the sanctity of his appearance, struck cold and ominous to the very heart of Wagner,—"and then, too, at the risk of becoming the prey of the terrible anaconda!"

"Thou sayest, holy hermit," exclaimed Fernand, endeavouring to conquer a feeling of unaccountable aversion which he had suddenly entertained towards the old man,—"thou sayest that thy cave is hard by. In the name of mercy! I beseech thee to spare me a few fruits and a cup of water—for I am sinking with fatigue, hunger, and thirst."

"Follow me, young man," said the hermit; and he led the way to a cave opening from a narrow fissure in the rock.

The anchorite's abode was, as Wagner had expected to find it, rude and cheerless. A quantity of dry leaves were heaped in one corner—evidently forming the old man's couch; and in several small hollows made in the walls of the rock, were heaps of fruit—fresh and inviting, as if they had only just been gathered. On the ground stood a large earthen pitcher of water.

Upon this last object did thirsty Wagner lay his left hand; but, ere he raised it, he glanced hastily round the cave in search of a crucifix, in the presence of which he might sign the form of the cross with his right hand.

But, to his astonishment, the emblem of Christianity was not there; and it now struck him for the first time that the anchorite wore no beads round his waist.

"Young man, I can divine thy thoughts," said the hermit, hastily: "but drink—eat and ask a blessing presently. Thou art famished—pause not to question my motives—I will explain them fully to thee when thy body is refreshed with that pure water and those delicious fruits."

"Water shall not pass my lips, nor fruits assuage the cravings of hunger, until I know more of thee, old man!" exclaimed Wagner, a terrible suspicion flashing to his mind: and, without another instant's hesitation or delay, he made the sign of the cross.

A yell of rage and fury burst from the lips of the false anchorite, while his countenance became fearfully distorted—his eyes glared fiercely—his whole aspect changed—and in a few moments he stood confessed, in shape—attire—and features, the demon who had appeared to Fernand in the prison of Florence.

"Fiend! what wouldst thou with me?" exclaimed Wagner, startled and yet subdued by this appearance of the Evil Spirit amidst that region of desolation.

"Mortal," said the Demon, in his deepest and most sonorous tones, "I am here to place happiness—happiness ineffable, within thy reach. Nay—benot impatient: but listen to me for a few moments. 'Twas my power that conducted thy ship, amidst the fury of the storm, which *He* whose name I dare not mention raised, to the shores of this island. 'Twas my influence which yesterday, as thou wast seated on the sunny bank, filled thine imagination with those delicious thoughts of Nisida. And it was I also who, by the wonders of the Mirage, showed thee the form of the only female inhabitant of this isle. And that one female, Wagner—that woman who is now as it were within thy reach—that lovely being whose presence on this island would teach thee to have no regret for the world from which you are separated, and *whose eyes would cast forth rays of joy and gladness upon everything around*—that charming lady, who has already *decked herself with those wild flowers which her fair hands have woven into wildly fantastic arabesques*,—that being is thy Nisida—the Island Queen!"

"Fiend! you mock—you deceive me!" cried Fernand, wildly hovering between joyous hope and acute fear.

"Did I deceive thee, Wagner, when I showed thee thy Nisida in the power of the corsairs?" asked the Demon, with a smile of bitter, sardonic triumph. "I tell thee, then, that Nisida is on this island—there, in the very region into which thou wouldst descend, but to which thou wilt find no avenue save by my aid!"

"Nisida is here—on this island!" exclaimed Fernand in an ecstacy of joy.

"Yes—and Stephano, the bandit, likewise!" added the Demon. "It was his doublet which you found—it was he who slaked his thirst with the juice of the fruits which I, then invisible, beheld thee contemplate with attention."

"Stephano here also!" cried Wagner, "Oh! Nisida—to thy rescue!"

And he bounded forth from the cave, and was rushing madly down one of the tortuous defiles leading towards the chasm, when the voice of the Demon suddenly caused him to stop short.

"Fool!—insensate mortal!" said the fiend, with a derisive laugh. "How canst thou escape from these mountains? But tarry a moment—and behold thy Nisida,—behold also her persecutor!"

Thus speaking, he handed Wagner a magic telescope,

which immediately brought the most remote objects to a distance of only a few yards.

Then what a delicious scene met Fernand's eyes!

He beheld Nisida bathing in the sea—sporting like a mermaid with the wavelets,—plunging into the refreshing depths—then wringing out the water from her long raven hair,—now swimming, and diving, then wading on her feet,—unconscious that a human eye beheld her!

At length she came forth from the sea, beauteous as a Venus rising from the ocean; and her toilette commenced upon the sand.

But scarcely had she decked herself with the flowers which she had gathered early in the morning for the purpose, when she started and rose up; and then Wagner beheld a man approaching her from the nearest grove.

"That is Stephano Verrina!" murmured the Demon in his ears.

Fernand uttered a cry of dismay, and threw down the telescope.

"You may save her—save her yet!" said the Demon, speaking in a tone of unusual haste. "In a few minutes she will be in his power—he is strong and desperate: be mine—and consent to serve me—and in a moment Nisida shall be clasped in thy arms—the arms of thee, her deliverer!"

"No—no! I will save her without thine aid, dread fiend!" exclaimed Wagner, a prey to the most terrible excitement.

Then, making the sign of the cross, he rushed forward to leap the yawning chasm: his feet touched the opposite side—but he lost his balance—reeled—and fell back into the tremendous abyss,—while the Demon, again baffled, and shrinking in horror from the emblem of Christianity, disappeared with cries of rage and vexation.

Down—down fell Wagner,—turning over and over in the hideous vacancy, and clutching vainly at the stunted shrubs and dead roots which projected from the rugged sides of the chasm.

In another moment he was swallowed up by the boiling torrent: but his senses did not leave him—and he felt himself hurried along with the furious speed of the mad waters.

Thus nearly a minute passed: and then his headlong course was suddenly arrested by the boughs of a tree, which, having given way at the root, bent over into the torrent.

He clung to the boughs, as if they were arms stretched out to rescue him;—he raised himself from amidst the turbid waters—and in a few moments reached a bank which shelved upwards to the edge of a dense forest.

Precisely on the opposite or inner side there was an opening in the rocks; and Wagner's eye could trace upwards a steep but still practicable path, doubtless formed by some torrent the spring of which was now dried up amidst the mountain above,—that path reaching to the very basis of the volcano.

Thus, had circumstances permitted him to exercise his patience and institute a longer search among the defiles formed by the crags and rocks around the conical volcano, he would have discovered a means of safe egress from that region without daring the desperate leap of the chasm,—desperate even to him, although he bore a charmed life, because his limbs might have been broken against the rugged sides of the precipice.

Between the opening to the steep path just spoken of, and the shelving bank on which Wagner now stood, there was so narrow a space, that the bent tree stretched completely across the torrent:—thus any one descending from the mountains by the natural pathway, might cross, by means of the tree, to the side which Fernand had gained.

"This, then, must have been the route by which the villain Stephano emerged from the mountains," he said to himself:—"and the fiend deceived me when he declared that I could not reach the plains below without his aid."

Such were his reflections as he hurried up the shelving bank; and when he reached the summit his glance embraced a scene already described to the reader.

For, flying on wildly towards the forest, was his beauteous Nisida, scattering flowers in her whirlwind progress,—those flowers that had ere now decked her hair, her neck, and her waist.

At some distance behind her was the bandit Stephano:—with sword in hand he still maintained the chase, though breathless and ready to sink from exhaustion.

Not an instant did Wagner tarry upon the top of that bank which he had reached: but darting towards Nisida, who was now scarce fifty yards from him, he gave vent to an ejaculation of joy.

She saw him—she beheld him: and her speed was checked in an instant with the overpowering emotions of wonder and delight.

Then, as he hurried along the verge of the forest to encounter her—to fold her in his fond embrace—to protect her,—she once more sprang forward with out-stretched arms, to fly into his, which were open to receive her.

But at that instant there was a horrible rustling amidst the foliage of the huge trees beneath which she was hastening on; a monstrous snake darted down with gushing sound, and in another moment the beauteous form of Nisida was encircled by its hideous folds.

Then fled that wondrous self-command which for long years she had exercised with such amazing success:—then vanished from her mind all the strong motives which had induced her to undertake so terrible a martyrdom as that of simulating the loss of two faculties most dear and most valuable to all human beings;—and, with a cry of ineffable anguish, she exclaimed, "*Fernand! save me—save me!*"

CHAPTER XLIII.

NISIDA AND WAGNER.

OH! with what astonishment and joy would Wagner have welcomed the sound of that voice so long hushed, and now so musical even in its rending agony,—had not such an appalling incident broken the spell that for years had sealed the lips of his beloved!

But he had no time for thought—there was not a moment for reflection:—Nisida lay senseless on the ground, with the monster coiled around,—its long body hanging down from the bough to which it was suspended by the tail.

Simultaneously with the cry of anguish that had come from the lips of Nisida, exclamations of horror burst alike from Wagner and Stephano.

The latter stood transfixed as it were for a few moments—his eyes glaring wildly on the dreadful spectacle before him; then, yielding to the invincible terror which had seized upon him, he hurled away the sword—knowing not what he did in the excitement of his mind—and fled!

But the gleaming of the naked weapon in the sunbeams met Wagner's eyes, as it fell; and darting towards it, he grasped it with a firm hand—resolving also to use it with a stout heart.

Then he advanced towards the snake, which was comparatively quiescent—that portion of its long body which hung between the tree and the first coil that it had made round the beauteous form of Nisida, alone moving; and this motion was a waving kind of oscillation, like that of a bell-rope which a person holds by the end and swings gently.

But from the midst of the coils, the hideous head of the monster stood out—its eyes gleaming malignantly upon Wagner, as he approached.

Suddenly the reptile—doubtless alarmed by the flashing of the bright sword—disengaged itself like lightning from the awful embrace in which it had retained the Lady Nisida, and sprang furiously towards Fernand.

But the blow that he aimed at its head was unerring and heavy: its skull was cloven in two—and it fell on the long grass, where it writhed in horrible convulsions for some moments—although its life was gone.

Words cannot be found to describe the delirium of joy which Wagner felt, when, thus having slain the terrible anaconda, he placed his hand on Nisida's heart and felt that it beat—though languidly.

He lifted her from the ground—he carried her in his arms to the bank of the limpid stream—and he sprinkled water upon her pale cheeks.

Slowly did she recover; and when her large black eyes at length opened, she uttered a fearful shriek, and closed them again—for with returning life, the reminiscence of the awful embrace of the serpent came back also.

But Wagner murmured words of sweet assurance and consolation—of love and joy in her ears; and she felt that it was no dream, but that she was really saved!

Then winding her arms round Fernand's neck, she embraced him in speechless and still almost senseless trance; for the idea of such a happy deliverance was almost overpowering—amounting to an agony which a mortal creature could scarcely endure.

"Oh, Nisida," at length exclaimed Wagner, "was it a delusion produced by the horrors of that scene?—or did thy voice really greet mine ears ere now?"

There was a minute's profound silence—during which as they sat upon the bank of the stream, locked in a fond embrace, their eyes were fixed with fascinating gaze upon each other,—as if they could not contemplate each other too long,—he in his tenderness, and she in her passion.

"Yes, Fernand," said Nisida, breaking that deep silence at last, and speaking in a voice so mellifluously clear—so soft, so silvery, and so penetrating in its tone, that it realized all the fond ideas which her lover had conceived of what its nature would be if it ever were restored,—"yes, Fernand, dearest Fernand," she repeated, "you did indeed hear my voice—and to you never again shall I be mute!"

Wagner could not allow her time to say more;—he was almost wild with rapture! His Nisida was restored to him,—and no longer Nisida the Deaf and Dumb,—but Nisida who could hear the fond language which he addressed to her, and who could respond in the sweetest—most melting and delicious tones that ever came from woman's lips.

For a long time their hearts were too full, alike for total silence or connected conversation; and, while the world from which they were cut off was entirely forgotten, they gathered so much happiness from the few words which they did exchange, and from the tender embraces in which they indulged, and from all that they read in each other's eyes, that the emotions which they experienced might have furnished sensations for a long life!

At length—she scarcely knew how the subject began, although it might naturally have arisen of its own spontaneous suggestion,—Nisida found herself speaking of the long period of deception which she had maintained relative to her powers of speech and hearing.

"Thou lovest me well, dearest Fernand," she said, in her musical Italian tones; "and thou wouldst not create a pang in my heart? Then never—never seek to learn wherefore, when at the still tender age of fifteen I resolved upon consummating so dreadful a sacrifice as to affect deafness and dumbness. The circumstances were indeed solemnly grave and strangely important, which demanded so awful a martyrdom. But well did I weigh all the misery and all the peril that such a self-devotion was sure to entail upon me. I knew that I must exercise the most stern—the most remorseless—the most inflexible despotism over my emotions,—that I must crush as it were the very feelings of my soul,—that I must also observe a caution so unwearied and so constantly wakeful, that it would amount to a sensitiveness the most painful,—and that I must prepare myself to hear the merry jest without daring to smile, or the exciting narrative of the world's stirring events without suffering my countenance to vary a hue! Oh! I calculated—I weighed all this: and yet I was not appalled by the immensity of the task! I knew the powers of my own mind; and I did not deceive myself as to their extent. But ah! how fearful was it at first to hear the sounds of human voices, and yet dare not respond to them; how maddening at times was it to listen to conversation in which I longed to join, and yet be compelled to sit like a passionless statue! But mine was a will of iron strength —a resolution of indomitable power! Even when alone —when I knew that I should not be overheard—I never essayed the powers of my voice—I never murmured a single syllable to myself, so fearful was I lest the slightest use of the glorious gift of speech might render me weak in my purpose. And strange as it may seem to you, dearest Fernand, not even on this island did I yield to the temptation of suddenly breaking that long—that awful silence which I had imposed upon myself; no—not even in the midst of these solitudes did I abandon myself to the temptation of removing the seal from my lips, and raising my voice to heaven in answer to the sweet notes of the birds, or the melody of the rippling stream, or the murmurs of the sea. And, until this day, one human being only, save myself, was acquainted with that mighty secret for ten long years: and that man was the generous-hearted—the noble-minded Dr. Duras. He it was who aided me in my project of simulating the forlorn condition of the Deaf and Dumb:—he it was who bribed the turnkeys to admit me unquestioned to your cell in the prison of the ducal palace. And for years, perhaps, should I have retained my wondrous secret, even from *you*, dearest Fernand; for through dangers of many kinds—in circumstances of the most trying nature—have I continued firm in my purpose,—abjuring the faculty of speech even when it would have saved me from much cruel embarrassment or from actual peril. Thus, when the villain Stephano Verrina bore me away by force from my native city, I maintained the seal upon my lips—trusting to circumstances to enable me to escape from his power without being compelled to betray a secret of such infinite value and importance to myself. But when I found that I was so narrowly watched at Leghorn that flight was impossible, I seriously debated in my own mind the necessity of raising an alarm in the house where I was kept a prisoner for two whole days: and then I reflected that I was in the power of a desperate bandit and his two devoted adherents, who were capable of any atrocity to forward their designs or prevent exposure. Lastly, when I was conveyed in the dead of the night on board the corsair-ship, the streets were deserted, and the pirates with whom Stephano was leagued thronged the port, I therefore resigned myself to my fate—trusting still to circumstances, and retaining my secret. But that incident of to-day—Oh! it was enough to crush energies ten thousand times more powerful than mine: it was of so horrifying a nature as to be sufficient to loose the bands which confine the tongue of one really dumb."

And a strong shudder convulsed the entire form of Nisida, as she thus, by her own words, recalled so forcibly to mind that terrific event which had broken a spell of ten long years' duration.

Fernand pressed her to his bosom, exclaiming, "Oh! beloved Nisida, how beautiful dost thou appear to me! how soft and charming is that dear voice of thine! Let us not think of the past—at least not now;—for I also have explanations to give thee," he added, slowly and mournfully: then, in a different and again joyous tone, he said, "Let us be happy in the conviction that we are restored to each other—let this be a holiday—nay, more," he added, sinking his voice almost to a whisper;—"let it be the day on which we join our hands together in the sight of heaven. No priest will bless our union, Nisida; but we will plight our vows; and God will accord us *His* blessing!"

The lady hid her blushing—glowing countenance on his breast, and murmured in a voice melodious as the music of the stream by which they sat, "Fernand, I am thine—thine for ever!"

"And I am thine, my beauteous Nisida—thine for ever, as thou art mine!" exclaimed Wagner, lifting her head and gazing on her lovely blushing face as on a vision from heaven.

"No! she is mine!" thundered the voice of the forgotten Stephano; and in a moment the bandit flung himself upon Wagner, whom he endeavoured to hurl into the crystal but deep river.

Fernand, however, caught the arm of the brigand, and dragged him along with him into the water, while a terrific scream burst from the lips of Nisida.

Then furious was the struggle that commenced in the depths of the stream: but Stephano lay beneath Wagner, who held him down on the pebbly bottom. In another moment Nisida herself plunged into the river, with the wild hope of aiding her lover to conquer his foe, or to rescue him from the grasp which the bandit maintained upon him with the tenacity than was strengthened, rather than impaired, by the agony of suffocation.

But she rose again to the surface in an instant, by the indomitable influence of that instinct for self-preservation which no human being, when immersed in the deep water, can resist, if the art of swimming have been attained.

Again she dived to succour her lover: but her aid—even if she could have afforded any—was no longer necessary; for Fernand rose from the crystal depths, and bore his Nisida to the bank, while the corpse of the drowned bandit was carried away by the current.

Wagner and Nisida were now the sole human inhabitants of that isle—the King and Queen of the loveliest clime on which the sun shone.

Towards the sea-shore they repaired, hand in hand; and, having partaken of the fruits which they gathered in their way, they set to work to form a hut with the planks, cordage, and canvas of the wreck. It will be remembered that Nisida had saved the carpenter's tools; and thus the task became a comparatively easy one.

By the time the sun went down, a tenement was formed—rude, it is true; but still perfect enough to harbour them in a clime where the nights were warm, and where the dews prevailed only in the verdant parts of the isle.

Then with what joyous feelings did Nisida deck the walls of the hut with a tapestry of flowers, and prepare the bridal-couch with materials which she had saved from the wreck!

Softly and sweetly shone the moon that night; and as its silver rays penetrated through the crevices of the little cottage so hastily and so rudely formed, they played kissingly upon the countenances of the happy pair who had wedded each other in the sight of heaven.

CHAPTER XLIV.

ALESSANDRO FRANCATELLI.

IN order that the reader should fully understand the stirring incidents which yet remain to be told, it is necessary for us to explain certain particulars connected with Alessandro Francatelli—the brother of the beautiful Flora.

It will be recollected that this young man accompanied the Florentine Envoy to Constantinople, in the honourable capacity of Secretary, some few years previously to the commencement of our tale.

Alessandro was strikingly handsome,—tall, well-formed, and of great physical strength. His manners were pleasing—his conversation agreeable to a degree. Indeed, he had profited so well by the lessons of the excellent-hearted Father Marco, that his mind was well stored with intellectual wealth. He was moreover a finished musician, and played the violin—at that period a rare accomplishment—to perfection. In addition to all these qualifications, he was a skilful versifier, and composed the most beautiful extemporaneous poetry apparently without an effort.

But his disposition was by no means light or devoted to pursuits which worldly-minded persons would consider frivolous. For he himself was worldly-minded—keen—shrewd—far-seeing—and ambitious. He deplored the ruin which had overtaken his family—and longed—ardently longed to rebuild its fortunes, adding thereto the laurels of glory and the honours of rank.

The situation which he enjoyed in the establishment of the Florentine Envoy appeared to him the stepping-stone to the attainment of these objects; but the Embassy had not been long settled in Constantinople, when Alessandro found that his master was one who, being ignorant himself, was jealous of the talents displayed by others. Great interest had alone procured the Envoy the post which he held as Negotiator Plenipotentiary with the Ottoman Porte on behalf of the Republic of Florence; and the Turkish Reis-Effendi, or Minister of Foreign Affairs, soon perceived that the Christian Ambassador was quite incompetent to enter into the intricacies of treaties and the complex machinery of diplomacy.

But suddenly the official notes which the Envoy addressed to the Effendi began to exhibit a sagacity and an evidence of far-sighted policy which contrasted strongly with the imbecility which had previously characterized those communications. It was at that period a part of the policy of the Ottoman Porte to maintain spies in the household of all the foreign ambassadors residing in Constantinople; and through this agency the Reis-Effendi discovered that the Florentine Envoy had condescended to avail himself of the brilliant talents of his Secretary, Alessandro Francatelli, to infuse spirit into his official notes.

The Reis-Effendi was himself a shrewd and sagacious man; and he recognised in the abilities evidenced by the youthful Secretary, those elements which, if properly developed, would form a great politician. The Turkish Minister accordingly resolved to leave no stone unturned in order to entice so promising an individual into the service of the Sultan.

To accomplish this object, indirect means were at first attempted; and the secret agents of the Minister sounded Alessandro upon the subject. He listened to them at first in silence—but not unwillingly. They grew bolder and their speech became more open. He encouraged them to lay bare their aims; and they hinted to him how glorious a career might be opened to him were he to enter the service of the high and mighty Sultan, Solyman the Magnificent, who then sat upon the proud throne of the Ottoman Empire.

The more attentively Alessandro listened, the less reserved became those who were instructed to undermine his fidelity towards his master, the Florentine Envoy. They represented to him how Christians, who had abjured their creed and embraced the Moslem faith, had risen to the highest offices—even to the post of Grand Vizier, or Prime Minister of the empire.

Alessandro was completely master of his emotions: he had not studied for some years in the school of diplomacy without learning how to render the expression of his countenance such as at any moment to belie the real state of his feelings. He did not suffer the spies and agents of the Reis-Effendi to perceive how deep an impression their words had made upon him: but he said and looked enough to convince them that the topics of their discourse would receive the most serious consideration at his hands. His mind was however already made up to accept the overtures thus made to him; but he affected to hesitate—for he saw that his services were ardently longed for, and he resolved to drive as advantageous a bargain as possible.

flashed through the two holes which were formed in the veil so as to permit the enjoyment of the faculty of sight, were gloriously brilliant, yet black as jet. Once, too, when the lady raised her delicate white hand, sparkling with jewels, to arrange the folds of that hated veil, Alessandro caught a rapid—evanescent glimpse of a neck as white as snow.

The little procession stopped at the door of a merchant's shop in the bazaar; the slaves assisted the lady to dismount, and she entered the warehouse followed by her dependants, the mule being left in charge of one of the numerous porters who thronged in the bezestein

AND HE BOUNDED TOWARDS HER WITH OUTSTRETCHED ARMS." (See p. 72.)

At length an incident occurred which hastened his decision.

He was one afternoon lounging through the principal bezestein, or bazaar, when he was struck by the elegant form, imposing air, and rich apparel of a lady who rode slowly along upon a mule, attended by four female slaves on foot. The outlines of her figure shaped the most admirable symmetry he had ever beheld; and though her countenance was concealed by a thick veil, in accordance with the custom of the East, yet he seemed to have been impressed with an instinctive conviction that the face beneath that invidious covering was eminently beautiful. Moreover, the eyes whose glances

Alessandro lingered near the door; and he beheld the merchant displaying various pieces of rich brocade before the eyes of the lady, who, however, scrupulously retained the dense veil over her countenance. Having made her purchases, which were taken charge of by one of the slaves, the lady came forth again; and Alessandro, forgetting that his lingering near now amounted almost to an act of rudeness, was chained to the spot—lost in admiration of her elegant gesture, her graceful yet dignified carriage, and exquisite contours of her perfect shape. Her feet and ankles, appearing beneath the full trousers, that were gathered in just at the commencement of the swell of the leg, were small and beautifully shaped; and so light was her tread, that she scarcely seemed to touch the ground upon which she walked.

As the lady issued from the door of the merchant's shop, she cast a rapid but inquiring look towards Alessandro, though whether in anger or curiosity he was unable to determine; for the eyes only could he see—and it was impossible for him to read the meaning of the glances they sent forth, when unassisted by a view of the general expression worn by her countenance at the same time.

Accident however favoured him far more than he could have possibly anticipated. At the very moment when the lady's head was turned towards him, she tripped over the cordage of a bale of goods that had shortly before been opened beneath the painted awning over the front of the shop,—and she would have fallen had not Alessandro sprung forward and caught her in his arms.

She uttered a faint scream—for her veil had shifted aside from its proper position; and her countenance was thus revealed to a man—and that man evidently a Christian.

Instantly recovering her self-possession, she readjusted her veil—gave a gentle but graceful inclination of the head towards Alessandro—mounted her mule by the assistance of the slaves—and rode away at a somewhat hasty pace.

Alessandro stood gazing after her until she turned the angle of the nearest street; and it struck him that her glance was for an instant cast rapidly back towards him, ere she disappeared from his view.

And no wonder that he stood thus rooted to the spot, following her with his eyes;—for the countenance which accident had revealed to him was already impressed upon his heart. It was one of those lovely Georgian faces, oval in shape, and with a complexion formed of milk and roses, which have at all times been prized in the East as the very perfection of female beauty,—a face, which, without intellectual expression, possesses an ineffable witchery and all the charms calculated to fascinate the beholder. The eyes were black as jet—the hair of a dark auburn, and luxuriantly rich in its massive beauty: the lips were of bright vermilion—and between them were two rows of pearl, small and even. The forehead was high and broad, and white as marble, with the delicate blue veins visible through the transparent complexion.

Alessandro was ravished as he reflected on the wondrous beauty thus for a moment revealed to him; but his raptures speedily changed to positive grief when he thought how improbable it was that this fair creature would ever cross his path again.

He entered the warehouse, made a small purchase, and inquired casually of the Turkish merchant if he knew who the lady was. The reply was in the negative; but the merchant informed Alessandro that he had no doubt the lady was of some rank, from the profound respect with which her slaves treated her, and from the readiness with which she paid the prices demanded of her for the goods she had purchased, Turkish ladies generally being notorious for their disposition to drive a hard bargain with traders.

Alessandro returned to the suburb of Pera, in which the mansion of the Florentine Embassy was situate,—his mind full of the beautiful creature whose countenance he had seen for a moment, and whose soft form he had also for a moment—a single moment, held in his arms. He could not apply himself to the duties of his office, but feigned indisposition and retired to the privacy of his own apartment. And never did that chamber seem so lonely—so cold—so cheerless. He could not sit down —and he grew only the more restless by pacing backwards and forwards. His entire disposition appeared to have become suddenly changed: he felt that the world now contained something the possession of which was positively necessary to his happiness. One sole idea absorbed all his thoughts: the most lovely countenance which in his estimation he had ever seen, was so indelibly reflected in the mirror of his mind, that his imagination could contemplate naught besides.

He knew not that whenever he went abroad he was watched by one of the spies of the Reis-Effendi; and he was therefore surprised when, on the following day, that secret agent of the Minister whispered in his ear, "Christian, thou lovest!—and it depends on thyself whether thou wilt be loved in return!"

Alessandro was stupefied at these words. His secret was known—or at least suspected. He questioned the individual who had thus addressed him; and he found that the incident of the preceding day was indeed more

than suspected—it was known. He besought to know who the lady was; but the spy would not, or could not satisfy him. He however promised that he would endeavour to ascertain a point in which Alessandro appeared to be so deeply interested.

The intriguing spirit of Turkish dependants is notorious: the reader will not therefore be surprised when we state that in a few days the spy made his appearance in Alessandro's presence with a countenance denoting joyous tidings. The young Italian was impatient to learn the result of the agent's inquiries.

"I know not who the lady is," was the reply; "but this much I have to impart to you, signor, —that she did not behold you the other day with indifference—that she is grateful for the attention which you displayed in offering your aid to save her from perhaps a serious accident—and that she will grant you a few moments' interview this evening, provided you assent to certain conditions to be imposed upon you, respecting the preliminary arrangements for your meeting."

"Name them! name them!" exclaimed Alessandro, with wild joy, and almost doubting whether he were not in the midst of a delicious dream.

"That you consent to be blindfolded while being conducted into her presence,—that you maintain the most profound silence while with those who will guide you to her abode,—and that you return from the interview under the same circumstances of precaution."

"I should be unworthy the interest which she deigns to manifest in my behalf, were I to refuse compliance with those terms," answered Alessandro.

"An hour after sunset," said the spy, "you will meet me at the gate of the Mosque of Selimya:"—and with these words he hurried away, leaving the young Florentine in a state of excited hope, amounting almost to a delirium of joy.

Alessandro was well aware that adventures, such as the one in which he found himself suddenly involved, were by no means uncommon in the East, and that ladies of the most unimpeachable virtue as well as of the highest rank, frequently accorded interviews of this private nature to those men who were fortunate enough to merit their attention,—such visits being the first step towards matrimonial connexions. But then he remembered that he was a Christian, and the fair object of his devotion was most probably of the Moslem faith. What, then, would be the result? Was some wealthy lady of high rank about to abandon her creed for his sake? or would the sacrifice of his faith be required as the only condition on which his complete happiness might be achieved?

He knew not—he cared but little; it was sufficient for him that he was to meet the charming being whose image had never once quitted his mind, from the first moment that he had seen her in the bezestein!

Even before the appointed hour, was Alessandro pacing the square in front of the splendid temple which the Sultan Selim, the conqueror of Egypt, had erected, and which bore his imperial name. At length the agent, for whom he waited, made his appearance. This man, though actually a Turkish dependant in the service of the Florentine Envoy, was, as before stated, neither more nor less than one of the numerous spies placed by the Reis-Effendi about the person of that ambassador. Alessandro was aware of this, in consequence of the offers and representations that had been made to him through the means of this agent; and though the youth suspected that the man knew more concerning the beauteous idol of his heart than he had chosen to admit, yet he had seen enough to convince him of the inutility of questioning him on that head.

It was therefore in silence that Alessandro followed his guide through several bye-streets, down to the margin of the waters of the Golden Horn. There a boat, in which two rowers and a female slave were seated, was waiting.

"Here must you be blindfolded," said the spy.

For a few moments Alessandro hesitated—in regret that he had gone so far with this adventure. He had heard fearful tales of dark deeds committed on the waters of the Bosphorus and the Golden Horn; and he himself, when roving during his leisure hours along the verdant banks of those waters, had seen the livid corse float by —with the tale-telling bow-string fastened round the neck.

The spy seemed to divine his thoughts.

"You hesitate, signor," he said: "then let us retrace our way. But remember," he added in a low tone, "that were treachery intended, it would be as easy to perform the deed where you now stand, as on the bosom of that star-lit gulf."

Alessandro hesitated no longer, but suffered himself to be completely hooded in a cap which the spy drew over his countenance. He was then conducted into the boat and guided to a seat next to the female slave. The spy leapt upon the strand—the boatmen plied their oars—and the skiff shot away from the bank, no one uttering a word.

CHAPTER XLV.

THE LADY OF CONSTANTINOPLE.

FOR upwards of half-an-hour did the boat skim the surface of the Golden Horn, the dip of the oars in the water and the rippling around the sharp prow alone breaking the solemn silence of the night.

At length the skiff stopped; and the female slave took Alessandro's hand, whispering in a low tone, "I will serve as thy guide, Christian; but speak not till thou hast permission."

She then led him from the boat, up a flight of steps, and through a garden—for he occasionally came in contact with the outstretching branches of shrubs, and there was moreover a delicious odour of flowers, as he proceeded in the total darkness of his blindfolding.

At the expiration of ten minutes, the guide stopped; and Alessandro heard a key turn in a lock.

"Enter there," said the slave, pushing him gently forward, and speaking in a low tone. "Take off the cap—attire yourself in the raiment you will find ready provided—and then pass fearlessly through the door at the farther end of the room. You will meet me again in the hall which you will thus reach."

And, without waiting for a reply, the slave closed and locked the door through which Alessandro had just passed.

Hastily did he remove the cap, which had indeed almost suffocated him; and he now found himself in a small apartment, elegantly furnished in the most luxurious oriental fashion, and brilliantly lighted. A table, spread with confectionery, cates, fruits, sherbet, and even wines,—though the fermented juice of the grape be expressly forbidden by the laws of the Prophet Mohammed,—occupied the centre of the room. Around the walls were the continuous sofas, or ottomans, so conducive to the enjoyment of a voluptuous indolence; the floor was spread with a carpet so thick that the feet sank into the silky texture, as into newly fallen snow; and whichever way he turned, Alessandro beheld his form reflected in vast mirrors set in magnificent frames. There were no windows on any side of this apartment; but there was a cupola, fitted with stained glass, on the roof; and Alessandro judged that he was in one of those voluptuous Kiosks usually found in the gardens of wealthy Turks.

Precisely as the slave had informed him, he found an elegant suit of Moslem garments set out on the sofa for his use; and he hastened to exchange his Italian costume for the oriental raiment. As he thus attired himself, it was necessary to contemplate himself in the mirror facing him, so as properly to adjust clothes to which he was totally unaccustomed; and it struck him that the garb of the infidel became him better than that of the Christian.

He did not, however, waste time in the details of his strange toilette; but as soon as it was completed, opened the door at the farther end of the room, in pursuance of the instructions he had received.

Alessandro now found himself in a large marble hall, from which several flights of stairs led to the apartments above. The place was refulgent with the light of numerous chandeliers, the glare of which was enhanced by the vast mirrors attached to the walls and the crystal pillars that supported the roof.

Not a human being met Alessandro's eyes; and he began to fear either that he had mistaken the directions he had received, or that some treachery was intended, when a door opened, and the female slave, wrapped in her veil, made her appearance.

Placing her forefinger upon that part of the veil which covered her lips, to enjoin silence, she led the way up the nearest staircase, Alessandro following her with a heart beating audibly. They reached a door at which a negro slave was stationed.

"The Hakim,"* said Alessandro's guide, laconically

---

* The Physician.

addressing herself to the negro, who bowed in silence and threw open the door.

The female slave conducted the pretended physician into a small but elegantly furnished ante-room, in which there were several other dependants of her own sex.

A door at the farther end was opened—Alessandro passed through into another, larger, and still more magnificently appointed room,—the door closed behind him, and he found himself alone with the idol of his adoration.

Half-seated—half-lying upon cushions of scarlet brocade, the glossy bright hue of which was mellowed by the muslin spread over it, appeared the beauteous creature whose image was so faithfully delineated in his memory. She was attired in the graceful and becoming dualma—a purple vest which set close to her form with a species of elasticity shaped itself so as to develop every contour. But, in accordance with the custom of the clime and age the dualma was open at the bosom, sloping from each lovely white shoulder to the waist, where the two folds joining, formed an angle at which the purple vest was fastened by a diamond worth a monarch's ransom. The sleeves were wide, but short—scarcely reaching to the elbow, and leaving all the lower part of the snowy arms completely bare. Her ample trousers were of purple silk, covered with the finest muslin, and drawn in tight a little above the ankles, which were naked. On her feet she wore crimson slippers cut very low, and each ornamented with a diamond. Round her person, below the waist, she wore a magnificent shawl, rolled up as it were negligently so as to form a girdle or zone, and fastened in front with two large tassels of pearls. Diamond bracelets adorned her fair arms; and her head-dress consisted of a turban, or shawl of light but rich material, fastened with golden bodkins, the head of each being a pearl of the best water. Beneath this turban her rich auburn hair, glowing like gold in the light of the perfumed lamps, and amidst the blaze of diamonds which adorned her, was parted in massive bands, sweeping gracefully over her temples and gathered behind the ears, then falling in all the luxuriance of its rich clustering folds over the cushion whereon she reclined.

Her finger-nails were slightly tinged with hennah—the rosy hue the more effectually setting off the lily whiteness of her delicate hand and full, round arm. But no need had she to die the lashes of her eyes with the famous kohol so much used by oriental ladies: for those lashes were by nature formed of the deepest jet—a somewhat unusual, but beauteous contrast with the colour of her hair.

The cheeks of the lovely creature were slightly flushed —or it might have been a reflection of the scarlet brocade of the cushion on which, as we have said, she was half-seated, half-lying, when Alessandro appeared in her presence.

For a few moments the young Italian was so dazzled by her beauty—so bewildered by the appearance of that lady whose richness of attire seemed to denote the rank of Sultana, that he remained rooted to the spot, uncertain whether to advance—to retire—or to fall upon his knees before her.

But in an encouraging tone, and in a voice musical as a silver bell, the lady said, "Approach, Christian!"— and she pointed to a low ottoman within a few paces of the sofa which she herself occupied.

Alessandro now recovered his presence of mind; and no longer embarrassed and awkward, but with graceful ease and yet profound respect, he took the seat indicated.

"Beauteous lady," he said, "how can I ever demonstrate the gratitude—the illimitable boundless gratitude which fills my heart, for the joy—the truly elysian delight afforded me by this meeting?"

"You speak our language well, Christian," observed the lady, smiling faintly at the compliment conveyed by the words of Alessandro, but evading a direct reply.

"I have for some years past been in the service of the Florentine Envoy, lady," was the answer; "and the position which I occupy at the Palace of the Embassy has led me to study the beauteous language of this clime, and to master its difficulties. But never—never did that language sound so soft and musical upon my ears as now when flowing from those sweet lips of thine."

"The Moslem maiden dares not listen to the flattery of the Infidel," said the beauteous stranger, in a serious but not severe tone. "Listen to me, Christian, with attention—for our meeting must not be prolonged many minutes. To say that I beheld thee with indifference when we first encountered each other in the bazaar, were to utter a falsehood, which I scorn: to admit that I can love thee—and love thee well," she added, her voice slightly trembling, "is an avowal which I do not blush to make. But never can the Moslem maiden bestow her hand on the Infidel. If thou lovest me—if thou wouldst prove thyself worthy of that affection which my heart·is inclined to bestow upon thee, thou wilt renounce the creed of thy forefathers, and embrace the Mussulman faith. Nor is this all that I require of thee, or that thou must achieve to win me. Become a True Believer—acknowledge that Allah is God and Mohammed is his Prophet—and a bright and glorious destiny will await thee. For, though thou wilt depart hence without learning my name—nor who I may be—nor the place to which you have been brought to meet me, though we shall behold each other no more until thou hast rendered thyself worthy of my hand, yet shall I ever be mindful of thee, my loved one! An unseen—an unknown influence will attend thee: thy slightest wishes will be anticipated and fulfilled in a manner for which thou wilt vainly seek to account,—and, as thou provest thy talents or thy valour, so will promotion open its doors to thee with such rapidity that thou wilt strain every nerve to rise to the highest offices in the State,—for then only mayst thou hope to receive my hand, and behold the elucidation of the mystery which up to that date will envelope thy destinies."

While the lady was thus speaking, a fearful struggle took place in the breast of Alessandro,—for the renunciation of his creed—a creed in which he must ever in his heart continue to believe, though ostensibly he might abjure it—such renunciation was an appalling step to contemplate. Then to his mind also came the images of those whom he loved, and who were far away in Italy—his aunt who had been so kind to him, his sister whom he knew to be so proud of him, and Father Marco, who manifested such deep interest in his behalf. But on his ears continued to flow the honied words and the musical tones of the charming temptress; and, as she gradually developed to his imagination the glorious destinies upon which he might enter, offering herself as the eventual prize to be gained by a career certain to be pushed on successfully through the medium of a powerful though mysterious influence,—Florence, relatives, and friends became as secondary considerations in his mind—and by the time the lady brought her long address to a conclusion—that address which had grown more impassioned and tender as she proceeded—Alessandro threw himself at her feet, exclaiming, "Lovely houri that thou art—beauteous as the maidens that dwell in the Paradise of thy Prophet—I am thine, I am thine!"

The lady extended her right hand, which he took and pressed in rapture to his lips.

But, the next moment, she rose lightly to her feet, and assuming a demeanour befitting a royal Sultana, said in a sweet though impressive tone, "We must now part—thou to enter on thy career of fame—I to set in motion every spring within my reach to advance thee to the pinnacle of glory and power! Henceforth thy name is *Ibrahim!* Go, then, my Ibrahim, and throw thyself at the feet of the Reis-Effendi; and that great Minister will forthwith present thee to Piri-Pacha, the Grand Vizier. Toil diligently—labour arduously—and the rest concerns me. Go, then, my Ibrahim, I say,—and enter on the path which will lead thee to the summit of fame and power!"

She extended her arms towards him—he snatched her to his breast, and covered her cheeks with kisses. In that paradise of charms he could have revelled for ever; but the tender caresses lasted not beyond a few moments: for the lady tore herself away from his embrace, and hurried into an adjacent apartment.

Alessandro—or rather the renegade Ibrahim—passed into the ante-room where his guide, the female slave, awaited his return. She conducted him back to the hall, and advanced towards the door of the voluptuous Kiosk where he had changed his raiment.

"Goest thou forth a Christian still, or a True Believer?" she asked, turning suddenly round.

"As a Mussulman," answered the renegade, while his heart sank within him, and remorse already commenced its torture.

"Then thou hast no further need of the Christian garb," said the slave. "Await me here."

She entered the Kiosk, and returned in a few moments with the cap, which, in obedience to her directions, he once more drew on his head and over his countenance. The slave then led him into the garden, which they

threaded in profound silence. At length they reached the steps leading down to the water; and the slave accompanied him into the boat, which immediately shot away from the bank.

Alessandro had now ample time for calm reflection. The excitement of the hurried incidents of the evening was nearly over; and though his breast was still occupied with the image of his beautiful Unknown, and with the brilliant prospects which she had opened to his view, he nevertheless shrank from the foul deed of apostacy which he had vowed to perpetrate. But we have already said that he was essentially worldly-minded, and, as he felt convinced that the petty jealousy of the Florentine Envoy would prevent him from rising higher in the diplomatic hierarchy than the post of Secretary, he by degrees managed to console himself for his renegadism on the score that it was the necessary—the indispensable stepping-stone to the gratification of his ambition.

Thus by the time the boat touched the landing-place where he had at first entered it, he had succeeded to some extent in subduing the pangs of remorse.

The female slave now bade him remove the cap from his face, and resume his turban. A few moments sufficed to make this change; and he was about to step on shore, when the woman caught him by the sleeve of his caftan, and, thrusting a small case of sandal-wood into his hand, said, "She who you saw ere now, commanded me to give thee this."

The slave pushed him gently towards the bank: he obeyed the impulse and landed—she remaining in the boat, which instantly darted away again, most probably to convey her back to the abode of her charming mistress.

On the top of the bank the renegade was accosted by the spy whom he had left there when he embarked in the skiff.

"Allah and the Prophet be praised!" exclaimed the man, surveying Alessandro attentively by the light of the lovely moon: "thou art now numbered amongst the Faithful!"

The apostate bit his lips to keep down the sigh of remorse which rose to them; and his guide, without uttering another word, led the way to the palace of the Reis-Effendi. There Alessandro—or Ibrahim, as we must henceforth call him—was lodged in a splendid apartment, and had two slaves appointed to wait upon him.

He, however, hastily dismissed them, and, when alone, opened the case that had been put into his hands by the female slave.

It contained a varied assortment of jewellery and precious stones, constituting a treasure of immense value.

But, oh! how utterly worthless—how miserably insignificant, were the diamonds in that case and even the bright eyes of her whose image was in his heart,—how dim, too, was all the prospective glory of those brilliant destinies opened to his view,—when compared with that jewel beyond all price, from the sphere of whose supernal lustre he had wantonly strayed,—the jewel—the inestimable jewel of the Christian faith!

CHAPTER XLVI.

THE APOSTATE IBRAHIM.

CONSTANTINOPLE, like haughty Rome, is built on seven hills—the houses being so disposed that they do not intercept the view commanded by each on the amphitheatrical acclivities. But the streets are narrow, crooked, and uneven; and the grand effects of the numerous stately mosques and noble edifices are subdued, or in many cases altogether lost, either by the insignificant width of the thoroughfares in which they stand, or by the contiguity of mean and miserable wooden tenements.

The mosque of Saint Sophia, once a Christian church, with its magnificent portico, supported by marble columns, its nine vast folding doors, adorned with bas-reliefs, and its stupendous dome, a hundred and twenty feet in diameter;—the mosque of the Sultan Solyman, forming an exact square with four noble towers at the angles, and with its huge cupola in the midst;—the mosque of the Sultan Ahmed, with its numerous domes, its tall minarets, and its tall colonnades supported by marble pillars; and the mosque of the Sultana Valida, or Queen Mother of Mohammed the Fourth, excelling all other Mussulman churches in the delicacy of its architecture and the beauty of its columns of marble and jasper, supplied by the ruins of Troy,—these are the most remarkable temples in the Ottoman Empire.

The Grand Bezestein, or Exchange, is likewise a magnificent structure,—consisting of a spacious hall of circular form, built of free-stone, and surrounded by shops displaying the richest commodities of oriental commerce.

In the Ladies' Bazaar there is a marble column of extraordinary height, and on the sides of which, from the foot to the crown are represented in admirable bas-reliefs, the most remarkable events which characterized the reign of the Emperor Arcadius, ere the capital of the Roman dominions of the East fell into the hands of the descendants of Osman.

number of buildings, constituting a complete town of itself. But within this enclosure dwell upwards of ten thousand persons—the entire court of the Sultan. There reside the great officers of state, the body guards, the numerous corps of bostandjis, or gardeners, and baltajis, or fire-wood purveyors,—the corps of white and black eunuchs, the pages, the mutes, the dwarfs,—the ladies of the harem, and all their numerous attendants.

There are nine gates to the palace of the Sultan. The principal one opens on the square of Saint Sophia, and is very magnificent in its architecture. It is this gate which is called the Sublime Porte—a name figuratively

"'FERNAND! SAVE ME—SAVE ME!'"   (See p. 75.)

But of all the striking edifices at Constantinople, that of the Sultan's palace, or seraglio, is the most spacious and the most magnificent.

Christian writers and readers are too apt to confound the seraglio with the harem, and to suppose that the former means the apartments belonging to the Sultan's ladies; whereas the word *seraglio*, or rather *serail*, represents the entire palace, of which the *harem*, or females' dwelling, is but a comparatively small portion.

The seraglio is a vast enclosure, occupying nearly the entire site of the ancient city of Byzantium, and embracing a circumference of five miles. It contains nine enormous courts of quadrangular form, and an immense

given to the Court of the Sultan, in all histories, records, and diplomatic transactions.

It was within the enclosure of the seraglio that Alessandro Francatelli—whom we shall henceforth call by his apostate name of Ibrahim—was lodged in the dwelling of the Reis-Effendi, or Minister of Foreign Affairs. But in the course of a few days the renegade was introduced into the presence of Piri-Pacha, the Grand Vizier—that high functionary who exercised a power almost as extensive and as despotic as that wielded by the Sultan himself.

Ibrahim, the apostate, was received by his highness Piri-Pacha at a private audience: and the young man exerted all his powers, and called to his aid all the accomplishments which he possessed to render himself agreeable to that great Minister. He discoursed in an intelligent manner upon the policy of Italy and Austria, and gave the Grand Vizier considerable information relative to the customs, resources, and condition of those countries. Then, where the Vizier touched upon lighter matters, Ibrahim showed how well he was already acquainted with the works of the most eminent Turkish poets and historians; and the art of music being mentioned, he gave the Minister a specimen of his proficiency on the violin. Piri-Pacha was charmed with the young renegade, whom he immediately took into his service as one of his private secretaries.

Not many weeks elapsed before the fame of Ibrahim's accomplishments and rare talents reached the ears of the Sultan, Solyman the Magnificent; and the young renegade was honoured with an audience of the ruler of the East. On this occasion he exerted himself to please even more triumphantly than when he was introduced to the Grand Vizier; and the Sultan commanded that henceforth Ibrahim should remain attached to his person, in the capacity of Keeper to the Archives.

We should observe that the despatches which the Florentine Envoy wrote to the government of the Republic contained but a brief and vague allusion to the apostacy of Alessandro Francatelli; merely mentioning that the youth had become a Mussulman, and entered the service of the Grand Vizier, but not stating either the name which he had adopted, nor the brilliant prospects which had so suddenly opened before him. The Florentine ambassador treated the matter thus lightly, because he was afraid of incurring the blame of his government for not having kept a more stringent watch over his subordinate, were he to attach any importance to the fact of Alessandro's apostacy. But he hoped that by merely glancing at the event as one scarcely worth special notice, the Council of Florence would be led to treat it with equal levity. Nor was the ambassador deceived in his calculations; and thus the accounts which reached Florence relative to Alessandro's renegadism—and which were not indeed communicated to the Council until some months after the occurrence of the apostacy itself—were vague and indefinite to a degree.

And had Ibrahim no remorse? did he never think of his lovely sister Flora, and of his affectionate aunt who, in his boyhood, had made such great and generous sacrifices to rear him honourably? Oh! yes;—but a more powerful idea dominated the remembrance of kindred and the attachment to home;—and that idea was ambition! Moreover, the hope of speedily achieving that greatness which was to render him eligible and worthy to possess the charming being whose powerful influence seemed to surround him with a constant halo of protection, and to smooth down all the asperities which are usually found in the career of those who rise suddenly and rise highly—this ardent longing hope not only encouraged him to put forth all his energies to make himself master of a glorious position, but also subdued to no small extent the feelings of compunction which would otherwise have been too bitter, too agonizing, to endure.

His mind was, moreover, constantly occupied. When not in attendance upon the Sultan, he devoted all his time to render himself intimately acquainted with the laws, polity, diplomatic history, resources, condition, and finances of the Ottoman Empire: he also studied the Turkish literature, and practised composition, both in prose and verse, in the language of that country which was now his own.

But think not, reader, that he was in his heart a Mussulman, or that he had extinguished the light of Christianity within his soul. No—oh! no: the more he read on the subject of the Mohammedan system of theology, the more he became convinced not only of its utter falsity, but also of its incompatibility with the progress of civilization. Nevertheless he dared not pray to the True God whom he had renounced with his lips; but there was a secret adoration, an interior worship of the Saviour, which he could not, and sought not to subdue.

Solyman the Magnificent was an enlightened prince, and a generous patron of the arts and sciences. He did not persecute the Christians, because he knew in his own heart that they were farther advanced in all humanizing ideas and institutions than the Ottomans. He was therefore delighted whenever a talented Christian embraced the Moslem faith, and entered his service; and his keen perception speedily led him to discern and appreciate all the merits and acquirements of his favourite Ibrahim.

Such was the state of things at Constantinople, when all those rapidly successive incidents, which we have already related, took place in Florence.

At this time immense preparations were being made by the Sultan for an expedition against the island of Rhodes, then in the possession of the Knights of St. John, commanded by their Grand Master, Villiers of Isle-Adam. This chieftain, aware of the danger which menaced him, despatched envoys to the courts of Rome, Genoa, Venice, and Florence, imploring those powers to send him assistance against the expected invasion of the Turks. Each of these states hastened to comply with this request; and numerous bodies of auxiliaries sailed from various ports of Italy to fight beneath the glorious banner of Villiers of Isle-Adam, one of the stanchest veteran champions of Christendom.

Thus, at the very time when Nisida and Wagner were united in the bonds of love on the island of which they were the possessors—while, too, Isaachar the Jew languished in the prisons of the Inquisition of Florence, at which city the chivalrous-hearted Manuel d'Orsini tarried to hasten on the trial and to give his testimony in favour of the Israelites—and moreover while Flora and the Countess Giulia dwelt in the strictest retirement with the young maiden's aunt—at this period, we say, a fleet of three hundred sail quitted Constantinople, under the command of the Kapitan-Pacha, or Lord High Admiral, and proceeded towards the island of Rhodes.

At the same time, Solyman the Magnificent crossed into Asia Minor, and placing himself at the head of an army of a hundred thousand men, commenced his march towards the coast facing the island, and where he intended to embark on his warlike expedition. His favourite Ibrahim accompanied him, as did also the Grand Vizier, Piri-Pacha, and the principal dignitaries of the empire.

It was in the spring of 1521,* that the Ottoman fleet received the army on board at the Cape in the Gulf of Macri, which is only separated by a very narrow strait from the island of Rhodes; and in the evening of the same day on which the troops had thus embarked, the mighty armament appeared off the capital city of the Knights of St. John.

CHAPTER XLVII.
THE SIEGE OF RHODES.

ON the following morning, salvoes of artillery throughout the fleet announced to the inhabitants and garrison of Rhodes that the Sultan was about to effect a landing with his troops.

The debarkment was not resisted; for it was protected by the cannonade which the ships directed against the walls of the city, and the Christians had no vessels capable of demonstrating any hostility against the mighty fleet commanded by the Kapitan-Pacha.

Villiers of Isle-Adam, the generalissimo of the Christian forces, had reduced to ashes all the circumjacent villages, and received their inhabitants into the city itself. But the Ottomans cared not for the waste and desolation thus created around the walls of the city; but while the artillery, alike on land and by sea, maintained an incessant fire on the town, they threw up works of defence, and established depots of provisions and ammunition.

The Sultan went in person, accompanied by Ibrahim, and attended by a numerous escort, to reconnoitre the fortifications, and inspect the position of his troops.

On the other side, Villiers of Isle-Adam distributed his forces in such a manner that the warriors of each nation defended particular gates. Thus the corps of Spaniards, French, Germans, English, Portuguese, Italians, Auvergnese, and Provencials, respectively defended eight of the gates of Rhodes; while the Lord General himself, with his body-guard, took his post at the ninth. For the knights of Rhodes comprised natives of nearly all Christian countries; and the mode in which Villiers thus allotted a gate to the defence of the warriors of each nation, gave an impulse to that emulative spirit which ever induces the soldiers of one clime to vie with those of another.

The Ottoman troops were disposed in the following

---

* To suit the plot of our tale we have been compelled to perpetrate a slight anachronism; it being really in July, 1522, when Solyman the Magnificent undertook the memorable siege of Rhodes.

manner:—Ayaz-Pacha, Beglerbeg (or governor) of Roumilia, found himself placed in front of the walls and gate defended by the French and Germans; Ahmed Pacha was opposed to the Spaniards and Auvergnese; Mustapha-Pacha had to contend with the English; Kasim, Beglerbeg of Anatolia, was to direct the attack against the bastion and gate occupied by the natives of Provence; the Grand Vizier, Piri-Pacha, was opposed to the Portuguese; and the Sultan himself undertook the assault against the defences occupied by the Italians.

For several days there was much skirmishing; but no advantage was gained by the Ottomans. Mines and counter-mines were employed on both sides; and those executed by the Christians effected terrible havoc amongst the Turks. At length, in pursuance of the advice of the renegade Ibrahim, the Sultan ordered a general assault to be made upon the city: and heralds went through the entire encampment, proclaiming the imperial command.

Tidings of this resolution were conveyed into the city by means of the Christians' spies; and while the Ottomans were preparing for the attack, Villiers of Isle-Adam was actively employed in adopting all possible means for the defence.

At day-break the general assault commenced; and the Aga (or colonel) of the Janizaries succeeded in planting his banner on the gate entrusted to the care of the Spaniards and Auvergnese. But this success was merely temporary in that quarter; for the Ottomans were beaten back with such immense slaughter, that fifteen thousand of their choicest troops were cut to pieces in the breach and ditch.

But still the assault was prosecuted in every quarter and every point; and the Christian warriors acquitted themselves nobly in the defence of the city. The women of Rhodes manifested a courage and zeal which history has loved to record as most honourable to them and to their sex. Some of them carried about bread and wine to recruit the fainting and refresh the wearied; others were ready with bandages and lint to stanch the blood which flowed from the wounded; some conveyed earth in wheel-barrows, to stop up the breaches made in the walls; and others bore along immense stones to hurl down upon the assailants.

Oh! it was a glorious, but a sad and mournful scene—that death-struggle of the valiant Christians against the barbarism of the East! And many, many touching proofs of woman's courage and daring characterized that memorable siege. Especially does this fact merit our attention:—The wife of a Christian captain, seeing her husband slain, and the enemy gaining ground rapidly, embraced her two children tenderly, made the sign of the cross upon their brows, and then, having stabbed them to the heart, threw them into the midst of a burning building near, exclaiming, "The Infidels will not now be able, my poor darlings, to wreak their vengeance upon you, alive or dead!" In another moment she seized her dead husband's sword, and plunging into the thickest of the fight, met a death worthy of a heroine.

The rain now began to fall in torrents, washing away the floods of gore which since day-break had dyed the bastions and the walls; and the assault continued as arduously as the defence was maintained with desperation.

Solyman commanded in person the division which was opposed to the gate and the fort entrusted by the Lord General of the Christians to the care of the Italian auxiliaries. But, though it was now past noon, and the Sultan had prosecuted his attack on that point with unabated vigour since the dawn, no impression had yet been made. The Italians fought with a heroism which bade defiance to the numerical superiority of their assailants: for they were led on by a young chieftain, who, beneath an effeminate exterior, possessed the soul of a lion. Clad in a complete suit of polished armour, and with crimson plumes waving from his steel helmet, to which no vizor was attached, that youthful leader threw himself into the thickest of the medley, sought the very points where danger appeared most terrible—and, alike by his example and his words, encouraged those whom he commanded to dispute every inch of ground with the Moslem assailants.

The Sultan was enraged when he beheld the success with which the Italian chieftain rallied his men again after every rebuff; and, calling to Ibrahim to keep near him, Solyman the Magnificent advanced towards the breach which his cannon had already effected in the walls defended so gallantly by the Italian auxiliaries. And now, in a few minutes, behold the Sultan himself,

nerved with wonderful energy, rushing on—scimitar in hand—and calling on the young Italian warrior to measure weapons with him. The Christian chieftain understood not the words which the Sultan uttered, but full well did he comprehend the anxiety of that great monarch to do battle with him; and the curved scimitar and the straight cross-handled sword clashed together in a moment. The young warrior knew that his opponent was the Sultan, whose imperial rank was denoted by the turban which he wore; and the hope of inflicting chastisement on the author of all the bloodshed which had taken place on the walls of Rhodes inspired the youth with a courage perfectly irresistible.

Not many minutes had this combat lasted before Solyman was thrown down in the breach, and the cross-handled sword of his conqueror was about to drink his heart's blood, when the renegade Ibrahim dashed forward from amidst the confused masses of those who were fighting around, and by a desperate effort hurled the young Italian warrior backwards.

"I owe thee my life, Ibrahim," said the Sultan, springing upon his feet. "But hurt not him who has combated so gallantly; we must respect the brave!"

The Italian chieftain had been completely stunned by his fall; he was, therefore easily made prisoner and carried off to Ibrahim's tent.

Almost at the same moment a messenger from Ahmed Pacha presented to the Sultan a letter, in which it was stated that the Grand Master, Villiers of Isle-Adam, anxious to put a stop to the fearful slaughter that was progressing, had offered to capitulate on honourable terms.

This proposition was immediately agreed to by the Sultan; and a suspension of hostilities was proclaimed around the walls. The Ottomans retired to their camp, having lost upwards of thirty thousand men during that deadly strife of a few hours; and the Christians had now leisure to ascertain the extent of their own disasters, which were proportionately appalling.

CHAPTER XLVIII.

THE PRISONER.

IN the meantime Ibrahim had ordered his prisoner, the young Italian chieftain, to be conveyed to his tent: and when the renegade's slaves had disencumbered the Christian of his armour, he began to revive.

As Ibrahim bent over him, administering restoratives, a suspicion, which had already struck him the moment he first beheld his face, grew stronger and stronger; and the apostate at length became convinced that he had seen that countenance on some former occasion.

Ordering his slaves to withdraw, Ibrahim remained alone with his prisoner, who was now able to sit up on the sofa and gaze around him.

"I understand it all!" he exclaimed, the blood rushing back to his pale cheek; "I am in the power of the barbarians!"

"Nay, call us not harsh names, brave chieftain," said Ibrahim, "seeing that we do not treat you unworthily."

"I was wrong," cried the prisoner; then, fixing his fine blue eyes upon the renegade, he added, "Were you not habited as a Moslem, I should conceive, by the purity with which you speak my native language, that you were a Christian, and an Italian."

"I can speak many languages with equal fluency," said Ibrahim, evasively, as a pang shot through his heart. "But tell me thy name, Christian—for thou art a brave man, although so young."

"In my own country," answered the youth, proudly, "I am called the Count of Riverola."

We have before stated that Ibrahim was the complete master of his emotions; but it required all his powers of self-possession to subdue them now, when the name of that family into which he was well aware his sister had entered fell upon his ears. His suspicion was well founded: he had indeed seen Francisco before this day—had seen him when he was a mere boy in Florence, for Alessandro was three or four years older than the young Count. But he had never, in his native land, exchanged a word with Francisco: he had merely occasionally seen him in public; and it was quite evident that even if Francisco had ever noticed him at that time, he did not recollect him now. Neither did Ibrahim wish the young Count to ascertain who he was; for the only thing which the renegade ever feared was the encounter of any one who had known him as a Christian, and who might justly reproach him for that apostacy which had led him to profess Mohammedanism.

"Lord Count of Riverola," said Ibrahim, after a short pause, "you shall be treated in a manner becoming your rank and your bravery. Such indeed was the command of my imperial master, the most glorious Sultan; but even had no such order been issued, my admiration of your gallant deportment in this day's strife would lead us to the same result."

"My best thanks are due for these assurances," returned Francisco. "But tell me how fares the war without?"

"The Grand Master has proffered a capitulation, which has been accepted," answered Ibrahim.

"A capitulation!" ejaculated Francisco. "Oh! it were better to die in defence of the cross than live to behold the crescent triumphant on the walls of Rhodes!"

"The motive of the Grand Master was a humane one," observed Ibrahim: "he has agreed to capitulate to put an end to the terrific slaughter that was going on."

"Doubtless the Lord General acts in accordance with the dictates of a matured wisdom!" exclaimed the Count of Riverola.

"Your lordship was the leader of the Italian auxiliaries?" said Ibrahim, interrogatively.

"Such was the honourable office entrusted to me," was the reply. "When messengers from Villiers of Isle-Adam arrived in Florence beseeching succour against this invasion, which has, alas! proved too successful, I panted for occupation to distract my mind from ever pondering on the heavy misfortunes which had overtaken me."

"Misfortunes!" exclaimed Ibrahim.

"Yes—misfortunes of such a nature that the mere thought of them is madness!" cried Francisco, in an excited tone. "First, a beauteous and amiable girl—one who, though of humble origin, was endowed with virtues and qualifications that might have fitted her to adorn a palace, and whom I fondly, devotedly loved—was snatched from me. She disappeared, I know not how! All trace of her was suddenly lost, as if the earth had swallowed her up and closed over her again! This blow was in itself terrible. But it came not alone. A few days elapsed, and my sister—my dearly beloved sister—also disappeared, and in the same mysterious manner. Not a trace of her remained—and what makes this second affliction the more crushing—the more overwhelming, is that she is deaf and dumb! Oh! heaven grant me the power to resist—to bear up against these crowning miseries! Vain were all my inquiries—useless was all the search I instituted to discover whither had gone the being whom I would have made my wife, and the sister who was ever so devoted to me! At length, driven to desperation, when weeks had passed and they returned not—goaded on to madness by bitter, bitter memories—I resolved to devote myself to the service of the cross. With my gold I raised and equipped a gallant band; and a favouring breeze wafted us from Leghorn to this island. The Grand Master received me with open arms; and, forming an estimation of my capacities far above my deserts, placed me in command of all the Italian axiliaries. You know the rest: I fought with all my energy, and your Sultan was within the grasp of death, when you rushed forward and saved him. The result is that I am your prisoner."

"So young—and yet so early acquainted with such deep affliction!" exclaimed Ibrahim. "But can you form no idea, Christian, of the cause of that double disappearance? Had your sister no attendants who could throw the least light upon the subject?" he asked, with the hope of eliciting some tidings relative to his own sister, the beauteous Flora.

"I dare not reflect thereon!" cried Francisco, the tears starting into his eyes. "For, alas! Florence has long been infested by a desperate band of lawless wretches—and, my God! I apprehend the worst—the very worst!"

Thus speaking, he rose and paced the spacious tent with agitated steps: for this conversation had awakened in his mind all the bitter thoughts and dreadful alarms which he had essayed to subdue amidst the excitement and peril of war.

A slave now entered to inform Ibrahim that the Sultan commanded his immediate presence in the imperial pavilion.

"Christian," said Ibrahim, as he rose to obey this mandate, "wilt thou pledge me thy word as a noble and a knight not to attempt an escape from this tent?"

"I pledge my word," answered Francisco, "seeing that thou thyself art so generous towards me."

Ibrahim then went forth; but he paused for a few moments outside the tent to command his slaves to serve up choice refreshments to the prisoner. He then hastened to the pavilion of the Sultan, whom he found seated upon a throne surrounded by the Beglerbegs, the Councillors of State, the Viziers, the Lieutenant-Generals of his army, and all the high dignitaries who had accompanied him on his expedition.

Ibrahim advanced and prostrated himself at the foot of the throne; and at the same moment two of the high functionaries present threw a caftan of honour over his shoulders—a ceremony which signified that the Sultan had conferred upon him the title of Beglerbeg, or "Prince of Princes."

"Rise, Ibrahim Pacha!" exclaimed Solyman; "and take thy place in our councils—for Allah and his Prophet have this day made thee their instrument to save the life of thy sovereign."

The newly-created Pacha touched the imperial slipper with his lips, and then rising from his prostrate position received the congratulations of the high functionaries assembled.

Thus was it that in a few months, protected by that secret influence which was hurrying him so rapidly along in his ambitious career, the Italian apostate attained to a high rank in the Ottoman empire: but he was yet to reach the *highest*, next to that of the sovereign, ere he could hope to receive the fair hand of his mysterious patroness as the crowning joy of his prosperity. For her image—her charming image ever dwelt in his mind; and an ardent fancy often depicted her as she appeared, in all the splendour of her beauty, reclining on the sofa at the dwelling to which he had been conducted with so much precaution, as detailed in a preceding chapter.

On the following day peace was formally concluded between the Ottomans and the Knights of Rhodes, the latter consenting to surrender the island to the formidable invaders. An exchange of prisoners was the result; and Francisco, Count of Riverola, again found himself free within twenty-four hours after his capture.

"Your lordship is now about to sail for your own clime," said Ibrahim, when the moment of separation came; "is there aught within my power that I can do to testify my friendship for one so brave and chivalrous as thou art?"

"Nothing, great Pacha!" exclaimed Francisco, who felt his sympathy irresistibly attached towards Ibrahim—he knew not why. "But, on the other hand, receive my heartfelt thanks for the kindness which I have experienced during the few hours I have been your guest."

"The history of your afflictions has so much moved me," said Ibrahim Pacha, after a brief pause, "that the interest I experience in your behalf will not cease when you shall be no longer here. If, then, you would bear in mind the request I am about to make, gallant Christian——"

"Name it!" cried Francisco: "'tis already granted!"

"Write to me from Florence," added Ibrahim; "and acquaint me with the success of thy researches after thy lost sister and the maiden whom thou lovest. The ships of Leghorn trade to Constantinople, whither I shall speedily return; and it will not be a difficult matter to forward a letter to me occasionally."

"I should be unworthy the kind interest you take in my behalf, great Pacha, were I to neglect this request," answered Francisco. "Oh! may the good angels grant that I may yet recover my beloved sister Nisida, and that sweetest of maidens—Flora Francatelli!"

Francisco was too much overpowered by his own emotions to observe the sudden start which Ibrahim gave, and the pallor which instantaneously overspread his cheeks, as the name of his sister thus burst upon his ears,—that sister who, beyond all doubt, had disappeared most strangely.

But, with an almost superhuman effort, he subdued any farther expression of the agony of his feelings; and, taking Francisco's hand, said, in a low, deep tone, "Count of Riverola, I rely upon your solemn promise to write to me—and write soon—and often! I shall experience a lively pleasure in receiving and responding to your letters."

"Fear not that I shall forget my promise to your highness," answered Francisco.

He then took leave of Ibrahim-Pacha, and returned into the city of Rhodes, whence he embarked on the same day for Italy, accompanied by the few Florentine auxiliaries who had survived the dreadful slaughter on the ramparts.

The bustle and excitement attending the preparations for departure from Rhodes, somewhat absorbed the grief which Ibrahim felt on account of the mysterious disappearance of his sister Flora. Solyman left a sufficient force, under an able commander, to garrison the island, which was speedily evacuated by Villiers of Isle-Adam and his knights; and by the middle of May, the Sultan, attended by Ibrahim and other dignitaries of the empire, once more entered the gates of Constantinople.

Not many days had elapsed when at a Divan, or State Council, at which Solyman the Magnificent himself presided, Ibrahim-Pacha was desired to give his opinion upon a particular question then under discussion. The renegade expressed his sentiments in a manner at variance with the policy recommended by the Grand Vizier; and this high functionary replied in terms of bitterness and even grossness, at the same time reproaching Ibrahim with ingratitude. The apostate delivered a rejoinder which completely electrified the Divan. He repudiated the charge of ingratitude on the ground of being influenced only by his duty towards the Sultan; and he then entered upon a complete review of the policy of the Grand Vizier, Piri-Pacha. He proved that the commerce of the country had greatly fallen off—that the revenues had diminished—that arrears were due to the army and navy—that several minor powers had not paid their usual tribute for some years past,—and, in a word, drew such a frightful picture of the effects of maladministration and misrule, that the Grand Vizier was overwhelmed with confusion, and the Sultan and other listeners were struck with the lamentable truth of all which had fallen from the lips of Ibrahim-Pacha. Nor less were they astonished at the wonderful intimacy which he displayed with even the minutest details of the machinery of the government: in a word, his triumph was complete.

Solyman the Magnificent broke up the Divan in haste, ordering the members of the council to return each immediately to his own abode.

In the evening a functionary of the imperial household was sent to the palace of the Grand Vizier to demand the seals of office; and thus fell Piri-Pacha.

It was midnight when the Sultan sent to order Ibrahim-Pacha to wait upon him without delay. The conference that ensued was long and interesting; and it was already near day-break when messengers were despatched to the various members of the Divan to summon them to the seraglio. Then, in the presence of all the rank and talent of the capital, the Sultan demanded of Ibrahim whether he felt sufficient confidence in himself to undertake the weight and responsibility of office.

All eyes were fixed earnestly upon that mere youth of scarcely twenty-three, who was thus solemnly adjured.

In a firm voice he replied that, with the favour of the Sultan, and the blessing of the Most High, he did not despair of being enabled to restore the Ottoman Empire to all its late prosperity and glory.

The astronomer of the Court declared that the hour was favourable to invest the new Grand Vizier with the insignia of office; and at the moment when the call to prayer, "*God is Great!*" sounded from every minaret in Constantinople, Ibrahim-Pacha received the imperial seals from the hand of the Sultan.

CHAPTER XLIX.

THE NEW GRAND VIZIER.

The call to prayer, "*God is Great*," sounded from every minaret in Constantinople, when Solyman the Magnificent raised the renegade, Ibrahim, to a rank second only to his own imperial station.

The newly-appointed Prime Minister received the congratulations of the assembled dignitaries of the empire; and, when this ceremony was accomplished, he repaired to the palace of the Viziership, which Piri-Pacha had vacated during the night.

A numerous escort of slaves and a guard of honour, composed of an entire company of Janizaries, attended Ibrahim to his new abode, the streets through which he passed being lined with spectators anxious to obtain a glimpse of the new Minister.

But calm—almost passionless—was the expression of Ibrahim's countenance: though he had attained to his present station speedily, yet he had not reached it unexpectedly; and, even in the moment of this, his proud

triumph, there was gall mingled with the cup of honey which he quaffed.

For, oh! the light of Christianity was not extinguished within his breast; and though it no longer gleamed there to inspire and cheer, it nevertheless had strength sufficient to burn with reproachful flame.

The multitudes cheered and prostrated themselves as he passed: but his salutation was cold and indifferent; and he felt at that moment that he would rather have been wandering through the Vale of Arno, hand-in-hand with his sister, than be welcomed in the streets of Constantinople as the Grand Vizier of the Ottoman Empire!

O crime! thou mayst deck thy brow with flowers and adorn thy garments with the richest gems,—thou mayst elicit the shouts of admiring myriads, and proceed, attended by guards ready to hew down those who would treat thee with disrespect,—thou mayst quit the palace of a mighty sovereign to repair to a palace of thine own, —and in thine hands thou mayst hold the destinies of millions of human beings; but thou canst not subdue the still small voice that whispers reproachfully in thine ear, nor pluck from thy bosom the undying worm.

Though Ibrahim-Pacha felt acutely, yet his countenance, as we before said, expressed nothing:—he was still sufficient master of his emotions to retain them pent up in his own breast; and if he could not appear completely happy, he would not allow the world to perceive that his soul harboured secret care.

He entered the palace now destined to become his abode, and found himself the lord and master of an establishment such as no Christian monarch in all Europe possessed. But as he passed through marble halls and perfumed corridors lined with prostrate slaves,—as he contemplated the splendour and magnificence, the wealth and the luxury, by which he was now surrounded,—and as he even dwelt upon the hope—nay, the more than hope, the conviction, that he should full soon be blest with the hand of a being whose ravishing beauty was ever present to his mental vision,—that still small voice which he could not hush, appeared to ask him of what avail it was for a man if he gain the whole world but lose his own soul?

But Ibrahim-Pacha was not the man to give way to the influence of even reflections so harrowing as these; and he immediately applied himself to the business of the State to divert his mind from unpleasurable meditations. Holding a levee that same day, he received and confirmed in their offices all the subordinate Ministers: he then despatched letters to the various governors of provinces to announce to them his elevation to the Grand Viziership; and he conferred the Pachalick of Egypt upon the fallen Minister, Piri-Pacha. In the afternoon he granted audiences to the Ambassadors of the Christian powers; but the Florentine Envoy, it should be observed, had quitted Constantinople some weeks previously—indeed at the time when the Sultan undertook his expedition against Rhodes; for the representative of the Republic had utterly failed in the mission which had been entrusted to him by his government.

In the evening, when it was quite dark, Ibrahim retired to his apartment; and hastily disguising himself in a mean attire, he issued forth by a private gate at the back part of the palace. Intent upon putting into execution a scheme which he had hastily planned that very afternoon, he repaired to the quarter inhabited by the Christians. There he entered a house of a humble appearance where dwelt a young Greek, with whom he had been on friendly terms at that period when his present greatness was totally unforeseen—indeed while he was simply private secretary of the Florentine Envoy. He knew that Demetrius was poor, intelligent, and trustworthy; and it was precisely an agent of this nature that Ibrahim required for the project which he had in view.

Demetrius—such was the young Greek's name—was seated in a small and meanly furnished apartment, in a desponding manner, and scarcely appearing to notice the efforts which his sister, a beautiful maiden of nineteen, was exerting to console him, when the door opened and a man dressed as a water-carrier entered the room.

The young Greek started up angrily, for he thought that the visitor was one of the numerous petty creditors to whom he was indebted, and whose demands he was unable to liquidate; but the second glance which he cast by the light of the lamp that burnt feebly on the table, towards the countenance of the meanly dressed individual, convinced him of his mistake.

"His Highness, the Grand Vizier!" ejaculated Demetrins, falling on his knees; "Calanthe!" he added, speaking rapidly to his sister, "bow down to the representative of the Sultan!"

But Ibrahim hastened to put an end to this ceremony, and assured the brother and sister that he came thither as a friend.

"A friend!" repeated Demetrius, as if doubting whether his ears heard aright; "is it possible that heaven has indeed sent me a friend in one who has the power to raise me and this poor suffering maiden from the depths of our bitter, bitter poverty?"

"Dost thou suppose that my rapid elevation has rendered me unmindful of former friendships?" demanded Ibrahim; although had he not his own purposes to serve, he would never have thought of seeking the abode, nor inquiring after the welfare of the humble acquaintance of his obscure days.

The young Greek knew not, however, the thorough selfishness of the renegade's character; and he poured forth his gratitude for the Vizier's kindness and condescension with the most sincere and heartfelt fervour; while the beauteous Calanthe's large dark eyes swam in tears of hope and joy, as she surveyed with mingled wonder and admiration the countenance of that high functionary, whose rapid rise to power had electrified the Ottoman capital, and whom she now saw for the first time.

"Demetrius," said Ibrahim, "I know your worth—I have ever appreciated your talents—and I feel deeply for the orphan condition of your sister and yourself. It is in my power to afford you an employment whereby you may render me good service, and which shall be liberally rewarded. You are already acquainted with much of my former history; and you have often heard me speak, in terms of love and affection, of my sister Flora. During my recent sojourn in the island of Rhodes, a Florentine nobleman, the Count of Riverola, became my prisoner. From him I learnt that he was attached to my sister, and his language led me to believe that he was loved in return. But, alas! some few months ago Flora suddenly disappeared; and the Count of Riverola instituted a vain search to discover her. Too pure-minded was she to fly of her own accord from her native city: too chaste and too deeply imbued with virtuous principles was she to admit the suspicion that she had fled with a vile seducer. No: force or treachery—if not *murder*," added Ibrahim, in a tone indicative of profound emotion, "must have caused her sudden disappearance. The Count of Riverola has doubtless ere now arrived in Italy; and his researches will most assuredly be renewed. He promised to communicate to me their result; but, as he knew not to whom that pledge was given—as he recognised not in me the brother of the Flora whom he loves—I am fearful lest he forget or neglect the promise. It is therefore my intention to send a secret agent to Florence,—an agent who will convey rich gifts to my aunt, but without revealing the name of him who sends them,—an agent, in a word, who may minister to the wants and interests of my family, and report to me whether my beloved sister be yet found, and, if so, the causes of her disappearance. It seems to me that you, Demetrius, are well fitted for this mission. Your knowledge of the Italian language—your discreetness—your sound judgment, all render you competent to enact the part of a good genius watching over the interests of those who must not be allowed to learn whence flow the bounties which suddenly pour upon them."

"Gracious lord," said the young Greek, his countenance radiant with joy, "I will never lose any opportunity of manifesting my devotion to the cause in which your Highness condescends to employ me."

"You will proceed alone to Italy," continued Ibrahim: "and on your arrival in Florence, you will adopt a modest and reserved mode of life, so that no unpleasant queries may arise as to your object in visiting the Republic."

Demetrius turned a rapidly inquiring glance upon Calanthe, who hastened to observe that she did not fear being left unprotected in the city of Constantinople.

Ibrahim placed a heavy purse and a case containing many costly jewels in the hands of Demetrius, saying, "These are in earnest of my favour and friendship:"—then, producing a second case, tied round with a silken cord, he added, "And this for my aunt, the Signora Francatelli."

Demetrius promised to attend to all the instructions which he had received; and Ibrahim-Pacha took his leave of the brother and the charming sister, the latter of whom conveyed to him the full extent of her gratitude

for his kindness and condescension to them in a few words uttered in a subdued tone, but with all the eloquence of her fine dark eyes.

"Did I not love my unknown protectress," murmured Ibrahim to himself, as he sped rapidly back to his palace, "I feel that Calanthe's eyes would make an impression upon my heart!"

Scarcely had he resumed his magnificent garb, on his return home, than a slave announced to him that his Imperial Majesty, the Sultan, required his immediate attendance at the seraglio, whither he was to repair in the most private manner possible.

A sudden misgiving shot through Ibraham's imagination. Could Solyman have repented of the step which he had taken in thus suddenly elevating him to the pinnacle of power? Was his Viziership to last but a few short hours? had the secret influence, which had hitherto protected him, ceased?

Considering the time and the country in which he lived, these fears were justifiable; and it was with a rapidly beating heart that the new Minister hastened, attended only by a single slave, to the dwelling of his imperial master.

But when he was ushered into the presence of the Sultan,—his own slave remaining in the ante-room,—his apprehensions were dissipated by the smiling countenance with which the monarch greeted him.

Having signalled his attendants to retire, Solyman the Magnificent addressed the Grand Vizier in the following manner:—

"Thy great talents, thy zeal in our service, and the salvation which I owed to thee in the breach of Rhodes, have been instrumental, O Ibraham! in raising thee to thy present high state. But the bounties of the Sultan are without end, as the mercy of Allah is illimitable! Thou hast doubtless heard that amongst my numerous sisters, there is one of such unrivalled beauty, — such peerless loveliness, that the world hath not seen her equal. Happy may that man deem himself on whom the fair Aischa shall be bestowed;—and you are the happy man, Ibrahim—and Aischa is thine!"

The Grand Vizier threw himself at the feet of his imperial master, and murmured expressions of gratitude;—but his heart sank within him—for he knew that in marrying the Sultan's sister, he should not be allowed the enjoyment of the Mussulman privilege of polygamy : and thus his hopes of possessing the beautiful unknown, to whom he owed so much, appeared to hover on the verge of annihilation. But might not that unknown lady and the beauteous Aischa be one and the same person? The unknown was evidently the mistress of an influence almost illimitable; and was it not natural to conceive that she, then, must be the sister of the Sultan? Again, —the Sultan had many sisters; and the one who had exerted herself for Ibrahim might not be the Princess Aischa who was now promised to him!

All these conjectures and conflicting speculations passed through the mind of Ibrahim in far less time than we have taken to detail their nature; and he was cruelly the prey to mingled hope and alarm when the Sultan exclaimed, "Rise, my Vizier Azem,* and follow me."

The apostate obeyed with a beating heart; and Solyman the Magnificent conducted him along several passages and corridors to a splendidly furnished room, which Ibrahim instantly recognised as the very one in which he had been admitted, many months previously, to an interview with the beauteous unknown. Yes—that was the apartment in which he had listened to the eloquence of her soft, persuasive voice;—it was there that, intoxicated with passion, he had abjured the faith of a Christian and embraced the creed of the false Prophet Mohammed.

And, reclining on the very sofa where he had first seen her—but attended by a troop of female slaves,—was the fair unknown—his secret protectress—more lovely, more bewitching than she appeared when last they met!

An arch smile played upon her lips, as she rose from the magnificent cushions,—a smile which seemed to say, "I have kept my word—I have raised thee to the highest dignity save one in the Ottoman Empire — and I will now crown thine happiness by giving thee my hand!"

And, oh! so beauteous—so ravishingly lovely did she appear, as that smile revealed teeth whiter than the orient pearls which she wore, and as a slight flush on her damask cheek and the bright flashing of her eyes betrayed the joy and triumph which filled her heart,—so elegant and graceful was her faultless form, which the gorgeous Ottoman garb so admirably became, that Ibrahim forgot all

---

* "My Prime Minister."

his recent compunctions—lost sight of home and friends—remembered not the awful apostacy of which he had been guilty,—but fell upon his knees in adoration of that charming creature, while the Sultan, with a smile which showed that he was no stranger to the mysteries of the past, exclaimed in a benignant tone, "Vizier Azem! receive the hand of my well-beloved sister, Aischa!"

CHAPTER L.

THE COUNT OF ARESTINO.—THE PLOT THICKENS.

RETURN we now to the fair city of flowers,—to thee, delightful Florence—vine-crowned queen of Tuscany.

The summer has come; and the gardens are brilliant with dyes and hues of infinite variety; the hills and the valleys are clothed in their brightest emerald garments,—and the Arno winds its peaceful way between banks blushing with the choicest fruits of the earth.

But, though gay that July scene—though glorious in its splendour that unclouded summer sun—though gorgeous the balconies filled with flowers, and brilliant the parterres of Tuscan roses,—yet gloomy was the countenance and dark were the thoughts of the Count of Arestino, as he paced with agitated steps one of the splendid apartments of his palace.

That old man was naturally endowed with a good—a generous—a kind—and a forgiving disposition; but the infidelity of his wife—the being on whom he had so doated, and who was once his joy and his pride—that infidelity had warped his best feelings—soured his temper—and aroused in his soul the dark spirit of Italian vengeance.

"She lives! she lives!" he murmured to himself, pausing for a moment to press his feverish hand to his heated brow: "she lives!—and doubtless under the protection of her paramour! But I shall know more presently. Antonio is faithful—he will not deceive me!"

And the Count resumed his agitated walk up and down the room.

A few minutes elapsed, when the door opened slowly, and Antonio—whom the reader may remember to have been a valet in the service of the Riverola family—made his appearance.

The Count hastened towards him, exclaiming, "What news, Antonio? speak—hast thou learnt any more of—of *her?*"

"My lord," answered the valet, closing the door behind him, "I have ascertained everything. The individual who spoke darkly and mysteriously to me last evening has within this hour made me acquainted with many strange things."

"But the Countess?—I mean the guilty, fallen creature who once bore my name?" ejaculated the old nobleman, his voice trembling with impatience.

"There is no doubt, my lord, that her ladyship lives—and that she is still in Florence," answered Antonio.

"The shameless woman!" cried the Count of Arestino, his usually pale face becoming perfectly death-like through the violence of his inward emotions. "But how know you all this?" demanded his lordship, suddenly turning towards the dependant: "who is your informant? and can he be relied on? Remember, I took thee into my service at thine own solicitation—I have no guarantee for thy fidelity—and I am influential to punish as well as rich to reward!"

"Your lordship has bound me to you by ties of gratitude," responded Antonio: "for when discarded suddenly by the young Count of Riverola, I found an asylum and employment in your lordship's palace. It is your lordship's bounty which has enabled me to give bread to my aged mother; and I should be a villain were I to deceive you."

"I believe you, Antonio," said the Count: "and now tell me how you are assured that the Countess escaped from the conflagration and ruin of the institution to which my just vengeance had consigned her,—how, too, you have learnt that she is still in Florence."

"I have ascertained, my lord, beyond all possibility of doubt," answered the valet, "that the assailants of the convent were a terrible horde of banditti, at that time headed by Stephano Verrina, who has since disappeared no one knows whither,—that the Marquis of Orsini was one of the leaders in the awful deed of sacrilege,—and that her ladyship the Countess and a young maiden, named Flora Francatelli, were rescued by the robbers from their cell in the establishment. These ladies and the Marquis quitted the stronghold of the banditti together, blindfolded, and guided forth by that same

Stephano Verrina whom I mentioned just now, Lomellino (the present captain of the horde), and another bandit."

"And who is your informant? how learnt you all this?" demanded the Count, trembling with the excitement of painful reminiscences re-awakened, and with the hope of speedy vengeance on the guilty pair—his wife and the Marquis.

"My lord," said Antonio, "pardon me if I remain silent on that head: but I dare not compromise the individual who——"

"Antonio!" exclaimed the Count, wrathfully, "you are deceiving me! Tell me who was your informant—I command you—hesitate not——"

"My lord!—my lord!" ejaculated the valet; "is it not enough that I prove my assertions—that I——"

"No!" cried the nobleman; "I have seen so much duplicity where all appeared to be innocence—so much deceit where all wore the aspect of integrity, that I can trust man no more. How know I for certain that all this may not be some idle tale which you yourself have forged, to induce me to put confidence in you—to entrust you with gold to bribe your pretended informant, but which will really remain in your own pocket? Speak, Antonio—tell me all, or I shall listen to you no more, and your servitude in this mansion then ceases."

"I will speak frankly, my lord," replied the valet: "but in the course which you may adopt——"

"Fear not for yourself nor for your informant, Antonio," interrupted the Count, impatiently. "Be ye both leagued with the banditti yourselves—or be ye allied to the fiends of hell," he added with bitter emphasis, "I care not so long as I can render ye the instruments of my vengeance!"

"Good, my lord!" exclaimed Antonio, delighted with this assurance: "and now I can speak fearlessly and frankly. My informant is that *other bandit* who accompanied Stephano Verrina and Lomellino when the Countess, Flora, and the Marquis were conducted blindfold from the robbers' stronghold. But while they were yet all inmates of that stronghold, this same bandit, whose name is Venturo, overheard the Marquis inform Stephano Verrina that he intended to remain in Florence to obtain the liberation of a Jew who was imprisoned in the dungeons of the Inquisition; and this Jew, Venturo also learnt by subsequent inquiry from Verrina, is a certain Isaachar ben Solomon."

"Isaachar ben Solomon!" ejaculated the Count, the whole incident of the diamonds returning with all its painful details to his mind. "Oh! no wonder," he added bitterly, "that the Marquis has so much kindness for him! But, proceed—proceed, Antonio."

"I was about to inform your lordship," continued the valet, "that Venturo from whom I have spoken, happened the next day to overhear the Marquis inform the Countess that he should be compelled to stay for that purpose in Florence; whereupon Flora Francatelli offered her ladyship a home at her aunt's residence, whither she herself should return on her liberation from the stronghold. Then it was that the maiden mentioned to the Countess the name of her family; and when Venturo represented all these facts to me just now, I at once knew who this same Flora Francatelli is and where she dwells."

"You know where she dwells!" cried the Count joyfully. "Then Giulia—the false, the faithless, the perjured Giulia is in my power! Unless, indeed," he added more slowly,—"unless she may have removed to another place of abode——"

"That, my lord, shall be speedily ascertained," said Antonio. "I will instruct my mother to call, on some pretext, at the cottage inhabited by Dame Francatelli; and she will soon learn whether there be another female resident there besides the aunt and the niece Flora."

"Do so, Antonio," exclaimed the Count. "Let no unnecessary delay take place. Here is gold—much gold, for thee to divide between thyself and the bandit informant. See that thou art faithful to my interests, and that sum shall prove but a small earnest of what thy reward will be."

The valet secured about his person the well-filled purse that was handed to him, and then retired.

The Count of Arestino remained alone to brood over his plans of vengeance. It was horrible—horrible to behold that aged and venerable man, trembling as he was on the verge of eternity, now meditating schemes of dark and dire revenge. But his wrongs were great,—wrongs which, though common enough in that voluptuous Italian clime, and especially in that age and city of licentiousness and debauchery, were not the less sure to be followed by a fearful retribution where retribution was within the reach of him who was outraged.

"Ha! ha!" he chuckled fearfully to himself, as he now paced the room with a lighter step—as if joy filled his heart: "all those who have injured me are within the reach of my vengeance! The Jew in the Inquisition—the Marquis open to a charge of diabolical sacrilege—and Giulia assuredly in Florence! I dealt too leniently with that Jew—I sent to pay for the redemption of jewels which were my own property! All my life have I been a just—a humane—a merciful man: I will be so no more. The world's doings are adverse to generosity and fair dealing. In my old age I have learnt this! Oh! the perfidy of woman towards a doating a confiding—a fond heart, works strange alterations in the deceived one! I, who but a year,—nay, six months ago, would not harm the meanest reptile that crawls, now thirst for vengeance—vengeance," repeated the old man, in a shrieking, hysterical tone, "upon those who have wronged me! I will exterminate them at one fell swoop—exterminate them all—all!"

And his voice rang screechingly and wildly through the lofty room of that splendid mansion.

CHAPTER LI.

A MEETING.

On the bank of the Arno, in a somewhat retired situation, stood a neat cottage in the midst of a little garden, surrounded by no formal pile of bricks to constitute a wall, but protected only by its own sweet hedge of fragrant shrubs and blooming plants.

Over the portico of the humble but comfortable tenement twined the honeysuckle and the clematis; and the sides of the building were almost completely veiled by the vines amidst the verdant foliage of which appeared large bunches of purple grapes.

At an open casement on the ground-floor, an elderly female, very plainly but very neatly attired, and wearing a placid smile and a good-natured expression upon a countenance which had once been handsome, sat watching the glorious spectacle of the setting sun.

The orb of day went down in a flood of purple and gold, behind the western hills; and now the dame began suddenly to cast uneasy glances towards the path that led along the bank of the river.

But the maiden for whose return the good aunt felt anxious, was not far distant:—indeed, Flora Francatelli, wearing a thick veil over her head, was already proceeding homeward after a short ramble by the margin of the stream, when the reverie in which she was plunged was interrupted by the sounds of hasty footsteps behind.

Ever fearful of treachery since the terrible incident of her imprisonment in the Carmelite convent, she redoubled her speed, blaming herself for having been beguiled by the beauty of the evening to prolong her walk farther than she had intended on setting out,—when the increasing haste of the footsteps behind her excited the keenest alarms within her bosom—for she now felt convinced that she was pursued.

The cottage was already in sight, and a hundred paces only separated her from its door, when a well-known voice—a voice which caused every fibre in her heart to thrill with surprise and joy—exclaimed, "Flora! beloved one; fly not! Oh! I could not be deceived in the symmetry of thy form—the gracefulness of thy gait: I knew it was thou!"

And in another moment the maiden was clasped in the arms of Francisco, Count of Riverola.

Impossible were it to describe the ecstatic bliss of this meeting,—a meeting so unexpected on either side; for a minute before, and Flora had deemed the young nobleman to be far away, fighting in the cause of the Cross: while Francisco was proceeding to make inquiries at the cottage concerning his beloved, but with a heart that scarcely dared nourish a hope of her re-appearance.

"Oh! my well-beloved Flora!" exclaimed Francisco; "and are we indeed thus blest? or is it a delusive dream? But tell me, sweet maiden, tell me whether thou hadst ceased to think of one from whose memory thine image has never been absent since the date of thy sudden and mysterious disappearance?"

Flora could not reply in words—her heart was too full for the utterance of her feelings: but, as she raised the veil from her charming countenance, the tears of joy which stood upon her long lashes, and the heavenly smiles which played upon her lips, and the deep blushes which overspread her cheeks, spoke far more eloquently of unaltered affection than all the vows and pledges which might have flowed from the tongue.

"Thou lovest me—lovest me still!" exclaimed the enraptured Count, again clasping her in his arms, and now imprinting innumerable kisses on her lips, her cheeks, and her fair brow.

Hasty explanations speedily ensued: and Francisco now learnt for the first time the cause of Flora's disappearance—her incarceration in the convent—and the particulars of her release.

"But who could have been the author of that outrage?" exclaimed the Count, his cheeks flushing with indignation and his hand instinctively grasping his sword: "whom could you, sweet maiden, have offended? what fiend thus vented his infernal malignity on thee?"

"Hold, my lord!" cried Flora, in a beseeching tone: "perhaps you——"

And she checked herself abruptly.

"Call me not 'my lord,' dearest maiden," said the Count: "To thee I am Francisco, as thou to me art Flora—my own beloved Flora! But wherefore didst thou stop short thus? Why not conclude the sentence that was half uttered? Oh! Flora—a terrible suspicion strikes me! Speak—relieve me from the cruel suspense under which I now labour: was it my sister—my much lamented sister who did thee that wrong?"

"I know not," replied Flora, weeping; "but—alas! pardon me, dear Francisco—if I suspect aught so bad of any one connected with thee—and yet heaven knows how freely, how sincerely I forgive my enemy——"

Her voice was lost in sobs; and her head drooped on her lover's breast.

"Weep not, dearest one!" exclaimed Francisco: "Let not our meeting be rendered mournful with tears. Thou knowest, perhaps, that Nisida disappeared as suddenly and as mysteriously as thou didst; but could she also have become the victim of the Carmelites? and did she alas! perish in the ruins of the convent?"

"I am well assured that the Lady Nisida was not doomed to that fate," answered Flora; "for had she been consigned to the convent, as a punishment for some real offence or on some groundless charge, she must have passed the ordeal of the Chamber of Penitence, where I should have seen her. Yes, Francisco—I have heard of her mysterious disappearance; and I have shed many—many tears when I have thought of her, poor lady! although," added the maiden, in a low and plaintive tone, "I fear, Francisco, that it was indeed she who doomed me to that monastic dungeon! Doubtless, her keen perception--far more keen than in those who are blessed with the faculties which were lost to her—enabled her to penetrate the secret of that affection with which you had honoured me, and in which I felt so much happiness——"

"I confessed my love to Nisida," interrupted Francisco; "but it was not until after your disappearance. I was driven to despair, Flora—I was mad with grief—and I could not, neither did I attempt to conceal my emotions. I told Nisida all, and well—oh! well—do I recollect the reply which she conveyed to me, giving fond assurance that my happiness should alone be consulted."

"Alas! was there no double meaning in that assurance?" asked Flora, gently. "The Lady Nisida knew well how inconsistent, with your high rank—your proud fortunes—your great name, was that love which you bore for a humble and obscure girl——"

"A love which I shall not be ashamed to declare in the presence of all Florence," exclaimed Francisco, in an impassioned tone. "But if Nisida were the cause of that cruel outrage on thee, my Flora, we will forgive her—for she could have acted only through conscientious, though most mistaken motives. Mistaken, indeed! for never, never could I have known happiness again, hadst thou not been restored to me! It was to wean my mind from pondering on afflictions which goaded me to despair, that I embarked in the cause of Christendom against the encroachments of Moslem power. Thinking that thou wast for ever lost to me—that my sister had also become the victim of some murderous hand,—harassed by doubts the most cruel, and uncertainty the most agonizing,—I sought death on the walls of Rhodes; but the destroying angel's arrow rebounded from my corslet—his sword was broken against my shield? During my voyage to Italy—after beholding the crescent planted on the walls where the Christian standard had floated for so many, many years—a storm overtook the ship: and yet the destroying angel gave me not the death I courted. This evening I once more set foot in Florence. From my own mansion Nisida is still absent; and no tidings have been received of her. Alas! is she then lost to me for ever? Without tarrying even to change my travel-soiled garments, I set off to make inquiries concerning *another* whom I loved—and that other is thyself! Here, thanks to a merciful heaven! my heart has not been doomed to experience a second and equally cruel disappointment: for I have found thee at last, my Flora—and henceforth my arm shall protect thee from peril!"

"How have I deserved so much kindness at thine

bursting into tears; "but it was not my fault! On the night following the one in which the banditti stormed the convent, as I ere now detailed to your ears, I returned home to my aunt. When the excitement of our meeting was past, and when we were alone together, I threw myself at her feet, confessed all that had passed between thee and me, and implored her advice. '*Flora,*' she said, while her tears fell upon me as I knelt, '*no happiness will come to thee, my child, from this attachment which has already plunged thee into so much misery. It is beyond all doubt certain that the relations of the Count were the authors of thy imprisonment: and their persecu-*

"AND SHE POINTED TO A LOW OTTOMAN." (See p. 79.)

hands?" murmured the maiden, again drooping her blushing head. "And, oh! what will you think, Francisco—what will you say, when you learn that I was there—there at that cottage—with my aunt—when you called the last time to inquire if any tidings had been received of me——"

"You were there!" exclaimed Francisco, starting back in surprise not unmingled with anger: "you were there, Flora—and you knew that I was in despair concerning thee—that I would have given worlds to have heard of thy safety,—I, who thought that some fiend in human shape had sent thee to an early grave!"

"Forgive me, Francisco—forgive me!" cried Flora,

tions would only be renewed were they to learn that the Count was made aware of your reappearance in Florence. For thy sake, then, my child, I shall suffer the impression of thy continued absence and loss to remain on the minds of those who may inquire concerning thee; and should his lordship call here again, most especially to him shall I appear stricken with grief on account of thee. His passion, my child, is one of boyhood—evanescent, though ardent while it endures. He will soon forget thee; and when he shall have learnt to love another, there will no longer be any necessity for thee to live an existence of concealment.' Thus spoke my aunt, dear Francisco; and I dared not gainsay her. When you came the last time, I heard your voice—I listened from my chamber door to all you said to my aunt—and I longed to fly into your arms. You went away—and my heart was nearly broken. Some days afterwards we learnt the strange disappearance of the Lady Nisida; and then I knew that you must have received a severe blow,—for I was well aware how much you loved her. Two or three weeks elapsed; and then we heard that you were about to depart to the wars. Oh! how bitter were the tears that I shed—how fervent were the prayers that I offered up for thy safety."

"And those prayers have been heard on high, beloved one!" exclaimed Francisco, who had listened with melting heart and returning tenderness to the narrative which the maiden told so simply but so sincerely, and in the most plaintive tones of her musical voice.

"Can you forgive me now?" asked the blushing maiden, her swimming eyes bending on her lover glances eloquently expressive of hope.

"I have nothing to forgive, sweet girl," replied Francisco. "Your aunt behaved with a prudence which in justice I cannot condemn; and you acted with an obedience and submission to your venerable relative, which I could not be arbitrary enough to blame. We have both endured much for each other, my Flora; but the days of our trials are passed; and your good aunt shall be convinced that in giving your young heart to me, you have not confided in one who is undeserving of so much love. Let us hasten into her presence. But one question have I yet to ask you," he added, suddenly recollecting an idea which had ere now made some impression on his mind. "You informed me how you were liberated from the convent, and you mentioned the name of the Countess of Arestino, whom circumstances had made your companion in that establishment, and to whom your aunt gave an asylum. Know you not, dearest Flora, that fame reports not well of that same Giulia of Arestino—and that a woman of tarnished reputation is no fitting associate for an innocent and artless maiden such as thou?"

"During the period that the Lady of Arestino and myself were companions in captivity," responded Flora, with a frankness as amiable as it was convincing, "she never in the most distant manner alluded to her love for the Marquis of Orsini. When the Marquis appeared in the convent, in company with the robbers, I was far too much bewildered with the passing events, to devote a thought to what might be the nature of their connexion; and even when I had more leisure for reflection, during the entire day which I passed in the stronghold of the banditti, I saw naught in it save what I conceived to be the bond of close relationship. I offered her ladyship an asylum at the abode of my aunt, as I should have given a home, under such circumstances, to the veriest wretch crawling on the face of the earth. But in that cottage the Countess and myself have not continued in close companionship; for my aunt accidentally learnt that fame reported not well of the Lady of Arestino, and in a gentle manner she begged her to seek another house at her earliest leisure. The Countess implored my venerable relative to permit her to remain at the cottage, as her life would be in danger were she not afforded a sure and safe asylum. Moved by her earnest entreaties, my aunt assented; and the Countess has almost constantly remained in her own chamber. Sometimes—but very rarely—she goes forth after dusk, and in a deep disguise: the Marquis has not, however, visited the cottage since my aunt made that discovery relative to the reputation of the Lady of Arestino."

"Thanks, charming Flora, for this explanation!" cried the young Count. "Let us now hasten to thine aunt; and in her presence will I renew to thee all the vows of unalterable and honourable affection which my heart suggests, as a means of proving that I am worthy of thy love."

And, hand-in-hand, that fine young noble and that beauteous, blushing maiden proceeded to the cottage.

*   *   *   *   *   *   *

*   *   *   *   *   *

Two persons, concealed in an adjacent grove, had overheard every syllable of the above conversation.

These were the valet Antonio, and his mother, Dame Margaretha, at whose dwelling, it will be recollected, the unfortunate Agnes had so long resided, under the protection of the late Count of Riverola.

"This is fortunate, mother!" said Antonio, when Francisco and Flora had retired from the vicinity of the grove. "You are spared the trouble of a visit to the old

Signora Francatelli; and I have heard sufficient to enable me to work out all my plans alike of aggrandizement and revenge. Let us retrace our way into the city; thou wilt return to thy home—and I shall thence straight to the Lord Count of Arestino."

CHAPTER LII.

THE GREEK PAGE.—SONG OF THE GREEK PAGE.—A REVELATION.

THREE months had now elapsed since Ibrahim-Pacha had risen to the exalted rank of Grand Vizier, and had married the sister of Solyman the Magnificent. The Sultan daily became more attached to him; and he, on his part, rapidly acquired an almost complete influence over his Imperial Master. Vested with a power so nearly absolute that Solyman signed without ever perusing the hatti-sheriffs, or decrees, drawn up by Ibrahim,—and enjoying the confidence of the Divan, all the members of which were devoted to his interests,—the renegade administered according to his own discretion the affairs of that mighty empire. Avaricious and ever intent upon the aggrandizement of his own fortunes, he accumulated vast treasures; but he also maintained a household and lived in a style unequalled by any of his predecessors in office."

Having married a sister of the Sultan, he was not permitted a plurality of wives:—but he purchased the most beauteous slaves for his harem, and plunged headlong into a vortex of dissipation and pleasure.

For some weeks he had manifested the most ardent and impassioned attachment towards Aischa, who, during that period, was happy in the belief that she alone possessed his heart. But the customs of the East, as well as the duties of his office, kept them so much apart, that he had no leisure to discover the graces of her mind, nor to appreciate all the powers of her naturally fine and indeed well cultivated intellect; so that the beauty of her person constituted the only basis on which his affection was maintained. The fervour of such a love soon cooled with satiety; and those female slaves whom he had at first procured as indispensable appendages to his rank and station, were not long in becoming the sources of new pleasure and voluptuous enjoyment.

Aischa beheld his increasing indifference, and strove to bind him to her by representing all she had done for him. He listened coldly at first; but when, on several occasions, the same remonstrances were repeated, he answered angrily.

"Had it not been for my influence," she said to him one day, when the dispute had become more serious than preceding quarrels of the kind, "you might still have been a humble Secretary to a Christian noble."

"Not so," replied the Grand Vizier; "for at the very time when I first beheld thee in the Bezestein, certain offers had been secretly conveyed to me from the Reis-Effendi."

"In whose service you would have lingered as a mere subordinate for long, long years," returned Aischa. "It was I who urged you on! Have I not often assured you that your image dwelt in my memory after the accident which first led to our meeting,—that one of my faithful women noticed my thoughtful mood,—and that when I confessed to her the truth, she stated to me that, by a strange coincidence, her own brother was employed by the Reis-Effendi as an agent to tempt you with the offers to which you have alluded? Then, inquiries which my slave instituted, brought to my ears the flattering tidings that you also thought of me—and I resolved to grant you an interview. From that moment my influence hurried you on to power; and when you became the favourite of the mighty Solyman, I confessed to him that I had seen and that I loved you. His fraternal attachment to me is great—greater than to any other of his sisters, seeing that himself and I were born of the same mother, though at a long interval. Thus was it that my persuasion made him think higher and oftener of you than he would else have done:—and now that you have attained the summit of glory and power, she who has helped to raise you is neglected and loved no longer."

"Cease these reproaches, Aischa!" exclaimed Ibrahim, who had listened impatiently to her long address; "or I will give thee less of my company than heretofore. See that the next time I visit thee, my reception may be with smiles instead of tears—with sweet words instead of reproaches."

And in this cruel manner the heartless renegade quitted

his beauteous wife, leaving her plunged in the most profound affliction.

But as Ibrahim traversed the corridors leading to his own apartments, his heart smote him for the harshness and unfeeling nature of his conduct; and as one disagreeable idea, by disposing the spirits to melancholy, usually arouses others that were previously slumbering in the cells of the brain, all the turpitude of his apostacy was recalled with new force to his mind.

Repairing to a small but magnificently-furnished saloon in a retired part of the palace, he dismissed the slaves who were waiting at the door, ordering them, however, to send into his presence a young Greek page who had recently entered his service.

In a few minutes the youth made his appearance, and stood in a respectful attitude near the door.

"Come and sit at my feet, Constantine," said the Grand Vizier; "and thou shalt sing to me one of those airs of thy native Greece with which thou hast occasionally delighted mine ears. I know not how it is, boy—but thy presence pleases me, and thy voice soothes my soul, when oppressed with the cares of my high office."

Joy flashed from the bright black eyes of the young Greek page as he glided noiselessly over the thick carpet, and proceeded to place himself on a footstool near the sofa whereon his master was reclining; but that emotion of pleasure was instantly subdued by the youth, and his countenance again became settled into an expression of the deepest deference.

"Proceed, Constantine," said the Grand Vizier; "and sing me that plaintive song which is supposed to depict the woes of one of the unhappy sons of Greece."

"But may not its sentiments offend your Highness," asked the page, speaking in a soft and even feminine tone—"seeing that they are unfriendly to the Moslem domination in Greece?"

"It is but a song, Constantine," responded Ibrahim. "I give thee full permission to sing those verses, and I should be sorry were you to subdue aught of the impassioned feelings which they are well calculated to excite within thee."

The page turned his strikingly handsome countenance up towards the Grand Vizier, and commenced in melodious, liquid tones, the following song:—

SONG OF THE GREEK PAGE.

I.

Oh! are there not beings condemned from their birth
To drag without solace or hope, o'er the earth,
    The burden of grief and sorrow?
Doomed wretches who know, while they tremblingly
        say,
"The star of my fate appears brighter to-day,"
That it is but a brief and a mocking ray
    To make darkness darker to-morrow.

II.

And 'tis not to the vile and the base alone
That unchanging grief and sorrow are known,
    But as oft to the pure and guileless;
And he, from whose fervid and generous lip
Gush words of the kindliest fellowship,
Of the same pure fountain may not sip
    In return, but is sad and smileless!

III.

Yes; such doomed mortals, alas! there be;
And mine is that self-same destiny—
    The fate of the lorn and lonely:
For e'en in my early childhood's day,
The comrades I sought would turn away;
And of all the band from the sportive play
    Was I thrust and excluded only.

IV.

When fifteen summers had passed o'er my head,
I stood on the battle-plain strewed with the dead,—
    For the day of the Moslem's glory
Had made me an orphan child—and there
My sire was stretched—and his bosom bare
Showed a gaping wound—and the flowing hair
    Of his head was damp and gory.

V.

My sire was the chief of the patriot band
That had fought and died for their native land,
    When her rightful prince betrayed her

On his kith and kin did the vengeance fall
Of the Mussulman foes—and each and all
Were swept from the old ancestral hall,
    Save myself, by the fierce invader.

VI.

And I was spared from that blood-stained grave
To be dragged away as the Moslem's slave,
    And bend to the foe victorious:
But, O Greece! to thee does my memory turn
Its longing eyes—and my heart-strings yearn
To behold thee rise in thy might, and spurn,
    As of yore, the yoke inglorious!

VII.

But, oh! whither has Spartan courage fled:—
And why, proud Athens! above thine head
    Is the Mussulman crescent gleaming?
Have thine ancient memories no avail?
And art thou not fired at the legend tale
Which reminds thee how the whole world grew pale
    And recoiled from thy banners streaming?

"Enough, boy!" exclaimed Ibrahim; then, in a low tone, he murmured to himself, "The Christians have indeed much cause to anathematise the encroachments and tyranny of the Moslems."

There was a short pause, during which the Grand Vizier was absorbed in profound meditation, while the Greek page never once withdrew his eyes from the countenance of that high functionary.

"Boy," at length said Ibrahim, "you appear attached to me. I have observed many proofs of your devotion during the few months that you have been in my service. Speak—is there aught that I can do to make you happy? have you relations or friends who need protection? If they be poor I will relieve their necessities."

"My lips cannot express the gratitude which my heart feels towards your Highness," returned the page, a rich crimson glow suffusing itself over his olive countenance; "but I have no friends in behalf of whom I might supplicate the bounty of your Highness."

"Are you yourself happy, Constantine?" asked Ibrahim.

"Happy in being permitted to attend upon your Highness," was the reply, delivered in a soft and tremulous tone.

"But is it in my power to render you happier?" demanded the Grand Vizier.

Constantine hung down his head—reflected deeply for a few moments—and then murmured, "Yes."

"Then, by heaven!" exclaimed Ibrahim-Pacha, "thou hast only to name thy request, and it will be granted. I know not wherefore, but I am attached to thee much; I feel interested in thy welfare, and I would be rejoiced to minister to thy happiness."

"I am already happier than I was—happier, because mine ears have drunk in such kind words flowing from the lips of one who is exalted as highly as I am insignificant and humble," said the page, in a voice tremulous with emotions, but sweetly musical. "Yes—I am happier," he continued; "and yet my soul is filled with the image of a dear—a well-beloved sister, who pines in loneliness and solitude, ever dwelling on a hapless love which she has formed for one who knows not that he is so loved, and who perhaps may never—never know it."

"Ah! thou hast a sister, Constantine!" exclaimed the Grand Vizier. "And is she as lovely as the sister of a youth so handsome as thou art ought to be?"

"She has been assured by those who have sought her hand, that she is indeed beautiful," answered Constantine. "But of what avail are her charms, since he whom she loves may never whisper in her ear the delicious words, 'I love thee in return.'"

"Does the object of her affections possess so obdurate a heart?" inquired the Grand Vizier, strangely interested in the discourse of his youthful page.

"It is not that he scorns my sister's love," replied Constantine; "but it is that he knows not of its existence. It is true that he has seen her once—yet 'twere probable that he remembers not there is such a being in the world. Thus came it to pass, my lord:—An officer, holding a high rank in the service of his Imperial Majesty, the great Solyman, had occasion to visit a humble dwelling wherein my sister resided. She—poor silly maiden! was so struck by his god-like beauty—so dazzled by his fascinating address—so enchanted by the sound of his voice, that she surrendered up her heart suddenly and secretly—surrendered it beyond all power of reclamation. Since then she has never ceased to ponder upon this fatal passion—this unhappy love: she has nursed his image in her mind, until her reason has rocked with the wild thoughts, the ardent hopes, the emotions of despair—all the conflicting sentiments and feelings, in a word, which so ardent and so strange a love must naturally engender. Enthusiastic, yet tender—fervent, yet melting is her soul; and while she does not attempt to close her eyes to the conviction that she is cherishing a passion which is preying upon her very vitals, she, nevertheless, clings to it as a martyr to the stake! Oh! my lord, canst thou marvel if I feel deeply for my unhappy sister?"

"But wherefore doth she remain thus unhappy?" demanded Ibrahim-Pacha "Surely, there are means of conveying to the object of her attachment an intimation how deeply he is beloved? and he must be something more than human," he added, in an impassioned tone, "if he can remain obdurate to the tears and sighs of a beauteous creature, such as thy sister doubtless is."

"And were he to spurn her from him—oh! your Highness, it would kill her!" said the page, fixing his large, eloquent eyes upon the countenance of the Grand Vizier. "Consider his exalted rank and her humble position——"

"Doth she aspire to become his wife?" asked Ibrahim.

"She would be contented to serve him as his veriest slave," responded Constantine, now strangely excited, "were he but to look kindly upon her: she would deem herself blest in receiving a smile from his lips, so long as it was bestowed as a reward for all the tender love she bears him."

"Who is this man that is so fortunate as to have excited so profound an interest in the heart of one so beautiful?" demanded the Grand Vizier. "Name him to me—I will order him to appear before me—and, for thy sake, Constantine, I will become an eloquent pleader on behalf of thy sister."

Words cannot express the joy which flashed from the eyes of the page, and animated his handsome though softly feminine countenance, as, casting himself on his knees at the feet of Ibrahim-Pacha, he murmured, "Great lord, that man whom my sister loves, and for whom she would lay down her life, is thyself."

Ibrahim was for some minutes too much overcome by astonishment to offer an observation—to utter a word; while the page remained kneeling at his feet.

Then suddenly it flashed to the mind of the Grand Vizier that the only humble abode which he had entered since he had become *an officer holding a high rank in the service of Solyman*, was that of his Greek emissary, Demetrius; and it now occurred to him, for the first time, that there was a striking likeness between the young page and the beautiful Calanthe, whom he had seen on that occasion.

"Constantine," he said at length, "art thou, then, the brother of that Demetrius whom I despatched three months ago to Florence?"

"I am, my lord—and 'tis our sister Calanthe of whom I have spoken," was the reply. "Oh! pardon my arrogance—my presumption, great Vizier!" he continued, suddenly rising from his kneeling position, and now standing with his arms meekly folded across his breast—"pardon the arrogance, the insolence of my conduct," he exclaimed; "but it was for the sake of my sister that I sought service in the household of your Highness. I thought that if I could succeed in gaining your notice—if in any way I could obtain such favour in your eyes, as to be admitted to speak with one so highly raised above me as thou art, I fancied that some opportunity would enable me to make those representations which have issued from my lips this day. How patiently I have waited that occasion, heaven knows! how ardent have been my hopes of success, when from time to time your Highness singled me out from amongst the numerous free pages of your princely household to attend upon your privacy—how ardent, I say, these hopes have been, your Highness may possibly divine! And now, my lord, that I *have* succeeded in gaining your attention, and pouring this secret into your ears, I will away to Calanthe and impart all the happiness that is in store for her. Though the flowers may hold up their heads high in the light of the glorious sun, yet she shall hold hers higher in the favour of your smile. Generous master," he added, suddenly sinking his voice to a lower tone, and re-assuming the deferential air which he had partially lost in the excitement of speaking, "permit me now to depart."

"This evening, Constantine," said the Grand Vizier, fixing his dark eyes significantly upon the page, "let your sister enter the harem by the private door in the garden. Here is a key: I will give the necessary instructions to the female slaves to welcome her."

Constantine received the key, made a low obeisance, and withdrew, leaving the Grand Vizier to feast his voluptuous imagination with delicious thoughts of the beauteous Calanthe.

CHAPTER LIII.

THE SULTANA-VALIDA.—THE THREE BLACK SLAVES.

IN the meantime the Princess Aischa, the now neglected wife of the Grand Vizier, had repaired to the imperial seraglio to obtain an interview with her brother, Solyman the Magnificent.

The Sultan, as the reader has already learnt, was deeply attached to Aischa. Their mother, the Sultana-Valida, or Empress-Mother, was still alive, and occupied apartments in the seraglio. Her children entertained the greatest respect for her; and her influence over the Sultan, who possessed an excellent heart, though his sway was not altogether unstained by cruelties, was known to be great.

It was therefore to her mother and her brother that the beautiful Aischa proceeded; and when she was alone with them in the Valida's apartment, and removed her veil, they immediately noticed that she had been weeping.

Upon being questioned relative to the cause of her sorrow, she burst into an agony of tears, and was for some time unable to reply.

At length, half regretting that she had taken the present step, Aischa slowly revealed the various causes of complaint against the Grand Vizier.

"By Allah!" exclaimed the Sultan, "the ungrateful Ibrahim shall not thus spurn and neglect the costly gift which I, his master, condescended to bestow upon him! What! when the Shah of Persia, the Khan of the Tartars, and the Prince of Karamania all sought thine hand, and despatched ambassadors laden with rich gifts to our Court to demand thee in marriage, did I not send them back with cold words of denial to their sovereigns? And was it to bestow thee, my sister, on this ungrateful boy, who was so late naught save a dog of a Christian, ready to eat the dirt under our imperial feet,—was it to bestow thee on such an one as he that I refused the princely offers of the Persian Shah? By the tomb of the Prophet! this indignity shall cease!"

"Restrain your wrath, my son," said the Sultana-Valida, "Ibrahim must not be openly disgraced: the effects of his punishment would redound on our beloved Aischa. No—rather entrust this affair to me; and fear not that I shall fail in compelling this haughty Pacha to return to the arms of his wife—aye, and implore her pardon for his late neglect."

"Oh! dearest mother, if thou canst accomplish this!" exclaimed Aischa, her countenance becoming animated with joy and her heart palpitating with hope, "thou wouldst render me happy indeed!"

"Trust to me, daughter," replied the Sultana Valida. "In the meantime seek not to learn my intentions; but, on thy return home, send me by some trusty slave thy pass-key to the harem. And thou, my son, wilt lend me thine imperial signet-ring for twelve hours."

"Remember," said the Sultan, as he drew the jewel from his finger, "that he who bears that ring possesses a talisman of immense power—a sign which none to whom it is shown dares disobey: remember this, my mother, and use it with caution."

"Fear not, my dearly beloved son," answered the Sultana-Valida, concealing the ring in her bosom. "And now, Aischa, do you return to the palace of your haughty husband, who, ere twelve hours be passed, shall sue for pardon at thy feet."

The Sultan and Aischa both knew that their mother was a woman of powerful intellect and determined character; and they sought not to penetrate into the secret of her intentions.

Solyman withdrew to preside at a meeting of the Divan; and Aischa returned to the palace of the Grand Vizier, attended by the slaves who had waited for her in an anderoon leading to her mother's apartments.

It was now late in the afternoon: and the time for evening prayer had arrived ere the Sultana-Valida received the pass-key to Ibrahim-Pacha's harem. But the moment it was conveyed to her, she summoned to her presence three black slaves belonging to the corps of the Bostandjis, or gardeners, who also served as executioners when a person of rank was to be subjected to the process of the bow-string, or when any dark deed was to be accomplished in silence and with caution. Terrible appendages to the household of Ottoman Sultans were the black slaves belonging to that corps :—like snakes, they insinuated themselves, noiselessly and ominously, into the presence of their victims ; and it were as vain to preach peace to the warring elements which God alone can control as to implore mercy at the hands of those remorseless Ethiopians !

To the three black slaves did the Sultana-Valida issue her commands ; and to the eldest she entrusted Solyman's signet-ring and the pass-key which Aischa had sent her.

The slaves bowed three times to the Empress-Mother—laid their hands on their heads to imply that they would deserve decapitation if they neglected the orders they had received—and then withdrew.

There was something terribly sinister in their appearance as they retired noiselessly but rapidly through the long, silent, and darkened corridors of the imperial harem.

*　　*　　*　　*　　*

It was night—and the moon shone softly and brightly upon the mighty city of Constantinople, tipping each of its thousand spires and pinnacles as with a star.

Ibrahim-Pacha, having disposed of the business of the day, and now with his imagination full of the beautiful Calanthe, hastened to the anderoon, or principal apartment of the harem.

The harem, occupying one complete wing of the Vizier's palace, consisted of three storeys. On the ground floor were the apartments of the Princess Aischa and her numerous female dependants. These opened from a spacious marble hall; and at the folding-doors leading into them were stationed two black dwarfs, who were deaf and dumb. Their presence was not in any way derogatory to the character of Aischa, but actually denoted the superior rank of the lady who occupied those apartments in respect to the numerous females who tenanted the rooms above. As she was the sister of the Sultan, Ibrahim dared not appear in her presence without obtaining her previous assent through the medium of one of the mutes, who were remarkably keen in understanding and conveying intelligence by means of signs. A grand marble staircase led from the hall to the two floors containing the apartments of the ladies of the harem ; and thus, though Aischa dwelt in the same wing as those females, her own abode was as distinct from theirs as if she were the tenant of a separate house altogether,

On the first floor there was a large and magnificently furnished room, in which the ladies of the harem were accustomed to assemble when they chose to quit the solitude of their own chambers for the enjoyment of each other's society. The ceiling of the anderoon, as this immense apartment was called, was gilt entirely over : it was supported by twenty slender columns of crystal ; and the splendid chandeliers which were suspended to it diffused a soft and mellow light, producing the most striking effects on that mass of gilding, those reflecting columns, and the wainscoted walls inlaid with mother-of-pearl and with ivory of different colours. A Persian carpet, three inches thick, was spread upon the floor. Along two opposite sides ran continuous sofas, supported by low white marble pillars, and covered with purple figured velvet, fringed with gold. In the middle of this gorgeous apartment was a large table, shaped like a crescent, and spread with all kinds of preserved fruits, confectionery, cakes, and delicious beverages of a non-alcoholic nature.

The room was crowded with beauteous women when the presence of Ibrahim was announced by a slave. There were the fair-complexioned daughters of Georgia —the cold, reserved, but lovely Circassians—the warm and impassioned Persians—the voluptuous Wallachians —the timid Tartars—the dusky Indians—the talkative Turkish ladies—beauties, too, of Italy, Spain, and Portugal, indeed, specimens of female perfection from many, many nations. Their various styles of beauty and their characteristic national dresses formed a scene truly delightful to gaze upon : but the Grand Vizier noticed none of the countenances so anxiously turned towards him to mark on which his eyes would settle in preference ; and the ladies noiselessly withdrew, leaving their master alone with the slave in the anderoon.

Ibrahim threw himself on a sofa, and gave some hasty instructions to the slave, who immediately retired.

In about a quarter of an hour he came back, conducting into the anderoon a lady veiled from head to foot. The slave then withdrew altogether ; and Ibrahim approached the lady, saying, " Calanthe—beauteous Calanthe ! welcome to my palace !"

She removed her veil ; and Ibrahim fixed his eager eyes upon the countenance thus disclosed to him :—but he was immediately struck by the marvellous resemblance existing between his page Constantine and the charming Calanthe.

It will be remembered that when he called, in a mean disguise, at the abode of Demetrius, he saw Calanthe for the first time, and only for a short period ; and though he was even then struck by her beauty, yet the impression it made was but momentary : and he had so far forgotten Calanthe as never to behold in Constantine the least resemblance to any one whom he had seen before.

But now that Calanthe's countenance burst upon him in all the glory of its superb Greek beauty, that resemblance struck upon him with all the force of a new idea ; and he was about to express his astonishment that so wondrous a likeness should subsist even between brother and sisters when the maid sank at his feet, exclaiming, " Pardon me, great Vizier !—but Constantine and Calanthe are one and the same being !"

" Methought the brother pleaded with marvellous eloquence on behalf of his sister," said Ibrahim, with a smile ; and raising Calanthe from her suppliant posture, he led her to a seat, gazing on her the while with eyes expressive of intense passion.

" Your Highness," observed the maiden, after a short pause, " has heard from my own lips how profound is the attachment which I have dared to conceive for you—how great is the admiration I entertain for the brilliant powers of your intellect. To be with thee, great Ibrahim ! will I abandon country, friends—aye, and even creed, shouldst thou demand that concession ; for in thee—and in thee only—are all my hopes of happiness now centred !"

" And those hopes shall not be disappointed, dearest Calanthe !" exclaimed Ibrahim, clasping her in his arms. " But a few minutes before you entered this room, a hundred women—the choicest flowers of all climes—were gathered here ;—and yet I value one smile on thy lips more than all the tender endearments that those purchased houris could bestow. For thy love was unbought, —it was a love that prompted thee to attach thyself in a menial capacity to my person——"

The impassioned language of the Grand Vizier was suddenly interrupted by the opening of the door ; and three black slaves glided into the anderoon—half crouching as they stole along—and fixing on the beauteous Calanthe, eyes, the dark pupils of which seemed to glare horribly from the whites in which they were set.

" Dogs ! what signifies this intrusion ?" exclaimed Ibrahim-Pacha, starting from the sofa, and grasping the handle of his scimitar.

The chief of the three slaves uttered not a word of reply, but exhibited the imperial signet-ring, and at the same time unrolled from the coil which he had hitherto held in his hand a long green silken bow-string.

At that ominous spectacle Ibrahim fell back, his countenance becoming ashy pale, and his frame trembling with an icy shudder from head to foot.

" Choose between this and her," whispered the slave, in a deep tone, as he first glanced at the bow-string and then looked towards Calanthe, who knew that some terrible danger was impending, but was unable to divine where or when it was to fall.

" Merciful Allah !" exclaimed the Grand Vizier ; and, throwing himself upon the floor, he buried his face in his hands.

In another moment Calanthe was seized and gagged, before even a word or scream could escape her lips ; but Ibrahim heard the rustling of her dress as she unavailingly struggled with the monsters in whose power she was.

The selfish ingrate ! he drew not his scimitar to defend her—he no longer remembered all the tender love she bore him ; but, appalled by the menace of the bow-string, backed by the warrant of the Sultan's signet-ring, he lay grovelling on the rich Persian carpet, giving vent to his alarms by low and piteous moans.

Then he heard the door once more close as softly as possible :—he looked up—glared with wild anxiety around—and breathed more freely on finding himself alone !

For the Ethiopians had departed with their victim !

Slowly rising from his supine posture, Ibrahim approached the table, filled a crystal cup with sherbet to the brim, and drank the cooling beverage which seemed to go hissing down his parched throat—so dreadful was the thirst which the horror of the scene just enacted had produced.

Then the sickening as well as maddening conviction struck to his very soul, that though the envied and almost worshipped Vizier of a mighty empire,—having authority of life and death over millions of human beings, and able to dispose of the governments and patronage of huge provinces and mighty cities,—he was but a miserable helpless slave in the eyes of another greater still—an ephemeron whom the breath of Solyman the Magnificent could destroy!

And overcome by the conviction, he threw himself on the sofa, bursting into an agony of tears,—tears of mingled rage and woe.

Yes; the proud—the selfish—the haughty renegade wept as bitterly as ever a poor weak woman was known to weep!

* * * * *

How calm and beautiful lay the waters of the Golden Horn beneath the light of that lovely moon which shone so chastely and so serenely above,—as if pouring its argent lustre upon a world where no evil passions were known—no hearts were stained with crime—no iniquity of human imaginings was in course of perpetration.

But, ah! what sound is that which breaks on the silence of the night?

Is it the splash of oars? No—for the two black slaves who guide yon boat which has shot out from the shore into the centre of the gulf, are resting on the slight sculls—the boat itself too, is now stationary—and not a ripple is stirred by its grotesquely-shaped prow.

What then was that sound?

'Twas the voice of agony bursting from woman's throat; and that boat is about to become the scene of a deed of horror, though one of frequent—alas! too frequent—occurrence in that clime, and especially on that gulf.

The gag has slipped from Calanthe's mouth: and a long, loud scream of agonizing despair sweeps over the surface of the water—rending the calm and moonlit air—but dying away ere it can raise an echo on either shore.

Strong are the arms and relentless is the heart of the black monster who has now seized the unhappy Greek maiden in his ferocious grasp—while the lustre of the pale orb of night streams on that countenance lately radiant with impassioned hope, but now convulsed with indescribable horror.

Again the scream bursts from the victim's lips; but its thrilling, cutting agony is interrupted by a sudden plunge—a splash—a gurgling and rippling of the waters—and the corse of the murdered Calanthe is borne towards the deeper and darker bosom of the Bosphorus.

* * * * *

The sun was already dispersing the orient mists when the chief of the three black slaves once more stood in the presence of the Grand Vizier, who had passed the night in the anderoon, alone and a prey to the most lively mental tortures,

So noiselessly and reptile-like did the hideous Ethiopian steal into the apartment, that he was within a yard of the Grand Vizier ere the latter was aware that the door had been opened.

Ibrahim started as if from a snake about to spring upon him—for the ominous bow-string swung negligently from the slave's hand, and the imperial signet still glistened on his finger.

"Mighty Pacha!" spoke the Ethiopian, in a low and cold tone; "thus saith the Sultana-Valida:—'Cease to treat thy loving wife with neglect. Hasten to her—throw thyself at her feet—implore her pardon for the past—and give her hope of affection for the future. Shouldst thou neglect this warning, then every night will the rival whom thou preferest to her, be torn from thine arms, and be devoted as food for the fishes. She whom thou didst so prefer this night that is passed, sleeps in the dark green bed of the Bosphorus. Take warning, Pacha; for the bow-string may be used at last. Moreover, see that thou revealest not to the Princess Aischa the incident of the night, nor the nature of the threats which send thee back repentant to her arms.'"

And with these words the slave glided hastily from the room, leaving the Grand Vizier a prey to feelings of ineffable horror.

His punishment on earth had begun—and he knew it!

What had his ambition gained? What had his apostacy accomplished? Though rich, invested with high rank, and surrounded by every luxury, he was more wretched than the meanest slave who was accustomed to kiss the dust at his feet!

But subduing the fearful agitation which oppressed him—composing his feelings and his countenance as well as he was able—the proud and haughty Ibrahim hastened to implore admittance to his wife's chamber; and when the boon was accorded, and he found himself in her presence, he besought her pardon in a voice and with a manner expressive of the most humiliating penitence!

Thus, at the moment when thousands—perhaps millions were envying the bright fortunes and glorious destinies of Ibrahim the Happy, as he was denominated—the dark and terrible despotism of the Sultana-Valida made him tremble for his life, and compelled him to sue at Aischa's feet for pardon.

And if, at that instant of his crushed spirit and wounded pride, there were a balm found to soothe the racking fibres of his heart, the anodyne consisted in the tender love which Aischa manifested towards him, and the touching sincerity with which she assured him of her complete forgiveness.

CHAPTER LIV.

NISIDA AND WAGNER ON THE ISLAND.—THE INCANTATION.

RETURN we again to that Mediterranean Island on which Fernand Wagner and the beauteous Nisida espoused each other by solemn vows plighted in the face of heaven, and where they have now resided for six long months.

At first how happy—how supremely happy was Nisida,—having tutored herself so far to forget the jarring interests of that world which lay beyond the sea, as to abandon her soul without reservation to the delights of the new existence on which she had entered.

Enabled once more to use that charming voice which God had given her, but which had remained hushed for so many years,—able also to listen to the words that fell from the lips of her lover, without being forced to subdue and crush the emotions which they excited,—and secure in the possession of him to whom she was so madly devoted and who manifested such endearing tenderness towards herself,—Nisida indeed felt as if she were another being, or endowed with the lease of a new life.

And at first, too, how much had Wagner and Nisida to say to each other,—how many fond assurances to give—how many protestations of unalterable affection to make! For hours would they sit together upon the sea-shore, or on the bank of the limpid stream in the valley, and converse almost unceasingly,—wearying not of each other's discourse, and sustaining the interest and enjoyment of that interchange of thoughts by flying from topic to topic just as their unshackled imaginations suggested.

But Fernand never questioned Nisida concerning the motive which had induced her to feign dumbness and deafness for so many years; she had given him to understand that family reasons of the deepest importance, and involving dreadful mysteries from the contemplation of which she recoiled in horror, had prompted so tremendous a self-martyrdom;—and he loved her too well to outrage her feelings by urging her to touch more than she might choose on that topic.

Careful not to approach the vicinity of large trees, for fear of those dreadful tenants of the isle who might be said to divide its sovereignty with them, the lovers—may we not venture to call them husband and wife?—would ramble, hand-in-hand, along the stream's enchanting banks, in the calm hours of moonlight which lent softer charms to the scene than when the gorgeous sun bathed all in gold.

Or else they would wander on the sands, to the musical murmur of the rippling sea,—their arms clasping each other's necks—their eyes exchanging glances of fondness—hers of ardent passion, his of more melting tenderness.

But there was too much sensuality in the disposition of Nisida to render her love for Wagner sufficient and powerful enough to ensure permanent contentment with her present lot.

The first time that the fatal eve drew near when he must exchange the shape of a man for that of a horrible wolf, he had said to her, "Beloved Nisida, I remember that there are finer and different fruits on the other side of the island, beyond the range of mountains ; and I should rejoice to obtain for thee a variety. Console thyself for a few hours during mine absence : and on my return we shall experience renewed and increased happiness, as if we were meeting again after a long separation." Vainly did Nisida assure him that she recked not for a more extensive variety of fruits than those which the nearest grove yielded, and that she would rather have his society than all the luxuries which his absence and return might bring her : he overruled her remonstrances—and she at length permitted him to depart. Then he crossed the mountains by means of the path which he had descried when he escaped from the torrent at the point where the tree stretched across the stream, as described in a preceding chapter ; and on the other side of the range of hills he fulfilled the fearful destiny of the Wehr-Wolf! On his return to Nisida—after an absence of nearly twenty-four hours, for the time occupied in crossing and re-crossing the mountains was considerable—he found her gloomy and pensive. His long absence had vexed her ; she, in the secrecy of her own heart, had already felt a craving for a change of scene—and she naturally suspected it was to gratify a similar want that Fernand had undertaken the transmontane journey. She received his fruits coldly ; and it was some time ere he could succeed in winning her back to perfect good humour.

The next interval of a month glided away : the little incident which had for a moment ruffled the harmony of their lives, was forgotten—at least by Nisida ;—and so devoted was Fernand in his attention, so tenderly sincere in his attachment towards her,—and so joyful, too, was she in the possession of one whose masculine beauty was almost superhumanly great,—that those incipient cravings for change of scene—those nascent longings for a return to the great and busy world, returned but seldom and were even then easily subdued in her breast.

When the second fatal date of their union on the island approached, Wagner was compelled to urge some new, though necessarily trivial excuse for again crossing the mountains ; and Nisida's remonstrances were more authoritative and earnest than on the previous occasion. Nevertheless, he succeeded in obtaining her consent ; but during his absence of four or five and twenty hours, the lady had ample leisure to ponder on home—the busy world across the sea—and her well-beloved brother Francisco. Fernand, when he came back, found her gloomy and reserved : then as he essayed to wean her from her dark thoughts she responded petulantly, and even reproachfully.

The ensuing month glided not away so happily as the two former ones : and though Fernand's attentions and manifestations of fondness increased, if possible, still Nisida would frequently sigh, and look wistfully at the sea, as if she would have joyed to behold a sail in the horizon.

The third time the fatal close of the month drew nigh, Wagner knew not how to act : but some petulance on the part of Nisida furnished him with an excuse to which his generous heart only had recourse with the deepest—the keenest anguish. Throwing back the harsh words at her whom he loved so devotedly, he exclaimed, "Nisida, I leave thee for a few hours until thy good humour shall have returned ;" and, without waiting for a reply, he darted towards the mountains. For some time the lady remained seated gloomily upon the sand ; but as hour after hour passed away, and the sun went down, and the moon gathered power to light the enchanting scene of landscape and of sea, she grew uneasy and restless. Throughout that night she wandered up and down on the sands, now weeping at the thought that she herself had been unkind—then angry at the conviction that Fernand was treating her more harshly than she deserved.

It was not until the sun was high in the heavens that Wagner re-appeared ; and though Nisida was in reality delighted to find all her wild alarms, in which the monstrous snakes of the isle entered largely, thus completely dissipated,—yet she concealed the joy which she experienced in beholding his safe return, and received him with gloomy hauteur.

Oh! how her conduct went to Wagner's heart! for he knew that, so long as the direful necessity which had compelled his absence remained unexplained, Nisida was justified in attributing the absence to unkind feelings and motives on his part. A thousand times that day was he on the point of throwing himself at her feet, and revealing all the details of his frightful destiny : but he

dared not—oh! no, he dared not;—and a profound melancholy seized upon his soul.

Nisida now relented—chiefly because she herself felt miserable by the contemplation of his unhappiness : and harmony was restored between them.

But during the fourth month of their union, the lady began to speak more frequently and frankly of the weariness and the monotony of their present existence ; and when Fernand essayed to console her, she responded only by deep-drawn sighs. *His* love was based on those enduring elements which would have rendered him content to dwell for ever with Nisida on that island, which had no sameness for him so long as she was there to be his companion : but *her* love subsisted rather sensually than mentally ; and now that her fierce and long pent-up desires had experienced gratification, she longed to return to the land of her birth, to embrace her brother Francisco—yes, even though she should be again compelled to simulate the deaf and dumb!

The close of the fourth month was now at hand, and Wagner was at a loss how to act. New excuses for a fresh absence were impossible ; and it was with a heart breaking with anguish, that he was compelled to seize an opportunity in the afternoon of the last day of the month, to steal away from Nisida and hasten across the mountain. Oh! what would she think of his absence now ?—an absence for which he had not prepared her, and which was not on this occasion justified by any petulance or wilfulness on her part ? The idea was maddening ; but there was no alternative!

It was noon on the ensuing day when Fernand Wagner, pale and careworn, again sought that spot on the strand where the rudely-constructed cottage stood : but Nisida was not within the hut. He roved along the shore to a considerable distance, but still he beheld her not. Terrible alarms now oppressed him. Could she have done some desperate deed to rid herself of an existence whereof she was weary ? or had some fatal accident befallen her ?

From the shore he hastened to the valley ; and there, seated by the side of the crystal stream, he beheld the object of his search. He ran—he flew towards her ; but she seemed not to observe him ; and when he caught a glimpse of her countenance, he shrank back in dismay— it was so pale, and yet so expressive of deep, concentrated rage !

But we cannot linger on this portion of our tale. Suffice it to say that Wagner exerted all his eloquence, all his powers of persuasion to induce Nisida to turn a kind glance upon him ; and it was only when, goaded to desperation by her stern silence and her implacable mien, he exclaimed, "Since I am no longer worthy of even a look or a syllable, I will quit thee for ever !"— it was only when these words conveyed to Nisida a frightful menace of loneliness, that she relented and gradually suffered herself to be appeased. But vainly did she question him relative to the cause of his absence on this occasion : he offered a variety of excuses, and she believed none of them.

The month that followed was characterized by many quarrels and disputes ; for Nisida's soul acquired all that restlessness which had marked it ere she was thrown on the island, but which solitude at first, and then the possession of Wagner, had for a time so greatly subdued.

Nevertheless, there were still occasions when she would cling to Wagner with all the confiding fondness of one who remembered how he had saved her life from the hideous anaconda, and who looked up to him as her only joy and solace in that clime the beauty of which became painful with its monotony :—yes, she would cling to him as they roved along the sands together—she would gaze up into his countenance—and, as she read assurances of the deepest affection in his fine dark eyes, she would exclaim rapturously, "Oh! how handsome—how godlike art thou, my Fernand! Pardon me—pardon me, that I should ever have nursed resentment against thee!"

It was when she was in such a mood as this, that he murmured in her ears, "Nisida, dearest, thou hast thy secret which I have never sought to penetrate. I also have my secret, beloved one, as I hinted to thee on that day which united us in this island ; and into that mystery of mine thou mayst not look. But at certain intervals I must absent myself from thee for a few hours, as I hitherto have done ; and on my return, O dearest Nisida! let me not behold that glorious countenance of thine clouded with anger and with gloom !"

Then ere she could utter a word of reply, he sealed her lips with kisses—he pressed her fervently to his heart—

and at that moment she thought he seemed so divinely handsome, and she felt so proud of possessing the love of a man invested with such superhuman beauty and such a splendid intellect, that she attempted not a remonstrance nor a complaint against words which were but the preface to a fifth absence of four-and-twenty hours.

And when Fernand Wagner re-appeared again, his Nisida hastened to meet him, as he descended from the mountains,—those mountains which were crossed even by a sure-footed and agile man with so much difficulty, and which he knew it would be impossible for him to traverse during that mad career in which he was monthly doomed to whirl along in his lupine shape;—yes, she hurried to meet him—received him with open arms—smiled tenderly upon him—and led him to the sea-shore, where she had spread the noon-day meal in the most inviting manner.

The unwearied and unchanging nature of his love had touched her heart; and, during the long hours of his fifth absence, she had reasoned with herself on the folly of marring the sweet harmony which should prevail between the only two human tenants of the island.

The afternoon passed more happily than many and many a previous day had done: Nisida thought that Fernand had never seemed so handsome, though he was somewhat pale—and Wagner fancied that his companion had never appeared so magnificently beautiful as now, while she lay half reclining in his arms, the rays of the setting sun faintly illuminating her aquiline countenance, and giving a glossy richness to the luxuriant black hair which floated negligently over her naked shoulders.

When the last beams of the orb of day died flickeringly in the far horizon, the tender pair retired to their hut, rejoicing in the serene and happy way in which the last few hours had glided over their heads.

Sleep was upon their eyelids as they lay in each other's arms,—the island and the sea were sleeping too in the soft light of the silver moon and the countless stars which gemmed the vault of heaven,—when a dark figure passed along the sand and stopped at a short distance from the door of the rudely-constructed tenement.

And assuredly this was no mortal being—nor wore it now a mortal shape: but Satan—in all the horrors of his ugliness, though still invested with that sublimity of mien which marked the fallen angel,—Satan, clothed in terrors ineffable, it was!

For a few moments he stood contemplating the hut wherein the sleepers lay:—dread lightnings flashed from his eyes—and the forked electric fluid seemed to play around his haughty brow—while his fearful countenance, the features of which no human pen may venture to describe, expressed malignant hate, anticipated triumph, and tremendous scorn.

Then, extending his right hand towards the hut, and speaking in that deep sonorous tone which, when heard by mortal ears, seemed to jar against the very soul, he chanted the following incantation:—

"Woman of wild and fierce desires!
 Why languish thus the wonted fires
That armed thine heart, and nerved thine hand
To do whate'er thy firmness plann'd?—
 Has maudlin love subdued thy soul,
 Once so impatient of control?
Has amorous play enslaved thy mind
Which erst no common chains confined?
 Has tender dalliance power to kill
 Thy wild, indomitable will?—
No more must love thus paralyse
And crush thine iron energies;—
 No more must maudlin passion stay
 Thy despot soul's remorseless sway:—
Henceforth thy lips shall cease to smile
Upon the beauties of this isle;—
 Henceforth thy mental glance shall roam,
 Over the Mediterranean foam,
Towards thy far-off Tuscan home!
Alarms for young Francisco's weal,
And doubts into thy breast will steal;—
 While retrospection carries back
 Thy mem'ry o'er Time's beaten track,
And stops at that dread hour when thou,
With burning eyes, and flushing brow,
 Call'd heaven to hear the solemn vow
 Dictated with the latest breath
Of thy fond mother on th' untimely bed of death!"

Thus spoke the Demon; and, having chanted the in-

cantation, full of menace and of deep design, he turned to depart.

Sleep was still upon the eyelids of Fernand and Nisida as they lay in each other's arms, the island and the sea, too, were still sleeping in the soft light of the silver moon and the countless stars which gemmed the vault of heaven,—when the dark figure passed along the sand, away from the rudely-constructed tenement!

CHAPTER LV.

THE FIRST EFFECTS OF THE INCANTATION.

WHEN the sun rose again from the orient wave, Fernand repaired to the grove, as was his wont, to gather fruits for the morning repast,—while Nisida bathed her fair form in the waters of the Mediterranean.

But there was a gloom upon the lady's brow, and there was a sombre flashing in her large dark eyes, which denoted an incipient conflict of emotions stirring within her breast.

She had retired to rest, as we have seen, on the previous evening, with a heart glowing towards her beloved and handsome Fernand,—she had fallen asleep with the tender sounds of his musical yet manly voice in her ears, and the image of his beautiful countenance in her mind:—but in the night—she knew not at what hour—strange dreams began to oppress her—ominous visions filled her with anxiety.

It seemed as if some being, having right to reproach and power to taunt, whispered to her as she slept stern remonstrances against the idle, voluptuous, and dreaming life she was leading,—mocking her for passing her time in the maudlin delights of love,—calling upon her to arouse her latent energies and shake off that luxurious lethargy, teaching her to look upon the island, beauteous though it were, as one vast prison in which she was confined, from whence there was nevertheless means of escape,—raising up before her mental vision all the most alluring and bustling scenes of her own native city of Florence,—then bitterly reproaching her for having allowed her soul to be more wrapped up in the society of Fernand Wagner, than solicitous, as it was wont to be, for the welfare of her brother Francisco,—creating, too, wild doubt in her imagination as to whether circumstances might not after all have united her brother and Flora Francatelli in the bonds of a union which for many reasons she abhorred,—and lastly, thundering in her ears the terrible accusation that she was perjured to a solemn and an awful vow pledged by her lips, on a dread occasion, and to the dictating voice of her dying mother!

When she awoke in the morning, her brain appeared to be in confusion;—but as her thoughts gradually settled themselves in the various cells of the seat of memory, the entire details of her long dream assumed the semblance of a connected chain, even as we have just described them.

For those thoughts had arisen in the nature and the order commanded by the Demon!

Fernand Wagner saw that the mind of his lovely companion—his charming bride—was ruffled; and as he embraced her tenderly, he inquired the cause. His caresses for the moment soothed her, and induced her to struggle against the ideas which oppressed her;—*for there are no thoughts that Satan excites within us, which we cannot wrestle with—aye, and conquer, if we will!*

Finding that Nisida became more composed, and that she treated her mournfulness and her agitation merely as the results of a disagreeable dream, Fernand rose—hastened to perform his own ablutions—and then repaired to the adjacent grove, as above stated.

But Nisida remained not long in the Mediterranean's mighty bath: the moment Wagner had departed from her presence, the thoughts which had so recently passed in sad procession through her brain, came back with renewed vigour—forcing themselves as it were upon her contemplation, because she offered but a feeble resistance to their returning invasion.

And as she stood on the shore, having donned her scant clothing, and now combing out her long, luxuriant hair, to the silken riches of which the salt water lent a more glorious gloss,—she became a prey to an increasing restlessness—an augmenting anxiety—a longing to quit that island and an earnest desire to behold her brother Francisco once again,—sentiments and cravings which gave to her countenance an expression of sombre lowering and concentrated passion, such as it was wont to exhibit in those days when her simulated deafness and dumbness forced her to subdue all the workings of her excited soul, and compress her vermilion lips to check the ebullition of that language which on those occasions struggled to pour itself forth.

"O Italy! Italy!" she exclaimed, in an impassioned tone; "shall I ever behold thee again? Oh! my beloved native land—and thou, too, fair city, whose name is fraught with so many varied reminiscences for me,—am I doomed never to visit ye more?"

"Nisida! dearest Nisida!" said Wagner, who had returned to her unperceived and unheard—for his feet passed noiselessly over the sand; "wherefore those pas-

volcano. My thoughts wander, in spite of myself, towards Italy: I think, too, of my brother—the young and inexperienced Francisco! Moreover, there is in our mansion at Florence, a terrible mystery which prying eyes may seek to penetrate,—a closet containing a fearful secret, which, if published to the world, would heap loathing execration and disgrace on the haughty name of Riverola! And now Francisco is the sole guardian of that mystery, which he himself knows not—at least, knew not, when last we were together. But it requires a strong and an energetic mind, like my own, to watch over that awful secret. And now, Fernand—dear Fer-

"'RECEIVE THE HAND OF MY WELL-BELOVED SISTER.'"   (See p. 87.)

sionate exclamations? why this anxious longing to revisit the busy, bustling world? Are not the calm and serene delights of this island sufficient for our happiness? or art thou wearied of me, who love thee so tenderly?"

"I am not wearied of thee, my Fernand!" replied Nisida: "nor do I fail to appreciate all thy tender affection towards me. But—I can conceal it from myself and from thee no longer,—I am overcome with the monotony of this isle. Unvaried sunshine during the day—unchanging calmness by night, pall upon the soul. I crave variety—even the variety that would be afforded by a magnificent storm, or the eruption of yon sleeping

nand, thou canst not blame me—thou wilt not reproach me, if I experience an irresistible longing to return to my native land!"

"And know you not, Nisida," said Wagner, in a tone of mingled mournfulness and reproach, "that, even if there were any means for thee to return to Florence, I could not accompany thee? Dost thou not remember that I informed thee, that being doomed to death, I escaped from the power of the authorities—it matters not how; and that were I to set my foot in Florence again, it would be to return to my dungeon?"

"Alas! all this I remember well—too well!" exclaimed Nisida. "And think not, my Fernand, that I feel no pang, when I lay bare to thee the state of my soul. But if it were possible for us to return to Italy, thou couldst dwell secretly and retiredly in some suburb of Florence ; and we should be together often—very often !"

"No—Nisida," answered Wagner, "that were impossible ! Never more may I venture into that city :—and if thou couldst find even the means to revisit thy native clime, thither must thou go and there must thou dwell *alone !*"

For Wagner knew full well that were the lady to return to Florence, she would hear of the frightful incident which marked his trial and also the day of his escape ; and, though when he had first become reunited to her on the island, he had intended, in the fulness of a generous confidence, to impart to her the terrible secret of his fate,—yet subsequent and more calm deliberation in his own mind had convinced him of the imprudence of giving her love a shock by such a tremendous—such an appalling revelation.

"Fernand," said Nisida, breaking silence after a long pause, during which she was wrapped in profound meditation, "thy words go to my heart like fiery arrows ! O my handsome—my beautiful—my beloved Fernand, why does destiny thus persecute us ? It is impossible for thee to return to Florence :—it is equally impossible for me to renounce the first opportunity which heaven may afford for me to repair thither ! My God ! wherefore do our fates tend in such opposite directions ? To separate from thee, were maddening—maddening : to abandon my brother Francisco—to desert the grave and solemn interests which demand my presence at home, were to render myself perjured to a vow which I breathed, and which heaven witnessed, when I knelt long years ago at the death-bed of my mother !"

"After all thou hast said, my beloved Nisida," exclaimed Fernand, in a voice expressive of the deepest melancholy, "I should be wrong—I should be even criminal to listen only to the whisperings of my own selfishness and retain thee here, did opportunity serve for thy departure. But on this island shall I remain—perhaps for ever ! And if the time should ever come when you grew wearied of that bustling world across the sea, and thy memory travelled to this lonely isle where thy Fernand was left behind thee,—haply thou wouldst embark to return hither and pass the remainder of thy days with one who can never cease to love thee !"

Tears came into the eyes of Nisida—of her who so seldom, so very seldom wept ;—and throwing herself into Wagner's arms, she exclaimed, " God grant that I may revisit my native land ; and believe me—oh ! believe me when I declare that I would come back to thee the moment the interests of my brother no longer demanded my presence !"

They embraced fondly ; and then sat down upon the sand to partake of their morning repast.

But the thoughts of both were naturally intent upon the recent topic of their discourse ; and their conversation, though each determined to force it into other channels, reverted to the subject which was now uppermost in their minds.

"What must my poor brother Francisco conjecture to be the cause of my prolonged, and to him mysterious absence ?" said Nisida, as her eyes were cast wistfully over the wide expanse of waters. "Methinks that I have already hinted to thee how the foolish passion which he had conceived for a maiden of low degree and obscure birth, compelled me—in accordance with his nearest and best interests—to consign the object of his boyish love to the Convent of the Carmelites ! Yes—and it was with surprise and dismay indescribable that I heard, ere I was torn away from Florence by the villain Stephano, how that convent was sacked and destroyed by unknown marauders——"

" Full intelligence of which terrible sacrilege you communicated to me by signs the second and last time you visited me in my dungeon," observed Wagner.

"And I heard also, and with increased fear," continued Nisida, "that some of the inmates of that convent had escaped ; and, being unable, in consequence of my simulated deafness and dumbness, to set on foot the necessary inquiries, I could not learn whether Flora Francatelli was amongst those who had so escaped the almost general ruin. Oh ! if she should have survived that fatal night—and if she should have again encountered my brother ! Alas ! thou perceivest, my Fernand, how necessary it is for me to quit this island on the first occasion which may serve for that purpose."

"And wouldst thou, Nisida," asked Wagner, reproach-

fully, "place thyself as a barrier between the Count of Riverola and her whom he loves ?"

" Yes !" ejaculated Nisida, her countenance suddenly assuming a stern and imperious expression : " for the most important interests are involved in the marriage which he may contract. But enough of this, Fernand," she added, relapsing into a more tender mood. " And now tell me—canst thou blame me for the longing desire which has seized upon me—the ardent craving to return to Florence ?"

"Nay—I do not blame thee, dearest Nisida !" he exclaimed ; "but I pity thee—I feel for thee ! Because," he continued, "if I understand rightly, though wilt be compelled to feign deafness and dumbness once more, in order to work out thy mysterious aims ;—thou wilt be compelled to submit to that awful martyrdom—that terrible privation—that tremendous duplicity, which thou wilt find so doubly painful and so difficult to resume after the full enjoyment and exercise of the blessed faculties of speech and hearing."

"Alas ! such will be my destiny !" murmured Nisida : " and, oh ! that destiny is a sad one ! But," she exclaimed, after a moment's pause, and as a reminiscence appeared suddenly to strike her, "dost thou not think that even such a destiny as that becomes tolerable, when it is fulfilled as the only means of carrying out the conditions of a vow breathed to a well-beloved and dying mother ? But wearisome—oh ! crushingly tedious was that mode of existence !—and the first bright day of real happiness which I enjoyed, was that when I first knew that thou didst love me ! And again, Fernand—oh ! again was I supremely happy when one evening—thou mayst remember well—it was the eve when my brother and the minion Flora exchanged tender words together in the room adjoining where we were seated—on that evening, Fernand, I besought by signs that thou wouldst breathe the words, ' *I love thee !*' and thou didst so—and I drank in those words as a person dying with thirst would imbibe the first drop of pure spring water which was placed to his lips !"

Fernand pressed Nisida to his heart ;—for he saw, in spite of her anxiety to return to Italy, that she really loved him.

CHAPTER LVI.

NISIDA AND THE DEMON.

BUT though sensual and impassioned feelings led the beauteous Nisida thus frequently to melt into softness and tenderness when she contemplated the wondrously handsome countenance of Fernand Wagner,—yet from this day forth her longings to return to Italy became more earnest—more irresistible ; and she would compel him to sit by her side for hours together on the shore, while she eagerly watched for the appearance of a sail in the horizon.

And Fernand, who divined her object, and knew full well wherefore those fine and eloquent black eyes were cast so wistfully over the sunny expanse,—Fernand himself now longed for the advent of a ship,—so sincere was his love for Nisida, that he was prepared to make any sacrifice—aye, even to suffer her to depart and leave him alone on the island—in order to promote her happiness.

Thus passed away the sixth month ; and on the afternoon of the last day thereof, when Wagner was about to observe to her that the time had now arrived for him to cross the mountains once again, she said of her own accord, " Fernand, my beloved, when next you visit the other side of the island, you would do well to raise some sign, or leave some permanent mark to show that there are inhabitants on this land. For a ship might touch in that point—the sailors might seek the shore for water—and they would then search to discover the spot where those who raised the signal-post are dwelling."

"Your wish shall be fulfilled, dearest," answered Wagner ; "and without delay will I seek the other side of the island."

Then they embraced tenderly ; and Fernand departed once more to fulfil his frightful doom !

Nisida watched his receding form until it was lost in the groves intervening between the plains and the acclivities of the range of mountains ; and then she seated herself again on the sand, wondering of what nature her husband's secret could be, and why it compelled him to absent himself occasionally from her.

Though *he* kept an accurate calculation of the lapse of time, and counted the passing days with unvarying precision,—yet she retained no such faithful calendar in her memory; and thus it had not yet struck her that his absence always occurred on the last day of the month.

The hour of sunset was now rapidly approaching; and as Nisida was wrapped up in thought, but with her eyes fixed wistfully upon the mighty bosom of the deep, a slight sound as of the rustling of garments fell upon her ears.

She started up, and glanced rapidly around.

But how ineffable was her astonishment—how great was her sudden joy—when she beheld the figure of a man approaching her:—for it instantly struck her that the same ship which had conveyed him thither, might bear her away from a scene which had latterly become insupportably monotonous.

The individual whose presence thus excited her astonishment and her delight, was tall, thin, and attired rather in the German, than in the Italian fashion: but as he drew nearer, Nisida experienced undefinable emotions of alarm, and vague fears rushed to her soul—for the expression of that being's countenance was such as to inspire no pleasurable emotions.

It was not that he was ugly:—no—his features were well formed, and his eyes were of dazzling brilliancy. But their glances were penetrating and reptile-like,—glances beneath which those of ordinary mortals would have quailed; and his countenance was stamped with a mingled sardonism and melancholy which rendered it painful to contemplate.

Nisida attributed her feeling of uneasiness and embarrassment to the shame which she experienced in finding herself half naked in the presence of a stranger; for so oppressive had become the heat of summer that her clothing was most scanty, and she had long ceased to decorate her person with garlands and wreaths of fantastically woven flowers.

"Fear not, lady," said the Demon—for he indeed it was: "I am come to counsel and solace—not to alarm thee."

"How knowest thou that I require counsel? and who art thou that talkest to me of solace?" asked Nisida, her sentiment of shame yielding to one of boundless surprise at hearing herself thus addressed by a being who appeared to read the inmost secrets of her soul.

"I am one who can penetrate into all the mysteries of the human heart," returned the fiend, in his sonorous, deep-toned voice; "and I can gather thine history from the expression of thy countenance—the attitude in which I first beheld thee, whilst thou wast still seated upon the strand—and the mingled emotions of surprise and joy with which thou didst mark my presence. Is it then, difficult to imagine that thou requirest counsel to teach thee how to proceed so as to obtain thine emancipation from this isle? or would it be extraordinary if, moved by thy sorrow, I offered to befriend thee? And is it not ever the way with mortals—poor weak, miserable beings that they are—to grow speedily dissatisfied with their lot? In the spirit of religion ye say that heaven controls your destinies according to its own wise purposes; —and when all goes well with ye, and you have your desires, ye pray and are thankful—because forsooth," added the Demon, with a smile of bitter scorn, "it is so easy to pray when ye are contented and happy, and so easy to be thankful when ye are pampered with all ye require. Here art thou, lady,—on an island teeming with the choicest fruits of the earth, and enjoying an eternal summer,—where all is pleasant to the view, and to whose silent shores the cares of the great world cannot come; and yet thou wouldst quit this calm retreat, and rush back into the vortex of evil passions—warring interests—conflicting pursuits! But I will not weary thee with my reflections;—although it is my nature first to taunt and upbraid those whom I intend to serve!"

"And who art thou, strange being, that reasoneth morally with the smile of scorn upon thy lips?" demanded Nisida, the vague alarms which had previously influenced her reviving with additional power: "who art thou, I say, that comest to reproach, and yet profferest thine aid?"

"No matter who I am," replied the fiend. "Some day thou mayst know me better if thou wilt——"

"But how camest thou hither? Where is the ship that brought thee—the boat that landed thee?" demanded Nisida, in a tone of feverish impatience.

"No ship brought me hither—no boat set me on the shore," answered the Demon, fixing his eyes—those piercing eyes upon Nisida's countenance, as if to read the impression which this strange revelation made upon her secret soul.

"Then who art thou?" exclaimed the lady, a cold shudder passing over her entire frame, although she retreated not, nor withdrew the glances which she through her wondrous state of mind, was enabled to retain fixed upon the Demon's countenance.

"Seek not to learn as yet whom I am," said the fiend. "Let it suffice for thee to know that I am something more than a mere mortal—a being gifted with powers which, in the hands of such an one as thou, would throw the entire world into convulsions; for there is much in thee after my own heart, beauteous Nisida of Riverola."

"Ah! thou art acquainted even with my name!" cried Nisida, again shuddering violently in spite of her powerful efforts to appear calm and fearless.

"I am acquainted with thy name, and with all that concerns thee and thine, Nisida," replied the fiend; "aye," he added, with a malignant chuckle,—even to the mystery of the closet in thy late father's chamber, and the contents of the terrible manuscript which taught thee such dreadful secrets! I know, too, all that thou hast done to serve thine aims—thy simulated deafness and dumbness—the assassination of Agnes—the imprisonment of Flora in the convent——"

"Then art thou indeed some superhuman power," interrupted Nisida in a tone of inexpressible alarm; "and I dare hold no further converse with thee!"

"One moment—and thou wilt think differently!" exclaimed the Demon. "But I will give thee an evidence of my power. Here, take this instrument,—'tis called a telescope—and use it for a single minute. Glance across the waters, and thou shalt behold a scene which will interest thee somewhat, I trow!"

The fiend handed her a telescope, and directed her to apply it to her eye. She obeyed him, though reluctantly; but intense curiosity overcame her scruples — and, moreover, her extraordinary strength of mind aided her in supporting the presence of one whom she knew to be invested with superhuman powers—but of what nature she feared to guess.

Nisida turned towards the sea, and used the magic telescope as directed, while the Demon stood behind her, his countenance expressing a diabolical triumph mingled with blighting scorn.

But, ah! what does Nisida behold?

The moment she applies the telescope to her eyes, she is transported, as it were to her own native city. She is in Florence—yes, in the fair capital of Tuscany. Every familiar scene is present to her again; and she once more views the busy crowds and the bustling haunts of men. She sweeps them all with a hurried glance; and then her looks settle upon a young couple, walking together in a secluded place on the banks of the Arno. But, oh; how terribly flash her eyes—how changed with wrath and concentrated rage suddenly becomes her countenance! For in that fond pair, wandering so lovingly together on the Arno's margin, she recognises her brother Francisco and the maiden Flora Francatelli!

"Thou hast seen enough!" cried the Demon, snatching the telescope from her hands. "And now, more than ever," he added, with a malignant smile of triumph, "dost thou long to revisit thy native land. It was to confirm that longing that I showed thee the scene!"

"And canst thou give me the means to return thither?" demanded Nisida, almost maddened by the spectacle that had met her eyes.

"Listen!" exclaimed the fiend; "and hear me patiently. I charge thee not to breathe to thy Fernand one word descriptive of this interview which thou hast had with me. Thou couldst simulate dumbness for ten long years or more, with a success which renders thee great and glorious in my eyes—for I love the hypocrite and the deceiver," he added, with one of his diabolical smiles, "although I myself deceive them! Be dumb, then; in all that relates to my visit here. But thou mayst so beset thy Fernand with earnest entreaties to give thee the means of departure from the island,—for he can do so, if he have the will,—that he shall be unable to resist thy prayers—thy tears—thine anguish, real or feigned, whichever that anguish may be! And should he not yield to thine impressions, then assail him on another point. Tell him that thou wilt never rest until thou shalt have discovered the cause of those periodical visits which he makes to the other side of yon mountains —threaten to accompany him the next time he goes thither! But I need not teach *thee* how to be energetic nor eloquent: I need not suggest the measures nor the language to be used in the furtherance of *thine* aims. For thou art a woman of iron mind and of persuasive tongue; and thy perseverance, as thy will, is indomitable.

Follow my counsel, then—and, though the future to a great extent be concealed from my view, yet I dare prophesy success for thee! And now farewell, Nisida—farewell!"

And the Demon retreated rapidly towards the forests, as if to seek the abode of those terrible serpents whose cunning was akin to his own.

Nisida was too much astonished by the nature of the counsel which his deep sonorous voice had wafted to her ear to be able to utter a word until his receding form was no longer visible; and then she exclaimed wildly, " I have assuredly seen Satan face to face!"

And her blood ran cold in her veins.

But a few moments were sufficient to enable that woman of wondrous energy to recover her presence of mind and collect her scattered thoughts; and she sat down on the sand to ponder upon the strange incident which had so terribly varied the monotony of her existence.

She thought too of the scene which she had beholden on the banks of the Arno:—her worst fears were confirmed; Flora had escaped from the ruin of the Carmelite Convent—was alive, was at liberty—and was with Francisco!

Oh! how she now longed for the return of Fernand Wagner;—but many hours must elapse—a night must pass—and the orb of day which had by this time gone down must gain the meridian once more ere he would come back.

And in the meantime—although she suspected it not—he must fulfil the awful doom of a Wehr-Wolf, as the reader will find by the perusal of the next chapter.

CHAPTER LVII.

THE WEHR-WOLF.

It was within a few minutes of sunset as Fernand Wagner, having crossed the mountains, hastened down that bituminous declivity constituting the scene of desolation which separated the range of volcanic hills from the delightful plains and verdant groves stretching to the sea-shore.

A shudder passed over his frame as he beheld the solitary tree in which he had seen the monstrous snake playing and gambolling on the morning when he was thrown upon this Mediterranean isle.

" Oh!" he exclaimed aloud, as he sped onwards, " what happiness and also what misery have I known in this clime! But—doomed and fated being that I am—such is my destiny—and so must it be, here or elsewhere—in whichever land I may visit—in whatever part of the earth I may abide! Oh! merciful heaven, can no prayer —no self-mortification remove the ban—the curse from my devoted head?"

He suddenly stood still—threw a horrified glance towards the west—and then fell upon his knees with a fearful yell of agony, as he saw the last beams of the sun flickering in that quadrature.

" Oh! just heaven," he exclaimed, stretching forth his arms towards the sky, and with ineffable anguish depicted on his up-turned countenance; " spare me— spare me? Have I not been punished enough? Oh! take away from me this appalling doom—let me become old, wrinkled, forlorn, and poor once more,—let me return to my humble cot in the Black Forest,—or let me die, Almighty power! if thou wilt,—but spare me—spare me now! Wretch—wretch that I was to be dazzled by thy specious promises, O Faust! But I am justly punished—thy vengeance, O heaven! is well deserved— sinner, sinner that I am!"

And, as he uttered these words in a tone of bitter lamentation, and while his handsome face grew horrible with the dread workings that distorted it, some unseen but irresistible influence hurled him prostrate on the green sward; and yet again he shrieked, as the moment of an agonizing transformation was at hand, " Spare me, great heaven! though thy vengeance be most just."

Those were the last human sounds he uttered for several hours;—for, scarcely had they escaped his lips, when the horrible change began—and in a few moments a wild yell rent the air, and a monstrous wolf sprang from the spot where Wagner had fallen down in such agonizing writhings.

Away—away went the ferocious animal, headlong towards the sea, careering, thundering on, as if intent on plunging into the silent depths, and there ending its dreadful course in a watery grave.

But, no:—death yawns not for the Wehr-Wolf! Scarcely have its feet touched the verge of the water,

when the monster wheels round, and continues its whirlwind way without for an instant relaxing one tittle of its speed.

Away—away, through the fruit-bearing groves,—clearing for itself a path of ruin and havoc—scattering the gems of the trees, and breaking down the richly-laden vines,—away, away flies the monster, hideous howls bursting from its foaming mouth.

The birds scream and whistle wildly, as, startled from their usually tranquil retreats, they spread their gay and gaudy plumage, and go with gushing sound through the evening air.

Madly—furiously over nature's carpeting of flowers— rapidly—headlong through the groups of verdant evergreens and the thickets of fragrant shrubs—spurning the rich herbage and tracing a path of woful destruction, —speeds on the howling animal.

He reaches the banks of a stream, and bounds along its pleasant margin,—trampling to death noble swans which vainly seek to evade the fury of the rushing monster.

Away—away towards the forests hurries the Wehr-Wolf—impelled, lashed on by an invisible scourge, and filling the woods with its appalling yells,—while its mouth scatters foam like thick flakes of snow.

Hark! there is an ominous rustling in one of the trees of the forest; and the monster seems instinctively to know the danger which menaces it. But still its course is not changed:—it seems not to exercise its own will in shaping its course: it obeys an influence unseen—not understood—though fatally irresistible;—and its howlings now grow more frightful—more horrible than ever.

Down the tremendous snake flings itself from the tree —and in an instant its hideous coils are wound round the foaming, steaming, palpitating body of the wolf. The air is rent with the yell of agony that bursts from the throat of the horrified monster, as it tumbles over and over, as if it had run to the length of a tether—for the snake clings with its tail to the bough from which it has darted down.

But the yielding of the wolf is only momentary: up— up it springs again—and away, away it careers,—more madly—more desperately—more ferociously, if possible, than before.

And the snake? Oh! poor, weak, and powerless was even that dread reptile of forty feet in length when combating with a monster lashed on and also protected by invisible fiends. For, as the wolf sped on again, the boa was dragged as if by a thousand horses from its coiling hold upon the bough,—and shaken, lacerated, and affrighted, the hideous reptile unwound itself from the ferocious animal, and fell powerless on the grass, where the vermin of the forest attacked it with their greedy maws ere its pestilential breath had ceased.

Away—away towards the mountains rushes the Wehr-Wolf,—those mountains which constitute the barrier of safety to protect Nisida from the fangs of the animal that would mangle her fair form were she to cross its path.

Yes—even she would be sacrificed to the indomitable and irresponsible rage of the monster, obedient only to the unseen scourge and the invisible influence that hurries him on,

But, ah! he rushes up the acclivity—he clears rugged rock and jutting crag with wondrous bounds:—just heaven! will he pass those heights?—will he cross the range of volcanic hills?

Oh! Nisida, who art on the other side of that range, —little dreamest thou of the peril that menaces thee!

Joy! joy! the danger has passed;—the wolf turns aside from a loftier impediment of crag than had yet appeared in its course; and down—down again towards the groves and valleys—over the bituminous waste made by the volcano—on, on goes the monster.

Away—away, through the verdant scenes once more,— fresh havoc—fresh desolation—fresh ruin marking his maddened course,—away—away the Wehr-Wolf speeds.

The moon rises to give a stronger and purer light to the dreadful spectacle—a light stronger and purer than that of the night itself, which is never completely dark in the tropics.

Away—away—and still on, on—outstripping time— running a race with the fleeting moments, till hours and hours of unrelaxing speed are numbered—thus goes the wolf.

And now he snuffs the morning air; the fresh breeze from the east raises the foam of the Mediterranean waves, and allays the heat of that on the body of the careering—bounding—and almost flying monster.

His howling grows less ferocious—his yells become less terrible; and now his pace is a trifle more measured—that relaxation of a whirlwind speed gradually increasing.

'Tis done: the course is over—the race is run;—and the Wehr-Wolf falls in writhing agonies upon the fresh grass, whence in a few moments rises Fernand Wagner—a man once more!

But as he throws a glance of horror around on the scene of his night's dread employment, he starts back with mingled aversion and alarm;—for there—with folded arms, eyes terrible to gaze upon, and a countenance expressing infernal triumph and bitter scorn—stood the Demon,

all the sobs and sighs that tell of human agony,—then multiply the aggregate by ten million, million times its sum,—and go on multiplying by millions and millions till thou wast tired of counting,—thou wouldst not form even an idea of that huge amount of human misery which could alone appease me! For on man do I visit the hate wherewith my own fall has animated me:—powerless on high,—where once I was so powerful,—I make my kingdom of earth and of hell—and in both my influence is great and is terrible!"

"Yes—yes: too great—too terrible!" exclaimed Wagner. "But why dost thou persecute me with thy

"AGAIN THE SCREAM BURSTS FROM THE VICTIM'S LIPS." (See p. 94.)

"Fiend! what wouldst thou with me?" demanded Wagner. "Are not the sufferings which I have just endured enough to satisfy the hatred of all human beings? are not the horrors of the past night sufficient to glut even thine insatiate heart?"

"Mortal!" said the Demon, speaking in his profound and awe-inspiring tones,—"didst thou take all the miseries which at this moment afflict thy race,—combine all the bitter woes and crushing sorrows that madden the brains of men,—mix up all the tears and collect

presence? I did not call thee—I did not invoke thine aid."

"No—but thou requirest it!" said the Demon, with a satirical smile. "Thinkest thou to be enabled to dream away thine existence in this island, with thy warm, impassioned Nisida? No, mortal, no! Already does she pine for her own native Italian clime; and she will end by loathing thee and this land if she continue to dwell here, and with only thee as her companion. But it is in thy power to make Nisida forget Italy—Francisco—Flora—and all the grave interests and dreadful mysteries which seem to demand her presence in the busy world;—it is in thy power to render her happy and contented in this island—to attach her to thee for the remainder of thine existence—to provide her with the means of preserving her youth and her beauty unimpaired, even as thine own—to crush for ever all those pinings and longings which now carry her glances and her thoughts wistfully across the sea,—in a word, to bend her mind to all thy wishes—her soul to all thy purposes! Yes:—it is in thy power to do all this--and the same decision which shall place that amount of ineffable happiness within thy reach will also redeem thee from the horrible destiny of a Wehr-Wolf—leaving thee thy youth and thy beauty, and investing thee with a power equal to that enjoyed by thy late master, Faust."

"And doubtless on the same conditions?" said Wagner, half ironically, and half in horror at the mere idea of surrendering his soul to Satan.

"Art thou blind to the means of promoting thine earthly happiness?" demanded the Demon, fixing on Fernand a glance intended to appal and to intimidate, but at which he on whom it was bent quailed not. "Hast thou not received sufficient experience of the terrific sufferings which twelve times a year thou art doomed to endure? Knowest thou not on each occasion thou destroyest human life, where mortal beings are in thy path—or that thou ravagest the fair scenes which HE whose name I dare not mention has created? and art thou ignorant of the tremendous horror and loathsome obloquy which attach themselves to the name of a Wehr-Wolf? See—thou art already wearied of travelling through the various climes of the earth; thou no longer delightest in cultivating thine intellect, so marvellously adapted to receive knowledge of all kinds;—and thy power to create whole mines of wealth is exercised no more. But thou wouldst fix thine abode in this island for ever—were Nisida to remain thy companion! Well—and if thou losest her? for assuredly a vessel will some day touch on these shores. What wouldst thou do, then? All lonely—desolate—forlorn, thou wouldst curse the day that gave thee regenerated life—thou wouldst seek death—and to thee death may not come yet for many, many years! Fernand, thou art worse than mad not to embrace my offers. Consent to become mine—mine eternally, when thy mortal breath shall have left thy body,—and in the meantime I promise thee power illimitable—happiness such as no human being ever yet enjoyed——"

"No—no!" exclaimed Wagner, his better feelings rising dominant from the awful struggle that took place in his breast while the fiend thus spoke: "no—no! Rather the destiny of the Wehr-Wolf—rather lose my Nisida for ever—rather the solitude of this island for the remainder of my days—than resign all chance of salvation! And that mine immortal soul is as yet safe, the very temptations thou offerest with such eloquent persuasion fully proves! Oh! heaven, in its infinite mercy, will receive the dreadful sufferings 'tis mine to endure each month, as an atonement for that hour of weakness—madness—folly, when dazzled by the words of Faust, and overwhelmed by a weight of miseries, I accepted a regenerated existence. Yes—heaven will forgive me yet: and, therefore, avaunt—fiend!—avaunt! avaunt!"

And, as he uttered these words in an excited and impassioned manner, he made the sign of the cross, and the Demon fled howling into the adjacent wood, his form rapidly losing its mortal shape and assuming an appearance too horrible to describe.

Wagner turned aside in dismay, and sank upon the ground, as if blasted by the lightnings that marked with their forked and vivid flashes the transformation of the Prince of Darkness.

A deep sleep fell on Fernand's eyes; and in his dreams he thought that he heard a solemn but rejoicing strain of music filling the air—the harmony of the spheres! And that divine melody seemed to speak a language eloquent and intelligible, and to give him hope and promise of a deliverance from the dreadful destiny which his weakness and his folly had entailed upon him. Then a luminous mist appeared to collect around him—enveloping him in its glorious halo. The music grew fainter and fainter; and at the moment when it died away altogether, a heavenly and radiant being rose in the midst of the lustrous cloud—an angel, clad in white and shining garments, and with snowy wings closed and drooping gracefully from his shoulders. Looking benignly upon the sleeping Wagner, the angel said in a soft and liquid tone, "Thrice hast thou resisted the temptations of the enemy of mankind: once in thy dungeon at Florence—a second time amidst the defiles of

yon mountains—and now on this spot. He will appear to thee no more, unless thou thyself shalt summon him. Much hast thou already done in atonement for the crime that endangered thy soul when, withdrawing thy faith from heaven, thou didst accept new life on the conditions proposed to thee by the agent of Satan :—but much more must thou yet do, ere the atonement will be complete!" The form ceased to speak, and gradually became fainter and fainter, until it disappeared with its glorious halo altogether.

Then Fernand awoke—and his dream was vividly impressed upon his memory.

Assuming a kneeling posture, he clasped his hands fervently together, and said aloud, "Merciful heaven! be the vision one divinely sent—or be it but the sport of an imagination fevered by a long night of suffering—I receive it as an emblem, and as a sign of hope and promise."

He arose :—the sun was now high in the heavens; and he hastened to the shore to perform his ablutions.

Refreshed in body with the bath which he took in the Mediterranean, and in mind with the influence of the vision, he retraced his way towards the mountains.

The range was passed in safety; and he once more set foot on that section of the island where Nisida was so anxiously awaiting his presence.

CHAPTER LVIII.

THE EFFECTS OF THE DEMON'S COUNSEL.

THE hour at which Fernand Wagner was accustomed to return after his periodical excursions beyond the mountains had long passed ;—for it will be remembered that he had fallen asleep and slumbered some time after his restoration to human shape and his encounter with the Demon.

Nisida was already a prey to the wildest alarms, which were not altogether untainted with selfishness; for the enemy of mankind had led her to believe that Wagner had within his reach certain means of enabling her to quit the island ;—and she trembled lest death might have intervened to snatch him away, and thus annihilate the hopes which had been so insidiously infused into her soul.

It is but, however, just to observe that she was also distressed at his prolonged absence on grounds more creditable to her heart; for she shuddered convulsively as the idea—the appalling idea flashed to her mind, that her handsome Fernand might at that moment be writhing in the coils of a horrible snake.

Then, arousing herself with that courage and iron resolution which constituted such essential features in her character, Nisida resolved to attempt the passage of the mountains, and seek for her lover; and at the time when this thought was uppermost in her mind, she vowed to rescue him, if possible—and if not, to die with him.

But as she drew near the rising ground leading towards the craggy mountains, she suddenly beheld the object of her anxiety approaching her; and in a few minutes they were locked in each other's arms.

"My Fernand," said Nisida at length, "I feared that some danger had befallen you, and I was hastening to join you on the other side of these heights, either to aid you in escaping from the peril, or to share its consequences with you."

"Beloved Nisida!" exclaimed Wagner, casting his arm around her waist, and conducting her back to the immediate vicinity of their rudely constructed cottage; "how welcome to me is this proof of thy regard—this earnest of thy love!"

"I can never cease to love you, dear Fernand," answered Nisida, turning her fine large eyes upon his handsome face, while the flush of ardent passion animated her own splendid countenance: then, while her bosom heaved with a profound sigh, she added, "Oh! that I should seek to quit thee, Fernand! The thought smites to the inmost recesses of my heart. And yet it is to some extent thy fault—for wherefore wilt thou not accompany me?"

"In the first place, beloved one," replied Wagner, "thou talkest as if a ship were already in sight, or a boat lay ready to launch from this shore: secondly, I have before assured thee that I dare not return to Florence, and that as I therefore cannot be thy companion thither, it would be better for me to remain on this island—to which, perhaps," he added in a mournful tone, "you might, after all, never come back!"

"Oh! Fernand, think not so ill of your Nisida!" she cried, throwing one of her snowy full arms round his neck, and looking earnestly, but yet tenderly on his countenance. "Never—never shall I know happiness again until I have revisited Florence. Each day that passes without giving me a hope to see this aim fulfilled, increases my misery—adds to my uneasiness—augments my anxiety—so that in a short time my suspense will become intolerable. It is nearly so already, Fernand; and I sometimes feel that even thy sweet caresses and kindness cannot soothe me. Oh! blame me not, Fernand—but pity me:—yes—and help me, if you can!"

"Dearest Nisida, willingly would I sacrifice my own inclinations to forward thine," exclaimed Wagner, in a tone of deep sincerity; "but how is it possible that I can aid thee? I have not wings to affix to thy fair shoulders—I have not a voice powerful enough to raise echoes on a shore whence assistance might be sent. Nay, look not sternly on me, beloved Nisida. I did not intend to vex thee with idle jestings;—but thou knowest that I cannot aid thee!"

"Fernand, you love me not!" exclaimed Nisida, suddenly withdrawing her arm from its fond position about his neck, and retreating a few paces. "No:—you do not love me as you were wont—or as I love you. You, doubtless, have some means of gratifying my ardent longings. A secret voice whispers me that if you chose to exert all your powers, you might render me happy—at least so happy as I could be when separated from you! I have assured you that naught save the most important interests would render me thus anxious to return to my native city;—and if you find me thus importunate, you should pity me—not refuse to aid me."

"Holy Virgin! this is maddening!" cried Wagner. "Nisida—be reasonable: how can I assist thee?—how can I enable thee to cross that sea which appears to us boundless? And thou accusest me of not loving thee, Nisida! Oh! this is too cruel!"

"No—it is thou who art cruel!" exclaimed Nisida, in an impassioned tone. "I know that you are not a being of an ordinary stamp—that your intellect is as wonderful as your person is god-like—and that you possess a mine of knowledge in the extent of which no mortal can equal thee. Is it strange—is it marvellous, then, that I should implore thee to exert thy powers—the vast powers of thy glorious intelligence, to forward my designs? Nay—seek not to interrupt me, Fernand; denial is vain! A secret voice continues to whisper within me that thou art able to do all I ask: I know not the means to be used—I seek not to know them; but that thou hast such means within thy reach, is a conviction firmly impressed upon my mind. Here, then, Fernand—at thy feet—on my knees, do I implore thee—beseech thee, not to refuse the boon which I—thy loving wife—crave at the hands of thee—my husband—as if I were a humble suppliant suing at the footstool of a throned king!"

"Nisida—Nisida!" cried Fernand, painfully excited by this sudden movement on her part, and endeavouring to raise her: "what means so strange a proceeding? Rise, dearest—rise: it is not to me that you must thus humble yourself!"

"No—I will not quit this suppliant attitude until you shall have granted my request—my prayer," said Nisida. "Refuse me not—my Fernand—oh! I implore you not to refuse me! Whatever means be within your reach, exert them on my behalf. A brother's interests—the remembrance of a solemn vow breathed to my lamented and much wronged mother—and the safeguard of a mystery, the discovery of which by curious and prying eyes would heap infamy and disgrace on the name of Riverola—all these reasons render me thus anxious to return to Italy. And if you keep me here, Fernand, I shall pine away—I shall perish before your eyes—and you will repent of your harshness when it is too late. Or else," she added, speaking with wild rapidity, "I shall be reduced to despair, and in a moment of excitement, shall seek death in those silent waters, or climb yon craggy mountains to fling myself headlong from their summit."

"Nisida, your menaces are maddening as your supplications to me are vain and useless!" said Wagner, himself now labouring under a fearful excitement. "Rise, I implore you—rise, and let us endeavour to converse more calmly—more rationally."

"Yes—I will rise," said Nisida, now affecting a sullen haughtiness, and preparing to wield another of the weapons which the Demon had placed in her hand: "I rise, Fernand, because I feel that I was wrong thus to abase myself—I, who bear the proud name of Riverola;" —and she tossed her head indignantly. "Well—it seems

that you are resolved to keep me chained to your side on this island. Be it so; but henceforth let there be no mistrust—no mystery—no secrets between us. If Italy must be forgotten for ever, then this isle shall become our world, and our thoughts shall travel not beyond its confines. All shall be mutual confidence—a reciprocal outpouring of our minutest thoughts. On that condition only will existence *here* be tolerable to us both. And now as a proof that thou wilt assent to this proposal—than which nothing can be more rational—let our new life of mutual confidence date from this moment. Tell me then, my Fernand," she proceeded, assuming a winning manner, and throwing as much pathos as possible into her sweetly musical voice—that voice which gave new and indescribable charms to the soft Italian language—"tell me then, my Fernand, wherefore thou quittest me at certain intervals—why thou invariably seekest on those occasions the opposite side of the island—and whether thou wilt in future suffer me to be the companion of those journeys?"

"Thou be my companion!—thou, Nisida!" exclaimed Wagner, his whole frame convulsed with mental agony. "Merciful heaven! what fiend hath prompted thee thus to speak? Nisida," he said, suddenly exercising a strong mastery over his emotions, as he seized her hand and pressed it with spasmodic violence—"Nisida, as thou valuest our happiness, seek not to penetrate into my secret—proffer not that mad request again!"

And, dropping her hand, he paced the shore with the agitation of reviving excitement.

"Fernand," said Nisida, approaching him, and once more speaking in a resolute and even severe tone—"listen to me! When we met upon this island, an accident of a terrible nature led me to forget my vow of self-imposed dumbness; and when the excitement occasioned by that accident had somewhat passed, you were in doubt whether you had really heard my voice or had been deluded by a fevered imagination. It would then have been easy for me to simulate dumbness again; and you would have believed that the bewilderment of the dread scene had misled you. But I chose not to maintain a secret from thee—and I confessed that my long supposed loss of two glorious faculties was a mere deed of duplicity on my part. At that time you said that you also had explanations to give:—and yet months and months have passed by, and confidence has not begotten confidence. Let this mistrust on your part cease. Reveal to me the cause of those frequent excursions across the mountains; or else, the next time that you set out on one of the mysterious journeys, I shall assuredly become your companion."

"Now, Nisida," exclaimed Wagner, his heart rent with indescribable tortures,—"it is you who are cruel—you who are unjust!"

"No, Fernand—it is you!" cried Nisida, in a thrilling, penetrating tone, as if of anguish.

"Merciful heavens! what misery is in store for us both!" said Wagner, pressing his hand to his burning brow. "Oh! that some ship would appear to bear thee away—or that my destiny were other than it is!"

And he flung himself upon the sand in a fit of black despair.

Nisida now trembled at the violence of those emotions which she had raised in the breast of him whom she loved; and for a minute she reproached herself for having so implicitly obeyed the counsel of the evil spirit.

Her own feelings were worked up to that pitch of excitement, which with woman—even in the strongest-minded—must have its vent in tears;—and she burst into an agony of weeping.

The sound of those sobs was more than the generous-hearted and affectionate Fernand could bear; and starting from the sand whereon he had flung himself, he exclaimed, "Nisida—my beloved Nisida, dry those tears—subdue this frantic grief! Let us say no more upon these exciting topics this evening; but I will meditate—I will reflect until the morrow,—and then I will communicate to thee the result of my deliberations."

"Oh! there is then hope for me yet!" cried Nisida joyfully; "and thou hast the means to grant my wishes—but thou fearest to use them. We will say no more this evening on subjects calculated to give us so little pleasure;—but to-morrow, my Fernand—to-morrow——"

And Nisida stopped her own utterance by pressing her lips to those of Wagner, winding her beauteous arms most lovingly round his neck at the same time, and pressing him to her bosom.

But that night and the ensuing morn were destined to wring the heart-chords of the unhappy Fernand; for the influence of the Demon—though unknown and unrecognised—was dominant with Nisida.

CHAPTER LIX

MUTUAL CONFESSIONS.

It was night—and Fernand was pacing the sand with even greater agitation than he had manifested during the crnel scene of the evening.

He was alone on the sea-shore; and Nisida slept in the hut.

Terrible thoughts warred in the breast of Wagner. Nisida's language had astonished and alarmed him; and he was convinced that Satan himself had inspired her with those ideas, the utterance of which had nearly goaded him to madness.

She had insisted on the belief that he was acquainted with the means of enabling her to return to Italy;—and yet Nisida was not a mere girl—a silly, whimsical being, who would assert the wildest physical impossibilities just as caprice might prompt her. No;—she really entertained that belief—but without having any ostensible ground to establish it.

"Such an impression could only have been made upon her mind by the fiend who seeks to entangle me in his meshes!" murmured Wagner to himself, as he paced the strand. "The Demon has failed to tempt me as yet—thrice has he failed;—and now he musters all his force to assail me,—to assail me, too, in the most vulnerable points! But, O heaven! give me strength to resist the dread influence thus brought to bear upon me! What course can I adopt? what plan pursue? If to-morrow must witness the renewal of that scene which occurred this evening, I shall succumb—I shall yield: in a moment of despair I shall exclaim, ' Yes, Nisida — I will sacrifice everything to acquire the power to transport thee back to Italy;—and I shall hurry to yon mountains. and seeking their wildest defile, shall evoke the Enemy of Mankind, and say, ' Come, Satan! I give thee my soul in exchange for the illimitable power thou offerest!'—And this will be the terrible result—the fearful catastrophe!"

Big drops of agony stood upon Fernand's brow as he uttered these words. He saw tLat he was hovering on the verge of a fearful abyss—and he trembled lest he should fall, so intense was his love for Nisida.

At one moment he thought of the soothing vision, full of hope and promise, which had occupied his slumber in the morning: at another he pondered on the tears, the prayers, and the threats of Nisida.

The conflicting thoughts were indeed sufficient to urge him on to a state of utter despair: his eternal salvation and the happiness of her whom he loved so tenderly were placed in such antagonistic positions, that they raised a fierce—a painful—an agonizing warfare in his breast.

Now he would fall upon his knees and pray—pray long and fervently, for strength to continue in the right path: —then he would give way to all the maddening influences of his bitter reflections: and, while in this mood, had Satan suddenly stood before him, he would have succumbed,—yes—he would have succumbed.

But the fiend had no longer any power to offer direct temptation to the wretched Wagner.

Oh! if he could die—if he could die that moment, how gladly would he release himself from an existence fraught with so much misery:—but death was not yet within the reach of him who bore the doom of a Wehr-Wolf!

The morning dawned; and Fernand Wagner was still pacing the sand,—dreading to meet Nisida again, and not daring to seek to avoid her. Were he to fly to the mountains or the forest; she would search after him; and thus he would only be leading her into perils amidst yawning precipices, or where she might become the prey of the terrible anaconda.

To remain were anguish—to fly were madness!

"Oh! wretch—miserable wretch that I am!" exclaimed Wagner, as he beheld the twilight—so short in the tropics—growing more powerful, and knew that Nisida would soon come forth from the hut.

In a few minutes the orb of day appeared above the orient wave—and almost at the same time the lady made her appearance on the shore.

"Fernand, thou hast not sought repose throughout the night just past!" she said, advancing towards him, and endeavouring to read upon his countenance the thoughts which filled his brain.

"Nisida," he replied, in a rapid and excited tone, "I have gone through so much during the last few hours, that 'tis a marvel reason has maintained its seat. If thou lovest me, let us forget all those topics which have so strongly excited us both; and let us unite our prayers that heaven will send thee the means to quit this isle and return to thy native land."

"Fernand," said Nisida, in a tone of deep disappointment and reproach, "I was not prepared for this. Your words imply that you possess the power to aid my departure hence, but you have resolved not to use it. Is that your decision?"

"I scorn to deceive thee, Nisida, by a direct falsehood in so serious a matter as this," exclaimed Wagner. "Knowest thou, my beloved, at what price must be purchased the power which alone can enable me to effect thy return to Italy? canst thou divine the immeasurable sacrifice which I must make to satisfy thy wishes?"

"Fernand," answered Nisida, in a reproachful and yet resolute tone, "there is no price that I would not pay to obtain the means of pleasing thee!—there is no sacrifice that I should shrink from were your happiness at stake."

"Nisida," ejaculated Wagner, in a tone of fearful excitement: "you drive me to despair! Have mercy upon me, Nisida—have mercy upon me! My God! if you taunt me—if you reproach me thus, I will do all that you command;—but force me not to believe, Nisida—my well-beloved Nisida—that, in espousing thee in the sight of heaven, I took to my bosom a fiend instead of a woman —a relentless demon in the most charming female shape that evil spirit ever wore. Oh! if you knew all, you would pity me as it is. So wretched on earth, you would not compel me to renounce every hope of salvation: for, know, Nisida," he added, his countenance wearing an expression of indescribable horror,—"know that in demanding of me this last sacrifice, you ordain that I should sell my immortal soul to Satan!"

For a moment Nisida appeared shocked and appalled at the words which met her ears;—but she rather recoiled from the manner of fearful excitement in which they were uttered, than from the intelligence which they conveyed.

"He who truly loves," said she coldly, as she recovered her equanimity, "would make even that sacrifice! And now, listen — Fernand," she continued her eyes flashing fire, and her naked bosom heaving convulsively as she spoke,—while her splendid form was drawn up to its full height, and her whole aspect was sublimely terrible and wondrously beautiful even in that fit of agitated passion, —"listen, Fernand!" she cried, in her musical, flute-like voice, which however assumed the imperious accent and tone of command: "thou art a coward, and unworthy such an earnest—such a profound—such a devoted love as mine, if thou refusest to consummate a sacrifice which will make us both powerful and great as long as we live! Consider, my Fernand!—the spirit with whom thou wouldst league thyself, can endow us with an existence running over centuries to come—can invest us with eternal youth—can place countless treasures at our disposal — can elevate us to the proudest thrones of Christendom! Oh! wilt thou spurn advantages like those? wilt thou refuse to avail thyself of gifts that must render us so supremely happy? No—no :—and then we can return together to my native city—we can enter Florence in triumph,—thou no longer fearing the terrors of the law—I no more compelled to simulate the doom of the deaf and dumb! Our enemies shall lick the dust at our feet—and we shall triumph wherever success may be desirable, Oh! I understand that beseeching, appealing look, Fernand: thou thinkest that I shall love thee less if this immense sacrifice be consummated—that I shall look upon thee with loathing! No—not so: and to convince thee that mine is a soul endowed with an iron will —that mine is an energy which can grapple even with a remorse, I will reveal to thee a secret which thou hast perhaps never even suspected. Fernand!" she exclaimed now becoming absolutely terrible with the excitement that animated her; "Fernand!" she repeated, "'twas I who murdered the girl Agnes in the garden of thy mansion at Florence!"

"Thou! — thou, Nisida!" almost shrieked Wagner wildly: "Oh! no—no! Recall that dreadful avowal! And yet—Oh! yes—I see it all—my former suspicions are confirmed! Wretched woman! what harm did the unfortunate Agnes do to thee?"

"I saw in her a rival, Fernand—or fancied that she was so," answered Nisida: "I overheard your conversation with her that morning in the garden—I saw her embrace thee tenderly—mine ears drank in her words—oh!

I remember them even now! She said, '*Oh! what a night of uneasiness have I passed! But at length thou art restored to me—thou whom I have ever loved so fondly; although I abandoned thee for so long a time.*' Were not those her very words? And thou didst speak to her in a tone equally tender. Ah! I have ever suspected that she was thy mistress—although thou didst swear upon the cross in thy dungeon that she was not! But so great was my love for thee, that I smothered the dread suspicion——"

"Suspicion!" repeated Wagner, in the penetrating tone of heartrending anguish,—an anguish so intense that his

easily to enact the spy upon my own father that I originally simulated the doom of the deaf and dumb. A purse of gold induced Dame Margaretha, Antonio's mother, to give me admission into her house; though she also believed that I was really deprived of the faculties of hearing and of speech. But often and often was I concealed in the chamber adjacent to that where my father passed many hours with his mistress;—and it was not without advantage that I so acted. For I discovered that, amongst the presents which he had given her were the jewels which had belonged to my sainted mother; that mother whose wrongs were so manifold, and whose

" SHE SWEEPS THEM ALL WITH A HURRIED GLANCE." (See p. 99.)

brain whirled, and he knew not what he said or did. "Oh! wretched woman! and thou didst slay Agnes on a mere suspicion?"

"I hated her—even before I entertained that suspicion," exclaimed Nisida, impatiently; "for she was the mistress of my father! Thinkest thou that my quick ears had not gleaned the mysterious whisperings which frequently passed between my sire and his valet Antonio, relative to the lady who dwelt in seclusion at the abode of that menial's mother? or thinkest thou that when I once obtained a clue to my father's degrading passion, I scrupled to watch him—to follow him—to learn all his proceedings? No:—for it was the more

sufferings were so great! Yes:—and I possessed myself of those jewels, leaving the girl the other gifts which she had received from my sire. And now, since I am involved in revelations of such import, I shall do well to inform thee, Fernand, that I had seen and loved thee before thou didst come as a visitor to our mansion in Florence. For it was my habit to proceed occasionally to the dwelling of the good Dr. Duras—the depositor of my grand secret of the feigned loss of faculties; and when wandering alone in his garden, I once beheld thee! And the moment I beheld, I loved thee. Often—often after that would I visit the kind physician's grounds, whereof I possessed a pass-key: and my admiration of thee led me to pass the slight boundary which separated his garden from thine. Then I would approach the windows of thy dwelling, and contemplate thee as thou was sitting in thy favourite apartment. On the night of my father's funeral—although so very late when all the subsequent business connected with the reading of the will was concluded—my mind was so perturbed and restless that I could not sleep;—and, quitting the Riverola mansion by a private door, I sought the fresh air with the hope that it would calm me. Some vague and indescribable sentiment of curiosity—or else something that I heard on the return of the mourners, relative to the strange scene enacted in the church, I know not which at this moment—led to the vicinity of your abode: and there—in your favourite room—I beheld you seated, listening attentively to some sweet words, doubtless, which Agnes was breathing in your ear. But she caught a glimpse of my countenance by the light of the lamps——"

"Enough! enough!" exclaimed Wagner; "thou hast indeed cleared up innumerable mysteries! But, oh! Nisida—would that thou hadst remained silent—that thou hadst not drawn aside the veil which my elevated opinion of thee had thrown over the suspicions that, I admit, from time to time——"

"And if I have told thee all this, Fernand," interrupted Nisida, impatiently, "it is that thou mayst be convinced not only of the natural energy of my mind, but also of the deep love which I bear thee. And now—now, that thou seest me in my true character—a murderess, if thou wilt," she added, with an emphasis of bitter scorn,—"now canst thou refuse the sacrifice?"

"Nisida! Nisida! enough crime has been perpetrated by both of us, heaven knows!" ejaculated Wagner, still writhing with the anguish produced by the avowal which had so lately met his ears. "Oh! accursed be the day —blotted from the annals of Time, be the hour, Nisida, when thy hand struck the fatal dagger into the heart of Agnes."

"What! this to my face!" cried Nisida, her countenance becoming crimson with indignation,—and not her face only, but her swan-like neck, her shoulders, and her bosom. "Then she was thy mistress, Fernand! And thou didst love her, while I fancied, false one that thou art! thine affections to be wholly and solely mine!"

"Nisida!" exclaimed Fernand, cruelly bewildered; "you drive me to despair! I know not whether to loathe thee for this avowal which thou hast made—or to snatch thee to my arms, abandon all hope of salvation, and sacrifice myself entirely to one so transcendently beautiful as thou art! But thy suspicions relative to Agnes are ridiculous—monstrous—absurd! For, as surely as thou art there, Nisida,—as surely as the heaven is above us, and the earth beneath us,—as surely as that I love thee so well as to be unable to reproach thee for the deed which thou hast confessed,—so surely, Nisida, was Agnes my own grand-daughter,—and I—I—Fernand Wagner—young, strong, and full of health as thou now beholdest me, am fourscore and fifteen years of age!"

Nisida started in affright—and then fixed a scrutinizing glance upon Fernand's countenance; for she feared that his reason had abandoned him—that he was raving,

"Ah, Nisida! I see that you do not credit my words," he exclaimed; "and yet I have told thee the solemn, sacred truth. But mine is a sad history and a dreadful fate; and if I thought that thou wouldst soothe my wounded spirit—console, and not revile me—pity, and not loathe me, I would tell thee all."

"Speak—Fernand—speak!" she cried; "and do me not so much wrong as to suppose that I could forget my love for thee—that love which made me the murderess of Agnes! Besides," she added, enthusiastically, "I see that we were destined for each other—that the dark mysteries attached to both our lives engender the closest sympathies—that we shall flourish in power, and glory, and love, and happiness together!"

Wagner threw his arms round Nisida's neck and clasped her to his breast. He saw not in her the woman who had dealt death to his grand-daughter;—he beheld in her only a being of ravishing beauty and wondrous mind,—so intoxicated was he with his passion—so great was the magic influence which she wielded over his yielding spirit!

Then, as her head reclined upon his breast, he whispered to her, in a few hurried but awfully significant words, the nature of his doom, the dread conditions on which he had obtained resuscitated youth, an almost superhuman beauty, a glorious intellect, and the power

of converting the very clods of the earth into gold and precious stones at will!

"And now, dearest," he added, in a low, plaintive, and appealing tone,—"and now thou canst divine wherefore on the last day of every month I have crossed these mountains: thou mayst divine, too, how my escape from the prison of Florence was accomplished;—and, though no mortal can abridge my days—and though the sword of the executioner would fall harmless on my neck, and the deadly poison would curdle not the blood in my veins —still man can bind me in chains—and my disgrace is known to all Florence!"

"But thou shalt return thither, Fernand," exclaimed Nisida, raising her countenance and gazing upon him— not with horror and amazement, but in pride and triumph:—"thou shalt return thither, Fernand—armed with a power that may crush all thine enemies, and blast with destructive lightning the wretches who would look slightingly on thee! Already thou art dearer—far dearer to me than ever thou wast before;—for I love the marvellous—I glory in the supernatural,—and thou art a being whom such a woman as myself can worship and adore. And thou repinest at thy destiny?—thou shudderest at the idea of that monthly transformation which makes thy fate so grand, because it is so terrible? Oh! thou art wrong—thou art wrong, my Fernand! Consider all that thou hast gained—how many, many years of glorious and magnificent beauty await thee! Think of the power with which thy boundless command of wealth may invest thee! Oh! thou art happy—enviable —blest! But I—I," she added, the impassioned excitement of her tone suddenly shaking into subdued plaintiveness, as her charming head once more fell upon his breast,—"I am doomed to fade and wither like the other human flowers of the earth! Oh! that thought is now maddening. While thou remainest as thou art now —invested with that fine manly beauty which won my heart when first I saw thee, and before I knew thee—I shall grow old and wrinkled, and thou wilt loathe me! I shall be like a corpse by the side of one endowed with vigorous life. Oh! Fernand—this may not be; and thou canst purchase the power to bestow unperishing youth, unchanging beauty upon me,—the power, moreover, to transport us hence, and to render us happy in inseparable companionship for long, long years to come!"

"Merciful heavens! Nisida," exclaimed Fernand, profoundly touched by the urgent—earnest appeal of the lovely syren whose persuasive eloquence besought him to seal his own eternal damnation,—"wouldst thou have me yield my soul to the Enemy of Mankind?"

"Do you hesitate?—can you even pause to reflect," cried Nisida, with whose tongue the Demon himself was as it were speaking. "Oh! Fernand—you love me not —you have never, never loved me!"

And she burst into a flood of tears.

Wagner was painfully moved by this spectacle, which constituted so powerful an argument to support the persuasive eloquence of her late appeal. His resolution gave way rapidly—the more agonizing became her sobs, the weaker grew his self-command;—and his lips were about to murmur the fatal assent to her prayer—about to announce his readiness to summon the Enemy of Mankind and conclude the awful compact,—when suddenly there passed before his eyes the image of the guardian angel whom he had seen in his vision—dim and transparent as the thinnest vapour, yet still perceptible and with an expression of countenance profoundly mournful.

The apparition vanished in a moment; but its evanescent presence was fraught with salvation.

Tearing himself wildly and abruptly from Nisida's embrace, Wagner exclaimed in a tone indicative of the horror produced by the revulsion of feeling in his mind, —"No—never—never!" and, fleet as the startled deer, he ran—he flew towards the mountains.

Frightened and amazed by his sudden cry and simultaneous flight, Nisida cast her eyes rapidly around to ascertain the cause of his alarm, thinking that some dreadful spectacle had stricken terror to his soul.

But, ah! what sees she?—why do her glances settle fixedly in one direction?—what beholds she in the horizon?

For a few instants she is motionless—speechless: she cannot believe her eyes. Then her countenance which has already experienced the transition from an expression of grief and alarm to one of suspense and mingled hope and fear, becomes animated with the wildest joy; —and, forgetting the late exciting scene as completely as if it had never taken place—but with all her thoughts and feelings absorbed in the new—the one idea which now engrosses her,—she turns her eyes rapidly round towards the mountains, exclaiming, " Fernand! dearest Fernand! a sail!—a sail!"

But Wagner hears her not: she stamps her foot with impatient rage upon the sand;—and in another moment the groves conceal her lover from her view.

CHAPTER LX.

THE FLEET.

YES:—Wagner looked not round—heard not the voice of Nisida invoking him to return—but continued his rapid flight towards the mountains,—as if hurrying in anguish and in horror from the meshes which had been spread to ensnare his immortal soul!

And now Nisida became all selfishness:—there was at length a hope—a sudden hope that she should be speedily enabled to quit the hated, monotonous island; and her fine large, dark eyes were fixed intently upon the white sails which gradually grew more and more palpable in the azure horizon.

She was not deceived: there was no doubt—no uncertainty as to the nature of the object which now engrossed all her thoughts and filled her heart with the wildest joy.

It was indeed a ship—and its course was towards the isle;—for, as she gazed with fixed and longing eyes, it by degrees assumed a more defined shape; and that which had at first seemed to be but one small white piece of canvas, gradually developed the outlines of many sails and showed the tapering spars,—until at last the black hull appeared, completing the form of a large and noble vessel!

Joy! joy!—she would yet be saved from the island!

And, ah!—do the chances of that hoped-for safety multiply? Is it indeed another ship which has caught her eye in the far-off horizon! Yes:—and not one only —but another—and another—and another,—until she can count seven vessels, all emerging from the mighty distance, spreading their snow-white canvas to the breeze which wafts them towards the isle!

Crowds of conflicting thoughts now rush to the mind of Nisida; and she seats herself upon the strand to deliberate as calmly as she may upon the course which she should adopt.

Alas! Fernand—thou wast not then uppermost in the imagination of thy Nisida—although she had not entirely forgotten thee!

But the principal topic of her meditations,—the grand question which demanded the most serious weighing and balancing in her mind,—was whether she should again simulate the deafness and dumbness which she had now for so many months been unaccustomed to affect?

Grave and important interests and a deeply-rooted attachment to her brother on the one side urged the necessity of so doing: but, on the other, a fearful disinclination to resume that awful duplicity—that dreadful self-sacrifice,—an apprehension lest the enjoyment of the faculties of hearing and speech for so long a period should have unfitted her for the successful revival and efficient maintenance of the deceit,—these were the arguments on the negative side.

But Nisida's was not a mind to shrink from any peril or revolt from any sacrifice which her interests or her aims might urge her to encounter;—and it was with fire-flashing eyes and a neck proudly arching, that she raised her head in a determined manner, exclaiming aloud, " Yes: it must be so! But the period of this renewed self-martyrdom will not last long. So soon as thine interests shall have been duly cared for, Francisco, I will quit Florence for ever—I will return to this island: —and here will I pass the remainder of my days with thee, my beloved Fernand! And that I *do* love thee still, Fernand—although thou hast fled from my presence as if I were suddenly transformed into a loathsome monster,—that I must ever continue to love thee, Fernand,—and that I shall anxiously long to return to thine arms, are truths as firmly based as the foundations of this island! Thine, then, shall be the last name, —thy name shall be the last word that I will suffer my lips to pronounce ere I once more place the seal upon them! Yes—I love thee, Fernand: oh! would to God that thou couldst hear me proclaim how much I love thee, my beauteous—my strangely-fated Fernand!"

It was almost in a despairing tone that Nisida gave utterance to these last words:—for as the chances of her escape from the island grew every moment less equivocal, by the nearer approach of the fleet, which was however still far from the shore, the intensity of her sensual passion for Wagner—that passion which she believed to be the purest and most firmly-rooted love— revived; and her heart smote her for her readiness to abandon him to the solitude of that island!

But as she was now acquainted with all the mystery of his fate—as she knew that he could not die for many, many years to come, nor lose that glorious beauty which had proved alike her pleasure and her pride,—her remorse and her alarms were to a considerable degree mitigated! for she thought within herself, *although she now spoke aloud no more*,—" Death will not snatch him from me— disease will not impair his god-like features and elegant form—and he loves me too well not to receive me with open arms when I shall be enabled to return to him!"

These were her thoughts: and, starting upon her feet, she compressed her lips tightly, as if to remind herself that she had once more placed a seal there—a seal not to be broken for some time!

An hour had now passed since Fernand Wagner and Nisida had separated upon the sea-shore;—and he did not come back. Meantime the fleet of ships had drawn nearer—and, though she more than once entertained the idea of hastening after Wagner, to implore him to accompany her whithersoever these vessels were bound, or at least to part with the embrace of tenderness, yet her fear lest the ships might sail past without touching at the isle, predominated over her softer feelings.

And now, having settled in her mind the course she was to adopt, she hastened to the stores which she had saved from the wreck of the corsair-vessel, and which had been piled up on the strand the day after she was first thrown on that Mediterranean isle.

It will be remembered that amongst the articles thus saved were changes of apparel, which Stephano Verrina had procured for her use at Leghorn ere the corsair-bark set sail on that voyage from which it never returned: —and, during Nisida's long sojourn on the island, she had frequently examined those garments, and had been careful to secure them from the effects of rain or damp, in the fond hope that the day would sooner or later come when she might assume them for the purpose of bidding adieu to that lovely but monotonous island.

And now that day had come; and the moment so anxiously longed for, appeared to be rapidly approaching!

Nisida accordingly commenced her toilette, as if she had only just risen from her couch and was preparing to dress to go abroad amongst the busy haunts of human beings.

Her dark luxuriant hair, which so long had floated negligently upon her ivory shoulders, was now gathered up in broad massive bands at the sides, and artistically plaited and confined at the back of her well-shaped head. The tight bodice was next laced over the swelling bosom; hose and light boots imprisoned the limbs which had so often borne her glancingly along in their nudity to the soft music of the stream in the vale or of the wavelets of the sea:—and the rich velvet robe, worked with curious embroidery, set off the fine form of Nisida in all the advantage of its glowing, full, and voluptuous proportions. Then the large black veil was fastened to the plaits of her hair, whence its ample folds swept over that admirable symmetry of person, and endowing her once more with the queen-like air which became so well her splendid, yet haughty style of beauty!

Yes: no longer subdued by simplicity of attire—no longer tender and soft, was the loveliness of Nisida; but grand, imperious, and dazzling did she now seem again, as erst she seemed ere her foot trod that island-shore.

Apparelled in handsome garments,—and with the rich carnation glow of health and animation on her cheeks, and with her eyes flashing the fires of hope,—but with the vermilion lips compressed, Nisida now stood on that strand where so oft she had wandered like a naiad, feeling no shame at her scant attire.

During the time occupied by her toilette, the fleet of seven ships had approached much nearer to the island, and now they were not more than three miles distant. The hulls, which at first had seemed quite black, shone, as they drew closer, with the gay colours in which they were painted, the gorgeous sun-light playing vividly on the gilding of the prows, the streaks of red and white along the sides, and the splendid decorations of the poop-lanterns.

Noble and mighty ships they were,—ships of a size such as Nisida had never seen before, and in comparison

with which all the merchant vessels she had beheld at
Leghorn, were but mere boats.

There was no need to raise a signal to invite them to
approach; for that gallant fleet was evidently steering
direct towards the island.

Whence did this fleet come? whither was it bound? to
what nation did it belong? and would those on board
treat her with attention and respect?

Such were the thoughts which now flashed across her
brain;—and her heart beat with anxiety for the arrival
of the moment which should solve those questions.

Absorbed as she was in the contemplation of the noble
ships—those mighty but graceful swans of the ocean,—
she did not forget to cast, from time to time, a rapid
glance around, to see if Fernand were retracing his way
towards her.

Alas! no—he came not,—and she must quit the isle
without embracing him—without assuring him of her
constant love—without renewing her oft-repeated promise to return!

Ah! a thought struck her: she would leave a note for
him in the hut!

No sooner was the project determined on than she set
about its execution; for there were writing materials
amidst the stores saved from the corsair-wreck.

A brief but tender letter was hastily penned, and then
secured in a place where she knew he must find it should
he revisit the tenement in which they had so often
reposed together.

And that he would revisit it, she both fondly hoped
and firmly believed,—revisit it as soon as the excitement
and the terror, under the influence of which he had
parted from her, should have subsided.

Her mind was now much easier; and her beauty was
wonderfully enhanced by the glow of animation which
suffused itself over her countenance, giving additional
light to her ever brilliant eyes, and rendering her noble
aquiline face resplendent to gaze upon.

The ships came to an anchor at a distance of about
two miles from the shore; and though the banners of
each were fluttering in the breeze, yet Nisida was not
well skilled enough in discriminating the flags of different nations to be enabled immediately to satisfy herself to which country that fleet belonged.

But as she stood with her eyes fixed on the foremost
vessel, which was also the largest, she observed that
there was a gilt crescent in the middle of the blood-red
standard that floated over her central poop-lantern: and
a chill struck to her heart—for the thought of African
pirates flashed to her mind!

This alarm was, however, as evanescent as it was
poignant; for another moment's reflection convinced
her that none of the princes of Africa could send so proud
a fleet to sea. Following up the chain of reasoning thus
suggested, and calling to her aid all the accounts she
had read of naval fights between the Christians and
Moslems, she at length remembered that the blood-red
banner, with the gilt crescent in the middle, denoted the
presence of the Kapitan-Pacha, or Lord-High Admiral of
the Ottoman Empire.

Confidently believing that peace existed between Italy
and Turkey, she had now no longer any fears as to the
treatment she was likely to experience at the hands of
the Mohammedans; and it was with unfeigned joy that
she beheld a boat, which had put off from the Admiral's
ship, at length approaching the shore.

As the magnificently painted and gorgeously gilt barge,
which twenty-four white-turbaned rowers urged along
with almost race-horse speed, neared the strand, Nisida
observed, beneath a velvet canopy in the stern, a personage, who by his splendid apparel, his commanding
demeanour, and the respect paid to him by the slaves
accompanying him, was evidently of exalted rank. She
accordingly conceived that this must be the Kapitan-
Pacha himself. But she was mistaken.

Her delight at the approach of the barge, which she
fondly hoped would prove the means of her deliverance
from the island, was equalled only by the surprise of
those on board at beholding a beautiful and elegantly-
dressed lady, unattended and alone, on the sea-shore, as
if awaiting their arrival. And during the few minutes
which now elapsed ere the barge touched the strand, it
was evident that the high functionary seated beneath
the canopy surveyed Nisida with increasing wonder and
admiration; while she, on her side, could not help notic-
ing that he was remarkably handsome, very young, and
possessing a countenance rather of an Italian than a
Turkish cast of features.

Meantime a profound silence, broken only by the

slight and uniform sounds produced by the oars, prevailed; and when the boat touched the strand, a long
and wide plank, covered with velvet, was so placed as to
enable the high functionary before alluded to, to land
conveniently.

Attended by two slaves, who followed at a respectful
distance, the Mussulman chief advanced towards Nisida,
whom he saluted in a manner which strengthened her
suspicion that he was not of Turkish origin, although
habited in the richest oriental costume she had ever seen,
and evidently holding some very superior office amongst
the Ottomans.

She returned his salutation with a graceful bow and a
sweet smile; and he immediately addressed her in the
Italian tongue—her own dear and delightful language—
saying, "Lady, art thou the queen of this island? or art
thou, as appearances would almost lead me to conjecture,
a solitary inhabitant here?"

For he saw that she was alone;—he beheld no traces
of culture;—and there was but one miserable dwelling,
and that such as she might have built up with her own
hands.

Nisida shook her head mournfully, making signs that
she was deaf and dumb.

The Mussulman chief uttered an ejaculation of mingled surprise and grief, and surveyed the lady with
additional interest and admiration. But in a few
moments his countenance assumed a sudden expression
of astonishment, as if a light had broken in upon him,
suggesting something more than a mere suspicion—nay,
indeed, a positive conviction; and having examined her
features with the most earnest attention, he abruptly
took his tablets from the folds of his garment, and wrote
something on them. He then handed them to Nisida;
and it was now her turn to experience the wildest surprise;—for on the page opened to her view, were these
words, traced in a beautiful style of caligraphy, and in
the Italian language:—"*Is it possible that your ladyship
can be the Donna Nisida of Riverola?*"

Nisida eyes wandered in astonishment from the tablets
to the countenance of him who had pencilled that question;
but his features were certainly not familiar to her!—and
yet she thought that there was something in the general
expression of that handsome face not altogether unknown
to her.

As soon as she had partially recovered from the surprise and bewilderment produced by finding that she at
least was partially known to the Ottoman functionary,
she wrote beneath his question the following reply:—"*I
am indeed Nisida of Riverola, who for seven long months
have been the only inhabitant of this island, whereon I was
shipwrecked; and I am most anxious to return to Italy—or
at all events to the first Christian port at which your fleet
may touch. Have mercy upon me, then; and take me
hence! but who are you, Signor, that I should prove no
stranger to you?*"

The Ottoman chief read these words, and hastened to
reply in the following manner:—"*I have the honour to
be the Grand Vizier of his Imperial Highness the glorious
Sultan Solyman, and my name is Ibrahim. A few months
ago I encountered your brother, Francisco, Count of
Riverola, who was then in command of a body of Tuscan
auxiliaries raised to assist in defending Rhodes against the
invading arms of the mighty Solyman. Your brother
became my prisoner; but I treated him worthily. He informed me, with bitter tears, of the strange and mysterious
disappearance of his well-beloved sister, who has the misfortune to be deprived of the faculties of hearing and speech.
Your brother was soon set free, after the fall of Rhodes;
and he returned to his native city. But from all he told me
of thee, lady, it was natural that I should ere now conjecture
who thou must be.*"

Ibrahim did not choose to add that he remembered to
have seen Nisida occasionally in their native city of
Florence, and that he was indeed the brother of her late
dependant, Flora Francatelli. But the explanation which
he did give was quite sufficient to renew her deepest surprise; as she now learnt for the first time that, during
her absence, her brother had been engaged in the perils
of warfare.

The Grand Vizier gently withdrew from Nisida's hands
the tablets on which her eyes were positively riveted;
but it was only to trace a few lines to afford her additional explanations.

When he returned the tablets to her again, she read as
follows:—"*By a strange coincidence, the glorious fleet
which has wafted me hither to deliver you from this beautiful but lonely isle, and which is under the command of
Kapitan-Pacha in person, is bound for the western coast*

of Italy. Its mission is at present known only to myself and a faithful Greek dependant; but your ladyship shall receive worthy attention and be duly conveyed to Leghorn. The squadron has been driven from its course by a tempest which assailed us off the island of Candia; our pilot lost his reckonings,* and when land was descried this morning, it was believed to be the coast of Sicily. Hast thou, lady, any means of enlightening us as to the geographical position of this island?"

Nisida answered in the ensuing manner :—" I have not the least notion of the geographical position of the island. An eternal summer appears to prevail in this clime, which would be a terrestrial paradise, were not the forests infested by hideous serpents of an enormous size."

Ibrahim-Pacha, having read this reply, summoned from the barge the officer in command : and to him he communicated the intelligence which he had just received from Nisida.

That officer's countenance immediately underwent a dreadful change ; and falling on his knees at Ibrahim's feet, he made some strong appeal, the nature of which Nisida could only divine, by its emphatic delivery, and the terrified manner of the individual,—inasmuch as he addressed the Grand Vizier in the Turkish language.

Ibrahim smiled contemptuously, and motioned the officer with an imperious gesture to rise and return to the barge. Then, again having recourse to the tablets, he conveyed the following information to Nisida :—" Lady, it appears that this is the Isle of Snakes, situate in the Gulf of Sictra, on the African coast. Horrible superstitions are attached to this clime; and I dare not remain longer on this abhorred shore, lest I should seriously offend the prejudices of those ignorant sailors. Come then, lady, and I will convey thee to the Admiral's ship, on board of which you will receive a treatment due to your rank, your beauty, and your misfortunes."

In the meantime the officer had returned to the barge, where whispers speedily circulated in respect to the land on which the boat had touched ; and the reader may imagine the extent of the loathing which the mere name of the isle was calculated to inspire in the breasts of the superstitious Mussulmans, when we observe that the existence of that island was well known to the Turks and also to the Africans, but was left uninhabited, and was never visited knowingly by any of their ships.

Nisida saw that the Grand Vizier was in haste to depart,—not through any ridiculous fears on his part, because he was too enlightened to believe in the fearful tales of mermaids, genii, gholes, vampires, and other evil spirits by which the island was said to be haunted: —but because his renegadism had been of so recent a date, that he dared not, powerful and exalted as he was, afford the least ground for suspecting that the light of Christianity triumphed in his soul over the dark barbarism of his assumed creed.

Seeing, then, that Ibraham-Pacha was anxious to yield to the superstitious feelings of the sailors, Nisida intimated, with a graceful bend of the head, her readiness to accompany him.

But, as she advanced towards the boat, she cast a rapid and searching glance behind her :—alas! Wagner appeared not !

A feeling of uneasiness—amounting almost to the pang of remorse—took possession of her, as she placed her foot upon the velvet-covered plank;—and for an instant she hesitated to proceed !

Could she abandon Fernand to the solitude of that isle ?—could she renounce the joys which his love had taught her to experience ? And might she not yet be enabled to persuade him to make that sacrifice which would invest him with a power that she herself would direct and wield according to her own pleasure and suitably to her own interests ?

But, oh! that hesitation lasted not more than a moment ;—for her feet were on the plank leading to the barge—and at a short distance floated the ship that would bear her away from the isle !

One longing—lingering look upon the shores of that clime where she had enjoyed so much happiness, even if she had experienced so much anxiety : one longing, lingering look, and she hesitated no more !

Ibrahim escorted her to a seat beneath the velvet canopy : the officer in command gave the signal—the

barge was shoved off—the rowers plied their oars—and the island was already far behind, ere Nisida had the courage to glance towards it again !

CHAPTER LXI.

WAGNER'S MENTAL STRUGGLES.—THE VISION.—THE SIGN FULFILLED.

LET us now return to Fernand Wagner, whom we left flying from his Nisida,—flying in horror and alarm from her whom he nevertheless loved so tenderly and devotedly.

He fled as if from the brink of the yawning pit of hell, into which the malignant fiend who coveted his soul was about to plunge him.

Not once did he look back: absorbed as his feelings were in the full conviction of the tremendous peril from which he had just escaped, he still found room for reflection that were he to turn and catch but one glimpse of the beauteous—oh ! too beauteous creature, from whom he had torn himself away, he should be lost !

His mind was bent upon the salvation of his immortal soul ; and he knew that the Enemy of Mankind was assailing him with a power and with an energy which nothing save the assistance of heaven could enable him to resist. He knew also that heaven helps only those who are willing and anxious to help themselves ; and of this doctrine he had received a striking and triumphant proof in the sudden and evanescent appearance of his guardian angel at the instant when, overpowered by the strong, the earnest, and the pathetic pleading of the syren Nisida, he was about to proclaim his readiness to effect the crowning sacrifice.

And it was to avoid the chance of that direful yielding —it was to fly from a temptation which became irresistible when embellished with all the eloquence of a woman on whom he doated, and urged in a voice which no music could surpass,—it was to seek safety, in fine, that Fernand Wagner sped with almost lightning rapidity towards the mountains.

He gained the barrier which divided the Island of Snakes into two equal parts :—he sprang wildly up the precipitous pathway ;—and he paused not until he reached the basis of the conical volcano.

There he sat down exhausted ; and as he found leisure for reflection—as his thoughts composed themselves and settled down into something like collected calmness—he felt a sensation of indescribable joy at having triumphed over the appalling temptations which had beset him. And in his soul a voice seemed to be singing an anthem of delight and gratitude : and he soon experienced a serenity of mind such as he had not known for many hours past !

When man, having yielded to temptation, succeeds in escaping the perils of the consequences, he beholds a strong motive for self-congratulation :—but how ineffably more sweet is it to be able to reflect that the temptation itself has been avoided in the first instance, and that the dangers of the results have never ever been risked.

Thus thought Wagner :—but not for a moment did he attribute to any strength of mind on his own part the escape which had just been effected from the snares set by the Evil One. No : he acknowledged within himself, and with all due humility, that the hand of the Almighty had sustained him in the most trying moment of peril ;— and ere he thought of resuming his journey to that side of the island of which Nisida was not, he knelt in fervent prayer.

Rising from his knees, his eyes accidentally swept the sea ;—and he was riveted to the spot from which he was about to turn away—for the white sails of the Ottoman fleet met his astonished view. He remained gazing on those objects for some time, until he was convinced they were nearing the island.

For a few moments a deep regret took possession of him :—he should lose his Nisida irrecoverably !

But his next impulse was to wrestle with this feeling— to combat this weakness. How could he have hoped ever to rejoin her without rendering himself again liable to the witchery of her syren tongue—the eloquence of her silver-toned voice—the persuasiveness of her graceful manners ? No : it were better that she should depart : it were preferable that he should lose her and preserve his immortal soul !

Thus reasoned he : and that reasoning was effectual.

He waited only long enough to assure himself that the fleet was positively approaching the island :—he then

---

* The compass, though known to all civilized nations at the period of which we are writing, was not used by the Turks, who associated with it some ridiculous superstition which forbade them from availing themselves of its benefit.

knew that she would not fail to seize that opportunity to depart;—and without permitting himself to yield again to the weakness which had for a few moments threatened to send him back within the sphere of Nisida's fatal influence, he tore himself away from that point amongst the heights which commanded the view of the side of the island where she was.

Hastening round the base of the volcano, he reached the defiles leading to that part of the isle where he had periodically fulfilled his dreadful destiny as a Wehr-Wolf.

It was past noon when he cleared the scene of desolation so frequently alluded to as existing on the acclivity separating the actual range of hills from the verdant portions and fruit-laden groves on that side of the Island of Snakes.

Carefully avoiding the outskirts of the forest, and the knots of large trees, he proceeded towards the shore; and his heart was rent with feelings of deep anguish as he everywhere beheld the traces of destruction left behind him by his recent run in the horrible form of a savage monster.

Then, too, when melancholy thoughts had once again entered his soul, the image of Nisida appeared to flit before him in the most tempting manner; and the more he endeavoured to banish from his memory the recollection of her charms, the more vividly delineated did they become.

At length jealousy took possession of him;—and, suddenly stopping short in his progress towards the shore, he exclaimed aloud, "What if she should be wooed and won by another? If she return to her native land, as assuredly she now will, she may meet some handsome and elegant cavalier who will succeed in winning her affections or exciting her passions;—and I—I, who loved her so well—shall be forgotten! Oh! this is madness! To think that another may possess her—clasp her in his arms—press his lips to hers—feel her fragrant breath fan his cheek—play with the rich tresses of her beauteous hair,—oh! no, no—the bare thought is enough to goad me to despair! She must not depart thus—we have separated, if not in anger, at least abruptly—too abruptly, considering how we have loved, and that we have wedded each other in the sight of heaven! Heaven!" repeated Wagner, his tone changing from despair to a deep solemnity: "Heaven! Oh! I rejoice that I gave utterance to the word;—for it reminds me that to regain my Nisida, I must lose heaven!"

And, as if to fly from his own reflections, he rushed on towards the sea; and there he stopped to gaze, as oft before he had gazed, on the mighty expanse, seeming, in the liquid sun-light, as it stretched away from the yellow sand, a resplendent lake of molten silver bounded by a golden shore.

"How like to the human countenance art thou, O mighty sea!" thought Wagner, as he stood with folded arms on the brink of the eternal waters. "Now thou hast smiles as soft and dimples as beautiful as ever appeared on the face of innocence and youth, while the joyous sun-light is on thee. But if the dark clouds gather in the heaven above thee, thou straightway assumest a mournful and a gloomy aspect, and thou growest threatening and sombre. And in how many varied voices dost thou speak, O treacherous and changeful sea! Now thou whisperest softly as if thy ripples conveyed faint murmurs of love;—but, if the gale arise, thou canst burst forth into notes of laughter as thy waters leap to the shore with bounding mirth;—and, if the wind grow higher, thou canst speak louder and more menacingly;—till, when the storm comes on, thou lashest thyself into a fury,—thou boilest with rage, —and thy wrathful voice vies with the rush of the tempest and the roar of the thunder! Deceitful sea—imaging the beauties, thoughts, and passions of the earth! Within thy mighty depths, too, thou hast gems to deck the crowns of kings and the brows of loveliness; and yet thou cravest for more—more,—and engulfest rich argosies with all their treasures,—thou insatiate sea! And in thy dark caverns are the skeletons of myriads of human beings whom thou hast swallowed up in thy fury; and those bones are trophies which thou retainest in thy fathomless depths, as the heart of man enshrineth the relics of those hopes which have wasted away and perished!"

Thus thought Wagner, as he stood gazing upon the sea, then so calm and beautiful, but which he knew to be so treacherous.

When wearied of the reflections which that scene inspired, and not daring to allow his mind to dwell upon the image of Nisida, he repaired to the nearest grove and refreshed himself with the cooling fruits which he plucked. Then he extended his rambles amongst the verdant plains, and strove strenuously to divert his thoughts as much as possible from the one grand but mournful idea—the departure of Nisida from the island! But vainly did he endeavour to fix his attention upon the enchanting characteristics of that clime:—the flowers appeared to him less brilliant in hue than they were wont to be—the fruits were less inviting—the verdure was of a less lively green—and the plumage of the birds seemed to have lost the bright gloss that rendered its colours so gorgeous in the sun-light. For, oh! the powers of his vision were almost completely absorbed in his mind; and that mind was a mirror wherein were now reflected with a painful vividness all the incidents of the last few hours.

But still he was sustained in his determination not to retrace his way to the spot where he had left Nisida; and when several hours had passed, and the sun was drawing near the western horizon, he exclaimed, in a moment of holy triumph, "She has doubtless by this time quitted the island, and I have been enabled to resist those anxious longings which prompted me to return and clasp her in my arms! O God! I thank thee that thou hast given me this strength!"

Wagner now felt so overcome with weariness, after his wanderings and roamings of many hours,—especially as the two preceding nights had been sleepless for him,—that he sat down upon a piece of low rock near the shore. A quiet, dreamy repose insensibly stole over him: —in a few minutes his slumber was profound.

And now he beheld a strange vision.

Gradually the darkness which appeared to surround him grew less intense; and a gauzy vapour that rose in the midst, at first of the palest blueish tint possible, by degrees obtained more consistency,—when its nature began to undergo a sudden change, assuming the semblance of a luminous mist. Wagner's heart seemed to flutter and leap in his breast, as if with a presentiment of coming joy;—for the luminous mist became a glorious halo, surrounding the beauteous and holy form of a protecting angel, *clad in white and shining garments, and with snowy wings drooping gracefully from her shoulders!* And ineffably—supernally benign and reassuring was the look which the angel bent upon the sleeping Wagner, as she said in the softest, most melodious tones, "The choir of the heavenly host have hymned thanksgivings for thy salvation! After thou hadst resisted the temptations of the Enemy of Mankind, when he spoke to thee with his own lips, an angel came to thee in a dream to give thee assurance that *thou hadst already done much in atonement for the crime that endangered thy soul*; but he warned thee then *that much more remained to be done ere that atonement would be complete.* And the rest is now accomplished, for thou hast resisted the temptations of the Evil One when urged by the tongue and in the melodious voice of lovely Woman! This was thy crowning triumph; and the day when thou shalt reap thy reward is near at hand;—for the bonds which connect thee with the destiny of a Wehr-Wolf shall be broken, and thy name shall be inscribed in heaven's own Book of Life! And I will give thee a sign that what thou seest and hearest now in thy slumber is no idle and delusive vision conjured up by a fevered brain. The sign shall be this: —On awaking from thy sleep, retrace thy way to the spot where this morning thou didst separate from her whom thou lovest; and there shalt thou find a boat upon the sand. That boat will waft thee to Sicily; and there, in the town of Syracuse, *thou must inquire for a man whose years have numbered one hundred and sixty-two;*—for that man it is who will teach thee how the spell which has made thee a Wehr-Wolf, may be broken." Scarcely had the angel finished speaking, when a dark form rose suddenly near that heavenly being; and Wagner had no difficulty in recognising the Demon. But the Enemy of Mankind appeared not armed with terrors of countenance nor with the withering scorn of infernal triumph: for a moment his features denoted ineffable rage—and then that expression yielded to one of the profoundest melancholy, as if he were saying within himself, "There is salvation for repentant man, but none for *me!*" A cloud now seemed to sweep before Wagner's eyes;—denser and more dense it grew—first absorbing in its increasing obscurity the form of the Demon, and then enveloping the radiant being who still continued to smile sweetly and benignly upon the sleeping mortal until the glorious countenance and the shining garments were no longer visible,—but all was black darkness around!

And Fernand Wagner continued to sleep.

Many hours elapsed ere he awoke; and his slumber was serene and soothing.

At length when he opened his eyes and slowly raised his head from the hard pillow which a mass of rock had formed, he beheld the rich red streaks in the eastern horizon, heralding the advent of the sun;—and as the various features of the island gradually developed themselves in his view, as if breaking slowly from a mist, he collected and re-arranged in his mind all the details of the strange vision which he had seen.

For a few minutes he was oppressed with a fear that this vision would indeed prove the delusive sport of his fevered brain; for there seemed to be in its component parts a wild admixture of the sublime and the fantastic. The solemn language of the angel appeared strangely diversified by the intimation that he would find a boat upon the shore,—that this boat would convey him to a place where he was to inquire for a man whose age was one hundred and sixty-two years,—and that this man was the being destined to save him from the doom of a Wehr-Wolf. Then, again, he thought that heaven worked out its designs by means often inscrutable to human comprehension; and he blamed himself for having doubted the truth of the vision. Feelings of joy therefore accompanied the reassurance of his soul; and, having poured forth his thanksgivings for the merciful intervention of Providence in his behalf, he tarried not even so break his fast with the fruits clustering at a short distance from him, but hastened to retrace his way across the mountains, no longer doubting to find the sign fulfilled and the boat upon the shore.

And now these thoughts rose within him:—Should he again behold Nisida? Was the fleet, which he had seen on the previous day, still off the island? Or had it departed, bearing Nisida away to another clime?

He expected not to behold either the fleet or his loved one;—for he felt convinced that the angel would not send him back within the influence of her temptations.

Nor was he mistaken;—for having traversed the volcanic range of heights, he beheld naught to break the uniform and monotonous aspect of the sun-lit sea. But, when drawing nearer to the shore, he saw a dark spot almost immediately in front of the little hut which Nisida and himself had constructed, and wherein they had passed so many, many happy hours.

But the beauteous form of Nisida met not now his eyes: and, deeply—profoundly—ardently as he still loved her, and felt he must ever love her so long as the tide of life should flow in his veins,—yet, to speak soothly, he deplored not that she was no longer there. The vision of the previous night had so firmly established hope in his soul, that he had prepared and tutored himself, during his journey across the mountains, to sacrifice all his happiness on earth to ensure the eternal felicity of heaven.

No:—Nisida was not there! But as he drew closer to the shore, he beheld, to his ineffable joy, the dark spot gradually assume that defined shape which left no room to doubt the truth of his vision, even were he inclined to be sceptical. For, there indeed, touching the strand,—but still so far in the water that a slight exertion would send it completely afloat,—was a large boat, curiously shaped, and painted in a wreath of fantastic colours. It had a mast standing—but the sail was lowered; and, on a close inspection, the boat proved to be altogether unimpaired.

"Heaven delights to effect its wise intentions by natural means," thought Wagner within himself. "But surely it could not have been through the agency of Nisida that this boat was left upon the shore? No," he added aloud, after a still closer inspection; "the rope fastened to the prow has been snapped asunder! Doubtless the boat became detached from one of the ships which appeared off the island yesterday—and which," he said in a low murmuring voice, "have afforded Nisida the means of departure hence!"

He now advanced, with a beating heart, to the hut. The door was closed:—was it possible that Nisida might be within?

Oh! how weak in purpose is the strongest-minded of mortals! For an instant a pleasing hope filled Wagner's breast;—and then again summoning all his resolution to his aid, he opened the door—resolved, should she indeed be there, to remain proof against all the appeals she might make to induce him to sacrifice to their mundane prosperity his immortal soul.

But the hut was empty.

He lingered in it for a few minutes; and the reminiscenses of happy hours passed therein swept across his brain.

Suddenly the note which Nisida had left for him met his eyes; and it would be representing him as something far more, or else far less than human, were we to declare that he did not experience a feeling of intense pleasure at beholding that memorial of her love. And tears flowed down his cheeks as he read the following lines:—

"The hour approaches, dearest Fernand, when, in all probability, I shall quit the island. But think not that this hope is unaccompanied by severe pangs. Oh! thou knowest that I love thee;—and I will return to thee, my own adored Fernand, as soon as my presence shall be no longer needed at Florence. Yes: I will come back to thee—and we will not part until death shall deprive thee of me—for I must perish first, and while thou still remainest in all the glory of thy regenerated youth! Alas! thou hast fled from me this morning in anger—perhaps in disgust: but thou wilt forgive me, Fernand, if yielding to some strange influence which I could not control, I urged an appeal so well calculated to strike terror into thy soul. Oh! that I could embrace thee ere I leave this isle; but, alas! thou comest not back—thou hast fled to the mountains! It is, however, in the ardent hope of thy return to this spot, that I leave these few lines to assure thee of my undying affection—to pledge to thee my intention to hasten back to thine arms as soon as possible—and to implore thee not to nourish anger against thy devoted

"NISIDA."

Wagner placed the letter to his lips, exclaiming, "Oh! wherefore did an evil influence ever prove its power on thee, thou loving—loved—and beauteous being! Why was thine hand raised against the hapless Agnes? wherefore did fate make thee a murderess? And why—oh! why didst thou assail me with prayers—tears—reproaches—menaces, to induce me to consign my soul to Satan? Nisida—may heaven manifest its merciful goodness unto thee, even as that same benign care has been extended to me!"

Fernand then placed the letter in his bosom, next to his heart; and, dashing away the tears from his long lashes, began to turn his attention towards the preparations for his own departure from the island. As he approached the pile of stores, he beheld the light drapery which Nisida had lately worn, but which she had laid aside previous to leaving the island; and he also observed that the rich dress, which he had often seen her examine with care, was no longer there.

"How beautiful she must have appeared in that garb!" he murmured to himself. "But, alas! she returns to the great world to resume her former character of the *Deaf and Dumb!*"

Nisida and himself had often employed themselves in gathering quantities of those fruits which form an excellent aliment when dried in the sun; and there was a large supply of these comestibles now at his disposal. He accordingly transferred them to the boat; then he procured a quantity of fresh fruits;—and lastly he filled with pure water a cask which had been saved by Nisida from the corsair-wreck.

His preparations were speedily completed; and he was about to depart, when it struck him that he might never behold Nisida again, and that she might really perform her promise of returning to the island sooner or later. He accordingly availed himself of the writing materials left amongst the stores, to pen a brief but affectionate note, couched in the following terms:—

"Dearest Nisida, I have found, read, and wept over thy letter. Thou hast my sincerest forgiveness, because I love thee more than man ever before loved woman. Heaven has sent me the means of escape from this island; and the doom at which my regenerated existence was purchased, will shortly lose its spell. But perhaps my life may be surrendered up at the same time; at all events, everything is dark and mysterious in respect to the means by which that spell is to be broken. Should we never meet again, but shouldst thou return hither and find this note, receive it as a proof of the unchanging affection of thy

"FERNAND."

This letter was placed in the hut, in precisely the same spot where the one written by Nisida had been left; and

Wagner then hastened to the boat, which he had no difficulty in pushing away from the shore.

Without being able to form any idea of the direction in which the Island of Sicily lay, but trusting entirely to the aid of heaven to guide him to the coast whither his destiny now required him to proceed, he hoisted the sail and abandoned the boat to the gentle breeze which swept the surface of the Mediterranean.

CHAPTER LXII.

THE KAPITAN-PACHA'S SHIP.—NISIDA AN EAVESDROPPER. —A HISTORY OF PAST OCCURRENCES IN FLORENCE.

THE state-cabins—they might more properly be called spacious apartments — occupied by the Grand Vizier, Ibrahim-Pacha, on board the ship of the Lord High Admiral, were fitted up in a most sumptuous and luxurious manner. They consisted of two large saloons in a suite, and from each of which opened, on either side, a number of small cabins, tenanted by the officers immediately attached to the Grand Vizier's person, and the pages and slaves in attendance on him.

The first of the two large saloons was lighted by a handsome conical skylight on the deck: the innermost had the advantage of the stern windows. The drapery—the curtains—the carpets—the sofas—and the hangings were all of the richest materials: the sides and ceilings of the cabins were beautifully painted and elaborately gilt, and the wood-work of the windows were encrusted with thin slabs of variously coloured marbles, on which were engraved the cyphers of the different Lord High Admirals who had hoisted their flags at any time on board that ship. For the state-apartments which we are describing, properly belonged to the Kapitan-Pacha himself; but they had been surrendered to the Grand Vizier, as a mark of respect to the superior rank of this Minister, during his stay on board.

The little cabins communicating with the large saloons, were in reality intended to accommodate the ladies of the Kapitan-Pacha's harem; but Ibrahim did not turn them to a similar use, because it was contrary to Ottoman usage for the Princess Aischa, being the Sultan's sister, to accompany her husband on any expedition; and he had received so menacing a warning, in the fate of Calanthe, not to provoke the jealousy of Aischa or the vengeance of her mother, the Sultana-Valida, that he had brought none of the ladies of his own harem with him. Indeed, since the violent death of Calanthe, that harem had been maintained at Constantinople rather as an appendage of his high rank, than as a source of sensual enjoyment.

Nisida of Riverola was treated with the utmost deference and attention by the Grand Vizier, Ibrahim-Pacha; and, on reaching the Lord High Admiral's ship, she was instantly conducted to the innermost saloon, which she was given to understand by signs would be exclusively appropriated to her use. The slaves occupying the small cabins opening therefrom were removed to another part of the ship; and the key of the door connecting the two saloons was handed by the polite Ibrahim to the lady, as a guarantee—or at least an apparent one—of the respect with which she should be treated and the security she might hope to enjoy.

The fleet weighed anchor and set sail again almost immediately after the return of the Grand Vizier to the Admiral's ship; and as she was wafted away from the Island of Snakes, Nisida sat at the window of her splendid saloon, gazing at the receding shores, and so strangely balancing between her anxiety to revisit Florence and her regrets at abandoning Fernand Wagner, that while smiles were on her lips, tears were in her eyes, and if her bosom palpitated with joy at one moment it would heave with a profound sigh at the next.

In the afternoon four male slaves entered Nisida's cabin, and spread upon the table a magnificent repast, accompanied with the most delicious wines of Cyprus and of Greece; and while the lady partook slightly of the banquet, two other slaves appeared and danced in a pleasing style for several minutes. They retired, but shortly returned, carrying in their hands massive silver censers, in which burnt aloes, cinnamon, and other odoriferous woods, which diffused a delicious perfume around. The four slaves who attended at table removed the dishes on splendid silver salvers, and then served sherbet and a variety of delicious fruits; and when the repast was terminated, they all withdrew, leaving Nisida once more alone.

The Island of Snakes had been lost sight of for some hours, and the fresh breeze of evening was playing upon the cheeks of the Lady Nisida as she sat at the open casement of her splendid saloon, watching the ships that followed in the wake of that in which she was, when the sounds of voices in the adjacent cabin attracted her attention; and as the partition was but slight, and the persons discoursing spoke in Italian, she could not help overhearing the conversation which there took place, even if she had possessed any punctilious feelings to have prevented her from becoming a willing listener.

"The Lady Nisida is a magnificent woman, Demetrius," observed a voice which our heroine immediately recognised to be that of the Grand Vizier. "Such a splendid aquiline countenance I never before beheld! Such eyes too—such a delicious mouth—and such brilliant teeth! What a pity 'tis that she has not the use of her tongue. The voice of such a glorious creature, speaking mine own dear native Italian language, would be music itself. And how admirably is she formed; upon somewhat too large a scale, perhaps, precisely to suit my taste, and yet the contours of her shape are so well rounded—so perfectly proportioned in the most harmonious symmetry, that were she less of the Hebe she would be less charming."

"Is your Highness already enamoured of Donna Nisida?" asked the person to whom the Grand Vizier had addressed the preceding observations.

"I must confess that I am, Demetrius," replied Ibrahim: "I would give a year of my life to become her favoured lover for one day. But considering that I hope to see my sister Flora become the wife of Donna Nisida's brother, Francisco, I must restrain this passion of mine within due bounds. But wherefore do you sigh thus heavily, Demetrius?"

"Alas! my lord, the mention you made of your sister reminded me that I once possessed a sister also," returned the Greek, in plaintive tone. "But when I returned to Constantinople, I sought vainly for her—and heaven knows what has become of her, and whether I shall ever see her more. Poor Calanthe! some treachery has doubtless been practised towards thee!"

"Do not give way to despair, Demetrius," said the Grand Vizier. "Who knows but that Calanthe may have espoused some youth on whom her affections were set——"

"Ah! my lord," interrupted the Greek, "it is considerate—it is kind on the part of your Highness to suggest such a consolatory belief; but Calanthe would not keep a honourable bridal secret. Yet better were it that she should be dead—that she should have been basely murdered by some ruthless robber—than that she should live dishonoured. However, I will not intrude my griefs upon your Highness, although the friendship and the condescension which your Highness manifests towards me, emboldens me to mention these sorrows in your presence."

"Would that I could really console thee, Demetrius!" exclaimed Ibrahim, with well-affected sincerity; "for thou hast shown thyself a sincere friend to my poor sister Flora. And now that we are alone together, Demetrius, for almost the first time since this hastily undertaken voyage began, let us recapitulate in detail all the occurrences which have led me to enter upon the present expedition, the real nature of which you alone know, save my imperial master. And moreover, let us continue to discourse in Italian; for thou canst speak that language more fluently than I can express myself in thy native Greek;—besides, it rejoices my heart," he added with a sigh, "to converse in a tongue so dear to me as that of the land which gave me birth. Ah! if Donna Nisida only knew that in the representative of the mighty Solyman she had beholden the brother of her late menial, Flora, how surprised would she be!"

"And it were not prudent that she should learn this fact, my lord," observed Demetrius, "for more reasons than one;—since, from sundry hints which the Signora Francatelli, your lordship's worthy aunt, dropped to me, it is easy to believe that the Donna Nisida was averse to the attachment which her brother Francisco had formed, and that her ladyship indeed was the means of consigning your Highness's sister to the Convent of the Carmelites."

"Albeit I shall not treat Count Francisco's sister the less worthily, now that she is in my power," said Ibrahim-Pacha: "indeed, her matchless beauty would command my forbearance, were I inclined to be vindictive. Moreover, deaf and dumb as she is, she could not obtain the least insight into my plans; and, therefore, she is unable to thwart them."

The reader may suppose that not one single word of all this conversation was lost upon Nisida, who had indeed learnt with extreme surprise—nay, with the most unbounded wonderment—that the high and mighty Grand Vizier of the Ottoman Empire—a man enjoying an almost sovereign rank, and who bore a title which placed him on a level with the greatest princes of Christendom—was the brother of the detested Flora Francatelli!

During a short pause which ensued in the dialogue between Ibrahim-Pacha and his Greek confidant, Nisida stole gently up to the door in the partition between the two saloons—so fearful was she of losing a single word of

Sipehsalar* of the armies of the Sultan, I am responsible for my actions to his Majesty alone—yet it is not a small thing, Demetrius, to march an invading force into the heart of Italy, and thereby risk a war with all Christendom. Therefore let us recapitulate and pause to reflect upon every detail of all those incidents which occurred two months ago at Florence."

"Good, my lord," said Demetrius. "I will therefore begin with my arrival in that fair city, to which I repaired with all possible despatch so soon as I received the instructions of your Highness. It would appear that the Lord Count of Riverola reached Florence the same

"THE COURSE IS OVER—THE RACE IS RUN." (See p. 101.)

a discourse that so deeply interested and nearly concerned her.

"But as I was saying ere now, Demetrius," resumed the Grand Vizier, who, young as he was, had acquired all the methodical habits of a wise statesman—"let us examine in detail the whole posture of affairs in Florence, so that I may maturely consider the precise bearings of the case, and finally determine how to act. For, although I have at my disposal a fleet which might cope with even that of enterprising England or imperious France—though twenty thousand well-disciplined soldiers on board these ships are ready to draw the sword at my nod—and though, as the Seraskier and

day as myself, he having been detained at the outset of his voyage home from Rhodes by contrary winds and a severe storm. It was somewhat late in the evening when I called at the cottage of the Signora Francatelli, your Highness's worthy aunt; for I previously passed a few hours in instituting by indirect means as many inquiries concerning her circumstances and welfare as could be prudently made without exciting suspicion. To my grief, however, I could not ascertain any tidings concerning your Highness's sister: and I therefore came

* Generalissimo alike of all the infantry and cavalry forces of the Ottoman Empire.

to the mournful conclusion that her disappearance still remained unaccounted for—in a word, that she was irrevocably lost to her anxious relatives. Pondering upon the sad tidings which, in this respect, I should have to forward to your Highness, and having already devised a fitting tale whereby to introduce myself to your lordship's aunt, I went to the cottage, which, as I heard in the course of a subsequent conversation, Don Francisco of Riverola had just quitted. Your Highness's aunt received me with as much cordiality as she could well show towards a stranger. Then, in accordance with my pre-arranged method of procedure, I stated that I was sent by the son of a debtor to the estate of the late Signor Francatelli, to repay to any of his surviving relations a large sum of money which had been so long—so very long owing, and the loss of which at the time had mainly contributed to plunge Signor Francatelli into embarrassment. I added that the son of the debtor having grown rich, had deemed it an act of duty and honour to liquidate this liability on the part of his deceased father. My tale was believed; the case of jewels, which I had previously caused to be estimated by a goldsmith in Florence, was received as the means of settling the fictitious debt; and I was forthwith 'a welcome friend at the worthy lady's abode."

"Thy stratagem was a good one, Demetrius," observed the Grand Vizier. "But proceed—and fear not that thou wilt weary me with lengthened details.".

"I stayed to partake of the evening's repast," continued the Greek: "and the Signora Francatelli grew confiding and communicative, as was nothing more than natural, inasmuch as I necessarily appeared in the light of the agent of a worthy and honourable man, who had not forgotten his obligation to a family that had suffered by his father's conduct. I assured the Signora that the person by whom I was employed to liquidate that debt would be rejoiced to hear of the prosperity of the Francatellis, and I ventured to make inquiries concerning the orphan children of the late merchant."

"Proceed, Demetrius," said the Grand Vizier: "I know wherefore you hesitate—but spare not a single detail."

"Your Highness shall be obeyed," returned the Greek, though now speaking with considerable diffidence. "The worthy lady shook her head mournfully, observing that Alessandro, the son of the late merchant, was in Turkey she believed;—and then she rose hastily, and opening a door leading to a staircase, called to her niece to descend, '*as there was only a friend present.*' I was overjoyed to learn, thus suddenly and unexpectedly, that the Signora Flora *had* reappeared : and when she entered the room, I could scarcely contain my delight beneath that aspect of mere cold courtesy which it became a stranger to wear. The young lady appeared perfectly happy;—and, no wonder! For when she had retired, after staying a few minutes in the room, her good aunt, in the fulness of her confidence in me, not only related all the particulars of the Signora Flora's immurement in the Carmelite Convent, as I have detailed them to your Highness on a former occasion, but also explained to me her motives for so long concealing the young lady's return home. Those motives I have likewise fully narrated to your Highness. The worthy aunt then proceeded to inform me that the Count of Riverola had only returned that same day from the wars—that he had made honourable proposals to her on behalf of the Signora Flora—and that it was intended to sustain the mystery which veiled the young lady's existence and safety in the cottage, until the marriage should have been privately effected, when concealment would be no longer necessary, as it would be then too late for the Count's friends to interfere or renew their persecutions against your lordship's sister. In the course of this conversation which I had with your Highness's aunt, she dropped hints intimating her suspicion that the Lady Nisida was the principal, if not indeed the sole means of those persecutions which had consigned the innocent young maiden to the Carmelite Convent. And the more I reflect upon this point—considering all I know of the affairs under discussion, and all I learnt in Florence relative to Donna Nisida's strange and resolute character—the more I am convinced that she really perpetrated that diabolical outrage."

"Were it not for young Francisco's sake, and that I should bring dishonour into a family with which my sister will, I hope, be soon connected by marriage-ties," exclaimed Ibrahim, "I would avenge myself and my sister's wrongs by forcing the cruel Nisida to yield herself to my arms. But, no—it must not be!"

And Nisida, who overheard every syllable that was uttered, curled her lip haughtily, while her eyes flashed brilliant fire, at the dark menace which the renegade Ibrahim had dared to utter, qualified though it were by the avowal of the motive which would prevent him from putting it into execution.

"No—it must not be," repeated Ibrahim-Pacha, after a pause. "And yet," he added in a musing tone, "she is so wondrously beautiful that I would risk a great deal —endure much—and sacrifice much, also, to win her love! But proceed, Demetrius :—we now come to that portion of the narrative which so nearly concerns my present proceedings."

"Yes, my lord—and God give your Highness success !" exclaimed the young Greek. "Having taken my leave of your excellent aunt, who invited me to visit her again, as I had casually observed that business would detain me in Florence for some time—and having promised the strictest secrecy relative to all she had told me —I repaired to the inn at which I had put up, intending to devote the next day to writing the details of all those particulars which I have thus related, and which I purposed to send by some special messenger to your Highness. But it then struck me that I should only attract undue attention to myself by conducting at a public tavern a correspondence having so important an aspect ; and I accordingly rose very early in the morning to sally forth and seek after a secluded but respectable lodging. I eventually, after many inquiries, obtained suitable apartments in the house of a widow known as Dame Margaretha. Her dwelling was situate in an obscure street near the cathedral ; and there I immediately took up my abode. Having written my letters to your Highness, I was anxious to get them expedited to Constantinople as speedily as possible ; for I was well aware that your Highness would be rejoiced to hear that your beloved sister was indeed in the land of the living—that she was in good health—and that a brilliant marriage was in store for her. I accordingly spoke to Dame Margaretha relative to the means of obtaining a trusty messenger, who, by being well recompensed—partly before he should quit Florence, and fully on his arrival at the place of destination—would undertake a journey to Constantinople. The old woman assured me that her son Antonio, who was a valet in the service of the Count of Arestino, would be able to procure me such a messenger as I required ; and in the course of the day that individual was fetched by his mother to speak to me on the subject. Having repeated my wishes to him, he asked me several questions which seemed to indicate a prying disposition and a curiosity as impertinent as it was inconvenient. In fact I did not like his manner at all ; but, conceiving that his conduct might arise from sheer ignorance and from no sinister motive, I still felt inclined to avail myself of his assistance to procure a messenger. Finding that he could not sift me, he at length said that he had no doubt a friend of his, whom he named Venturo, would undertake my commission ; and he promised to return with that individual in the evening. He then left me ; and, true to his promise, he came back shortly after dusk, accompanied by this same Venturo. The bargain was soon struck between us ; and Venturo promised to set off that very night for Rimini, whence vessels were constantly sailing for Constantinople. I gave him a handsome sum in advance, and also a sealed packet, addressed to your Highness's private secretary, but containing an enclosure, also well sealed, directed to your Highness ;—for I did not choose to excite the curiosity of those Italians by allowing them to discover that I was corresponding with the Grand Vizier of the Ottoman Empire. Venturo accordingly left me, promising to acquit himself faithfully of his mission."

"Your plans were all wisely taken," said the Grand Vizier ; "and no human foresight could have anticipated other than successful results. Proceed—for, although you have hastily sketched all these particulars before, yet I am anxious to consider them in more attentive detail."

"Having thus disposed of that important business," resumed the young Greek, "I went out to saunter through the streets of Florence, and while away an hour or two in viewing the splendid appearance of that charming city, when lighted up with the innumerable lamps of its palaces and casinos. At length, finding myself dazzled as it were by the illuminations denoting the dwellings of the rich, and sated with the display of magnificence and wealth in the gay quarters, I entered a dark and obscure street which I knew, by the direction wherein it lay, must lead towards the river. Feeling no inclination to return to my lodgings to seek repose, I resolved to enjoy the fresh breeze on the bank of the Arno. But I had not proceeded far down the street, when I heard the sound of many steps rapidly approaching from behind, as if of a patrol. I stepped aside under a deep archway, to afford sufficient room for the men to pass along the very narrow street; but as chance would have it they stopped short within a few paces of the spot where I was shrouded in the utter obscurity of the arch. I should have immediately passed on my way, but was induced to stop where I was by hearing a voice which I immediately recognised to be that of Venturo, whom I believed to be already some miles away from Florence. I was perfectly astounded at this discovery; and if I had entertained any doubts as to the identity of that voice, they were speedily cleared up by the conversation which ensued between the men. '*We had better separate here,*' said Venturo, '*and break into at least two parties; as at the bottom of this street we shall come within the blaze of the lights of the casinos on the Arno's bank.*'—'*Well spoken,*' returned a voice, which, to my increasing wonder, I recognised to be that of Antonio, my landlady's son: '*you and I, Venturo, will keep together; and our friends can go on first. We will follow them in a few minutes, and then unite again at the angle of the grove nearest to Dame Francatelli's cottage. What say you, Lomellino?*'—'*Just as you think fit, Antonio,*' returned a third person, who I naturally concluded to be the individual addressed as Lomellino. '*You, or rather your master, the Count of Arestino, pays for this business,*' he added; '*and so I am bound to obey you!*'—'*Listen, then,*' resumed Antonio: '*the young Count of Riverola, whom I have traced to the cottage this evening, will no doubt be coming away by about the time we shall all meet down there; and, therefore, we shall have nothing to do but to carry him off to the cave.*'—'*Why is the Count of Arestino so hostile to young Riverola?*' demanded the man who had answered to the name of Lomellino.—'*He cares nothing about young Riverola, either one way or the other,*' replied Antonio: '*but I have persuaded his lordship that if Francisco be left at large, he will only use his influence to mitigate the vengeance of the law against the Countess Giulia, who is the friend of Flora Francatelli; and so the Count of Arestino has consented to follow my advice and have Francisco locked up until the Inquisition has dealt with the Countess, her lover, the Marquis of Orsini, and the Francatellis, aunt and niece.*'—'*Then you have a spite against this Count Francisco of Riverola, Antonio?*' said Lomellino.—'*Truly have I,*' responded Antonio.—'*You remember that night when you, with Stephano Verrina and Piero, got into the Riverola palace some months ago? Well, I don't know who discovered the plot; but I was locked in my room, and next morning young Francisco dismissed me in a way that made him my mortal enemy. And, as a man and an Italian, I must have vengeance. For this purpose I have urged on the Count of Arestino to cause Flora Francatelli, whom Francisco loves and wishes to marry, to be included in the proceedings taken by the Inquisition at his lordship's instigation against the Countess Giulia and the Marquis of Orsini; and the old aunt must necessarily be thrown in, into the bargain, for harbouring sacrilegious persons.*'—'*And so young Francisco is to lose his mistress Flora, and be kept a prisoner in the cavern till she has been condemned along with the others?*' said Lomellino.—'*Neither more nor less than what you imagine,*' returned the villanous Antonio, with a hideous chuckle; '*and I only wish I had the Lady Nisida also in my power, for I have no doubt that she instigated her brother to turn me off suddenly like a common thief, because, from all you have since told me, Lomellino, I dare swear that it was she who got an inkling of our intentions to plunder the Riverola palace; though how she could have done so, being deaf and dumb, passes my understanding. After all, Flora might have detected the scheme and made it known to her mistress.*'—'*Well, well,*' growled Lomellino, '*it is no use to waste time in talking of the past: let us only think of the present. Come, my men: we will go on first, as already agreed.*'—Three or four armed ruffians then put themselves in motion, passing close by the place where I was concealed, but fortunately without discovering my presence."

"Oh! those miscreants would have assuredly murdered you, my faithful Demetrius," said the Grand Vizier.

"Of that, my lord, there is little doubt," returned the young Greek; "and I must confess that I shuddered more than once while listening to the discourse of the cold-blooded monsters. But Venturo and Antonio still remained behind for a few minutes; and the discourse which took place between them, when their comrades had separated from them, gave me a still farther insight into the characters of the gang. '*Well, Venturo,*' said Antonio, after a short pause, '*have you examined the packet which was entrusted to you?*'—'*I have; and the contents are written in Greek or Arabic, or some such outlandish tongue, for I could not read a word of them,*' answered Venturo; '*and so I thought the best thing was to destroy them.*'—'*You acted wisely,*' observed Antonio: '*by the Saints! it was a good thought of mine to introduce you to my mother's lodger as a trustworthy messenger! If he only knew that we had shared his gold and were laughing at him for his credulity, he would not be over well pleased. His purse appears to be well lined; and when we have got all our present business off our hands, we will devote our attention to the lodger. The Arno is deep, and a foreigner the less in the city will not be missed.*'—'*Not at all,*' answered Venturo: '*but let us now hasten to join our companions. At what time are the officers of the Inquisition to visit the cottage?*'—'*They are no doubt already in the neighbourhood,*' replied Antonio, '*and will pounce upon their victims as soon as young Francisco leaves the place. Another set of officers are after the Marquis of Orsini.*'—The two miscreants then departed, continuing their conversation in a low tone as they went along the street; but I overheard no more."

"The wretches!" exclaimed the Grand Vizier, in an excited voice. "But vengeance will light upon them yet."

"Heaven grant that they may not go unpunished!" said Demetrius. "Your Highness may imagine the consternation with which I had listened to the development of all the damnable plots then in progress; but I nevertheless experienced a material solace in the fact that accident had thus revealed to me the whole extent of the danger which menaced those whom your Highness held dear. Without pausing to deliberate, I resolved, at all risks, to proceed immediately to the cottage, and, if not too late, warn your aunt and lovely sister of the terrible danger that menaced them. Nay, more—I determined to remove them immediately from Florence—that very night—without an unnecesary moment's delay. Darting along the street, as if my speed involved matters of life and death, I succeeded in passing the two villains, Venturo and Antonio, before they had entered within the sphere of the brilliant illuminations of the casinos in the Vale of Arno: and I heard one say to the other, '*There's some cowardly knave who has just done a deed of which he is no doubt afraid.*' Convinced by this remark that they suspected not who the person that passed them so rapidly was, I hurried on with increasing speed, and likewise with augmenting hope to be enabled to save not only your lordship's aunt and sister from the officers of the Inquisition, but also the young Count of Riverola from the power of his miscreant enemies. Alas! my anticipations were not to be fulfilled! I lost my way amongst a maze of gardens connected with the villas bordering on the Arno; and much valuable time—time vitally valuable at such a crisis—was wasted in the circuits which I had to make to extricate myself from the labyrinth and reach the bank of the river. At length I drew within sight of the cottage; but my heart beat with terrible alarm as I beheld the lights moving rapidly about the house. '*It is too late!*' I thought; and yet I rushed on towards the place. But suddenly the door opened, and by the glare of a light within I saw *three* females, closely muffled in veils, led forth by several armed men. It instantly struck me that the *third* must be the Countess Giulia of Arestino to whom I had heard the miscreants allude. I stopped short—for I knew that any violent demonstration or interference on my part would be useless, and that measures of another kind must be adopted on behalf of the victims. As the procession now advanced from the cottage, I concealed myself in the adjacent grove, wondering whether Count Francisco had been already arrested, or whether he had managed to elude his enemies. The procession, consisting of the officers of the Inquisition, with their three female prisoners, who were dragged rather than led along, passed by the spot where I was concealed; and the deep sobs which came from the unfortunate ladies, gagged though they evidently were, filled my heart with horror and anguish. As soon as they had disappeared, I struck farther into the grove, knowing by its situation that the outlet on the other side would conduct me to the nearest road to the quarter of the city in which I lodged. But scarcely had I reached the outskirts of the little wood in the direction which I have named when I saw a party of men moving on in front of me through the obscurity of the night. It struck me that this party might consist of Antonio, Venturo, and the other worthies; and I determined to ascertain whether Count Francisco had fallen into their hands. I accordingly followed them as cautiously as possible, taking care to skirt the grove in such a manner that I was concealed by its deep shade, whereas those whom I was watching proceeded farther away from the trees. Thus the party in advance and myself continued our respective paths for nearly a quarter of an hour, during which I had ascertained beyond all doubt that the men whom I was following were really the villains of the Antonio gang, and that they had a prisoner amongst them who could be none other than the Count of Riverola. At length the grove terminated; and I was about to abandon farther pursuit, as dangerous,—when it struck me that I should be acting in a cowardly and unworthy manner not to endeavour to ascertain the locality of the cave of which I had heard the miscreants speak, and to which they were most probably conveying him who was so dear to the beautiful Signora Flora. Accordingly, by exercising the greatest caution, I managed to track the party across several fields to a grove of evergreens. Now my task of pursuit became far more difficult; and I confess that I trembled at the danger I was incurring in acting the spy upon such desperate men. But as they advanced without caring how they broke through the cracking thickets, the noise of their movements absorbed the far fainter sounds which accompanied my progress: and I moreover picked my way as carefully as possible. So successful was my undertaking, terribly hazardous as it was, that when the party at length stopped, about a quarter of an hour after having first entered this grove, I was within twenty paces of them. But it was profoundly dark amidst that dense foliage, through which I had tracked them by ear and not by eye; and I was unable to observe their movements. A few minutes elapsed, during which I computed the distance they were from me, and calculated so as to form an idea of the exact spot where they were standing; for, by an observation which one of the villains let drop, I learnt that they had reached the entrance to their cavern. It also struck me that I had heard a bell ring as if in the depths of the earth; and, granting the suspicion to be correct, I concluded that this was a signal made to obtain admittance or to give notice of their coming. While I was weighing all these matters in my mind, Lomellino suddenly exclaimed, ' Let the prisoner be taken down first; and have a care, Venturo, that the bandage is well fastened.'—' All right, Captain,' was the reply; and thus I ascertained that Lomellino was the chief of some band, most probably, I thought, of robbers—for I remembered the allusions which had been made that evening by Antonio to a certain predatory visit some months previously to the Riverola mansion.—' God help Francisco!' I said within myself, as I reflected upon the desperate character of the men who had him in their power: and then I was consoled by the remembrance that he was merely to be detained a prisoner for a period, and not harmed."

"Unfortunately such demons as those Florentine banditti are capable of every atrocity," observed the Grand Vizier.

"True, my lord," returned Demetrius: "but let us hope that all those in whom your Highness is interested will yet be saved. I shall however continue my narrative. Three or four minutes had elapsed since the robbers had come to a full stop, when I knew by the observations made amongst them, that they were descending into some subterranean place. I accordingly waited with the utmost anxiety until I was convinced they had all disappeared with their prisoner; and then I crept cautiously along to the place at which I had already reckoned them to have paused. I stooped down, and carefully felt upon the ground, until I was enabled to ascertain the precise point at which the marks of their footsteps had ceased. At this moment the moon shone forth with such extreme brilliancy, that its beams penetrated the thick foliage; and I now observed, with feelings of indescribable horror, that I had advanced to the very verge of a steep precipice, on the brink of which the grove suddenly ceased. Had not the moon thus providentially appeared at that instant, I should have continued to grope about in the utter darkness, and have assuredly fallen into the abyss. I breathed a hasty, but not the less fervent prayer for this signal deliverance, and then continued my researches. But not a trace of any secret entrance to a cavern could I find—no steps—no trap-door! Well aware that it would be dangerous for me to be caught in that spot, should any of the banditti emerge suddenly from their cave, I

was reluctantly compelled to depart. But before I quitted the place, I studied it so well, that I should have no difficulty in recognising it again. In fact, just at the precise spot where the footsteps of the banditti ceased, an enormous chestnut tree, which for years making more than a century must have continued to draw from the earth its mighty nourishment, slopes completely over the precipice, in the hard soil on the verge of which its roots are firmly fixed; while on the right of this tree, as you face the abyss, is a knot of olives, and on the left an umbrageous lime. These features of the spot I committed to memory, with the idea that such a clue to the robbers' retreat might not eventually prove useless."

" I will extirpate that nest of vipers—that horde of remorseless banditti!" exclaimed Ibrahim-Pacha, in a tone indicative of strong excitement.

"Your Highness has the power," responded Demetrius; " but the Florentine authorities must be completely impotent in respect to such a formidable horde of desperate and lawless men. The remainder of my narrative is soon told, my lord," continued the young Greek. " I returned to my lodgings in safety—but well-determined, for more reasons than one, not to remain there a single hour longer than was necessary. For apart from the resolve which I had formed already, in consequence of the various and unforeseen incidents which had occurred, to return to Constantinople without delay, the murderous designs of Antonio and Venturo, in respect to myself, would have hastened my removal, at all events, to another lodging. That night sleep never visited my eyes, so horrified and alarmed—so amazed and grieved was I at the calamities which had befallen those who were so dear to your Highness. Very early in the morning, I arose from a feverish bed, and in pursuance of plans which I had devised during the slumberless hours of night, I sallied forth to ascertain if I could learn any tidings of the Marquis of Orsini. ' For,' thought I, ' if this nobleman has escaped arrest by the officers of the Inquisition, he might be enabled to effect somewhat in aiding the female victims.'—But I heard at his dwelling that he had been arrested the previous evening on a charge of sacrilege, perpetrated with others, in respect to the Carmelite Convent. Frustrated in this quarter, I repaired to the principal clerk of the criminal tribunal, and inquired the name and address of a lawyer of eminence and repute. The clerk complied with my demand, and recommended me to Angelo Duras, the brother of a celebrated Florentine physician."

"Both of whom are well known to me by name," observed the Grand Vizier; "and Angelo Duras is a man of unblemished integrity. It delights me much to know that you have employed him."

"I found him, too," continued Demetrius, "a kind-hearted and benevolent man. He received me with affability; and I narrated to him as much as it was necessary for him to know of all the particulars which I have detailed to your Highness. Without stating by whom I was employed,—and, indeed, without making the least allusion to your Highness,—I merely represented to him that I was deeply interested in the Francatelli family, and that it was of the utmost importance to obtain a delay for at least two or three months in the criminal proceedings instituted against those innocent females,—as, in the meantime, I should undertake a journey to a place at some considerable distance, but the result of which would prove materially beneficial to the cause of the accused. He observed that the interest of the Count of Arestino, who would doubtless endeavour to hasten the proceedings in order to wreak speedy vengeance upon his wife and the Marquis of Orsini, was very powerful to contend against; but that gold could accomplish much. I assured him that there would be no lack of funds to sustain even the most expensive process; and I threw down a heavy purse as an earnest of my ability to bear the cost of the suit. He committed to paper all the particulars I had thought it prudent to reveal to him, and after some consideration said, ' I now see my way clearly. I will undertake that the final hearing of this case, at least so far as it regards the Francatellis, shall be postponed for three months. You may rely upon the fulfilment of this promise, let the Count of Arestino do his worst.' Thus assured I quitted the worthy pleader, and proceeded to visit Father Marco, who, as I happened to learn when in conversation with your Highness's aunt, was the family confessor. I found that excellent man overwhelmed with grief at the calamities which had occurred; and to him I confided, under a solemn promise of inviolable secrecy, who the present Grand Vizier of the Ottoman Empire really was, and how I had been employed by your Highness to visit Florence for the purpose of watching over the safety of your relatives. I however explained to Father Marco that his vow of secrecy was to cease to be binding at any moment when the lives of the Francatellis should be menaced by circumstances that might possibly arise in spite of all the precautions I had adopted to postpone the final hearing of their case; and that should imminent peril menace those lives, he was immediately to reveal to the Duke of Florence the fact of the relationship of the Francatellis with one who had power to punish any injury that might be done to them. Though well knowing, my lord, the obstinacy of the Christian States in venturing to beard Ottoman might, I considered this precaution to be at all events a prudent one; and Father Marco promised to obey my injunctions in all respects.''

"I was not mistaken in thee, Demetrius," said the Grand Vizier, "when I chose thee for that mission on account of thy discreetness and foresight.''

"Your Highness's praises are my best reward," answered the Greek. "I had now done all that I could possibly effect or devise under the circumstances which prompted me to think or act; and it grieved me that I was unable to afford the slightest assistance to the young Count of Riverola. But I dared not wait longer in Italy; and I was convinced that the authorities of Florence were too inefficient to root out the horde of banditti, even had I explained to them the clue which I myself obtained to the stronghold of those miscreants. I accordingly quitted Florence in the afternoon of the day following the numerous arrests which I have mentioned, and had I not been detained so long at Rimini, by adverse winds, your Highness would not have been kept for so many weeks without the mournful tidings which it was at length my painful duty to communicate in person to your lordship.''

"That delay, my faithful Demetrius," said the Grand Vizier, "was no fault of thine. Fortunately the squadron was already equipped for sea; and, instead of repairing to the African frontiers to chastise the daring pirates, it is on its way to the Tuscan coast, where, if need be, it will land twenty thousand soldiers to liberate my relations and the young Count of Riverola. A pretext for making war upon the Italian States has been afforded by their recent conduct in sending auxiliaries to the succour of Rhodes; and of that excuse I shall not hesitate to avail myself to commence hostilities against the proud Florentines, should a secret and peaceful negotiation fail. But now that thou hast recapitulated to me, in minute detail, all those particulars which thou didst merely sketch forth at first, it seems to me fitting that I anchor the fleet at the mouth of the Arno, and that I send thee, Demetrius, as an Envoy in a public capacity, but in reality to stipulate privately for the release of those in whom I am interested.''

Thus terminated the conference between Ibrahim-Pacha and his Greek dependant,—a conference which had revealed manifold and astounding occurrences to the ears of the Lady Nisida of Riverola.

Astounding indeed!

Francisco in the hands of the formidable banditti— Flora in the prison of the Inquisition—and the Ottoman Grand Vizier bent upon effecting the marriage of those two—a marriage which Nisida abhorred,—these tidings were sufficient to arouse all the wondrous energies of that mind which was so prompt in combining intrigues and plots, so resolute in carrying them out, and so indomitable when it had formed a will of its own.

Ominous were the fires that flashed in her fine large dark eyes, and powerful were the workings of those emotions which caused her heaving bosom to swell as if about to burst the bodice which confined it,—when, retreating from the partition door between the two saloons, and resuming her seat at the cabin-windows to permit the evening breeze to fan her fevered cheek, Nisida thought within herself, " It was indeed time that I should quit that accursed island, and return to Italy !"

CHAPTER LXIII.

THE GRAND VIZIER AND THE SPY.—THE SLEEPER IN THE BOAT.

THE roseate streaks, which the departing glories of a Mediterranean sunset left lingering for a few minutes in the western horizon, were yielding to the deeper gloom of evening,—a few days after the scene related in the preceding chapter,—as Nisida rose from her seat at the open windows of her splendid saloon on board the Ottoman Admiral's ship, and began to lay aside her apparel, preparatory to retiring to rest.

She was already wearied of the monotonous life of shipboard; and the strange revelations which the discourse between Ibrahim-Pacha and Demetrius had developed to her ears, rendered her doubly anxious to set foot once more upon her native soil.

The Grand Vizier had paid his respects to her every day since she first embarked on board the Turkish ship; and they exchanged a few observations, rather of courtesy than of any deeper interest, by means of the tablets.

Ibrahim's manner towards her was respectful;—but when he imagined himself to be unperceived by her, his eyes were suddenly lighted up with the fires of ardent passion, and he devoured her with his burning glances. She failed not to notice the effect which her glorious beauty produced upon him; and she studiously avoided the imprudence of giving him the least encouragement; —not from any innate feeling of virtue,—but because she detested him as a man who was bent on accomplishing a marriage between her brother and Flora Francatelli. This hatred she, however, concealed beneath an appearance of modest reserve; and even the eagle-sighted Ibrahim perceived not that he was in any way displeasing to the lovely Nisida.

With the exception of the Grand Vizier, and the slaves who waited upon her, the lady saw no one on board ship; for she never quitted the magnificent saloon allotted to her, but passed her time chiefly in surveying the broad sea and the other vessels of the fleet from the windows, or in meditating upon the course which she should pursue on her arrival in Florence.

But let us return to the thread of our narrative.

The last tints of sunset were, we said, fading away, when the lady Nisida of Riverola commenced her preparations for retiring to rest. She closed the casement, satisfied herself that the partition door between the two saloons was well secured, and then threw herself upon the voluptuous couch spread in one of the smaller cabins opening from her own spacious and magnificent apartment.

She thought of Fernand—her handsome Fernand, whom she had abandoned on the Isle of Snakes; and profound sighs escaped her. Then she thought of Francisco; and the idea of serving that much-loved brother's interests afforded her a consolation for having thus quitted the clime where she had passed so many happy days with Wagner.

At length sleep fell upon her, and closed over the large, dark, brilliant eyes the white lids, beneath the transparent skin of which the blue veins were so delicately traced; and the long jetty lashes reposed on the cheeks which the heat of the atmosphere tinged with a rich carnation glow.

And when the moon arose that night, its silver rays streamed through the window set in the port-hole of that small side-cabin,—streamed upon the beauteous face of the sleeper !

But, hark !—there is the light, light sound of a footfall in the saloon from which that cabin opens !

The treacherous Ibrahim possesses *two* keys to the partition door ;—and, having successfully wrestled with his raging desires until this moment, he is at length no longer able to resist the temptation of invading the sanctity of Nisida's sleeping-place.

Already has he set his foot upon the very threshold of the little side-cabin, having traversed the spacious saloon,—when a hand is laid upon his shoulder, and a voice behind him says in a low tone, " Your Highness has forgotten the fate of the murdered Calanthe !"

Ibrahim started—shook the hand from off him—and exclaimed, " Dog of a negro ! what and who have made thee a spy upon my actions ?"

At the same instant that Ibrahim felt the hand on his shoulder, and heard the well-known voice uttering the dreadful warning in his ears, Nisida awoke. Her first impulse was to start up ; but checking herself with wondrous presence of mind, as the part of the deaf and dumb which she had imposed upon herself to play, flashed with lightning velocity across her brain,—comprehending too in an instant, that the Grand Vizier had violated her privacy, but that some unknown succour was at hand, as the rapid exchange of the words above recorded met her ears,—she remained perfectly motionless, as if still wrapped up in an undisturbed slumber.

The grand Vizier, and the individual whom he had in his rage addressed as a " dog of a negro," retreated into the saloon, Nisida holding her breath so as not to lose a word that might pass between them should their dialogue be resumed.

"Your Highness asks me what and who have made me a spy upon your actions," said the negro, in his low monotonous voice, and speaking with mingled firmness and respect. "Those questions are easily answered! The same authority which ordered me to wrest from thine arms, some months past, the lady who might be unfortunate enough to please your Highness's fancy, exercises an unceasing supervision over you, even in this ship, and in the middle of the mighty sea. To that authority all your deeds and acts are matters of indifference, save those which would render your Highness faithless to an adoring wife. Remember, my lord, the fate of Calanthe —the sister of your dependant Demetrius,—she who was torn from your arms, and whose beauteous form became food for the fishes of the Bosphorus."

"How knew you *who* she was?" demanded the Grand Vizier, in a low hoarse voice, the powers of his utterance having been temporarily suspended by the rage that filled his soul at finding his iniquitous design in respect to Nisida thus suddenly baffled by the chief of *the three black slaves*, whose attendance in this expedition had been forced upon him by the Sultan, at the instigation of the Sultana-Valida:—"how knew you *who* she was?" he again asked.

"Rather demand, my lord, what can escape the prying eyes of those by whom your Highness has been surrounded ever since the seals of office were in your grasp!" returned the slave, in a cool, imperturbable manner.

"But you would not betray *that secret* to Demetrius who is now devoted to me—who is necessary to me—and who would loathe me, were he to learn the dreadful fate of his sister!" said the Grand Vizier, with rapid and excited utterance.

"I have no eyes and ears, great Pacha," answered the negro, "save in respect to those matters which would render you faithless to the sister of the Sultan."

"Would to heaven that you had neither eyes nor ears at all—that you did not exist, indeed!" exclaimed Ibrahim, unable to repress his wrath: then, in a different and milder tone, he immediately added, "Slave, I can make thee free—I can give thee wealth—and thou mayest dwell in happy Italy, whither we are going, for the remainder of thy days. Reflect, consider! I love that deaf and dumb Christian woman, who sleepeth there—I already love her to distraction! Thwart me not, good slave—and thou mayest command my eternal gratitude."

"My lord, *two other slaves* overhear every word that now passes between us," responded the Ethiopian, his voice remaining calm and monotonous; "and even were we alone in all respects, I would not betray the trust reposed in me. But not on your Highness would the effects of your infidelity to the Princess Aischa fall. No, my lord, I have no authority to harm *you*. Had your Highness succeeded in your purpose ere now, the bowstring would have for ever stifled the breath in the body of that deaf and dumb Christian lady; and her corpse would have been thrown forth from these windows into the sea. Such are my instructions, my lord; and thus every object of your sated passion must become its victim also."

"Better—better were it," exclaimed Ibrahim, in a tone denoting the profoundest mental anguish, "to be the veriest mendicant who implores alms at the gate of the Mosque of Saint Sophia, than the Grand Vizier of the Ottoman Empire!"

With these words, he rushed into the adjoining saloon, the negro following and fastening the door behind him.

Nisida now began to breathe freely once more.

From what perils had she escaped! The violation of her couch by the unprincipled Ibrahim, would have been followed by her immediate assassination at the hands of the Ethiopian whom the Sultana-Mother had placed as a spy on the actions of her son-in-law. On the other hand, she felt rejoiced that the incident of this night had occurred; for it had been the means of revealing to her a secret of immense importance in connexion with the Grand Vizier. She remembered the terms of grief and affection in which Demetrius had spoken of the disappearance of Calanthe: and she had heard enough on that occasion to convince her that the Greek would become the implacable enemy of any man who had wronged that much-loved sister. How bitter, then, would be the hatred of Demetrius—how dreadful would be the vengeance which he must crave against him whose passions had led to the murder of Calanthe! Yes—Ibrahim, thy secret

was now in the possession of Nisida of Riverola,—in the possession of that woman of iron mind and potent energy, and whom thou fondly believest to be deaf and dumb!

Nisida slept no more that night, the occurrences of which furnished her with so much food for profound meditation; and with the earliest gleam of dawn that tinged the eastern heaven, she rose from her couch.

Entering the saloon, she opened the windows to admit the gentle breeze of morning; and ere she commenced her toilette, she lingered to gaze upon the stately ships that were ploughing the blue sea in the wake of the Admiral's vessel wherein she was.

Suddenly her eyes fell upon what appeared to be a black speck at a little distance;—but as this object was moving rapidly along on the surface of the Mediterranean, it soon approached sufficiently near to enable her to discern that it was a boat impelled by a single sail.

Urged by an undefinable and yet a strong sentiment of curiosity, Nisida remained at the saloon window, watching the progress of the little bark, which bounded over the waves with extraordinary speed, bending gracefully to the breeze that thus wafted it onward.

Nearer and nearer towards the vessel it came, though not pursuing exactly the same direction:—and in five minutes it passed within a few yards of the stern of the Kapitan-Pacha's ship.

But, oh! wondrous and unaccountable fact! There—stretched upon his back in that bounding boat, and evidently buried in a deep slumber,—with the rays of the rising sun gleaming upon his fine and now slightly flushed countenance,—lay he whose image was so indelibly impressed upon the heart of Nisida—her handsome and strangely-fated Fernand Wagner.

The moment the conviction that the sleeper was indeed he struck to the mind of Nisida, she would have called him by name—she would have endeavoured to awake him, if only to exchange a single word of fondness,—for her assumed dumbness was for the instant forgotten;—but she was rendered motionless and retained speechless —stupefied, paralyzed as it were—with mingled wonder and joy,—wonder that he should have found the means to escape from the island, and joy that she was thus permitted to behold him at least once again?

But the pleasure which this incident excited in her mind, was transitory indeed; for the boat swept by, as if urged on by a stronger impulse than the gentle breeze of the morning—and in another minute Nisida beheld it no more!

CHAPTER LXIV.

THE TALKATIVE BARBER.

THE sun was setting behind the western hills of Sicily, as Fernand Wagner entered the squalid suburb which at that period stretched from the town of Syracuse to the sea.

His step was elastic, and he held his head high;—for his heart was full of joyous and burning hope.

Hitherto the promises of the angel who had last appeared to him were completely fulfilled. The boat was wafted by a favouring breeze direct from the Island of Snakes to the shore of Sicily; and he had landed in the immediate vicinity of Syracuse—the town at which a farther revelation was to be made in respect to the breaking of the spell which had fixed upon him the frightful doom of a Wehr-Wolf!

But little suspected Fernand Wagner that, one morning while he slept, his boat had borne him through the proud fleet of the Ottomans :—little wist he that his beloved Nisida had caught sight of him as he was wafted rapidly past the stern of the Kapitan-Pacha's ship!

For on that occasion he had slept during many hours: and when he had awakened, not a bark nor a sail save his own was visible on the mighty expanse of water.

And now it was with elastic step and joyous heart that the hero of our tale entered the town of Syracuse. But suddenly he remembered the singular nature of the inquiry which he was there to make,—an inquiry concerning *a man whose years had numbered one hundred and sixty-two!*

"Nevertheless," thought Wagner, "that good angel, who gave me a sign whereby I should become convinced of the reality of her appearance, and whose promises have been all fulfilled up to this point, could not possibly mislead me. No: I will obey the command which I received—even though I should visit every human dwelling in the town of Syracuse! For heaven works out its wise purposes in wondrous manners; and it is not for me to shrink from yielding obedience to its orders, nor to pause to question their propriety. And, oh! if I can but shake off that demon-influence which weighs upon my soul,—if I can but escape from the shackles which still enchain me to a horrible doom,—how sincere will be my thanks to heaven—how unbounded my rejoicings!"

As Wagner had reached this point in his meditations, he stopped at the door of a barber's shop of mean appearance,—the pole, with the basin hanging to it, denoting that the occupant of the place combined, as was usual in those times, the functions of shaver and blood-letter or surgeon.

Having hastily surveyed the exterior of the shop, and fancying that it was precisely the one at which his inquiries should commence,—barbers in that age being as famous for their gossiping propensities as in this,—Fernand entered, and was immediately accosted by a short, sharp-visaged, dark-complexioned old man, who pointed to a seat, saying in a courteous, or rather obsequious tone, "What is your will, signor?"

Fernand desired the barber-surgeon to shave his superfluous beard and trim his hair; and while that individual was preparing his lather and sharpening his razor in the most approved style of the craft, Wagner asked, in a seemingly careless tone, "What news have you, good master, in Syracuse?"

"Naught of importance, signor," was the reply; "mere every-day matters. Syracuse is indeed wretchedly dull. There were only two murders and three attempts at assassination reported to the Lieutenant of Police this morning; and that is nothing for a town usually so active and bustling as ours. For my part, I don't know what has come over the people! I stepped as far as the dead-house just now to view the body of a young lady, unclaimed as yet, who had her head nearly severed from the trunk last night; and then I proceeded to the great square to see whether any executions are to take place to-morrow; but really there is nothing of any consequence to induce one to stir abroad in Syracuse, just at this moment."

"Murders and attempts at assassination are matters of very common occurrence amongst you, then?" said Wagner, inquiringly.

"We get a perfect surfeit of them, signor," returned the barber, now applying the soap to his customer's face. "They fail to create any sensation now, I can assure you. Besides, one gets tired of executions."

"Naturally enough," said Fernand. "But I have heard that there are some very extraordinary personages in Syracuse; indeed that there is one who has lived to a most remarkable age——"

"The oldest person I know of is the Abbot of St. Mary's," interrupted the barber: "and he——"

"And he——?" repeated Wagner, with feverish impatience.

"Is ninety-seven and three months, signor—a great age truly," responded the shaver-surgeon.

Fernand's hopes were immediately cooled down: but thinking that he ought to put his inquiry in a direct manner, he said, "Then it is not true that you have in Syracuse an individual who has reached the wondrous age of a century three-score and two?"

"Holy Virgin have mercy upon you, signor!" ejaculated the barber, "if you really put faith in the absurd stories that people tell about the Rosicrucians!"

"Ah! then the people of Syracuse do talk on such matters?" said Wagner, conceiving that he had obtained a clue to the aim and object of his inquiry.

"Have you never heard, signor, of the Order of the Rosy Cross?" demanded the barber, who was naturally of a garrulous disposition, and who now appeared to have entered on a favourite subject.

"I have heard, in my travels, vague mention made of such an Order," answered Fernand: "but I never experienced any curiosity to seek to learn more—and, indeed, I may say that I know nothing of the Rosicrucians save their mere name."

"Well, signor," continued the barber, "for common pastime-talk it is as good a subject as any other; but no one shall ever persuade me either that there really is such an Order as the Brothers of the Rosy Cross, or that it is possible for human beings to attain the powers attributed to that fraternity."

"You interest me much by your remarks, good leech," exclaimed Fernand: "I pray you to give me further explanation."

"With infinite pleasure, signor,—since you appear to desire it," returned the barber, still pursuing his tonsorial duties. "You must know that there are many wild legends and stories abroad concerning these invisible beings denominated Rosicrucians. But the one which gains most general credence is that the Brotherhood was founded by a certain Christianus Rosencrux, a German philosopher, who fancied that the arts and sciences might be developed in such a manner as to confer the greatest possible blessings on the human race."

"Then the aims of Rosencrux were entirely good and philanthropic?" said Wagner, interrogatively.

"As a matter of course, signor," replied the barber: "and therefore, if such a man ever did live, he must have been an insane visionary—for who would believe that knowledge could possibly make us richer, happier, or better? All the philosophy in the universe would never convert this shop into a palace."

"But you are wandering from your subject, my good friend," observed Fernand, in a tone of gentle remonstrance.

"I crave your pardon, signor. Let me see? Oh! I recollect—we were talking of Christianus Rosencrux. Well, signor—this fabled philosopher was a monk, and a very wise as well as a very good man. I am only telling you the most generally-received legend, mind—and would not have you think that I believe it myself. So this Rosencrux, finding that his cloistral existence was inconvenient for the prosecution of his studies, travelled into the East, and spent many years in acquiring the knowledge handed down to the wise men of those climes by the ancient Magi and Chaldeans. He visited Egypt and learnt many wonderful secrets by studying the hieroglyphics on the Egyptian pyramids. I forget how long he remained in the East; but it is said that he visited every place of interest in the Holy Land, and received heavenly inspirations on the spot where our Saviour was crucified. On his return to Europe, he saw full well that if he revealed all his knowledge at once, he would be put to death by the Inquisition as a wizard, and the world would lose the benefit of all the learning he had acquired. So says the legend; and it goes on to recite that Christianus Rosencrux then founded the Order of the Rosy Cross, which is nothing more or less than a brotherhood of wise men whom he initiated in all his secrets, with the intention that they should reveal from time to time small portions thereof, and thus give to the world by very slow degrees that immense amount of knowledge which, he supposed, would have stupefied and astounded everybody if made public suddenly and all at once."

"Strange—most strange," thought Wagner within himself, "that I should never have gleaned all these details before, eager as my inquiries and researches in the pursuit of knowledge have been! But heaven has willed everything for the best; and it is doubtless intended that my salvation shall proceed from the very quarter that was least known to me, and concerning which I have ever manifested the most contemptuous indifference, in the sphere of knowledge!"

"You appear to be much interested, signor," said the barber, "in this same tale of Christianus Rosencrux. But there is too much intelligence depicted on your countenance to allow me to suppose that you will place any reliance on the absurd story. How is it possible, signor, that an Order could have existed for so many years without any one member ever having betrayed the secrets which bind them all together? Moreover, their place of abode and study is totally unknown to the world; and if they inhabited the deepest cavern under the earth, accident must sooner or later have led to its discovery. Believe me, signor, 'tis naught save a ridiculous legend; and, though a poor ignorant man myself, I hope I have too much good sense and too much respect for my father confessor, to suppose for a minute that there is on earth any set of men more learned than the holy ministers of the Church."

"How long ago is Christianus Rosencrux reported to have lived?" demanded Wagner, suddenly interrupting the garrulous and narrow-minded Sicilian.

"There we are again?" he ejaculated. "The credulous declare that Rosencrux discovered in the East the means of prolonging existence, and though he was born as far back as the year 1359, he is still alive."

Had not the barber turned aside at that precise instant to fill an ewer and place a towel for his customer's use, he would have been surprised by the sudden start and the expression of ineffable joy which denoted Fernand's emotions, as by a rapid calculation mentally made, our hero perceived that if Rosencrux were born in 1359, and were alive at that moment—namely in 1521—*his age would be exactly one hundred and sixty-two!*

"It is Christian Rosencrux, then," he said to himself, "whom I have inquired for—whom I am to see—and who will dissolve the spell that has been placed upon me! But where shall I seek him?—whither can I go to find his secret abode?"

The duties of the barber were completed; and Wagner threw down a piece of gold, saying, "Keep that coin, friend; for your discourse has greatly interested me—and has indeed well deserved it."

The poor old man had never possessed in all his life so much money at one time; and so vast was his joy, that he could only mutter a few broken sentences to express his gratitude.

"I require not thanks, my good friend," said Wagner. "But, one word ere I depart. Knowest thou the spot which rumour indicates as the abode of that sect of whom we have been speaking?"

"Nay, excellent signor," replied the barber; "there your question masters me; for in this case rumour goes not to such a length as to afford hints for an investigation which would prove its utter fallacy. All that I have ever heard, signor, concerning the Rosicrucians, you have learnt from my lips; and I know no more."

Wagner, finding that further inquiry in the quarter was useless, took leave of the old man, and, traversing the suburb, entered the town of Syracuse.

CHAPTER LXV.

THE ROSICRUCIANS.

FERNAND was now at a loss how to act. He felt convinced that it was useless to institute any further inquiry relative to the whereabouts of the secret Order of the Rosy Cross: because, had popular rumour ever hinted at any clue in that respect, the garrulous and inquisitive barber would have been sure to hear of it.

He was not, however, disheartened. No; very far from that;—for he was confident that the same supernal power which had hitherto directed him, and which was rapidly clearing away all obstacles in his path towards perfect emancipation from the influence of the Evil One, would carry him on to a successful and triumphant issue.

Throwing himself, therefore, entirely on the wisdom and mercy of heaven, he roamed about the town of Syracuse, without any settled object in view, until he was much wearied and it was very late. He then entered a miserable hostel, or inn—the best, however, that he could discover; and there, having partaken of some refreshment, he retired to the chamber allotted to him.

Sleep soon visited his eyes: but he had not long enjoyed the sweets of slumber, when that balmy repose was interrupted either by a touch or sound, he knew not which.

Starting up in his couch, he perceived a tall figure, muffled in a huge dark mantle, and wearing a slouched broad-brimmed hat, standing by the side of the bed.

"Rise, Fernand Wagner," said a mild but masculine voice; "and follow me. He whom thou seekest hath sent me to lead me to him."

Wagner did not hesitate to obey this mandate, which, he felt certain, was connected with the important business that had borne him to Syracuse. His apparel was speedily assumed; and he said, "I am ready to follow thee, stranger, whoever thou art, and whithersoever thou mayst lead; for my faith is in heaven."

"Those who have faith, shall prosper," observed the stranger, in a solemn tone.

He then led the way noiselessly down the steep staircase of the inn, and issued forth by the front gate, closely followed by Wagner.

In deep silence did they proceed through the dark, narrow, and tortuous streets,—leaving at length the town behind them,—and then entering upon a barren and uneven waste.

By degrees an object, at first dimly seen in the distance and by the uncertain moonlight which was constantly struggling with the dark clouds of a somewhat tempestuous night assumed a more defined appearance,—until a mass of gigantic ruins at length stood out from the sombre obscurity. In a few moments the moon shone forth purely and brightly; and its beams falling on decayed buttresses, broken Gothic arches, deep entrance ways, remnants of pinnacles and spires, the rich sculptures of a mighty oriel, and the massive walls of ruined towers, gave a wildly romantic and yet not unpicturesque aspect to the remains of what was evidently once a vast monastic institution.

The muffled stranger led the way amongst the ruins, and at last stopped at a gate opening into a small square enclosure formed by strong iron railings, seven feet high and shaped at the points like javelins.

Passing through the gateway, the guide conducted Wagner into a cemetery, which was filled with the marble tombs of the mitred abbots who had once held sway over the monastery and the broad lands attached to it.

"You behold around you," said the muffled stranger, waving his arm towards the ruins, "all that remains of a sanctuary once the most celebrated in Sicily for the piety and wisdom of its inmates. But a horrible crime, —a murder perpetrated under circumstances unusually diabolical, the criminal being no less a person than the last Lord Abbot himself, and the victim a beauteous girl whom he had seduced,—rendered this institution accursed in the eyes of God and man. The monks abandoned it; and the waste over which you have passed, is the now unclaimed but once fertile estate belonging to the abbey. The superstition of the Sicilians has not failed to invent terrific tales in connection with these ruins; and the belief that each night at twelve o'clock the soul of the guilty abbot is driven by the scourge of demons through the scene alike of his episcopal power and his black turpitude, effectually prevents impertinent or inconvenient intrusion."

The observation, with which the muffled stranger concluded his brief narrative, convinced Wagner that it was amongst those ruins the brethren of the Rosy Cross had fixed their secret abode.

But he had no time for reflection;—inasmuch as his guide hurried him on amidst the tombs on which the light of the silver moon now streamed with a power and an effect that no dark cloud could for the time have impaired.

Stopping at the base of one of the most splendid monuments in that cemetery, the muffled stranger touched some secret spring, and a large marble block immediately opened like a door, the aperture revealing a narrow flight of stone steps.

Wagner was directed to descend first—a command which he obeyed without hesitation, his guide closing the marble entrance ere he followed.

For several minutes the two descended in total darkness.

At length, a faint glimmering light met Wagner's view;—and as he proceeded, it grew stronger and stronger—until it became of such dazzling brilliancy that his eyes ached with the supernal splendour.

That glorious lustre was diffused from a silver lamp hanging to the arched roof of a long passage or corridor of masonry, to which the stone steps led.

"Fernand Wagner," said the guide, in his mild and somewhat monotonous voice, "thou now beholdest the Eternal Lamp of the Rosicrucians. For a hundred and twenty years has that lamp burnt with as powerful a lustre as that which it now sheds forth; and never once —no, not once during that period, has it been replenished. No human hand has touched it since the day when it was first suspended there by the great founder of our sect."

All doubt was now dispelled from the mind of Wagner —if doubt he had even for a moment entertained since the muffled stranger had summoned him from the inn: he was indeed in the secret abode of the holy sect of the Rosy Cross—his guide, too, was a member of that brotherhood—and there, almost too dazzling to gaze upon, burnt the Eternal Lamp, which was the symbol of the knowledge cherished by the Order!

Wagner turned to gaze in wonder and admiration upon his guide; and beneath the broad brim of the slouched hat he beheld a countenance venerable with years—imposing with intelligence—and benevolent with every human charity.

"Wise and philanthropic Rosicrucian!" exclaimed Wagner; "I offer thee my deepest gratitude for having permitted my feet to enter this sanctuary. But how camest thou to learn that I sought admittance hither? and wherefore hast thou so far trusted me as to unveil to my eyes the mysteries of this place?"

"We are the servants of holy angels who reveal to us in visions the will of the Most High!" answered the Rosicrucian; "and they who commanded me to bring thee hither will induce thy heart to retain our secret inviolable."

"Not for worlds," cried Wagner, with an enthusiasm which denoted his sincerity, "would I betray ye!"

"'Tis well," said the Rosicrucian with philosophic calmness—as if he put more faith in the protecting influence of heaven than in the promises of man. "I shall not accompany thee farther. Follow that passage: at the extremity there are two corridors branching off in different directions; but thou wilt pursue the one leading to the right. Proceed fearlessly, and stop not until thou shalt stand in the presence of the great founder of our sect."

Fernand hastened to obey these directions; and having

long, and white as snow: a century and three score years had not dimmed the lustre of his eyes; and his form, though somewhat bent, was muscular and well-knit.

He was seated at a table covered with an infinite variety of scientific apparatus; and articles of the same nature were strewed upon the ground. To the roof hung an iron lamp, which indeed burnt faintly after the brilliant lustre of the eternal flame that Wagner had seen in the passage; but its flickering gleam shone lurid and ominous on a blood-red cross suspended to the wall.

Fernand drew near the table, and bowed reverentially

"A QUIET, DREAMY REPOSE INSENSIBLY STOLE OVER HIM." (See p. 110.)

threaded the two passages, he entered a large and rudely-hollowed cavern, where the feelings of mingled awe and suspense with which he had approached it, were immediately changed into deep veneration and wonder as he suddenly found himself in the presence of one who, by his appearance, he knew could be none other than Christianus Rosencrux!

Never had Fernand beheld a being of such venerable aspect; and, though old—evidently very old, as indeed Wagner knew him to be,—yet the founder of the celebrated Rosicrucians manifested every appearance of possessing a vigorous constitution, as he was assuredly endowed with a magnificent intellect. His beard was

to the Rosicrucian chief, who acknowledged his salutation with a benignant smile.

"Wagner," he said, in a firm but mild tone, "I have been forewarned of thy coming, and am prepared to receive thee. Thy constant and unvarying faith in heaven has opened to thee the gates of salvation, and it is mine to direct thee how to act, that the dreadful doom which thou hast drawn upon thyself may be annihilated soon and for ever."

The venerable man paused, and Fernand again bowed lowly with profound respect.

"So soon as the morning's sun shall have revisited this hemisphere," continued Rosencrux, "thou must depart for Italy. Start not, Fernand—but prepare to obey that power which will sustain thee. On arriving in Italy, proceed direct to Florence; and fear not to enter that city even in the broad daylight. Thou wilt not be harmed! There await the current of those circumstances that must lead to the one grand event which is ordained to break the spell that has cast upon thee the doom of a Wehr-Wolf. For as thou didst voluntarily unite thyself in the face of heaven with Donna Nisida of Riverola, so it is decreed, for the wisest purposes, that a circumstance intimately connected with *her* destiny must become a charm and talisman to change *thine own*. On thine arrival in Florence, therefore, seek not to avoid the Lady Nisida;—but rather hasten at once to her presence—and, again I say, a supernal power will protect thee from any baneful influence which she might still exercise over thee! *For the spell that the Evil One hath cast upon thee, Fernand Wagner, shall be broken only on that day and in that hour when thine eyes shall behold the bleached skeletons of two innocent victims suspended to the same beam!*"

Having uttered these words in a louder and more hurried, but not the less impressive tone, than he had at first used, Christianus Rosencrux motioned impatiently for Wagner to depart.

And Fernand, amazed and horrified at the dreadful words which had met his ears, retreated from the cavern, and sped rapidly back to the spot where he had quitted his guide, whom he found waiting his return beneath the nudying lamp.

The Rosicrucian conducted Wagner in silence from that deep and mysterious subterranean beneath the tomb: thence through the cemetery—amidst the ruins of the monastery—and across the wild waste, back to Syracuse;—nor did the muffled brother of the Rosy Cross take leave of Fernand until they reached the door of the hostel.

There they parted—the Rosicrucian invoking a blessing upon the head of Wagner, who regained his chamber without disturbing the other inmates of the house,—but with the conflicting emotions of ardent hopes and appalling fears, vague doubts, and holy aspirations filling his breast.

By degrees, however—as he was enabled to reason to himself with increasing calmness—the fears and the doubts became fainter and fainter, while the hopes and the aspirations grew stronger and stronger: and at length, throwing himself upon his knees, he exclaimed fervently, "O Lord, deal with me as thou wilt: thy will be done!"

CHAPTER LXVI.

NISIDA AT HOME AGAIN.

It was late in the afternoon of a sultry day, towards the close of September,—or, to be more particular, on the 25th of this month,—that a numerous and brilliant cavalcade, on emerging from a grove which bounded one of the sinuosities of the Arno, came within sight of the towers and pinnacles of Florence.

On the white felt turbans of a hundred and fifty Ottoman soldiers glistened the crescent—the symbol of Islamism; and their steel-sheathed scimitars and the trappings of their horses sent forth a martial din as they were agitated by the rapidity of the march.

Forty-eight slaves, also mounted on steeds procured at Leghorn, followed the soldiers with a short interval between the two corps; and in the space thus left, rode the Greek Demetrius and the Lady Nisida of Riverola.

The latter wore the garb of her sex, and sat upon her horse with the grace and dignity of an Amazonian Queen.

The moment the cavalcade came in sight of the fair City of Flowers, a flush of joy and triumph suddenly diffused itself over Nisida's countenance; and her lips were simultaneously compressed to prevent the utterance of that exclamation of gladness which her heart sent up to her tongue.

Demetrius now commanded a temporary halt: and, addressing himself to a Turkish youth who had been attached to his person in the capacity of secretary, he said, "Yakoub, hie thou in advance, with an escort of two soldiers and two slaves, and push on to Florence, there seek an immediate interview with the President of the Council of State, and acquaint that high functionary with the tidings of my approach. Thou wilt inform him that I am about to enter Florence in the peaceful capacity of Envoy from the puissant and most glorious

Ibrahim-Pacha, the Vizier of the Sultan, to treat on divers matters interesting to the honour of the Ottoman Porte and the welfare of all Italy. In the meantime, I shall so check our speed that we may not reach the city until after sunset, which arrangement will afford you two full hours to accomplish the mission which I now entrust to thee."

Yakoub bowed, and hastened to obey the commands which he had received,—speeding towards Florence, attended by two soldiers and two slaves.

Demetrius then ordered his party to dismount and rest for a short space upon the banks of the Arno. Some of his slaves immediately pitched a tent, into which he conducted Nisida; and refreshments were served to them.

When the repast was concluded, and they were left alone together for a few minutes, Nisida's manner suddenly changed from calm patrician reserve to a strange agitation,—her lips quivered—her eyes flashed fire;—and then, as if desperately resolved to put into execution the idea which she had formed, she seized Demetrius by the hand, bent her head towards him, and murmured in the faintest whisper possible, "Start not to hear the sound of my voice! I am neither deaf nor dumb. But this is not the place for explanations. I have much to tell you —much to hear—for I can speak to thee of Calanthe, and prove that he whom thou servest so zealously is a wretch meriting only thy vengeance."

"My God! my God!—what marvels are now taking place!" murmured the Greek, surveying Nisida in astonishment and alarm.

"Silence—silence, I implore you!" continued she, in the same rapid, low, and yet distinctly audible whisper: "for *your* sake—for *mine*, betray me not! Deaf and dumb must I appear—deaf and dumb must I yet be deemed for a short space. But to-night—at twelve o'clock—you will meet me, Demetrius, in the garden of the Riverola mansion; and then I will conduct you to an apartment where we may confer without fear of being overheard—without danger of interruption."

"I will not fail thee, lady," said the Greek, scarcely able to recover from the amazement into which Nisida's sudden revelation of her power of speech and hearing had thrown him: then, as an oppressive feeling seized upon his soul, he demanded, "But Calanthe, lady—in the name of heaven! one word more—and let that word give me hope that I may see my sister again!"

"Demetrius," answered Nisida, her countenance becoming ominous and sombre, "you will never behold her more. The lust of Ibrahim-Pacha—nay, start not violently — brought destruction and death upon Calanthe?"

The features of the young Greek were at first distorted with anguish, and tears started from his eyes: but, in the next moment, their expression changed to one denoting fierce rage and a determination to be avenged.

Nisida understood all that was passing in his soul; and she bent upon him a significant glance, which said more eloquently than language could have done—"Yes; vengeance thou shalt have!"

She then rose from the velvet cushions which had been spread upon the ground within the tent, and waving her hand in token of temporary farewell to Demetrius, hastened forth—mounted her horse—and departed, alone and unattended, towards Florence.

Great was the surprise that evening of the numerous servants and dependants at the Riverola mansion, when Donna Nisida suddenly reappeared, after an absence of nearly seven months—and that absence so unaccountable to them! Although her haughty and imperious manner had never been particularly calculated to render her beloved by the menials of the household,—yet her supposed affliction of deafness and dumbness had naturally made her an object of interest; and, moreover, as close upon three months had elapsed since Count Francisco himself had disappeared in a strange and alarming way, two days only after his return from the wars, the domestics were pleased to behold at least one member of the lost family come back amongst them.

Thus it was with sincere demonstrations of delight that the dependants and menials welcomed Donna Nisida of Riverola; and she was not ungracious enough to receive their civilities with coldness!

But she speedily escaped from the ceremonies of this reception; and, intimating by signs to the female minions who were about to escort her to her own apartments, that she was anxious to be alone, she hurried thither, her heart leaping with joy at the thought of being once more beneath the roof of the palace of her forefathers.

And, Fernand—wast thou forgotten? Oh! no—no: in spite of all her revived schemings and new plots, Nisida —thy well-beloved Nisida—had room in her heart for thine image!

On reaching her own suite of apartments, the key of which had been handed to her by one of the female dependants, Nisida found everything in the same state as when she was last there; and it appeared to her a dream—yes, a very wondrous dream—that she had been absent for nearly seven months, and during that period had seen and experienced such strange vicissitudes.

The reader need scarcely be informed that Nisida's first impulse, on entering her own suite of apartments in the Riverola mansion, was to hasten and gaze once more upon the portrait of her mother:—and intent—earnest—enthusiastic was the upraised look now fixed on that portrait,—even as when we first saw Nisida contemplating the sweet and benignant countenance, in the second chapter of our narrative!

Yes:—and again was her gaze indicative of a devotion—an adoration—a worship!

"Oh! my sainted mother," thought Nisida within her breast, "I have not proved ultimately faithless to the solemn vows I pledged to thee upon thy death-bed! No: if for a time I yielded to the voluptuous idlesse of love and passion in that now far-off Mediterranean isle,—yet at last did I arouse myself to energy for young Francisco's sake—and I came back so soon as heaven sent me the means of return to the place where my presence may best serve his interests and carry out thy wishes! For, oh! when thou wast alive, my worshipped, my adored mother, how good—how kind—how affectionate wast thou towards me! And that tenderness of a mother for her offspring—ah! how well can I comprehend it now! —for I also shall soon become a mother! Yes—Fernand, within the last week I have received the conviction that a being bearing thine image will see the light in due time;—and the honour of the proud name of Riverola requires that our child must not be born of an unwedded mother! But wilt thou seek *me* out, Fernand?—Oh! where art thou now?—whither was the bark, in which I beheld thee last, wafting thee away?"

And, all the while that these thoughts were agitating within her mind, Donna Nisida kept her eyes intently fixed on her mother's portrait;—but, on reflecting a second time that should she fail to meet with Wagner soon again, or should he prove faithless to her,—or if, indeed, he should nurse resentment and loathing for her on account of her unworthy conduct towards him on the island,—and that her child should be born of an unwedded mother,—when, we say, she thought of this dread probability a second time, she burst into tears, and turned away from the contemplation of her mother's countenance.

And Nisida so seldom wept, that when tears did escape the usually sealed up springs of her emotions, they came in torrents, and were most bitter and painful to shed.

But she at length triumphed over her feelings—or rather, their outpouring relieved her; and now the remembrance of another duty which she had resolved upon performing the moment she should reach home again, was uppermost in her mind.

She contemplated a visit to the mysterious closet—the dark cabinet of horrible secrets,—in order to ascertain whether curiosity had triumphed over Francisco's prudence, or if any one indeed had violated the loneliness of that chamber in which the late Count of Riverola had breathed his last.

She accordingly took a lamp in her hand,—for it was now far advanced in the evening,—and proceeded to the apartment where a father's dying injunctions had been given to her brother, and which that father and that brother had so little suspected to have been heard and and greedily drunk in by her ears.

The door of the room was locked; Nisida accordingly proceeded forthwith to her brother's chamber: and there, in a secret place where she knew he had been accustomed to keep papers or valuables, she found the key of the chamber containing the mysterious closet—but not the key of that closet itself.

Of this latter circumstance she was glad; inasmuch as she conceived that he had adopted her counsel to carry it invariably secured about his person, so that no prying domestic might use it in his absence. Returning, therefore, with the one key which she had found, she entered the apartment where her father had breathed his last.

Unchanged was its appearance,—in mournfulness and gloom unchanged,—in arrangements and features precisely the same as when she last was there, on the night when she intercepted the banditti in their predatory visit. She drew aside the hangings of the bed,—a cloud of dust flew out;—and for a few moments she stood gazing on the couch where the dark spirit of her sire had fled its mortal tenement for ever!

And as she still lingered near that bed, the remembrance of the death-scene came so vividly back to her mind, that for an instant she fancied she beheld the cold, stern, relentless countenance of the late Count of Riverola upon the pillow,—and she turned away more in loathing and abhorrence than in alarm—for though her brain flashed, in dread association with his memory, the awful words—"*And as the merciless scalpel hacked and hewed away at the still almost palpitating flesh of the murdered man, in whose breast the dagger remained deeply buried,—a ferocious joy—a savage hyena-like triumph filled my soul; and I experienced no remorse for the deed I had done!*"

Yes:—she turned aside—and was advancing rapidly towards the mysterious closet, when—holy God! was it reality, or imagination?—was it a human being or a spectre from another world?

For a tall dark form—muffled apparently in a long cowl,—or it might have been a cloak, but Nisida was too bewildered to discriminate aright,—glided from the middle of the room where her eyes first beheld it—and was lost to her view almost as soon as seen.

Strong-minded as Nisida was—indomitable as was her courage—and far away as she was from being superstitious,—yet now she staggered—reeled—and would have fallen, had she not come in contact with the mysterious closet, against which she leaned for support. She gasped for breath—and her eyes were fixed wildly upon the door by which the figure had disappeared. Nevertheless she had so far retained her presence of mind as to grasp the lamp firmly in her hand: for, at that moment—after such a fright—in the room where her father had died—and in the close vicinity of the fearful cabinet—even Nisida would have fainted with terror to be left in darkness.

"'Twas imagination—naught but imagination!" she thought within herself as she exerted all her power to surmount the alarms that had seized upon her. "But—no! I remember to have closed the door carefully behind me—and now it is open!"

As that reminiscence and conviction flashed to her mind, she nerved herself so as to advance into the passage: but all was silent, and not a soul was there save herself.

Scarcely knowing what to think—yet ashamed to give way to superstitious fears—Nisida retraced her steps into the apartment, and proceeded to examine the door of the closet. She was satisfied that it had never been opened since she herself had visited it on the night of her father's death: for the seals which she had induced Francisco to place upon the lock next day were still there, and those seals she knew at once, without any unusual effort of the memory, to be the same which had been so affixed in her presence.

But all the while she was thus scrutinizing the door, the lock, and the seals, she could not help occasionally casting a furtive glance around, to convince herself that the tall, dark, muffled form was not standing behind her: and, as she retraced her way to her own suite of apartments, she stopped now and then through dread that *other* footsteps besides her own echoed in the long and lonely corridors of the old mansion.

She however regained her chamber in safety, and fell into a deep reverie respecting the tall figure she had seen.

Were it not for the fact—of which she was confident—relative to having closed the door, on entering the room where her father had died, she would have speedily come to the conclusion that her imagination had deluded her: but that fact was positive—and she now feared lest she might be watched by spies for some unknown and hostile purpose. It was perplexing, to say the least of it;—and Nisida determined to adopt all possible precautions against her secret enemies, whoever they might be.

She accordingly rose from her seat—put off her upper garment—donned her thin but strong corslet—and then assumed the black velvet robe which reached up to her throat, concealing the armour beneath. Her flexible dagger—that fatal weapon which had dealt death to the unfortunate Agnes—was next thrust into the sheath formed by the wide border of her stomacher;—and Nisida smiled with haughty triumph, as if in defiance to her foes.

She then repaired to one of the splendid saloons of the mansions; and ere she sat down to the repast that was served up, she despatched a note acquainting Dr. Duras with her return, and requesting his immediate presence.

In about half an hour the physician arrived; and his joy at beholding Nisida again was only equalled by his impatience to learn the cause of her long absence, and all that had befallen her during the interval.

She made a sign for the old man to follow her to the retirement of her own apartments; and then, having carefully closed the doors, she said to him in a low tone, "Doctor, we will converse by means of signs no more; for, though still forced to simulate the Deaf and Dumb in the presence of the world, yet *now*—with you, who have all along known my terrible secret—our discourse must be too important to be carried on by mere signs."

"Nisida," returned Duras, also in a low and cautious tone, "thou knowest that I love thee as if thou wast my own daughter; and thy voice sounds like music upon my ears. But when will the dreadful necessity which renders thee dumb before the world—when will it cease, Nisida?"

"Soon—soon, doctor—if thou wilt aid me," answered the lady.

A long and earnest conversation then ensued:—it is not necessary to give the details to the reader, inasmuch as their nature will soon transpire. Suffice it to say that Nisida urged a particular request, which she backed by such explanations, and we must also say *misrepresentations*, as she thought suitable to her purpose; and that Dr. Duras eventually, though not without much compunction and hesitation, at length acceded to her prayer.

She then gave him a brief account of her abduction from Florence by the villain Stephano—her long residence on the Island of Snakes—and her deliverance from thence by the Ottoman fleet, which was now moored off the coast of Leghorn. But she said nothing of Fernand Wagner; nor did she inform the physician that she was acquainted with the cause of Francisco's disappearance and the place where he was detained.

At length Dr. Duras took his leave; but ere he left the room, Nisida caught him by the hand, saying in a low yet impressive tone, "Remember your solemn promise, my dear friend, and induce my brother to leave Flora Francatelli to her fate."

"I will—I will," answered the physician. "And, after all you have told me, and if she be really the bad, profligate, and evil-disposed girl you represent her, it will be well that the Inquisition should hold her tight in its grasp."

With these words Dr. Duras departed, leaving Nisida to gloat over the success which her plans had thus far experienced.

CHAPTER LXVII.
NISIDA AND DEMETRIUS.

IT was verging towards midnight, and the moon was concealed behind dark clouds, when a tall figure, muffled in a cloak, climbed over the iron railings which enclosed one portion of the spacious gardens attached to the Riverola palace.

This person was Fernand Wagner.

He had arrived in Florence two days before that on which Nisida returned once more to the ancestral dwelling:—he had entered the city boldly and openly by the joyous sunlight—and yet no one molested him. He even encountered some of the very sbirri who had arrested him in the preceding month of February: they saluted him respectfully, thus showing that they recognised him —but offered not to harm him. His trial, his condemnation, and his escape appeared all to have been forgotten. He repaired to his own mansion: his servants, who had remained in possession of the dwelling, received him with demonstrations of joy and welcome, as if he had just returned, under ordinary circumstances, from a long journey. Truly, then, he was blessed by the protection of heaven! And—more wondrous still—on entering his favourite room, he beheld all his pictures in their proper places, as if none of them had ever been removed—as if the confiscation of several by the criminal tribunal had never taken place. Over the *one* which had proclaimed the secret of his doom to the Judges and the audience on the occasion of his trial, still hung the black cloth; and an indefinable curiosity—no, not a sentiment of curiosity, but one of hope—impelled him to remove the covering. And how exquisite was his joy—how great his amaze-

ment—how sincere his thanksgivings, when he beheld but a blank piece of canvas! The horrible picture of the Wehr-Wolf—a picture which he had painted when in a strangely morbid state of mind—had disappeared! Here was another sign of heaven's goodness—a farther proof of celestial mercy!

On instituting inquiries, Fernand had learnt that Donna Nisida had not yet come back to Florence; but he employed trusty persons to watch and give him notice of her arrival, the instant it should occur. Thus Nisida had not been half an hour at the Riverola mansion when Fernand was made acquainted with her return.

From the conversation which had taken place between them at various times on the island, and as the reader is well aware, Wagner felt convinced that Nisida would again simulate deafness and dumbness; and was therefore desirous to avoid giving her any surprise, by appearing abruptly before her—a proceeding which might evoke a sudden ejaculation, and thus betray her secret. Moreover, he knew not whether circumstances would render his visits, made in a public manner, agreeable to her;— and perhaps—pardon him, gentle reader!—perhaps he was also curious to learn whether she still thought of him, or whether the excitement of her return had absorbed all tender feelings of that nature.

Influenced by these various motives, Wagner muffled himself in a long Tuscan cloak, and repaired to the vicinity of the Riverola mansion. He passed through the gardens without encountering any one; and, perceiving a side door open, he entered the building. Ascending the stairs, he thought that he should be acting in accordance with the advice given him by Rosencrux and also consistently with prudence, were he at once to seek an interview with Nisida privately. He therefore repaired in the direction of the principal saloons of the palace; but, losing his way amidst the maze of corridors, he was about to retire, when he beheld the object of his search—the beautiful Nisida—enter a room with a lamp in her hand. He now felt convinced that he should meet her alone; and he hurried after her. In pursuance of his cautious plan, he opened the door gently, and was already in the middle of the apartment, when he perceived Nisida standing by the side of a bed and with her head fixed in that immovable manner which indicates intent gazing upon some object. Instantly supposing that some invalid reposed in that couch, and now seized with a dreadful alarm lest Nisida, on beholding him, should utter a sudden ejaculation which would betray the secret of her feigned dumbness, Fernand considerately retreated with all possible speed; nor was he aware that Nisida had observed him—much less that his appearance there had excited such fears in her breast, those fears being greatly enhanced by his negligence in leaving the door open behind him.

Oh! had Nisida known it was thou, Fernand Wagner— how joyous—how happy she would have been ;—for the conviction that she bore within her bosom the pledge of your mutual loves, had made her heart yearn that eve to meet with thee again.

And was it a like attraction on thy part—or the mysterious influence that now guided all thy movements, which induced thee, at midnight, to enter the Riverola gardens again, that thou mightest be as it were upon the same spot where she dwelt, and scent the fragrance of the same flowers that perfumed the atmosphere which she breathed? Oh! doubtless it was that mysterious influence;—thou hadst now that power within thee which made thee strong to resist all the blandishments of the syren, and to prefer the welfare of thine own soul to aught in this world beside!

We said, then—at the commencement of this chapter— that Fernand entered the Riverola gardens shortly before midnight.

But scarcely had he crossed the iron railings and turned into the nearest path formed by shrubs and evergreens, when he was startled by hearing *another* person enter the grounds in the same unceremonious manner. Fernand accordingly stood aside, in the deep shade of the trees; and in a few moments a figure, muffled like himself in a cloak, passed rapidly by.

Wagner was debating within himself what course he should pursue—for he feared that some treachery was intended towards Nisida—when, to his boundless surprise, he heard the mysterious visitant say in a low tone, "Is it you, lady?—to which query the unmistakable and never-to-be-forgotten voice of his Nisida answered, "'Tis I, Demetrius. Follow me noiselessly—and breathe not another word for the present!"

Fernand was shocked and grieved at what he had just heard, and which savoured so strongly of an intrigue. Had not his ears deceived him? was this the Nisida from whom he had parted but little more than three weeks back, and who had left him that tender note which he had found in the hut on the island?

But he had no time for reflection!—the pair were moving rapidly towards the mansion—and Wagner unhesitatingly followed, his footsteps being soundless on the damp soil of the borders of flowers, and his form being concealed by the shade of the tall evergreens which he skirted.

He watched Nisida and her companion until they disappeared by a small private door at the back of the mansion; and this door was by them incautiously left unlocked, though shut close. It opened readily to Wagner's hand, and he found himself at the foot of a dark staircase, the sound of ascending steps on which met his ears. Up that narrow flight he sped, noiselessly but hastily; and in a few moments he was stopped by another door which had just closed behind those whom he was following.

Here he was compelled to pause, in the hope that the partition might not be so thick as completely to intercept the sound of their voices in the chamber: but, after listening with breathless attention for a few minutes, he could not catch even the murmuring of a whisper. It now struck him that Nisida and her companion might have passed on into a room more remote than the one to which that door had admitted them; and he resolved to follow on. Accordingly, he opened the door with such successful precaution that not a sound—not even a creaking of the hinge, was the result: and he immediately perceived that there was a thick curtain within; for it will be recollected that this door was behind the drapery of Nisida's bed. At the same time a light, somewhat subdued by the thick curtain, appeared; and the sounds of voices met Fernand's ears.

"Signor," said the melodious voice of Nisida, in its sweetest, softest tones, "it is due to myself to tender fitting excuse for introducing you thus into my private chamber; but the necessity of discoursing together without fear of interruption and in some place that is secure from the impertinence of eaves-droppers, must serve as an apology."

"Lady," replied Demetrius, "it needed no explanation of your motive in bringing me hither to command on my part that respect which is due to you."

A weight was removed from Wagner's mind:—it was assuredly no tender sentiment that had brought Nisida and the Greek together this night; and the curiosity of Fernand was therefore excited all the more strongly.

"We will not waste time in unnecessary parlance," resumed Nisida, after a short pause; "nor must you seek to learn the causes—the powerful causes, which have urged me to impose upon myself the awful sacrifice involved in the simulation of loss of speech and hearing. Suffice it for you to know that, when on board the Kapitan-Pasha's ship, I overheard every syllable of the conversation which one day took place between the apostate Ibrahim and yourself,—a conversation wherein you gave a detailed account of all your proceedings at Florence, and in the course of which you spoke feelingly of your sister Calanthe."

"Alas! poor Calanthe!" exclaimed Demetrius, in a mournful tone: "and is she really no more?"

"Listen to me while I relate the manner in which I became aware of her fate," said Nisida.

She then explained the treacherous visit of the Grand Vizier to the cabin wherein she had slept on board the Ottoman Admiral's ship—the way in which the Ethiopian slave had interfered to save her—and the conversation that had taken place between Ibrahim and the negro, revealing the dread fate of Calanthe.

"Is it possible that I have served so faithfully a man possessed of such a demon-heart!" cried Demetrius. "But I will have vengeance, lady—I will have vengeance: —yes—the murdered Calanthe shall be avenged!"

"And I too must have vengeance upon the proud and insolent Vizier who sought to violate all the laws of hospitality in respect to me," observed Nisida, "and who seeks to marry his sister, the low-born Flora—the sister of the base renegade—to the illustrious scion of the noble house of Riverola! Vengeance, too, must I have upon the wretch Antonio—the base pander to my father's illicit and degrading amours—the miscreant who sought to plunder this mansion, and who even dared to utter threats against me in that conversation with his accomplice Venturo, which you, signor, overheard in the

streets of Florence. This same wretch it is, too, who consigned my brother to the custody of banditti;—and though, for certain reasons, I deplore not that captivity which Francisco has endured, inasmuch as it has effectually prevented him from interesting himself on behalf of Flora Francatelli,—yet as Antonio was animated by vengeance only in so using my brother, he shall pay the penalty due on account of all his crimes."

"And in the task of punishing Antonio, lady," said Demetrius, "shall I be right glad to aid—for did not the villain deceive me infamously in respect to the despatches which I sought to forward to Constantinople when last I was at Florence? and, not contented with that vile treachery, he even plotted with his accomplice Venturo against my life."

"Vengeance, then, upon our enemies, Demetrius!" exclaimed Nisida. "And this is how our aims shall be accomplished," she continued, in a lower and less excited tone:—"The ambitious views of Ibrahim-Pacha must experience a signal defeat; and, as he is too powerful to be personally injured by us, we must torture his soul by crushing his relations—we must punish him through the medium of his sister and his aunt. This evening I had a long discourse with Dr. Duras, who is devoted to my interests, and over whom I wield a wondrous power of persuasion. He has undertaken to induce his brother, Angelo Duras, to abandon the cause of the Francatellis; and the Inquisition will therefore deal with them as it lists. Father Marco I can also manage as I will: he understands the language in which the deaf and dumb converse, for he has so long been confessor to our family. To-morrow I will undertake to send him to Rome on some charitable mission connected with the Church. Thus the only persons whom you secured, when last you were in Florence, in the interests of the Francatellis, will cease to watch over them; and as they are accused of being accomplices in the sacrilege perpetrated in the Carmelite Convent, naught will save them from the flames of the auto-da-fé."

"Oh! spirit of the murdered Calanthe," exclaimed Demetrius, with savage joy, "thou wilt be avenged yet! And thou, false Vizier, shalt writhe in the anguish of bitter feelings while thy relatives writhe in the flames at the stake!"

"Now, as for Antonio, and the rest of the banditti who stormed the convent and gave freedom to the hated Flora—who have likewise captured my brother—and who have so long been a terror to Florence," continued Nisida, "we must annihilate them all at a blow: not a soul of the gang must be spared!"

Nisida knew full well that at least some of the banditti were acquainted with the fact that she was the murderess of Agnes, and that they could also tell an awkward tale of how she sought to bribe them to rescue Fernand Wagner in case of an adverse judgment on the part of the criminal tribunal. The total annihilation of the horde was consequently the large aim at which she aspired; and her energetic mind shrank not from any difficulties that might appear in the way towards the execution of that object.

"The design is grand, but not without its obstacles," observed Demetrius. "Your ladyship will moreover adopt measures to rescue the Lord Count of Riverola first."

"By means of gold everything can be accomplished amongst villains," returned Nisida; "and the necessary preliminaries to the carrying out of our project lie with you, signor. To-morrow morning must you seek Antonio. He knows not that you suspect his villany; and, as you will say nothing relative to the failure in the arrival of your despatches at Constantinople, he will rest secure in the belief that you have not yet discovered that deed of treachery. You must represent yourself as the mortal enemy of the Count of Riverola, and so speak as to lead Antonio to confess to you where he is, and offer to become the instrument of your vengeance. Then bribe Antonio heavily to deliver up Francisco into your power to-morrow night at a particular hour, and at a place not far from the spot where you know the secret entrance of the banditti's stronghold to be."

"All this, lady," said Demetrius, "can be easily arranged. Antonio would barter his soul for gold;— much more readily, then, will he sell the Count of Riverola to one who bids high for the possession of the noble prisoner."

"But this is not all," resumed Nisida: "'tis merely the preface to my plan. So soon as the shades of to-morrow's evening shall have involved the earth in obscurity, a strong party of your soldiers, properly disguised, but well armed, must repair, in small sections, or even singly, to that grove where you have already obtained a clue to the entrance of the robbers' strong-hold. Let them conceal themselves amidst the trees in the immediate vicinity of the enormous chestnut that overhangs the precipice. When the robbers emerge from their lurking-place with Francisco, your soldiers will immediately seize upon them. Should you then discover the secret of the entrance to the stronghold, the object will be gained,—your men will penetrate into the sub-terranean den,—and the massacre of the horde will prove an easy matter. But should it occur that those banditti who may be employed in leading forth my brother do shut up the entrance of their den so speedily that your dependants discover not its secret, then must we trust to bribery or threats to wrest that secret from the mis-creants. At all events Antonio will be present to accompany Francisco to the place which you will appoint to meet them; and as the villain will fall into your power, it will perhaps prove less difficult to induce him to betray his comrades, than it might be to persuade any of the banditti themselves."

"Lady, your plan has every element of success," ob-served Demetrius; "and all shall be done as you suggest. Indeed, I will myself conduct the expedition. But should you thus at once effect the release of Don Francisco, will he not oppose your designs relative to the condemnation of Flora Francatelli by the Inquisition?"

"Dr. Duras is well acquainted with the precise position of that process," answered Nisida; "and from him I learnt that the third examination of the prisoners will take place to-morrow, when judgment will be pronounced should no advocate appear to urge a feasible cause of delay."

"The arrests took place on the 3rd of July," said Demetrius; "and Angelo Duras undertook to obtain the postponement of the final hearing for three months. To-morrow, lady, is but the 26th of September."

"True," responded Nisida; "but were a delay granted, it would be for eight days,—and thus you perceive how nicely Angelo Duras had weighed all the intricacies of the case, and how accurately he had calculated the length of the term to be gained by the exercise of all the subtleties of the Inquisitorial law. Therefore, as no advocate will appear to demand the delay, Flora is certain to be condemned to-morrow night, and the release of Francisco may take place simultaneously;—for when once the Grand Inquisidor shall have pronounced the extreme sentence, no human power can reverse it. And now," added Nisida, "but one word more. The Grand Vizier commanded you to despatch a courier daily to Leghorn with full particulars of all your pro-ceedings: see that those accounts be of a nature to lull the treacherous Ibrahim into security; for, were he to learn that his aunt and sister are in dread peril, he would be capable of marching at the head of all his troops to sack the city of Florence."

"Fear not on that subject, lady," answered Demetrius. "I will so amuse the demon-hearted Grand Vizier by my despatches, that he shall become excited with joyous hopes,—so that the blow,—the dread blow which we are preparing for him—may be the more terribly severe!"

The Greek then rose to take his leave of Donna Nisida: and Wagner, having closed the secret door as noiselessly as he had opened it, hurried away from the Riverola mansion, bewildered and grieved at all he had heard—for he could now no longer conceal from himself that a very fiend was incarnate in the shape of her whom he had loved so madly!

*   *   *   *   *
*   *   *   *   *

Having tossed on a feverish couch for upwards of an hour,—unable to banish from his mind the cold-blooded plot which Nisida and Demetrius had resolved upon in order to consign Flora Francatelli and her equally innocent aunt to the stake,—Wagner at last slept through sheer exhaustion.

Then Christian Rosencrux appeared to him in a dream, and addressed him in the following manner:—"Heaven hath chosen thee as the instrument to defeat the iniquitous purposes of Nisida of Riverola in respect of two guiltless and deserving women. Angelo Duras is an upright man; but he is deluded and misled by the representations made to him by Nisida, through his brother the physician, relative to the true character of Flora. In the evening, at nine o'clock, hie thou to Angelo Duras—command him, in the name of justice and humanity, to do his duty towards his clients—and he will obey thee. Then, having performed this much,

speed thou without delay to Leghorn, and seek the Grand Vizier, Ibrahim-Pacha. To him shalt thou merely state that Demetrius is a traitor, and that tremendous perils hang over the heads of the Vizier's much-loved relatives. Manifest no hatred to the Vizier on account of his late treacherous intention with regard to the honour of Nisida: for vengeance belongeth not to mortals. And in these measures only, of all the deeply ramified plots and designs which thou didst hear discussed between Nisida and Demetrius, shalt thou interfere. Leave the rest to heaven!"

The founder of the Rosicrucians disappeared; and when Fernand awoke late in the day—for his slumber had been long and deep—he remembered the vision which he had seen, and resolved to obey the orders he had received.

CHAPTER LXVIII.
THE INQUISITION.

BENEATH the massive and heavy tower of the Palazzo del Podesta, or Ducal Palace of Florence, was the tri-bunal of the Holy Inquisition.

Small, low, and terribly sombre in appearance was this court,—with walls of the most solid masonry, an arched roof, and a pavement formed of vast blocks of dark-veined marble.

Thither the light of heaven never penetrated;—for it was situate far below the level of the earth, and at the very foundations of that tower which rose, frowning and sullen, high above.

Iron lamps diffused a lurid lustre around, rendering ghastly the countenances alike of the oppressors and the oppressed; and when it was deemed necessary to invest the proceedings with a more awe-inspiring solemnity than usual, torches, borne by the Familiars, or officers, of the Inquisition, were substituted for those iron lamps.

Over the judgment-seat was suspended a large crucifix.

On one side of the court were three doors,—one com-municating with the corridor and flight of stone steps leading to and from the tribunal; the second affording admission into the Torture-chamber; and the third opening to the prisons of the Inquisition.

It was about seven o'clock in the evening, on the 26th of September, that Flora Francatelli and her aunt were placed before the Grand Inquisidor to be examined for the second time.

When the Familiars, habited in their long black eccle-siastical dresses with the strange cowls or hoods shading their stern and remorseless countenances, led in the two females from the separate cells in which they had been confined, the first and natural impulse of the unhappy creatures was to rush into each other's arms:—but they were immediately torn rudely asunder, and so stationed in the presence of the Grand Inquisidor as to have a con-siderable interval between them.

But the glances which the aunt and niece exchanged, gave encouragement and hope to each other;—and the sentiments which prompted those glances were really cherished by the persecuted females; inasmuch as Father Marco, who had been permitted to visit them occasionally, had dropped sundry hints of coming aid, and powerful though at present invisible protection,—thereby cheering their hearts to some little extent, and mitigating the intensity of their apprehensions.

Flora was very pale;—but never, perhaps, had she appeared more beautiful,—for her large blue eyes ex-pressed the most melting softness, and her dark brown hair hung dishevelled over her shoulders, while her bosom heaved with the agitation of suspense.

"Women," said the Grand Inquisitor, glancing first to the aunt and then to the niece, his eyes however lingering longer upon the latter, "know ye of what ye are accused? Let the younger speak first."

"My lord," answered Flora, in a firmer tone than might have been expected from the feelings indicated by her outward appearance, "when on a former occasion I stood in the presence of your Eminence, I expressed my belief that secret enemies were conspiring, for their own bad purposes, to ruin my beloved relative and myself: and yet I call heaven to witness my solemn declaration that knowingly and wilfully we have wronged no one by word or deed!"

"Young woman," exclaimed the Grand Inquisidor, "thou answerest my question evasively. Wast thou not an inmate of that most holy sanctuary, the Convent of Carmelite Nuns?—wast thou not there the companion of

Giulia of Arestino?—did not a sacrilegious horde of miscreants break into the convent, headed, or at least accompanied, by a certain Manuel d'Orsini, who was the lover of the Countess?—was not this invasion of the sacred place undertaken to rescue that guilty woman? and did she not find an asylum at the abode of your aunt, doubtless with your connivance, until the day of her arrest?"

"None of these circumstances, my lord," replied Flora, "do I attempt to deny: but it is so easy to give to them a variety of colourings, some of which, alas! may seem most unfavourable to my venerable relative and to myself. Oh! my lord, do with me what thou wilt," exclaimed Flora, clasping her hands together in a sudden paroxysm of anguish; "but release that aged woman,—suffer not my beloved aunt—my more than mother to be thus persecuted! Have mercy, my lord, upon her—oh! have mercy, great judge, upon her."

"Flora—dearest Flora," cried Dame Francatelli, the tears trickling fast down her countenance, "I do not wish to leave you—I do not seek to be set free—I will stay in this dreadful place so long as you remain a prisoner also; for, though we are separated——"

"Woman," exclaimed the Grand Inquisidor, not altogether unmoved by this touching scene, "the tribunal cannot take heed of supplications and prayers of an impassioned nature. It has to do with facts, not feelings."

At this moment there was a slight sensation amongst the Familiars stationed near the door of the judgment-hall; and an individual who had just entered the court, and who wore the black robe and the cap or tocque of a counsellor, advanced towards the Grand Inquisidor.

"My lord," said the advocate, with a reverential bow, "the day after the arrest of these females I submitted to the Council of State a memorial setting forth certain facts, which induced the President of the Council to issue his warrant to order the postponement of the second examination of the two prisoners now before your Eminence, until this day."

"And the case has been postponed accordingly," answered the Grand Inquisidor. "It will now proceed, unless reasonable cause be shown for farther delay. The prisoners are obstinate. Instead of confessing their heinous crimes and throwing themselves on the mercy of heaven,—for past the hope of human mercy they assuredly are,—they break forth into impassioned language savouring of complaint. Indeed, the younger attributes to the machinations of unknown enemies the position in which she is placed. Yet have we positive proof that she was leagued with those who perpetrated the sacrilege which ended in the destruction of the Carmelite convent; and the elder prisoner gave refuge not only to the young girl her niece, but also to a woman more guilty still—thus rendering herself infamous as one who encouraged and concealed the enemies of the Church, instead of giving them up to the most Holy Inquisition. Wherefore," continued the Grand Inquisitor, "it remaineth only for me to order the prisoners to be put to the torture, that they may confess their crimes, and receive the condemnation which they merit."

At the terrible word "*torture,*" Dame Francatelli uttered a cry of agony—but it was even more on account of her beloved niece than herself; while Flora, endowed with greater firmness than her aunt, would have flown to console and embrace her, had not the Familiars cruelly compelled the young maiden to retain her place.

"My lord," said Angelo Duras—for he was the advocate who appeared on behalf of the prisoners, "I formally and earnestly demand a delay of eight days ere this examination be proceeded with."

"It is impossible," returned the Grand Inquisidor, while his words went like ice-shafts to the hearts of the unhappy women. "In addition to the charges against them which I have already glanced at, it appeareth that one Alessandro Francatelli, who is nearly related to them both, hath abjured the Christian faith and become a Mussulman. This fact was reported many months ago to the Council of State; and in the cottage lately inhabited by the prisoners, was found a costly set of jewels, ornamented with sundry Moslem devices and symbols, all of which are hateful to the true Catholic. It is therefore natural to suppose that they themselves have secretly abjured their country's religion, and have already received the reward of their apostacy."

"No—never, never!" exclaimed the aunt, clasping her hands together, and showing by her tone and manner that she felt herself to be more outraged by this cruel suspicion than by any other portion of the treatment which she had received at the hands of the Inquisition.

On her side, Flora appeared to be astounded at the accusation made against her aunt and herself by the Grand Inquisidor.

"My lord," said Angelo Duras, "the very statement which has just been put forth by your Eminence furnishes a new ground whereon I base my requisition for a delay of eight days, in order to prepare a fitting defence on behalf of the prisoners. The Council of State is now sitting in deliberation on certain demands made by the newly arrived Ottoman Envoy, and should your Eminence refuse my requisition for a delay, it will be my duty forthwith to apply to that august body."

The Grand Inquisidor endeavoured to reason with the advocate on the inconvenience of obstructing the business of the tribunal;—but Angelo Duras, knowing that he had the law on his side, was firm; and the judge was finally compelled to accord the delay.

Flora and her aunt were accordingly conveyed back each to her separate cell; while Angelo Duras retired, murmuring to himself, "I shall doubtless offend my brother by my conduct in this respect, after my solemn promise to him to abandon the cause of the Francatellis: but I prefer having obeyed that young man of god-like aspect and persuasive manner who visited me ere now to adjure me not to neglect my duty."

The next case that occupied the attention of the Grand Inquisidor on the present occasion, was that of the Jew, Isaachar ben Solomon.

The old man was indeed a miserable spectacle. His garments hung loosely about his wasted and attenuated form;—his countenance was wan and ghastly;—but the fire of his eyes was not altogether quenched. He was heavily chained;—and, as he walked between the two Familiars who led him into the tribunal, he could scarcely drag himself along. For the persecuted old man had been confined for nearly seven months in the prison of the Inquisition; and during that period he had suffered acutely with the damps of his dungeon—the wretched food doled out to him—and the anguish occasioned by conscious innocence unjustly accused of a dreadful crime.

"Jew," said the Grand Inquisidor, "when last thou wast examined by me, thou didst obstinately refuse to confess thy grievous sins. This is the day for the final investigation of thy case: and thou mayst produce witnesses in thy favour, if thou canst."

"My lord," replied Isaachar ben Solomon, in a weak and tremulous tone, "unless heaven should work a miracle in my favour, I have no hope in this life. I do not fear death, my lord;—for, persecuted—reviled, despised—accused as I am, I can yet lay my hand on my heart, and say, *I have never injured a fellow-creature.* But, my lord," he continued, his voice growing stronger with excitement, "it is sufficient that I am a Jew to ensure my condemnation;—and yet strange indeed is that Christian faith—or rather should I say most inconsistent is the conduct of those who profess it—in so far as this ruthless persecution of my race is concerned. For where, my lord, is your charity—where is your tolerance—where is your mercy? If I be indeed involved in mental darkness, 'tis for you to enlighten me with argument, not coerce me with chains. Never have I insulted a Christian on account of his creed: wherefore should I be insulted in respect to mine? Granting that the Jew is in error, he surely deserves pity—not persecution. For how came I by the creed which I profess? Even as your lordship obtained yours, which is that of a Christian. Our parents reared us each in the belief which they respectively professed; and there is no more merit due to your Eminence for being a Christian than there is blame to be attached to me for being a Jew. Had all the religions of the earth been submitted to our consideration, when we were children—and had it been said to each of us, '*Select a faith for yourself*;'—then there might be some merit in choosing the one most popular and the most assuredly conducive to personal safety. But such was not the case, my lord; and I am a Jew for the same reason that you are a Christian—and I cling to the creed of my forefathers even as you adhere tenaciously to that faith which your ancestors have handed down to you. Reproach me not, then, because I am a Jew. And now I will pass to another subject, my lord," continued Isaachar, becoming more and more animated as he proceeded. "I am accused of a fearful crime—of murder. The evidence rests upon the fact that stains of blood were observed upon the floor of a room in my house. The answer is simple. Two men—one of noble birth, the other a robber—fought in that room; and the blood of one of them flowed from a slight wound. This is the truth—and yet I know that I am not believed. Merciful heavens! of what would you accuse me? Of murder!—and it was hinted, when last I stood before your Eminence, that the Jews have been known to slay Christian children as an offering to heaven. My lord, the Jews worship the same God as the Christians—for the Christians adopt that book in which the Jews put faith. Then I appeal to your Eminence whether the God whom the Christians worship would delight in such sacrifices; and as you must answer 'Nay,' the reply acquits the Jew also of the hideous calumny sought to be affixed upon us. The Jews, my lord, are a merciful and humane race. The records of your tribunals will prove that the Jews are not addicted to the shedding of blood. They are too patient—enduring—and resigned, to be given to vengeance. Behold how they cling to each other—how they assist each other in distress;—and charity is not narrowed to small circles, my lord—it is a sentiment which must become expansive, because it nourisheth itself and is cherished by those good feelings which are its only reward. Think you, my lord, that if I saw a fellow-creature starving in the street, I should wait to ask him whether he were a Christian, a Jew, or a Mussulman? Oh! no—no: the world's bread was given for men of all nations and all creeds."

Isaachar would have continued his address to the Grand Inquisidor; but sheer exhaustion compelled him to desist—and he would have sunk upon the cold marble, had not the Familiars supported him.

"By his own words is he convicted of disbelief in the most holy Catholic faith," said the Grand Inquisidor. "But I find by a memorial which was addressed to me many months ago,—indeed, very shortly after the arrest of this miserable unbeliever,—and signed by Manuel, Marquis of Orsini, that the said Marquis hath important evidence to give on behalf of the Jew. Now, though Manuel d'Orsini be himself a prisoner of the Holy Office, yet as he hath not yet been judged, he is a competent witness."

Orders were then given to introduce the Marquis; and Isaachar ben Solomon murmured to himself. "Is it possible that the young man can have felt sympathy for me? Ah! then I was not mistaken in him: methought, in spite of his dissipation and his wildness, that he possessed a generous heart."

In a few minutes the Marquis of Orsini was led into the judgment hall. He was chained;—but he carried his head erect—and, though his countenance was pale and care-worn, his spirit was not crushed.

He bowed respectfully, but not cringingly, to the Grand Inquisidor, and bestowed a friendly nod of recognition upon the Jew.

"This memorial, dated in the month of March last, was signed by you?" said the Grand Inquisidor interrogatively, as he displayed a paper to the Marquis.

"That memorial was signed by me," answered Orsini, in a firm tone; "and I rejoice that your Eminence has at length granted me an opportunity of explaining the matter hinted at therein. Your Eminence sits there, it is presumed, to administer justice: then let justice be done towards this innocent man—albeit that he is a Jew, —for solemnly do I declare that the blood which stained the floor in Isaachar's house, flowed from my right arm. And it may not be amiss to observe," continued the Marquis, "that the worthy Jew there did not only bind the wound for me with as much care as if I myself had been an Israelite, or he a Christian—but he moreover offered me aid of his purse: and therefore am I under obligations to him which I can never wholly discharge. In good sooth, my lord," added Manuel, in whom neither a lengthened imprisonment nor the awful solemnity of the present scene could entirely subdue the flippancy which was habitual to his speech,—"in good sooth, my lord, he is a splendid specimen of a Jew—and I pray your Eminence to discharge him forthwith."

"This levity ill becometh you, Manuel d'Orsini," said the Grand Inquisidor; "for you yourself are in terrible danger."

Then, upon a signal given, the Familiars conveyed the Marquis back to his dungeon; but ere he left the judgment-hall, he had the satisfaction of beholding the Jew's eyes fixed upon him with an expression of boundless gratitude and deep sympathy. Tears too, were trickling down the cheeks of the Israelite; for the old man thought within himself, "What matters it if the rack dislocate my limbs? But it is shocking—oh! it is shocking to reflect that thy fellow-creatures, noble youth, shall dare to deface and injure that god-like form of thine!"

"Jew," suddenly exclaimed the Grand Inquisidor, "I put no faith in the testimony of the witness who hath just appeared in thy favour. Confess thy sins—avow openly that thou hast murdered Christian children to obtain their blood for use in thy sacrifices—and seek forgiveness from heaven by embracing the faith of Jesus!"

The unhappy Israelite was so appalled by the open, positive, and undisguised manner in which an atrocious charge was revived against him, that he lost all power of utterance, and stood stupefied and aghast.

"Away with him to the Torture-Chamber!" cried the Grand Inquisidor, in a stern and remorseless tone.

"Monster!" exclaimed the Jew, suddenly recovering his speech, as that dreadful mandate warned him that he would now require all his energy—all his presence of mind:—"monster!" he repeated, in a voice indicative of loathing and contempt:—"and thou art a Christian!"

The Familiars hurried Isaachar away to the Torture-Chamber, which, as we before stated, opened from the tribunal. And terrible, indeed, was the appearance of that earthly hell—that terrestrial Hades, invented by fiends in human shape—that den of horrors constituting, indeed, a fitting foretaste of trans-Stygian torment!

The Grand Inquisidor followed the victim and the Familiars into this awful place; and on a signal being given by that high functionary, Isaachar was stripped of all his upper clothing, and stretched upon the accursed rack.

Then commenced the torture—the agonizing torture by means of that infernal instrument,—a torture which dislocated the limbs, appeared to tear the members asunder, and produced sensations as if all the nerves of the body were suddenly being drawn out through the brain!

"Dost thou confess? and wilt thou embrace the Christian faith?" demanded the Grand Inquisidor from time to time.

"I have nothing to confess—I will not renounce the creed of my forefathers!" answered Issachar in a tone of bitter agony, as he writhed upon the rack, while every fresh shock and jerk of the infernal engine seemed as if it would tear the very life out of him.

But the old man remained firm in the declaration of his innocence of the dreadful crime imputed to him; staunch also to his creed did he remain;—and, having endured the full extent of that special mode of torture, he was borne back to his dungeon—cruelly injured—with dislocated limbs—blood streaming from his mouth and nostrils—and these terrible words of the Grand Inquisidor ringing in his ears—"*Obstinate and impenitent one, Satan claims thee as his own: therefore art thou condemned to death by fire at the approaching auto-da-fé!*"

*   *   *   *   *

Half an hour afterwards another human being lay stretched upon that accursed rack:—and agonizing—oh! most agonizing were the female shrieks and rending screams which emanated from the lips of the tortured victim, but which reached not beyond the solid masonry of those walls and the massive iron-plated door.

The white and polished arms were stretched out, in a position fearfully painful, beyond the victim's head: and the wrists were fastened to a steel bar by means of thin cord, which cut through flesh, muscle, and nerve to the very bone!

The ankles were attached in a similar manner to a bar at the lower end of the rack,—and thus from the female's hands and feet thick clots of gore fell on the stone pavement. But even the blood flowed not so fast from her lacerated limbs as streamed the big drops of agony from her distorted countenance—that countenance erst so beautiful, and so well beloved by thee, Manuel d'Orsini!

For, oh! upon that rack lay stretched the fair and half-naked form of Giulia of Arestino,—its symmetry convulsing in matchless tortures—the bosom palpitating awfully with the pangs of that earthly hell—and the exquisitely modelled limbs enduring all the hideous pains of dislocation, as if the fibres that held them in their sockets were drawn out to a tension at which they must inevitably snap in halves!

But who gazes on that awful spectacle?—whose ears drink in those agonizing screams, as if they made a delicious melody?

With folded arms—compressed lips—and remorseless, though ashy pale countenance, the old Lord of Arestino stands near the rack;—and if his eyes can for a moment quit that feast which they devour so greedily, it is but to glance with demoniac triumph towards Manuel d'Orsini, whom an atrocious refinement of cruelty, suggested by the vengeful Count himself, has made a spectator of that appalling scene!

And terrible are the emotions which rend the heart of the young Marquis! But he is powerless—he cannot stretch forth a hand to save his mistress from the hellish torments which she is enduring: nor can he even whisper a syllable to inspire her with courage to support them. For he is bound tightly—the Familiars, too, have him in their iron grasp—and he is gagged!

the infernal vengeance of the old Italian noble;—for the remorseless judge urges on the fullest extent;—and while the creaking sound of wheels mingles with the cracking noise of dislocating limbs, the Count of Arestino exclaims, "I was once humane and benevolent, Giulia:—but thy conduct has made me a fiend!"

"A fiend!" shrieked the tormented woman: "Oh! yes—yes—thou art a fiend—a very fiend—I have wronged thee—but this vengeance is horrible—horrible—mercy—mercy!—oh! for one drop of water—mercy—mercy!"

The rack gave the last shock of which its utmost power was capable—a scream more dreadful, more

"NEVER HAD FERNAND BEHELD A BEING OF SUCH VENERABLE ASPECT." (See p. 121.)

Nevertheless he can see—and he can hear;—he can behold the rending tortures of the rack—and he is compelled to listen to the piercing screams which the victim sends forth!

If he close his eyes upon the horrible spectacle, imagination instantly makes it more horrible even still; and moreover, in the true spirit of a chivalrous heart, he seeks by the tenderness of glances to impart at least a gleam of solace to the soul of her who has undergone so much, and is suffering now so much more, through her fatal love of him!

The Grand Inquisidor, who is an intimate friend of the Count of Arestino, ministers well and faithfully to

agonizing, more piercing than any of its predecessors, rent this time the very walls of the Torture-Chamber; and with that last outburst of mortal agony, the spirit of the guilty Giulia fled for ever!

Yet was not the vengeance of the Count of Arestino satisfied; and the Grand Inquisidor was prepared to gratify the hellish sentiment to its fullest extent.

The still warm and palpitating corpse of the Countess was hastily removed from the rack; and the Familiars stripped—nay, tore off the clothing of Manuel d'Orsini. The countenance of the young nobleman was now terribly sombre, as if the darkest thoughts were occupying his inmost soul; and his eyes were bent fixedly on the dreadful engine to the tortures of which it appeared to be his turn to submit.

The Familiars, in order to divest him of his garments, and also to stretch him in such a way on the rack that his arms might be fastened over his head to the upper end of that instrument, had removed the chains and cords which had hitherto bound him.

And now the fatal moment seemed to be at hand; and the Familiars already grasped him rudely to hurl him on the rack, when, as if suddenly inspired by a superhuman strength, the young nobleman dashed the men from him; then, with lightning speed, he seized a massive iron bar that was used to move the windlass of the rack,—and in another instant, before a saving arm could intervene, the deadly implement struck down the Count of Arestino at the feet of the Grand Inquisidor, who started back with a cry of horror!

The next moment the Marquis was again powerless and secure in the grasp of the Familiars:—but he had accomplished his purpose—he had avenged his mistress and himself—and the old Lord of Arestino lay, with shattered skull, a corpse upon the cold pavement of the Torture-Chamber!

"Back—back with the murderer to his dungeon!" exclaimed the Grand Inquisidor, in a tone of fearful excitement and rage. "We must not afford him a chance of dying upon that engine of torture. No—no: the lingering flames of the auto-da-fé are reserved for the Marquis d'Orsini!"

And in pursuance of the sentence thus pronounced, Manuel was hurried away to his dark and solitary cell, there to remain a prey to all the dreadful thoughts which the occurrences of that fatal evening were so well calculated to marshal in horrible array to his imagination.

CHAPTER LXIX.

THE EXPEDITION OF DEMETRIUS AGAINST THE BANDITTI.

WHILE these awful scenes were being enacted in the subterranean of the Holy Inquisition, Demetrius was actively engaged in directing those plans and effecting those arrangements which the scheming disposition of Nisida of Riverola had suggested.

We should observe that in the morning he had sought and found Antonio, with whom he had so expertly managed that the villain had fallen completely into the snare spread to entrap him, and had not only confessed that he held at his disposal the liberty of the Count of Riverola, but had also agreed to deliver him up to the Greek. In a word, everything in this respect took place precisely as Nisida had foreseen.

Accordingly, as soon as it was dark in the evening, sixty of the Ottoman soldiers quitted by twos and threes the mansion which the Florentine Government had appropriated as a dwelling for the Envoy and his suite. The men, whom Demetrius thus entrusted with the execution of his scheme, and whose energy and fidelity he had previously secured by means of liberal reward, and promise of more,—were disguised in different ways, but were all well armed. To be brief, so well were the various dispositions taken, and so effectually were they executed, that those sixty soldiers had concealed themselves in the grove indicated by their master without having excited in the minds of the Florentine people the least suspicion that anything unusual was about to take place.

It was close upon eleven o'clock at night, when Demetrius, after having obtained a hasty interview with Nisida, whom he acquainted with the progress of the plot, repaired to the grove wherein his men were already distributed, and took his station in the midst of the knot of olives on the right of the huge chestnut tree which overhung the chasm.

Nearly a quarter of an hour elapsed; and naught was heard save the waving of the branches and the rustling of foliage, as the breeze of night agitated the grove: but at the expiration of that brief period, the sound of voices was suddenly heard close by the chestnut tree,—not preceded by any footsteps nor other indication of the presence of men,—and thus appearing as if they had all at once and in an instant emerged from the earth.

Not a moment had elapsed—no, not a moment—ere those individuals whose voices were thus abruptly heard, were captured and secured by a dozen Ottoman soldiers, who sprang upon them from the dense thickets around or dropped amongst them from the branches overhead:—and so admirably was the swoop made, that five persons were seized, bound, and held powerless and incapable of resistance ere the echo of the cry of alarm which they raised, had died away in the mazes of the grove.

And, simultaneously with the performance of this skilfully executed feat, a shrill whistle was wafted from the lips of Demetrius through the wood; and, as if by magic, a dozen torches were seen to light up, and numbers of men, with naked scimitars gleaming in the lurid rays of those firebrands, rushed towards the spot where the capture had been made. The effect of that sudden illumination—those flashing weapons—and that convergence of many warriors all towards the same point, was striking in the extreme, and, as the glare of the torches shone on the countenances of the four men in the midst of whom was Francisco (the whole five however being held bound and powerless by the Ottoman soldiers), it was evident that the entire proceeding had inspired the guilty wretches with the most painful alarm.

Demetrius instantly knew that the tall, handsome, and noble-looking young man in the midst of the group of captives and captors, must be Don Francisco of Riverola: and he also saw at a glance that one of the ruffians with him was Antonio. But he merely had leisure at the moment to address a word of re-assurance and friendship to Nisida's brother—for lo! the secret of the entrance to the robbers' stronghold was revealed—discovered! Yes—there, at the foot of the tree, and now rendered completely visible by the glare of the torch-light, was a small square aperture, from which the trap-door had been raised to afford egress to the captured party.

"Secure that entrance!" cried Demetrius hastily: "and hasten down those steps, some dozen of you, so as to guard it well!"—then, the instant this command was obeyed, he turned towards Francisco, saying, "Lord of Riverola—am I right in thus addressing you?"

"Such is my name," answered Francisco; "and if you, brave chief, will but release me and lend me a sword, I will prove to thee that I have no particular affection for these miscreants."

Demetrius gave the necessary order—and in another moment the young Count of Riverola was not only free, but with a weapon in his hand.

The Greek then made a rapid, but significant—fatally significant sign to his men; and—quick as thought—the three robbers and their confederate Antonio were strangled by the bow-strings which the Ottomans whipped around their necks. A few stifled cries—and all was over.

Thus perished the wretch Antonio—one of those treacherous, malignant, and avaricious Italians who bring dishonour on their noble nation,—a man who had sought to turn the vindictive feelings of the Count of Arestino to his own purposes, alike to fill his purse and to wreak his hateful spite on the Riverola family!

Scarcely was the tragedy enacted, when Demetrius ordered the four bodies to be conveyed down the steps disclosed by the trap-door:—"For," said he, "we will endeavour so to direct our proceedings that not a trace of them shall be left above ground; as the Florentines would not be well pleased if they learnt that foreign soldiers have undertaken the duties which they themselves should perform."

Several of the Ottomans accordingly bore the dead bodies down the steps; and Demetrius, accompanied by Francisco, followed at the head of the greater portion of the troops, a sufficient number, however, remaining behind to constitute a guard at the entrance of the stronghold.

While they were yet descending the stone stairs, Demetrius seized the opportunity of that temporary lull in the excitement of the night's adventures, to give Francisco hasty but most welcome tidings of his sister; and the reader may suppose that the generous-hearted young Count was overjoyed to learn that Nisida was not only alive, but also once more an inmate of the ancestral home. Demetrius said nothing relative to Flora; and Francisco, not dreaming for a moment that his deliverer even knew there was such a being in existence, asked no questions on that subject. His anxiety was not however the less to fly to the cottage;—for it must be remembered that he was arrested first on the 3rd of July, and had yet to learn all the afflictions which had fallen upon Flora and her aunt,—afflictions of the existence whereof he had been kept in utter ignorance by the banditti during his long captivity of nearly three months in their stronghold.

But while we are thus somewhat digressing, the invaders are penetrating farther into that stronghold. Headed by Demetrius and Francisco, and all carrying their drawn scimitars in their hands, the corps proceeds along a vast vaulted subterranean, paved with large flag-stones, until a huge iron door, studded with nails, bars the way.

"Stay," whispered Francisco, suddenly recollecting himself: "I think that I can devise a means to induce the rogues to open this portal—or I am much mistaken."

He accordingly seized a torch and hurried back to the foot of the stone steps; in the immediate vicinity of which he searched narrowly for some object. At last he discovered the object of his investigation—namely a large bell hanging in a niche, and from which a strong wire ran up through the ground to the surface. This bell Francisco set ringing, and then hurried back to rejoin his deliverers.

Scarcely was he again by the side of Demetrius, when he saw that this stratagem had fully succeeded; for the iron door swung heavily round on its hinges and in another moment the cries of terror which the two robber sentinels raised on the inner side, were hushed for ever by the Turkish scimitars.

Down another flight of steps the invaders then pre-cipitated themselves, another door, at the bottom, having been opened in compliance with the same signal which had led to the unfolding of the first;—and now the alarm was given by the sentinels guarding that second post,—those sentinels flying madly on, having beholden the im-molation of their comrades.

But Demetrius and Francisco speedily overtook them, just as they emerged from another long vaulted and paved cavern-passage, and were about to cross a plank which connected the two sides of a chasm in whose depths a rapid stream rushed gurgling on.

Into the turbid waters the two fugitive sentinels were cast: over the bridge poured the invaders,—and into another caverned corridor, hollowed out of the solid rock, did they enter,—the torch-bearers following im-mediately behind the Greek and the young Count.

It was evident that neither the cries of the surprised sentinels nor the tread of the invaders had alarmed the main corps of the banditti; for, on reaching a barrier formed by massive folding-doors, and knocking thereat, the portals instantly began to move on their hinges;—and in rushed the Ottoman soldiers, headed by their two gallant Christian leaders.

The robbers were in the midst of a deep carouse in their magnificent cavern-hall, when their festivity was thus rudely interrupted.

"We are betrayed!" thundered Lomellino, the captain of the horde: "to arms! to arms!"

But the invaders allowed them no time to concentrate themselves in a serried phalanx;—and a tremendous carnage ensued. Surprised and taken unaware as they were, the banditti fought as if a spell were upon them, paralysing their energies and warning them that their last hour was come. The terrible scimitars of the Turks hewed them down in all directions :—some, who sought to fly, were literally cut to pieces;—Lomellino fell be-neath the sword of the gallant Count of Riverola;—and within twenty minutes after the invaders first set foot in the banqueting-hall, not a soul of the formidable horde was left alive!

Demetrius abandoned the plunder of the den to his troops; and when the portable part of the rich booty had been divided amongst them to their satisfaction, they followed their leaders back to the grove into which the entrance of the stronghold opened.

When the subterranean was thus entirely cleared of the living, and the dead alone remained in that place which had so long been their home, and was now their tomb, Demetrius ordered his forces to disperse and return to their quarters in Florence in the same prudent manner which had characterized their egress thence a few hours before.

Francisco and Demetrius, being left alone together in the grove, proceeded by torch-light to close the trap-door, which they found to consist of a thick plate of iron covered with earth so prepared, by glutinous substances, no doubt, that it was as hard as rock; and thus, when the trap was shut down, not even a close inspection would lead to a suspicion of its existence, so admirably did it fit into its setting and correspond with the soil all around. It required, moreover, but a slight exercise of their imaginative powers, to enable Demetrius and Francisco to conjecture that every time any of the banditti had come forth from their stronghold, they were accustomed to strew a little fresh earth over the entire

spot, and thus afford an additional precaution against the chance of detection on the part of any one who might chance to stray in that direction. We may also add that the trap-door was provided with a massive bolt which fastened inside, when closed, and that the handle of the bell-wire, which gave the signal to open the trap, was concealed in a small hollow in the old chestnut tree.

Having thus satisfied his curiosity by means of these discoveries, Demetrius accompanied Francisco to the city; and during their walk thither, he informed the young Count that he was an Envoy from the Ottoman Grand Vizier to the Florentine Government—that he had become acquainted with Nisida on board the ship which delivered her from her lonely residence on an island in the Mediterranean—and that as she had by some means or other learnt where Francisco was imprisoned, he had undertaken to deliver him.

The young Count renewed his warmest thanks to the chivalrous Greek for the kind interest which he had manifested in his behalf; and they separated at the gate of the Riverola mansion, into which Francisco hurried to embrace his sister, while Demetrius repaired to his own abode.

CHAPTER LXX.
ANOTHER STEP IN THE VENGEANCE OF NISIDA.

THE meeting between Nisida and her brother Francisco was affecting in the extreme; and for a brief space the softer feelings of the lady's nature triumphed over those strong, turbulent, and concentrated passions which usually held such indomitable sway over her. For her attachment to him was profound and sincere; and the immense sacrifices she had made in what she conceived to be his welfare and interests, had tended to strengthen this almost boundless love.

On his side, the young Count was rejoiced to behold his sister, whose strange disappearance and long absence had filled his mind with the worst apprehensions. Yes—he was rejoiced to see her once more beneath the ancestral roof; and, with all a fond brother's pride, he surveyed her splendid countenance, which triumph and happiness now invested with an animation that rendered her sur-passingly beautiful!

A few brief and rapidly given explanations were ex-changed between them, by means of the language of the fingers,—Francisco satisfying Nisida's anxiety in respect to the success of her project by which the total extermi-nation of the banditti had been effected,—and she convey-ing to him as much of the outline of her adventures during the last seven months as she thought it prudent to impart.

They then separated, it being now very late; and more-over Nisida had still some work in hand for that night!

The moment Francisco was alone, he exclaimed aloud, "Oh! is it possible that this dear sister who loves me so much, is really the bitter enemy of Flora? But to-morrow—to-morrow I must have a long explanation with Nisida; and heaven grant that she may not stand in the way of my happiness! O Flora—dearest Flora, if you knew how deeply I have suffered on your account during my captivity in that accursed cavern! And what must you have thought of my disappearance—my absence? Alas! did the same vengeance which pursued me, wreak its spite also on thee, fair girl?—did the miscreant Antonio, who boastingly proclaimed himself to my face the author of my captivity, and who sullenly refused to give me any tidings of those whom I cared for, and of what was passing in the world without,—did he dare to molest thee? But suspense is intolerable—I cannot en-dure it even for a few short hours!—No—I will speed me at once to the dwelling of my Flora, and thus assuage her grief and put an end to my own fears at the same time!"

Having thus resolved, Francisco repaired to his own apartment, enveloped himself in a cloak, secured weapons of defence about his person, and then quitted the mansion, unperceived by a living soul.

Almost at the same time, but by another mode of egress—namely, the private staircase leading from her own apartments into the garden, and which has been so often mentioned in the course of this narrative—Donna Nisida stole likewise from the Riverola palace.

She was habited in male attire; and beneath her doublet she wore the light but strong cuirass which she usually donned ere setting out on any nocturnal enter-prise, and which she was now particularly cautious not to omit from the details of her toilette, inasmuch as the mysterious appearance of the muffled figure, which had alarmed her on the preceding evening, induced her to adopt every precaution against secret and unknown enemies.

Whither was the Lady Nisida now hurrying, through the dark streets of Florence?—what new object had she in contemplation?

Her way was bent towards an obscure neighbourhood in the immediate vicinity of the cathedral; and in a short time she reached the house in which Dame Margaretha, Antonio's mother, dwelt.

She knocked gently at the door, which was shortly opened by the old woman, who imagined it was her son that sought admittance; for, though in the service of the Count of Arestino, Antonio was often kept abroad late by the various machinations in which he had been engaged, and it was by no means unusual for him to seek his mother's dwelling at all hours.

Margaretha, who appeared in a loose wrapper hastily thrown on, held a lamp in her hand; and when its rays streamed not on the countenance of her son, but showed the form of a cavalier handsomely apparelled, she started back in mingled astonishment and fear. A second glance, however, enabled her to recognise the Lady Nisida; and an exclamation of wonder escaped her lips.

Nisida entered the house—closed the door behind her —and motioned Dame Margaretha to lead the way into the nearest apartment. The old woman obeyed trembling; for she feared that the lady's visit boded no good; and this apprehension on her part was not only enhanced by her own knowledge of all Antonio's treachery towards Count Francisco, but also by the imperious manner, determined looks, and strange disguise of her visitress.

But Margaretha's terror speedily gave way to indescribable astonishment, when Nisida suddenly addressed her in a language which not for many, many years had the old woman heard flow from that delicious mouth!

"Margaretha," said Nisida, "you must prepare to accompany me forthwith! Be not surprised to hear me thus capable of rendering myself intelligible by means of an organ on which a seal was so long placed! A marvellous cure has been accomplished in respect to me, during my absence from Florence. But you must prepare to accompany me, I say: your son, Antonio——"

"My son!" ejaculated the woman, now again trembling from head to foot, and surveying Nisida's countenance in a manner denoting the acutest suspense.

"Your son is wounded—mortally wounded in a street-skirmish——"

"Wounded!" shrieked Margaretha. "Oh! dear lady —tell me all—tell me the worst! What has happened to my unfortunate son? He is dead—he is dead! Oh! I know that he is dead! Your manner convinces me that hope is past!"

And she wrung her hands bitterly, while tears streamed down her wrinkled cheeks.

"No—he is not dead, Margaretha!" exclaimed Nisida; "but he is dying—and he implored me, by everything I deem sacred, to hasten hither, and fetch you to him, that he may receive your blessing and close his eyes in peace."

"In peace!" repeated the old woman bitterly: then, to herself she said, "Donna Nisida suspects not his perfidy—knows not all his wickedness."

"Delay not!" urged the lady, perceiving what was passing in her mind. "You are well aware that my brother, who, alas! has disappeared most mysteriously, dismissed Antonio abruptly from his service many months ago: but, whatever were the cause, it is forgiven at least by me. So, tarry not—but prepare to accompany me!"

Margaretha hastened to her bed-room, and re-appeared in a few minutes, completely dressed and ready to issue forth.

"Keep close by me," said Nisida, as she opened the house-door; "and breathe not a word as we pass through the streets. I have reasons of my own for assuming a disguise, and wish not to be recognised."

Margaretha was too much absorbed in the contemplation of the afflicting intelligence which she had received, to observe anything at all suspicious in these injunctions; and thus it was that the two females proceeded in silence through the streets leading towards the Riverola mansion.

By means of a pass-key Nisida opened the wicket-gate of the spacious gardens; and she traversed the grounds, Margaretha walking by her side.

In a few minutes they reached a low door, affording admission into the basement-storey of the palace, and of which Nisida also possessed the key.

"Go first," said the lady, in a scarcely audible whisper: "I must close the door behind us."

"But wherefore this way?" demanded Margaretha, a sudden apprehension starting up in her mind. "This door leads down to the cellars."

"The officers of justice are in search of Antonio—and I am concealing him for your sake," was the whispered and rapid assurance given by Nisida. "Would you have him die in peace in your arms, or perish on the scaffold?"

Margaretha shuddered convulsively, and hurried down the dark flight of stone steps upon which the door opened. Terrible emotions raged in her bosom—indescribable alarms, grief, suspicion, and also a longing eagerness to put faith in the apparent friendship of Nisida.

"Give me your hand," said the lady;—and the hand that was thrust into hers was cold and trembling.

Then Nisida hurried Margaretha along a narrow subterranean passage, in which the blackest night reigned; and, though the old woman was a prey to apprehensions that increased each moment to a fearful degree, she dared not utter a word either to question—to implore—or to remonstrate.

At length they stopped; and Nisida, dropping Margaretha's hand, drew back heavy bolts which raised ominous echoes in the vaulted passage. In another moment a door began to move stubbornly on its hinges; and almost at the same time a faint light gleamed forth —increasing in power as the door opened wider, but still attaining no greater strength than that which a common iron lamp could afford.

Margaretha's anxious glances were instantly plunged into the cellar or vault to which the door opened, and whence the light came; but she saw no one within. It however appeared as if some horrible reminiscence, connected with the place, came back to her startled mind; for, falling on her knees, and clinging wildly to her companion, she cried in a piercing tone, "Oh! lady, wherefore have you brought me hither?—where is my son?— what does all this horrible mystery mean? But, chiefly *now* of all—why, why are we *here*—at this hour?"

"In a few moments you shall know more!" exclaimed Nisida;—and, as she spoke, with an almost superhuman strength she dragged—or rather flung the prostrate woman into the vault,—rushing in herself immediately afterwards, and closing the door behind her.

"Holy God!" shrieked Margaretha, gazing wildly around the damp and naked walls of solid masonry, and then up to the lamp suspended to the arched ceiling, "is this the place? But, no—you are ignorant of all *that* —it was not for *that* that you brought me hither! Speak, lady—speak! Where is Antonio?—what have I done to merit thy displeasure? Oh! mercy—mercy! Bend not those terrible glances upon me! Your eyes flash fire! You are not Nisida—you are an evil spirit! Oh! mercy —mercy!"

And thus did the miserable woman rave, as, kneeling upon the cold damp ground, she extended her tightly clasped hands in an imploring manner towards Nisida, who, drawn up to her full height, was contemplating the grovelling wretch with eyes that seemed to shoot forth shafts of devouring flame!

Terrible, indeed, was the appearance of Nisida! Like to an avenging deity was she,—no longer a woman in the glory of her charms and the elegance of her disguise— but a fury—a very fiend—an implacable demoness— armed with the blasting lightnings of infernal malignity and hellish rancour!

"Holy Virgin! protect me," shrieked Margaretha, every nerve thrilling with the agony of ineffable alarm.

"Yes—call upon heaven to aid you, vile woman!" said Nisida, in a thick, hoarse, and strangely altered voice: "for you are beyond the reach of human aid! Know ye whose remains—or rather, the mangled portions of whose remains—lie in this unconsecrated ground? Ah! well may you start in horror and surprise—for I know all— all!"

A terrific scream burst from the lips of Margaretha; and she threw her wild looks around as if she were going mad!

"Detestable woman!" exclaimed Nisida, fixing her burning eyes more intently still on Margaretha's countenance; "you are now about to pay the penalty of your complicity in the most odious crimes that ever made nights terrible in Florence! But I must torture, ere I slay ye! Yes—I must give thee a foretaste of that hell to which your soul is soon to plunge down! Know, then, that Antonio—your son Antonio—is no more. Not three hours have elapsed since he was slain—assassinated

—murdered, if you will so call it,—and by my commands!"

"Oh! lady, have pity upon me—pity upon me, a bereaved mother!" implored the old woman, in a voice of anguish so penetrating, that, vile as she was, it would have moved any human being save Nisida. "Do not kill me—spare me—and I will end my miserable days in a convent! Give me time to repent of all my sins—for they are numerous and great! Oh! spare me, dear lady—have mercy upon me—have mercy upon me!"

"What mercy had you on them whose mangled remains are buried in the ground beneath your feet?" demanded Nisida, in a voice almost suffocated with rage. "Prepare for death—your last moment is at hand!"—and a bright dagger suddenly flashed in the lamp-light.

"Mercy—mercy!" exclaimed Margaretha, springing forward, and grasping Nisida's knees.

"I know not what mercy is!" cried the terrible Italian woman, raising the long, bright, glittering dagger over her head.

"Holy God! protect me! Lady—dear lady, have pity upon me!" shrieked the agonizing wretch, her countenance hideously distorted, and appallingly ghastly, as it was raised in such bitter earnest appeal towards that of the avengeress. "Again I say, mercy—mercy!"

"Die, fiend!" exclaimed Nisida: and the dagger, descending with lightning speed, sank deep into the bosom of the prostrate victim.

A dreadful cry burst from the lips of the wretched woman; and she fell back—a corpse!

"Oh! my dear—my well-beloved—and never-to-be-forgotten mother!" said Nisida, falling upon her knees by the side of the body, and gazing intently upward—as if her eyes could pierce the entire building overhead, and catch a glimpse of the spirit of the parent whom she thus apostrophised;—"pardon me—pardon me for this deed! Thou didst enjoin me to abstain from vengeance: but when I thought of all thy wrongs, the contemplation drove me mad,—and an irresistible power—a force which I could not resist—has hurried me on to achieve the punishment of this wretch who was so malignant an enemy of thine! Dearest mother, pardon me—look not down angrily on thy daughter!"

Then Nisida gave way to all the softer emotions which attended the reaction that her mind was now rapidly undergoing, after being so highly strung as for the last few hours it was;—and her tears fell in torrents.

For some minutes she remained in her kneeling position, and weeping, till she grew afraid—yes, afraid of being in that lonely place, with the corpse stretched on the ground,—a place, too, which for other reasons awoke such terrible recollections in her mind.

Starting to her feet—and neither waiting to extinguish the lamp which she herself had lighted at an earlier period of the night, nor to withdraw her dagger from the bosom of the murdered Margaretha—Nisida fled from the vault, and regained her own apartment in safety and unperceived.

* * * * * *

When morning dawned, Nisida rose from a couch in which she had obtained two hours of troubled slumber, and, having hastily dressed herself, proceeded to the chamber of her brother Francisco.

But he was not there—nor had his bed been slept in during the past night.

"He is searching after his Flora!" thought Nisida. "Alas! poor youth—how it grieves me thus to be compelled to thwart thee in thy love! But my oath—and thine interests, Francisco demand this conduct on my part. And better—better is it that thou shouldst hear from strangers the terrible tidings that thy Flora is a prisoner in the dungeons of the Inquisition, where she can issue forth only to proceed to the stake! Yes—and better too, is it that she should die, than that this marriage shall be accomplished!"

Nisida quitted the room, and repaired to the apartment where the morning repast was served up.

A note, addressed to herself, lay upon the table. She instantly recognised the handwriting of Dr. Duras—tore open the billet—and read the contents as follows:—

"My brother Angelo came to me very late last night, and informed me that a sense of imperious duty compelled him to change his mind relative to the two women Francatelli. He accordingly appeared on their behalf, and obtained a delay of eight days. But nothing can save them from condemnation at the end of this period, unless, indeed, immense interest is made on their

account with the duke. My brother alone deserves your blame, dear friend, let not your anger fall on your affectionate and devoted servant,

"JERONYMO DURAS."

Nisida bit her lip with vexation. She now regretted that she had effected the liberation of Francisco before she was convinced that Flora was past the reach of human mercy;—but, in the next moment, she resumed her haughty composure, as she said within herself, 'My brother may essay all *his* influence : but mine shall prevail!'

Scarcely had she established this determination in her mind, when the door was burst open, and Francisco—pale, ghastly, and with eyes wandering wildly—staggered into the apartment.

Nisida, who really felt deeply on his account, sprang forward—received him in her arms—and supported him to a seat.

"Oh! Nisida, Nisida!" he exclaimed aloud, in a tone expressive of deep anguish : " what will become of your unfortunate brother? But it is not you who have done this! No—for you were not in Florence at the time which beheld the cruel separation of Flora and myself!"

And, throwing himself on his sister's neck, he burst into tears.

He had apostrophised her in the manner just related, not because he fancied she could hear or understand him ; but because he forgot, in the paroxysms of his grief, that Nisida was (as he believed) deaf and dumb!

She wound her arms around him—she pressed him to her bosom—she covered his pale forehead with kisses ; while her heart bled at the sight of his alarming sorrow.

Suddenly he started up—flung his arms wildly about—and exclaimed in a frantic voice, "Bring me my steel panoply! give me my burgonet—my cuirass—and my trusty sword ;—and let me arouse all Florence to a sense of its infamy in permitting that terrible Inquisition to exist! Bring me my armour, I say—the same sword that I wielded on the walls of Rhodes—and I will soon gather a trusty band to aid me !"

But, overcome with excitement, he fell forward—dashing his head violently upon the floor, before Nisida could save him.

She pealed the silver bell that was placed upon the breakfast-table, and assistance soon came. Francisco was immediately conveyed to his chamber—Dr. Duras was sent for—and on his arrival, he pronounced the young nobleman to be labouring under a violent fever. The proper medical precautions were adopted ; and the physician was in a few hours able to declare that Francisco was in no imminent danger, but that several days would elapse ere he could possibly become convalescent.

Nisida remained by his bed-side, and was most assiduous—most tender—most anxious in her attentions towards him ; and when he raved, in his delirium, of Flora and the Inquisition, it went to her very heart to think that she was compelled by a stern necessity to abstain from exerting her influence to procure the release of one whose presence would prove of far greater benefit to the sufferer than all the anodynes and drugs which the skill of Dr. Duras might administer !

CHAPTER LXXI.

THE SICK ROOM.—FLORENCE IN DISMAY.

IT was about an hour past daybreak on the 1st of October,—five days after the incidents related in the three preceding chapters.

Nisida, worn out with long watchings and vigils in her brother's chamber, had retired to her own apartment ; but not before she had seen Francisco fall into a sleep which, under the influence of a narcotic ordered by the physician, promised to be long and soothing.

The lady had not quitted the chamber of the invalid ten minutes, when the door was slightly opened, and some one's looks were plunged rapidly and searchingly into the room,—then the visitor, doubtless satisfied by the result of his survey, stole cautiously in.

He advanced straight up to the table which stood near the bed—drew a small phial from the bosom of his doublet—and poured its crystal contents into the beverage prepared to quench the thirst of the invalid.

Then, as he again secured the phial about his person, he murmured, "The medicaments of Christian Rosencrux will doubtless work greater wonders than those of of Dr. Duras, skilled though the latter be !"

Having thus mused to himself, the visitor shook Francisco gently ; and the young Count awoke, exclaiming petulantly that he was athirst. A goblet of the beverage containing the Rosicrucian fluid was immediately conveyed to his lips; and he drank the refreshing draught with eagerness.

The effect was marvellous indeed;—a sudden tinge of healthy red appeared upon the cheeks a moment before so ashy pale—and fire once more animated the blue eyes —and Francisco recovered complete consciousness and self-possession for the first time since the dread morning when he was attacked with a dangerous illness.

He closed his eyes for a few minutes; and when he opened them again, he was surprised to perceive by his bedside a young, well-attired, and very handsome man, whose countenance appeared to be familiar to him.

"Count of Riverola," said the visitor, bending over him, and speaking in a low but kind tone, "despair not! Succour is at hand—and ere forty-eight hours shall have passed away, your well-beloved Flora will be free!"

Joy lighted up the countenance of the young nobleman as these delightful words met his ears;—and, seizing his consoler's hand, he exclaimed, "A thousand thanks for this assurance! But, have we not met before?—or was it in those wild dreams which have haunted my imagination, that I have seen thee?"

"Yes—we have met before, Count," was the reply. "Dost thou not remember Fernand Wagner?"

Francisco passed his hand across his brow, as if to collect his scattered thoughts: then, at the expiration of a few moments, he said, "Oh, yes—I recollect you well! But where have you been so long? Do you know that I had conceived a great friendship for you, when some strange incident—I cannot remember what, and it is of no matter—parted us?"

"Do not excite yourself too much, by racking your memory to decipher the details of the past," returned Wagner. "I dare not stay another minute with you now: therefore listen attentively to what more I have to say. Yield yourself not up to despondency—on the contrary, cherish every hope that is dear to you. Within a few days Flora shall be yours! Yes—solemnly do I assure you that all shall take place as I affirm. But *your* agency is not needed to ensure her liberation: heaven will make use of *other* means. Compose your mind, then,—and suffer not yourself to be tortured by vain fears as to the future. Above all, keep my visit to thee a profound secret—intimate not to thy sister Nisida that thou hast seen me. Follow my counsel in all these respects—and happiness is in store for thee!"

Fernand pressed the young Count's hand warmly as he terminated these rapidly delivered injunctions, and then retreated from the chamber ere the invalid had time to utter a syllable indicative of his gratitude.

But how different was Francisco now—how different did Nisida find him, on her return to his room, from what he was when she had left him two hours before! Nor less was Dr. Duras astonished, at his next visit, to perceive that his patient had made in those two hours as rapid strides towards convalescence as he could barely have hoped to see accomplished in a week.

In obedience to a hint rapidly conveyed by a signal from Nisida to the physician, the latter touched gently upon the subject of Flora Francatelli: but Francisco, resolute in his endeavours to follow the advice of Fernand Wagner, and to avoid all topics calculated to excite, responded briefly, and immediately spoke on another matter.

But he did not think the less deeply on that interesting subject. No: he cherished the image of his Flora, and the hope of being yet united to her, with an enthusiasm which a love so ardent as his passion alone could feel.

And Nisida congratulated herself on the conviction which she now very naturally entertained, that he had resigned himself to the loss of the young maiden, and was exerting his utmost to banish her altogether from his memory!

Throughout that day Francisco continued to improve rapidly; and on the following morning he was enabled to leave his couch. Indeed, his recovery was so marvellously quick, that Dr. Duras considered it to be a perfect phenomenon in the history of medicine; and Nisida looked upon the physician, whom she conceived to be the author of this remarkable change, with unfeigned admiration.

*   *   *   *   *   *   *

It was verging towards the hour of sunset, on the 2nd of October, when a rumour of a most alarming nature circulated with the celerity of wildfire throughout the city of Florence. At first the report was received with contemptuous incredulity;—but by degrees—as circumstances tended to confirm it,—as affrighted peasants came flying into the town from their country homes, bearing the dread tidings,—the degenerate and voluptuous Florentines gave way to all the terrors which, in such a case, were too well adapted to fill the hearts of an emasculated people with dismay.

For, while the dwellers in the City of Flowers were thinking only of the gay festivals which invariably commenced their winter season,—while the noble and wealthy burghers were whiling their time pleasantly in the regilding and decoration of their palaces or mansions,—while the Duke was projecting splendid banquets, and the members of the Council of State were dreaming of recreation and enjoyment, rather than of the duties of office,—while, too, preparations were being made for the approaching *auto-da-fé*—that terrible spectacle which the Inquisition annually offered to the morbid tastes of a priest-ridden people,—while, in a word, Florence seemed wrapped up in security and peace,—at such a moment the astounding intelligence arrived, that a mighty army was within a few hours' march of the sovereign city of Tuscany!

Yes:—these were the news that suddenly spread confusion and dismay throughout Florence,—the news which told how the Ottoman fleet, for some days past moored off the port of Leghorn, had vomited forth its legions,— and how the formidable force was approaching at a rapid rate, under the command of the Grand Vizier in person —the Seraskier and Sipehsalar of the armies of the Sultan!

The moment these tidings were bruited abroad in the city, Demetrius, the Greek, fled secretly—for he too well understood that his treacherous intentions had, in some unaccountable manner, transpired, and reached the ears of Ibrahim-Pasha. Nisida was perfectly astounded; and, for the first time in her life, she felt all her energies paralysed—all her powers of combination suddenly laid prostrate. As for Francisco—he could not help thinking that the invasion of Italy by the Turks was connected with the succour so mysteriously, but confidently promised by Wagner; although he was not only ignorant of the relationship subsisting between the Grand Vizier and his beloved Flora, but was even unaware of the fact that this high functionary was the same Ibrahim whose prisoner he had been in the Island of Rhodes.

The Council of State assembled to deliberate upon the proper course which should be adopted at so critical a moment; but when the resources of Florence and the means of resisting the invaders were scrutinized—when it was discovered that there were not three thousand soldiers to defend the place, nor arms sufficient to equip more than fifteen hundred volunteers in addition to the regular force—all idea of attempting to make a stand against an army which was in reality twenty thousand strong, but which the exaggerations of fear had trebled in amount, was ultimately abandoned.

The sun went down, and was succeeded by no illuminations that night. Florence was in mourning. A spell had fallen upon the City of Flowers: her streets were deserted:—and within the houses, those who possessed wealth were busily engaged in concealing their gold and jewels in cellars, holes dug in the ground, or at the bottom of wells. The general consternation was terrific indeed; and the solemn stillness which prevailed throughout the town so lately full of animation and happiness, was even more dreadful than that which had accompanied the plague two centuries before!

It was near midnight when messengers from the Grand Vizier, who was now within three miles' march of the city, arrived at the western gate, and demanded admission that they might obtain an immediate audience of the Duke. The request was directly complied with; and the envoys were conducted to the Palazzo, where the Prince immediately assembled the Council of State to receive them, himself presiding.

The audience was in other respects strictly private; but the nature of the interview was soon proved to have been most unexpectedly pacific; for two hours after the reception of the envoys, criers proceeded throughout the city, proclaiming the joyful news that the Grand Vizier had of his own accord proposed such terms as the Council of State had not hesitated to accept.

Thus, at two o'clock in the morning, were the Florentines at first alarmed by hearing the monotonous voices of the criers breaking upon the solemn stillness; but their fears changed into gladness ineffable, ere those functionaries had uttered a dozen words of the proclamation which they were entrusted to make.

What the terms were did not immediately transpire ;—but two circumstances which occurred ere it was daybreak, and which, though conducted with considerable secrecy, nevertheless soon became known,—these circumstances, we say, afforded ample scope for comment and gossip.

The first was the occupation of the Riverola palace by Ottoman soldiers who had accompanied Demetrius as an escort, and whom he had left in Florence;—and the second was the fact that two females, closely muffled up, were removed from the prison of the Inquisition, and delivered over to the charge of the Grand Vizier's messengers, who conveyed them out of the city.

But the curiosity excited by these incidents was absorbed in the general anxiety that was evinced by the Florentine people to feast their eyes with the grand, interesting, and imposing spectacle which the dawn of day revealed to their view.

For, far as the eye could reach, on the western side of Florence, and commencing at the distance of about a quarter of a mile from the city, a mass of innumerable tents and pavilions showed where the Ottoman army was encamped! Myriads of banners, of all colours, floated from the tall javelins to which they were affixed before the entrances of the chief officers' tents ; and in front of the entire encampment waved, at the summit of a spear planted in the ground, the three horse-tails which invariably preceded the march of a Turkish army. The sunbeams glittered on thousands of bright crescents ; and the brazen pommels of the mounted sentinels' saddles shone like burnished gold. It was, indeed, a grand and imposing spectacle ;—and the din of innumerable voices mingling with the sounds of martial music reached the ears of those Florentines, who, more daring than the rest, advanced nearly up to the outposts of the encampment.

But, in the meantime, a scene of profound and touching interest had taken place in the gorgeous pavilion of the Grand Vizier.

CHAPTER LXXII.

THE PAVILION OF THE GRAND VIZIER.

WHILE it was yet dark—and ere that martial panorama of tents and pavilions developed itself to the admiring and astonished eyes of the Florentines—two females closely muffled in handsome cachmere shawls, which had been presented to them for the purpose, were threading the Ottoman encampment, under the guidance of messengers, to whom they had been consigned.

It is hardly necessary to inform the reader that these females were the elder Signora Francatelli and her beautiful niece, Flora.

Their sudden and most unexpected deliverance from the terrible dungeon of the Inquisition, and the profound respect with which they were treated by those into whose charge the Familiars of the Holy Office had surrendered them, inspired them with the most lively joy ; and their congratulations were expressed by frequent pressures of each other's hands as they proceeded in company with their guides. But they knew not by whom, nor how, nor wherefore they had been released ; —and yet a vague suspicion, founded solely on the fact that their conductors wore the Ottoman garb, that Alessandro must be in some way connected with the matter, had entered their minds. It was, at all events, clear that no harm was intended them—for they were not treated as prisoners :—and thus they hastened on in confidence and hope.

It was not until they had left the city some distance behind, that the bright moon showed them a confused mass of white objects in front; and they were both marvelling what the strange and unknown spectacle could be, when their party was suddenly challenged by the sentries of an outpost. The leader of the little escort gave the watchword ; and now as the two females drew near to the encampment, the mass of white objects became more shapely — until, in a few minutes, the pointed tops of the tents and pavilions stood out in strong relief against the purple sky.

What could this unusual spectacle mean ? They were till in the dungeons of the Inquisition when the alarm caused by an approaching army had circulated through Florence; and the rumour had not reached their ears. For the first time since the moment of their release they now hung back, and manifested signs of fear.

"Be not terrified, ladies," said the chief of the escort, speaking in excellent Italian; "ye have no cause for apprehension! Before you spread the innumerable tents of the Ottoman army ; and it is to the presence of this mighty host that ye are indebted for your freedom."

"But whither are you taking us?" inquired Flora, scarcely reassured.

"To the pavilion of his Highness, Ibrahim-Pacha, the Grand Vizier of the glorious Sultan Solyman," answered the Turk : "and at the hands of that powerful Minister ye will receive naught but honourable and kind treatment."

"Know you, signor," inquired Flora, "if there be in the Ottoman camp, a young man, who when a Christian," she added with a profound sigh, "bore the name of Alessandro Francatelli ?"

"There is such a young man," responded the Turkish messenger; "and you will see him presently."

"Oh! is it then to him that we owe our deliverance ?" demanded the beauteous maiden, her heart fluttering with varied emotions at the idea of meeting her brother. "Is he attached to the person of that mighty chief whom you denominate the Grand Vizier ?—and shall we see him in the pavilion of his Highness ?"

"You will see him in the pavilion of his Highness," answered the Turk.

"And the Grand Vizier himself—is he a good, a kind man ?" asked Flora. "Is my brother—I mean Alessandro—a favourite with him ?"

"I believe that the mighty Ibrahim loves no man more than Alessandro Francatelli, lady," said the Turk, highly amused by the questions which were put to him, although his manner was respectful and calm.

"Then there is a chance that Alessandro will rise in the service of the Sultan ?" continued Flora, naturally anxious to glean all the information she could relative to her brother.

"There is not a more enviable personage in the imperial service than he whom you style Alessandro Francatelli."

"Heaven be thanked that he is so prosperous, poor boy!" exclaimed the aunt, who had been an attentive listener to the preceding discourse. "But your Grand Vizier, signor, must be very powerful to have a great army at his disposal ?"

"The Grand Vizier, lady," returned the Ottoman envoy, "is second only to the Sultan—and in him we see a reflection of the imperial Majesty. At a sign from the great and potent Ibrahim, every scimitar throughout this host of twenty thousand men, would leap from its sheath in readiness to strike where and at whom he might choose to order. Nay more, lady—he has the power to gather together armies so numerous that they would inundate Christendom as with a desolating sea. Allah be thanked! there is no limit to the power of the mighty Ibrahim, so long as he holdeth the seals of his great office."

The two females made no farther observation aloud; but they thought profoundly on all they had just heard, for in a short time they were to stand in the presence of this puissant chief whom the Ottomans seemed to worship as a god, and who wielded a power which placed him on a level with the proudest potentate in the Christian world.

In the meantime the little party had entered the precincts of the Ottoman encampment—a complete city of tents and pavilions, ranged in the most admirable order, and with all the regularity of streets.

A solemn silence prevailed throughout the camp, interrupted only by the measured pace and the occasional challenge of sentinels.

At length Flora and her aunt perceived, in the clear moonlight, a pavilion loftier, larger, and more magnificent, than any other which they had yet seen. The pinnacle glittered as if it were tipped with a bright star ; the roof was of dazzling whiteness ; and the sides were of dark velvet, richly embroidered with gold. It stood in the midst of a wide space, the circumjacent tents forming a complete circle about it. Within this enclosure of tents the sentries were posted at very short intervals ; and, instead of walking up and down, they stood motionless as statues, their mighty scimitars gleaming in the moonlight.

In profound silence did the little party proceed towards the entrance of the vast pavilion, which the females had no difficulty in discerning to be the habitation of the potent and dreaded chief into whose presence they were now repairing. In front of this splendid tent floated two large banners, each from the summit of a tall javelin, the head of which was of burnished gold. One of these enormous flags was green; the other was blood-red. The first was the sacred standard of the Prophet Mahommed, and accompanied the Grand Vizier in his capacity of representative and vicegerent of the Sultan; and the latter was the banner which was always planted in front of the pavilion inhabited by the Seraskier, or commander-in-chief of an Ottoman army.

At the entrance of the vast tent stood four mounted sentinels, horses and men alike so motionless that they seemed to be as many equestrian statues.

"In a few moments," whispered the leader of the little escort to the two females, "you will be in the presence of the Grand Vizier, who will receive you alone."

"And Alessandro Francatelli?" inquired Flora, in a tone of disappointment: "will he not be there also?"

"Fear not—you shall behold him shortly," answered the Turk; and, passing behind the mounted sentinels, he drew aside a velvet curtain, at the same time bidding Flora and her aunt enter the pavilion.

A blaze of light bursting forth from the interior of the magnificent tent, dazzled and bewildered them, as the Ottoman pushed them gently onward—for they hung back in vague and groundless alarm.

The curtain was instantly closed behind them; and they now found themselves inside the gorgeous abode of the Grand Vizier. The pavilion was decorated in the most sumptuous manner. Crystal chandeliers were suspended to the spars which supported the canvas ceiling; and the pillars which propped up those spars were gilt and inlaid with mother-of-pearl. Rich sofas placed around the sides—vases, some containing flowers, others delicious perfumes—tables laden with refreshments of the most exquisite kind,—in a word, all the evidences of enormous wealth and all the accessories of luxurious splendour were displayed in that sumptuous abode.

At the farther end of the pavilion was seated an individual, whom, by the intimation they had already received, and by the magnificence of his attire, Flora and her aunt immediately knew to be the Grand Vizier. He was reclining on a sofa raised on a dais, and apparently in a pensive mood—for his countenance was shaded by his hand.

Slowly and timidly did the two females advance towards the mighty chieftain, whose apparel glittered all over with precious stones. A beautiful plume of feathers, fastened to the front of his turban, by a diamond clasp, waved gracefully above his head; and two rows of precious stones, gleaming resplendently, traced the outlines of his sabre sheath.

But wherefore retained he his hand thus over his countenance? was he unaware of the presence of Flora and her aunt, as noiselessly they advanced upon the thick carpet which was spread over the ground?

And now at length they paused—for they stood within a few yards of the dais on which stood the sofa, or divan, whereon the Vizier reclined.

"Mighty lord," said Flora, in her soft, musical tones, "behold before you the Christian women who are doubtless indebted to the generous intervention of your Highness——"

But she stopped short suddenly;—for Ibrahim raised his head—tears were trickling down his cheeks,—and his countenance—his well-known countenance—was mournful in the extreme.

"Alessandro — my brother Alessandro!" exclaimed Flora, after a pause of a few moments, during which she surveyed him with the most earnest attention, her own features the while expressing indescribable astonishment: then, springing towards him, she cried, "Yes—'tis he, 'tis he!"—and she threw herself into his arms.

Long and fervent was that embrace; and the tears of the brother and sister were commingled—but they were now as much tears of joy as of bitterness—joy on account of this meeting, and bitterness at the renegadism which had invested Ibrahim with that power whereby it was brought about. Nevertheless, long and fervent, we say, was that embrace; and longer it might have been, had not the good aunt also sought her turn to testify her unaltered affection for her nephew.

When the excitement of this affecting scene had somewhat subsided, the Grand Vizier made his relatives sit down, one on either side; and then, in as succinct a manner as possible, he unfolded to them the circumstances of his rapid rise in the Ottoman service, and his proud elevation. Then Flora and her aunt learnt, for the first time, that the Turkish chief whose prisoner Francisco had become at Rhodes, was none other than

Ibrahim himself; and that Demetrius was an agent whom he had despatched to Florence to watch over the interests of his relatives. The Grand Vizier also informed them how he had undertaken this expedition on purpose to rescue them from the persecution of their enemies—how he had rescued Donna Nisida of Riverola from her sojourn on the Island of Snakes—and how he had received information, through the kindness of Fernand Wagner, that Demetrius was playing a perfidious game, which information had induced him to march without delay to Florence.

Flora and her aunt were astonished at the varied and interesting tidings which the Grand Vizier thus imparted to them; but the young maiden's manner was frequently mournful and abstracted while her brother was speaking.

Ibrahim knew full well what was passing in her mind; and he hastened to reassure her, as soon as he had brought his explanations and disclosures to an end.

"Droop not, dearest sister," he said, "nor abandon thyself to melancholy thoughts. It is in my power to render thee completely happy; and it is in accordance with my will to accomplish that aim. Thy misfortunes —thy persecutions, from whatever quarter they come, are at an end; and not a single soul in yon proud city of Florence shall dare to menace my beloved relatives with mischief! No," exclaimed Ibrahim proudly, as he laid his jewelled hand upon that sword-hilt which glittered with diamonds worth a monarch's ransom: "no need have ye now to fear secret enemies nor diabolical inquisitors! For, were even a breath to threaten ye with insult, twenty thousand scimitars should gleam on yonder walls, and the very Duke himself should fall upon his knees to implore your pardon. Yes—ye are both safe; and happiness awaits you!"

Thus speaking, the Grand Vizier clapped his hands together, and a slave entered the pavilion from behind the elevated seat on the dais. Ibrahim asked him a question in a language which his relatives did not comprehend: and he seemed pleased by the reply which the menial gave him. He then issued certain orders, and the slave, after making a low obeisance, withdrew.

"Again I say, dearest Flora," continued the Grand Vizier, pressing his sister's hand affectionately, "abandon not thyself to mournful thoughts. For well—Oh! full well can I divine what is now passing in your mind; and in a few moments you shall see if I have rightly conjectured!"

Flora gazed on him with astonishment; for as yet he had said nothing which led her to believe that he was acquainted with her love for the Count of Riverola.

Her eyes were still fixed upon his countenance, while the blushes were rising to her cheeks; when the curtain behind the dais was once more drawn aside, and an exclamation of joy burst from the lips of him who now entered the pavilion by that means of ingress.

"Francisco!" cried Flora, in an ecstacy of joy; and in another moment the lovers were clasped in each other's arms.

"Dearest aunt," whispered Ibrahim to his relative, "if I have sinned deeply in order to open to myself the avenues which lead to power, thou wilt at least admit that the almost sovereign rank which I enjoy has been of some utility in enabling me to bestow happiness on those whom I love."

"My heart is too full of delightful feelings to permit me to utter a single reproach," returned the good dame, in a similarly subdued tone.

"Oh! my beloved Flora!" exclaimed Francisco; "what marvel—what enchantment has thus brought us together once again?"

"And no more to part, Count of Riverola!" said a voice which caused the young nobleman to turn in amazement towards the speaker.

"Pacha! is it indeed you?" cried Francisco, grasping the hand that was extended to him. "It rejoices me much to meet with thee again, that I may renew my thanks for the kind treatment I experienced from thee in Rhodes. But this is an epoch of miracles and mysteries; for 'tis doubtless to thee that I am indebted for this meeting with one whom I so sincerely love—and yet am I at a loss to conceive wherefore you should manifest such interest in either herself or me. Moreover, methought it was into the presence of the Grand Vizier that I was about to enter."

"And you were rightly informed, my lord," said Ibrahim, laughing: "and as for the miracles and the mysteries whereof you speak, they are readily explained in one word. I am the brother of Flora, whom you love!"

"Great and generous prince, how deeply am I indebted to thee!" exclaimed Francisco. "But one boon I implore—and that is on behalf of my sister Nisida! For when the Ottoman soldiers ere now occupied our mansion, they retained her a prisoner, whereas me they sent under escort hither. I beseech your Highness, then, to send forthwith, and order that my sister be restored to perfect freedom——"

"Fear not that she will be treated unworthily," interrupted Ibrahim. "There is some ground to believe that my sister was consigned to the Carmelite Convent solely on account of the attachment subsisting between your

"Can your Highness suppose that I balance for one moment between the alternatives?" exclaimed Francisco, enthusiastically. "Oh! my lord, the greatest boon you can confer upon me is the hand of your sister! And, much as I love Nisida—deeply as I am attached to her—grateful as I feel for all her goodness towards me—yet I cannot permit her to rule me in a matter so closely regarding my life's happiness as this."

"Flora is yours," said the Grand Vizier: "and may all possible felicity await you both!"

Francisco took the blushing maiden's hand, and pressed it to his lips, while the aunt shed tears of joy.

"'LET JUSTICE BE DONE TOWARDS THIS INNOCENT MAN.'" (See p. 128.)

lordship and herself, and that the Lady Nisida was the authoress of that outrage. The offence is freely forgiven; and if I mention it now, it is but to explain the motives which have prompted me to act as I have done in ordering her ladyship to be watched and guarded for the present. But it depends upon you, my lord, whether she be set free so soon as a messenger can speed hence to the Riverola palace, or whether she be retained a prisoner for a few hours longer. In a word, 'tis for your lordship to decide at once whether my sister Flora shall remain in Florence as the Countess of Riverola; or whether she shall bid adieu to her native city for ever, and accompany me to Constantinople."

"And now you understand," resumed Ibrahim, "wherefore I have ordered the Lady Nisida to be retained a prisoner in the Riverola palace—that she may not become acquainted with this alliance until it shall be too late to prevent it. It now remains with your lordship to determine how long your sister shall thus be kept under coercion."

"I am too fearful of losing this jewel, through some misfortune as yet unforeseen," said Francisco, taking Flora's hand again, "not to be anxious to secure possession of it as soon as possible. Our union may be celebrated privately and without useless pomp and ceremony: a few hours hence may see us allied to part no more. I have a friend in Florence—Fernand Wagner——"

"And if he be your friend, Count, you cannot possess one more likely to be sincere," exclaimed Ibrahim-Pacha.

"He has, indeed, proved a warm friend to me," continued Francisco. "Two days ago I was stretched upon a bed of sickness—delirious—my mind wandering—reason gone——"

"Merciful heavens!" cried Flora, shuddering from head to foot, and contemplating her intended husband with the deepest solicitude.

"Yes—I was indeed in a desperate state," said the Count. "But Wagner came—he breathed words of hope in my ears, and I recovered rapidly—so rapidly and so completely that I feel not as if I had ever known indisposition save by name. I was, however, about to observe that there is an oratory in Signor Wagner's mansion; and there may the holy ceremony be performed. Fernand is moreover well acquainted with the language by which the deaf and dumb communicate their ideas; and through friendship for me, he will break the tidings of my marriage to my sister."

"Be it as you propose," said the Grand Vizier; then, after a moment's pause, he added, speaking in a low and mysterious whisper, "And if you will not shrink from the contact of the renegade at the altar of God—a renegade in name only and not in heart—a renegade to suit his worldly purposes, and not from conviction—then shall I be present at the ceremony. Yes!" he continued, perceiving that his aunt, his sister, and the young Count surveyed him with mingled amazement and pleasure;—yes—in a deep disguise will I quit the encampment and enter Florence; for it would grieve me—grieve me deeply to be excluded from the solemn scene."

"Dearest Alessandro—for thus you will permit me still to call you," exclaimed his aunt, "your words have made my happiness complete. Oh! you are still a Christian in heart—thank God! The Holy Virgin be praised!"

"Not for worlds would I that you should be absent from the ceremony which makes your sister the Countess of Riverola!" exclaimed Francisco.

The arrangements, so happily come to and so amicably digested, were now to be carried into effect. The expectant bridegroom accordingly took a temporary leave of the Grand Vizier, Flora, and the aunt, and returned into the city to seek his friend, Fernand Wagner, it being understood that those whom he had just left should meet him at that signor's mansion by mid-day.

For the morning was now breaking; and every roof-top in Florence was crowded with persons anxious to obtain a view of the encampment, as we stated at the close of the preceding chapter.

CHAPTER LXXIII.

THE APPROACH OF THE CATASTROPHE.

IT was an hour past mid-day; and Nisida was seated at the window of one of the splendid saloons in the Riverola palace—apparently gazing upon the parterres of variegated flowers in the garden beneath, but in reality pondering on the sudden and alarming check which her grand schemes had received by the presence of Ibrahim-Pacha and the Ottoman army before Florence.

For, full well could she divine wherefore she was placed under restraint—wherefore the mansion had been occupied by Turkish guards, and herself kept a prisoner within its walls, while her brother had been hurried away! Moreover, without having positively heard that Flora and her aunt had been released from the dungeons of the Inquisition, she naturally felt certain that this deliverance of the captives would immediately take place, either by fair means or foul; and she could not close her eyes upon the disagreeable fact, nor shut out from her mind the mortifying—nay, the maddening conviction, that the hated Grand Vizier would succeed in effecting an alliance between his sister and the young Count of Riverola!

Yes—he would succeed in his object; and Nisida was powerless! Even were there no guards in the corridors—no sentries beneath the windows—even were she free to quit the mansion at will, what plan could she adopt—what weapon could she wield—what artifice or subtlety would now avail her, to counteract the intentions of one who came with a mighty army at his back?

Tremendous was the rage that filled the soul of Nisida—that proud, haughty, and indomitable soul which rebelled against constraint, as a lioness chafes in her cage. The flashings of the lady's brilliant black eyes were terrible—terrible; and could Wagner have beheld her now, he would have fancied that the time must have been a mere dream when he saw those glorious orbs speak the eloquent language of love! Her bosom heaved like the stormy ocean; and she sat, with her hands clasped and her lips compressed—a very Juno in the imposing majesty of her ire!

By insensible degrees, and without any actual encouragement on her part, a thread of ideas and reminiscences connected with Wagner interwove itself amidst the tangled skein of her thoughts. Her mind appeared to possess the attribute of duality; for while her meditation upon baffled schemes and blasted aims lost no portion of its painful intensity, she also found herself pondering, with a distinctness not impaired by this simultaneousness of two separate trains of thought, on all the pleasure and felicity she had enjoyed on the island with Fernand Wagner!

Her affection for him rapidly revived with all its original ardour; she mentally reviewed every feature of his wondrously handsome countenance—the remembrance of his strange and wild destiny awoke a powerful interest in her bosom—and she was just giving way to an earnest hope of soon meeting him again, when—lo, she suddenly beheld his tall, graceful, and manly form advancing along the path that led through the gardens to the principal entrance of the mansion!

She started from her seat in boundless astonishment and thrilling joy, and waved her hand to bid him quicken his pace.

He saw the signal—he recognised Nisida—and he did hasten his steps: but his heart felt not towards her as enthusiastically as it once had done;—for the conviction that she was cruel and relentless, selfish and vindictive in disposition, was now more deeply seated in his mind.

The sentinels at first refused admittance to Fernand Wagner; for they had received positive orders not to allow any one, save her female attendants, to approach Nisida until further instructions should be issued :—but he displayed the signet-ring of the Grand Vizier—and that was a talisman which made the points of scimitars sink towards the ground and heads bow in respectful recognition of the undisputable passport.

In a few minutes Wagner was alone with Nisida.

She threw herself into his arms, and embraced him so fervently—so ardently—so enthusiastically, that she failed to perceive, in the excitement of her soul, that he returned not her caresses with an equal ardour.

"Oh! my beloved Fernand," she whispered in a tone scarcely audible, "how rejoiced am I that we thus meet again! I have been longing for this happy moment;—but why—oh! why did we ever part? Alas! it was my fault—I left thee—I abandoned thee, for the sake of projects which will now most probably experience complete frustration! Fernand," she added, in a slower and more solemn tone, as she buried her blushing countenance in his breast, "had I known then that I was in a way to become a mother, I do not believe that I should ever have had the heart or the courage to leave thee!"

"Nisida! is it possible?" said Wagner, also speaking in as low a tone as he could—for he saw that his mistress still maintained the simulation of deafness and dumbness in respect to the world generally: but he was greatly affected at the tidings which had just met his ears—for he was to become a father, and his own fate was as yet involved in such uncertainty that he knew not how soon he might have to surrender up his breath!

"Yes, Fernand," continued Nisida, hanging to his neck in so loving and tender a manner that he could not repulse her, although he no longer derived pleasure from the contact of that woman of glorious beauty: "in a few months I shall become a mother—and our child must bear its father's name! I am already wearied of my return to the great world—I long to go back to the Mediterranean isle where we passed so many happy days—and if my dear brother Francisco should escape that snares that are now laid to force him into a marriage which——"

"Nisida," interrupted Fernand, now gently disengaging himself from her embrace, but taking her hand kindly,—"prepare yourself to receive tidings——"

"Ah! I understand you," she said abruptly, her entire countenance undergoing a sudden change; and for a moment she seemed as if she were choking :—but subduing her emotions with an amazing effort, she added slowly, as she fixed her flashing eyes upon Wagner, "Francisco is then already united to the hated Flora!"

"Nisida, I implore you to crush this spite—to stifle

this animosity against a young lady who has never done you harm, and whom you should now tutor yourself to love as a sister!" urged the generous-hearted Wagner.

But she whom he thus addressed made no reply :—with her eyes now bent upon the floor, and one hand remaining listlessly in that of Fernand, she was wrapped up in a reverie of the most absorbing nature.

Wagner pressed her hand gently to recall her attention to himself, that he might pursue the theme which he had entered upon ; but, suddenly starting, as if some new idea flashed to her mind, Nisida said, in a deep-toned though whispering voice, "When will the bridegroom bring his bride hither ?—for that I may expect them soon, I am well convinced !"

"They are even now on their way to the mansion," answered Wagner ; "and they are coming alone,—not as the Count and Countess of Riverola should come on such an occasion—but without attendants—without retainers —that they may escape observation——"

"Enough !" said Nisida, in a tone so strange, mysterious, and foreboding, that Fernand surveyed her with curiosity and alarm. "I can well divine wherefore Francisco is bringing hither his bride in such haste," she added, while her countenance assumed an expression awfully fiendish and unearthly in its rancorous hate : "my brother will fulfil his father's dying injunctions,— and Flora—the detested Flora will view a spectacle, and, if she survive it, receive a warning which will make her repent—bitterly repent her entrance into the family of Riverola ! But, come, Fernand—come !—I have no secrets from thee !" she said, in a whisper that hissed snake-like between her half-compressed lips.

It was evident to Wagner that his mistress was labouring under the influence of emotions as terrible as her last words were unintelligible but appallingly ominous ; and, not knowing how to act—nor what to say,—urged on, too, by some secret influence which prompted him to obey her, but which he could not resist, —he suffered her to lead him hastily away from the apartment.

On they went—through the long corridors and winding passages of the spacious mansion,—past the Turkish sentries, who fell back with a low obeisance as Wagner showed them the signet-ring of the Grand Vizier,—on— on, until Nisida conducted her companion into a chamber, the door of which she closed behind them.

Fernand started—for it was the one into which, when muffled up in his cloak, he had penetrated a few nights previously ; and he knew not why—but he felt that kind of oppressive sensation—that action of a mental presentiment on the physical condition, which serves as a warning to mortals of some grand and important event being at hand !

Nisida observed not that Wagner evinced agitation ; for she herself was fearfully excited ;—and her eyes seemed to flash fire.

Still retaining his hand firmly locked in her own, she led him behind the thick, ample, and flowing drapery of the couch ; and when they were both concealed in that place, she said in a hurried, hollow whisper, "Move not, Fernand—remain quiet as the dead,—suspend even your very breathing! For—hark—footsteps approach! Silence—silence—silence !"

And she pressed his hand violently, in the physical convulsiveness of her own awful emphasis.

And Wagner—stupefied, astounded—was motionless as a corpse !

In a few moments the door opened slowly—gave admittance to two persons—and was then closed and locked by one of them.

"Flora, my beloved Flora," said the well-known voice of Francisco, "it is in obedience to the dying commands of my father that I have brought thee hither now— hither into the very chamber where he breathed his last !"

"Francisco, you are pale—very pale !" exclaimed the bride, in a tone tremulous with anxiety. "Oh ! what is the meaning of this mysterious visit to the room where his late lordship gave up the ghost "

"Fear not, my adored bride—for such, thank heaven, you now are," replied Francisco ; "but grant me your attention for a few minutes ! You are well aware—for it was a matter of common gossip in the household—that yon cabinet, whereon my seals are set, has long been closed :—but it is now to be opened by us—by us, who are alone in this chamber together ! Tremble not, my beloved : what cause can we have to fear ? Doubtless the contents of that cabinet will prove of service to us in some way or another ;—for thus spoke my father to me

on his death bed :—' *Upon the day of your marriage, when-ever such an event may occur, I enjoin you to open the door of that closet. You must be accompanied by your bride—and by no other living soul. I also desire that this may be done with the least possible delay after the matrimonial ceremony, the very day—the very morning—within the very hour after you quit the church. That closet contains the means of elucidating a mystery profoundly connected with me—with you—with the family,—a mystery, the development of which may prove of incalculable service alike to yourself and to her who may share your title and wealth. But should you never marry, then must the closet remain unvisited by you ; nor need you trouble yourself concerning the eventful discovery of the secret which it contains, by any persons into whose hands the mansion may fall after your death. It is also my wish that your sister should remain in complete ignorance of the instructions which I am now giving you. Alas ! poor girl—she cannot hear the words which fall from my lips ; neither shall you communicate their import to her by writing, nor by the language of the fingers. And remember that while I bestow upon you my blessing—my dying blessing—may that blessing become a withering curse—the curse of hell upon you—if in any way you violate one tittle of the injunctions which I have now given you.'* Thus spoke my father on his death-bed, dearest Flora," added Francisco, in a tone of deep emotion : "the words are impressed on my memory as if they still rang in my ears ;—and now we have come to do his bidding !"

"Oh, yes," murmured the Countess-bride, trembling from head to foot ; haste thou, my Francisco, to obey your lamented sire's commands—and avoid, oh ! avoid the consequence of that withering curse !"

"Thou speakest like one who is as sensible as she is tender and loving," replied Francisco : "and heaven grant that the contents of this mysterious closet may indeed prove of incalculable service to us both !"

The young Count took his charming wife's hand, and led her up to the very door of that mysterious cabinet, the seals of which he hastily broke off :—then, taking the key from the bosom of his doublet, he said, in a tone indicative of the most acute suspense and profound curiosity, "Now, my beloved Flora, for the grand secret !"

At the same moment—impelled by some irresistible influence—Wagner advanced his countenance from behind the hangings of the couch, in such a way that he was enabled to obtain a full view of the mysterious cabinet, the door of which was about to open !

CHAPTER LXXIV.

THE key grated in the lock of the mysterious cabinet— the door was opened—the young Countess of Riverola uttered a dreadful scream, while her husband gave vent to an ejaculation of horror and wild amazement :—for appalling was the spectacle which burst upon their view.

Nor were that scream and that ejaculation the only expressions of fearfully excited emotions which the opening of the closet called forth :—for, at the same instant, a cry of mingled wonder and joy burst from the lips of Fernand Wagner ; and, forgetting that he was betraying the presence of Nisida, as well as his own—forgetting all and everything save the prophecy of the Rosicrucian chief and the spectacle now before him—he sprang from behind the curtain—rushed towards the open cabinet—and, falling on his knees, exclaimed triumphantly, "I am saved! I am saved!"

For, behold ! in that closet, two bleached and perfect skeletons were suspended to a beam ;—and a voice whispered in Wagner's ear, that the spell of the Demon was now broken for ever,—while his inmost soul seemed to sing the canticle of a blessed salvation !

Yes : there—in that cabinet—suspended side by side— were the two skeletons,—horrible—hideous to gaze upon !

It is scarcely possible to convey to the reader an adequate idea of the wild emotions—the conflicting thoughts—and the clashing sentiments, which the dread revelation of that ghastly spectacle suddenly excited in the hearts of the four persons now assembled together— stirring up and agitating terribly all their acutest feelings, as the hurricane, abruptly bursting forth, takes up the withered leaves and scattered straws, and whirls them round and round as if they were in the eddies of the Maelstroom.

Here was Flora clinging to her husband in speechless

horror,—there was Wagner on his knees before the open cabinet: here was Francisco gazing in astonishment on his sister,—and there was Nisida herself, wrapt up in the stupefaction of bewilderment at the conduct of her lover!

But, oh! wondrous—amazing—and almost incredible sight!—what change comes over the person of Fernand Wagner?

There—even there, as he kneels,—and now—even now, as his looks remain bent upon the ghastly skeletons which seem to grin with their fleshless mouths, and to look forth with their eyeless sockets,—yes—even there and even now—is an awful and a frightful change taking place in him whom Nisida loves so well:—for his limbs rapidly lose their vigour, and his form its uprightness—his eyes, bright and gifted with the sight of an eagle, grow dim and failing—the hair disappears from the crown of his head, leaving it completely bald—his brow and his cheeks shrivel up into countless wrinkles—his beard becomes long, flowing, and white as threads of silver—his mouth falls in, brilliant teeth sustaining the lips no more —and with the hollow moan of an old, old man, whose years are verging fast towards a century, the dying Wagner sinks upon the floor!

"Merciful God!" exclaimed Nisida, in a paroxysm of dreadful anguish, mingled with amazement and alarm; then, as if overwhelmed by the blow which the sudden fate of her lover inflicted upon her, she likewise sank down, her heart-strings cracking with burning grief.

For a few moments Francisco and Flora were so astounded by the unsealing of Nisida's lips, that they were riveted to the spot with a stupefaction which rendered them powerless and motionless.

"Take me away from him—bear me hence!" shrieked Nisida, endeavouring to raise herself from the floor, and averting her head with ineffable loathing from the changed form of him whom she had loved so madly. "Bear me hence, I say—Francisco—my brother—take me hence! take me hence!"—then, falling back again, while a ghastly pallor overspread her entire countenance, and her bosom palpitated so violently with her painful gaspings, that it seemed as if the corsage of her dress must burst, she exclaimed, "Holy Virgin! I am dying!"

"Say not so, my beloved sister!" cried Francisco, now springing forward to assist her; while Flora, recovering her self-possession somewhat at the same moment, hastened to aid her husband in raising his wretched sister.

"No—no!" said Nisida, extending her arms to repulse the proffered services of the amiable young Countess, on whom the malignant woman darted glances of burning hate; "keep off—keep off! Touch me not! I would sooner die here—*here*," she added, pointing to the immediate vicinity of Wagner, who lay at the point of death on the floor.

Flora fell back, tears streaming down her cheeks—for this demonstration of Nisida's aversion cut her to the very soul. But, as her eyes fell on Wagner, she forgot her own emotions—brushed away her tears—and, kneeling down, supported the head of that old—old man, who was dying rapidly with a smile on his countenance,—a heavenly smile of ineffable hope!

Francisco conveyed his sister to the couch on which their father had breathed his last; and, in a hasty whisper, he intimated his intention of sending for medical assistance.

"No—no," murmured Nisida, seizing him by the hand: "not yet—not yet! You have not yet performed all that yourself and your bride have to fulfil in respect to yon cabinet. Behold—on a little shelf in that closet—there is a manuscript," she added in a faint and tremulous tone; "'tis for you and Flora to read—to study it—together!"

"But you, my dear sister—you, who have so marvellously recovered the faculties of speech and hearing—oh! I must save you," cried Francisco, bending over her, and pressing his lips to her heated brow; "for you are ill—dangerously ill—the shock was too much—"

At that moment Flora uttered a faint scream; Francisco turned his eyes hastily towards her; and a single glance showed him that she was now supporting the head of the lifeless Wagner, as she knelt upon the floor.

Francisco pressed his sister's hand in silent assurance that he would return to her side in a few moments; and he then hastened to raise his horror-striken bride from her kneeling posture, and to remove her from contact with the corpse.

Leading her to the door, he said in a rapid but tender manner, "Retire for a short time, my beloved one! God knows how innocent I am of having prepared all these accumulated horrors for our bridal day! Retire and compose yourself, dearest Flora: I will join thee presently!"

"Feel not alarmed on my account—not grieved, my Francisco!" answered his charming wife, in a low and melting tone: "for that old man, who doubtless was a saint in mortal guise, promised us long years of happiness —yes, gave me that assurance with his dying breath, and I believe him!"

She then pressed her husband's hand affectionately, and hurried from the room.

Francisco immediately took his handkerchief, and threw it over the countenance of Fernand Wagner's corpse,—that countenance which still appeared to wear the bland and heavenly smile of a soul filled with sure and certain hope of eternal salvation!

Then, advancing towards the closet, he possessed himself of the manuscript which, as Nisida had declared, lay rolled up on a little shelf: and, having secured it about his person, he hastily shut and locked the door which had revealed so frightful—so appalling a spectacle.

In the meantime Nisida lay, stretched out upon her side, on the couch to which her brother had transported her. She was motionless—but alive:—and she kept her eyes closed that she might the better prevent her thoughts from settling themselves entirely on the dreadful change which had rendered her lover loathsome to her in his last moments. For as she lay in her present position—and being unable, through the sudden paralysis which had seized on her lower extremities, to move herself round—her looks must have fallen on the corpse of Wagner, had she not maintained her eyes shut.

"Nisida—my sister!" said the low and flute-like voice of Francisco, as he bent over her again: "arouse thyself —there is naught now to horrify thee, my sweet sister— I have covered over the face of the departed one;—and, even if I had not, its lineaments are those of a saint, and there is nothing terrible in them!"

The lady opened her large black eyes, the fire of which was already dimmed; and, pressing her hand to her brow as if to collect her thoughts, she appeared to struggle against the numbness and the stupefying influence that had come over her a few moments before, when she lay with her lids closed.

"Francisco," she said at length, removing her hand from her forehead and extending it to him, "I have a boon—a favour to implore of thee; and perchance—if thou wilt grant it—I may yet recover from the dreadful shock which I experienced through the transformation of that man whom I so fondly loved."

"Didst thou then love Fernand Wagner, dearest sister?" asked Francisco, receiving this announcement with unfeigned surprise.

"I loved him madly—passionately!" exclaimed Nisida, her eyes again recovering their wonted fire—but only for a short time. "Of *that*, however, let me not speak now," she added, her tone suddenly becoming mournful and plaintive. "I said that I required a favour at thy hands——"

"'Tis granted already, dear sister, even before the words which explain it pass thy lips!" cried Francisco. "Name thy demand, my beloved Nisida—thou who art, if possible, doubly dear to me, now that the tones of thy sweet voice fall upon my ears!"

"Thou hast not yet fulfilled the wishes of thy father, Francisco," said Nisida, raising her eyes towards him almost in a reproachful manner. "'Tis for thee and thy bride to make yourselves, together and at the same time, acquainted with all the mysteries which that dread cabinet was intended to reveal; and this wast thou commanded to do with the least possible delay after thy nuptials. The boon, I crave, then, is that thou wilt at once fulfil the last injunctions of thy departed sire,— here—in this room—and by the side of this bed whereon I am stretched, and where our father breathed his last!"

"Holy Virgin! Nisida," exclaimed Francisco, "wouldst thou have me again open that frightful depository of a horrible mystery——"

"No: I would have thee elucidate that mystery!" interrupted Nisida, her voice becoming stronger with the excitement of her feelings. "Did not our father declare that yourself and your bride must through the medium of that cabinet's contents, learn a secret of value and utility to you both? and did you not swear to obey all his injunctions?"

"That is true—perhaps too true!" said Francisco, mournfully. "And the manuscript——"

"Will reveal your father's meaning!" exclaimed Nisida. "It is penned by his own hand, and contains the sad and shocking narrative of our dear mother's fate!" she ad'ed, suddenly sinking her voice to a low and plaintive whisper. "Go, then, Francisco," she continued, her tone again becoming excited: "fetch hither thy newly-married Flora—fear not that I shall receive her harshly *now*—for a sacred duty is to be performed, and she must be present!"

"It shall be as you say, Nisida," returned Francisco, after a few moments' profound reflection: "and may the readiness which my amiable bride will manifest in yielding compliance with this requisition—may it, I say, find favour for her in your eyes."

The Count of Riverola then quitted the room;—and the moment the door closed behind him, Nisida's countenance became suddenly animated with an infernal triumph; and, clasping her hands together in the excitement of a savage hope, she murmured to herself, "Now, Flora, shalt thou hear revelations so awful, the narrative of deeds so appalling, that if thy spirit be not crushed, and if thy heart be not broken by the overwhelming details of that accursed history—then art thou indeed worthy to bear the name of Riverola! And now, too, Flora—hated, detested Flora—wilt thou hear the whole of that manuscript whereof thy base curiosity once prompted thee to read a few lines—and those lines of such terrible import!"

Scarcely had Nisida reached this point in her dreadful musings, when Francisco returned, leading into the room his lovely bride, whose countenance was very pale, and who approached the bed with downcast eyes.

"Draw chairs close to the couch, Francisco," said Nisida; "and seat yourselves near me. There! and now prepare, both of ye, to hear the revelation of the most tremendous secret that was ever nourished in the bosom of an Italian family."

Francisco cast a rapid and imploring glance upon Flora,—a glance which besought her to nerve herself with all her courage to endure the disclosure of a mystery which the ominous words of Nisida promised to be very dreadful.

The beauteous bride responded by a look which reassured her anxious husband: and Nisida having made a sign of impatience, Francisco began to read aloud that fearful document, the contents of which will be found in the ensuing chapter.

CHAPTER LXXV.

THE MANUSCRIPT.

"In order that you, Francisco—and she who as your bride, shall accompany you on your visit to the secret cabinet wherein you are destined to find this manuscript, —in order, I say, that you may both fully comprehend the meaning of the strange and frightful spectacle there prepared to meet your eyes, it is necessary that I should enter into a full and perfect detail of certain circumstances, the study of which will I hope prove beneficial to the lady whom you may honour with the proud name of RIVEROLA.

"In the year 1494 I visited Naples on certain pecuniary business, an intimation of which I found amongst the private papers of my father, who had died about ten months previously. I was then just one-and-twenty, and had not as yet experienced the influence of the tender passion. I had found the Florentine ladies so inveterately given to intrigue, and had seen so many instances in which the best and most affectionate of husbands were grossly deceived by their wives, that I had not only conceived an abhorrence at the idea of linking my fortunes with one of my own fellow country-women, but even made a solemn vow that if ever I married, my choice should not fall on a Tuscan. It was with such impressions as these that I quitted Florence on the business to which I have alluded; and I cared not if I never returned thither—so shallow, heartless, and superficial did its gay society appear to me.

"On my arrival at Naples I assumed the name of Cornari, and representing myself as a young man of humble birth and moderate fortunes, mixed in the best society that would receive a stranger of such poor pretensions. I had already learnt at Florence that the fair sex are invariably dazzled by titles and riches, and I had a curiosity to try whether I should be at all sought after when apparently unpossessed of such qualifications. Not that I had any serious thoughts of matrimony; for indeed I was far from being so romantic as to suppose that any beautiful lady of high birth would fall in love with me so long as I passed as plain *Signor Cornari*. No: it was a mere whim of mine;—would that I had never, never undertaken to gratify it!

"I was altogether unattended by any retinue, having quitted Florence with only a single valet, who died of sudden illness on the road. Thus did I enter Naples alone, with my packages of necessaries fastened to the saddle of the steed that bore me. I put up at a small but respectable hostel; and the first few days of my residence in the Neapolitan capital were passed in making inquiries concerning the individual whose large debt to my deceased father had been the principal cause of my journey thither. I found him at length; but perceiving that he was totally unable to liquidate my claim upon him, I did not discover my real name, and took my leave, resolving to think no more of the matter. Returning to the inn, I happened to pass through one of the most squalid and miserable parts of the city, when my attention was suddenly fixed upon the most charming female figure I had ever seen in my life. The object of my interest was respectably but plainly clad: indeed, she appeared to belong to the class of petty tradespeople. Her form was most perfect in its symmetry; her gait was peculiarly graceful, and her manners were evidently modest and reserved—for she looked neither to the right nor to the left, but pursued her way with all the unobtrusiveness of strict propriety. I longed to behold her face; and, quickening my steps, presently passed her. I then had an opportunity of beholding the most beautiful countenance that ever adorned a woman. Heaven seemed to smile through the mirror of her mild black eyes; and there was such an indescribable sweetness in the general expression of her face, that it might have served a limner to copy for the countenance of an angel!

"She saw that I gazed intently upon her, and instantly turned aside into another street; for I should observe that females of the lower orders in Naples are not permitted to wear veils. I stood looking after her until she was lost to my view; and then I went slowly back to the inn, my mind full of the image of the beauteous unknown. Day after day did I rove through that same quarter of the city in the hope of meeting her again; and every evening did I return to my lonely chamber chagrined with disappointment. My spirits sank—my appetite fled—and I grew restless and melancholy. At length I one morning beheld her in the flower-market: and I stood gazing on her with such enthusiastic, and yet respectful admiration, that though she turned away, still methought it was not with resentment. I was transfixed to the spot for some minutes; and it was not until she had disappeared amidst the crowd gathered in that quarter, that I could so far collect my scattered thoughts as to curse my folly for having omitted such an opportunity of accosting her. I however inquired of an old woman, of whom she had purchased some flowers, who she was; but all the information I could glean was that she had recently been in the habit of buying a few flowers every Wednesday of that same old woman. I went away more contented than I had felt for many days; because I now felt certain that I knew where to meet the lovely creature again. Nevertheless, during the six succeeding days I rambled about the flower-market and the squalid quarter of the city where I had first seen her; but my search was unsuccessful—and the greater the disappointment I experienced, the more powerful grew my love. Yes:—it was indeed love which I now felt for the first time, and for a being to whom I had never spoken—whom I had only seen twice, and on each of those occasions but for a few minutes—and whom I knew by her garb to belong to the poorer orders.

"But on the following Wednesday I saw her for the third time; and when she beheld me standing near the old woman's flower-stall, she appeared vexed and surprised, and was about to turn away. I, however, approached her, besought her to accept of the choicest nosegay which I had been able to find, and continued to speak to her in so ardent yet respectful a manner, that she no longer viewed me with resentment, but with something approaching to interest. And if I had been charmed by her beauty when as yet I had seen her at a comparative distance, how enraptured was I now by a nearer contemplation of that heavenly countenance. I assured her that her image had never been absent from my heart since I first saw her—that I should never know happiness again unless she would give me some hope—

and that I would sooner die than have her construe my words into an insult. She was touched by the earnestness and evident sincerity of my manner; and, encouraged somewhat even by her silence, I proceeded hastily to inform her that my name was Cornari—that I was a young man of humble birth—but that I possessed a modest competency, and was my own master. I then pressed her to accept my nosegay; but suddenly bursting into tears, she exclaimed, '*Oh, signor, you know not whom you have thus honoured with your notice*,' and hurried away, leaving me absolutely stupefied with astonishment and grief.

"It immediately struck me that she was a lost and degraded creature who dared not respond to a virtuous love. But a few minutes' reflection told me that such innocence—such artlessness—such candour never could be assumed—never feigned: no—they were most natural! And this conviction, added to the intense curiosity which now inspired me to fathom the mystery of her singular remark, rendered me more anxious than ever to meet with her again. Several weeks passed without seeing the gratification of my wish; and I was becoming seriously ill with disappointment and defeated hope, when accident led me to encounter her once more. She would have avoided me; but I absolutely compelled her to stop, Seizing her hand, I said, 'Look at me—behold to what I am reduced—mark these pale and sunken cheeks—and have pity upon me!' 'And I, too,' she murmured, 'have been very miserable since last we met.'—'Then you have thought of me?' I exclaimed, retaining her hand still in mine, and reading love in the depths of her large dark eyes.—'I have, I have,' she answered bitterly, withdrawing her hand at the same time; then in a tone of deep anguish, she added, 'I implore you to let me proceed on my way; and if you value your own happiness you will never seek me more.' —'But my happiness depends on seeing you often,' I exclaimed; 'and if the offer of an honest heart be acceptable, I have that to give.'—She shuddered dreadfully from head to foot.—'Surely you are not married already?' I said, rendered almost desperate by her strange and incomprehensible manner.—'I married!' she absolutely shrieked forth: then, perceiving that I was perfectly amazed and horrified by the wild vehemence of her ejaculation, she said in a subdued and profoundly melancholy tone, 'I adjure you to think of me no more!' —'Listen, beauteous stranger,' I exclaimed; 'I love and adore you. My happiness is at stake. Repeat that cruel adjuration, and you inflict a death-blow. If I be loathsome to your sight, tell me so: but leave me not a prey to the most horrible suspense. If you have a father, I will accompany you to him, and make honourable proposals.'—'My father!' she murmured, while her countenance was suddenly swept by a passing expression of anguish so intense that I began to tremble for her reason. I implored her to speak candidly and openly, and not in brief sentences of such ominous mystery. She scarcely appeared to listen to my words, but seemed totally absorbed in the mental contemplation of a deeply seated woe. At length she suddenly turned her large dark eyes upon me, and said in a low, plaintive, profoundly touching tone, 'Signor Cornari, again I adjure you to think of me no more. But, for my own sake, I would not have you believe that unmaidenly conduct on my part is the cause of the solemn prayer I thus make to you. No, no; I have naught wherewith I can reproach myself: but there are reasons of terrible import that compel me to address you in this manner. Nevertheless,' she added more slowly and hesitatingly, 'if you really should continue to entertain so deep an interest in me as to render you desirous to hear *the last explanation* from my lips, then you may rely upon meeting me on this spot, and at the same hour, fifteen days hence.' —And she hurried away.

"How that fortnight passed I can scarcely tell. To me it appeared an age. I was deeply—madly enamoured of that strange, beauteous, and apparently conscientious being; and the mystery which involved her threw around her a halo of interest that fanned the flame of my passion. I was prepared to make any sacrifice rather than abandon all hope of calling her my own. The proud title of Riverola was nothing in my estimation when weighed in the balance against her charms—her bewitching manner—her soft, retiring modesty. I moreover flattered myself that I loved her all the more sincerely, because I reflected, that if she gave her heart to me, it would be to the poor and humble Cornari, and not to the rich and mighty Lord of Riverola. At length the day—the memorable day came; and she failed not to keep her appointment. She was pale—very pale, but exquisitely beautiful; and she smiled in spite of herself when she beheld me. She endeavoured to conceal her emotions; but she could not altogether subdue the evidence of that gratification which my presence caused her. 'You have disregarded my earnest prayer?' she said in a low and agitated tone.—'My happiness depends upon you,' I answered: 'in the name of heaven keep me not in suspense: but tell me, can you and will you be mine?'—'I could be thine, but I dare not,' she replied in a voice scarcely audible.—'Reveal to me the meaning of this strange contradiction, I implore you,' said I, again a prey to the most torturing suspense. 'Do you love another?'—'Did I love another,' she exclaimed, withdrawing her hand which I had taken, 'I should not be here this day.'—'Pardon me,' I cried; 'I would not offend thee for worlds! If you do not love another, can you love me?'—Again she allowed me to take her hand! and this concession, together with the rapid but eloquent glance she threw upon me, was the answer to my question.—'Then, if you can love me,' I urged, 'why cannot you be mine?'—'Because,' she replied in that tone of bitterness which did me harm to hear it, 'you are born of parents whose name and calling you dare mention; whereas you would loathe me as much as you now declare that you love me, were you to learn who my father is! For mother, alas! I have none: she has been dead many, many years.'—And tears streamed down her cheeks. I also wept, so deeply did I sympathise with her.—'Beloved girl,' I exclaimed, 'you wrong me! What is it to me if your father be even the veriest wretch, the greatest criminal that crawls upon the face of the earth, so long as you are pure and innocent?'—'No, no,' she cried hastily, 'you misunderstand me! There breathes not a more upright man than my father!—'Then wherefore should I be ashamed to own my marriage with his daughter?' I asked in an impassioned manner.—'Because,' she said, in a tone of such intense anguish that it rent my heart as she began to speak; 'because,' she repeated slowly and emphatically, 'he is viewed with abhorrence by that world which is so unjust; for that which constitutes the awful stigma is an hereditary office in his family—an office that he dares not vacate under pain of death; and now you can too well comprehend that my sire is the PUBLIC EXECUTIONER OF NAPLES!'

"This announcement came upon me like a thunderbolt. I turned sick at heart—my eyes grew dim—my brain whirled—I staggered, and should have fallen had I not come in contact with a wall. It appeared to me afterwards that sobs of ineffable agony fell upon my ears, while I was yet in a state of semi-stupefaction— and methought likewise that a delicate, soft hand pressed mine convulsively for a moment. Certain it was that when I recovered my presence of mind,—when I was enabled to collect my scattered thoughts,—the executioner's daughter was no longer near me. I was in despair at the revelation which had been made,—overwhelmed with grief, too, at having suffered her thus to depart—for I feared that I should never see her more. Before me was my hopeless love—behind me, like an evil dream, was the astounding announcement, which still rang in my ears, though breathed in such soft and plaintive tones! Three or four minutes were wasted in the struggles of conflicting thoughts, ere I was sufficiently master of myself to remember that I might still overtake the maiden who had fled from me, It struck me that her father's dwelling must be near the criminal prison; and this was in the squalid quarter of the town where I had first encountered her. Thither I sped—into the dark streets, so perilous after dusk, I plunged: and at length I overtook the object of my affection just as she was skirting the very wall of the prison. I seized her by the hand, and implored her to forgive me for the manner in which I had received the *last explanation* to which I had urged her.—'It was natural that you should shrink in loathing from the bare idea,' she said in a tone which rent my heart. 'And now leave me, signor; for farther conversation between us is useless.'—'No,' I exclaimed; 'I will not leave you, until I shall have exacted from you a promise that you will be mine! For I could not live without you; and most unjust should I be, most unworthy of the name of a man, if I were to allow a contemptible prejudice to stand in the way of my happiness.'—She returned no answer, but the rapidity of her breathing and the ill-subdued sobs which interrupted her respiration at short intervals, convinced me that a fierce struggle was taking place within her bosom. For it was now quite dark, and I could not see her face: the hand, however, which I held clasped in my own, trembled violently.—' Beautiful maiden,' I said after a long pause, ' wherefore do you not reply to me? Were I the proudest peer in Christendom, I would sacrifice every consideration of rank and family for your sake. What more can man say? What more can he do?'—' Signor Cornari,' she answered at length, ' prudence tells me to fly from you; but my heart prompts me to remain. Alas! I feel that the latter feeling is dominant within me!'—' And you will be mine?' I demanded eagerly.—' Thine for ever!' she murmured, her head sinking upon my breast.

" But I shall not dwell unnecessarily upon this portion of my narrative. Suffice it to say that we parted, having arranged another meeting for the next evening. It was on this occasion that I said to her, ' Vitangela, I have thought profoundly upon all that passed between us yesterday; and I am more than ever determined to make you my wife. Let us away to your father, and demand his consent to our union.'—' Stay,' she said, in an emphatic tone ; ' and hear me patiently ere you either renew the promise to wed me or reiterate your desire to seek my father. You must know,' she continued, while I listened with painful suspense, ' that my father will not oppose a step in which his daughter's happiness is involved. But the very moment that sees our hands joined will behold the registry of the marriage in the great book kept by the Lieutenant of Police; and thereby will be constituted a record of the name of one who, if need be, must assume the functions of that office which my sire now fills!'—' What mean you, Vitangela?' I demanded, horrified by the dim yet ominous significance of these words.—' I mean,' she continued, ' that the terrible post of Public Executioner must remain in our family as long as this family shall exist; and that those who form marriages with us are considered to enter into the family. When my father dies, my brother will succeed him; but should my brother die without having a son old enough to take his place, *you*, signor, if you become my husband, will be forced to assume the terrible office.'—' But I am not a Neapolitan,' I exclaimed : ' and I should hope that when we are united, you will not insist upon dwelling in Naples.'—' I would give worlds to leave this odious city,' she said, emphatically.—' Nothing detains me here another day, nor another hour,' I cried : ' let the priest unite our hands, and we forthwith set off for Florence. But why should not our marriage take place privately, unknown even to your father? and in that case no entry need be made in the books of the Lieutenant of Police.' —' You have expressed that desire which I myself feared to utter, lest you should think it unmaidenly,' she murmured. ' For your sake I will quit home and kindred without farther hesitation,'—I was rejoiced at this proof of affection and confidence on her part; and it was arranged between us that we should be married on the ensuing evening, and in the most private way possible. Before we parted, however, I drew from her a solemn pledge that, when once she should have become my wife, she would never even allude to her family—that she would not communicate to them the name of her husband nor the place of our abode under any circumstances, —*in a word, that she would consider her father and her brother as dead to her*. With streaming eyes and sobbing breast, she gave me the sacred promise I required, ratifying it with an oath which I made her repeat to my dictation.

" On the ensuing evening Vitangela met me according to the appointment: and it was then that I revealed to her my real name and rank. ' Dearest girl,' I said, ' you gave me your heart, believing me to be a poor and humble individual; and you have consented to abandon home and kindred for my sake. Profoundly, then, do I rejoice that it is in my power to elevate you to a position of which your beauty, your amiability, and your virtue render you so eminently worthy; and in my own native Florence, no lady will be more courted, nor treated with greater distinction than the Countess of Riverola.'—She uttered an exclamation of mingled astonishment and sorrow, and would have fallen to the ground had I not supported her.—' Oh!' she murmured, ' I should have been happier were you indeed the humble and the poor Signor Cornari!'—' No: think not thus,' I urged: ' wealth and rank are two powerful aids to happiness in this life. But at all events, beloved Vitangela, you now recognise more than ever the paramount necessity which exists to induce you to maintain inviolate your solemn vow of yesterday.'—' I require no such inducement to compel me to keep that pledge,' she answered. ' Think not that I will bring disgrace on the name, whether

humble or lofty, with which you have proposed to honour me! Oh! no—never, never!'

" I embraced her fondly; and we proceeded to the dwelling of a priest, by whom our hands were united in the oratory attached to his abode. At daybreak we quitted Naples ; and in due time we reached Florence, where my bride was received with enthusiastic welcome by all the friends of the Riverola family. My happiness appeared to have been established on a solid foundation by this alliance; and the birth of Nisida in 1495—just one year after the marriage—was a bond which seemed to unite our hearts more closely, if possible. Indeed, I can safely assert that not a harsh word ever passed between us, nor did aught occur to mar our complete felicity for some years after our union. But in 1500 a circumstance took place which proved to be the first link in a chain of incidents destined to wield an important influence over my happiness.

" It was in the month of April, of that year—oh! how indelibly is the detested date fixed on my memory—that Duke Piero de Medici gave a grand entertainment to all the aristocracy of Florence. The banquet was of the most splendid description; and the gardens of the palace were brilliantly illuminated. The days of Lorenzo the Magnificent seemed to have been revived for a short period by his degenerate descendant. All the beauty and rank of the Republic were assembled at this festival ; but no lady was more admired for the chaste elegance of her attire, the modest dignity of her deportment, and the loveliness of her person than Vitangela, Countess of Riverola. After the banquet, the company proceeded to the gardens, where bands of music were stationed; and while some indulged in the exhilarating dance, others sauntered through the brilliantly lighted avenues. I need scarcely inform you that no husband, unless he were anxious to draw down upon himself the ridicule which attaches itself to extreme uxoriousness, would remain linked to his wife's side all the evening at such an entertainment as the one of which I am speaking. I was therefore separated from the Countess, who was left in an arbour with some other ladies, while I joined the group which had assembled around the Prince. I know not exactly how it was that I happened to quit my companions, after a lively conversation which had probably lasted about an hour : certain, however, it is that towards midnight I was proceeding alone down a long avenue in which utter darkness reigned, but outside of which the illuminations shone brilliantly. Suddenly I heard voices near me ; and one of them appeared to be that of the Countess of Riverola—but they were speaking in so subdued a tone that I was by no means confident in my suspicion. The voices approached; and a sentiment of curiosity, unaccountable at the time, as I believed Vitangela to be purity itself, impelled me to listen attentively. To conceal myself was not necessary ; I had but to remain perfectly still for my presence to be unknown, utter darkness prevailing in the avenue.

" The persons who were conversing advanced. ' You know,' said the soft and whispering voice which I believed to be that of the Countess,—' you know how sincerely, how tenderly I love you; and what a frightful risk I run in even thus according you a few moments' private discourse?'—The voice of a man gave some reply, the words of which did not reach my ears : then the pair stopped, and I heard the billing sound of kisses. Oh! how my blood boiled in my veins! I grasped the handle of my sword;—but I was nailed to the spot—my state of mind was such that though I longed—I thirsted for immediate vengeance, yet I was powerless—motionless—paralyzed. To the sounds of kisses succeeded those of sobbing and of grief on the part of the lady whose voice had produced such a terrible effect upon me. ' Holy Virgin!' I thought : ' she deplores the fate that chains her to her husband ; she weeps because she has not the courage to fly with her lover!'—and now I experienced just the same sensations as those which stunned and stupefied me on that evening at Naples when I first heard that Vitangela was the daughter of the Public Executioner. Several minutes must have passed while I was in this condition of comparative insensibility—or rather while I was a prey to the stunning conviction that I was deceived by her whom I had loved so well and deemed so pure!

" When I awoke from that dread stupor all was still in the dark avenue—not a footstep, not a whispering voice was heard. I hurried along amidst the trees, my soul racked with the cruellest suspicions. And yet I was not confident that it was positively my wife's voice that I had heard; and the more I pondered upon the circumstance, the more anxious was I to arrive at the conviction that I had indeed been deceived by some voice closely resembling hers. I accordingly hurried back to the arbour where I had last seen her in the company of several Florentine ladies. Joy animated my soul when I beheld Vitangela seated in that arbour, and in the very spot too where I had beheld her upwards of an hour previously. But she was now alone. 'Where are your friends?' I asked, in a kind tone, as I approached and took her hand.—'Indeed I know not,' she replied, casting a hurried glance around, and now appearing surprised to find that there was not another lady near her. She seemed confused—and I also observed that she had been weeping very recently. The joy which had for a moment animated me was now succeeded by a sudden chill that went to my heart death-like—icy. But, subduing my emotion, I said, 'Your ladyship has not surely remained here ever since I last saw you, more than an hour?'—'Yes,' she responded, without daring to raise her eyes to meet mine, —I knew that she lied, most foully lied; her confusion—her whole manner betrayed her. But I exercised a powerful mastery over my mind: the suspicion which I had all along entertained was strengthened greatly, but not altogether confirmed—and I resolved to wait for confirmation ere I allowed my vengeance to burst forth. Moreover, it was necessary to discover who the gallant might be,—the favoured one who had superseded me in the affections of Vitangela! I, however, promised myself that when once my information was complete, my revenge should be terrible;—and this resolution served as a solace for the moment, and as an inducement for me to conceal alike the suspicions I had imbibed and the dreadful pain they had caused me. Presenting my hand, therefore, to Vitangela, I escorted her to that part of the grounds where the company were now assembled, and where I hoped that some accident might make known to me the person of the gallant with whom she had walked in the avenue, Anxiously, but unsuspectedly, did I watch the manner of the Countess every time she returned the salutation of the various nobles and cavaliers whom we encountered in our walk: but not a blush—not a sign of confusion on her part—not one rapidly dealt but significant glance afforded me the clue which I sought. And yet it struck me that she often cast furtive and uneasy, or rather searching looks hither and thither, as if to seek and single out some one individual amidst the multitudes moving about the illuminated gardens. She was certainly preoccupied and mournful: but I affected not to observe that a cloud hung over her spirits; and, in order to throw her completely off her guard, I talked and laughed as gaily as was my wont.

"To be brief, the festivities terminated a little before sunrise; and I conducted the Countess back to our mansion.

"From that night forth I maintained the strictest watch upon her conduct and proceedings: I appointed Margaretha, the mother of my page Antonio, to act the spy upon her;—but weeks and months passed, and nothing transpired to confirm the terrible suspicion that haunted me night and day. I strove to banish that suspicion from my mind—heaven knows how hard I struggled to crush it. But it was immortal—and it beset me as if it were the ghost of some victim whom I had ruthlessly murdered. Vitangela saw that my manner had somewhat altered towards her; and she frequently questioned me on the subject. I, however, gave her evasive replies; for I should have been ashamed to acknowledge my suspicion if it were false, and it was only by keeping her off her guard that I should ever receive confirmation of it if it were true. Thus nearly nine months passed away from the date of the ducal banquet: and then you, Francisco, were born.

"The presence of an heir to my name and wealth was the subject of much congratulation on the part of my friends; but to me it was a source of torturing doubts and racking fears. You never bore the least—no, not the least resemblance, either physical or mental, to me; whereas the very reverse was the case with Nisida, even in her infancy. From the moment of your birth—from the first instant that I beheld you in the nurse's arms,—the most agonizing feelings took possession of my soul. Were you indeed *my* son?—or were you a pledge of adulterous love? Merciful heavens! in remembering all I suffered when those terrible thoughts oppressed me, I wonder that you, Francisco, should now be alive—that I did not strangle you as you lay in your cradle. And, O God! how dearly I could have loved you, Francisco, had I felt the same confidence in my paternity as in that of

your sister Nisida! But, no—all was at least doubt and uncertainty in that respect;—and, as your cast of features and physical characteristics developed themselves, that hideous doubt and that racking uncertainty increased until there were times when I was nearly goaded to do some desperate deed. Those mild blue eyes—that rich brown hair—that feminine softness of expression which marked your face—oh! those belonged not to the family of Riverola!

"Time wore on—and my unhappiness increased. I suspected my wife, yet dared not proclaim the suspicion. I sought to give her back my love—but was utterly unable to subdue the dark thoughts and crush the maddening uncertainties that agitated my soul. At last I was sinking into a state of morbid melancholy, when an incident occurred which revived all the energies of my mind. It was in 1505—Nisida being then ten years old, and you, Francisco, four—when Margaretha one evening informed me that the Countess had received a letter which had thrown her into a state of considerable agitation, and which she had immediately burnt. By questioning the porter at the gate of the mansion, I learnt that the person who delivered the letter was a tall, handsome man, of about thirty-two, with brown hair, blue eyes, and a somewhat feminine expression of countenance. Holy Virgin! this must be the gallant—the paramour of my wife—the father of the boy on whom the law compelled me to bestow my own name! Such were the ideas which immediately struck me; and I now prepared for vengeance—deadly vengeance. Margaretha watched my wife narrowly; and, on the evening following the one on which the letter had been delivered, Vitangela was seen to secure a heavy bag of gold about her person, and quit the mansion by the secret staircase of her apartmest—that apartment which is now the sleeping chamber of your sister Nisida. Margaretha followed the Countess to an obscure street, at the corner of which the guilty woman encountered a tall person, enveloped in a cloak, and who was evidently waiting for her. To him she gave the bag of gold; and they embraced each other tenderly. They then separated—the Countess returning home, unconscious that a spy watched her movements.

"Margaretha reported all that had occurred to me; and I bade her redouble her attention in watching her mistress. Now that the lover is once more in Florence, I thought, and well provided with *my* gold to pursue his extravagances, there will soon be another meeting—and then for vengeance—such a vengeance as an Italian must have! But weeks and months again passed without affording the opportunity which I craved: yet I knew that *the day* must come—and I could tutor myself to await its arrival, if not with patience, at least with so much outward composure as to lull the Countess into a belief of perfect security. Yes—weeks and months,—aye, and years too: and still I nursed my hopes and projects of vengeance, the craving for which increased with the lapse of time!

"And now I come to the grand—the terrible—the main incident in this narrative. It was late one night, in the month of January, 1510—Nisida being then fifteen, and you, Francisco, nine—that Margaretha came to me in my own apartment, and informed me that she had seen the tall gallant traverse the garden hastily, and obtain admission to the Countess's chamber by means of the secret staircase. The hour for vengeance had at length come! Margaretha was instantly despatched to advertise two bravoes, whose services I had long secured for the occasion, that the moment had arrived when they were to do the work for which they had been so well paid in advance, and by the faithful performance of which they would still farther enrich themselves. Within half-an-hour all the arrangements were completed: Margaretha had retired to her own chamber—and the bravoes were concealed with me in the garden. Nor had we long to wait. The private door opened shortly: and two persons appeared on the threshold. The night was clear and beautiful—and, from my hiding-place, I could discern the fondness of the embrace that marked their parting. And they parted, too, never to meet again in life! Vitangela closed the door—and her lover was passing rapidly along amidst the trees in the garden, when a dagger suddenly drank his heart's blood. That dagger was mine, and wielded by my hand!

"He fell without a groan—dead, stone-dead at my feet. Half of my vengeance was now accomplished: the other half was yet to be consummated. Without a moment's unnecessary delay the corpse was conveyed to a cellar beneath the northern wing of the mansion; and the two bravoes then hastened to Vitangela's chamber, into which they obtained admission by forcing the door of the private staircase. In pursuance of the orders which they had received from me, they bound and gagged her: and they conveyed her through the garden to the very cellar where, by the light of a gloomy lamp, she beheld her husband close by a corpse! 'Bring her near!' I exclaimed, unmoved by the looks of indescribable horror which she threw around;—but when her eyes caught sight of the countenance of that lifeless being, they remained fixed with frenzied wildness in their sockets—and even if there had been no gag between her teeth, I do not believe that she could have uttered a syllable.

"And now commenced the second act in this appalling form so loved by thee! Now hack away at the countenance—deface that beauty—pick out those mild blue eyes!'—and I laughed madly—madly! The Countess fainted, and I ordered her to be carried back to her apartment, where Margaretha was already waiting to receive her. Indeed, I had naturally foreseen that insensibility would result from the appalling spectacle which I compelled Vitangela to witness, and Margaretha was prepared to breathe dreadful menaces in her ear the moment she should recover,—menaces of death to herself and both her children if she should ever dare to reveal, even to her father confessor, one tittle of the scene which had that night been enacted!

"APPALLING WAS THE SPECTACLE WHICH BURST UPON THEIR VIEW." (See p. 139.)

tragedy! While one of the bravoes held the Countess in his iron grasp, in such a manner that she could not avert her head, the other, who had once been a surgeon, tore away the garments from the corpse and commenced the task which I had beforehand assigned to him. And as the merciless scalpel hacked and hewed away at the still almost palpitating flesh of the murdered man, in whose breast the dagger remained deeply buried,—a ferocious joy—a savage hyena-like triumph filled my soul; and I experienced no remorse for the deed I had done! Far—very far from that;—for as the work progressed, I exclaimed, 'Behold, Vitangela, how the scalpel hews that

"The surgeon-bravo did his work bravely; and the man who had dishonoured me was reduced to naught save a skeleton! The flesh and the garments were buried deep in the cellar: the skeleton was conveyed to my own chamber, and suspended to a closet where you, Francisco, and your bride are destined to behold it—*along with another!* My vengeance was thus far gratified—the bravoes were dismissed—and I locked myself up in my chamber for several days, to brood upon all I had done, and occasionally to feast my eyes with the grim remains of him who had dared to love my wife. During these days of seclusion I would see no one save the servant who brought me my meals. From him I learnt that the Countess was dangerously ill—that she was indeed dying, and that she besought me to visit her, if only for a moment. But I refused—implacably refused! I was convinced that she craved my forgiveness; and *that* I could not give. Dr. Duras, who attended upon her, came to the door of my chamber, and implored me to grant him an interview:—then Nisida besought a similar boon:—but I was deaf to each and all! Yes—for there was still a being on whom I yet longed to wreak my vengeance;—and that being was yourself, Francisco! I looked upon you as the living evidence of my dishonour—the memorial of your mother's boundless guilt! But I recoiled in horror from the idea of staining my hands with the blood of a little child:—yet I feared that if I came near you—if I saw you clinging affectionately to Vitangela—if I heard you innocently and unconsciously mock me by calling me '*Father!*'—Oh! I felt that I should be unable to restrain the fury of my wrath!

"I know not how long I should have remained in the seclusion of my own chamber—perhaps weeks and months: but one morning, shortly after day-break, I was informed by the only servant whom I would admit near me, that the Countess had breathed her last during the night, and that Nisida was so deeply affected by her mother's death, that she—poor girl! was dangerously ill. Then I became frantic on account of my daughter; and I quitted my apartment, not only to see that proper aid was administered to her, but to complete the scheme of vengeance which I had originally formed. Thus, in the first place, Dr. Duras was enjoined to take up his abode altogether in the Riverola palace, so long as Nisida should require his services!—and, on the other hand, a splendid funeral was ordered for the Countess of Riverola. But Vitangela's remains went not in the velvet-covered coffin to the family vault:—no—her flesh was buried in the same soil where rotted the flesh of her paramour—and her skeleton was suspended to the same beam to which his bones had been already hung! For I thought, within myself, ' This is the first time that the wife of a Count of Riverola has ever brought dishonour and disgrace upon her husband: and I will take care that it shall be the last. To Nisida will I leave all my estates—all my wealth, save a miserable pittance as a provision for the bastard Francisco. She shall inherit the title; and the man on whom she may confer her hand, shall be the next Count of Riverola. Their wedding-day shall be marked by a revelation of the mystery of this cabinet; and the awful spectacle will teach *him*, whoever he may be, to watch his wife narrowly—and will teach *her* what it is to prove unfaithful to a fond husband! To both the lesson will be as useful as the manner of conveying it will be frightful; and they will hand down the tradition to future scions of the family of Riverola! Francisco, too, shall learn the secrets of this cabinet;—he shall be taught why he has been disinherited—why I have hated him; and thus even from the other world shall the spirits of the vile paramour and the adulterous wife behold the consequences of their crime perpetuated in this!'

"Such were my thoughts—such were my intentions. But an appalling calamity forced me to change my views. Nisida, after a long and painful illness, became deaf and dumb; and Dr. Duras gave me no hope of the restoration of her lost faculties. Terrible visitation! Then was it that I reasoned with myself—that I deliberated long and earnestly upon the course which I should pursue. It was improbable that, afflicted as Nisida was, she would ever marry; and I felt grieved—deeply grieved to think that you, Francisco, being disinherited, and Nisida remaining single, the proud title of Riverola would become extinct! I therefore resolved on the less painful alternative of sacrificing my intention of disinheriting you altogether; and I accordingly made a will by which I left you the estates, with the contingent title of Count of Riverola, under certain conditions which might alienate both property and rank from *you*, and endow therewith your sister Nisida. For should she recover the faculties of speech and hearing by the time she shall have attained the age of even thirty-six, she will yet be marriageable and may have issue: but should that era in her life pass, and still see her deaf and dumb, all hope of her recovery will be dead. Thus, if she be still so deeply afflicted at that age, you, Francisco, will inherit the vast estates and the lordly title which, through the circumstances of your birth, it grieves me to believe will ever devolve upon you!

"Such were my motives for making that will which you are destined to hear read, doubtless, before the time comes for you to peruse this manuscript. And having

made that will, and experiencing the sad certainty that my unfortunate daughter will never become qualified to inherit my fortune and title, but that the name of Riverola must be perpetuated through *your* marriage, I have determined that to *you* and *your bride* alone, shall the dread secrets of the cabinet be revealed!"

Thus terminated the manuscript.

CHAPTER LXXVI.

NISIDA'S EXPLANATIONS.

POWERFUL in meaning and strong in expression as the English language may be rendered by one who has the least experience in the proper combination of words, yet it becomes totally inadequate to the task of conveying an idea of those feelings—those harrowing emotions—those horrifying sentiments, which were excited in the breasts of Francisco di Riverola and his beautiful Countess, Flora, by the revelations of the manuscript.

At first the document begat a deep and mournful interest, as it related the interviews of the late Count with Vitangela in the streets of Naples: then amazement was engendered by the announcement of that lovely and unhappy being's ignominious parentage;—but a calmness was diffused through the minds of Francisco and Flora, as if they had found a resting-place amidst the exciting incidents of the narrative, when they reached that part which mentioned the marriage.

Their feelings were, however, destined to be speedily and most painfully wrung once more; and Francisco could scarcely restrain his indignation—yes, his indignation even against the memory of his deceased father—when he perused those injurious suspicions which were recorded in reference to the honour of his mother. Though unable to explain the mystery in which all that part of the narrative was involved, yet he felt firmly convinced that his mother was innocent; and he frequently interrupted himself in the perusal of the manuscript to give utterance to passionate ejaculations expressive of that opinion.

But it was when the hideous tragedy rapidly developed itself, and the history of the presence of the two skeletons in the closet was detailed,—it was then that language becomes powerless to describe the mingled wrath and disgust which Francisco felt, or to delineate the emotions of boundless horror and wild amazement that were excited in the bosom of his Flora. In spasmodic shuddering did the young Countess cling to her husband when she learnt how fearfully accurate was the manner in which the few lines of the manuscript which she had read many months previously in Nisida's boudoir fitted in with the text,—and how appalling was the tale which the whole made up! She was cruelly shocked—and her heart bled for that fine young man whom she was proud to call her husband, but whom his late father had loathed to recognise as a son!

And Nisida—what were *her* feelings as she lay stretched upon the couch, listening to the contents of the manuscript which she had read before? At first one hope—one idea was dominant in her soul,—the hope that Flora would be crushed even to death by the revelations which were indeed almost sufficient to overwhelm a gentle disposition and freeze the vital current in the tender and compassionate heart. But as Francisco read on, and when he came to those passages which described the sufferings and the cruel fate of his mother, then Nisida became a prey to the most torturing feelings—dreadful emotions were expressed by her convulsing countenance and wildly glaring eyes—and she muttered deep and bitter anathemas against the memory of her own father! For well does the reader know that she had loved her mother to distraction; and thus the horrifying detail of the injuries heaped upon the head and on the name of that revered parent, aroused all the fiercest passions of rage and hate, as completely as if that history had been new to her, and as if she were now becoming acquainted with it for the first time.

Indeed, so powerful—so terrible was the effect produced by the revival of all those dread reminiscences and heartrending emotions on the part of Nisida, that, forgetting her malignant spite and her infernal hope with regard to Flora, she threw her whole soul into the subject of the manuscript; and the torrent of feelings to which she thus gave way, was crushing and overwhelming to a woman of such fierce passions, and who had received so awful a shock as that which had stretched her on the couch where she now lay. For the fate of him whom she had loved with such ardour, and the revulsion that her affections experienced on account of the ghastly spectacle which Wagner had presented to her view in his dying moments,—the disgust and loathing which had been inspired in her mind by the thought that she had ever fondled that being in her arms and absolutely doted on the almost superhuman beauty which had changed to such revolting ugliness,—it was all this that had struck her down—paralysed her—inflicted a mortal, though not an instantaneous blow, upon that woman lately so full of energy, so strong in moral courage, and so full of vigorous health!

Thus, impressed with the conviction that her end was approaching, the moment the perusal of the manuscript was concluded, the Lady Nisida said in a faint and dying tone, "Francisco, draw near—as near as possible—and listen to what I have now to communicate; for it is in my power to clear up all doubt—all mystery relative to the honour of our sainted mother, and to convince thee that no stigma attaches itself to thy birth!"

"Alas! my beloved sister," exclaimed the young Count, "you speak in a faint voice—you are very ill! In the name of the Holy Virgin! I conjure you to allow me to send for Dr. Duras!"

"No, Francisco," said Nisida, her voice recovering somewhat of its power as she continued to address her brother: "I implore you to let me have my own way—to follow my own inclinations! Do not thwart me, Francisco; already I feel as if molten lead were pouring through my brain—and a tremendous weight lies upon my heart! Forbear, then, from irritating me, my well-beloved Francisco——"

"Oh! Nisida," cried the young Count, throwing his arms round his sister's neck and embracing her fondly; "if you love me now—if you have ever loved me, grant me one boon! By the memory of our sainted mother I implore you—by your affection for her I adjure you, Nisida——"

"Speak—speak, Francisco," interrupted his sister, hastily: "I can almost divine the nature of the boon you crave—and—my God!" she added, tears starting from her eyes, as a painful thought flashed across her brain,—"perhaps I have been too harsh—too severe! At all events, it is not now—on my death-bed——"

"Your death-bed!" echoed Francisco, in a tone indicative of acute anguish, while the sobs which convulsed the bosom of the young Countess were heard alike by him and his sister.

"Yes, dearest brother—I am dying!" said Nisida, in a voice of profound but mournful conviction: "and therefore let me not delay those duties and those explanations which can alone unburden my heart of the weight that lies upon it! And first, Francisco, be thy boon granted —for I know that thou wouldst speak to me of her who is now thy bride. Come to my arms, then, Flora—embrace me as a sister—and forgive me, if thou canst—for I have been a fierce and unrelenting enemy to thee!"

"Oh! let the past be forgotten, my friend—my sister!" exclaimed the weeping Flora, as she threw herself into Nisida's outstretched arms.

And the young wife and the dying woman embraced each other tenderly—for deep regrets and pungent remorse at last attuned the mind of Nisida to sweet and holy sympathy!

"And now," said Nisida, "sit down by my side, and listen to the explanations which I have promised. Give me your hand, Flora—dear Flora: let me retain it in mine—for at the last hour, and when I am about to leave this fair and beauteous earth, I feel an ardent longing to love those who walk upon its face, and to be loved by them in return. But, alas—alas!" she added, somewhat bitterly; "reflections and yearnings of this nature come too late! O Flora! the picture of life is spread before you—while from me it is rapidly receding and dissolving into the past. Like our own fair city of palaces and flowers, when seen from a distance beneath the glorious lights of morning, may that picture continue to appear to thee:—and mayst thou never draw near enough to recognise the false splendours in which gorgeous hues may deck the things of this world,—mayst thou never be brought so close to the sad realities of existence, as to be forced to contemplate the breaking hearts that dwell in palaces, or to view in disgust the slime upon flowers!"

"Nisida," said Francisco, bending over his sister and speaking in a voice indicative of deep emotion, "the kind words you utter to my beloved Flora shall ever—ever remain engraven upon my heart."

"And on mine also," murmured the young Countess,

pressing Nisida's hand with grateful ardour, while her eyes, radiant with very softness, threw a glance of passionate tenderness upon her generous-hearted and handsome husband.

"Listen to me," resumed Nisida, after a short pause, during which she gave way to all the luxury of those sweet and holy reflections which the present scene engendered;—and these were the happiest moments of the lady's stormy life! "Listen to me," she repeated; "and let me enter upon and make an end of my explanations as speedily as possible. And, first, Francisco, relative to our sainted — our innocent — our deeply-wronged and much injured mother! You have already learnt that she was the daughter of the Public Executioner of Naples; and you have heard that ere she became our father's wife, she swore a solemn oath; she pledged herself in the most sacred manner, *that she would never even allude to her family—that she would not communicate to them the name of her husband nor the place of his abode, under any circumstances—in a word, that she would consider her father and her brother as dead to her!* And yet she had a tender heart; and after she became the Countess of Riverola, she often thought of that parent who had reared her tenderly and loved her affectionately; she thought also of her brother Eugenio, who had ever been so devoted to his sister. But she kept her promise faithfully for five years, until that fatal date of April, 1500, which our father has so emphatically mentioned in his narrative. It was in the gardens belonging to the ducal palace, that she suddenly encountered her brother Eugenio——"

"Her brother!" ejaculated Francisco, joyfully: "oh! I knew—I felt certain that she was innocent!"

"Yes—she was indeed innocent," repeated Nisida. "But let me pursue my explanations as succinctly as possible. It appeared that the old man—the Executioner of Naples—was no more; and Eugenio, possessing himself of the hoardings of his deceased father, had fled from his native city to avoid the dread necessity of assuming the abhorrent office. Accident led the young adventurer to Florence in search of a more agreeable employment as a means whereby to earn his livelihood; and, having formed the acquaintance of one of the Duke's valets, he obtained admittance to the gardens on that memorable evening when the grand entertainment was given. In spite of the strict injunctions which he had received not to approach the places occupied by the distinguished guests, he drew near the arbour in which our mother had been conversing with other ladies, but where she was at that moment alone. The recognition was immediate; and they flew into each other's arms. It would have been useless, as well as unnatural, for our mother to have refused to reveal her rank and name: her brilliant attire was sufficient to convince her brother that the former was high—and inquiry would speedily have made him acquainted with the latter. She accordingly drew him apart, into a secluded walk, and told him all: but she implored him to quit Florence without delay; and she gave him her purse and one of her rich bracelets, thereby placing ample resources at his disposal. Five years passed away—and during that period she heard no more of her brother Eugenio. But at the expiration of the interval, she received a note stating that he was again in Florence—that necessity had alone brought him thither—and that he would be at a particular place, at a certain hour, to meet either herself or any confidential person whom she might instruct to see him. Our mother filled a bag with gold, and put into it some of her choicest jewels; and, thus provided, she repaired in person to the place of appointment. It grieved her—deeply grieved her generous heart thus to be compelled to meet her brother secretly, as if he were a common robber or a midnight bravo: but for her husband's peace, and in obedience to the spirit of the oath which imperious circumstances had alone led her in some degree to violate, she was forced to adopt that sad and humiliating alternative!"

"Alas — poor mother!" sobbed Francisco, deeply affected by this narrative.

"Again did five years elapse without bringing tidings to our mother of Eugenio," continued Nisida; "and then he once more set foot in Florence. The world had not used him well—Fortune had frowned upon him—and though a young man of fine spirit and noble disposition, he failed in all his endeavours to carve out a successful career for himself. Our mother determined to accord him an interview in her own apartment. She longed to converse with him at her ease—to hear his tale from his own lips—to sympathise with and console him. Oh!

who could blame her if in so doing she departed from the strict and literal meaning of that vow which had bound her to consider her relations as dead to her? But the fault—if fault it were—was so venial, that to justify it is to invest it with an importance which it would not have possessed save for the frightful results to which it led. You have already heard how foully he was waylaid—how ruthlessly he was murdered! Holy Virgin! my brain whirls when I reflect upon that hideous cruelty which made our mother the spectatress of his dissection: for, even had he been a lover—even were she guilty—even if the suspicions of our father had been well founded——"

"Dwell not upon this frightful topic, my beloved Nisida!" exclaimed Francisco, perceiving that she was again becoming dreadfully excited,—for her eyes dilated and glared wildly—her bosom heaved in awful convulsions—and she tossed her arms frantically about.

"No: I will not—I dare not pause to ponder thereon," she said, falling back upon the pillow, and pressing her hands to that proud and haughty brow behind which the active, racking brain appeared on fire.

"Tranquillize yourself, dearest sister," murmured Flora, bending over the couch and pressing her lips on Nisida's burning cheek.

"I will—I will, my Flora, whom I now love as much as I once hated!" exclaimed the dying lady. "But let me make an end of my explanations. You already know that our dear mother was gagged when she was compelled to witness the horrible deed enacted in the subterranean charnel-house by the dim light of a sickly lamp; but even had she not been, no word would have issued from her lips—as the manuscript justly observes. During her illness, however, she besought an interview with her husband, for the purpose of proving to him her complete innocence by revealing the fact that his victim was her own brother! But he refused all the entreaties proffered with that object; and our unfortunate mother was forced to contemplate the approach of death with the sad conviction that she should pass away without the satisfaction of establishing her guiltlessness in the eyes of our father. Then was it that she revealed everything to me—to me alone—to me, a young girl of only fifteen when those astounding facts were breathed into my ears. I listened with horror—and I began to hate my father; for I adored my mother! She implored me not to give way to any intemperate language or burst of passion which might induce the inmates of the mansion to suspect that I was the depositress of some terrible secret. 'For,' said our mother, when on her death-bed, 'if I have ventured to shock your young mind by so appalling a revelation, it is only that you may understand wherefore I am about to bind you by a solemn vow to love, protect, and watch over Francisco, as if he were your own child rather than your brother. His father, alas! hates him: this I have observed almost ever since the birth of that dear boy: but it is only by means of the dread occurrence of the other night that I have been able to divine the origin of that dislike and unnatural loathing. Your father, Nisida,' continued my mother, 'believes that I have been unfaithful, and suspects that Francisco is the offspring of a guilty amour. With this terrible impression upon his mind, he may persecute my poor boy—he may disinherit him—he may even seek to rid him of life. Kneel, then, by my bed-side, Nisida, and swear by all you deem sacred—by the love you bear me—and by your hopes of salvation, that you will watch unweariedly and unceasingly over the welfare and the interests of Francisco—that you will make any sacrifice, incur any danger, or undergo any privation to save him from the effects of his father's hate—that you will exert all possible means to cause the title and fortune of his father to descend to him, and that you will in no case consent to supplant him in those respects—and lastly, that you will keep secret the dread history of my brother's fate and your knowledge of your father's crime.'—To all these conditions of the vow I solemnly and sacredly pledged myself, calling heaven to witness the oath. But I said to our mother, ' My father will not for ever remain locked up in his own apartment: he will come forth sooner or later, and I must have an opportunity of speaking to him. May I not justify you, my dear mother, in his eyes? may I not assure him that Eugenio was your own brother? He will then cease to hate Francisco, and may even love him as much as he loves me; and you need then have no fears on his account.'—' Alas! the plan which you suggest may not be put into execution,' replied our dying mother; 'for were your father to be aware that I had revealed the occurrences of that dread night to you, Nisida, he would feel that he must be ever looked upon as a murderer, by his own child! Moreover, such appears to be the sad and be-

nighted state of his mind, that he might peradventure deem the tale relative to Eugenio a mere excuse and vile subterfuge. No: I must perish disgraced in his eyes unless he should accord ere I die, the interview which yourself and the good Dr. Duras have so vainly implored him to grant me.'—Our dear mother then proceeded to give me other instructions, Francisco, relative to yourself: but these," added Nisida, glancing towards Flora, "it would now be painful to unfold. And yet," she continued hastily, as a second thought struck her, "it is impossible, my sweet Flora, that you can be weak-minded—for you have this day seen and heard enough to test your mental powers to the extreme possibility of their endurance. Moreover, I feel that my conduct towards you requires a complete justification; and that justification will be found in the last instructions which I received from the lips of my mother!"

"Dearest Nisida," said the young Countess, "no justification is needed—no apology is required in reference to that subject: for your kind words—your altered manner towards me now—your recognition of me as a sister, made so by my union with your brother,—oh! all this would efface from my mind wrongs ten thousand times more terrible than any injury which I have sustained at your hands. But," continued Flora, in a slow and gentle tone, "if you wish to explain the nature of those instructions which you received from the lips of your dying parent, let not my presence embarrass you."

"Yes—I do wish to render my explanation as complete as possible, dearest Flora," replied Nisida; "for if I have acted severely towards you, it was not to gratify any natural love of cruelty nor any mean jealousy or spite;—on the contrary, the motives were engendered by that imperious necessity which has swayed my conduct, modelled my disposition, and regulated my mind, ever since that fatal day when I knelt by my mother's death-bed and swore to obey her last words! For thus did she speak, Flora—these were her instructions, Francisco :— ' Nisida, there is one more subject relative to which I must advise you, and in respect to which you must swear to obey me. My own life furnishes a sad and terrible lesson of the impropriety and folly of contracting an unequal marriage. All my woes—all my sorrows—all the dreadful events which have occurred may be traced to the one grand fact that the Count of Riverola espoused a person of whose family he was ashamed. Nisida,' she continued, her voice becoming fainter and fainter, ' watch you narrowly and closely over the welfare of Francisco in this respect. Let him not marry beneath him: let him not unite himself to one whose family contains a single member deserving of obloquy or reproach. Above all, see that he marries not until he shall have reached an age when he may be capable of examining his own heart through the medium of experience and matured judgment. If you see him form a boyish attachment of which you have good and sufficient reason to disapprove, exert yourself to wean him from it: hesitate not to thwart him :—be not moved by the sorrow he may manifest at the moment;—you will be acting for his welfare—and the time will speedily come when he will rejoice that you have rescued him from the danger of contracting a hasty, rash, and ill-assorted marriage.' Those were the last instructions of our mother, Francisco; and I swore to obey them. Hence my sorrow, my fears, and my anger when I became aware of the attachment subsisting between yourself and your dear brother, and you, my sweet Flora;—and that sorrow was enhanced — those fears were augmented—that anger was increased, Flora, when I learnt that your brother, Alessandro, had renounced the creed of the true God, and that your family thereby contained a member deserving of obloquy and reproach. But that sorrow, those fears, and that anger have now departed from my soul: I recognise the finger of heaven—the will of the Almighty, in the accomplishment of your union, despite of all my projects—all my intrigues to prevent it ;—I am satisfied, moreover, that there is in this alliance a fitness and a propriety which will ensure your happiness;—and may the spirit of my sainted mother look down from the empyrean palace where she dwells, and bless you both, even as I now implore the divine mercy to shed its bounties and diffuse its protecting influence around you!"

Nisida had raised herself up to a sitting posture as she uttered this invocation so sublimely interesting and solemnly sincere; and the youthful pair, simultaneously yielding to the same impulse, sank upon their knees to receive the blessings of one who had never bestowed a blessing on mortal being until then! She extended her hands above those two beautiful, bending heads; and her voice as she adjured heaven to protect them, was plaintively earnest and tremulously clear — and its musical sound seemed to touch the finest chords of sympathy, devotion, and love that vibrated in the hearts of that youthful noble and his virgin-bride!

When this solemn ceremony was accomplished, an immense weight appeared to have been removed from the soul of Lady Nisida of Riverola; and her countenance wore a calm and sweet expression, which formed a happy contrast with the sovereign hauteur and proud contempt that were wont to mark it.

"I have now but little more to say in explanation of my past conduct," she resumed after a long pause. "You can readily divine wherefore I affected the loss of those most glorious faculties which God has given us. I became enthusiastic in my resolve to carry out the injunctions of my dear and much loved mother; and while I lay upon a bed of sickness—a severe illness produced by anguish and horror at all I had heard from her lips, and by her death so premature and sad—I pondered a thousand schemes the object of which was to accomplish the great aims I had in view. I foresaw that I—a weak woman—then, indeed, a mere girl of fifteen—should have to constitute myself the protectress of a brother who was hated by his own father; and I feared lest that hatred should drive him to the adoption of some dreadful plot to rid himself of your presence, Francisco—perhaps even to deprive you of life. I knew that I must watch all his movements and listen to all his conversations with those unprincipled wretches who are ever ready to do the bidding of the powerful and the wealthy. But how was all this to be accomplished?—how could I remain constantly on the alert?—how was I to become a watcher and a listener—a spy ever active, and an eaves-dropper ever awake—without exciting suspicions which would lead to the frustration of my designs, and perhaps involve both myself and my brother in ruin! Then was it that an idea struck me like a flash of lightning;—and as a flash of lightning was it terrible and appalling, when breaking on the dark chaos of my thoughts. At first I shrank from it—recoiled from it in horror and dismay:—but the more I considered it—the longer I looked that idea in the face—the more I contemplated it, the less formidable did it seem. I have already said that I was enthusiastic and devoted in my resolves to carry out the dying injunctions of my mother;—and thus by degrees I learnt to reflect upon the awful sacrifice which had suggested itself to my imagination, as a species of holy and necessary self-martyrdom. I foresaw that if I affected the loss of hearing and speech, I should obtain all the advantages I sought and all the means I required to enable me to act as the protectress of my brother against the hatred of my father. I believed also that I should not only be considered as unfit to be made the heiress of the title and fortune of the Riverola family, but that our father, Francisco, would see the absolute necessity of treating you in all respects as his lawful and legitimate son, in spite of any suspicions which he might entertain relative to your birth. There were many other motives which influenced me, and which arose out of the injunctions of our mother,—motives which one can well understand, and which I need not detail. Thus was it that, subduing the grief which the idea of making so tremendous a sacrifice excited, on the one hand—and arming myself with the exultation of a martyr, on the other,—thus was it that I resolved to simulate the character of the Deaf and Dumb. It was however necessary to obtain the collusion of Dr. Duras; and this aim I carried after many hours of argument and persuasion. He was then ignorant—and still is ignorant—of the real motives which prompted me to this self-martyrdom: but I led him to believe that the gravest and most important family interests required that moral immolation of my own happiness;—and I vowed that unless he would consent to aid me, it was my firm resolve to shut myself up in a convent and take the veil. This threat, which I had not the least design of carrying into effect, induced him to yield a reluctant acquiescence with my project; for he loved me as if I had been his child. He was moreover consoled somewhat by the assurance which I gave him, and in which I myself felt implicit confidence at the time, that the necessity for the simulation of deafness and dumbness on my part would cease the moment my father should be no more. In a word, the good—the kind Dr. Duras promised to act in accordance with my wishes; and I accordingly became NISIDA THE DEAF AND DUMB!"

"Merciful heavens! and that immense—that immeasurable sacrifice was made for me!" cried Francisco, throwing himself into the arms of his sister, and imprinting a thousand kisses on her cheeks.

"Yes—for your sake, and in order to carry out the dying commands of our mother, the sainted Vitangela!" responded Nisida. "I shall not weary you with a description of the feelings and emotions with which I commenced that long career of duplicity; by the very success that attended the part which I had undertaken to perform, you may estimate the magnitude and the extent of the exertions which it cost me thus to maintain myself a living—a constant—and yet undetected lie! Ten years passed away—ten years, marked by many incidents which made me rejoice, for your sake, Francisco, that I had accepted the self martyrdom which circumstances had suggested to me. At length our father lay upon his death-bed: and then—Oh! then, I rejoiced, yes, rejoiced, though he was dying;—for I thought that the end of my career of duplicity was at hand. Judge, then, of my astonishment—my grief—my despair, when I heard the last injunctions which our father addressed to you, Francisco, on that bed of death. What could the mystery of that closet mean? Of that I then knew nothing. Wherefore was I to remain in complete ignorance of the instructions thus given to you? And what was signified by the words relative to the disposal of our father's property? For you may remember that he spoke thus, addressing himself of course to you:—'You will find that I have left the whole of my property to you. At the same time my will specifies certain conditions relative to your sister Nisida, for whom I have made due provision only in the case—which is, alas! almost in defiance of every hope, of her recovery from that dreadful affliction which renders her so completely dependant on your kindness.'—These ominous and mysterious words seemed to proclaim defeat and overthrow to all the hopes that I had formed relative to the certainty of your being left the sole and unconditional heir alike to title and estate. I therefore resolved to maintain the character of the Deaf and Dumb until I should have fathomed the secrets of the closet, and have become acquainted with the conditions of the will. Oh! well do I remember the glance which the generous-hearted Duras cast towards me, when, returning to the chamber, he inquired by means of that significant look whether the words of our dying father were prognostic of hope for me—whether, indeed, the necessity of sustaining the dreadful duplicity would cease when he should be no more. And I remember also, that the look and the sign by which I conveyed a negative answer was expressive of the deep melancholy that filled my soul."

"Alas! my dear—my self-sacrificed sister!" murmured Francisco, tears trickling down his cheeks.

"Yes—my disappointment was cruel indeed," continued Nisida. "But the excitement of the scenes and incidents which followed rapidly the death of our father, restored my mind to its wonted tone of fortitude—vigour—and proud determination. That very night, Francisco, I took the key of the cabinet from your garments, while you slept—I sped to the chamber of death—I visited the depository of horrible mysteries—and for the first time I became aware that the two skeletons were contained in that closet! And whose fleshless relics they were, the dreadful manuscript speedily revealed to me! Then was it also for the first time that I learnt how Margaretha was the detestable spy whose agency had led to such a frightful catastrophe in respect to Eugenio and Vitangela;—then became I aware that our mother's corpse slept not in the vault to which a coffin had been consigned:—in a word, the full measure of our sire's atrocity—O God! that I should be compelled thus to speak—was revealed to me! But on Margaretha have I been avenged," added Nisida, in a low tone, and with a convulsive shudder, produced by the recollection of that terrible night when she immolated the miserable old woman above the grave where lay a portion of the remains of her mother and of Eugenio.

"You have been avenged on Margaretha, sister?" ejaculated Francisco, surveying Nisida with apprehension.

"Yes," she replied, her large black eyes flashing with a scintillation of their former fires: "that woman—I have slain her! But, start not, Flora—look not reproachfully upon me, Francisco: 'twas a deed fully justified—a vengeance righteously exercised—a penalty well deserved! And now let me hasten to bring my long and tedious explanations to a conclusion—for they have occupied a longer space than I had at first anticipated, and I am weak and faint! Little, however, remains to be told. The nature of our father's will compelled me to persist in my self-martyrdom; for I had sworn to my dying mother not to accept any conditions or advantages which could have the effect of disinheriting you, Francisco!"

"Oh! what a deep debt of gratitude do I owe thee, my beloved sister!" exclaimed the young Count, powerfully affected by the generous sacrifices made by Nisida on his behalf.

"And think you that I have experienced no reward?" asked the lady in a sweet tone, and with a placid smile: "do you imagine that the consciousness of having devoted myself to the fulfilment of my adored mother's wishes, has been no recompense? Yes—I have had my consolations and my hours of happiness, as well as my sufferings and periods of profound affliction. But I feel a soft and heavenly repose stealing over me—'tis a sweet sleep—and yet it is not the slumber of death! No, no: 'tis a delicious trance into which I am falling—'tis as if a celestial vision——"

She said no more: her eyes closed—she fell back and slept soundly.

"Merciful heavens! my sister is no more," exclaimed Francisco, in terror and despair.

"Fear not, my beloved husband," said Flora; "Nisida sleeps—and 'tis a healthy slumber! The pulsations of her heart are regular—her breath comes freely. Joy—joy, Francisco—she will recover!"

"The Holy Virgin grant that your hopes may be fulfilled!" returned the young Count. "But let us not disturb her. We will sit down by the bedside, Flora,—and watch till she shall awake!"

But scarcely had he uttered these words, when the door of the chamber opened, and an old man of venerable aspect, and with a long beard as white as snow, advanced towards the newly married pair.

Francisco and Flora beheld him with feelings of reverence and awe; for something appeared to tell them that he was a mortal of no common order.

"My dear children," he said, addressing them in a paternal manner—and his voice was firm but mild; "ye need not watch here for the present. Retire—and seek not this chamber again until the morning of to-morrow. Fear nothing, excellent young man—for thou hast borne arms in the cause of the cross:—fear nothing, amiable young lady—for thou art attended by guardian angels!"

And as the venerable man thus addressed them severally, he extended his hands to bless them;—and they received that blessing with holy meekness, and yet with a joyous feeling which appeared to be of glorious augury for their future happiness.

Then, obedient to the command of the stranger, they slowly quitted the apartment—urged to yield to his will by a secret influence which they could not resist, but which nevertheless animated them with a pious confidence in the integrity of his purpose.

The door closed behind them:—and Christian Rosencrux remained in the room with the dead Wagner and the dying Nisida.

CHAPTER LXXVII.

THE GRAND VIZIER IN FLORENCE.

WHILE the incidents related in the last few chapters were taking place at the Riverola Palace, the Council of State had assembled to receive the Grand Vizier—the mighty Ibrahim—who had signified his intention of meeting that august body at three o'clock in the afternoon.

Accordingly, so soon as he had witnessed the marriage ceremony which united his sister to the Count of Riverola, he returned from Wagner's mansion to his own pavilion in the midst of the Ottoman encampment. There he arrayed himself in a manner becoming his exalted rank; and mounting his splendidly caparisoned steed, he repaired with a brilliant escort to the ducal palace.

The streets of the city of Florence were thronged with multitudes anxious to gain a sight of the representative of the Sultan,—a view of the man whose will and pleasure swayed the greatest empire in existence at that period of the world's age!

And as Ibrahim passed through those avenues so well known to him—threading those thoroughfares each feature of which was so indelibly impressed upon his memory—and beheld many, many familiar spots, all of which awakened in his mind reminiscences of a happy childhood, and of years gone by,—when too he reflected that he had quitted Florence, poor, obscure, and unmarked amidst the millions of his fellow-men—and that now as he entered the beauteous city, multitudes came forth to gaze upon him, as on one invested with a high

rank, and enjoying a power mighty to do much—when he thought of all this, his bosom swelled with mingled emotions of pride and tenderness, regret and joy: and while tears trembled upon his long black lashes, a smile of haughty triumph played on his lips.

On—on the procession goes, through the crowded streets and across the spacious squares—watched by the eyes of transcendent beauty and proud aristocracy from the balconies of palaces and the casements of lordly mansions,—on—on, amidst a wondering and admiring populace, grateful, too, that so mighty a chief as Ibrahim should have spared their city from sack and ruin!

At length the Grand Vizier, attended by the great Beglerbegs and Pachas of his army, entered the square of the ducal palace; and as his prancing steed bore him proudly beneath the massive arch, the roar of artillery announced to the City of Flowers that the Ottoman Minister was now within the precincts of the dwelling of the Florentine sovereign.

The Duke and the Members of the Council of State were all assembled in the court of the Palazzo to receive the illustrious visitor, who, having dismounted, from his horse, accompanied the Prince and those high dignitaries to the Council-Chamber.

When the personages thus assembled had taken their seats around the spacious table, covered with a rich red velvet cloth, the Grand Vizier proceeded to address the Duke and the councillors.

"High and mighty Prince, and noble and puissant Lords," he said, in the tone of one conscious of his power, "I am well satisfied with the manner in which my demands have been fulfilled up to this moment. Two ladies, in whom I feel a deep and sincere interest, and who were most unjustly imprisoned to suit the vindictive purposes of the Count of Arestino, have been delivered up to me; and ye have likewise agreed to make full and adequate atonement for the part which Florence enacted in the late contest between the Christians and Mussulmans in the Island of Rhodes. I have therefore determined to reduce my demands upon the Republic, for indemnity and compensation, to as low a figure as my own dignity and sense of that duty which I owe to my sovereign (whom God preserve many days!) will permit. The sum that I now require from your treasury, mighty Prince and puissant lords, is a hundred thousand pistoles;* and in addition thereto, I claim peculiar privileges for Ottoman vessels trading to Leghorn—a guarantee of peace on the part of the Republic for three years—and the release of such prisoners now in the dungeons in the Inquisition, whom it may seem good to me thus to mark out as deserving of your mercy."

"A hundred thousand pistoles, my lord, would completely exhaust the treasury of the Republic," said the Duke, with dismay pictured upon his countenance.

"Think you," cried the Grand Vizier angrily, "that I shall dare to face my imperial master, on my return to Constantinople, unless I be able to place at his feet a sum adequate to meet the expenses incurred by this expedition of a great fleet and a powerful army?"

"Your Highness will at least accord us a few days wherein to obtain the amount required," said the Duke; "for it will be necessary to levy a tax upon the Republic."

"I grant you until sunset, my lord—until sunset this evening," added the Grand Vizier, speaking with stern emphasis. "And if you will permit me to tender my advice, you will at once command the Grand Inquisidor and the Count of Arestino to furnish the sum required; for the former, I am inclined to suspect, is a most unjust judge—and the latter, I am well convinced, is a most cruel and revengeful noble."

"The Count of Arestino is no more, your Highness," answered the Duke. "The Marquis of Orsini murdered him before the very eyes of the Grand Inquisidor, and will therefore head the procession of victims at the approaching auto-da-fé."

"By the footstool of Allah! that shall not be," exclaimed Ibrahim. "The machinations of the Count of Arestino threw into the Inquisition dungeons those two ladies whom ye delivered up to me last night; and it was my intention when I spoke of releasing certain prisoners ere now, to stipulate for the freedom of those whom the vengeance of that Count had immured in your accursed prison-house. See then, my lords, that all those of whom I speak be forthwith brought hither into our presence."

It may be proper to inform the reader that Flora had

---

* 350,000l. in English money—an immense sum at that period.

solicited her brother to save the Marquis of Orsini and the Countess Giulia, to whom the young wife of Francisco had been indebted for her escape from the Carmelite Convent; for, as the secrets of the Torture Chamber were never suffered to transpire, she was of course ignorant of the death of the guilty Giulia and of the assassination of the Count of Arestino by the Marquis of Orsini.

At the command of Ibrahim-Pacha, who spoke in a firm and resolute manner, the Duke summoned a sentinel from the corridor adjoining the Council-chamber, and issued the necessary orders to fulfil the desire of the Grand Vizier.

Nearly a quarter of an hour elapsed, during which one of the councillors drew up the guarantee of peace and of the commercial privileges demanded by Ibrahim.

At length the door opened and several Familiars made their appearance, leading in Manuel d'Orsini and Isaachar ben Solomon, both heavily chained.

The former walked with head erect, and proud bearing: the latter could scarcely drag his wasted, racked, and tottering limbs along, and was compelled to hang upon the arms of the Familiars for support. Nevertheless, there was something so meek—so patient—and so resigned in the expression of the old and persecuted Israelite's countenance, that Ibrahim-Pacha's soul was touched with a sentiment of pity in his behalf.

"But these are not all the prisoners," exclaimed the Grand Vizier, turning angrily towards the Duke: "where is the Countess Giulia of Arestino?"

"My lord, she is no more," answered the Prince.

"And heaven be thanked that she is indeed no more!" cried Manuel d'Orsini, in a tone of mingled rage and bitterness. "Fortunate is it for her that Death has snatched her away from the grasp of miscreants in human shape, and who call themselves Christians. My lord," he continued, turning towards Ibrahim,—"I know not who you are—but I perceive by your garb that you are a Moslem, and I imagine that your rank is high by the title addressed to you by the Duke——"

"Presume not thus to intrude your observations on his Highness, the Grand Vizier!" exclaimed one of the councillors in a severe tone.

"On the contrary," said Ibrahim-Pacha, "let him speak—and without reserve. My lord of Orsini, fear not —I will protect you!"

"The remark I was about to make, illustrious Vizier," cried Manuel, "is brief, though it may prove not palatable to the patrons of the Inquisition and the supporters of that awful engine of despotism and cruelty," he added, glancing fiercely at the Duke and the assembled councillors. "I was anxious to observe that the Christian Church has founded and maintained that abhorrent institution; and that there is more true mercy—more genuine sympathy—and more of the holy spirit of forgiveness in the breast of this reviled, despised, and persecuted Jew, than in the bosoms of all the miserable hypocrites who have dared to sanction the infernal tortures which have been inflicted upon him. For myself I would not accept mercy at their hands; and I would rather go in the companionship of this Jew to the funeral pile, than remain alive to dwell amongst a race of incarnate fiends, calling themselves Christians."

"This insolence is not to be borne!" exclaimed the Duke, starting from his seat, his countenance glowing with indignation.

"Your Highness and all the councillors now assembled, well merit the reproaches of the Marquis of Orsini," said the Grand Vizier, sternly. "But it is for *me* to command here—and for *you* to obey, proud Prince. Let the chains be removed from those prisoners forthwith."

The Duke sank back into his chair; and, subduing his rage as well as he was able, he made a sign to the Familiars to set the Jew and the Marquis at liberty.

"Great Vizier," exclaimed Manuel, "the life and the liberty which, at your all-powerful nod, are restored to me, will prove irksome and valueless if I be compelled to remain in a Christian land. Confer not favours by halves, my lord—render me completely grateful to you! Take me into your service—even as a slave, if your Highness will; but let me accompany to a Mussulman country a Mussulman who can teach the Christians such a fine lesson of mercy and forgiveness."

"You shall go with me to Constantinople, Manuel—but not as a slave," returned Ibrahim, profoundly touched by the sincere tone and earnest manner of the young noble: "no—you shall accompany me as a friend."

"A thousand thanks, great Vizier, for this kindness—

this generosity!" said the Marquis, deeply affected: then, as a sudden idea struck him, he turned towards the Jew, exclaiming, "But we must not leave this old man here behind us. 'Twere the same as if we were to abandon a helpless child in the midst of a forest inhabited by ferocious wolves."

"Yes—yes—let me accompany you, excellent young man!" murmured Isaachar, clinging to the arm of the Marquis—for their chains were now knocked off. "You were the first Christian who ever spoke kindly to me; and I have no kith—no kindred on the face of the earth. I am a lone—desolate old man : but I have wealth—much wealth, Manuel di Orsini—and all that I have shall be thine."

"The Jew shall accompany us, my lord," said Ibrahim, addressing himself to the Marquis : then, turning towards the Duke, he exclaimed, in a severe tone, "But a few hours remain until sunset, and the ransom of a hundred thousand pistoles must be paid to me; or I will deliver up this proud palace and the homes of all the councillors now assembled, to the pillage of my troops."

"Nay—nay, my lord!" cried the Jew, horror-struck at the threat : "bring not the terrors of sack, and storm, and carnage into this fair city! A hundred thousand pistoles, your Highness says—a hundred thousand pistoles," he added, in a slower and more musing tone: "'tis a large sum—a very large sum! And yet—to save so many men, and their innocent families, from ruin—from desolation——Yes—yes, my lord," he exclaimed, hastily interrupting himself,—"I—I will pay you the ransom-money!"

"No—by Allah!" ejaculated Ibrahim; "not a single pistole shall be thus extorted from thee! Sooner shall the Florentine Treasury grant thee an indemnification for the horrible tortures which thou hast endured, than thy wealth be poured forth to furnish this ransom-money. Come, my lord of Orsini—come, worthy Jew," continued the Grand Vizier, rising from his seat; "we will depart to the Ottoman encampment."

"Patience, your Highness, for a few hours," urged the Duke; "and the hundred thousand pistoles shall be counted down before thee."

"This poor old man," answered the Grand Vizier, indicating the Jew with a rapid glance, "has been so racked and tortured in your accursed prison-house, that he cannot be too speedily placed under the care of my own chirurgeon. For this reason I depart at once : see thou that the ransom be despatched to my pavilion ere the sun shall have set behind the western hills."

With these words the Grand Vizier bowed haughtily to the Duke, and quitted the Council-Chamber. Manuel of Orsini followed, supporting Isaachar ben Solomon; and, on reaching the court, one of Ibrahim's slaves took the Jew up behind him on his steed. The Marquis was provided with a horse; and the cavalcade moved rapidly away from the precincts of the ducal palace.

Profiting by the hint which Ibrahim-Pacha had offered them, the Duke and the councillors instantaneously levied a heavy fine upon the Grand Inquisidor; and the remainder of the money required to make up the amount demanded, was furnished from the public treasury.

Thus by the hour of sunset the ransom was paid.

* * * * * * *

At an early hour on the ensuing morning, Francisco di Riverola and his beautiful, blushing bride quitted the chamber where they had passed the night in each other's arms, and repaired to the apartment where so many terrible mysteries had been revealed to them and so many dreadful incidents had occurred on the preceding day.

Hand in hand they traversed the passages and the corridors leading to that room in which they had left Christian Rosencrux with the dead Wagner and the dying Nisida : hand in hand and silently they went—that fine young noble, and that charming bride!

On reaching the door of the chamber, Francisco knocked gently; and the glance of intelligence which passed between himself and Flora showed that each was a prey to the same breathless suspense—the same mingled feelings of bright hopes and vague fears.

In a few moments the door was slowly opened; and the venerable old man appeared, his countenance wearing a solemn and mournful aspect.

Then Francisco and the young Countess knew that all was over; and tears started into their eyes.

Christian Rosencrux beckoned them to advance towards the bed, around which the curtains were drawn close; and as they entered the room, the rapid and simultaneous glances which they cast towards the spot where Fernand

Wagner fell down and surrendered up his breath, showed them that the corpse had been removed.

Approaching the bed, with slow and measured steps, Rosencrux drew aside the drapery; and for a moment Francisco and Flora shrank back from the spectacle which met their view—but at the next instant they advanced to the couch, and contemplated with mournful attention the scene presented to them.

For there—upon that couch,—side by side, lay Fernand Wagner and Nisida of Riverola—stiff, motionless, cold.

"Grieve not for her loss, my children," said Christian Rosencrux: "she has gone to a happier realm—for the sincere repentance which she manifested in her last hours has atoned for all the evils she wrought in her life-time. From the moment, young lady, when she banished from her soul the rancour long harboured there against thee —from the instant that she received thee in her arms, and called thee sister—the blessing of heaven was vouchsafed unto her. She was penitent—very penitent, while I administered to her the consolations of religion; and a complete change came over her mind. Grieve not, then, for her: happy on earth she never could have been again—but happy in heaven she doubtless now is!"

Francisco and the young Countess knelt by the side of the couch, and prayed for a long time in silence, with their faces buried in their hands.

When they again raised their heads, and glanced around, the venerable old man no longer met their eyes.

Christian Rosencrux had departed unperceived, leaving Francisco and Flora in complete ignorance of his name; but they experienced a secret conviction that he was something more than an ordinary mortal; and the remembrance of the blessing which he had bestowed upon them on the preceding day shed a soothing and holy influence over their minds.

———

CONCLUSION.

LITTLE now remains to be said: a few brief observations and a rapid glance at the eventual fortunes and fates of the leading characters in the tale will acquit us of our task.

Nisida and Wagner were entombed in the same vault; and their names were inscribed upon the same mural tablet. The funeral was conducted with the utmost privacy—and the mourners were few, but their grief was sincere. And amongst them was Dr. Duras, who had loved Nisida as if she had been his own child!

On the night following the one on which those obsequies took place, another funeral procession departed from the Riverola Palace to the adjacent church; and two coffins were on this occasion, as on the former, consigned to the family tomb. But the ceremony was conducted with even more privacy than the first; and one mourner alone was present. This was Francisco himself; and thus did he perform the duty of interring in sacred ground the remains of his ill-fated mother Vitangela and her brother Eugenio.

The manuscript of the late Count of Riverola was burnt: the closet which had so long contained such fearful mysteries was walled up; and the chamber where so many dreadful incidents had occurred, was never used during the lifetime of Francisco and Flora.

The Grand Vizier remained with his army a few days beneath the walls of Florence; and during that time Isaachar ben Solomon so far recovered his health and strength, under the skilful care of an Egyptian physician, as to be able to visit his dwelling in the suburb of Alla Croce, and secure the immense wealth which he had amassed during a long life of activity and financial prosperity.

When the day of the Grand Vizier's departure arrived, he took a tender farewell of his sister Flora and his aunt, both of whom he loaded with the most costly presents; and in return, he received from Francisco a gift of several horses of rare breed and immense value. Nor did this species of interchange of proofs of attachment end here: for every year, until Ibrahim's death, did that great Minister and the Count of Riverola forward to each other letters and rich presents, thus maintaining to

the end that friendship which had commenced in the Island of Rhodes, and which was cemented by the marriage of Francisco and Flora.

Isachaar ben Solomon and Manuel d'Orsini accompanied the Grand Vizier to Constantinople, and were treated by him with every mark of distinction. But the Jew never completely recovered the tortures which he had endured in the prison of the Inquisition, and in less than two years from the date of his release, he died in the arms of the Marquis, to whom he left the whole of his immense fortune. Manuel d'Orsini abjured Christianity, and entered the Ottoman service, in which his success was brilliant and his rise rapid, thanks to the favour of the Grand Vizier. The reader of Ottoman history will find the name of Mustapha-Pacha frequently mentioned with honour in the reign of Solyman the Magnificent;—and Mustapha-Pacha, Beglerbeg of the mighty province of Anatolia, was once Manuel d'Orsini.

For nearly sixteen years did Ibrahim-Pacha govern the Ottoman realms in the name of the Sultan:—for nearly sixteen years did he hold the imperials seals which had been entrusted to him at a period when the colossal power of the Empire seemed tottering to its fall. During that interval he raised the Ottoman name to the highest pinnacle of glory—extended the dominions of his master —and shook the proudest thrones in Christendom to their foundation. Ferdinand, King of Hungary, called him "brother," and the Emperor Charles the Fifth of Germany, styled him "cousin," in the epistolary communications which passed between them. But a Greek, who had long—long cherished a deadly hatred against the puissant Grand Vizier, at last contrived to enter the service of the Sultan in the guise of a slave; and this man, succeeding in gaining that monarch's ear, whispered mysterious warnings against the ambition of Ibrahim. Solyman became alarmed; and, opening his eyes to the real position of affairs, perceived that the Vizier was indeed far more powerful than himself.

This was enough to ensure the immediate destruction of a Turkish Minister.

Accordingly, one evening Ibrahim was invited to dine with the Sultan, and to sleep at the imperial palace. Never had Solyman appeared more attached to his favourite than on this occasion; and Ibrahim retired to the chamber prepared for him, with a heart elated by the caresses bestowed upon him by his imperial master.

But in the dead of night he was awakened by the entrance of several persons into the room; and, starting up in terror, the Grand Vizier beheld *four black slaves*, headed by a Greek, creep snake-like towards his couch. And that Greek's countenance, sinister and menacing, was immediately recognised by the affrighted Ibrahim— though more than fifteen years had elapsed since he had last set eyes upon those features!

Short and ineffectual was the struggle against the messengers of death: the accursed bow-string encircled the neck of the unhappy Ibrahim;—and at the moment when the vindictive Greek drew tight the fatal noose, the last words which hissed in the ears of the Grand Vizier were—"The wrongs of Calanthe are avenged!"

Thus perished the most powerful Minister that ever held the imperial seals of Ottoman domination;—and the long pent-up but never subdued vindictive feelings of Demetrius were assuaged at length!

Dame Francatelli had long been numbered with those who were gone to their eternal homes, when the news of the death of Ibrahim-Pacha reached Florence. But the Count and Countess of Riverola shed many, many bitter tears at the sad and untimely fate of the Grand Vizier.

Time, however, smooths down all grief; and happiness again returned to the Riverola Palace. For when Francisco and Flora looked around them, and beheld the smiling progeny which had blessed their union,—when they expressed the sweet solace of each other's sympathy, the outpouring of two hearts which beat as one, ever in unison, and filled with a mutual love which time impaired not,—then they remembered that it was useless and wrong to repine against the decrees of Providence; and, in this trusting faith in heaven, and in the enjoyment of each other's unwearying affection, they lived to a good old age—dying at length in the arms of their children.

THE END

BIBLIOGRAPHY

The following bibliography lists first appearances of the individual works of G. W. M. Reynolds. Its primary intention, however, is not to provide bibliographic points about first editions, but to establish the canon of Reynolds's works in chronological order. It does not list reprints, unless there is a special reason for doing so. Quite possibly it is not complete; there may well be unrecorded short pieces in minor periodicals.

The following observations should be made:

(1) Most of Reynolds's works were issued and reissued so many times that it would be both pointless and impossible to try to list all later appearances. Library collections are lamentably weak where G. W. M. R. is concerned, and bibliographic references are fractional and sometimes wrong. Either Reynolds did not bother to deposit copies of his writings in the statutory libraries, or they have since been lost.

(2) Dates for the appearance of Reynolds's part fiction have been taken from his official announcements. Unfortunately, these announcements are not always above reproach, and the real dates may occasionally be a week or two distant from the official dates first announced. In some cases the first installment appeared late; in a couple of cases Reynolds skipped an issue, thereby throwing the chronology off. Worse yet, Reynolds often did not make any announcements at all, especially for the ending of his serials. Approximations have been given for such instances. Presumably his distribution was so secure that he did not have to concern himself greatly with publicity.

(3) For bibliographic convenience, the title under which a story was first published has been accepted as basic. No heed has been paid to variant subtitles; these were often changed with reissues. Variant titles, however, have been listed for purposes of identification.

(4) Reynolds's part fiction, after his contracts with Vickers expired with *Faust* and *The Mysteries of London, Second Series*, was published through his own offices, and printed by John Dicks. These items have been designated Reynolds-Dicks, although the actual legend varies over the years. Place of publication is London, unless otherwise indicated.

(5) The technique of publishing in parts: Reynolds usually issued the first two installments of one of his novels bound together, for the price of a single issue, a penny. This was followed by weekly parts, until the novel was finished. In addition to the weekly parts there were also monthly issues, which gathered up the story as already printed for the current month. On occasion, if the work sold extremely well, the first parts would be reissued before the story was

finished, and the whole sequence would start over again. Usually within a couple of weeks after the parts had finished, the complete story would be issued in paper wrappers, retaining the form (though without mastheads) of the original issues. These complete novels were then printed and reprinted as long as the demand for them continued. At a later date Dicks reissued Reynolds's novels several times, and also serialized them in *Dicks's English Library*.

(6) American editions of Reynolds's works: these are an almost impossible problem. While Long of New York issued an authorized edition of certain of Reynolds's novels in the 1850's, most American publishers simply pirated Reynolds's work. Peterson of Philadelphia, Dick and Fitzgerald of New York, Stringer and Townsend of New York, and Brady of New York were the most important early pirates. Many of these editions were abridged or otherwise altered, so that the American reader should prefer the British editions for an authentic text. For the bibliographer, too, these American editions pose problems, since the Americans often changed the title of the work, and equally often divided it into several parts, each published separately as a complete book with a new title. The situation became chaotic, especially in the 1870's and 1880's when the dime-novel publishers took up Reynolds. None of these reprints was registered bibliographically, and their existence becomes known only when a copy actually turns up in a shop or collection. Libraries do not own them. I have tried to identify as many of these alternate titles as possible, but I am sure that there are many others that I do not happen to have come upon.

(7) Spurious works: The Americans, in addition to pirating Reynolds's fiction, which was not illegal at the time, committed a much worse offense: they deliberately published under Reynolds's name novels that he did not write. This was not an uncommon practice among American publishers of the day, and other writers than Reynolds suffered from it. More than a dozen such novels are known to exist, and there are probably more. Reynolds disavowed a couple, but either lost interest or was not aware of others. These spurious novels often remained in print under Reynolds's name well into the twentieth century. I have located copies of some of these spurious works, but not all.

(8) Previous bibliographies. A curious aftermath to this authorial indifference and publishing chicanery arose in Great Britain. When the British *Bookseller* wanted a listing of Reynolds's works, back in the 1860's and 1870's, they discovered that there were no records in England. (Why they did not ask Reynolds or why they did not do some simple research I do not know.) They turned to American publishers' lists for information, and created "standard" bibliographies that list spurious works as by Reynolds and duplicate books with American variant or segmental titles. This confusion is still perpetuated, as can be seen by the *New Cambridge Bibliography of English Literature*. I have tried to clear it away.

FICTION

THE YOUTHFUL IMPOSTER. 3 vols. Librairie des Estrangers. Paris. 1835. Novel. A revised, enlarged edition, *The Parricide, or a Youth's Career of Crime*, Reynolds-Dicks, weekly parts beginning Jan. 2, 1847. This is not to be confused with *The Parricide, A Domestic Romance*, by Frederic Mansel Reynolds.

THE BARONESS. In *Monthly Magazine*, Sept. 1837 through Apr. 1838. Short novel. Started under pseud. Parisianus, signed G. W. M. R. at end. Alternate title: *The Baroness of Grandmanoir*.

PICKWICK ABROAD, OR THE TOUR IN FRANCE. In *Monthly Magazine*, Dec. 1837 through June 1838,

then continued in monthly parts, 20 altogether, Sherwood & Co. Novel with intercalated stories: "The Gendarme's Tale"; "The Pont Neuf"; "The Public Accuser"; "The Gambler"; "The Chevalier"; "The Self-Devoted"; "Rose Sevigne"; "St. Aubyn"; "The Blind Beauty of Montaigle"; "The Fair Stranger"; "The History of Anastasie de Volage"; "The Tower of St. Jacques." The last three stories were published together at a later date by Dicks under the title *Tales from France*.

ALFRED DE ROSANN. In *Monthly Magazine*, July 1838 through Dec. 1838, then taken over by Willoughby. Novel. Alternate titles: (British) *Alfred, or The Adventures of a French Gentleman;* (American) *Life in Paris, or The Adventures of Alfred de Rosann in the French Metropolis* (slightly abridged).

THE FATHER. In *Monthly Magazine*, Sept. 1838. Short story. Alternate title: "The Mysterious Manuscript."

MARY HAMEL. In *Monthly Magazine*, Oct. 1838. Short story. Alternate title: "The Fatal Glove."

THE BROKEN STATUE. In *Monthly Magazine*, Nov. 1838. Short story. Alternate title: "The Sculptor of Florence."

(Other fiction in *Monthly Magazine*, same period as above. Much of the unsigned fiction is probably by Reynolds. Only acknowledged stories have been listed above.)

THE APPOINTMENT, A TALE. In *The Isis*. 1839. Short story.

GRACE DARLING, OR THE HEROINE OF THE FERN ISLANDS. George Henderson. 1839. Novel with intercalated stories. Reprinted as title member of collections (not seen in this form): *Grace Darling and Other Stories* and *Grace Darling and Tales of a Gendarme*. The second probably includes intercalated tales from *Pickwick Abroad*.

ROBERT MACAIRE IN ENGLAND. 3 vols. T. Tegg. 1840. Novel. The 1839 edition that Summers (*Gothic Bibliography*) cites is an error. Alternate title (American): *Robert Macaire, or The French Bandit in England*.

NOCTES PICKWICKIANAE. In *The Teetotaler*, June 27, 1840 through Aug. 8, 1840. Fictionalized tract.

THE STEAM PACKET, A TALE OF THE RIVER AND OCEAN. Willoughby. 1840. Novel.

THE DRUNKARD'S TALE. In *The Teetotaler*, June 27, 1840 through Nov. 28, 1840. Novel. Alternate title: *The Drunkard's Progress*.

PICKWICK MARRIED. In *The Teetotaler*, Jan. 23, 1841 through June 19, 1841. Short novel. Alternate titles: (a) *The Marriage of Mr. Pickwick* (slightly revised); (b) *The Worries of Mr. Chickpick* (greatly revised, abridged).

(Other fiction in *The Teetotaler*. Some of the unsigned fiction may be by Reynolds. Only acknowledged material has been listed above.)

MASTER TIMOTHY'S BOOKCASE, OR THE MAGIC LANTHORN OF THE WORLD. W. Emans. Monthly parts starting July 15, 1841. Novel with intercalated tales: "The Baronet"; "The Two Sisters"; "The Engraver"; "A Legend of Granier"; "The Fatal Glove"; "The Three Friends"; "The Family Conspiracy"; "The Man with the Iron Mask"; "The Baroness of Grandmanoir"; "The Warrior's Love"; "The Broken Statue"; "The Death of Murad"; "The Duchess of Cavalcanti"; "The Duke of Cavalcanti" (originally published as "The Sisters" in *Monthly Magazine*, and attributed to Mrs. Reynolds); "The Odalisk"; "The Gipsy-Boy"; "The Mysterious Manuscript"; "The Marriage of Mr. Pickwick." Later editions, Reynolds-Dicks, middle 1850's on, omit "The Baroness of Grandmanoir"; "The Warrior's Love"; "The Broken Statue"; "The Death of Murad"; "The Odalisk"; "The Gipsy-Boy"; "The Mysterious Manuscript"; "The Marriage of Mr. Pickwick."

THE MYSTERIES OF LONDON (First Series). George Vickers. Weekly parts, Oct.(?) 1844 through Sept. 26(?) 1846. Novel. Alternate titles (American): divided into (a) *Life in London* and (b) *Ellen Munroe (Monroe)*.

THE ASSASSIN. In *London Journal*. Mar. 29, 1845. Short story.

MARGARET CATCHPOLE. In *London Journal*. Apr. 5, 1845. Short story.

FAUST, A ROMANCE. In *London Journal*, Oct. 4, 1845 through July 18, 1846. Novel. Alternate title (American): *Faust and the Demon*. The variant, *Faust, a Romance of the Second Empire*, of the *Cambridge Bibliography of English Literature* seems to be imaginary.

THE MYSTERIES OF LONDON, SECOND SERIES. George Vickers. Weekly parts, Oct. 3, 1846 through Sept. 16, 1848. Novel. Alternate titles (American): divided into (a) *Esther de Medina* and (b) *The Reformed Highwayman*.

WAGNER, THE WEHR-WOLF, A ROMANCE. In *Reynolds's Miscellany*, Nov. 6, 1846 through July 24, 1847. Novel. A dramatic version was performed in Dublin.

A TALE FOR CHRISTMAS. In *Reynolds's Miscellany*, Dec. 26, 1846. Short story.

THE MATRIMONIAL ADVERTISEMENT. In *Reynolds's Miscellany*, Jan. 30, 1847. Short story.

THE DAYS OF HOGARTH, OR THE MYSTERIES OF OLD LONDON. In *Reynolds's Miscellany*, May 29, 1847 through April 29, 1848. Novel. Alternate titles: (a) *Mysteries of Old London*; (b) *Old London*.

THE CORAL ISLAND, OR THE HEREDITARY CURSE. In *Reynolds's Miscellany*, July 15, 1848 through Mar. 31, 1849. Novel. Alternate titles (American): (a) *Queen Joanna, or The Mysteries of the Court of Naples;* (b) *Mysteries of the Court of Naples* (abridged).

THE MYSTERIES OF THE COURT OF LONDON, FIRST SERIES. Reynolds-Dicks. Weekly parts, Sept. 9, 1848 through Aug. 17, 1850. Novel. Alternate titles (American): Peterson (Phila.), divided into (a) *The Court of London* (also *Mysteries of the Court of London*); (b) *Rose Foster*. Stein (Chicago), divided into (a) *Mysteries of the Court of London;* (b) *Life and Trials of Rose Foster;* (c) *Caroline Walters;* (d) *Pauline Clarendon*. Oxford Society (N.Y.?), divided into *The Works of G. W. M. Reynolds*, volumes 1 through 5: *Pauline Clarendon; Rose Foster* (2 vols.); *Mrs. Fitzherbert; Caroline Walters*.

THE PIXY, OR THE UNBAPTIZED CHILD. Reynolds-Dicks. 1848. Short novel.

THE BRONZE STATUE, OR THE VIRGIN'S KISS. In *Reynolds's Miscellany*, Mar. 31, 1849 through Mar. 14, 1850. Novel. Alternate title (American): *Angela Wildon, or The Mysteries of Altendorph Castle*.

THE CASTELLAN'S DAUGHTER. In *Reynolds's Miscellany*, June 22 and 29, 1850. Short story.

THE GREEK MAIDEN, OR THE BANQUET OF BLOOD. In *Reynolds's Miscellany*, July 27, 1850. Short story. (Not a vampire story, as is sometimes stated)

THE SEAMSTRESS, OR THE WHITE SLAVES OF ENGLAND. In *Reynolds's Miscellany*, Mar. 23, 1850 through Aug. 10, 1850. Novel. Started serially under the title *The Slaves of England*. Alternate titles (American): (a) *Virginia Mordaunt, the Seamstress* and (b), possibly, *The Palace of Infamy* (not seen).

POPE JOAN, OR THE FEMALE PONTIFF. In *Reynolds's Miscellany*, Aug. 10, 1850 through Jan. 25, 1851. Novel.

THE MYSTERIES OF THE COURT OF LONDON, SECOND SERIES. Reynolds-Dicks. Weekly parts, Aug. 24, 1850 through May(?) 1852. Novel. Alternate titles (American): Peterson (Phila.), divided into (a) *Caroline of Brunswick* and (b) *Venetia Trelawney*. Stein (Chicago), divided into (a) *Venetia Trelawney, the Lady of Many Loves;* (b) *Louisa Stanley, a Lamb in the Lions' Den;* (c) *Caroline of Brunswick, or The Drama of a Night;* (d) *Ariadne Varian, or The Secrets of a Picture Gallery*. Another American publication, no publisher cited, *The Court of London* series, divided into (a) *Venetia Trelawney;* (b) *Clara Stanley;* (c) *Caroline of Bruns-*

wick; (d) *Florence Eaton, or The Secrets of a Picture Gallery*. Oxford Society (N.Y.?), *The Works of G. W. M. Reynolds*, volumes 6 through 10, *Venetia Trelawney*.

THE JANIZARY, OR THE MASSACRE OF THE CHRISTIANS. In *Reynolds's Miscellany*, Nov. 2 and 9, 1850. Short story.

THE PROPHECY, OR THE LOST SON. In *Reynolds's Miscellany*, Dec. 7 through 21, 1850. Short story.

KENNETH, A ROMANCE OF THE HIGHLANDS. In *Reynolds's Miscellany*, Jan. 25, 1851 through Dec. 27, 1851. Novel.

THE NECROMANCER, A ROMANCE. In *Reynolds's Miscellany*, Dec. 27, 1851 through July 31, 1852. Novel. Alternate title (American): *Musidora, or The Necromancer*.

MARY PRICE, OR THE MEMOIRS OF A SERVANT GIRL. Reynolds-Dicks. Weekly parts, Nov. 1, 1851 through Oct.(?) 1852. Novel. Alternate titles (American): divided into (a) *Mary Price* and (b) *Eustace Quentin, A Sequel to Mary Price*.

THE MYSTERIES OF THE COURT OF LONDON, THIRD SERIES. Reynolds-Dicks. Weekly parts, May 1, 1852 through Dec. 23, 1853. Novel. Alternate titles (American): Peterson (Phila.), divided into (a) *Lord Saxondale, or Life among the London Aristocracy* and (b) *Count Christoval, a Sequel to Lord Saxondale*. Stein (Chicago), divided into (a) *Lady Saxondale, or Fashionable Depravities;* (b) *Lady Bess, the Female Highwayman;* (c) *Lady Castelmaine, or The Warfare of Duplicities;* (d) *Lady Florina, or Mysteries Unraveled*. Oxford Society (N.Y.?), *The Works of G. W. M. Reynolds*, volumes 11 through 15, *Lady Saxondale's Crimes*.

THE MASSACRE OF GLENCOE, A HISTORICAL TALE. In *Reynolds's Miscellany*, July 31, 1852 through June 18, 1853. Novel. Alternate title (American): *Roderick the Brave, or The Massacre of Glencoe*.

THE SOLDIER'S WIFE. Reynolds-Dicks. Weekly parts, Nov. 12, 1852 through June(?) 1853. Novel. Alternate title (American): *The Degraded Deserter*.

THE RYE HOUSE PLOT, OR RUTH, THE CONSPIRATOR'S DAUGHTER. In *Reynolds's Miscellany*, June 18, 1853 through Aug. 19, 1854. Novel. Alternate titles (American): (a) *The Royal Favorite, or Mysteries of the Court of Charles II;* (b) *Mysteries of the Court of Charles II;* (c) *Mysteries of the Merry Monarch's Court*.

JOSEPH WILMOT, OR THE MEMOIRS OF A MAN SERVANT. Reynolds-Dicks. Weekly parts, July 29

1853 through July 4, 1855. Novel. Alternate titles (American): Peterson (Phila.), divided into (a) *Joseph Wilmot* and (b) *The Banker's Daughter, or The Lost Witness.* F. Tousey (N.Y.), divided into (a) *Joseph Wilmot* and (b) *The Greek Corsair.*

ROSA LAMBERT, OR THE MEMOIRS OF AN UNFORTUNATE WOMAN. Reynolds-Dicks. Novel. Weekly parts, Nov. 4, 1853 through Oct.(?) 1854.

THE MYSTERIES OF THE COURT OF LONDON, FOURTH SERIES. Reynolds-Dicks. Weekly parts, Dec. 30, 1853 through Dec. 5, 1855. Novel. Alternate titles (American): Peterson (Phila.), divided into (a) *Isabella Vincent, or The Two Orphans;* (b) *Vivian Bertram, or A Wife's Honor;* (c) *The Countess of Lascelles;* (d) *The Duke of Marchmont.* F. Tousey (N.Y.), divided into (a) *The Mysteries of the Marchmonts (The Mysteries of Marchmont);* (b) *Bertram Vivian;* (c) *The Countess of Lascelles;* (d) *The Doom of the Burker.* Stein (Chicago), divided into (a) *(The) Duke of Marchmont, an Unscrupulous Aristocrat;* (b) *(The) Earl of Lascelles, or The Hindoo Princess and the Duke;* (c) *The Love Affairs of Lord Octavian Meredith;* (d) *Lord Clandon, or The Explanation of a Plot.* Oxford Society (N.Y.?), *The Works of G. W. M. Reynolds,* volumes 16 through 20, *The Fortunes of the Ashtons.*

MAY MIDDLETON, THE HISTORY OF A FORTUNE. In *Reynolds's Miscellany,* Aug. 19, 1854 through Jan. 6, 1855. Novel.

OMAR, A TALE OF THE CRIMEAN WAR. In *Reynolds's Miscellany,* Jan. 6, 1855 through Jan. 5, 1856. Novel. Alternate titles (American): divided into (a) *Omar Pasha, or The Vizier's Daughter;* (b) *Catherine Volmar, or a Father's Revenge;* (c) *The White Lady, a Romance of Love and War.* (?)

THE LOVES OF THE HAREM, A ROMANCE OF CONSTANTINOPLE. Reynolds-Dicks. Weekly parts, Feb. 3, 1855 through July 7(?), 1855. Novel.

ELLEN PERCY, OR THE MEMOIRS OF AN ACTRESS. Reynolds-Dicks. Weekly parts, July 21, 1855 through Sept.(?) 1857. Novel. Alternate title (American): *Mary Glentworth* (possibly only a segment; not seen).

AGNES, OR BEAUTY AND PLEASURE. Reynolds-Dicks. Weekly parts, Dec. 12, 1855 through Jan(?) 1857. Novel. Alternate titles (American): Peterson (Phila.), divided into (a) *Agnes Evelyn;* (b) *The Countess and the Page, a Tale of Florentine Society;* (c) *Ciprina, or The Secrets of a Picture Gallery.* F. Tousey (N.Y.) further divided *Ciprina* into (a) *Ciprina* and (b) *The Secrets of a Picture Gallery.*

LEILA, OR THE STAR OF MINGRELIA. In *Reynolds's Miscellany,* Jan. 5, 1856 through July 5, 1856. Novel. Alternate titles (American): divided into (a) *Leila* and (b) *Karaman, or The Bandit Chief* (abridged and altered).

MARGARET, OR THE DISCARDED QUEEN. In *Reynolds's Miscellany,* July 5, 1856 through July 11, 1857. Novel. Alternate title (American): *The Discarded Queen.*

THE EMPRESS EUGENIE'S BOUDOIR. Reynolds-Dicks. Weekly parts, Feb. 4, 1857 on. Novel with intercalated tales. Alternate title (American): *The Mysteries of the Court of France.*

THE YOUNG DUCHESS, OR MEMOIRS OF A WOMAN OF QUALITY, A SEQUEL TO ELLEN PERCY. Reynolds-Dicks. Weekly parts, June 17, 1857 through June 9, 1858. Novel. Alternate titles (American): F. A. Brady (N.Y.), divided into (a) *The Young Duchess;* (b) *Imogen (Imogene) Hartland, or The Star of the Circus;* (c) *Ethel Trevor, or the Duke's Victim.*

CANONBURY HOUSE, OR THE QUEEN'S PROPHECY. In *Reynolds's Miscellany,* July 11, 1857 through May 1, 1858. Novel. Alternate titles (American): divided into (a) *The Mysteries of the Court of Queen Elizabeth* or *Canonbury House, or The Queen's Prophecy;* (b) *Ada Arundel, or The Secret Corridor;* (c) *Olivia, or The Maid of Honor.*

MARY STUART, QUEEN OF SCOTLAND. In *Reynolds's Miscellany,* May 14, 1859 through Dec. 24, 1859. Novel.

TWO CHRISTMAS DAYS. In *Reynolds's Miscellany,* Dec. 29, 1860. Short story.

THE YOUNG FISHERMAN, OR THE SPIRITS OF THE LAKE. In *Reynolds's Miscellany,* Oct. 5, 1861 through Nov. 9, 1861. Short novel. Dicks later published *The Young Fisherman and Other Stories* (not seen in this form), which contained "The Young Fisherman"; "Two Christmas Days"; "The Baroness of Grandmanoir"; "The Warrior's Love"; "The Odalisque"; "The Broken Statue"; "The Gipsy-Boy"; "The Worries of Mr. Chickpick"; and "The Dangers of Circumstantial Evidence." Earlier publications for the last two items have not been located.

MISCELLANEOUS WORKS

THE ERRORS OF THE CHRISTIAN RELIGION EXPOSED, BY A COMPARISON OF THE GOSPELS OF MATTHEW AND LUKE. R. Carlile. London. 1832.

SONGS OF TWILIGHT. Librairie des Estrangers. Paris. 1836. (Translation of Victor Hugo's *Chants du Crépuscule*.)

THE MODERN WRITERS OF FRANCE. 2 vols. George Henderson. London. 1839. (Started serially in *Monthly Magazine*, 1838. Second edition omits the Preface, in which sexual realism was defended.)

THE LAST DAY OF A CONDEMNED. George Henderson. London. 1840. (Translation of Victor Hugo's *Dernier Jour d'un Condamné*.) Alternate title: *The Last Day of a Condemned Man*.

SISTER ANNE. George Henderson. London. 1840. (Translation of Paul de Kock's *Soeur Anne*. Later incorporated in part into *The Empress Eugenie's Boudoir*.)

THE ANATOMY OF INTEMPERANCE. United Temperance Union. London. 1840. Planned to comprise 8 weekly parts. Parts 1 through 4 were published, but it is not certain if the work was completed. No copies known to survive.

THE HISTORY OF THE OTTOMAN EMPIRE, Part I. Announced as "nearly ready," Oct. 3, 1840, *The Teetotaler*. Questionable if ever published. "Foundation of the Ottoman Empire" in *Reynolds's Miscellany*, Feb. 18 & 25, 1854, may be a portion of this.

A SEQUEL TO DON JUAN. Paget & Co. London. 1843.

THE FRENCH SELF-INSTRUCTOR. Reynolds-Dicks. London. 1846.

MARY PRICE. (A play performed at the Royal Queen's Theatre, under the management of Mr. C. J. James, 1850. The printed play, *Mary Price; or, The Adventures of a Servant Girl. A domestic drama in two acts*, in Lacy's Acting Edition, #52, is cited as "founded on the popular work by G. W. M. Reynolds." There is little resemblance.)

THE SELF-INSTRUCTOR. Reynolds-Dicks. London. 1861. (A compilation of lessons which had appeared in *Reynolds's Miscellany*: spelling, punctuation, metrics, vocabulary, French pronunciation, etc.)

(Each issue of Reynolds's magazines had a certain amount of editorial matter, some of which must have been written by Reynolds. Most of it is unsigned, however, and the possibility exists that his subeditors (John W. Ross, *London Journal*; Edwin F. Roberts, *Reynolds's Miscellany*) may have written individual pieces. Signed material by Reynolds, too trivial to list separately, includes various announcements and apologies, "Letters to the Industrious Classes" (in part), an etiquette column, occasional letterpress for illustrations, and in later years features for Christmas and Valentine's Day.

The question of translations accomplished by Reynolds is particularly vexing. His magazines featured many translations from the French, all unsigned. It is tempting to assume that Reynolds made some of them, but one cannot be positive about any individual work. The translation of *Mysteries of the Inquisition* by Paul Féval, which appeared in the *London Journal*, has often been attributed to Reynolds—presumably from the title—but there is no proof of this. The only unsigned translation that there is evidence for assigning to Reynolds is *Martin the Foundling* by Eugène Sue; there the translator in footnotes puffs for Reynolds's works.)

JOURNALISM

THE LONDON AND PARIS COURIER. Paris. Jan. through Aug., 1836. Partial owner; editor for later months. No files located.

THE MONTHLY MAGAZINE OF POLITICS, LITERATURE, AND THE BELLES-LETTRES. London. Editor, exact dates not known, 1837 to end of 1838.

THE TEETOTALER, A WEEKLY JOURNAL DEVOTED TO TEMPERANCE, LITERATURE AND SCIENCE. London. June 27, 1840 through Sept. 25, 1841; all published. Editor, partial owner.

THE LONDON JOURNAL AND WEEKLY RECORD OF LITERATURE, SCIENCE AND ART. London. Editor, March 1845 (first issue) probably through Nov. 1846.

REYNOLD'S MISCELLANY OF ROMANCE, GENERAL LITERATURE, SCIENCE AND ART. (Earliest issues titled *Reynolds's Magazine* . . . .) Editor and proprietor, possibly part proprietor after 1862, Nov. 7, 1846 (first issue) through 1869.

REYNOLDS'S POLITICAL INSTRUCTOR. London. Nov. 10, 1849 through May 11, 1850. Editor and proprietor.

REYNOLDS'S WEEKLY NEWSPAPER. London. Aug. 18, 1850 (first issue) on, to his death. Proprietor (possibly part proprietor after 1862) and editor. No files available in U.S.A.

BOW BELLS. London. Reynolds edited *Bow Bells* for John Dicks, the co-proprietor, in later years, of *Reynolds's Miscellany* and *Reynolds's Weekly Newspaper*. Dates not known, but Reynolds seems to have been editor from the first volume of the New Series, 1864, through at least 1868.

MISATTRIBUTIONS AND SPURIOUS WORKS

THE CHILD OF WATERLOO, OR THE HORRORS OF THE BATTLE FIELD, by G. W. M. Reynolds. Obviously not Reynolds's work; author unknown.

EDGAR MONTROSE, OR THE MYSTERIOUS PENITENT, by G. W. M. Reynolds. Obviously not Reynolds's work; author unknown.

THE FIRST FALSE STEP, OR THE PATH OF CRIME, by G. W. M. Reynolds. Disavowed by Reynolds. Summers, *Gothic Bibliography*, attributes this to T. P. Prest. This is not correct; J. M. Rymer is probably the author.

GRETNA GREEN, by Mrs. Susannah F. Reynolds. Erroneously attributed to G. W. M. Reynolds in *English Catalogue*.

THE GIPSY CHIEF, by G. W. M. Reynolds. Peterson, c. 1855–8. This is much the most interesting of the spurious works, since it involves a skillful, deliberate attempt on the part of Peterson to deceive the public. The publisher printed on the title page a long review of the book (described as Reynolds's work) purported to come from the London (Weekly) *Dispatch*, a periodical with which Reynolds had once been associated. Summers has identified this novel, obviously without having seen it, with *The Gipsey Chief* by Hannah M. Jones. This is incorrect. It is an adaptation of *The Mysteries of London* by Thomas Miller, originally published by Vickers as a follow-up to Reynolds's *The Mysteries of London, Second Series*, when Reynolds and Vickers broke off their relationship.

PICKWICK IN AMERICA, by Bos. Attributed to Reynolds by Haynes, *Pseudonyms of Authors*, followed by Halkett and Laing. A bibliographic error, probably suggested by *Pickwick Abroad*. Other Bos items have been tentatively attributed to Reynolds, as by Block, but this attribution is not acceptable. The authorship of the Bos pastiches is not known, although T. P. Prest is a good possibility.

PRACTICAL RECIPES. (Full title: *The Household Book of Practical Recipes* by Mrs. Susannah F. Reynolds and others.) A bibliographic error in Allibone and Summers, *Gothic Bibliography*.

REYNOLDS'S DIAGRAM OF THE STEAM ENGINE [AND BOILER WITH POPULAR DESCRIPTION]. Attributed to G. W. M. R. in various bibliographies. Really by James Reynolds, a technical author and publisher.

THE RIVAL BEAUTIES, OR LOVE AND DIPLOMACY. Published in *The New York Dutchman* by Griffin and Farnworth, N.Y. Disavowed by Reynolds in *Reynolds's Miscellany*, Feb. 11, 1854.

THE ROBBER'S WIFE, A DOMESTIC ROMANCE. By the Author of *Rose Somerville, The First False Step*, etc. etc. Stringer & Townsend, c. 1860. Obviously not Reynolds's work; author unknown.

ROBERT BRUCE, THE HERO KING OF SCOTLAND, by G. W. M. Reynolds. The author is Gabriel Alexander. Originally a Reynolds-Dicks publication in England.

ROSE SOMERVILLE (SOMMERVILLE), OR A HUSBAND'S MYSTERY AND A WIFE'S DEVOTION, by G. W. M. Reynolds. Disavowed by Reynolds. According to Summers, *Gothic Bibliography*, this is the same as *Rose Summerville* by Ellen T——.

THE UNKNOWN, OR THE MYSTERIES OF LONDON. F. Tousey, *Brookside Library*. Attributed to G. W. M. Reynolds. This is really the American translation (*Mysteries of London*, c. 1845) of the French *Mystères de Londres* by Paul Féval.

WALLACE, THE HERO OF SCOTLAND, by G. W. M. Reynolds. The author is Gabriel Alexander. Originally a Reynolds-Dicks publication in England.

THE WOMAN IN RED by G. W. M. Reynolds. N. L. Munro, #106 *Munro's Library*. Obviously not Reynolds's work; author unknown.

QUESTIONABLE WORKS

The following books were attributed in America to Reynolds, either published under his name or as "by the author of . . . ." Some may be alternate titles for genuine works or segments of works by Reynolds; others may be spurious. I have not been able to locate copies of them, and they are known to me only from announcements and advertising. The editions listed below are not necessarily first printings; they are simply the editions that I happen to have identified. The abbreviation "r." is for "reported."

CLIFFORD AND THE ACTRESS, OR THE REIGNING FAVORITE. Peterson. r. 1860.

THE COUNTESS OF ARNHEIM. Dick & Fitzgerald. r. 1865.

DEGRADED AND DESERTED. Hurst, *Hawthorne Series*. r. 1905. (Note similarity to alternate title for *The Soldier's Wife.*)

THE MAID OF HONOR. F. A. Brady. r. 1860. (Probably from *Canonbury House.*)

MARY GLENTWORTH. Dick & Fitzgerald. r. 1865. (Probably a portion of *Ellen Percy.*)

THE MISER'S WILL, OR THE DOOM OF THE POISONER. Pollard & Moss. 1888. #45 in the *Echo Series.*

THE OPERA DANCER, OR MYSTERIES OF FEMALE LIFE IN LONDON. Peterson. r. 1860. (From *Ellen Percy* or *The Young Duchess*, probably.)

THE PALACE OF INFAMY, OR THE SLAVE WOMAN OF ENGLAND. F. Tousey, *Brookside Library* #306. c. 1885. (Note similarity to subtitle of *The Seamstress.*)

RAVENSDALE, OR THE FATAL DUEL. By the Author of *The First False Step, Rose Sommerville*, etc. Dick & Fitzgerald. r. 1857. (This is probably the book of the same title by Ellen T——, London, 1847.)

THE RIVAL LOVERS. Stringer & Townsend. r. 1855. Possibly the same work as *The Rival Beauties* in "Misattributions and Spurious Works."

THE RUINED GAMESTER. Peterson. r. 1860. (The first chapter of *The Robber's Wife*—cf. *Misattributions and Spurious Works*—is entitled "The Ruined Gamester." It may be the same work.)

TRAGIC SCENES IN THE LIFE OF A LONDON PHYSICIAN. F. Tousey, *Brookside Library* #367. c. 1885. (This title is suggestive of Samuel Warren's *Passages from the Diary of a Late Physician.*)

E.F.B.